NOW
I RISE

NOW I RISE

KIERSTEN WHITE

CORGI BOOKS

CORGI BOOKS

UK | USA | Canada | Ireland | Australia
India | New Zealand | South Africa

Corgi Books is part of the Penguin Random House group of companies
whose addresses can be found at global.penguinrandomhouse.com.

www.penguin.co.uk
www.puffin.co.uk
www.ladybird.co.uk

First published in the United States of America by Delacorte Press,
an imprint of Penguin Random House LLC, 2017

First published in Great Britain by Corgi Books 2017

001

Set in 11.74/15.06pt Centaur MT
Printed in Great Britain by Clays Ltd, St Ives plc

A CIP catalogue record for this book is available from the British Library

ISBN: 978–0–552–57375–7

All correspondence to:
Corgi Books
Penguin Random House Children's
80 Strand, London WC2R 0RL

For Christina, who will never have time to
read this book, but who gave me
the gift of time to write it

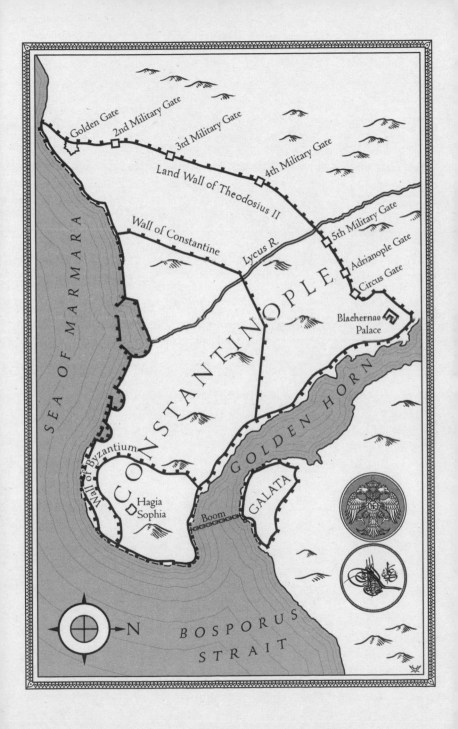

1

January 1453

HELL WAS A PARTY.

At least, Radu was fairly certain that whatever hell there was would certainly resemble this party.

Music drifted like perfume on the air, enough to sweeten but not overwhelm. Groups of musicians were scattered across the island; they could be glimpsed among the hardy green that had survived the winter months. Though the main meal would come later, blue-clad servants floated through the crowds with food-laden trays shaped like lily pads. On either side of the island, the Tunca River flowed leisurely by.

Whatever else he had been, Murad—Mehmed's dead father and Radu's onetime benefactor—had not been one to skimp on luxury. The harem complex he built on the island had been out of use since his death, but it had not faded in glory. The tiles gleamed. The carved stones of the walls promised luxury and peace. The fountains tinkled in cheery companionship with the surrounding river.

Radu wandered between buildings painted like geometric

gardens, pulled along as surely as the course of the river. He knew it was useless, knew that it would not make him feel better. But still he looked.

And there—next to the bathhouse. Radu was drawn to him like a leaf spun on the river current. Mehmed wore his now-constant deep-purple robes and a swirling golden turban. A jeweled chain fastened a cloak around his broad shoulders. Radu tried to remember Mehmed's full lips parting in a smile, his eyebrows rising in mirth rather than mockery. The two young men, both having finally finished growing, were the same tall, lean height. But lately Radu felt small when Mehmed looked at him.

He would have taken even that today. But Mehmed did not look in his direction, immune to the connection Radu could not escape.

"Truly glorious," Halil Vizier said to Mehmed, his hands on his hips as he looked up at the new bathhouse complex. Three connected buildings, with domed roofs echoing those of mosques, had been added in the past few months. They were the first new construction anticipating Mehmed's grand palace complex. It would rival anything his father had ever built— anything *anyone* had ever built. To celebrate this investment in the capital of the Ottoman Empire, Mehmed had invited everyone who mattered.

Ambassadors from various European countries mingled freely with the Ottoman elite. Mehmed stood apart, but was free with his smiles and sweeping promises of future parties at his palace. Along with his usual attendants, he was joined by Ishak Pasha, one of his most powerful spahi; Kumal Pasha, Radu's brother-in-law; and, as always, like a bitter taste that could not be swallowed, Halil Vizier.

Radu hated thinking of his old enemy Halil Pasha as Halil Vizier. He hated even more that it had been his own plan to put Halil in a place of trust and power to keep a closer eye on him. Maybe Lada had been right. Maybe they should have killed him. Things would be easier, or at least they would be more pleasant. That should be Radu's place at Mehmed's side.

As though sensing Radu's poisonous envy, Halil Vizier looked at him. His mouth curled in a sneering smile. "Radu the Handsome," he said. Radu frowned. He had not heard that title since the end of fighting in Albania, when Skanderberg, their foe, had coined it. Mehmed glanced over, then away as soon as their eyes met. Like a butterfly alighting on a flower and finding it lacking.

"Tell me," Halil said, that nasty smile still on his bearded face. "Is your pretty wife aware this is not a functioning harem yet? I fear she has false hopes about entering it."

The men around Halil snickered. Kumal frowned, then opened his mouth. Radu shook his head, a minute movement. Kumal looked sadly away. Mehmed did not acknowledge the insult—the implication that Radu's wife would enter Mehmed's harem to divorce Radu—but he did nothing to refute it, either.

"My wife is not—"

A gentle hand came down on Radu's arm. He turned to find Nazira. Nazira, who was not supposed to be here. "His wife is not pleased with anyone else monopolizing his attention." Beneath her translucent veil, her smile was far brighter than the winter sun. She wore the colors of springtime. Still, Radu felt cold looking at her. What was she doing?

Nazira turned Radu away from the men and led him down a path draped in more silk than most people would ever see in their lives. It was extravagant, excessive, absurd, like everything about this party. A reflection of a sultan too young and foolish to think of anything beyond appearances and his own pleasure.

"What are you doing here?" Radu whispered urgently.

"Come on a boat ride with me."

"I cannot! I have to—"

"Endure mockery from Halil Vizier? Try to regain the favor of Mehmed? Radu, what has happened?" Nazira pulled him into the shadows of one of the buildings. To onlookers it would appear as though he were stealing a moment with his beautiful wife.

He gritted his teeth, looking at the wall above her head. "I have business."

"Your business is my business. You do not write us, you never visit. I had to learn from Kumal that you have fallen out with Mehmed. What happened? Did you . . . does he know?" Her dark eyes were heavy with meaning, the weight of it too much for Radu.

"No! Of course not. I— It is much more complicated than that." He turned away, but she grabbed his wrist.

"Fortunately for you, I am very clever and can understand even the most complicated things. Tell me."

Radu ran the fingers of his free hand along the edges of his turban, tugging at it. Nazira reached up, taking his fingers in her own. Her sharp eyes softened. "I worry about you."

"You do not need to worry about me."

"I do not worry because I need to. I worry because I care about you. I want to see you happy. And I do not think *Edirne* holds any happiness for you." She emphasized *Edirne*, making it clear that it was not the capital she spoke of, but what—or rather, whom—that capital held.

"Nazira," Radu hissed, "I cannot talk about this right now."

He almost wished he could. He was desperate to talk to someone, anyone. But no one could help him with that problem. Radu wondered, sometimes, what Lazar could have told him if they had ever talked openly about what it meant for one man to love another. Lazar had been anything but discreet about his openness to something ... more ... with Radu. And Radu had rewarded Lazar's loyalty and friendship with a knife. Now he had no one to talk to, to ask these desperate questions. It was wrong, was it not? For him to love this way?

But when Radu looked at Nazira and Fatima, he did not feel anything other than happiness that they had found each other. Their love was as pure and true as any he had ever observed. Thoughts like this made his mind turn around in circles upon itself, until not even prayer could calm it.

Radu looked down at Nazira's hands on his. "The palace may not hold my happiness. But I cannot look anywhere else."

Nazira released him with a sigh. "Will you come back with me? Spend some time at home? Fatima misses you. It might do you good to be away."

"There is too much to do."

"Too much dancing? Too many parties?" Her voice teased, but her eyes lacked an accompanying sparkle of sincerity. Her words stung him.

"You know I am more than that."

"I do. I simply worry you might forget. You do not have to do this to yourself."

"I am not doing it to myself, or for myself. I— Damn. Damn, damn, damn." Radu watched as a man in naval uniform—a sturdy cape, a tighter, smaller turban than the ones worn by ordinary soldiers, and a sash of Mehmed's colors— walked past. He was accompanied by one of Halil Vizier's trusted friends.

"What?" Nazira followed Radu's gaze.

"I need to talk to that man. Without anyone else being able to hear. It is the only reason I am here."

She was suddenly excited. "You do? Is he—" She raised her eyebrows suggestively.

"No! No. I just need to speak with him. In secret."

Nazira's smile turned into a thoughtful frown. "Can you be seen together?"

"Yes, but it cannot look like we met on purpose or are discussing anything of importance. I was hoping to find some quiet moment, but there are so many people here. He has not been alone since he came to the capital. Halil Vizier has seen to it."

"Your party attendance is more complicated than I thought, then."

Radu gritted his teeth. "Much."

"Well, you are very fortunate you married so well." Nazira put a hand on his arm and steered him onto the walkway. "Tell me about him."

"His name is Suleiman, and he is the newly promoted admiral of the navy."

Nazira laughed. "This will be easy."

She danced effortlessly from group to group with a coy smile and a word of greeting for all. Radu was on the fringes of these parties lately, a contrast to when he had been a shining focal point. But with Nazira on his arm, more people were willing to stop for a moment of conversation. He craned his neck for a view of Suleiman. Nazira pinched his arm, hard.

"Patience," she whispered.

After several more stops to chat with the uncle of her deceased father's best friend, the cousin of Kumal's deceased wife, and any number of other people Nazira treated with delight and deference regardless of their place in the Ottoman social hierarchy, they plowed directly into Suleiman. Somehow Nazira had managed to turn and walk so that Radu knocked the man over.

"Oh!" Nazira squeaked, putting her hands over her veiled mouth. "I am so sorry!"

Radu held out a hand to help the man up. They had never met before, but Suleiman's eyes lingered on the boat-shaped gold pin on Radu's cloak. "Please forgive me."

"Of course." Suleiman bowed. "I am Suleiman Baltoghlu."

Radu bowed as well. "Radu."

"Radu . . . ?" Suleiman paused expectantly.

"Simply Radu." Radu's smile was tight. Lada had left him behind under the mantle of the Draculesti family. But Radu had rejected his father's name. He would not take it up again, ever. "This is my wife, Nazira."

Suleiman took her hand, bowing even deeper. "They make wives prettier in Edirne than they do in Bursa."

Nazira beamed. "That is because the wind blows too hard in harbor cities. The poor women there have to expend all their energy merely staying upright. There is no time left for being pretty."

Suleiman laughed, a loud burst of sound that drew attention. But the attention was focused on him and Nazira, not on him and Radu.

"Tell me, what do you do in Bursa?" she asked.

"I am an admiral."

"Boats! Oh, I adore boats. Look, did you see?" Nazira pointed to the collection of delicate boats bobbing in the river. They were carved in fanciful shapes. One had a prow like the head of a frog, and its oars had webbed feet carved into their ends. Another looked like a war galley, tiny decorative oars sticking out both its sides. "Radu is afraid if we take a boat out, he will not make it back to shore. But surely if we had an admiral with us . . ." Nazira looked up at Suleiman through her thick eyelashes.

"I am at your service." Suleiman followed them to the dock, helping Nazira into a boat carved like a heron. A head on a slender neck pointed their way forward, and silk wings extended on either side. The tail was a canopy arching overhead to protect passengers from the sun, though it was not quite warm enough to be necessary.

"This is lovely!" Nazira sighed happily, leaning over to trail one hand in the water. Radu was not quite so pleased—he hated boats—but he shared a secret smile with Nazira. She had done his job for him.

Suleiman took the oars. Radu sat gingerly in the back of the small boat.

"I am going to chatter very brightly, waving my hands a lot," Nazira said as they pulled away from the shore, and away from any prying ears. "In fact, I am going to talk the whole time, and you two will be unable to get a word in edgewise."

She continued her one-sided conversation—a silent one. Her head bobbed up and down, she laughed, and her hands punctuated imaginary sentences. Any onlookers would see her entertaining Suleiman while Radu tried his best to keep his stomach.

"How soon can you build the new galleys?" Radu muttered, clutching the sides of the boat.

Suleiman shrugged like he was trying to loosen up his shoulders for rowing. "We can build ships as fast as he can fund them."

"No one can know how many ships we really have."

"We will build a few galleys in Bursa for show, so it looks like I am doing something. The rest will be built in secret, in a private shipyard along the Dardanelles. But I still need men. We can have all the ships in the world, but without trained sailors, they will be as much use as the boat we are in now."

"How can we train that many men in secret?" Someone would notice if they conscripted men for a navy. A few new boats could be attributed to a foolish whim of an immature sultan. An armada, complete with the men to sail it, was another thing entirely.

"Give me the funds to hire Greek sailors, and I will give him the finest navy in the world," Suleiman said.

"It will be done." Radu leaned over the side, barely avoiding heaving.

Suleiman laughed at some new pantomime of Nazira's. "Whatever you do, keep this one around. She is truly a treasure."

This time Nazira's laugh was real. "I am."

Radu did not have to feign relief when Suleiman finished their loop around the island and pulled them back to the dock.

He stumbled onto it, grateful for the solid wood beneath his feet.

"Your husband has a weak stomach," Suleiman said as he helped Nazira out of the boat.

"Yes. It is a good thing he is so handsome." Nazira patted Radu's cheek, then waved prettily at Suleiman. "Our navy is in most capable hands!"

Suleiman laughed wryly. "My little bird boats will be the terror of the seas!" He bowed theatrically, then strode away.

"Thank you," Radu said, letting Nazira take him back through the party, then into a secluded corner. They sat on a bench with their backs to the bathhouse wall. "That was brilliant."

"Yes, I am. Now tell me what is really going on."

"I am— We are— This is very secret."

Nazira rolled her eyes, exasperated.

"I am helping Mehmed with his plans to take Constantinople. We have to work in secret so that Halil Pasha—" Radu paused, grimacing. Halil's new title always tasted foul on his tongue. *Why* had he insisted Halil be elevated from a pasha to a vizier? "So that he does not discover our plans with enough time to sabotage them. We know he is still in league with Emperor Constantine. My elimination from Mehmed's inner circle was deliberate. I need to appear unimportant; that way, I can organize things Mehmed cannot be seen to care about, like the navy. Everything we do in public is to divert attention from his true goals. Even this party is a farce, to show that Mehmed is frivolous and cares only about Edirne. Why would he invest so much money in a palace if he intends to make his capital elsewhere?"

"But if everything you are doing is in secret, could you not do all that and still be one of his advisors?"

"My actions would draw too much attention if I were constantly at Mehmed's side."

"Not if it were widely known that you were merely his friend. Sultans can have close friends who are not necessarily important, but are merely beloved." Nazira looked down, her expression pained but determined. "Do you never wonder if, perhaps . . . Mehmed understands more than you think he does? And this separation is not so much a strategy as a kindness?"

Radu stood so quickly he nearly lost his balance. "No."

"He is not a fool. If I saw in one evening how you felt, surely he has seen the same over the years you have spent together."

Radu put a hand up, wishing he could make Nazira swallow the words so they had never been spoken. If Mehmed truly understood how he felt, then . . . It was too much to think about. There were too many questions that had no answers Radu wanted.

"Maybe your sister was wise to leave. She realized a sultan could never give her what she needed."

Mehmed's plan made sense. It was the only path. That was why Mehmed had chosen it. "I am staying because my life is here," Radu said. "Lada left because she wanted the throne, and she got it."

Sometimes he wondered what would have happened if he had not pushed Lada to abandon them last year. Because he had chosen that, too. Chosen to say exactly what she needed to hear to decide to leave Mehmed—and Radu. It had been a dark, desperate move. A move he thought would bring him closer to Mehmed. Radu held back a bitter laugh.

He had pushed Lada away, and she had ridden to Wallachia and glory. To everything she had ever wanted, without a second glance for the man she allegedly loved. Or for her pathetic brother. For all his supposed cleverness, Radu could not secure the same happy ending for himself that he had tricked his sister into.

If Lada were still here, would this plan of enforced distance be his life? Or would Lada have come up with another way to subvert Halil? A way that let Radu keep his friendship with Mehmed? A way that did not leave Radu alone every night, wondering when his future would be what he hoped it to be? Wondering what those hopes even were?

Hope was an arrow that never ceased piercing his heart.

Plans notwithstanding, Mehmed could have done things as Nazira said. He could have made excuses so he and Radu were able to speak face to face instead of via covert, hidden messages. There were many things Mehmed could do but did not, and probably never would. If Radu let himself dwell on those things, he would surely go mad.

He avoided Nazira's gaze. "It is fine. Everything is as it ever was, and as it will ever be. Once we have taken Constantinople, I will be at his side again. As his friend." Radu's voice wavered on the last word, betraying him.

"Will it be enough?" she asked.

"It will have to be." Radu tried to smile, but it was useless to be false with Nazira. Instead he bent and placed a kiss on his wife's forehead. "Give my love to Fatima. I have work to do."

Nazira stood, taking his elbow firmly. "Not without me. You need an ally."

Radu sighed. He really did. He had been so lonely, so lost.

He did not want to ask this of her. But then again, he had not asked. She had simply shown up and told him how things would be. That was her signature, he supposed. And he was grateful for it. "Thank you."

Together, they walked back into the party. It felt less like hell and more like a game. Nazira deliberately greeted the people least likely to speak to Radu now that he was out of favor. She did it to annoy them, and he adored her for it. It was delightful to watch those who had once clamored for his favor and then shunned him squirm as they tried to be polite. Radu was actually enjoying himself. *And* he had good news for Mehmed, which meant an excuse to sneak into his rooms to leave a message.

He was laughing as he turned and came face to face with ghosts from his past.

Aron and Andrei Danesti. His childhood rivals. Memories of fists in the forest, stopped only by Lada's ferocity. Radu had been powerless to face them on his own. But he had figured out another way. The last time he had seen them, they were being whipped in public for theft. He had set them up in retaliation for their cruelty.

Time had stretched them, built them new forms. Aron was thin and sickly-looking. His mustache and beard were sparse and patchy. Andrei, broad-shouldered and healthy, had fared better, though there was something wary in his expression that had not been there before Radu's trick. Radu felt a brief pang of guilt that his actions had carved that onto someone else's face. Aron smiled, and Radu saw something in the man's eyes he had never seen as a child: kindness.

But apparently time had been more exacting on Radu than

it had on his Danesti foes. That, or his turban and Ottoman dress disguised him completely. Their smiles—Andrei's guarded, Aron's kind—held no spark of recognition.

Nazira cheerfully introduced herself. Radu resisted the urge to shield her from them. Surely they were not the same bullies they had been in childhood. "Where are you from?" she asked.

"Wallachia," Andrei answered. "We are here with our father, the prince."

A noise like the roaring of wind filled Radu's ears.

Nazira lit up. "Oh, what a coincidence! My husband is—"

Radu tugged her arm. "Apologies, we have to leave." He walked away so quickly Nazira had to run to keep up. As soon as he had rounded a corner, Radu leaned against the wall, overcome. Their father. A Danesti. The Wallachian prince. Which meant that Lada was not on the throne.

And if they were here paying respects, Mehmed *knew* Lada was not on the throne.

What else did Mehmed know? What other secrets was he keeping from Radu?

For once, though, the biggest question did not revolve around Mehmed. All these months, Radu had never written Lada, because she had never written him. And because he hated her for getting what she wanted and leaving him with nothing, as always.

But apparently he had been wrong about that.

Where was Lada?

2

February 1453

IT TOOK ONLY THREE fingers smashed beyond recognition before the would-be assassin screamed the name of Lada's enemy.

"Well." Nicolae raised his eyebrows, once singular but now bisected by a vicious scar that failed to fade with the passage of time. He turned away as Bogdan slit the young man's throat. The heat of life leaving body steamed slightly in the frigid winter air. "That *is* disappointing."

"That the governor of Brasov betrayed us?" Bogdan asked.

"No, that the quality of assassins has fallen this low."

Lada knew Nicolae meant to make the situation palatable through humor—he never liked executions—but his words struck deep. It was certainly a blow that the governor of Brasov wanted her dead. He had promised her aid, which had given her the first shred of hope in months.

Now she had none. Brasov was the last of the Transylvanian cities she had tried to find an ally in. None of the noble Wallachian boyar families would so much as respond to her letters. Transylvania, with its fortified mountain cities crushed between Wallachia and Hungary, was heavily Wallachian. But Lada saw now that the ruling class of Saxons and Hungarians treated her people like chaff, and considered her worthless.

But almost worse than losing her last chance at an ally was that *this* was the most they could be bothered to spare for her: an underfed, poorly trained assassin barely past boyhood.

That was all the fear she instilled, all the respect she merited.

Bogdan kicked the body over the edge of the small ravine bordering their encampment. Just as when they were children, he never had to be asked to clean up her messes. He wiped the blood from his fingers, then tugged his ill-fitting gloves back on. A misshapen hat was worn low, hiding the ears that stuck out like jug handles.

He had grown broad and strong. His fighting was not flashy but was brutally efficient. Lada had seen him in action, and had to bite back the admiring words that sprang to her lips. He was also fastidiously clean—a quality emphasized by the Ottomans that not all her men had retained. Bogdan always smelled fresh, like the pine trees they hid among. Everything about him reminded Lada of home.

Her other men crouched over their fires, scattered in groups among the thick trees. They were as misshapen as Bogdan's hat, their once pristine Janissary uniformity long since abandoned. They were down to thirty—twelve lost when they had met an unexpected force from the Danesti Wallachian prince as they attempted to cross the Danube River into the country, eight more lost in the months since, spent hiding and running and desperately seeking allies.

"Do you think Brasov is in league with the Danesti prince or with the Hungarians?" Nicolae asked.

"Does it matter?" Lada snapped. All sides were set against her. They smiled to her face and promised aid. Then they sent assassins in the dark.

She had bested vastly superior assassins on Mehmed's behalf. Meager comfort, though, and worse still that she found it only by remembering her time with Mehmed. It seemed as though anything she might look on with pride had happened when she was with him. Had she been so diminished, then, by leaving the person she was at his side?

Lada lowered her head, rubbing the unceasing tightness at the base of her neck. Since failing to take the throne, she had neither written to nor received word from Mehmed or Radu. It was too humiliating to lay bare her failure before them and anticipate what they might say. Mehmed would invite her to return. Radu would console her—but she questioned whether he would welcome her back.

She wondered, too, how close they had become in her absence. But it did not matter. She had chosen to leave them as an act of strength. She would never return to them in weakness. She had thought—with her men, with her dispensation from Mehmed, with all her years of experience and strength—that the throne was hers for the taking. She had thought that she would be enough.

She knew now that nothing she could do would ever be enough. Unless she could grow a penis, which did not seem likely. Nor particularly desirable.

Though it did make for an easier time relieving oneself

when perpetually hiding in the woods. Emptying one's bladder in the middle of the night was a freezing, uncomfortable endeavor.

What, then, was left to her? She had no allies. She had no throne. She had no Mehmed, no Radu. She had only these sharp men and sharp knives and sharp dreams, and no way to make use of any of them.

Petru leaned against a winter-bare tree nearby. He had grown thicker and quieter in the past year. All traces of the boy he had been when he joined Lada's company were gone. One of his ears had been mangled, and he wore his hair longer to cover it. He had also stopped shaving. Most of her men had. Their faces were no longer the bare ones that had indicated their station as Janissaries. They were free. But they were also directionless, which increasingly worried Lada. When thirty men trained to fight and kill had nothing to fight and kill for, what was there to keep them bound to her?

She pulled a branch from the fire. It was a burning brand, searing her eyes with its light. She sensed more than saw the attention of her men shift to her. Rather than feeling like a weight, it made her stand taller. The men needed something to do.

And Lada needed to see something burn.

"Well," she said, spinning the flaming stick lazily through the air, "I think we should send our regards to Transylvania."

———◆———

It is easier to destroy than to build, her nurse had been fond of saying when Lada would pull all the blossoms off the fruit trees, *but empty fields make hungry bellies.*

As a child, Lada had never understood what her nurse

meant. But now she thought she might. At least the part about destroying being easier than building. All her time spent writing letters or standing in front of minor nobles attempting to forge alliances had been wasted. It had been nothing but struggle for the past year. Struggle to arrange meetings, struggle to be seen as more than a girl playing at soldier, struggle to find the right ways to work within a system that had always been foreign to her.

They were closer to the city of Sibiu than to Brasov. For efficiency's sake, Lada decided to stop there first. It took less time to herd hundreds of Sibiu's sheep into the icy pond to drown than it had for a servant to inform her that the governor would not be meeting with her. The Wallachian shepherds, who would no doubt be killed for their failure to save the sheep, were quietly folded into her company.

That accomplished, Lada and her men passed through the slumbering, unprotected outer city of Sibiu, harming nothing and no one. Ahead of them rose the walls of the inner city, where only Transylvanian nobles—never Wallachians—were allowed to sleep. She imagined they dreamed deeply, pampered and protected by the sweat of Wallachian brows.

They had neither the time nor the numbers to launch an attack on inner Sibiu. And they were not here to conquer. They were here to destroy. As each volley of flaming arrows arced high over the walls and down into the maze of roofs, Lada's smile grew simultaneously brighter and darker.

A few days later, they waited outside Brasov for the sun to go down. The city was set in a valley ringed with deep green growth. Towers stood at intervals along the inner city walls, each maintained by a different guild. If she were planning a siege, it would be a challenge.

But, as with Sibiu, they did not want to keep this city. They merely wanted to punish it.

At twilight, Nicolae returned from a scouting trip. "Terror spreads faster than any fire. Rumors are everywhere. You have taken Sibiu, you lead ten thousand Ottoman soldiers, you are the chosen servant of the devil."

"Why must I always be a man's servant?" Lada demanded. "If anything, I should be partners with the devil, not his servant."

Bogdan scowled, crossing himself. He still clung to some bastard version of the religion they had been raised with. His mother—Lada and Radu's nurse—had wielded Christianity like a switch, lashing out with whichever stories suited her needs at the time. Usually the ones about naughty children being eaten by bears. Lada and Radu had also attended church with Bogdan and his mother, but Lada remembered very little from those infinite suffocating hours.

Bogdan must have carried his religion with him through all his years with the Ottomans. Janissaries were converted to Islam. There were no other options. The rest of her men had dropped Islam like their Janissary caps, but they had not replaced it with anything else. Whatever faith they had had in their childhood had been trained out of them.

Lada wondered what it had cost Bogdan to hold on to Christianity in spite of so much opposition. Then again, he had always been stubborn both in grudges and loyalty. She was grateful for the latter, as his loyalty to her had been planted young and deep in the green forests and gray stones of their childhood in Wallachia. Before he had been taken from her by the Ottomans.

Impulsively she reached out and tugged on one of his ears like she had when they were children. An unexpected smile bloomed on his blocky features, and suddenly she was back with him, tormenting Radu, raiding the kitchens, sealing their bond with blood on dirty palms. Bogdan was her childhood. Bogdan was Wallachia. She had him back. She could get the rest.

"If you are working for the devil, can you tell him to pay us? Our purses are empty." Matei held up a limp leather pouch to illustrate. Lada startled, turning away from Bogdan and the warmth in her chest. Matei was one of her original Janissaries, her oldest and most trusted men. They had followed her in Amasya, when she had had nothing to offer them. And they still followed her, with the same result.

Matei was older even than Stefan, with years of invaluable experience. Not many Janissaries lived to his age. When they had been surprised on the border, Matei had taken an arrow in the side protecting Lada. He was graying and gaunt, with a perpetually hungry look about him. That look had grown hungrier still during their sojourn in the mountain wildernesses of Transylvania. Lada valued that hunger in her men. It was what made them willing to follow her. But it was also what would drive them away if she did not do something more, soon. She needed to keep Matei on her side. She needed his sword and, in a less tangible but just as important way, she needed his respect. Bogdan she had no matter what. Her other men she was determined to keep.

Lada kept her eyes fixed on the walls of the city beneath them, watching as lights appeared like tiny beacons. "When your work is done, Matei, take anything you wish."

Brasov had sealed its gates, allowing no one in after dark. Matei and Petru led five men each to scale the walls under cover of darkness. After waiting for them to get where they needed to be, Lada lit the base of a bone-dry dead tree. It greeted the flames hungrily, pulling them so quickly to the top that she and her men had to run from the heat.

The bases of the two towers on the opposite end of the city were engulfed in a matching bright blaze. Lada watched as panicked guards ran around atop the tower nearest her and peered over the edge. "Are you Wallachian?" she called out in her native tongue.

One of them shot an arrow. Lada twisted to the side, and it glanced off the chain mail shirt she wore. Bogdan fired a return arrow. The man tipped silently over the tower's edge.

"Are you hurt?" Bogdan said, voice desperate as his big hands searched for a wound . . . around her breasts.

"Bogdan!" She slapped his hands away. "If I were, it would certainly not be a wound for you to see to!"

"You need a woman, then?" he asked, looking around as though one would magically appear.

"I am fine!"

Another man waved a piece of cloth above the edge of the tower. "Yes, we are Wallachian!" he shouted, voice quavering.

Lada considered it. "Let us in and you can run. Or you can join us."

She counted her heartbeats. It took only ten before the

tower door opened and seven men filed out. Three skulked silently into the trees. Four stayed. She walked past them and climbed the stairs to the top of the tower. It was circular, with a thick stone railing that she leaned over to view the city.

Already, panic spread like disease within the walls. People flooded the streets, women screaming, men shouting directions. It was chaos.

It was perfect.

Three days later, stray remnants of smoke still wrote Lada's anger across the sky above the crippled city. She and her men had camped brazenly close by, drunk on soot and revenge, secure in the knowledge that every man in the city was spent with the effort of saving what had not already been lost. They were also more than a little drunk on the cart full of wine that Matei had somehow managed to bring back.

It was there that Stefan slid in, silent and anonymous as a shadow. He, too, had been with Lada since the beginning. He had always been the best at gathering information: a blank and unremarkable face making him a half-forgotten memory even as he stood in front of someone. One day, Lada thought, the world would know she was deserving of an assassin such as him.

"What news from Tirgoviste?" she asked. Her throat was still raw from breathing in so much smoke, but her hoarseness did not disguise her excitement. "Did you kill the prince?"

"He was not there."

Lada scowled, hopes of announcing her rival's death to her men dashed. His death would not have meant the throne was hers—he had two heirs her own age, and she still needed the damnable boyars to support her claim as prince—but it would have been satisfying. "Then why have you returned?"

"Because he is in Edirne. At Mehmed's invitation."

Though Lada knew her internal fire should have blazed to white-hot fury at this information, she was filled instead with cold, bitter ashes. Her pride had not allowed her to ask Mehmed for help. But all this time she had held him tightly in her heart, knowing that somewhere out there, Mehmed and Radu still believed in her.

And now even that was taken from her.

3

January

MEHMED HAD NOT LEFT a letter in the potted plant where they exchanged messages. Radu always took the secret passage—the same one that Lada had run through the night of Ilyas and Lazar's betrayal. And Radu always wished that *this* time Mehmed would be waiting in the chamber where Radu and Lada had saved his life. But Mehmed was never there. Radu lived for the few brief sentences he spent in Mehmed's company. His eyes devoured the aggressive lines of Mehmed's script, lingering on the few curving flourishes. They never signed or addressed the messages. Radu would have liked to see his own name, just once, in Mehmed's hand.

But today, the dirt was as empty as Radu's life. Mehmed had to know that Radu knew about the Danesti prince. Radu had not been technically invited to that party—meeting Suleiman there had been a desperate, last-minute plan—but Mehmed had seen him. And so, rather than leaving his own message about the navy and then slipping away to wait until Mehmed decided to address the matter of Lada's fate, Radu sat. He hoped that . . .

Well, he no longer knew what to hope for. He sat, and waited.

As the sun set, Radu tried not to dwell on the horrors this room had held, but with Lada so firmly in his mind he could think of little else. He had been so certain she would take the Wallachian throne, he had not considered the possibility that she might fail. His sister did not fail. Was she even still alive? He could not imagine that Mehmed would withhold news of his sister's death.

But Mehmed *had* kept the knowledge of their father's and brother's deaths from Lada. Who was to say he was not doing the same with Radu? And if he was, what did that mean? That he was trying to protect Radu? Or that he was trying to keep him focused on their goals with Constantinople and feared what this news would do? Or that Mehmed cared so little that Lada was dead, he had not even found the time to pass along the information . . . ?

No. Radu could not believe the last one.

Unable to settle on any peaceful train of thought, Radu turned to the only solace in his life. He prayed, losing himself to the words and the motion. Whatever else was happening, had already happened, or would happen, he had God. He had prayer.

By the time he finished, a veil of peace had drifted over his harried mind. Drawing it tightly around himself, Radu opened the door and walked into the central hall of Mehmed's sprawling apartments. He could do nothing to change the past. He could only do what he felt best for the future. And to do that, he needed more information.

All the rooms were dark. Radu found a chair in the corner of Mehmed's bedchamber. He avoided looking at the bed, which threatened to tear his veil of peace.

Some time later, a girl around Radu's age came in and lit the lamps, then slid silently back out. Radu was so still she did not notice him.

Neither did Mehmed when he finally walked in. The same girl followed him. Radu would have been afraid of seeing something he had no wish to, but the girl wore the plain clothing of a servant, not the silks and scarves of a concubine or a wife. Mehmed held out his arms and she carefully took off his robes, one luxurious layer at a time. Radu knew he ought to look away.

He did not.

When Mehmed was down to his underclothes, the servant set his robes aside and slid a nightshirt painted with verses of the Koran over his head. Then, bowing, she backed out of the room. As soon as the door shut behind her, the sultan melted away. All the darkness and fear that had nestled in Radu's heart disappeared along with the sultan. There was Mehmed. *His* Mehmed, not the stranger who inhabited the throne.

Mehmed rubbed the back of his neck and sighed. Then he sat on the edge of the bed and unwound his voluminous turban. His hair was longer than Radu had ever seen it. Curling toward his shoulders, it was black in the dim light, though Radu knew it would shine with chestnut colors in the sun. Radu did not know what it would feel like to touch it, but he desperately wanted to.

"Is my sister dead?" Radu asked.

Mehmed stiffened, one hand going to his waist, where his dagger would normally be. Then he relaxed, shoulders sloping downward.

"You should not be here," he said, without turning.

"You should not be meeting with the Danesti Wallachian *prince* without telling me what happened."

Mehmed sighed, rubbing the back of his neck again. "She is not dead."

Unexpected tears pooled in Radu's eyes as he let out a sharp breath of relief—relief both that Lada was not dead and that his immediate reaction was not one of disappointment. He was not yet so evil, then, that he would begrudge his sister her life. Merely her place in Mehmed's affections.

"What happened? I thought you gave her the throne."

"I did. Apparently Wallachia disagreed with me."

"And yet you support her rival?"

Mehmed lifted his hands helplessly. He was still facing away from Radu. Radu yearned to see his face, his expression. But he could not cover the distance between them. After this long, he did not trust himself to be close to Mehmed.

"What can I do? You know I need all my borders secure. I cannot fight a war on two fronts. If we are to take Constantinople, we need peace everywhere else. Hungary looms as a threat, with Hunyadi harassing me at every opportunity. I cannot afford to lose any territory in Europe, and I cannot start a war there without risking a crusade. The Danesti prince accepted all my terms."

It made sense. It was a perfect explanation. And yet . . . Mehmed still would not look at him. "Is that all? Or do you keep Lada from the throne in the hopes that she will return here in her failure?" All Radu's frustration and loneliness of the past year climbed out his throat, lacing his words with accusation.

Mehmed laughed, darker than the night pressing against the

balcony. "Do you see her here? Have you heard from her even once? If she had asked for help, Radu, I would have sent it. I would have gone to war at one word from her. But *she* left *us*. She rejected us, and I will be damned if I follow without an invitation."

Again, the explanation made sense. But none of the information felt as though it should have been withheld like a secret. "How long have you known Lada was not on the throne?"

Mehmed grunted away the question with a noncommittal sound in his throat. "Does it matter?"

"It matters to me. She is my sister. Why would you keep information about her from me?"

Finally, *finally*, Mehmed turned to him. In the dim light of the lamp, his face was thrown into sharp relief, nose and cheekbones golden, lips teased into view and then tipped back into darkness. "Maybe I was afraid."

"Of what?"

"Afraid that if you knew she struggled, you would go to help her."

Radu laughed in shock. "What do you think I could do to help her?"

Mehmed tilted his head to one side, half his face in shadow, the other in light. "You are asking sincerely?"

Radu looked at the floor, intensely uncomfortable. He longed for an answer, and feared one. What if Mehmed could think of no reasons that didn't sound like anything more than empty words?

"I was always better with a bow and arrow." Radu smiled wryly.

"Lada does not need a perfectly aimed arrow. She needs a

perfectly aimed smile. Perfectly aimed words. Perfectly aimed manners."

Radu finally dared to look back up. "Her aim in those matters *has* always been off."

"And your aim never errs. Do not devalue what you can do merely because it is not what Lada excels at. You two are a balanced pair." Mehmed stared into the space between them, eyes no longer focused on Radu. "Or you were, at least."

In that moment Radu knew Mehmed was not seeing him but the absence of his sister. "Do not keep secrets from me," he said.

Mehmed refocused sharply on him. "What?"

"When you keep things secret, it gives them more power, more weight. I assumed the worst as soon as I discovered your deception. I was willing to risk our friendship being found out simply to talk with you. Be open with me in the future." Radu paused, knowing he had spoken to Mehmed as a friend and not as a sultan. In the past he would not have noticed. But now—now there was a distance. And he wondered if maybe the pretend distance had grown into something more. Frightened of this unknown element between them, he added a gentle "Please."

"And you are open with me in all things?" There was a note in Mehmed's voice, a subtle teasing lilt that terrified Radu in a different way. *Was Mehmed asking what it seemed like he was asking?*

"I— You know I work only for you, and—"

Mehmed dispelled the terror with one raised corner of his lips. "I know. And I was foolish to doubt your loyalties to our cause. But you cannot blame me for selfishly wanting to have you only to myself."

"No," Radu croaked, his mouth suddenly parched. "Of course not." But the words that wanted to leave his mouth were *"I am yours. Always."* He swallowed them painfully.

Mehmed shifted on the bed. "Do you have further plans for this evening?"

Radu's heart pounded so loudly he wondered if Mehmed heard it. "What? What do you mean?"

Mehmed gestured toward the door. "Any idea how you are going to sneak out without being seen?"

The sweat that had broken out on Radu's body turned cold and suffocating. He was a fool. "No."

"I will go out and make certain any guards follow me to the first antechamber. You should be able to slip into the passageway then." Mehmed stood, and Radu followed. Too close. He bumped into the other man.

Mehmed paused, then turned and clasped Radu's arms. "It is good to see you again, my friend."

"Yes," Radu whispered. And then Mehmed was gone.

———

A letter from Nazira waited for him on his desk. She wrote that she and Fatima would be staying in the city in the modest home Kumal kept there. And, she informed Radu, he would be joining them for regular meals.

Radu was both annoyed and pleased. She did not need to fuss over him, but it would be nice to have someone to talk with who expected nothing from him. If he imagined the perfect sister, Nazira would be close to what he would create for himself.

The guilt resurfaced. He had been able to dismiss thoughts of Lada because he assumed she had everything she wanted.

Now he knew otherwise. With a weary sigh, he pulled out a piece of parchment and a quill.

Beloved sister, he wrote. One of those words was true, at least.

Three days later, Radu walked toward an inn close to the palace, swinging his arms in time to his steps. A gathering of pashazadas—sons of pashas who were unimportant enough to still welcome him—had been talking about a foreign woman trying to be seen by the sultan. They joked she wanted to join his harem and had brought a cart full of cannons to make up for her homely face.

It was the cart that sparked Radu's curiosity. And his concern. If a foreign woman was in the city with weapons, trying to meet the sultan, Radu wanted to know why. The other men might dismiss her as crazy, but he knew firsthand that women could be every bit as violent as men.

Turning a corner, Radu ran right into a woman. He managed to catch her, but her bundle of parchments tumbled to the ground. She swore loudly and vehemently in Hungarian. It made Radu oddly homesick for his stuffy, stuttering tutor running through their lessons in the middle of a forest. And then he realized this had to be *her*. The foreign woman trying to meet Mehmed.

"Forgive me," Radu said, his Hungarian sliding into place despite years of neglect. He practiced his other languages—Latin, Greek, Arabic, anything that Mehmed had learned with Radu at his side—regularly, but Hungarian and Wallachian had not been on his tongue since Lada had left. "I was distracted."

The woman looked up, surprised. She was young, older

than him but only by a few years. She wore European-style clothing, sturdy skirts and blouses designed for travel. "You speak Hungarian?"

"Among other things." Radu handed her the parchments. Her fingers were blunt and blackened, her hands shiny with scars from old burns.

"I do not speak Turkish. Can you help me?" She said it crossly, more demanding than pleading. "No one in this damnable city will let me have a conference with the sultan."

Radu felt this wise of the damnable city. "Where are your servants? Your father?"

"I travel alone. And I am about to be kicked out of my inn for just that. I have nowhere to stay." She rubbed her forehead, scowling. "All this travel wasted."

"Are you trying to join the sultan's harem?"

Her look of murderous outrage was so sudden and severe it reminded him of Lada. He liked the woman more for it, and was also alarmed. Maybe she *was* here to kill Mehmed.

"I would sooner join his stables and let him ride on my back than join his harem and let him ride on my front."

Radu felt his cheeks burn and he cleared his throat. "Then what do you need?"

"I have a proposition for him. I went to Constantinople first, and they would not see me, either."

"You come from Constantinople?" If she was an assassin, she was a stupid one, admitting this up front.

She lifted one of the parchment rolls. "That ass of an emperor would not so much as let me show him my work. He laughed and said even if my claims were true, he could not afford me."

"Afford you for what?"

She finally smiled, showing all her fine teeth. "I can build a cannon big enough to destroy the walls of Babylon itself. I would have done it for the sultan, if he would have seen me. Now it appears I have to go home, every bit as disgraced as my father and mother said I would be." She shook her head bitterly and turned to walk away.

"Wait! What is your name?"

"Urbana. Of Transylvania."

"I am Radu. And I think we may be able to help each other." He took the bundle of parchments from her. "Go get your things, and I will introduce you to my wife."

Urbana raised an eyebrow. "I have no intention of joining *anyone's* harem."

Radu held back a laugh. It might have been misinterpreted as mean. "I assure you that is the last thing on my mind. I was born in Transylvania, and I know what it is to be a stranger in a new land. Allow me to help you as I would want someone to help my own sister."

"If you try anything unseemly, I am fully capable of blowing up your home."

This time Radu let himself laugh. "My sister would accept help in much the same spirit. Come, I will take you to my home. You are going to love my wife."

With Nazira's help, he would be able to determine whether Urbana could be trusted. If so, Radu had a creeping, joyful suspicion he was about to once again prove to Mehmed just how valuable he could be.

4

February

L ADA KNEW PUNISHING TRANSYLVANIA for everything that had gone wrong in the past year did not make
perfect strategic sense. But it felt better than anything else, and
so Transylvania burned.

Lada was not happy, but she was busy, and that was almost
the same.

"God's wounds," she whispered, trying to fasten binding
cloth tightly enough around her breasts so that they would not
chafe against her chain mail. It was difficult to dress herself in
the woods. But this arrangement was far preferable to the one
the governor of Brasov had proposed—*before* he sent an assassin
after her. After agreeing to see what men and funds he could
free up to support Lada's bid for the throne, he had suggested
she stay with him rather than going back "where no lady belongs."

She belonged with her men. Even if it *was* freezing. She
shivered behind the blanket she had hung to give herself some
privacy. She nearly had the binding cloth right, but her cold

fingers fumbled the knot. She threw the cloth to the ground and shrieked in rage.

"Lada?" Bogdan asked. He hovered on the other side of the blanket. "Do you need help?"

"Not from you! Leave me alone!" After a few more infuriating minutes, she finally had everything in place. She pulled on a tunic—clean, which was a novelty—and rejoined her men.

"You need help," Bogdan said, his voice low so no one would overhear.

"I do not need *help*.".

"You are a lady. You should not have to do these things for yourself."

Lada gave him a flat, angry stare. "Bogdan, when have I ever been a lady?"

He returned her angry look with a soft, shy smile. "You have always been a lady to me."

"Maybe you do not know me very well after all."

Bogdan put one rough hand out, holding it palm up to show the scar from when they had "married" as children. "I know you."

Before Lada could decide how to respond—or how to feel—Petru drew her attention.

The last caravan they robbed had been filled with fine clothing, pieces of which were strewn about their camp. Trousers hung from trees, shirts danced in the breeze. The bright colors on bare branches gave everything a festival air.

Petru wrestled with an intricately brocaded vest, struggling to get it across his shoulders. He spun in one direction and then the other. Nicolae watched, lips a single straight line but eyes dancing with mirth.

"That would fit better if it were designed for a man," Matei said as he walked by. Matei's purse was full now, but he still looked hungry.

Petru stopped spinning and ripped off the vest in horror. Nicolae burst into laughter. "You could have told me!" Petru said.

"But it set off the color of your eyes so nicely."

Petru glared murderously. Then he looked over at Lada and held the vest out. She raised a single eyebrow at the delicate colors and needlework. Muttering to himself, Petru threw the vest at Nicolae's head and walked away.

Lada wore a long tunic over trousers, all black except for a red sash tied at her waist. A thick black cloak, lined with glorious fur, kept her warmer than she had been in months. Her boots—finely tooled leather decorated with delicate patterns—were the only women's clothing she wore. She had grown accustomed to wearing her hair tied in cloth, but instead of Janissary white, she used black. Over that, she wore a fur cap.

They had all ceased wearing the Janissary caps and uniforms long ago. But some kept a few reminders of their lives as slaves: a sash here, a knife there. Bogdan used the white cloth from his cap to clean his weapons. Many of the men used theirs for much less savory cleaning.

"Has Stefan returned?"

Nicolae finished buttoning his vest, then drew his cloak closed. "Not yet. Must we wait for him before having any fun? We have plenty of men."

"Tonight is not a night for plenty. Tonight is a night for speed and secrecy."

Bogdan shifted closer to Lada. "I will come."

"Not you."

His face fell. Gritting her teeth, Lada continued, "I need to leave you in charge of the camp."

He shrugged and stomped away. She did not know if he stomped because he was angry, or simply because he was large. The truth was, she could not bring Bogdan tonight because he would object to what she had in mind. Nicolae might as well. Petru, she did not know. But Matei . . .

"Matei, just the two of us."

"What are you going to do?" Nicolae asked.

Lada sheathed her knives. One at either wrist, one at her right ankle. A large container of lamp oil hung from a strap slung over her shoulder. "I am going to visit the governor of Brasov."

"Is that really necessary?"

"He betrayed me. Why promise me aid and then try to have me killed? He must have been gathering information. And when he passed that information along, the return instruction was to eliminate me. Either he is working for Hungary or in league with the Danesti prince. I want to know which one. If it is the Danesti prince, we have nothing to fear. We already know he wants us dead. If it is the Hungarians, we have a new problem."

"How are you going to get to him? The city will be well guarded."

Lada met Matei's eyes. He nodded grimly. He would be up for the task. And Lada knew she was up for anything, always.

They slid through the night-black streets of the Wallachian section. It was a rambling warren of shacks pushed up to the very edge of the walls. Some of the homes were built against the wall itself, using the stones as an outer wall. A few times Lada and Matei heard patrols, but it was a simple matter of altering course to avoid detection.

The shacks built against the wall provided a benefit. Bracing against two homes within spitting distance of each other, they pushed their way to a roof. Matei boosted Lada up onto the wall itself. After a few tense breaths to make certain she was undetected, she lowered a rope so Matei could follow.

Within the walls of the inner city, even the air felt different. Cleaner. Wealthier. More privileged, with fewer desperate mouths pulling at it. But the scent of charred wood lurked beneath everything. It filled Lada with something like peace.

Lada knew exactly where to go, but it took two hours for them to make a journey of a dozen streets. They skirted the now-cold ruins of the homes that had burned, hiding in them when necessary. It was good that Lada had dressed in black, because the char would have ruined anything else.

Patrols tromped through the streets with aggravating consistency. Finally making it close to the governor's house did not simplify things, though. Three guards were stationed at the door, while others ringed the perimeter. Lada had counted on breaking in through a first-floor window, but that was not possible.

Matei waited in silence, but she could feel the question pulsing off him. *What now?*

Lada raised her eyes to the night sky to curse the stars, but the lines of the roofs caught her attention. The houses were built close together, elbowing each other for space. Sometimes the alleys between them were so narrow one had to turn sideways to make it through.

She did not need to break into the governor's house. She just needed to break into one of his less-protected neighbors' homes.

"How do you feel about churches?" she whispered.

Matei frowned at her in the dark.

"Did you notice how, in the countryside, all the churches are fortified? They provide shelter for everyone during an attack. But here in the heart of the city, the church is beautiful and cold. They do not let any of the Wallachians in to worship. I think we should warm up the church." She held out her container of oil. Understanding lit Matei's face as he took it from her.

He disappeared into the darkness. Though Lada had more men now, she always trusted her first few above all others. Matei would do the job. Nicolae and Bogdan might have balked at setting fire to a holy building, but how could something be holy if it was denied to Wallachians?

She slid from her shadowed nook and raced through an exposed alley. Four houses from the governor's was a three-story home with large windowsills, perfect for flower boxes in the spring.

Lada stepped onto a windowsill and pulled herself up to the second story, then the third. The roof had an awkward angle and jutted out too far for her to catch hold. Above her, tantalizingly out of reach, was a small attic window that would give her easy jumping access to the next roof.

The window in front of her was not sealed shut. One corner was lifted enough to slide a knife in. Lada worked it open, each tiny creak or protest of the wood making her certain she would be discovered. When it was wide enough, she pushed herself in feetfirst.

A girl sat in bed, staring directly at Lada. She could not be older than ten, her hair pinned beneath a cap, her nightshirt white.

"If you scream," Lada said, "I will murder your whole family in their sleep."

The girl was solemn—and silent—in her terror.

"Show me how to get into the attic."

The girl climbed out of bed, shivering, her small feet soundless on the wood floor. She eased open the bedroom door, looking both ways before gesturing for Lada to follow. At the end of the hallway was another door. Lada braced herself to face a foe, but the room was empty save for a jumble of old furniture and a ladder.

The girl pointed up.

Lada put one hand on the ladder, then paused. She turned back to the girl, who watched her in the same wide-eyed silence she had maintained since Lada first entered her bedroom.

Lada reached into her boot and pulled the small knife free. She turned it hilt out and bent down. "Next time someone comes into your room in the middle of the night, you should be prepared. Here."

The girl took the knife, staring at it like it was a puzzle. Then she gripped the hilt and nodded.

"Good. I am leaving now. Go back to sleep." Lada climbed up the ladder and eased open the trapdoor to the attic. The attic window, though, would not open. Cursing her luck, Lada grabbed a chair with a broken leg and smashed the window. She hoped Matei's work had begun in earnest, distracting anyone who might raise an alarm.

After pushing the jagged remnants of glass free, Lada climbed out and crouched on the sill. Beneath her the night waited, dizzying and dark. She jumped.

The roof slammed up to meet her faster than she had anticipated, and she nearly rolled off before she caught herself. Then she ran. Up and over the peak, gaining momentum before launching herself across the void yearning to claim her. Another roof. This one was angled the opposite way, and the roof after that was several feet higher. Lada ran along the peak, put on a burst of speed, and jumped.

Her hands found the edge of the next roof. Her legs dangled, her weight threatening to drag her down. Swinging from side to side, she hooked a knee onto the roof and pulled herself up.

One more.

This time she crept carefully across the tiles. Though the air was icy, her body itched with sweat. The governor's roof was higher than the one she was on, but it was not her goal. She prowled along the edge between the houses until she found what she was looking for—a window with a small ledge beneath it. She had planned on breaking in, but luck was finally on her side.

The casement window was flung wide, and a balding head leaned out, looking down toward the city center and the shouts echoing from that direction. There was a faint glow, and the distant sound of shattering glass.

For the eternal space between one breath and the next, Lada paused. He looked old and soft and vulnerable in his baggy nightshirt. He was a husband. A father. Then he cleared his throat with that same phlegmy rattle he had made while promising to help her and already planning to betray her.

Lada jumped the distance, slamming into the governor. They rolled together into the room. Lada recovered immediately and knelt on his chest, her knife to his throat.

"Who wanted me dead?"

He trembled, eyes crossing when they tried to focus on the knife.

She pressed her knife, drawing blood. The governor whimpered the words to a prayer.

"God is not here tonight," Lada said. "It is only you and me and my knife. Who wanted me dead?"

"The prince!" he said. "The prince of Wallachia."

"Why?"

"Because you are a threat."

Lada smiled. She knew that should not please her, but it did. The prince thought her a big enough threat to warrant an assassin. She still had a chance. Where there was fear, there was power.

She withdrew the knife and placed it next to the governor's head. He did not move. "A gift for the *prince*. Tell him I send my regards, and I will see him soon. And tell your god to make less flammable churches."

Lada slipped out the window, followed by the relieved sobs of the governor. She carried them with her like a gift as she ran across the rooftops, away from the center of Brasov and toward her men.

5

February

URBANA WAS A DECIDEDLY odd houseguest. In the week she had been living with Nazira and Fatima in Kumal's city house, she had not stopped talking.

"If she is a spy," Nazira said, sitting with an exhausted sigh next to Radu in the garden, "she is the worst spy that ever lived. How can she gain any information if she never lets anyone else talk?"

"What does she talk about?" Radu had made himself scarce at the house, wary of drawing too much attention before he was certain the risk was worthwhile.

"Her horrible cannons. Nothing else. She pulls sticks from the stove to draw diagrams—on the walls, Radu, the lovely white walls. And then she expects Fatima to wash them, because we have to pretend that Fatima is nothing but a servant."

"I am sorry." Radu knew it was asking much of the two women to let someone else into their private life.

Nazira waved a hand. "I do most of the cleaning after Urbana retires for the night. Fatima understands."

"So what do you think?"

"I think Urbana is insane, but she may also be a genius. I know nothing of cannons, but no one could fake what she is doing. And she is not lying when she says she will build them for anyone willing to fund her. She has been pursuing this her whole life, and rejected at every turn. Her only loyalty is to creating the most stunningly large and effective means of killing people the world has ever seen."

Radu tried to temper his excitement. "So you think I should move forward?"

"She is an incredible find. She may even prove invaluable."

Radu could not help his delighted smile. If Radu brought Mehmed something—someone—invaluable that he had found on his own? If Radu was the reason that Mehmed finally realized his dream of Constantinople?

Nazira put a hand on Radu's cheek. "Where are you right now?"

Radu shook his head. "Sorry."

"What about the navy? How is that progressing?"

"As well as can be hoped. Most of the galleys are built and Suleiman has found sailors to hire. I thought it would be difficult, but the men flocked to him. They foam at the mouth for the riches of Constantinople." Radu sighed. "I hear it among all the soldiers when Constantinople comes up. The golden apple at the center of the city, held by the statue of Justinian. The churches bricked in gold and decorated with jewels. They care nothing for our destiny to have the city, as declared by the Prophet, peace be upon him." Radu frowned. He also heard much darker talk that focused on the wealth and spoils to be found among citizens of the city. Right now it was spoken half in jest, as no one knew Mehmed meant to go for the city immediately. But it left a bad taste in Radu's mouth.

"But that is not why we have to take the city."

Radu had not really spoken with Nazira about Constantinople before. He was surprised that she had an opinion. "What do you mean?"

"People think it is prophesied because it will bring us wealth and fortune. But why would God care about that? I think the city will be ours because we need it to be. As long as Constantinople exists, it will draw crusades. More people who come into our land and kill us simply for being Muslim. I think Constantinople's fall will bring safety and protection. God will give us the city so we can worship in peace."

Radu closed his eyes, lifting his face to the sun. He had been so focused on *how* to help Mehmed take the city, he had stopped thinking about *why*. Nazira was right. This was not just for Mehmed; this was holy work. He would do it to help protect the faith that had given him so much.

"What is the timeline?" Nazira asked, pulling him back to the present.

"We are getting close. Everything is nearly in order. But Mehmed will not move until he is certain of all his borders. Hungary still troubles him. Hunyadi is a threat."

"And the Italians?"

Radu was glad he had opened up to Nazira. It was such a relief to discuss this openly with someone who understood all the pieces in play and who reminded him of what the actual purpose was. "They are too busy quarreling with each other to defend a city with as much history of animosity as Constantinople. Once we secure the waterways, they cannot send aid even if they decide to."

Nazira sighed. "I know it must be done, but I do not look forward to the day that will claim both my brother and my husband for their destinies at the walls of Constantinople. I fear the outcome."

Radu drew her close. "You know I will make certain you are taken care of. No matter what."

Nazira laughed sadly against his chest. "There you go again, assuming I am worried for myself. You never account for others loving you for *you*, Radu, rather than what you can do for them. It is my greatest prayer that someday you will know enough of love to recognize when it is freely given."

Radu had no answer. Sometimes Nazira offered *too much* insight. "I am going to speak with Urbana, then. Thank you." He kissed Nazira's hand.

As he walked inside, he passed Fatima. "Thank you for enduring this," he whispered. "Nazira is in the garden, and I will be occupying Urbana for the next few hours. Go spend some time with your wife."

She briefly met his gaze, a grateful smile shaping her kind face. "Good luck," she said.

———•———

"Your wife may be infertile," Urbana said as she and Radu sat down for a midafternoon meal.

Radu choked in surprise. "What?"

"You have been married more than a year. How often do you copulate?"

Radu raised his eyes to the ceiling, searching for answers

there as he felt his cheeks burning hotter than the furnaces of the foundry. "Are you also an expert in these matters?" he asked, trying for a teasing tone.

Urbana frowned. "No. But I wonder about the practicality of continuing on a course that is yielding no results. What about the maid?"

Radu panicked. Apparently they had underestimated Urbana's perceptiveness. "Fatima?" he asked, stalling. How would he explain this? What if she told someone?

"She is your servant. I am not unaware of customs here. If she bore you a son, he would be an acceptable heir. And it would be a nice thing for her, too. She would have legal status and you would not be able to sell her to someone else. I like Fatima. You should consider it."

Radu's voice came out strained, both with relief that Urbana did not realize the truth of his marriage and embarrassment that this was a conversation she thought appropriate. "I prefer to remain faithful to my wife."

"Is that why you have not tried to join my bed? I would have rebuffed you, violently if necessary, but it has puzzled me."

"I want to talk about your cannons!" Radu said, desperate to wrestle the topic away from babies and beds.

Urbana's face fell; then she brought her thick eyebrows together as though bracing for pain. "If you would just let me talk to your sultan, I can—"

"I want you to make them."

Her eyebrows lifted in surprise. "What?"

"I want you to make them. All of them. Your Babylon crusher, yes, but also every cannon you have time and dreams for. I want you to create the greatest artillery the world has ever seen."

Urbana's delight quickly shifted to tired disappointment. "I want that, too, but neither of us has a foundry or materials or the money to acquire them."

"Can you keep a secret?"

She licked her lips, pulling them thoughtfully between her teeth. "No, not really."

Radu laughed drily. Urbana might become invaluable, but not if he was unable to keep her hidden from Halil Vizier. Nothing could be easy in his life, apparently. He rubbed his forehead beneath his turban. "Well, that is a problem, then. Tell me, would it be possible to create these cannons without drawing a lot of attention?"

"Not with the amount of ore we will need. And we will need men—lots of men. I cannot do it alone. And I cannot do it just anywhere. That is why I came here—Edirne and Constantinople have the only foundries big enough for me to make my cannons in."

Radu had too many secrets. They were overflowing. And he did not know how he could build an artillery without being noticed. Besides which, the weight of secrets was wearing on him. He doubted everything now. Even Mehmed, which hurt. If Mehmed hid his dealings with the Wallachian prince, hid Lada's plight, what else might he be keeping from Radu?

Secrets gave everything more power, more potential for devastation and destruction.

Radu stood and walked to the window. Nazira and Fatima lay on a blanket in the garden, whispering and laughing. If he had seen them without knowing the truth of their relationship, he would have assumed they were very dear friends. No one questioned why Fatima was always with Nazira, why they were happy to live out in the countryside with no one else around.

They hid their love in plain sight.

"Urbana," Radu said, an idea forming that he liked the shape of, "how do you feel about parties?"

"I hate them," she said.

"What if I said that going to a lot of parties is the price you will have to pay to make your cannons?"

Her voice was flat but determined. "What should I wear?"

6

THE TREK BACK FROM interrogating the governor of Brasov was a frigid and lonely one. Lada looked for Matei on the way to camp. At every sound she whipped around, expecting to find him.

He did not appear.

She was nearly there, the fires in the distance promising rest and warmth, when a horse whinnied in the darkness to her right. She dropped into a crouch, cursing her generosity with the little girl that left her with only one knife out of the three she had brought. Why had she felt compelled to give the brat one?

The daughter of Wallachia wants her knife back.

She shuddered at the distant memory. Her father had given her a knife, and it had changed her life. She only hoped her own gift would change that little girl's life, because Lada might very well die for the gesture.

"Quiet, boys," a man whispered exaggeratedly, his voice carrying through the night. He spoke Hungarian. "We seem to have found a small predator. They are very dangerous when cornered."

Lada backed up against a tree so at least she could face whatever was coming. Her muscles were tight with the cold. She flexed her hands rapidly, trying to work some blood back into them.

She heard someone dismount. He made no attempt at hiding his footfalls as he approached. He sat close enough for Lada to see him, but too far for hand-to-hand combat. She would not throw her last knife. If she missed, she would be weaponless.

With a groan, he picked up a rock from beneath him and tossed it to the side.

"I have been looking for you, Ladislav Dragwlya. You are terrorizing the Transylvanians. It is in very poor taste."

Lada lifted her chin defiantly. "I owe them nothing."

"You were born here."

"And will I die here?"

The man laughed, pulling something from his vest. Lada tensed, but he leaned forward, striking flint until it caught on a pile of tinder. He fed the fire a few sticks pulled from the frozen forest floor. As the flames grew, the face of her enemy revealed itself. The face of the man who had driven her father from Tirgoviste and into the arms of the sultan, where he had abandoned his children. The face of the man who had returned to kill her father and her older brother.

Lada leaned back. She did not relax her grip on the knife, but it was an odd relief to have a connection to the man who would be her undoing. "Hunyadi."

His auburn hair gleamed as red as the fire. His forehead was broad, his eyebrows were strong, and his nose bore the evidence of multiple breakings. He did not seem to have grown older since Lada had last seen him in the throne room at Tirgoviste. He was around the same age her father would have been, if Hunyadi had not killed him. It was not fair that Hunyadi had remained unchanged when his actions had altered Lada in unimaginable ways.

Hunyadi dipped his head in acknowledgement. "What mischief have you been up to tonight?"

Lada saw no advantage to lying. "Arson. Threats of death. Gathering information."

Hunyadi sighed. "You have had a very full night. What did you burn?"

"The cathedral."

He coughed in surprise. "I paid for the new altar."

"It was a poor investment."

He snorted. "I suppose so. I was vaivode of Transylvania for a few years. I have never been so happy to be relieved of power. *Saxons.*" He shook his head, breath fogging the night in a silent laugh. Then he put an elbow on one knee, reclining to the side. "Tell me, what did burning the church give you?"

Lada touched her index finger to the point of her knife. "Distraction so I could accomplish my task. And satisfaction."

"Hmm. Somehow I doubt that anything here is going to satisfy you. I know you were sent for the Wallachian throne. Are you still in league with the sultan?"

Lada twirled her knife. "Does it look like I serve the Ottomans?"

"So you are not sending updates to him on where you are and what you are doing?"

Lada was glad the firelight covered her flush of humiliation. Write to Mehmed and admit her failures? Never. "No."

"He has been keeping track of you." Hunyadi held out a thin sheaf of parchment. It was crowded with spidery writing. One corner was blotted and darkened with a few large splashes of ink.

Lada squinted. Not ink. Blood.

"We found this on a wounded man following you. It is a letter to the sultan, detailing everything you are doing."

"Matei," Lada said. So that was why he had not caught up to her. He could not. She breathed something as close to a prayer of relief as she was capable of that she had left Bogdan behind. It surprised her, how glad she was that he was safe. She did not dwell on it. "What did you do with my man?"

"He fought. We killed him."

Lada nodded numbly. Matei was dead. Wounded in Brasov, finished by Hunyadi. And carrying a letter to Mehmed. How long had he been updating Mehmed on her? How much did Mehmed know? And whom should she be most angry with— Mehmed, for spying on her, Matei, for betraying her, or herself, for trusting Matei?

Or herself, for having so many miserable failures to write of?

Matei's betrayal cut deep, though. She had chosen Wallachians precisely because she assumed they would be as eager as she was to sever their Ottoman ties. But apparently Matei's hunger had extended beyond what Lada could provide. "I did not know he reported to Mehmed."

"I thought as much from the contents of the letter. So you are not working for the sultan. But you call him by his name. You know him, his temperament, his tactics."

This felt both dangerous and promising. "Better than any-one."

"In that case, I have another letter for you." Hunyadi dropped Matei's letter in the fire. Lada's fingers reflexively stretched toward it. She wanted to know how her life would read when being looked at by Mehmed. But it was too late.

Hunyadi reached into his vest and withdrew an envelope. He tossed it in front of Lada.

Puzzled, she picked it up. The seal was broken.

"We got this one off a Turk asking around for your where-abouts. It is from your brother." Hunyadi spoke as pleasantly as if they were discussing the weather over a meal. "He wonders how you fare, and fears for your safety. He even suggests re-turning to Edirne. He says they are having the most wonderful parties under Mehmed's rule."

Lada snorted. "He says that only because he knows nothing could keep me farther away than the promise of parties." Still, Lada tucked the letter into her shirt, against her heart. Beneath the necklace Radu had given her. Did he know everything, too? Were none of her humiliations private?

Hunyadi stood, holding out a gloved hand. He was close enough to strike. One quick thrust of her knife and she could avenge her father. And her older brother Mircea. Blood for her blood.

For his betrayal, Matei could go unavenged.

"Come," Hunyadi said. "I have an offer for you."

Lada's knife paused. Her father had died doing what he al-ways did—running—and she had never cared for Mircea any-way. She took Hunyadi's hand.

7

EVERYONE WHO MATTERED IN Edirne was around the massive table: valis, beys, pashas, viziers, and a smattering of their wives. Even a few daughters, hopeful of catching the eye of someone important. One such daughter had been trying to attract Radu's attention all evening. But he knew her father was already firmly in support of Mehmed, so there was no reason to be cruel and indulge her.

Salih, too, was here. Halil's second son. The only person Radu had ever kissed. But Salih had long since given up trying to speak to Radu. Radu could not even look at him without feeling a sick twist of guilt, and so he had gotten very good at letting his eyes pass over the other man's head.

They all reclined on pillows, a sumptuous spread laid out in front of them. Next to Radu, Urbana kept shifting, trying to get comfortable in her stiff European clothing. She stood out terribly, scowling and muttering to herself in Hungarian. If she caught anyone's eye, it was definitely not in a flirtatious way. She looked like she wanted to strangle someone. It made Radu miss Lada.

"Sit still," Radu whispered, looking toward the head of the table. He was seated far from where Mehmed lounged on a higher level than anyone else. A servant fanned the sultan, while behind him lingered the lonely stool attendant. And on the sultan's right, Halil Vizier.

Radu waited, anxious to the point of giddiness.

"What is this?" Urbana complained, dipping a finger in one of the cool, creamy sauces for the meat. "I am tired of these parties. Why do I have to be here when I could be working?"

Radu hushed her as Mehmed stood. "My friends," Mehmed said, extending his arms to take in the entire room, "this is a night for celebration! Tonight, I honor three of my greatest advisors. Their wisdom gives me strength. Their guidance builds my legacy. And tonight, I dedicate that legacy to the world. Zaganos Pasha. Sarica Pasha." He nodded at the two men to his immediate left, men Radu knew to be deeply loyal and committed to the cause of taking Constantinople. Kumal was gone, already on-site. "And my most important advisor, Halil Vizier."

Halil flushed a deep red, his expression that of a child who has gotten away with some feat of naughtiness. He bowed his head and put a hand over his heart.

"To honor you, my three wisest, I am building a fortress with a tower named for each of you. Your might will reach up to the very sky. Your wisdom will watch over our land forever. You three will be my towers of strength, my sentinels."

The three men bowed even deeper.

"For this honor, I would pay everything I own," Zaganos Pasha said.

Mehmed laughed brightly. "Well, that is good to hear,

because you will each be in charge of financing and constructing your tower. I would not trust your legacies with anyone else."

Halil Vizier looked slightly less pleased, but displeasure marred his visage only briefly. This was a tremendous honor, and further proof that his hold on Mehmed was tighter than ever. That Mehmed announced it in front of every important person in the empire doubtless did not escape Halil's notice. Halil nodded. "Of course, my sultan."

"Yours will be the most vital tower, and the largest." Mehmed took Halil's hand, squeezing it warmly. For him to touch another man was a gesture of the highest regard. Halil swept his eyes across the room, exulting in the moment.

Mehmed released Halil's hand and sat. His tone became less formal. "We begin construction immediately. The fortress will be called the Rumeli Hisari."

Halil's eyebrows drew together. "Rumeli Hisari. Like your grandfather's fortress on the Bosporus Strait, the Anadolu Hisari."

"Yes, precisely!" Mehmed gestured to a servant to refill his glass. "I have already moved the men into place, and the stones are being brought in as we speak. Kumal Pasha is there to direct construction."

"Where—" Halil wiped at his forehead, where sweat was beginning to bead beneath his turban. "Where will the Rumeli Hisari be built?"

Mehmed waved dismissively with the flatbread in his hand. "Across from the Anadolu Hisari."

"Across— But that is Constantinople's land."

Mehmed let out a burst of laughter. "It belongs to a few

scrappy goats. There is nothing there. Yet. But soon the foundation of a fortress honoring you will displace those goats! The fortresses will wink at each other from across the water of the Bosporus Strait. Their cannons could meet in the middle, I think." Mehmed laughed again. "We will have to try it out after your tower has been built."

This time, the deep flush on Halil's face was not one of pleasure. His mouth opened and closed as he struggled to find a way out of the trap Radu and Mehmed had set.

But it was too late. He had agreed to the fortress in front of everyone, had shown nothing but support. He had even agreed to pay for it. If he backed out now, he would have to say why. And he could not challenge Mehmed on Constantinople outright. He had no solid proof that Mehmed meant to attack, and he had to keep his own connections to Emperor Constantine secret.

Halil's options were dwindling, and would dwindle further when his allies in Constantine's court heard that a tower built on their land bore Halil's name.

Secrets made information more powerful and suspect. The best way to keep the fortress safe from Halil's machinations was to make him intimately—and inescapably—involved in its construction. It was the same method Radu was applying to the artillery, inspired by Nazira and Fatima's relationship. Hiding in plain sight.

"What is so funny?" Urbana said, scowling. "I did not understand any of that. Why are you smiling?"

"Because I am pleased with tonight's events."

She sighed, picking at the bones of the unfortunate fowl on

her plate. "I still do not understand why I have to be here. We never even speak to the sultan."

"You are here so that everyone sees you are my special project. I want the whole city gossiping about how foolish I am, hiring a woman to make the largest cannon in the world to try to impress the sultan. I intend to subject us both to ridicule."

Her scowl deepened. "Why would you do that?"

"So that no one pays any attention until we succeed."

For the first time that night, Urbana smiled. She snapped a bone off the chicken.

Radu nudged her with his elbow. "Imagine how surprised they will be when the sultan has the most advanced artillery in the world, built by a woman and the most handsome and useless foreigner in the empire." He stood. "Come. I need to introduce you to everyone, and tell them how we are designing a cannon so big it could puncture a hole in the bottom of the Black Sea and drain it dry."

Urbana grimaced but nodded. "Lead on."

———— · ————

Later that week, Radu pulled aside the tapestry to leave his update on Urbana's progress and the navy's readiness. He was so shocked to find Mehmed sitting in the room that he barely stifled a cry.

"Radu." Mehmed grinned. "You are very late."

"I— What is wrong?"

"Nothing. I have something for you." Mehmed held out a letter.

It was addressed to Radu in a hand like someone had taken

a blade and dipped it in ink. The part of his heart that was permanently vacant hurt as it beat again. He turned the parchment over to find it had been sealed by a knife tip pressed into wax.

"Lada," he whispered, running his fingers over the red seal.

"It arrived this morning." Mehmed's voice was carefully neutral. "Did you write her?"

"Yes, after I found out she was not on the throne. I had given up hope that the messenger would ever find her."

Radu would have preferred to read privately, but he could not bear to leave this gift of time with Mehmed. But the way Mehmed's eyes were fixed on the letter, like a starving man on a circle of bread, hurt. All this time they had spent apart, all these times he had never been waiting for Radu.

Mehmed was here only for Lada.

He was still in love with her. They never spoke of her, but it was inescapable. Perhaps, since she left before Mehmed could claim her, he would long for her forever. The same way he was fixated on Constantinople, simply because it was not his but he felt it should be.

According to Islam, though, Mehmed could not consummate his relationship with Lada. It was forbidden outside of marriage or official concubines. Lada had been inside Mehmed's harem, though, which legally made her part of it.

There was always a way forward for Mehmed and Lada.

Radu hung his head. What did he hope his future would be? To stand forever at Mehmed's side, beloved friend, trusted advisor? He had told Nazira it would be enough. It would never be enough.

Mehmed put a hand on Radu's shoulder. The jolt of the

touch went so much deeper than the light pressure of his fingers. "Are you well, my friend?"

Radu cleared his throat, nodding. He tore open the letter with more force than was needed. It was addressed, in typically sentimental style, to *My only brother, Radu.* It had been more honest than his greeting to her.

"What does she say?" Mehmed asked, perfectly still. He may as well have been bounding around the room, for all his stillness hid his anxiety.

Radu read aloud, his voice flat from the exhaustion of his emotions.

"I was surprised to receive your letter. I am sorry to report that the messenger you sent is dead. I did not kill him. I suppose, in a way, you did, for sending him here."

Radu paused, narrowing his eyes in annoyance both at Lada's words and at the fact that she might have a point. Had he sacrificed a life simply to send a letter to his sister?

"She teases you," Mehmed said. "I am sure the messenger is fine. Go on."

"In turn, I will surprise you by telling you I am with Hunyadi. He found me in Transylvania and we declined to murder each other. I wondered if I was being disloyal to our father and brother, but they are dead and so cannot complain. He invited my company to join his.

"I do not know his motives, but I accepted. I will finally have an ally worth something. If I can convince Hunyadi to support me, I can take the throne. I know it. But after that, I do not have the skill for nobility. I am a blunt weapon. I need a surgeon.

"I am tired of being the right hand to powerful men. I want you as my right hand. I have seen you move among nobility as easily as a hawk cuts

through the air. Cut through the boyars for me. Come home, Radu. Help me. Wallachia belongs to us, and I will not be complete without you."

Radu paused, shocked. "And then she signs her name." He did not say how she signed it.

Lada, on the ice and in need of your hand this time.

With one line she had dragged him back to his helpless childhood, when he had needed rescuing after going out too far on the ice. And—he could not quite believe it—she was asking him for help.

She recognized that he was good at something she was not. Mehmed had been right. Lada needed him to secure her path to power. For a few silent, painful moments, he considered it. She was his sister. She had never asked him for anything. She had expected him to come along initially, because she thought he should, not because she wanted him to.

Now, though . . .

"Will you go to her?"

Radu looked up, surprised. Mehmed's voice was as quiet as his own had been, as carefully devoid of emotion. But Radu knew his friend's face better than anything on earth. He had studied it, worshipped it. And Mehmed could not hide his fear and anguish.

It was balm to Radu's soul, such a tremendous relief that Radu let out a shaky laugh. Lada was not the only Dracul who mattered to Mehmed.

"No. No, of course not."

Mehmed's shoulders relaxed, the tension draining from his face. He again put a hand on Radu's shoulder, then took the letter from him.

And Radu was happy, standing there with his friend. Because as much as it meant to be valued by his weapon of a sister, it was not where he belonged. She wanted him to achieve *her* goals. But, as always, she discounted his feelings. He had worked too long and hard here to abandon it all in pursuit of her dream. It had never been his dream.

Lada would be hurt by his decision. The thought made him feel oddly powerful. He hated that about himself, but he could not avoid it. Lada wanted him, *and* Mehmed wanted him. He would choose Mehmed. He could not do anything else.

Mehmed tapped his finger against the page. "It is very interesting that she is in Hunyadi's inner circle. After everything he did to your father and brother."

Radu was surprised, too. But it made a sort of sense. "Lada only holds grudges that are useful to her. In a way, our father's death freed her. She might even be grateful to Hunyadi. Regardless, if she can learn from him and use him to gain power, she will forgive him anything."

"Hmm," Mehmed said. His finger traced Hunyadi's name.

Radu wanted the letter back. He wanted to read again how he could do things his strong, vicious sister never could. He wanted to hold the letter and remember the fear on Mehmed's face when he thought Radu would choose to leave. That fear was enough to give Radu hope.

He might have his own dream yet.

8

February

A WEEK INTO LADA'S TRAVELS with the Hungarians, Hunyadi rode along the edge of camp where her men had set up. He shouted a command in Hungarian to pack up. No one responded. He looked to Lada.

They had not spoken much, and Lada was beginning to question her rashness in sending Bogdan to find someone to carry a letter to Radu. Maybe she had written too soon of Hunyadi as her ally. And if anything happened to Bogdan, she would never forgive herself. He was the one piece of her childhood she had managed to hold on to. She could not bear to lose him, too.

The absence of Bogdan reminded Lada of the absence of the other two men who mattered most to her. But soon Radu would receive her letter and join them. The other man she chose not to dwell on.

Hunyadi shouted the order again. "Why do your men not obey?" he asked.

Lada raised an eyebrow. "They do not speak Hungarian."

He shouted the same command in Turkish. As one, the men looked at him. No one moved.

Lada narrowed her eyes. "And they do not answer to Turkish."

Hunyadi frowned, tugging at his beard. "Then how do I command them?"

"You do not. I do." In Wallachian, she commanded her men to pack up. Immediately they sprang into efficient, well-practiced action. Hunyadi watched, his expression thoughtful. Lada rode with more cheer after that. She would prove herself to him yet.

Later that day, Hunyadi found Lada riding next to Stefan and Nicolae near the back of the company. Stefan veered his horse away, giving Hunyadi space.

"Your men are very disciplined," Hunyadi said, scratching his beard. He toyed with it constantly. Lada wondered if it was because as a young man he had not been allowed a beard. He had fought long and hard to move from being the son of peasant farmers to one of the strongest leaders on the borders of the Ottoman Empire. She supposed he had every right to be amused by and affectionate toward his beard.

Or perhaps beards were just itchy.

"We were well trained," Lada answered in Wallachian.

Hunyadi responded in the same language. "I always prefer fighting spahis to Janissaries. Janissaries are so much fiercer."

Nicolae smiled wryly. "That is one of the benefits of a slave force that can have neither possessions nor families. It is easy to be fearless when you have nothing to lose."

Hunyadi grunted. Pointing to Nicolae's prominent scar, he

asked, "Where did you get that?" His Wallachian accent was so bad that it hurt Lada to hear him speak.

Nicolae's smile broadened, stretching his scar tight and white. "At Varna. From a Hungarian. Right before we killed your king."

Lada's hands went to her wrists, ready to defend Nicolae. To her surprise, Hunyadi laughed. "Oh, Varna. That was a disaster." He shifted back into Hungarian. "Set me back a few years. We still have not recovered from the loss of our king. Our new one, Ladislas Posthumous, is not exactly ideal." His expression grew faraway and thoughtful. "He could be replaced."

Lada pounced on his tone before she could think better of it. "You?" Hunyadi had been a prince of Transylvania. He was beloved by his people, and a fearsome military force. If he were king—and her ally—

The path to the throne of Wallachia opened before her, bathed in golden light.

Until Hunyadi laughed, puncturing her hopes and bringing darkness crashing back down. "Me, king? No. I have tried a throne. It turns out I am not fond of sitting, no matter what the seat may be."

Lada slouched moodily in her saddle. Hunyadi would still be a strong ally. But a king was better. "Your people would be fortunate to have such a man as their king."

Hunyadi clapped a hand on her shoulder. "I am a soldier. I am not made for politics and courts. My son Matthias, on the other hand, has been raised in them. He will go far, and do greater things than I ever could." Hunyadi beamed. "He is my greatest triumph. And he is very handsome."

Lada frowned, unsure what that had to do with Matthias's merits. She had seen, though, how many doors opened for Radu because of his face. "I am sure that will be useful to him."

"He needs a strong wife. Someone who can temper his . . . extravagances. Help steer him."

"He will need a good alliance." If Matthias wanted to continue to rise within the Hungarian courts, he would have to bring some sort of power with him. Hunyadi had no family name, no history. He had land and wealth, yes, but they were new. And newness was not something to be proud of in the world of nobility.

Hunyadi patted her shoulder again. "I am less concerned with alliances. Those come and go. But strength of character—that cannot be valued enough."

Hunyadi rode away, with Lada staring at his back in confusion.

"Does he want me to find his son a wife?" she asked, turning to Stefan, who had been leaning over to Nicolae and whispering. Stefan pretended not to speak Hungarian, but he understood it.

Nicolae's face was purpling from the effort of holding something back. Finally, it escaped in a strangled, airy laugh. "Lada, my darling dragon, he wants you to *be* his son's wife."

"The devil take him," she snapped. Anger and humiliation washed through her. All this time Hunyadi had been viewing her as merely a womb. How could she make the world see her as she saw herself? "And the devil take his son, too." She rubbed her forehead wearily. No wonder he had tried to command her men. He probably already viewed them as his own, some sort of dowry. "Where exactly are we?"

Nicolae pulled closer to her. "Near Bulgaria."

Staring bleakly at the winter-dead trees around them, Lada did not know what to do. Kill Hunyadi and move on? Marry his son for a chance at the Hungarian throne? Would that bring her closer to Wallachia, or take her even further away? It was the same choice she had faced before, the only choice ever given to her: take what little power you can through a man.

If she had known this would be her fate, over and over, she would have stayed with Mehmed. At least with him she had that spark, that burning. If Matthias was as smart and handsome as his father said, he would have no use for a wife such as her. And she did not want to be a wife.

Never a wife.

She had left behind love and ridden off to a future devoid of power. "I have nothing," she whispered.

Nicolae nudged his horse even closer to hers, until their legs brushed. "You still have us," he said, his voice soft with understanding. "We will figure something out."

Lada nodded, trying not to let her despair show. How much longer could she hope to keep Nicolae? Stefan? Petru and the rest of her men? Would they choose to stay loyal to her over someone with a reputation and power like Hunyadi's? Not if they remained with him for much longer.

"We break from Hunyadi at the first opportunity." She did not know how he would react, but he had more men than she did. She would not risk their lives against him. Until the right opportunity came up, she would grit her teeth and dodge all talk of marriage.

At camp two days later, Hunyadi huddled with three of his men. Though Lada had been avoiding him, the intensity of the men's conversation hinted at something new. It might be an opportunity for her men to make an exit. Or it might mean she was in trouble.

Lada marched over and shouldered her way in. "What is happening?"

Hunyadi looked up, surprised. "There is an armed force of Bulgars coming our way. They are in a canyon. If we let them get out, they can spread and form ranks. Our best option is to ride and meet them."

"But you do not have enough time to plan."

"Attack is my favorite form of defense."

Lada let the phrase turn over in her mind. It reminded her of something. Tohin—the Ottoman woman who had taught her how to use gunpowder in combat. She had spoken of the need to constantly be on the attack so that other countries did not invade Ottoman lands. Push out so no one can push in. *A dealer of death*, that was what Tohin had said one must become. Deal enough death elsewhere to keep it away from your own home.

"What kind of force?" Lada asked.

One of Hunyadi's men let out a dismissive huff of air at Lada's inclusion in the conversation, but Hunyadi answered. "Mounted, heavily armored."

Hunyadi had some armored men who could meet such a force head-on. But Lada's men wore light mail, unsuited to direct combat. Hunyadi must have followed her thoughts. "This is not a battle for your Janissaries. I will keep them in the rear."

Lada bristled. She knew her men were worth twice

Hunyadi's. He would know that, too, were he not so focused on her as a marriage prospect. But she bit her tongue before she could argue. If Hunyadi was engaged in a canyon, and her men were in the rear, it was as good an opportunity as any to flee.

She sighed, feeling these new threads to the throne snap one by one. She was left, as always, with her only thread of power: herself.

They rode fast through flat, open farmland until they came to the threat. Canyon walls rose before them, a narrow gash through a leagues-long line of rocky, steep hills—the only easy passage for mounted troops.

Lada saw immediately why Hunyadi needed to stop the Bulgars before they exited the canyon. Once through, they had a straight shot to anywhere in Hungary they wanted.

Shouts drifted to Lada on the sharp breeze. Hunyadi was riding his horse back and forth in front of his men. A scout appeared, his horse heaving and frothing. Lada saw Hunyadi's shoulders tense as he listened to the report. He said something, then pointed at her. The scout nodded.

Raising a fist, Hunyadi roared. His men roared in response and charged after him into the canyon.

Had he told the scout to make certain she did not leave? Lada smiled grimly. She would welcome that. She rode to meet the scout. He trembled atop his trembling horse.

"What is it?" she demanded.

"Hunyadi asks that you watch. If Bulgars begin to come through, ride hard for the nearest village and get the people out." He pointed to the east, where Lada could see hearth smoke lazily marking the village's location.

"Does he expect the Bulgars to break through?"

The man shrugged wearily. "More men than we thought. Too many."

"Why did he go in, then?"

"If they get through, they will burn the village and take all the winter stores. The people will starve."

Lada frowned. "But it is one village."

The man smiled bleakly. "It is *his* village, though. He grew up there."

Lada rode her horse slowly back to her men, the information nagging at her. They could leave. No one could stop them. But Hunyadi could have left, too. Regrouped elsewhere. Let one small village fall.

"Damn his honor," Lada grumbled, staring back into the canyon. Hunyadi's forces had already disappeared around a bend. It would not be long before they met the enemy. Both would be trapped and constricted by the canyon. It would be a slaughter on both sides.

It was not her problem.

But her eyes went to the rim of the canyon. It would be impassable for heavily armored mounted soldiers. But that did not mean it was impassable for everyone.

She needed an ally. She needed more threads of power. And if she could prove to Hunyadi what she was capable of, then maybe she would have them. She could run—again—or seize this chance.

Lada jumped off her horse and grabbed her weapons. "Dismount! Take everything you can easily carry. Nicolae, take men up the other side in case this one is impassable."

"What are we doing?" Petru asked, already following her lead.

"We are going to take a look."

They ran up the hill, scrambling between trees and boulders. Everyone found a different path and fanned out. Lada led the way, running and sliding and climbing. It was not easy going, but they made good time. The sound of men and horses screaming drew them closer to their goal.

Finally, scraped and sweating, they reached the rim of the canyon immediately above the fighting. Both sides had bottlenecked, leaving only a few men in front to fight. When those men died, the next went at it. Lada looked down the Bulgar line. It stretched too far. They could push harder and longer.

Hunyadi was not far beyond the front line. Everyone there would die. He had to know that—had to have known it going in.

But he had left Lada's men behind. If she had been in charge, she would have sacrificed someone else's men to wear down the other side. Instead, he had kept them out of the battle with a charge to protect the village if his efforts failed.

Hunyadi had killed her father and brother. Before that, he had been the reason her father ransomed her to the Ottomans. And he had invited her to join his troops with only a marriage in mind. She had every reason to let him die, even if she was grateful he had protected her men. But Wallachia called to her, and she had to answer. How could she win this for him?

"They will all be killed," Petru said, frowning.

Lada and her men were too high up for accuracy with arrows and bolts. And the Bulgars wore heavy armor. They would waste all their ammunition with very little effect.

But . . .

"Have you ever heard the story of David and Goliath?" Lada remembered that one. She only really cared for the old stories, the ones about battles and lions and armies. She had no use for Jesus with his parables and healing. She liked the wrathful god, the god of vengeance and war. She picked up a large stone, tossing it in the air a few times.

Lada looked across the canyon at Nicolae. She hefted the rock, then pointed at the rear of the Bulgar line. There was an area of the hill that spoke of years of rockslides—no trees, dirt recently churned up—and at the canyon's rim a collection of boulders waited patiently for time and the elements to free them.

Lada mimed pushing, then let the rock fall from her hands. Nicolae looked at the boulders. He waved an arm, then ran with Stefan and several men toward the boulders.

Lada waited, Petru crouching next to her. The sound of the battle beneath them was terrible. She had never seen one this big, this close. She watched, fascinated. It was not what she had expected. Her only experience with hand-to-hand combat had been with assassins or in practice. She saw how Hunyadi directed his men, how even from the ground he acted as though he had an aerial view.

She also saw how, in spite of his intelligence, he would lose. He had chosen honor instead of practicality. He should have sacrificed her men to slow the Bulgars, then regrouped elsewhere, ignoring the threat to his village.

But he had not counted on her.

A clatter that shifted to a rumble snapped Lada's attention back to Nicolae's work. The boulders crashed down, accompanied by a huge plume of dust. The fallen boulders were not enough to fully block the canyon, but they were enough to make it impossible to get more than one man at a time back the way they had come.

Hunyadi looked up. Catching sight of Lada, he shouted something, gesturing angrily toward the rocks. Lada laughed, knowing what it looked like. They had just guaranteed that the Bulgars could only go forward, into Hunyadi.

Lada picked up a rock, so heavy she had to use both arms. Then, with a loud whoop, she threw it.

The rock sailed downward, landing with a metallic *thunk* on the helmeted head of a soldier in the middle of the Bulgar ranks. He slumped in his saddle, then slid to the ground.

On either side of the canyon, Lada's men set to work. There was no shortage of rocks. The Bulgars were packed in so tightly that there was no need to aim. Throw a rock, hit something. It was as simple as that.

The Bulgars started to panic, trying to shift out of the way, but there was nowhere to go. Their horses screamed. Soldiers dismounted and tried to climb up the sides of the canyon. They were met with rocks. A few kept their wits and pulled out crossbows, but the distance was too great and Lada's men had too much cover.

The Bulgars in front made a desperate push, but Hunyadi had grasped that his role was to block them. He set up a firm line impervious to the chaotic attacks of the Bulgars, and then waited.

By evening, Lada's arms screamed with weariness as she tossed a last rock down. Then, exhausted, she sat. Nicolae and her men on the other side of the canyon followed suit. There were so few Bulgars left, it would be easy for Hunyadi's men to pick them off with crossbow bolts. It looked as though a careless god had passed through, tossing bodies aside like refuse. Men and horses clogged the path, broken and tangled together.

When Lada and her men stumbled down from the hills, they were greeted with roaring fires and waiting food. Hunyadi's men cheered, welcoming them with open arms. Hunyadi pushed through to Lada. He picked her up and spun her in a circle. "That was brilliant!" he shouted, laughing.

She waited until he put her down. Then she met his gaze with an unsmiling and unflinching one of her own. "Yes," she said. "It was. You are no king, and I am no wife. I am a leader and a ruler, and I want your support."

Hunyadi nodded solemnly, his fingers once again disappearing into his beard. "You have much value outside of marriage." He did not say it jokingly or dismissively. Lada could see in his eyes that he considered her differently now.

She stood a little straighter. She had done something good. She had secured an ally through her own merits. And she would use him however she could to destroy her enemies.

9

March

IT WAS A FESTIVE day in the port city of Bursa.
Ribbons adorned everything, whipping gaily in the perpetual wind that blew from the Sea of Marmara and through the streets. Children laughed, darting through the press of people. Vendors called out their goods—mostly food, and most of that fish—over the noise of the crowds.

Radu let the crowd pull them along. Nazira pointed out a young girl carrying a screaming toddler nearly as big as herself. The toddler managed to wriggle out of her arms. The little girl grabbed his wrist and dragged him on determinedly.

"Does that make you miss your sister?" Nazira asked.

Radu shook his head. "Lada would never have been so tender."

"I wish I had gotten to know her better."

"No, you do not."

Nazira stopped, looking into Radu's eyes. "Yes, I do. Because she is important to you, and you are important to me, so she is important to me."

Radu shifted away from acknowledging Lada's importance

to him. He tried not to think about it, or whether he was actually important to her. He had made his choice. Again. "You would not like her. And she would not like you."

Nazira sniffed, lifting her nose haughtily. "*Everyone* likes me. Just because you could not make your terror of a sister be civil does not mean I would have fared so poorly. I am the sweetest person alive. Or have you not heard?"

Radu laughed, taking her hand and rushing through a brief opening in the square. "I have heard, and received ample evidence to support the rumor."

After a few stops for Nazira to purchase ribbons for waving, they reached the docks. It took some time to find a spot to stand, but people tended to make way once they noticed Radu and Nazira's fine clothing. Radu still dressed the part of a frivolous member of the court, with bright robes and as much jewelry as he owned. Nazira wore her status with the easy grace of one born to it.

The day was brilliantly sunny, the warmth cut through by the wind. Light reflected off the churning water, and small waves slapped at the dock they stood on.

Out on the water were Radu's ships. Well, the empire's ships. But Radu felt a flush of pride looking at them. He had visited the construction docks under the pretense of going to his country estate with Nazira. Suleiman was ambitious but practical. Under his hand, everything went according to schedule. And now, before them, were the fruits of their labors.

It was a glorious sight to behold.

Nazira pointed out the different types. "Three of the big ones! What are they called?"

"Galleys. The largest ships the empire has ever owned, all brand-new."

"And those five medium ones?"

"Also galleys. Three are older, two are new."

Nazira sniffed in disappointment. "They should really be cleverer with naming than that. Big galleys and medium galleys. What about the smaller ones moving between them?"

Radu laughed. "You are going to be disappointed."

"Galleys?"

"Yes."

She scowled crossly. "I should have been consulted. Still, it is amazing! Look at them all! How can the water hold that much weight? Oh! They are moving."

Sails unfurled. Though the ships were too far out for Radu to see their decks, he knew the sailors would be scrambling to tie things off and adjust the sails to capture the wind. There would be even more men on benches manning the long, heavy oars for navigating rivers.

The boats danced on the water, cutting through the waves or skimming on top of them, depending on their size. Every time a boat maneuvered particularly well, the crowd cheered. After a few minutes, all the galleys lined up near the shore and stopped there, close enough for the onlookers to see the flurry of on-deck activity. And then the cannons fired across the water, away from the bank.

Though the ships could not bear the load of too much heavy artillery, the sound was terrible and impressive. Babies and children cried in fear and surprise. Everyone else clapped and waved their ribbons in the air. Never before had the Ottomans had such a navy. Never before had any of them seen such a demonstration.

Radu smiled, because he knew the truth: this was only half of their fleet. The other half was hidden in a boatyard on a little-used section of one of the tributary rivers.

"There he is." Nazira's quiet voice broke through the noise. Radu turned to see Mehmed, standing on a balcony. He wore deepest purple, with a red turban and a blindingly white cape. Nazira and Radu were not the only ones to notice him. Much of the crowd turned to cheer and wave their ribbons at him. Radu was too far away to be sure, but he thought Mehmed smiled.

Radu pretended that the smile was for him, and joined the cheering.

———— ✦ ————

"We should take more holidays together," Nazira said, leaning back in their carriage. "Fatima does not like to go to new places. It was all I could do to persuade her to stay in Edirne for this long. She loves familiar things, routine." Nazira smiled fondly. "She has settled in nicely there, though. As long as she does not have to go out among crowds."

"I did not know she had such a hard time with them." Radu watched the countryside pass by. He tried to hold on to the happy pride of seeing his work dance on the water. But the same scene kept playing out in his mind. Instead of being on the dock with Nazira, he had been on the balcony, at Mehmed's side. As Mehmed watched the triumph of Radu's planning, he shifted closer and closer. And then their hands, at their sides, brushed.

Instead of pulling away, Mehmed's fingers linked with Radu's, and they stood like that, watching the ships, together.

"Yes," Nazira said, puncturing Radu's fantasy. Which was just as well. It was poisonous, dwelling on such things. "Fatima does not— You see, when she was very young, she—" She paused, frowning. "I do not think it is my story to tell."

"I understand." He took Nazira's hand, which felt nothing like Mehmed's had in his imagination. "I wonder if anyone gets through childhood without being broken. I certainly did not."

"Oh, I had a wonderful childhood! Our parents died when I was too young to understand it. Kumal made certain that my life was filled with love and joy. And then, when I discovered Fatima shared my feelings, I had even more love and joy. And then, when you married me, even more. I sometimes think I am the most blessed woman in all of creation. I pray God gives me an opportunity to repay all the kindness He has shown me."

They had entered the city. The buildings rose around them like guests at a party—familiar, all of them, but hiding so much.

Radu squeezed Nazira's hand. "You have nothing to repay. Your life is filled with the goodness you attract because of your own goodness."

Nazira laughed, then grew solemn. "I do wish to do more, though. *Be* more. Maybe, someday . . ." She looked down, blushing, holding her stomach.

"Are you feeling ill? We have been in the carriage too long." They had left Bursa earlier than anticipated. They were back in the city a full day before planned. He was heading straight for the foundry to check in on Urbana.

She looked up, blinking rapidly. "Ill? No. No, I am well. Radu, I wondered . . ." She paused, sucking in her round lips. "Would you join us for a meal, a special family meal, next week?"

The carriage stopped in front of the narrow street leading to the foundry. Radu gave Nazira a quick kiss on the cheek. "Of course. Give my love to Fatima."

"And give mine to Urbana?"

Radu laughed. "Urbana would not care in the slightest for your love, unless it came with extra supplies of bronze, or a new furnace."

Though Radu did not like the intense heat of the foundry, he visited as often as he could. And it was a good thing he had come back when he did. Urbana was screaming in Hungarian at several confused workers. Radu jumped in as translator, though he left out most of what she said. He did not think telling the workers that they were "more useless than the rotting carcasses of a thousand dead dogs" would help morale.

Later that afternoon, he leaned against the entrance and watched a small caravan approach. Urbana had told him they were expecting a delivery, but Radu did not anticipate the grizzled woman who showed up with the gunpowder.

She climbed down from her cart, her back arched like a crescent moon. Radu moved to help her, but she waved him away. "I can manage, you young fool."

A bit stung by her dismissiveness—older women usually loved him—he directed two men to begin unloading the barrels of gunpowder. The woman watched warily. Another cart pulled up behind hers. A man jumped out to aid the unloading process.

"How many, Mother?" he called.

"All of it." She shook her head. "That ass cannot keep a number greater than three in his head."

Radu frowned at her lack of maternal softness. She turned her critical eye on him, taking in his robes. He had taken to wearing jewel tones lately, bright and bold colors to combat how he felt on the inside.

"Who put you in charge of so much gunpowder?" she asked.

Radu tried on his best smile, but it slid off his face. It would make no difference with this woman. "We are building the largest cannon in the world. It could take down the walls of Babylon itself."

The woman snorted. "Nothing quite so useful as an imaginary cannon to defeat a city that no longer exists. I can see all my work and travel has been useless. One of these days I will be asked to do another stupid thing, and I will finally hit my limit on idiocy. I have a husband and three sons, so my limit is very high, but even I cannot bear all things. And on that day, there will be an explosion to take down the walls of every *actual* city in the world."

Radu shifted on his feet, wishing the men would hurry up so this horrible woman would leave.

"You are not Turkish," she said.

Radu shook his head. "Wallachian."

She nodded, toying with several long white hairs on her

chin. "Not a lot of Wallachians in the empire. Too stupid to be useful. But I met a good Wallachian a few years ago. Made an impression on me. I never forgot her."

With a shock like a cannon burst, Radu tuned in to the woman's words. "'Her'?"

"Mean little bitch." The woman smiled with tenderness, an emotion that looked out of place on her. "Clever as anyone. It was out in— Where was it? I forget."

"Amasya," Radu said softly.

"That was it. You know her?"

"Lada. My sister."

Her gaze grew even more critical as she looked him up and down. "You do not seem like siblings."

Radu smiled tightly. "I am aware of that."

"Well. I always wondered what she might do, a bright, vicious mind like that. And those men followed her without question. She made me feel younger."

A sprig of affection rose in Radu's chest. It was strange, talking to someone who had known Lada and admired her. Not in the way Mehmed admired her. That did not ever make Radu happy. But this gnarled old woman's memories made Radu miss his sister.

"Where is she now?" the woman asked.

"In Hungary, I believe."

"What is she doing there?"

"That is anyone's guess."

"Well, whatever it is, it will not end well for anyone who gets in her way. The world will destroy her in the end. Too much spark leads to explosions." She patted a barrel of gunpowder that had not yet been unloaded. "But your sister will destroy as much as she can before she goes out."

The old woman's eerie prophecy rubbed at Radu like an ill-fitting collar. "Perhaps she will find a balance."

"No. She will go down in flames and blood." The woman smiled fondly. "If you write her, tell her Tohin sends her regards." Then, her eye catching something else, she shouted at her son, "Timur! Did you check the way they are storing them?"

"Yes, Mother," Timur said.

Tohin stomped toward the storage building. Timur shook his head, giving Radu a long-suffering smile. "I have three children of my own, and she would still dress me if she could. You know how mothers are."

Radu's return smile was reflexive. He did not, in fact, know how mothers were. But he knew what it was to have someone watching out for him. He stared at the remaining barrels, wondering. Lada was already playing with fire, taking up with Hunyadi. She might respect the man, but he had never shown kindness to their family. Who knew what purpose he had in taking her in?

Radu had been flattered and angry when she demanded he come help her. But perhaps he should have been afraid. For Lada to ask for help, surely she was teetering on the edge of the destructive end the old woman saw for her. And though she had never asked for Radu's help growing up, he had helped her. He had worn away her edges, talked their way out of trouble she would have welcomed. Maybe ... maybe she had always needed him. And he always chose Mehmed.

Someone shouted his name, and he hurried back to his duties.

His duties to his God. His duties to the Ottoman Empire. His duties to Mehmed. Lada would have to figure it out on her own. He owed her nothing.

But the promise of the guilt he would carry if she died without his help clung to his skin like a shadow.

10

February

LADA TRACKED A GROUP of fifty Janissaries. They were a long-range frontier group, used for enforcing the empire's will in vassal states. Hunyadi had no particular reason to attack the Janissaries, but he demanded no reason to kill Turkish forces.

Up until now they had only fought more Bulgars, brief flashes of blood and screaming and swords breaking up monotonous riding, camping, sleeping outside.

Lada was proud of her men. They were as good as or better than any that Hunyadi rode with. And he noticed. After their canyon victory, Hunyadi frequently consulted with Lada and asked her advice.

She had studied his tactics, but only on paper and in theory. Watching him in the field was something else entirely. He always thought three days ahead—food, water, defensible locations. But he was not so set on plans that he could not respond with lightning-fast force to an unexpected threat or opportunity.

This Janissary group was one such opportunity. Lada looked uneasily at Nicolae next to her.

"What do you think?" she asked.

"I think they could have been me."

She looked back at the men they stalked. He was right. They were the same—boys stolen and turned into soldiers who served another land and another god.

"We let them go, then," Lada said. She could not help imagining Nicolae on the other side of the meadow. Or Bogdan. Or Stefan, or Petru, or any of her men. She did not want to feel this companionship with the Janissaries, but it could not be avoided.

The Janissaries came to a sudden stop. Lada tensed, fearing they had discovered her ten men tracking them. Instead, they shifted direction and started heading straight for Hunyadi's camp.

Lada gestured sharply. Her men ran, silent and low to the ground. She pantomimed drawing crossbows. Still running, they fixed their bolts. If the Janissaries did not already know the camp was there, they would in a few minutes. Hunyadi would be caught unaware. Lada gestured to her men to head back to the camp.

"Go warn them," Lada whispered to Nicolae.

"What are you going to do?"

"Delay them, idiot. Now go!"

Nicolae disappeared into the woods. Lada stood. "The sultan is the son of a donkey!" she shouted in Turkish.

The Janissaries turned as one, arrows already nocked to bows and pointed in her direction. She had cover, but it would not take them long to find her. She darted to another tree. "I am sorry. I should not have said that about the sultan. It is an offense to donkeys, which are perfectly serviceable creatures."

Lada peeked around the tree. Their weapons still at the ready, the Janissaries were searching the dense foliage for threats. Lada laughed loudly, the sound ringing through the trees. "Are you Janissaries? I have heard that Janissaries are not fit to lick the dust from spahi boots."

"Who is there?" an angry voice shouted, while another cursed her. Their leader barked an order for them to be quiet. Then he called out, "Show yourself, woman!"

"Why do Bulgars make terrible farmers?" she answered.

There was silence. She peered from behind the trunk, amused to see the Janissaries trading confused looks. Most of them had lowered their bows when no attack came.

"What?" the commander shouted.

"I said, why do Bulgars make terrible farmers?"

One of the Janissaries in front sheathed his sword. "I do not know."

The commander barked at him for silence, but the Janissary shrugged. "I want to know."

"So do I," another called. Most of them nodded, a few grinning at this odd forest interlude.

"Because they confuse the pigs for Bulgar women, and cannot bear to slaughter their wives."

A chorus of snickering laughs broke out.

"Who are you?" one of the men called. "You should not be in these woods. It is not safe."

A volley of arrows rained from the sky onto the men.

"I know," Lada said, coming from behind the tree and letting her shaft join the others.

After, when the work of killing was done, Lada took no pleasure in the white-capped bodies on the ground. Stepping over
the corpses, Hunyadi found her and clasped her hand in his.
"How did you think to distract them like that?"

She lifted a shoulder as they walked back toward camp.
"They are soldiers. They depend upon routine, and anything
out of the ordinary will give them pause. And they are men.
They hate to be insulted, but they love to hear others mocked.
And they are fools, because they cannot imagine that a woman
alone in the woods would be a threat."

Later, around a campfire, Lada sat next to Hunyadi. Nicolae was on her other side. The men traded stories like coins,
each trying to make his the most valuable, the brightest. Petru
mimed being struck through the eye with an arrow so dramatically he nearly fell into the fire.

Lada remembered a time not so long ago when some of
these same men had come back from fighting and she had been
forced to listen to stories she feared she would never be part of.
Now she was at the center, truly belonging.

"How did you find your men?" Hunyadi asked. He spoke
Turkish around her men as a courtesy, since most of them did
not speak Hungarian and his Wallachian was dreadful.

"*We* found *her*," Nicolae said, beaming proudly. "Or I did,
at least. It is a funny story. When Lada was this small . . ." He
held his hand close to the ground, then squinted at her. "Well,
she is still that small."

Lada punched him in the shoulder. Hard.

He rubbed it, grimacing. "When Lada was not the towering
giantess of a woman that she is today, she was in Amasya as the

playmate of the little zealot. Back then no one knew he would be sultan. He was just a brat."

Lada nodded, then quickly erased the wistful smile threatening to break through her expression.

"She was spying on us while we trained. We caught her. Then when she beat up poor Ivan—" Nicolae paused. "Whatever happened to Ivan?"

"I killed him," Lada said without thinking.

"You—you *killed* him? I thought he was moved to a different city! Why did you kill him?"

Lada realized the low, steady hum of conversation around them had died. All eyes were on her. Most of her men had never known Ivan. She wished she had not, either. He had been stupid and cruel, had always hated her. In the end, he had tried to force himself on her as proof she was nothing but a girl. Something he could take. Something he could break.

She lifted her chin. "That is none of your concern."

Hunyadi laughed. "Spoken like a true leader," he said in Hungarian.

She met his gaze and he gave her a slight nod, something fierce and proud in his eyes. She saw how he sat straight, even while relaxing with his men. He was still in charge, still slightly apart. She mimicked his posture. She was their leader. She did not owe them explanations. Especially not for traumas of the past.

"Wait," Petru said, concern pulling down his features and making him look like a puppy. "Did you kill Bogdan, too? Is that why he is gone?"

Lada sighed in exasperation. "No, I did not kill Bogdan.

But I might kill you if you act out that stupid arrow-through-the-eye death one more time."

———•———

Bogdan found them.

How he tracked them down Lada did not know. But the next week he walked into camp with a grin so giddy she could not understand how his blocky features managed it. Lada ran to him.

Her first impulse was to throw her arms around him. Her second was to hit him for taking so long. Instead, she stood in front of him, glaring at his beloved stupid face and his beloved stupid ears and his beloved stupid self. "Where have you been?"

"I brought something you need."

"More men?" She looked behind Bogdan, but only one person followed him. And that person was not a man. She walked with solid assurance. Her long hair trailed down her back in a braid, showing off two ears sticking out like jug handles.

"Lada!" her old nurse said, rushing forward and embracing her. Lada's arms were pinned to her sides by the woman's hug. How Bogdan had found his mother, Lada could not begin to fathom. But he was Bogdan. He stayed loyal to the women in his life.

Lada looked at him. "*Why* did you bring her?"

"To help," he said, shrugging. "You needed someone who could help you with . . . girl things." He paused, blushing. "Woman things."

Lada clenched her jaw, grinding her teeth together. "I do not need anyone's help with anything."

"Where is your brother?" the nurse asked. "He should be here. I thought you would take better care of him."

Anger flared. Who was this woman to tell Lada how to take care of Radu? The nurse had not been there in Edirne. She had not seen what they had gone through, what Lada had had to do to survive. "He is coming," Lada said through still-gritted teeth. She extricated herself from her nurse's arms.

"Let me brush your hair," the nurse said, reaching for Lada's snarls.

The sensation made Lada feel like a child again. She stumbled back, flinging her hands up to deflect the woman's touch. "I do not need a nurse!"

"You said the same when you were five. But at least your hair was presentable then."

"Take yourself to the devil," Lada snapped.

Bogdan looked hurt, but her nurse just laughed. The woman's eyes shone with something. Mirth or affection, neither of which were tolerable to Lada. Worst of all, Hunyadi was sitting nearby, watching the whole encounter.

"Where is my cloak?" she snapped, yanking clothes out of her saddlebag.

"Let your nurse help you find it," Nicolae teased. He and Petru were sitting at the campfire. Had no one missed this spectacle? What had Bogdan been thinking?

"She is not my nurse!"

Petru shrugged. "You are lucky. I wish I had someone to take care of me. Maybe I should find a wife."

"Maybe you could marry the nurse," Lada spat out.

Giving up on the cloak, she threw herself onto her horse and left camp. They had moved from the location of the slaughtered Janissaries and were working their way toward the capital. The increasingly frequent sections of frosted farmland made Hunyadi's hands twitch. When asked where they were going, he would merely shrug. "The castle." It sounded like a foreign word when he said it.

Today, though, they were in a heavily forested section of the countryside. They had not seen another soul all day, but that did not mean they were alone. Lada scanned the trees as a matter of habit, one hand always on her sword.

The trees were as bare and cold as the air. The sun was overhead, but all it did was blind her. How could something be so bright and give so little warmth? After so long in the temperate climate of Amasya, she had forgotten what winter felt like.

Right now, she wanted nothing more than to be back there. *No!* she screamed at her traitorous heart. She did not mean back in the empire. She meant back at camp. Around a fire, with her men.

The nurse would be there, lingering, hovering, much like a fly that buzzed incessantly, but at least a fly Lada could swat. She did not need another woman. She did not need to be taken care of. That woman was not her mother. Her own mother had fled to her home country of Moldavia when Lada was four. That was what mothers did. Nurses, apparently, were more dependable. And embarrassing.

Hunyadi pulled his horse alongside hers. "It might be good to have someone to help."

"I do not see your nursemaid following you around, combing your hair."

Hunyadi ran his fingers through his thick auburn locks. "I

would not object!" His tone softened. "All leaders need help. Let someone do the mundane tasks so you can focus on the bigger ones. Surely Mehmed does not do anything himself."

Lada rolled her eyes. "He has a man whose only role is to follow after him carrying a stool."

"Does he even clean his own ass, I wonder?"

Lada grimaced. "Why would you put such an image in my mind?"

Hunyadi laughed loudly. Then he settled more deeply into his saddle, sighing happily. "This is a beautiful part of my country."

"It reminds me of the forests outside Tirgoviste. I used to make our tutor take us out there to study. The castle was an oven in the summer and an icebox in the winter. I always suspected the architect was a cook."

"Do you miss it?"

Lada frowned as she followed the trail of a dark bird across the pale blue sky. "Miss what?"

"Tirgoviste."

"I never cared for Tirgoviste. I prefer the mountains."

"But you still want the throne."

"I want Wallachia."

Hunyadi huffed a laugh. "Is that all?"

"It is far less than what Mehmed—" She stopped, biting off the rest of the sentence. How dare he slip out of her mouth uninvited.

Hunyadi leaned closer to Lada, his horse following the movement and nearly brushing its flanks against her legs. "So he does mean to go for Constantinople, then."

Lada had avoided talking about Mehmed's plans. It felt

disloyal, which made her angry. He had shown no loyalty to her by entertaining the usurper Danesti prince.

Hunyadi pressed on. "The general opinion is that he is young and easily swayed. More interested in lavish parties and well-stocked harems than expansion."

If Lada flinched at the mention of the harem, Hunyadi pretended not to notice. He continued. "Everyone has solidified advantageous treaties with him. No one fears him. Murad's death was seen as the end of Ottoman expansion. But I wonder. I think the sultan is settling us all down so his way to Constantinople is clear."

The word *harem* still rang in Lada's ears. Obviously Mehmed was not loyal to her. He spied on her. He supported her rivals. She owed him nothing, and would cut this traitorous impulse to protect him out of her heart. "Constantinople is his only desire. Everything he does, however innocent seeming or counterintuitive, is to achieve that goal and that goal only. He will not stop until it is his capital, until he is both sultan of the Ottoman Empire and Caesar of Rome."

Hunyadi breathed out heavily, slumping in his saddle. "Do you think he can do it?"

"If any man can, he will."

"I feared as much." He rubbed his face, tugging on the ends of his graying mustache. "When do you think he will move?"

"As soon as possible. This spring or next."

"That changes everything. We will head to Hunedoara tonight. I have letters to write and a crusade to plan."

"You would defend Constantinople?"

"Of course."

"But it is not your city, not your people. And it is no closer to Hungary's borders than the Ottomans already are, so there is no increased military threat."

Hunyadi smiled. "I am Christian, Lada. It is my duty to rally to Constantinople's cause. It is the last we have of the mighty Roman empire. I will be damned if I let the Turks take it." He pulled his horse to a stop, then paused before turning. "I would be honored if you were at my side. I think together we could hold off the very forces of hell."

Lada was glad he was not facing her. The warm flush of pride at his words was something she wanted to keep private.

11

Late March

"WHEN WILL IT BE ready?" Radu demanded, the air shimmering with heat.

"When it is ready!" Urbana wiped sweat from her forehead as she used giant bellows to adjust the temperature of the flames in the nearest furnace.

"I need it now!"

She laughed, a sound like a hammer ringing against an anvil. "You need it now? I have needed it my whole life! The Basilica is *my* legacy, my genius. I will not risk blowing us all up with a faulty cannon so your schedule can be maintained!"

Radu wiped the sweat that was dripping into his eyes. "Can you at least show me? We have both invested so much in it."

Huffing, Urbana led him to the back of the sweltering building. She pointed to a pit of sand that stretched more than four times longer than Radu was tall. "There it is."

"When will it be cool enough?"

"Two days." Urbana leaned against the wall, staring at the sand as though she could succeed by sheer force of will. "If there are no cracks or fissures—if, God willing, it actually worked this time—we can demonstrate it for your precious sultan in two days." She patted a six-hundred-pound stone cannonball with the tender affection of a mother.

"It will work," Radu said. It had to. It would prove, once and for all, that he was the better Dracul sibling. The more valuable. The more deserving of love. And it would prove to himself that he had made the right choice in staying.

———————

The ambassadors from Constantinople arrived the next day. Radu no longer stood next to Mehmed in the receiving hall, but near the back and off to the side.

Normally, Radu would have liked to see the ambassadors squirming. Mehmed was still acting the silly, spoiled sultan. But it was all so tiresome. He was ready for this interminable waiting period to be over. Constantinople needed to fall. When they marched, then everything would be better. Everything would be revealed. Radu would reclaim his place next to Mehmed. They would take the walls together.

And Lada would be nowhere near, either physically or in Mehmed's thoughts. When Constantinople fell, Mehmed would have what he wanted most. He would forget the girl who had left them behind. He would know who had been with him, helping him every step of the way.

He would finally see Radu's whole worth.

Radu refocused on what was being said. Though the ambassadors kept trying to steer the conversation back to the fortress Mehmed had built on their side of the strait, Mehmed could not be trapped.

"We should have a feast! A party." He smiled distractedly,

leaning over to whisper to a man taking notes, "Fish. No, lamb. No, fish. Both!"

The lead ambassador cleared his throat. "But we must discuss the matter of the land. You killed citizens from a nearby village."

Mehmed waved dismissively. "Our men defended themselves against attack. It is nothing. Tell me, do you like dancing? What style of dance do they favor in Constantinople now?"

The lead ambassador, who wore a blue coat that was open to reveal a bright red vest, shifted from foot to foot. "At the very least, we must demand payment for the land you took." The other five ambassadors remained perfectly still.

Mehmed's smile chilled even Radu. "Yes. Payment. We would say a great deal is owed Constantinople. Very soon every debt will be erased."

A silence as thick as blood had descended on the room.

Mehmed laughed, suddenly the bright, happy young sultan again. He clapped his hands. "A party! Tonight. You can show us how they dance in Constantinople. We will make you all dance."

Mehmed leaned toward Kumal, engaging him in conversation and effectively ignoring the ambassadors. They stayed where they were, shuffling their feet or clearing their throats. Mehmed had not dismissed them, so they could not leave. Radu could not see their faces from where he stood, but he did not imagine they looked happy.

Then one, the nearest to him, turned. It was the ambassador with the gray eyes who had delivered a gift—a book—to Mehmed upon his coronation. Radu was surprised at how easily he recognized the young man after more than a year. And it appeared the ambassador recognized him as well. His eyebrows lifted in shock, and then he smiled grimly, shrugging his shoulders toward the throne.

Radu answered with a similar smile.

To Radu's surprise, the ambassador took it as an invitation. He left his companions and made his way to Radu's side.

"You stood next to the sultan before," the ambassador said without preamble.

"Things change."

"They do. I am Cyprian."

"Radu."

Cyprian clasped Radu's hand, holding on for a few seconds more than seemed necessary. Radu was always deeply aware of touching, nervous to do anything out of the ordinary. As though someone might figure out he was not normal by the way he lingered in a hug, or drew too close while standing. Cyprian did not seem to have this same worry. He leaned in close, his unusual eyes piercing Radu. They were the color of the sea on a stormy day, and had a similar effect on Radu as that of stepping onto a boat. The floor swam beneath him for a moment, until Cyprian looked away.

"Tell me, is there somewhere we could get a meal outside the palace?" the ambassador asked. "It is far colder here than I remembered."

It was, in fact, quite warm in the room in spite of the season. But Radu did not think Cyprian referred to the temperature.

"I am sorry." Radu found to his surprise that he actually was. "We have a party to prepare for."

"I will find you there, then." Bowing his head, Cyprian smiled, his eyes crinkling until they nearly disappeared. Radu thought Mehmed's smile the best in the world, but he could not deny that something about Cyprian's transformed his whole face in a way that made Radu feel some hope for the first time in days.

———— ·•· ————

As Radu was changing for the party, a knock came at his door.

Opening it, he was shocked to find Mehmed standing there. Exactly as he had hoped and dreamed. "Mehm— My sultan?" Radu bowed low.

"Stay here," Mehmed said to the Janissary guards who always accompanied him. He brushed past Radu and waited for him to close the door.

Radu's heart raced, so loudly that he again wondered if Mehmed could hear it. "What is it?"

Mehmed paced the small length of Radu's receiving room. His hands were clasped behind his back, his brows drawn tight. "I have an idea."

"Oh?" Radu watched him. His presence filled the room. Mehmed did not talk further. Radu needed him to talk, needed to keep him here. "I have good news! Urbana said we can test the Basilica tomorrow. I wonder if we should make a demonstration of it. We could even invite the ambassadors. Let them run back with tales of your astonishing artillery."

Mehmed's gaze was on the floor, and though he nodded, he did not seem to have really heard Radu. "I sent forces into the Peloponnese today. They will keep the emperor's brothers from going to his aid in Constantinople. As soon as our troops set up a line there, we have effectively declared war. But I think I will do it sooner."

Radu wished there was enough room to pace by Mehmed's side. He would burst if he had to remain by the door. "The cannon demonstration would be the perfect moment!" He could see it playing out. Everyone lining up, watching. The shock and awe of the court. The fear of the ambassadors. Mehmed looking at him with secret, joyful pride. And it was all Radu's doing. Without him, no one would have helped Urbana. The cannon was his project alone. Radu's triumph would be used to declare war, and they could finally end this pretense at distance.

Mehmed stopped. He narrowed his eyes at Radu, expression unreadable. "I saw that ambassador seeking you out."

"I— What?"

"The young one. He sought you out the first moment he could. Why?"

Radu scrambled to adjust the trajectory of his thoughts. "I do not know, actually. He wanted to take a meal together."

"Was that all he said?"

"He remarked on the difference in my post from last time, when I stood at your side."

Mehmed smiled. It had none of the warmth of Cyprian's smile. "That was what I had hoped. Radu, I need you to do something. Something I can trust no one else to do. Something only you can do for me. For the empire. For the cause of our God."

Radu's heart beat even faster. Something only *he* could do for Mehmed. "Yes. Anything. You know I would do anything."

"At the party, seek out the ambassador. Tell him you want to leave me. Tell him you want to aid Constantine with your knowledge of my plans. Tell him you wish to be a traitor."

Radu could not process what was being asked. "But . . . then I will be *in* the city. How will I get back in time to join you?"

"You will be more valuable to me behind the walls than any man on my side of them."

Radu could not pick which path of thought to follow. Happiness that he would be the most valuable man in the world to Mehmed? Fear of what he was being asked to do? Or disappointment that after all his planning and work, he would not stand with Mehmed at the wall?

"How will I convince them? And if I do, what do you want me to tell Constantine?"

"Tell him anything you wish. In fact, tell him the truth. Tell him I am better prepared than anyone who has led forces against the wall. Tell him of my navy, my cannons, my legions of men. Tell him Constantinople will fall. Or, tell him that he has hope still. Either way, give him verifiable information and tell him you wish to fight at his side against the people who kidnapped you and stole your childhood."

"But I do not think that!"

Mehmed put his hands on Radu's shoulders, steadying him, forcing Radu to meet his eyes. "I know. But he does not. You will be my eyes and hands behind the wall."

"I wanted to be with you." Radu heard the longing in his own voice, but could not hide it. The idea of another separation—for a length of time no one could predict—was as cruel as a knife in his chest.

"I need you elsewhere. Do you think you can do it?"

Radu nodded, his head bobbing almost of its own volition.

"The ambassador will trust you. He seemed to . . . like you."

Radu came back to himself sharply. He searched Mehmed's face for a hint that there was something behind his words. Mehmed leaned closer, so close Radu could feel the other man's breath on his own lips. "Do not forget where your loyalties lie. Promise me."

It would be only a matter of leaning in to kiss. Radu managed to whisper, "I could never forget."

"Good." Mehmed pressed his lips against Radu's forehead. Radu closed his eyes and resisted tipping his face up. Mehmed's lips were so close to his own. Would it be so bad? Would Mehmed resist, be surprised? Or would he answer with his own lips in a way Radu never dared allow himself to imagine?

And then Mehmed pulled back. "I know you will accomplish this. Visit the cathedral of the Hagia Sophia for me. I will see you inside the walls of Constantinople."

"Inside the walls," Radu echoed hollowly as Mehmed released him and left as quickly as he had come.

12

Late February

If Lada had to endure this torture, the least her tormentor could do was pretend not to be so happy about it. Her nurse hummed and sang tunelessly as she finally got her way with Lada's hair.

"I could kill Bogdan for finding you again," Lada said.

"It was not easy. My boy is cleverer than he looks." Her nurse paused. "But not by much."

Lada snickered. Then she cursed as her head was yanked sideways, hair caught on the comb. "If he wanted his mother, that is fine. But I do not understand why you are still pretending to be my nurse."

"You silly child, Bogdan did not bring me for himself. He had barely greeted me before telling me that you needed someone to take care of you while you 'saved Wallachia.' Which he absolutely believes you will do. Ever since you could talk, he has belonged to you. He would do anything for you then, and he will do anything for you now."

Lada did not have a response to that. She had taken Bogdan's loyalty for granted as a child. When they found each other again, falling back into the same patterns had been effortless. But she knew now, after Matei, that loyalty was not a given. "I did not ask him to find you."

"Well, Radu was the one who loved me. But I love you enough for both of us." The comb caught on another snarl.

"God's wounds, Nurse, I—" Lada paused, gritting her teeth against the pain. "I cannot keep calling you Nurse. What is your name?"

The nurse paused, her fingers on Lada's temple. She stroked once, so lightly Lada wondered if it had been intentional. "Oana."

"Fine. Oana, when will you be finished?"

The nurse—no, Oana—laughed. She had lost most of her teeth in the years since they had parted. Lada had always thought her old, but now she realized Oana must have been a very young woman when she began taking care of her and Radu. In truth, Lada could not believe the woman was still alive. In Lada's mind, she had ceased existing once they were taken to Edirne. But Oana was strong and sturdy, as capable as ever.

Tonight, Lada both loved and hated her for that.

"It is easier to destroy than to build," Oana said. "And you have been destroying your looks for a long time now."

Lada could not enjoy the irony of hearing her nurse's— Oana's—favorite phrase used in relation not to the burning of Transylvania, but to the styling of hair.

"What does it matter? I am swearing loyalty to a foreign king as a soldier, not as a girl."

"These things matter, little one. Now hold still." Oana smacked the hard wooden edge of the comb against Lada's temple. Lada was certain it had been intentional.

The tiny room they had been given in the castle at Hunedoara had no fire. The stones themselves seemed to have been carved out of ice. Twice Oana had had to break the frozen top layer of the water bowl. Lada shivered violently, but not as violently as her thoughts were turning under the continued assault of the comb.

Finally satisfied, Oana helped her dress. The replacement king, Ladislas, had gifted her with a dress. Lada knew it would be disrespectful and even dangerous to reject it. Still, it was a good thing the room had no fire. Otherwise the dress would be feeding it.

Lada slapped Oana's hands away when she tied the underclothes too tight. Oana slapped Lada's hands away in return. By the end, they were both red-faced and sweating, having fought a more intense battle over getting Lada into the dress than Lada had ever endured.

"I cannot breathe in this damnable thing." Lada tried to lift her arms, but the sleeves were not made for her broad shoulders or thick arms. She could barely move. Oana had had to let out the waist some, and Lada's breasts still spilled out from the top of the bodice. Oana tucked extra fabric in there, trying to cover the soft mounds.

"This weighs more than my chain mail." Lada tugged at the layers of material that made up the skirts, and something stiffer sewn in to keep their shape.

"Think of it as armor."

Lada's lip curled in a sneer. "What could this possibly protect me from?"

"Mockery. Ridicule. Your men are used to you, but this is a court. You have to do things a certain way. Do not mess this up." Oana yanked on one of Lada's curls as she tucked it back into the elaborate style. A lacy kerchief went over the top of it all.

"Radu should be here." Lada stared down in despair. "I do not know how to talk to these people."

"He was always better at that. How did he fare when you left? I worried for him. I thought they would kill you, and break Radu's heart." There was a wistful tenderness in Oana's voice.

Lada took a deep breath. Or tried to—she could not manage it in this abomination of a dress. She and her nurse had not really spoken of Radu since Oana had asked where he was. The truth was as cold and brittle as the ice in her water bowl. "He grew into a new man. Smart. Sly. Too handsome. And, eventually, into a stranger to me." She had had no word from Radu, no news. She wanted to tell Oana that Radu was coming, but it had been so long. What if he was not? "When I left, he chose the Ottomans. So you were wrong. I survived, and Radu grew a new heart."

"Did you have nothing in common, then?"

A strangled laugh escaped the prison of her bodice. "Well, one thing." Lada wondered, yet again, whether her absence had granted Radu the portion of Mehmed's attention and love that he so desperately craved.

And, yet again, she forced herself not to think on it.

Lada tugged at the bodice, trying to shift it to make it more comfortable. She missed her Ottoman finery. At least those draped layers of tunics and robes were comfortable. "I am going to give the wrong impression, wearing this."

"You mean a good impression?"

"Yes, exactly."

Oana surveyed her with a critical eye, then threw her hands up in surrender. "This is the best we can hope for, at least as far as your looks. As far as everything else, tonight, pretend you are Radu."

A small pang hit just above Lada's heart. Did Oana wish that it were Radu and not Lada she had been reunited with? Everyone always loved Radu best. And now Radu and Mehmed had each other, and all Lada had was this woman who wielded a comb as a weapon.

Well. Lada could be Radu for one night. She grimaced, then smiled broadly and opened her large eyes as wide as she could. It was her best imitation of him.

Oana recoiled. "That is terrifying, girl. I was wrong. Be yourself."

Lada let her hooded eyelids drop low. She had never been able to be anyone else.

———— · ————

The castle at Hunedoara was small compared with anything in Edirne, but bigger than Tirgoviste. A moat surrounded it, with a hill on the back side of the castle that dropped off steeply. Lada liked looking out over the wall at the winter landscape stretching into the hazy distance. She pretended she could see Wallachia from there.

But tonight there was no time for that. She left her tiny room and traversed the back tower's serpentine stairs. For a few terrifying moments she thought the dress would actually be the death of her, but she managed to make it to the bottom. Stefan met her there. He was the only one of her men who spoke Hungarian—though no one else knew it. He would gather information as he always did, snatching pieces and organizing them into a whole for her.

They walked across the open courtyard in the center of the castle, then through a massive wooden door into the throne room. The floor was brightly tiled—though no tile was impressive to Lada here. After Edirne, everything except churches seemed drab. The walls of this castle were whitewashed and hung with elaborate tapestries and gilded, framed paintings of mournful-looking Hungarian royalty.

Lada had gotten used to large, lovely windows during her time in Edirne. She had forgotten that castles elsewhere were not for ornamentation, but rather for defense. To compensate, chandeliers dripped with light, and two fireplaces roared cheerily.

If her room had been freezing, the throne room was stifling. Lada had always thought it weakness when women fainted, but now she understood. It was not their bodies—it was their clothes.

She was not the only thing on the schedule for the evening. After interminable droning speeches in Hungarian, it was finally her turn. Kneeling in front of the king was a relief, if only to get off her feet. As she knelt, there were some tittering laughs and shocked whispers. The man who went before her had knelt.

What was she expected to do instead? To her horror, she realized there was nothing she *could* do. In her dress, she could not get up again on her own. Her face burning, she looked up at the king.

Ladislas Posthumous, the painfully young replacement for the previous monarch, trembled. At first Lada had thought him cold or frightened, but the trembling continued unabated. He was stricken with some sort of palsy, his illness showing in his every movement. Lada did not have to be ruthless to see that this was a king who would not last.

Younger than her, physically weaker than her, and still he was more important than her. So she bowed her head and murmured the words. She vowed to protect the Transylvanian frontier—no one objected that she had come directly from terrorizing it—and to keep the borders safe from the Ottoman threat. Finally, she swore her fealty to him and the crown of Hungary.

The crown that was nowhere to be seen. Certainly not on Ladislas's trembling head.

When Lada had finished, she stayed where she was, utterly humiliated. She could not get up, and she could not ask for help. A hand at her elbow rescued her. Stefan smiled wanly at her as he steadily guided her back to her feet. Hoping her expression hid her relief, she nodded at him as gracefully as she could manage. They walked back to their position at the rear of the room.

After the official business ended, everyone remained. Apparently there was always an informal reception afterward. Lada leaned against a wall for support. Every part of her hurt from being held in an unfamiliar position by her dress. No one spoke to her. She knew she should try to strike up conversations, try to gain allies, but she could not smile. She was gritting her teeth too hard to manage it. She was as likely to kill anyone who talked to her as she was to make a friend.

No. She was *far* more likely to kill someone than to make a friend.

Only when she could not place her source of vague disappointment did she come to a horrible realization. She had thought if she looked like a noblewoman, men would talk to her. Of course she would have rejected their flirtations, but she had been preparing herself to do that.

She had not prepared herself to remain utterly invisible while wearing a dress and with her hair combed. Or maybe she was so unbelievable in a dress, or had humiliated herself so completely by kneeling, that no one would ever believe she belonged among nobility.

Lada was taken back to Mehmed's wedding. Standing alone, always alone, without a place and without worth. She drew a ragged breath. This was not the same. She was not that person. She had more than just Mehmed and Radu now.

But she did not have *them* anymore. Tonight, she felt the full weight of that loss. The loss of a brother who would have stood at her side and fought this battle of manners and politics for her. The loss of a man who would have laughed at her dress and her hair but also been desperate to be alone so he could undo it all for her.

Perhaps she had never stopped being that girl lost in a place where she could never have power.

It took Lada several minutes to realize Stefan had returned from his rounds. "What did you find?" she asked, relieved and grateful for a familiar face. Even one as anonymous and blank as Stefan's.

"The crown," he said, nodding toward where Ladislas spoke with several priests and a tall, confident-looking older man. The rest of the royalty revolved around two men and a regal woman. The woman was glorious, Lada had to admit. She truly wore her elaborate clothes as armor, not something to wilt under like Lada did. The way she commanded the attention of everyone around her, shooting frequent sharp glances at the king, reminded Lada of Huma, Mehmed's mother. Huma had been so sick when Lada left, surely she was dead by now. The thought of Huma's death made Lada oddly mournful. The woman had been a threat, and a murderer, too. But she had been so *good* at everything she did.

The woman in layered, gold-embroidered finery briefly met Lada's eyes. Lada felt herself weighed and summarily dismissed. It stung.

"Where is the crown?" Lada asked, glad Stefan was here to distract her.

"After Varna, the Polish king took it for safekeeping. But no one can truly be king of Hungary without the crown. Elizabeth is trying everything she can to secure it."

"Elizabeth?"

Stefan nodded toward the glittering woman. Suddenly it all made sense. "She is his mother?" Lada asked

"She is the true ruler of Hungary. But she does not have the money to buy the crown back. And until Ladislas has it, his rule is illegitimate. The man next to him is Ulrich, his regent. Between him and Elizabeth, this country is run."

"I suspect Ladislas's rule will be as short in stature as he is."

"No one speaks outright of killing him. They do not speak of him at all. He does not matter. Elizabeth is the throne."

"And Ulrich?"

"The most likely successor. The connection to the royal line is distant, but there. He is modest, just, and well liked."

"How do you know?"

"I spoke with his servants. It is the best way to get a sense of a man. And the other—"

They were interrupted by silence, which was followed by a wave of noise. Lada followed the crowd's eyes to a doorway in which Hunyadi stood. The day before, he had ridden out to the Transylvanian border, to respond to a problem there. Judging by the riding cloak he wore on his shoulders and the weariness on his face, he had only now returned. A chorus of cheers filled the room as he smiled and lifted one hand. People surged forward to speak with him. Elizabeth watched with narrowed eyes. Then the crowd parted for her, and she greeted Hunyadi with a lingering embrace.

"He could have it all," Lada said.

Stefan shook his head. "He will not take it. But he controls the soldiers, which means he has more power than anyone else in this castle."

It was similar in Wallachia. The prince was allowed no troops of his own, permitted no fortresses or defense. He was entirely dependent on the boyars, each of whom kept his own soldiers at the ready. It did not make for powerful leaders.

King Ladislas waved to Hunyadi. Hunyadi did not see it. Lada pitied the king then, but more than that, she hated him for being weak. This was his country, and he let another man have all the power. He deserved to lose everything. Lada did not understand why Elizabeth depended on a feeble son rather than taking the throne herself.

Huma had played the same game, and in the end it had seen her banished. Power through sons was no more secure than power through husbands.

"You said there was another contender for the throne?" Lada asked Stefan.

One man had not moved forward to greet Hunyadi. He stood alone, dark eyes calculating as he watched everyone who mattered in Hungary clamoring for a moment of Hunyadi's attention. Though he was far leaner than Hunyadi and dressed in more finery than Hunyadi would ever wear, Lada saw the same determined jaw, the same confident brow. But where Hunyadi's eyes were bold and honest, his son's were calculating and secretive.

"Matthias," Stefan said.

———— • ————

Lada watched Matthias throughout the evening. He never so much as glanced her way, so she had ample time to study him without fear of being caught. He wore a smile as ostentatiously as he wore the gold chain at his neck and the jeweled pins on his vest. It was ornamentation, meant to dazzle. But always his eyes were narrowed and shrewd as he spoke to this person or another or, in many cases, did *not* speak to them.

Hunyadi had been drawn into a corner, trapped by an impassable wall of dresses. Lada did not envy him. He was a widower, and the most powerful man in the country. The fact that he had no family name paled in comparison to his wealth. She wished he could break free so they could speak. Of what, it did not matter. But he was her only ally here, and she might as well have been alone.

Nicolae sidled up to Lada. He had secured some clothes nice enough to gain him access. She did not know where or how he had obtained the clothing, and she did not care. It was a relief to see him.

"You should dance. Or at least speak to someone," he said.

Lada shook her head. "It will do no good. I belong here as much as a pig in a dress does, and everyone will know as soon as I open my mouth."

"I actually saw several pigs in dresses as I came in. Not a single one got past the door. You are definitely doing better than they are."

Shaking her head, Lada let Nicolae lead her away from the wall. "Look, no one is speaking to the king." Nicolae nudged her in that direction. "Talk to him."

"No one speaks to him because he does not matter. I have pledged my loyalty for nothing."

Something in Lada's tone must have warned Nicolae, because he immediately turned them both around and steered Lada out of the throne room and into the freezing night air of the courtyard. He smiled and nodded to everyone they passed, quickly taking them through the gate and across the bridge. Lada leaned heavily against one of the stone pillars.

"I knelt in there and swore fealty to another king—a foreign king—for nothing, Nicolae. He will not help me get my throne. He cannot even get his own crown. What have I accomplished?"

Nicolae took her hands in his. "You do what you must. It is no different from what the little zealot does, making treaties and creating alliances that mean less than the paper they are written on. Your brother would have done the same. You must survive, and Hungary has welcomed you. Take advantage of it. Hunyadi is a powerful ally. In spite of your best efforts, he cares about you. This is a good situation. It is certainly better than hiding in the woods, picking on Transylvania."

"But it is not what we came for."

Nicolae shrugged, stamping his feet against the cold. "I came to get away from the Ottomans. We all did. You gave that to us."

"Matei was spying on me," she said. She had told no one, holding the information close out of shame, anger, and, perhaps, a bit of guilt over his death. "He was reporting to Mehmed."

Nicolae uttered a sad oath, his breath fogging into the night air. "Matei was a fool, then. I will keep a sharper eye on everyone. But I know this—you have done many things for us already. We are in a good position. You fight at Hunyadi's side. Foreign kings accept your allegiance. Your men respect and are loyal to you." He smiled. "That is quite a bit for a little dragon from Wallachia."

Lada knew he was trying to help her, and she was comforted that her men were satisfied. She had gotten them out of slavery. Led them successfully in battle. Earned the respect of one of the greatest men of her time.

She stared numbly into the night. The Hungarian night. Not the Wallachian night.

It was not enough.

Never enough.

13

Late March

RADU HAD ONLY AN hour before the party, before he would need to persuade Cyprian that he was ready to betray Mehmed and join Emperor Constantine's cause. He hurried to Kumal's house. Kumal was not there, but he was not whom Radu needed to speak with.

"Nazira?" he called, bursting through the front door. "Fatima? Nazira?"

Nazira rushed into the front room, Fatima close behind her. Nazira held a cloth in her hands, dripping water along the floor. Concern pinched her face. "What is it?"

"I am leaving. For Constantinople."

"They march already? So soon?"

"No. No. I—" Radu paused, looking around the room. "Are we alone?"

"Yes, of course."

Radu sat, suddenly exhausted. He looked down at his hands. "Mehmed has asked me to defect. I am to convince an ambassador that I wish to aid Emperor Constantine. If all goes to plan, I will run tonight."

Nazira covered her mouth with the wet cloth, then dropped it. "Tonight?"

"Yes."

"But what if they find out you are still loyal to Mehmed?"

"They cannot. I have to pretend to want a new life with them. They must think I am never coming back. I do not know what Mehmed will tell Kumal, but I wanted you to know the truth. I will not be able to write or communicate in any way."

A sudden determination hardened Nazira's face. "That will not be a problem. I am coming with you."

"What? No. You cannot!" Radu stood again in disbelief.

"I can, and I will. You have taken care of us all this time. Now it is my turn to repay you. It is too much to bear this secret alone. I will go as your wife."

"It is too dangerous! If they discover me, they will kill us both!"

"Which is exactly why I need to come! Why would a man put his beloved wife in that much danger? My mere presence will sell your loyalty in a way nothing else could. Besides, I have spent all these years studying Greek. It is about time I got to use it."

Radu shook his head, aghast. He turned to Fatima for support. "Tell her this is insane."

Fatima looked as though she wanted to cry, but she shook her head instead. "Nazira is right," she whispered. "It is the best way to keep you safe. We will come."

"But you hate to travel!" Radu looked back at Nazira, triumphant. "You cannot ask Fatima to come."

"I am not." Nazira turned to Fatima, cupping her face gently in her hands. She put her lips to the other girl's ear, whispering something Radu could not hear. Then she said, "You understand?"

Fatima shook her head, silent tears streaming down her face. "I can come," she whispered. "I want to be wherever you are."

"And I want to be wherever you are. But I need you to be safe." Nazira regarded Fatima with a tenderness that hurt Radu to see. "I can weather this storm for both of us, but only if I have the shelter in my heart of knowing that my Fatima is well."

Fatima shook her head again, then nodded, crying.

"I will come back to you. Always." Nazira closed the distance between their mouths in the exact way Radu had imagined Mehmed doing with him. But this kiss was infinitely more sweet, more intimate than any Radu had ever managed to dream of. He looked away, unwilling to intrude on the two women's love and heartbreak.

Nazira cleared her throat. Radu turned back to find her still holding Fatima close. Fatima hid her face in Nazira's shoulder, but Nazira's face was ferocious. "When do we leave?"

———— • ————

Cyprian was waiting outside the grand doors to Mehmed's party. Though the ambassador had carefully composed himself, his nerves showed in the way his fingers tapped unceasingly against his blue-clad leg. Radu did not care for the styles out of Constantinople. He found the deliberate exposing of multiple layers of clothes to be gaudy and vain. But unlike that of the other ambassadors, Cyprian's layers were coordinated and less jarring. Radu supposed he himself would be wearing clothes like that soon.

He did not realize he was running his fingers along his turban until they caught in one of the folds.

And prayer. When would he pray? Being cut off from prayer with his brothers would be like being cut off from sleep. He could already feel his soul wearing thin and tired simply from contemplating it. He would find a way to pray. He had to. Even if he could only pray in his heart, God would understand.

Light and music spilled from the doorway, a jarring accompaniment to Radu's bleak thoughts. There was no use in delay. He crossed the hall to Cyprian, whose visage flashed a brief look of happiness before worry claimed it once more.

"You came," Cyprian said. "I had begun to fear you would not."

"We are all of us slaves to the whims of the sultan." Radu hated the way the words flowed smoothly out of his mouth, as though they belonged there. "Cyprian, this is Nazira, my wife."

A momentary twist of confusion distorted Cyprian's face as he finally noticed Nazira at Radu's side. "Your wife?" With movements formed by years of habit, Cyprian reached out and took her hand, bowing and kissing it.

"Hello," Nazira said, her voice strained. She looked over her shoulder constantly. Radu did not know how much of it was nerves, and how much was acting to sell their deception to Cyprian.

"I—I did not expect you to have a wife." Cyprian frowned, then shook his head. "I mean, you are so young. My age."

Radu smiled tightly. "When you find someone like Nazira,

you do not wait." He looked past Cyprian toward the party, and then back down the hall. "Can we speak in private?" he asked in a low voice.

"Of course." Cyprian followed them out into a side garden. The same side garden Radu had come to so many times to read and then destroy Mehmed's secret notes. In the face of what he was moving toward, he longed to have even that level of closeness again.

As soon as they were far enough into the garden, Radu turned to Cyprian. "We want to leave."

"What?"

"Right now. We cannot pretend to support Mehmed anymore. His father kidnapped me, tortured me, stole my entire childhood. I cannot stand by and watch as Mehmed takes Constantinople the same way."

Cyprian wilted. "So he does mean to attack."

"As soon as he is ready. Can you get us to the city, to the emperor? I will do whatever I can. I grew up with Mehmed and served him; I am familiar with his true temperament and many of his plans. I can help you."

Cyprian nodded. Mehmed had been right. Cyprian must have planned to try to get information from Radu. Why else would he be so quick to trust them? "We should leave right now," he said.

"We are ready." Radu pulled his and Nazira's traveling bags from behind a stone bench.

"She is coming?" Cyprian's surprise was confirmation of what Nazira had said. No one turning spy would risk the life of an innocent woman. *Please*, Radu prayed, *please let Nazira come through this safely.* It was one thing to gamble with his own life for Mehmed's cause. He felt sick knowing he was also risking Nazira's.

"Radu is my husband." Nazira gripped his hand. Some of Radu's fear was soothed. It was selfish to draw any amount of happiness from her sacrifice, but he could not help it. "Where he goes, I go."

"Very well." They followed Cyprian to the guest stables, where he found one of the ambassadors' servant boys. The boy was small, with intelligent eyes and black hair thick and tangled like thatch. After a quick, whispered conversation, the boy saddled three horses.

Though Radu knew perfectly well they would not be followed, Cyprian's paranoia was contagious. Radu found himself glancing over his shoulder as they rode through the city. His last view as they crested the hill outside Edirne was the same as the first he had ever had of the empire. Spires and minarets were black points against the starlit sky.

He bid them a silent farewell, praying that they would watch over the city in his absence.

14

Early March

LADA WAS NOT CERTAIN which was more surprising: that
she had been invited to one of Hunyadi's inner-circle coun-
cils, or that his son Matthias had not.

Hunyadi sat at the head of the table, with several similarly
grizzled men around him. At the opposite end of the table sat
two priests. The seat next to Hunyadi was empty. He stood
and gestured for Lada to sit there. The sting of invisibility that
had plagued her in the week since swearing her loyalty disappeared as she sat at Hunyadi's right hand. As soon as she was
settled, he leaned forward, slamming a fist against the table.

"Constantinople!" he roared. "Once again it faces a threat.
Perhaps the greatest threat it has ever known. We cannot let
the heart of Christendom, Rome of old, fall to the infidels.
If Constantinople succumbs to the Muslim plague, what is to
stop them from spreading over the whole world?"

One of the priests nodded vehemently. The other remained
impassive. A few of the men were engaged, but several leaned
away from the table as though distancing themselves from
the topic.

"What are you suggesting?" the excited priest asked.

"We crusade, as we have before. We gather the righteous until we swell around the walls like God's own wave, to forever drown the infidel threat."

The other priest smiled drily. "I believe the last successful Christian crusade actually *sacked* Constantinople."

Hunyadi huffed, waving away the words with his hands. "Italians. They have no honor. If we let the Muslims take Constantinople, the heart of Eastern Christendom, what is next? Transylvania? Hungary? Long have we stood between Islam's expansion and the rest of Europe. As defenders of Christ, we cannot ignore the plight of Constantinople."

Lada watched, trying to figure out Hunyadi's angle. The Ottoman Empire already surrounded Constantinople. If the city fell, it gave them a virtually impregnable capital, but it did not move them any closer to Hungary or the rest of Europe. The threat was merely spiritual, not physical. It would be demoralizing to lose the great city, but not damaging. At least not to Hungary.

"You have led us against a sultan before," said one of the men, his head shiny and bald, but his beard still dark. "We fought with you at Varna. We lost. We lost our king. Hungary still suffers the consequences and will continue to until the crown is once again stable. Why would we risk that again for Constantinople?"

"It is not about Hungary. It is about Christianity. Have you heard of the priest who led peasants—ordinary peasants!—against the Ottomans? They drove them back with the ferocity of their faith! They won a decisive and shocking victory, because Christ was on their side."

"Yes," the bald man said, rubbing his face wearily. "And then the priest caught the plague and most of the peasants froze to death."

Lada watched as Hunyadi tugged on his beard, trying to impose his intensity on the other men. He had no angle, she realized. There was no political advantage for him, personally, at Constantinople. If anything, he stood to lose all he had worked so hard to build here for himself and his son.

Listening to him talk and argue, Lada could not help but be stirred. He was passionate and charming, utterly adamant in his belief that defending Constantinople was the right thing to do. She weighed it against Mehmed's fervent desire for the city. She knew others thought he did it for gain—even his own men wanted the city only for the rumored riches—but that was not what moved Mehmed. Mehmed felt the weight of prophecy and the burden of his god on his shoulders. That would not disappear until he took the city or died trying.

Lada wondered how the world could survive with men such as Mehmed and Hunyadi on opposite sides. Or perhaps that was how it did survive. If they served the same purpose, she could not imagine any nation not falling before their combined might.

Each god, Christian and Muslim, had champions, keeping the other at bay.

Whose side would she fall on? Could she join Hunyadi? Could she go against Mehmed?

———

That evening Lada walked, Stefan at her side. He did not have much to report, other than that the king's mother did not like Hunyadi and was trying to either subvert or marry him.

"What do you think about Constantinople?" Lada asked, looking up through the bare branches at the twilight sky.

"Hunyadi does not have enough support to go fight, but he will. The king's mother is encouraging him. She hopes he will die there, and solve some of her problems. She will make certain he has the forces and the funding he needs."

"I mean you. What do you think? What do the men think? If I asked them to march with Hunyadi and defend the walls . . . would they?"

Stefan was quiet for a long time. Then he lifted his shoulders. "I think they would."

"But it is not our goal. It is not what has kept us together."

"Goals change," he said simply. "If you ask, most will follow."

"Will you?"

A ghost of a smile disrupted the blank space of his face. "I do not know."

Lada nodded, looking back up at the sky. "That is fine. I do not know, either."

———◆———

Two weeks after the council about Constantinople, Hunyadi invited Lada to dine in the castle. She always ate with her men, so this was unusual. Against her better judgment, she agreed, but only after Hunyadi said she did not have to wear a dress. She would not put herself through that again.

She entered the dining room with her back as straight as a sword, hair tied in a black cloth in defiance of the elaborate styles of the Hungarian court.

She need not have worried so much. Dress or trousers, curls or cloth, she was still invisible.

As dishes of food were passed by servants, Lada tried to listen to the conversations around her. Her dinner companions spoke of people she did not know, of matters that did not concern her. Nowhere was there anything for her to contribute to or even enjoy. The familiarity of it all exhausted her. It was the same as what she had grown up with: circles of gossip, words and favors traded for power, deals made for which the nobility would see none of the work and all of the benefit.

Since she had nothing to offer anyone, no one paid her the slightest mind. Hunyadi fared better. He was wildly popular, regaled with requests to tell stories of his conquest. But his otherness was inescapable. He was a soldier, through and through, and though he was undeniably charming, there was a gruff directness to him that was out of place here. The nobles deferred to him with a certain patronizing arrogance. The king's mother, Elizabeth, asked him for story after story, each circling back to his childhood.

Lada realized with a spike of anger what it was: Hunyadi was their pet. They were proud of his accomplishments, boastful of what he had done, but they would never, ever see him as their equal. And Elizabeth made certain no one forgot where he came from.

He was worth more than every glittering waste of a person in this whole castle.

Though Hunyadi never drank when they were campaigning or riding, Lada watched as he downed glass after glass of wine. She revised her previous thought that he was doing better than she. He was miserable. As the meal broke up and people stood in groups to talk, Hunyadi suggested dancing several times. Lada had seen him dance—he was a wonderful dancer—and she understood his need to do something with his body. Movement was freedom. But there were no musicians, and his suggestions were met with laughter, as though he jested.

Lada stomped across the room and took his elbow. "I need him," she snapped at the courtesans polluting the air with their aggressive perfume. They pouted, protesting mildly that he had not finished his story, but as soon as Lada removed Hunyadi they filled the space as though he had never existed.

"Thank you," Hunyadi said, swaying slightly. "These people are more terrifying than a contingent of Janissaries."

"And far more ruthless."

Lada guided him toward the door, but he stumbled to a stop, a smile of true joy parting the haze of alcohol on his expression. "Matthias!"

Matthias, his own auburn hair oiled and carefully styled, unlike his father's mane, paused in his conversation with several other men. Lada knew he had heard Hunyadi, but he continued as though he had not.

"Matthias!" Hunyadi barreled over, clapping his hands on the young man's shoulders. Matthias's answering smile was as carefully styled as his hair.

"Father."

"Matthias, I wanted you to meet Lada Dracul." Hunyadi turned back to her and gestured at Matthias with unabashed pride. Matthias's answering whisper of a sneer made Lada wish to run her sword through him.

He gave her a perfunctory bow. "So you are the feral girl of Wallachia he has taken under his wing." The men around him laughed. One made an obscene gesture behind Hunyadi's back.

Their opinion of her relationship with him was evident. Lada sensed that Matthias had never been privy to his father's idea of marrying them.

"Lada single-handedly defeated a whole Bulgar contingent. Saved my life. And she grew up with Sultan Mehmed. Invaluable insight. Very clever." Hunyadi smiled at Lada with the same level of pride as he had shown for his son, and something inside her broke.

"Is that so?" One of the men leaned forward, leering. "Tell me, is it true what they say? That he has one thousand women in his harem, and another harem made up entirely of boys?"

Lada felt the familiar stab of anger that always accompanied mention of the harem, and a brief spike of fear. A male harem? Was such a thing possible? Was Radu ... She shoved those feelings down with an unexpected defensiveness on her brother's behalf. How must Radu, already tormented by the impossibility of his love, feel when he heard such insinuations used as slander?

Besides, these men did not know Mehmed. How dare they speak of him this way? She raised an eyebrow coolly. "If you are so interested in male harems, I can introduce you to the sultan. Though you are not quite pretty enough for his tastes."

The man's face turned a dangerous shade of red. Hunyadi let out a barking burst of laughter and clapped Matthias on the back. His son cringed, then carefully reset his face. "I believe Elizabeth would like to speak to you," he said to his father.

Hunyadi groaned.

The leering man spoke again. "I believe she would like to do more than speak with you." Matthias pretended outrage, but it was all in jest. Hunyadi was embarrassed. Response was impossible. He could not impugn Elizabeth's honor, nor did he want to criticize Matthias's friends.

Lada could bear no more. "The room is too warm. Will you see me out?" Hunyadi nodded graciously, offering his arm. She steered him once more toward the door and grabbed a bottle of wine on their way. She handed it to him wordlessly. They walked through the center courtyard, then over the bridge, descending the bank to a bare weeping willow. Hunyadi slipped several times, nearly taking them both down.

Lada's thoughts were on Mehmed. It was so strange, hearing accounts of the Mehmed that the world saw—seemingly infinite versions of the same person, each distorted and exaggerated. But she knew the real him.

Or did she?

He had spied on her. He had sent her to Wallachia with his support, and then supported her rival. He had married and fathered children, all while professing his love for her. And through it all, he had never taken his sights off Constantinople. He would not, could not. Not even for her.

Could she really consider fighting for Constantinople, knowing it would be going directly against Mehmed and everything he had been to her? She did not think she could raise a sword against him. As much as she loved Hunyadi and hated the Ottomans, it would not be the Ottomans she would truly be fighting. It would be Mehmed.

She remembered those warm nights together, cocooned in her room, plotting and planning the attack on the city. It had felt like playing pretend. But it had never been pretend for Mehmed. Constantinople was his dream, the one thing he would not give up. Everything was to that end. Including supporting her rival on the Wallachian throne. He had sacrificed her dreams for his.

Maybe she *would* go to defend the walls.

"Did you see him?" Hunyadi said, once they were sitting.

Lada startled out of her thoughts. "Mehmed?"

Hunyadi laughed. "No! My son! He looks like a king."

Lada thought that was not a thing to be proud of. She weighed her next words as judiciously as she could. "He is nothing like you."

Hunyadi smiled, nodding. "I know. I do not understand him. But I have worked with blood and sweat my whole life so he could have access to everything that I never could. My sword has cut a way to the courts for him. He never has to do what I have done. I gave him that." Hunyadi lowered his head, closing his eyes. "I think he has a chance at the throne. Can you imagine? I am the son of peasants, and my son could be king. Everything I have done, all that I have lost, all the struggle and death. It was for him."

Lada remembered the look of pride he had given her. Matthias did not deserve Hunyadi. "I wish you had been my father," she said. If Hunyadi were her father, everything would be easier. She would jump at the chance to crusade with him, to fight at his side.

If Hunyadi were her father, she would never have known Mehmed, never had her loyalties twisted and tugged into strange new shapes. And her heart would not have to constantly shield itself from the part that missed Mehmed so desperately.

Hunyadi would have protected Radu, too. And Radu would have appreciated him in a way Matthias was incapable of.

Hunyadi patted her arm with his heavy hand. "Do not wish away what you are. If you were my daughter, I would have extinguished your fire long ago. I would have given you the best tutors and the finest clothes and made you into a pretty doll to be traded away in marriage. I did the same with my son; I made him into someone I do not know, and it fills me with both pride and sadness. That is the best we can do for our children—turn them into strangers with better hopes than we ever had. Your father was a fool and a coward, but his choices shaped you into the fearsome creature you are. I do not want to imagine a world in which you are not you."

For years Lada had nurtured only hatred for her father, to take away the pain that loving him had left her with. But that night in her tent as she drifted to sleep, she let some of it go. Because she, too, was grateful for who she was. She would not wish any part of herself away.

Which meant she was still left with the question of what to do with the parts that loved Mehmed and the parts that wanted to fight at Hunyadi's side.

15

Late March

THREE HOURS AFTER LEAVING Edirne, Radu, Cyprian, and Nazira heard a horse galloping madly toward them. They pulled their horses to the side of the road. Cyprian drew his sword, and Radu copied him, though he could not imagine who might be pursuing them. Certainly not Mehmed's forces. Perhaps one of the ambassadors had somehow discovered their deception, and was riding to warn Cyprian?

The horse, lathered and shivering, was drawn to an abrupt stop in front of them. "He has killed them!" the rider shouted.

"Valentin?" Cyprian sheathed his sword. It was the thatch-haired boy who had helped them in the stables.

Valentin tried to dismount, but fell roughly to the ground instead. "He killed them!"

Cyprian jumped from his horse, grabbing Valentin. "What do you mean? Why are you here?"

"He killed them! At the party. The sultan killed them. He killed them all."

Cyprian looked up at Radu and Nazira in horror. "Did you know?"

Radu shook his head, numb with shock. He had not known. This, then, was Mehmed's declaration of war. Radu knew that lives would be lost—of course they would, that was the price of a siege—but this felt so personal. So . . . excessive. It felt more like murder than war. He had no doubt Mehmed had his reasons, and if Mehmed could explain them, Radu would understand.

Unbidden, the image of the ambassadors lying on the gleaming tile floor, blood pooling around them, came to Radu's mind. Sour acid rose in his throat, threatening to come out. Surely there had been a reason. "I did not know," he whispered.

Cyprian cradled the boy, still looking up at Radu and Nazira. "Your timing saved my life. I owe you everything, and will call you friends to my dying day."

Nazira and Radu looked at each other as the full weight of what they were in the middle of finally descended on their shoulders.

Three days later, Radu's assumption that Nazira would require a lot of help on the road was heartily disproved. She had packed not only her essentials but also provisions. Radu had not even thought of it, a fact that was not lost on Nazira. She batted her eyes slyly at him as she started a fire effortlessly and pulled out food from a saddlebag. "We wives are very useful things to have around," she said.

Radu huddled close to the fire, grateful for the heat and for Nazira's skills. "And all this time I thought you were merely decorative."

Cyprian gave a small laugh, while Radu and Nazira traded

a secret smile over how true her decorative role actually was. It was good to hear Cyprian laugh. He had understandably been in a pall since receiving news of the murders.

Assassinations, Radu corrected himself. Political, not personal. That made them assassinations, not murders. Which he found easier to stomach, though neither was pleasant.

"How much farther to the city?" Radu asked.

"We should be there tomorrow." They had taken a wandering route, fueled by the servant Valentin's terror and Cyprian's fear of pursuit. Radu and Nazira could not very well assure their traveling companions that Mehmed wanted them all to arrive safely, so they toiled along little-used roads and through backcountry.

Nazira dished out soup and then settled in next to Radu.

"You even remembered spices?" Radu said. The soup was deliciously hot on his tongue.

"You married extremely well, Radu." She leaned against his free arm. Radu looked up to see Cyprian watching them with a forlorn, wistful expression.

Nazira noticed it, too. "Are you married, Cyprian?"

He shook his head as though coming out of a daze and looked down at his bowl. "No."

"I wondered if you were going home to a wife. Did you grow up in Constantinople?"

He nodded, soaking the now-stale flatbread in the soup to soften it.

Nazira continued asking questions, pumping Cyprian for information. Radu was both proud of her and sad that it was necessary. "Do you have family there still?"

"Yes. Sort of." Cyprian's smile twisted and did not touch his eyes. "My father is Demetrios."

"The despot?" Radu asked, surprised. Constantine's two brothers, Demetrios and Thomas, ruled other areas in the Peloponnese. They were often at odds with each other, enemies as frequently as they were allies. Radu could not understand why one of them would allow his son to be an ambassador. It was a job of dubious prestige, thankless and, frankly, dangerous. Ambassadors were as likely to be killed by foreign courts as their own if they brought back undesirable reports.

Cyprian nodded. "I am, unfortunately, a bastard. My mother was his mistress. So I am not as valuable as his legitimate sons. Constantine took me in and gave me a position in his court as a favor to my mother."

"Was she from Cyprus?" Nazira asked.

Cyprian's expression softened. "She named me after her island. She always said I was her home wherever she was."

Nazira sighed prettily. "I like her very much already. Have you ever been to Cyprus? I hear it is beautiful."

"No. My mother died four years ago. I have meant to go and see her birthplace, but Constantine's need has been greater than my whims."

"Is he so demanding, this uncle emperor of yours?" Nazira's tone was light and teasing. Radu leaned back, wondering how else Nazira would prove he had drastically underestimated her.

Cyprian laughed. "No. That is what keeps me at his side. I would fear for my soul if I had it in me to repay all his kindness by abandoning him in his time of greatest need." His expression turned dark once again. "I worry for how he will mourn if news of the ambassadors' deaths reaches him before we do. He will think me murdered, and will blame himself. It was not his fault. I requested to go."

Radu frowned. "Why would you do that?"

Cyprian took a moment to drain his soup, looking into the bowl like he could make more appear. "I liked my first visit. Edirne seemed to me very beautiful and . . . intriguing. I did not anticipate how things would have changed." He looked back up, another attempt at a smile moving his lips but not changing the sad shape of his eyes. "Besides, I had taken all that time to learn Turkish. It seemed a pity to waste it."

"If I had known, I would have warned you all." Even as he said it, Radu knew it was not true. He would have wanted to warn them. But he would not have gone against what Mehmed thought best.

Cyprian leaned forward as though he would grasp Radu's shoulder. Then he sat back. "It is for the best you did not. It would have alerted the sultan to your disloyalty, and you would have died with us. No, it is better this way. I will mourn my companions, buoyed by the hope that you have brought us."

The soup had turned sour in Radu's stomach.

16

Early March

"AMBASSADORS ARE HERE. FROM Edirne." Stefan had hardly finished speaking when Lada ran from their camp to the castle. Radu would be with them. She had a lot to speak with him about, and she anticipated with delight presenting Oana to him.

She pushed toward the throne room, trying to see over heads of others trying to get in. Two guards would not let her past. Hunyadi found her there, arguing with them.

"My brother will be with the ambassadors," she said.

Hunyadi shook his head. "No, they are all Turkish. But they brought this." He held a letter addressed to her. Unlike last time, he gave it to her unopened.

Lada clasped Hunyadi's hand, trying to hide her disappointment and frustration. "It is from Radu. I asked his aid. If there is news of value, I will bring it to you."

He nodded, smiling. "I know."

She took the letter and retreated beneath the bridge, where the heavy weeping branches of willows cocooned her and she could pretend to be far from the poisonous castle. There were many reasons why Radu might not have come. He was ill. He was delayed. He was dead. Or he finally had what he wanted, and nothing could tempt him to leave.

Lada only marginally preferred the last option to his death. She split the seal and opened the letter. It took her a moment to process that it was not from Radu, telling her whether he would join her in her quest for Wallachia.

It was from Mehmed.

Her face flushed as she read and then reread the first few lines, horrified.

> I dream of her neck, slender and unadorned as the gazelle,
> I long to see her tresses, draping a cloth between us and our nakedness,
> Her breasts like smooth mirrors, her legs like slender reeds bent by the
>   water,
> At eventide she lightens the shadows, a lamp against the night,
> And I will not forswear that fire nor the passion it alights in my body,
> Swift and taut as an arrow at the ready, with her, my target.

"What has he shat out on this page?" Lada muttered, scowling at the words. Mehmed had tried to read her poetry before, and she always stopped him. It was a waste of words and breath. Who had ever looked with lust upon a gazelle? And her breasts had nothing like the mirror about them.

She skimmed the rest of the poem. When he had finally finished comparing her body to various objects and animals, he moved on to business.

> I know you have not been successful in your attempts at the throne. I wish I could help. However, I have a proposition.

Lada scowled. He did not wish that he could help—he had very clearly demonstrated he wished no such thing. She braced herself for his suggestion that she return to him.

Do whatever you must to persuade Hunyadi to stay out of Constantinople, and I will be able to part with enough men to give you the strength you need to reclaim your throne. Send word back with my ambassadors. Once I have it, I will wait for you in the south of Transylvania, where it meets Serbia and Wallachia.

Lada dropped the letter in her lap. Whatever she had thought Mehmed might write, whatever sly attempts to lure her back or to remind her she had made the wrong choice, they were not there.

She did not know if that disappointed her. But she had found something she had not expected. Support. He wanted her to succeed. And he was offering her help.

Her way to the throne had opened up again. All she had to do was betray Hunyadi.

It was dark by the time Lada walked in a daze back to camp. Her men still lived outside, with no room for them in the barracks. It suited them fine, and it suited her as well. She preferred a tent to the stone prison of Hunedoara.

When she entered her tent, she found Oana sitting on the rug next to a lamp, mending in her lap. As a child, Lada had sometimes wondered if her nurse came with sewing supplies permanently attached. Lada collapsed onto her bedroll with a sigh. "What are you doing in here?" she asked Oana.

"Bogdan snores. This is my reward for carrying his great weight for nine months and nearly dying bringing him into the world. My beautiful little boy turned into a great hulking man who sounds like a dying pig when he sleeps."

Lada could not help laughing. "Have you walked the camp at night? An army of boars would make less noise than my men do."

Oana nodded, squinting, then set aside her work. "It is too dark for my old eyes."

"Sleep." Lada stripped some of the furs from her bedroll and tossed them at Oana. "Or, if you want, I can probably get you a bed in the castle."

"Lada, my dear one, you got me my Bogdan back. You do not need to get me anything ever again." The nurse sounded dangerously close to crying. "Though," she said, her voice turning gruff, "I would very much like to get out of Hungary. They all have marbles in their mouths. I cannot understand one word in five."

"You may get your wish soon enough."

"Back to Wallachia?"

Lada let out a breath heavy with the weight of the future. "No. Hunyadi plans to defend Constantinople."

"Why would we go there?"

"Because he thinks it is the right thing to do."

The nurse made a derisive sound. "The devil take Byzantium and all its glory. It never did anything for us."

Lada listened as the nurse lay down and shifted around, making all the small noises tired bodies make. It was annoying, but there was also something comforting about having another woman present. Someone she knew cared for her.

"Which way is the wrong way?" Lada asked. "How much should I give if it means getting back to Wallachia?" She could lie to Mehmed, tell him she had persuaded Hunyadi to stay out of Constantinople. He would not discover her duplicity until she already had the troops. There would be hell to pay after, though, and her castle was already filled with enemies.

Hunyadi's love and trust was a valuable thing; it meant more to Lada than she had thought possible. But he could not get her the throne. And she did not feel the pull of Constantinople that all the men in her life seemed to. Hunyadi, she cared about. Constantinople was only a city.

Wallachia, though. Wallachia was everything.

As though hearing Lada's thoughts, her nurse echoed, "Everything. There is no cost too high for your people, for your land."

"Even if it means betraying someone who trusts me? Or making deals with the empire that took your son from you?"

"You brought him back. You brought yourself back. Wallachia needs you, and you deserve Wallachia. Let your loyalty be only where your heart is. Everything else can fall by the road and be trodden underfoot as we pass to our home." Oana patted Lada's arm. "My fierce little girl. You can do anything."

Lada did not know if it was permission or prophecy, but she believed it either way.

Though manipulating people was Radu's area of expertise, Lada found the opportunity to do so handed to her with all the poetic grace of a gazelle's neck.

Hunyadi paced in front of her. He had called her to the meeting room in the castle, but this time only the two of them were present. "What about Serbia?" he asked.

Lada shook her head. "I know for a fact Mara Brankovic, one of Murad's wives, made a new treaty for Serbia. If you go to Constantinople, you will fight against Serbians, not with them." Lada wondered briefly what Mara Brankovic was doing with her cleverly purchased freedom. Mara had taken an offer of marriage from Constantine himself and used it to forge a deal between Mehmed and her father, the Serbian prince— creating a new, permanently single life for herself.

"Damn." Hunyadi leaned back with a sigh. "What do you think of the Danesti prince? I know you hate him, but will he aid us? Maybe he will die at the wall, which would be very convenient for you."

Lada dragged a knife along the tabletop, scoring the wood deeply. "He is a worm. And not long ago he was in Edirne, delivering his loyalty to Mehmed in person."

"How do you know?"

"Because I had someone in Tirgoviste trying to kill him at the time."

Hunyadi shook his head, but his expression was more amused than shocked.

"Besides," Lada continued, "he cannot commit troops without the boyars giving him support. They will bide their time and twiddle their thumbs until any usefulness has passed, and then they will send their condolences."

"The Wallachian boyars like me, though."

"Yes, and they fear Mehmed. Which do you think will be a stronger motivator among that pack of cowards?"

Hunyadi nodded grudgingly. "I have some support, though. Elizabeth encourages me to go. And I have you and your men. It will be good for you to have something to do."

Lada already had something to do. She respected Hunyadi, but he could not give her the throne. Mehmed could. He could also take it from her afterward, if she failed to uphold her end of their bargain.

"Elizabeth is exactly why you need to stay," Lada said, working her knife back and forth along the gash she was carving into the table.

"What do you mean?"

"Hungary is in turmoil. Ladislas will not live long, and Elizabeth knows you are a threat to her power. Matthias has a chance at the throne. Your son could be *king.*" She paused, letting the word hang in the air between them. "He will never have a better chance at the throne. If you go to Constantinople, Elizabeth will maneuver him out of the castle. You *must* see how much your strength and reputation buoy his popularity. All your toil and blood will be wasted if you shed it for misplaced loyalty to the emperor of a dead land."

The lines in Hunyadi's face deepened. "But I go for Christianity."

"Serve Christianity here. Protect the borders. Keep Mehmed from pushing farther into Europe. He will not be satisfied with taking Constantinople. As soon as the city falls, his eyes will turn toward Hungary. You cannot leave it under a weak child king and his conniving mother." Lada paused, as though thinking. "Besides, you will not make a difference at the walls."

She knew that was false. If Mehmed was willing to trade troops for the promise that Hunyadi would stay out, he understood that Hunyadi's experience and reputation were both weapons that could tip the city out of Ottoman reach forever.

Hunyadi would absolutely make a difference to the defense of the city. And Lada could not let that happen.

"But the infidels—"

"If even the pope does not see this as a threat to Christianity, I hardly think you need worry about it. Cities fall. Borders change. God endures." Lada finally dared look at Hunyadi, and what she saw nearly destroyed her resolve.

He looked older than he had when he began speaking, and infinitely more tired. "I already told Emperor Constantine I would fight for him. He depends on my aid. Matthias can manage without me."

Lada saw her opening, and she struck deep. "Then you are no better than my father. He sold our future for his own selfish desires, just as you would sell Matthias's to satisfy your soldierly pride."

Hunyadi held his hands apart, palms up, and looked down at them. They were thick and callused hands, with knotted joints. Then he dropped them to his sides, his shoulders drooping. "You are right. It is selfish of me to seek glory elsewhere. My duty is here."

Lada wanted to embrace him. She wanted to offer him comfort. She wanted to confess that she cared nothing for Matthias or Constantinople, but that she did care for Hunyadi. And she had manipulated him anyway.

Instead, she let him walk away, alone. Then she drafted her letter to Mehmed. His ambassadors were leaving the next day and would carry it to him. They would deliver her betrayal—and her future—to Mehmed.

Wallachia was waiting.

17

Late March

THE NEXT DAY THEY passed Rumeli Hisari, Mehmed's new fortress. Radu strained his neck to see as much as he could from the road. The fortress loomed, three soaring towers watching over the Bosporus. Cyprian regarded it with sad, solemn eyes. Valentin spat in its direction. They paused as a series of stakes came into view. Lining the banks of the Bosporus, decapitated bodies stood sentry.

"What happened?" Nazira whispered.

Cyprian's gaze darkened. "Someone must have tried to get through the blockade. This is the sultan's warning that the strait is closed."

They rode on, silent and disturbed. Radu remembered all too well his first lesson in Mehmed's father's court. He and Lada had been forced to watch as the head gardener had impaled several men. It was the beginning of many such lessons in the absolute rule of law. Radu had been able to forget them—mostly—since being taken under Mehmed's wing. But apparently Mehmed had received the same tutelage.

It was not long before they saw the patrol riding from

Rumeli Hisari. One of the ironies of a secret mission was that Radu was as liable to be killed by his own side as he was the enemy.

Cyprian drew his sword.

"No," Radu said. "Let me talk to them. I think I can get us past."

He scanned the soldiers' faces desperately as they got closer, but he knew none of them. Radu sat as straight and commandingly on his horse as he could manage after three days on the road. They were not in open war with Constantinople yet. He could make this work.

He had to.

"Who is your commander?" he asked, his tone both lazy and imperious, as though he had nothing to fear and every right to make demands.

The men slowed, fanning out to surround the small group. Their horses trotted a slow circle around them. "What business do you have in the city?" asked a man in front. Missing teeth beneath his clean-shaven lip gave him a lisp. Under other circumstances, it might have struck Radu as funny. But the man had his sword drawn, which dampened any humor.

Radu lifted an eyebrow. "I bring a message to Constantine from our glorious sultan, the Hand of God on Earth, the Blessed Mehmed."

"What message?"

Radu curled his upper lip, channeling Lada. "I was not aware you had been made emperor of Constantinople."

The man jutted out his chin angrily. "How do I know you are telling the truth?"

"By all means, detain me and take the time to send word to

the sultan. I am sure he will look kindly on you interfering with his express wishes."

The soldier looked less sure of himself and pulled his horse back sharply. "Who are you, then? I will send a message that we have seen you."

"My name is Radu."

The man frowned, then a mean smile revealed all the gaps in his teeth again. "Radu the Handsome? I have heard of you."

Radu pretended he was not surprised by this unusual title. "Then you know you should get out of my way."

The man gestured to the other soldiers, and they moved to the side. The gap-toothed soldier spoke in a low, ugly tone as Radu rode past, "Are you sure you are not a gift for the emperor? Maybe he has a taste for pretty boys, too."

The soldiers laughed, the sound hitting Radu's back like blows. But he did not cringe and he did not turn around, riding straight and steady toward the city.

"Well done," Cyprian said, alongside him. "I thought we were all dead."

"There are some benefits to being notoriously handsome, after all," Nazira said. She tried to pass it off as a joke, but Radu heard the strain beneath her voice.

He was more troubled by the soldier's insinuation. How had he heard of Radu? And what did he mean, that the emperor might have a taste for beautiful boys, *too*? The implication was that Radu had been the beautiful pet of another man.

He could think of only one man this rumor might be directed at. He tried to shake the thought off, but it lay heavier across his back than his winter cloak.

"Look," Nazira said, pointing. "Ships." The road curved and a view of the Bosporus strait opened up. Seven large, beautiful ships were sailing at a brisk clip toward the twin fortresses. Radu wondered where they were going, and envied the sailors' obvious skill. He had not seen such masterful maneuvering among their own navy. It planted a seed of doubt deep inside.

Cyprian cried out. "No!"

"What? What has happened?" Radu whipped around, certain his lie had been revealed and the gap-toothed soldier was coming for them. But the road was empty. Cyprian looked out at the water.

"Those are Italian ships. They must have hundreds of men aboard. They flee the city." Cyprian's shoulders fell, his head hanging heavy. "They abandon us. News of war has outpaced us. Come. We must hurry to console my uncle."

They spurred their tired horses forward. The wall, so long at the forefront of Mehmed's mind, and therefore Radu's, was . . . anticlimactic. Miles and miles of stone, worn and patched with jumbles of mismatching rocks, cut through farmland. Radu could not fathom how anyone was able to man the wall. It was too long. But it was also too high—easily five times taller than him. Any advance could be seen and met. There was nowhere to hide, no point more vulnerable to attack than any other. And behind the outer wall was another one.

"Stop gaping so," Nazira said, elbowing him. "You look like a slack-jawed boy from the country." Her smile was a tight warning. He had been scanning the walls as an invader. He was fortunate Cyprian focused only on the path ahead.

Radu had waited so long to be here, but he had never anticipated being escorted through a gate with a salute from soldiers
posted there. Just like that, they were within the outer walls.
Radu risked one look back as the gate closed behind them. He
did not know when—or if—he would leave again.

He glanced at Nazira, who rode tall and proud on her horse,
a hopeful smile pasted onto her face. He copied her confidence.
Cyprian was far enough ahead that he dared speak. He leaned
closer to her. "How are you so good at this?"

She lifted a hand in the air, gesturing toward herself. "When
you spend your whole life learning how to show people only
what you want them to see so your truest self remains safe,
you become quite adept at it." She smiled sadly at Radu. "You
understand."

He nodded. She was right. He knew how to do this. It
would work. "I am glad to have you with me."

She laughed. "Of course you are. Now put on a sorrowful
but curious expression, and let us go see the city that is our
sultan's destiny."

Radu faced forward again as they drew closer to the smaller
wall that barred the way into the city. It felt like his whole life
had been leading him here. If this was not how he had expected
to enter, well, he would simply make the best of it. After all,
Constantinople was the greatest city in the world.

———•———

Constantinople was not the greatest city in the world.

Compared with Edirne, it was a city of ruins. A city of
ghosts. More than half the narrow, crowding houses they passed

had an air of dereliction about them. Refuse filled the streets and pushed against foundations. Doors hung askew on some houses or were missing altogether from others. They passed entire blocks without seeing a soul. Unless scraggly stray cats and mean-looking mangy dogs had souls, in which case they passed many souls.

As Radu's group moved from the outskirts, things improved slightly. More of the homes appeared lived-in. A few stalls with vendors popped up here and there, the men halfheartedly soliciting them as they passed. Women hurried through the streets, dragging children and darting furtive glances at their mounted procession.

Radu had expected more soldiers patrolling, especially if word of war had already reached the city, but they had seen no one aside from the guards at the gates.

And he had seen nothing of the fabled wealth of Constantinople. He had always known, rationally, that the streets were not paved in gold, but he had expected something more. Even Tirgoviste had glittered brighter than this.

Finally they came to a quarter that showed more life. They pulled to an abrupt stop as a priest crossed their path, swinging a censer and trailing scented smoke in his wake. He sang hauntingly in Greek. Behind him was a parade of people. It took several minutes before the citizens, eerily silent save for the singing priest, finally passed and their way was clear again.

"What was that?" Radu asked.

"A procession." Cyprian looked troubled. "There is no small amount of internal strife. Most of it centers around Orthodoxy versus the Catholic Church. I will explain later. Come."

Bells tolled, their clanging echoing through the city. Cyprian looked up, then sighed. "I had forgotten the day. My uncle will be in the cathedral. We cannot speak with him there. Come, I will get you settled. I have a home near the palace."

"We cannot intrude," Nazira said. "Surely there is someplace else?"

Cyprian waved her worries away. "I have many bedrooms and only one me. We could all live there and never see one another. Much like this city, my home is in need of a much higher population."

Cyprian's house was not far. It was a handsome, well-maintained building. The houses in Constantinople practically shared walls, narrow gaps between them sometimes disappearing where the roofs met. He pulled out a key and opened the front door. They were greeted with a wall of frigid air.

"Valentin, go start the fires." The boy nodded and ran inside. Cyprian frowned. "I have a maid. Where is that girl? The main room should have a fire going already. Maria? Maria!" There was no response. "Well, come in. It will warm up soon enough." He led them to a small sitting room, where Valentin had already succeeded in lighting a fire.

They heard footsteps on the stairs. "Maria?"

"Just me," Valentin called out. "No one else here."

Cyprian looked troubled. Nazira put a hand on his. "Your home is lovely. Thank you so much. I hope you know your kindness is not unappreciated."

"Of course!" Cyprian covered her hand with his other hand. "I am sorry. I have been so caught up in my own worries and fears, I have scarcely thought how you must be feeling. You have left your home, your country, all your possessions." He turned to Radu. "Both of you have."

Radu thought of what Lada might have said in response. "Edirne was my prison, not my home. Nazira's is the true sacrifice."

She nodded, looking down. "I will miss my garden. But I no longer recognize the landscape of the empire under this new sultan. And I do not think I belong there anymore." She stood straighter, brightening. "And I have my Radu."

Radu tried to imagine what Fatima must be doing right now, alone in the home that she shared with Nazira. How she must worry. If his separation from Mehmed was agony, how much worse to be separated from someone with whom you shared everything, including your heart?

He held out his arms. Nazira met him, resting her head against his chest. Cyprian watched them with the same look of longing Radu had seen before. Then he cleared his throat. "I will see to some food and send a message to the palace to find out when the emperor can meet with us."

He left them alone. Radu stroked Nazira's back one last time, and then they sat, side by side, staring into the fire.

"I like him," Nazira said, and it sounded like a eulogy.

"Me too," Radu echoed.

18

Late March

LADA'S MEN HAD NEARLY finished breaking camp when Hunyadi rode up. His horse pranced and shifted beneath him, picking up on his agitation.

"You have heard, then?" he asked Lada.

She paused in tightening her saddle straps. "Heard what?" she asked, careful not to reveal anything by her tone.

"Rumors of Ottoman troops massing in Belgrade, with designs on our Serbian border. You were right about Serbian loyalties. Housing the infidels in their own capital!"

Lada whipped around. How had Mehmed been this stupid? They were to meet in southern Transylvania. Surely he would not have come close to the Hungarian border. She had accepted that she needed Mehmed's help, but she would be damned if she let Hunyadi know what she had done.

"Are you certain?"

Hunyadi shook his head. "One report. And the scout saw nothing himself. But I cannot risk this. Not with Matthias so close to the throne. You were wise to counsel me to stay." He smiled at her, his eyes sad. "My duty is here. I cannot turn my back on Matthias for Constantinople. When will your men be ready to ride?"

Lada was seized with a sudden need to recheck every strap on her saddle. "You want us to ride into Serbia?"

"No. I want you in Transylvania. Protect the passes in case the Ottomans try to go through Transylvania and come into Hungary that way."

Hunyadi had aided her yet again, giving her the simplest way to disguise her true goals: Mehmed and Wallachia. She nodded. "We will go to Transylvania. But after, we are not coming back. We will continue on when the way is clear." She let her words imply that she would continue after the Ottomans were gone, though she meant she would continue once the Ottomans had cleared a way for her. "We go to Wallachia."

Hunyadi put out his hand to stop Lada's frantic tugging on an already-tight buckle. His voice was soft with concern. "What awaits you there?"

"I do not know what will happen. But I know that it is my country. I spent too many years in exile. I cannot continue to exile myself. We go back to whatever fate holds for us. Live or die, I want it to be on Wallachian ground."

"Give me more time. Let me secure our borders, address this rumor of a threat. Once Matthias is on the throne, we can help you."

Lada shook her head. Though a few weeks ago she would have clung to that offer, now she knew better. A promise of help that might never materialize was worth less than a sultan already waiting with troops. She had to do this. For Wallachia.

Her thoughts lingered on Mehmed. Her Mehmed, waiting for her. She pretended that was not a factor in her desperation to go, but her heart knew her to be a liar of the worst sort.

"Wallachia," she whispered firmly to herself.

Before she could think better of it, she threw her arms around Hunyadi. "Thank you," she said, "for everything."

He patted her back. "Be careful, little dragon. You and I were made for battlefields, not royal courts. Do not start fights you have no weapons for."

He kissed her forehead, then got back on his horse. "May God be with you."

Lada smiled, and this time it was genuine. "God only sees me when I am in Wallachia."

Hunyadi laughed. "Give him my regards, then." He turned his horse and rode away, much slower than he had come. Lada watched him go, her smile disappearing. Her nurse, carrying their bedrolls, caught her eye and gave her a sharp nod.

It was time to go home.

19

Late March

CYPRIAN RETURNED, CARRYING A basket of bread and cheese and a skinny chicken with its neck already snapped. He motioned them to follow him into the kitchen. Radu and Nazira had been sitting in silence in front of the fire, both consumed with private strife. Radu had no doubt Nazira's revolved around thoughts of Fatima, but his was an endless cycle of worrying over what Mehmed was doing and how Radu could prove his worth to him.

Nazira gently edged Cyprian out of the way. "Show me where the dishes are and make a fire in the stove."

Cyprian nodded and gave her a tour of the kitchen. It appeared to be his first tour as well. "Oh, look! That is a lot of pots. Why do we need so many pots?"

Laughing, Nazira pointed at the table. "Go sit, you oaf. I can figure it out better on my own anyhow."

Cyprian did as he was told. "I solved the mystery of my missing maid. Apparently word of my death has spread far and wide. She considered it notice of termination of her employment, and fled not only my house but also the city. So many have. I hope she will be all right." He sighed, rubbing his face wearily. "I will try to find a replacement, but I do not think it will be easy."

"We can manage quite well," Nazira said. She smiled at Valentin, who had materialized and was helping stoke the fire in the stove. "Valentin is more than capable, and I am not unfamiliar with kitchens. I think we will do very nicely without extra bodies in the house." She caught Radu's eyes. She was right, of course. The fewer people watching them in close quarters, the better.

"Thank you," Cyprian said. His relief was visible, a relaxing of the tightness around his eyes and the strain in his shoulders.

There was a knock at the door. Valentin left and then returned, accompanied by a liveried servant wearing a vest with the double-headed eagle crest of the emperor. "The emperor wishes to see you immediately."

Radu stood. "I am at his disposal. We will go at once."

Radu and Cyprian fastened their cloaks as they stepped out into the chilly afternoon. The servant walked at a pace so brisk he was almost running.

"Is there anything I should know before I go in?" Radu asked, seized with nerves. This first meeting was the most important. If he could gain the emperor's trust now, he would be positioned perfectly. If he could not . . .

Well, that would be a much more unfortunate position.

Cyprian put a hand on Radu's shoulder. "You have nothing to fear."

Radu could not agree with that.

Constantine, just like the city he ruled, was not what Radu had expected. He was older, nearer to fifty than forty. His hair had thinned on top. In place of an elaborate crown, he wore a simple metal circlet on his head. Though every other man adhered to the fashion of layers, the emperor did not follow suit. His white shirt and purple breeches were simple, even austere. He seemed utterly devoid of pretense.

What a luxury honesty was.

Radu and Cyprian stood at the back of the crowded room. Constantine paced near the front, his tall, thin body leaning into the movement so that his head led the way with every step. With a start, Radu realized the emperor's feet were bare. He stifled a surprised laugh at the absurdity of the emperor of Rome walking around without even stockings.

"What of the Golden Horn and the seawall?" the emperor asked.

"We have nothing to fear there," a man said, waving dismissively. He was tall and broad, his body a blunt instrument of war. "A handful of poorly trained ships against my Italian sailors is nothing. We are perfectly safe on the seawall."

Radu saw his opportunity. Telling Constantine the truth, and about something easily confirmed, would solidify his status. Knowing what they faced would not magically replace the seven ships that had already fled, or line their walls with men that were not coming.

"You are not safe there," Radu said. Every face turned to him with curiosity. "When I left, Admiral Suleiman had six large galleys. Ten regular. Fifteen small. Seventy-five large rowboats for transporting men and navigating small spaces. Twenty horse transports."

The change in the air was palpable. "Who are you?" the Italian man demanded.

"Radu of—" Radu paused, again not knowing what name to give himself. "Radu most recently of Edirne, where I served at Mehmed's—the sultan's—side these last several years. Most particularly overseeing the secret development of his navy."

Cyprian put a hand on Radu's shoulder. "This is the man who saved my life, Uncle."

Constantine pointed at a man near the door. "Send word to the governor of Galata. Tell him we are drawing the chain across the horn to block all entry." No one moved. "Now!" he shouted.

The man stood, bowing, and ran from the room.

"Is that to be his main point of attack, then?" Constantine asked.

Radu shook his head. "He means to press you on all sides. If he can get through on the seaward side, he will. But his focus is the land walls."

"The walls will stand," a priest said. "They have always stood. They will always stand."

"They have always withstood attacks before, but attacks change," Radu said. "The sultan spares no expense on new methods and weapons. He has studied the walls, has even been here in person. He means to focus on the Lycus River Valley and the section outside the palace."

A man near the front frowned. He wore clothes closer in fashion to the Ottomans than to the Byzantines. "Those are obvious choices. We already know this."

"Orhan is right," the Italian man said. Radu startled, looking closer at the oddly dressed man who had just spoken. Orhan was the false heir to the Ottoman Empire—a man whom Constantinople had used to threaten Mehmed's rule since before it began. Even now, Mehmed had to send money periodically or else Constantine would send Orhan into the empire to stir up civil war.

Orhan had been and was an actual, active threat to Mehmed's life. Anger flared in Radu's heart. He wanted something to hurt these people, to make them feel the fear they should. "He has artillery."

"We have seen artillery!" a portly man shouted. "So he throws some stones. Our stones are bigger." Laughter echoed through the room. Encouraged, the man continued. "The Ottomans have never had stones as big as ours."

Radu offered a tight smile in response to the man's dirty bravado. "They have a cannon four times my height that can shoot a six-hundred-pound ball over a mile."

No one laughed at that, though several scoffed visibly. Constantine sighed. "We may as well bring in food. And I hope someone is writing all this down?" He gestured for Radu to take an empty seat nearby.

Radu sat. He was in, for good or ill.

Constantine looked at the ceiling as though an answer were there. "What if we relinquish Orhan's claim?"

Radu looked at the pretend heir. Orhan stared down at his hands, which were soft and pale. Not warrior's hands, like Constantine's or the Italian's. Orhan nodded.

Constantine reached out and squeezed the other man's shoulder. "We release any threat against Mehmed's legitimacy.

We graciously decline payment for the land the Rumeli Hisari is built on. We increase our payments to him."

Radu wondered if he should encourage that. Perhaps Mehmed would want it. But he would still attack. And everything here would be Mehmed's in the end, so it did not matter. Radu would tell the truth. "His mind is set on the city with a singular focus. He has spoken and dreamed of little else since he was twelve. I do not think anything will deter him now. You can offer, but short of surrender, you should prepare for siege." Radu dared to hope that after hearing his tales of men and cannons, they *would* surrender. He could deliver the city, unharmed, directly to Mehmed!

Constantine turned to the Italian, eyebrows raised expectantly. "Giustiniani?"

Giustiniani's Greek was heavily accented, but he spoke with a command and even a joviality that demanded confidence. "We are nearly settled, your grace. We stretched your purse as far as we could. All the food and water is stored. We have enough to last for a year, with minimal supplementation." He smiled bitterly. "There are advantages to so many leaving, after all."

Radu wilted inside. No easy surrender, then.

Giustiniani continued. "We may be outmatched in artillery, boats, and men—overwhelmingly outmatched in men—but rest assured, Constantinople is still the best-defended city in the world. It will not fall easily. Tell me, Radu: do you think we can outlast Mehmed?"

Radu weighed the truth. Surrender was not on their minds yet. And they were right to make an effort. Even speaking the words felt disloyal, but acknowledging reality would not change it. "If you can draw out the siege long enough, you have a chance. The Ottomans have come against Constantinople before, and they have always failed. They are superstitious; they will see portents of doom in any delay or failed initiative. Mehmed will be fighting time and morale. He is better prepared than anyone who has ever come before, but he is betting his throne and his legacy on this single assault. If you can outlast him, he will never be able to amass the support to make another attempt."

"So if we do this, the city is safe from him."

Radu nodded. "I do not doubt that if Mehmed fails at the wall, he will not live long afterward. There are too many powerful men who do not like him." The thought terrified Radu. Halil Vizier was still with Mehmed, working against him at every possible turn. How could Radu protect Mehmed from here?

Constantine stared blankly at the floor, his expression far away. "All we have to do is outlast him, then."

It was as simple and as impossible as that.

20

Late March

"WHERE ARE YOU GOING?" Bogdan asked.

Lada whipped around, knives in her hands. Taking a deep breath, she put them away. It was near midnight. She had thought her furtive exit from camp would go unmarked. She should have known Bogdan would mark it, as he did all her movements. He had a way of tracking her, watching her without watching. His childhood loyalty had grown as broad and strong as he had. Usually Lada found comfort in that. But lately it felt far more serious, like he was not only looking for her but also looking for something *from* her.

She had been deliberately vague about their purpose on the shared border of Hungary, Transylvania, and Wallachia. None of her men had questioned her disobeying Hunyadi's directive and leaving the Transylvanian passes they were supposed to guard.

Lada did not know how her men would feel about taking up with the Ottomans yet again. Some harbored less ill will toward their onetime captors and benefactors; others hated them. Doubtless some would prefer to fight for Constantinople than at the sides of Ottomans. But she was their leader. They joined her to take back Wallachia, and she did not need permission to make decisions. If they did not like it, they were welcome to make their own way.

Her way was forward, to the throne, however she got there.

"You are supposed to be patrolling on the other end of camp," she snapped.

Though she could not see his face, she could practically feel Bogdan's blunt smile. "You did not answer my question."

"Because I do not have to. I am leaving. I will be back. That is everything you need to know."

"Something is wrong."

"Nothing is wrong!" All day she had been on edge, knowing how close Mehmed was. She was not certain of the precise location of his camp, but she knew it was within a few miles of where she stood now. Mehmed was within a few miles, not separated by rivers and countries and the year that had come between them. She thought she had hidden her agitation well, but apparently not.

"I will go with you."

"No!" Not Bogdan. Anyone but Bogdan. Lada could not face him if he found out what she was doing. Admitting it felt like asking permission, and she refused to do that. Besides, she remembered Bogdan's thinly veiled distaste for Mehmed. She did not want to bring that along with her. "I must go alone."

"Why?"

"Get back to your patrol."

Bogdan stood, unmoving, for five eternally long breaths. Then he walked off into the night.

Lada hurried through the dark, knives back in both hands. She had a lot of ground to cover. It would have been easier on a horse, but that would have drawn even more attention to her departure. Still, after an hour crisscrossing through the terrain, looking for signs of a camp, Lada found herself slowing down. She wished she could enjoy walking alone—solitude was not a luxury she had much of lately—but she knew what awaited her.

Who awaited her.

And she did not know how to feel about seeing him again after so long apart. She had not been able to sort through her feelings, to separate what was real and what was merely a reaction to the circumstances of her childhood. What if she saw Mehmed and felt nothing? Worse, what if she saw Mehmed and felt everything as acutely as she had when they were together? It had been a hard thing, leaving him. Would this reopen the wound?

Before she could settle her emotions, she saw the familiar white cap of a Janissary. It glowed in the moonlight. Annoyance flickered through Lada. They should know better than to wear those white caps at night. If she were an assassin, this sentry would already be dead.

A slow, vicious smile spread across her face. She had planned on walking into the camp and announcing herself. She was not expected tonight—Mehmed had merely said where they would be. There had been no specific time to meet established.

It was a night to play "Kill the Sultan."

She generously decided not to hurt any sentries. They would

probably be punished for their failure to detect her, but they deserved that. The first was easily skirted. The second and third announced their approach with a cacophony of snapping twigs. Closer to camp, the going was more difficult. The tents were packed close, and under cover of trees. Between the trees and the darkness, Lada could not get a sense for how many men Mehmed had brought. It did not seem like enough. He probably had them spread out, though. That was what she would have done.

She pressed into the deeper darkness behind a tent as two Janissaries walked by, talking in quiet voices. She had an odd stirring of something that felt like nostalgia at hearing Turkish again. Scowling, she gripped her knives harder.

Mehmed's tent might as well have had his name painted on it. It was the largest, made of sumptuous cloth in what she assumed would be red and gold in the sunlight. That was another mistake. If she were in charge, he would be sleeping in one of the small, anonymous tents. Make an assassin look through every tent, rather than boldly advertising the target.

He really did make this too easy.

Lada peered around the edge of a soldier's tent from which gentle snores emanated. The entrance to Mehmed's grand tent was manned by two Janissaries, both awake and alert. Lada slipped around to the back of the tent, which was guarded only by her friend darkness.

She darted forward, not hesitating as she stabbed a knife into the tent and dragged it down. With only the barest whisper of material, she had her own private entrance.

Inside, it was dim, a coal brazier in the corner giving only a faint glow. Lada wondered who had to carry the furniture

Mehmed traveled with: a desk, a stool, a full table, an assortment of pillows, and a bed. No bedrolls for the sultan, whose body was too precious for the ground.

And whose body was in that bed, breathing softly.

Lada crept forward with her knife raised. And then she stopped, looking down at Mehmed.

She had forgotten the thick sweep of his black lashes. His full lips were turned down at the corners, as though his dreams troubled him. His hair, so often covered by turbans the past few years, was draped on his pillow, one strand lying across his forehead. Lada was filled with a sudden tenderness. She reached out and brushed the hair from his skin.

He awoke with a start, grabbing her wrist. His eyes were wide, body tensed for a fight. Lada leaned closer. She had never seen this ferocity in his face. She wanted to taste it.

Mehmed kept his painful grip on her wrist. "Lada?" he asked, blinking rapidly.

"I have just killed you. Again."

He pulled her down, meeting her lips with desperate hunger. She dropped the knife. She had forgotten what it was to be kissed, to be desired. She had thought she did not need it.

She had been wrong.

Mehmed moved from her lips to her neck, his hands in her hair. "When you left, you took my heart with you. Kill me, Lada," he said, with so much longing she could not keep her own hands off him. He rolled so she was beneath him. His hands explored her body, alternating between rough greediness and softness so gentle it nearly hurt her.

He put his mouth against her ear. "I have learned some things," he said, voice teasing, "about pleasure."

Before she could wonder where he had learned those things—things she had accused him of not caring about aside from his own satisfaction—he moved down her body. Her back arched as his hands slid under her tunic and up her torso. She grabbed his hair, not knowing whether she wanted to pull him away or draw him closer. She feared if he continued, she would lose control. She had never let herself lose control before.

His hands found the space between her legs and she cried out with the shock and intensity of it. He responded with greater eagerness, kissing her stomach, her breasts. He pulled her tunic up higher, and, impatient with his clumsiness, she tugged it off herself. They had done this much before, but absence had made every sensation stronger. This was where she had always stopped him, where she had always drawn the line so that she stayed in charge of what they did. So that she remained hers, and hers alone.

She did not stop him.

He pulled off his own nightshirt. He wore nothing underneath.

He unlaced her trousers and pulled them off. She thought he would try to put himself inside her, and thought—maybe— she wanted him to.

Instead, he lifted her legs and kissed her, and kissed her, and kissed her where she had never imagined being kissed. Lada's control fled on the wave of pleasure, and she did not miss it. She cried out like a wounded thing, but Mehmed put a hand over her mouth as he shifted on top of her.

She let him.

21

Late March

"HOW MANY ANGELS CAN dance on the head of a pin?" a man shouted, a sneer deforming his pockmarked face.

Another man jabbed his finger into the first man's chest, screaming something about the Father and the Son. The pockmarked man threw a punch, and then they were wrestling on the muddy street, biting and kicking.

Cyprian did not even pause as he steered Radu around them. "People here are very ... religious?"

Cyprian laughed darkly. "To all our downfall. There she is." He pointed. With nothing else to do for the day, Radu had asked to see more of the city. He wanted to see the fabled Hagia Sophia cathedral in particular. Mehmed had told him to visit. It had been his only actual instruction. And until Constantine called for him again, there was not much he could do besides wander with his eyes and ears open.

The street led to a courtyard, where the massive cathedral loomed. It was darker than Cyprian's laugh. Everywhere they had passed churches with bells ringing, a near-constant stream of people going in and out. But the Hagia Sophia, the jewel of Constantinople, the church so magnificent that stories said it had converted the entire population of Russia to Orthodoxy, sat cold and empty in the late-afternoon rain.

"Why is no one here?" Radu asked. They walked up to the gate, and Cyprian pushed experimentally against the door. It was locked.

"We had Mass in Latin here a few weeks ago."

Radu knew that Orthodox services were conducted in Greek, but he did not follow Cyprian's meaning.

A dog ran past them, followed by a young boy with bare feet. "Rum Papa!" he shouted. "Stop, Rum Papa! Come back right now!"

"Did that boy call his dog the Roman pope?"

Cyprian rapped his knuckles against the beautiful lacquered wood of the Hagia Sophia door. "Yes. Half the dogs in the city are called that. While my uncle appeals to the pope for help, people curse his name. My uncle pushed for union between the two churches, and even held Mass here to celebrate the official reunion, the ending of the schism between East and West. And now the most beautiful church in Christendom is silent and abandoned because it was tainted by watered wine, Catholic wafers, and worship in Latin." Cyprian sighed, resting the palm of his hand reverently against the door. "And for all her sacrifice, the Hagia Sophia brought us nothing. The pope sends no aid." He shook his head. "Come. We can see some relics. That is always fun."

"You and I have different opinions of fun."

Cyprian laughed, this time a bright sound at odds with the

dreary, wet day. "We take our relics very seriously in this city. They protect us." He winked.

"Do you really believe that?"

"Does it matter? If the people believe it, then it gives them strength, which gives the city strength, which means the relics worked."

"That is very circular."

"We Byzantines love circles. Time, the moon, arguments, and, most of all, coins. All good things are circular."

They passed another empty section of the city. As they walked, Cyprian cheerfully gave the history of this pillar or that crumbling foundation. The whole city was steeped in heritage, and falling down around them.

They were almost to another church when the ground rumbled beneath their feet. Radu stumbled, and Cyprian caught him. A sliding noise came from above. "Run!" Cyprian shouted, tugging Radu away from the walls of a house next to them. Slate crashed down with shattering force where they had just been standing. The two men dove onto the muddy street.

Radu breathed heavily, his arms tangled up in Cyprian's. Cyprian's eyes met his own, black pupils nearly swallowing the gray. Then he shook his head and stood. They brushed as much of the mud from their clothes as they could, but it was a lost cause.

"Thank you," Radu said. "Your quick instincts saved us both."

Cyprian smiled shyly, reaching out to flick away some mud on Radu's shoulder. "Consider it partial payment against the debt I owe you."

Guilt seeped the color from the world. Radu swallowed,

turning away. "Does that happen often? The earth shaking like that?"

"More and more lately. We have also had unseasonable storms, and a miserable winter and a torturous spring. You can imagine how much that boosts the morale of people looking for signs and portents in everything around them."

They heard someone shouting up ahead. Radu wondered if it was another fight, but the cadence suggested a performance. They made their way toward the voice, crossing a couple of streets until they found a crowd gathered around a man standing on the wall outside a shrine.

"Wretched Romans, how you have been led astray! You have trusted in the power of the Franks, rather than the hope in your God. You have lost the true religion, and our city will be destroyed for your sins!" The man, who wore rough-woven brown robes, lifted his arms to the cloud-laden skies and tipped his head back. "O Lord, be merciful to me. I am pure and innocent of blame for the corruption of this city." He snapped his head upright to stare down at the crowd and swept a hand over their heads. "Be aware, miserable citizens, of what you have done by betraying your faith in God for the promises of the pope. You have denied the true faith given to you by your fathers. You have accepted the slavery of heresy. In doing so, you have confessed all your sins to God. Woe to you when you are judged!"

Women cried out, beating at their chests. Men held children up, begging for blessings. Vicious, ugly shouts against Constantine, the pope, and all of Italy tore through the air.

Cyprian made a rude gesture, then took Radu's arm and pulled him away. "That fool hates the pope more than he hates the sultan. He would love nothing more than to see the city burn, welcoming hell with open arms as proof that he was right all along."

"How can they hate Constantine for doing whatever he must to protect them?"

Cyprian rubbed his face wearily, then looked down at his still-muddy hands. "This is Constantinople. We are more concerned with the purity of our souls than the survival of our bodies. Come. There is nothing left worth seeing here."

After they had washed, and eaten dinner with Nazira, Cyprian excused himself to attend to his uncle. Constantine's main duties seemed to be an endless campaign of letter writing, his weapon the pen, his ammunition empty promises and desperate pleading. Radu wished that Cyprian had invited him to come along.

"Patience," Nazira reminded him, squeezing his shoulder as he cleaned the dishes. "You will find ways to help. The best thing we can do now is become a part of the city."

Radu turned to see her wearing clothes in the style of the women in Constantinople: a stiff and structured bodice, with tight sleeves and excessive skirts. He raised his eyebrows. Twirling in a circle, she smirked. "Do you like it? I feel like a flower in the wrong petals."

"You always look lovely. Are you going somewhere?"

"Oh, yes. I met the wife of one of Emperor Constantine's advisors today in the market. She felt very sorry for me when I confessed I did not know how to cook with the food here. I am invited to supper with her."

"But we just had supper—and it was very good."

Nazira's smirk grew. "But she does not know that. And at this supper, I will meet all the other wives of important men, and they will gossip about all the mistresses of the important men, and in such a way I will soon have a larger net than you."

"I did not realize it was a competition."

Nazira laughed, rising up on her toes to kiss Radu on both cheeks. "It is. It is a competition to see who can find out the most the fastest so that we can go home."

She said it lightly, but Radu could hear the longing in her voice. Nazira never spoke of Fatima, and he was too ashamed of having separated them to bring her up. But if he missed his aching, one-sided relationship with Mehmed every day, how much more must she miss the woman who loved her back?

"I would place all my bets on you and your gossip, then. You are a terrifying creature."

Curtsying prettily, Nazira left. Radu was restless and itchy with anticipation. Alone for the first time since he had come to the city, he slipped out of Cyprian's home and into the evening-dark streets. He drew his cloak close against the bite of the cold drifting up from the stones beneath his feet.

Terrifying thoughts nipped at his heels. Nazira already had plans in motion. All Radu had was one meeting with Constantine in which he had merely told the truth. The fear he had been avoiding wrapped itself around him even tighter than his cloak.

He had no idea what he was doing.

This whole thing had been a mistake. Even if he got crucial information, pulled from Cyprian or Constantine, he had no way of communicating it to Mehmed. They had no code, no ways of trading messages. Unless Radu found some brilliant form of sabotage within the city, his being here as a spy was almost pointless. He did not want to fail Mehmed, but he could not shake the worry that Mehmed had failed him. Why had he sent Radu here with so little instruction, so little preparation? Radu would have been much better used at his side.

Or maybe that was simply what Radu was desperate to believe, because Mehmed's side was the only place he wanted to be. Was he really so expendable?

Or ... had Mehmed suspected Radu's true feelings, and deliberately sent him far away? Radu knew he should not feel the way he did about another man. There were many things that could be justified. But he did not know of anything that allowed for what he wanted from Mehmed.

Would this love separate him both from the most important person in his life and from the God that brought him solace in his loneliness?

He had meant to wander and get a better idea of the lay of the city, but he found himself back at the dark Hagia Sophia. Even now, he followed Mehmed's requests without conscious thought.

No one was in the streets. Radu removed some tools from a secret pocket in his vest and carefully picked the lock. After a few patient minutes, he was rewarded with a click. He slipped inside. It took his eyes some time to adjust to the darkness. He jumped at a rustling noise, fearing discovery, but it was the clacking of pigeon wings. They, too, had come to the empty church to worship.

Releasing all his exhaustion and fear with a long exhalation, he prayed. He had not been able to fully pray since arriving in Constantinople. Going through the movements was more comforting than slipping into a warm bath, and equally cleansing. He released everything he had been holding. His focus was singular, his faith a bright point in the dark building.

Reluctant to leave when he was done, he climbed the stairs to the gallery where the women would stand during services. Eventually, he found a small door that led to another flight of stairs, and then to a ladder. Pushing against the trapdoor at the top, he emerged onto the roof. Constantinople unfolded beneath him. He could see the palace, a hulking structure where Constantine worked into the night.

It would be enough to be here, waiting. He would get close to Constantine, and trust that a way to help Mehmed would reveal itself. He would trust that Mehmed had a plan for him. He would trust that God would help him in this mission.

Radu tried to draw that trust closer than the fear. Looking out over the city, he wondered at each of the lights. Who lived there? What were they thinking? Were they, too, praying for peace? For direction? For protection?

And whose god was listening?

He sat on the edge of the roof, his feet dangling in the void beneath him. It echoed the one that had opened up inside him. He felt close to falling—or to flying. He did not know which it would be, but had no doubt time would tell.

22

Early April

MEHMED LAY WITH AN ease so complete he seemed like a different person. Lada wondered . . . No, she would wonder nothing. Think about nothing. If he could exist in this space like he needed nothing more in the whole world than what he had just had, she could do the same.

That lasted about two minutes. She squirmed, pushing him away from her. "Do you always sweat this much?"

He laughed, pulling her close and nuzzling his face against her neck. His hand found somewhere else. "Would you like me to make you sweat more?"

She shrieked, half from delight, half from the shock of his wandering fingers, and pushed him. Before she could realize her mistake in making so much noise, the tent's front flap opened and two Janissaries rushed in. Mehmed shifted so that Lada was hidden behind him.

"Leave," Mehmed said, his voice coldly imperious and so different from the one he had been using moments before.

"We heard—"

"Leave."

The Janissaries bowed. One paused. "Your grace, we have reports of a skirmish, with Hunyadi, on the Serbian-Hungarian border."

"Reports that can wait until the morning! Do not come back in here for any reason."

The Janissaries nearly fell over as they bowed low and backed out in a rush.

Lada propped herself up on an elbow and drew the blanket up over her bare chest. "You do have troops there, then?"

Mehmed tried to pull her back down. "You are letting all the cold air in."

She scooted farther away. "Why do you have men on the Hungarian border?"

There was a studied casualness to Mehmed's voice that made the hairs on the back of Lada's neck rise. "As a reminder to Hunyadi that he is still needed in Hungary."

"But I persuaded Hunyadi to stay out of Constantinople. I told you I had. Do you not trust me?"

"Of course I trust you! But I cannot risk anything. It was extra assurance, is all."

It made sense, Lada supposed. But the fact that he felt he had to double up on work she had already done bothered her. And she worried for Hunyadi's safety. He was one of the few people in the world she considered family.

Family. Lada had not even thought to ask about Radu yet. "Where is Radu? Did he come?" He had not come with the ambassadors, but where Mehmed was, Radu would be, too.

Mehmed stopped trying to coax her back down. He flopped

flat onto his back, raising an arm over his face as though tired. "No, Radu did not come."

"He did not come," she repeated, her voice flat with disappointment and shock. She needed her brother. He had a way with people like the boyars. Hunyadi had been right—she did not have the weapons for that kind of combat. Radu did. How dare he reject her again. "Did he say why?"

Mehmed shook his head.

"Where is he now?" What was important enough to keep him away from both Lada and Mehmed?

Mehmed shrugged. He was avoiding answering her. She grabbed the arm that covered his face and pulled it down so he could not hide his expression from her. "Where is my brother, Mehmed?"

He looked at the ceiling of the tent. "Constantinople."

"The siege has already started?" The siege had started, and Mehmed was here. With her. She was warm with pleasure over finally outranking that stupid city.

"No."

Her pleasure fled, leaving her cold. "Then what is he doing in Constantinople? Did you make him an ambassador? You know how dangerous that is!"

"I needed someone there, inside."

Lada sat up, the blankets dropping. He had not answered her question about Radu being an ambassador. He had dodged it with something that sounded like an answer, but obviously was not. Not an ambassador, then. "You sent him as a *spy*!"

"I needed someone I could trust absolutely."

"I do not care what you needed! He was supposed to be

here, with me! Or at the very least at your side during the siege, where he would no doubt be perfectly safe."

Mehmed sat up, too, eyes flashing dangerously. "What do you mean by that?"

"I mean that wherever you are during the siege will be the safest place in the world. Which is where my brother should be as well! How could you throw him into so much danger?"

"It was the best choice."

"For him, or for you?"

"For the empire."

"Oh, for the empire! Well, that makes everything better." Lada threw back the blankets and got out of bed. She began tugging her discarded clothes on.

"Radu will be fine. He is smarter and stronger than you have ever given him credit for," Mehmed said.

Lada jabbed a finger against his bare chest. "Do not dare tell me you know my brother better than I do."

Mehmed laughed. "But I do."

Words she knew she would always regret saying halted on the tip of her tongue. If Mehmed did not know how Radu felt about him, he would not learn of it from her. "You ask too much of him."

"I ask only what he is willing to do. Nothing more."

"Then I do know him better, you fool. Radu would do *anything* for you."

Mehmed looked away, a dark flush spreading across his cheeks.

"You know . . ." Lada's eyes narrowed to thin slits, her fists clenched so tightly they ached. "You know that he is in love with you."

Mehmed tilted his head to the side, as though brushing something off his shoulder. "Your brother is very important to me."

"But he will never be as important to you as you are to him. Mehmed, release him. You must release him from this false hope he carries."

He shook his head. "I cannot. I care for Radu. And I need him."

"But you will never love him the way he loves you."

Mehmed stood, reaching for Lada's fisted hands. "How could I? I love you."

Lada closed her eyes against the way his words struck her. Radu felt like a ghost in the room, looming in the whisper of a breeze against the back of her neck. She had what he wanted, and she did not even know what to do with it.

"Bring him back. He could die."

Mehmed released her hands. "I have no one else better suited to the task. It is a risk, yes. But it is an acceptable risk. He knows the dangers, and he agreed. He cares as much as I do about Constantinople."

Lada let out a harsh bark of laughter. "No one cares about anything so much as you do that accursed city."

"You care about Wallachia that much."

"Because it is mine! What claim do you have to Constantinople that justifies risking Radu's life?"

Mehmed shook his head. He sat on the edge of the bed, shoulders curved inward as he ran his fingers through his hair. "I promise Radu will come out unharmed. And then we will all be together."

"You cannot promise that. And how will we be together? He will always choose your side over mine."

"Not if my side is your side as well." He smiled up at her, exhaustion pooling in the hollows beneath his eyes. "I cannot do this alone. You were right to leave before. I did not know your value, and I would have left you behind. But I know now." His smile turned tender. "And you know now, too. I need you with me. I *want* you with me. Stand by my side at the walls. Help me claim my destiny. And then ... rule it. With me. As empress of Rome."

Lada took a small step back, overwhelmed. "Empress."

Still naked, Mehmed stood before her, completely open and vulnerable, with his hands out, palms up. "Take the city with me. Take the crown. Take *me*, Lada."

A memory long since forgotten played out in front of her. Huma, Mehmed's terrifying mother, telling her the story of Theodora. The actress, the prostitute, the powerless woman who found the love of the emperor and rose to be emperor with him. Saving him and the city, changing everything to her vision of how it should be based only on her strength.

And the strength of the man who loved her.

Could Lada be that woman?

But Mehmed had not said *emperor.* He had said *empress.* Emperor consort. She would still owe her power and her position to a man. And she was no lowly prostitute, no actress. She already had a birthright of her own.

"What about Wallachia?"

"Forget about Wallachia! Why be vaivode of a worthless country when you can be empress of the greatest empire in the world?"

She stepped back from him. "Because if I do not lead Wallachia, no one will."

Mehmed brushed a hand through the air. "We will make certain Wallachia is always taken care of."

Lada shook her head slowly. The offer was tempting. But she was so close to Wallachia. She could feel it nearby, just as she had Mehmed. She could not turn her back on her country now. "Where are the troops? I can—we can discuss this after. When I have Wallachia secured, and you have Constantinople, then . . . then, I do not know. Maybe there will be a way for us. After we have accomplished what we need to."

Hurt reshaped Mehmed's face into something younger, softer. "Is that the only reason you came?"

"Of course it is!" Lada snapped.

His vulnerability was replaced with cold, stony features and imperious brows. He grabbed his nightshirt and pulled it over his head. "There are no troops."

"What do you mean?"

"I need every man I have. I cannot spare them to destabilize a country I already control. I have a treaty with the Danesti prince."

Lada staggered back. "But you could spare men to harass Hunyadi. You did not need to do that. You could have trusted me and given me those forces instead. Were there ever any troops? Did you ever mean to help me?"

"I *am* helping you! You are destined for bigger things! With me." He stepped toward her and she put her hands up.

"You did not write me. Not once, not until after I wrote Radu about having Hunyadi's trust. You saw an opportunity, and you used me. I betrayed Hunyadi for you." In all her life, Lada had never felt as small and miserable as she did then. She had sold Hunyadi's kindness for nothing. All her justifications and rationalizing amounted to nothing. She was no closer to Wallachia in spite of all her sacrifices. "You tricked me."

"I did you a favor! Even if I sent you the troops, even if you took the throne, you could never keep it. They would never follow a woman as prince. Abandon this delusion, Lada. It will destroy you. Come with me. Fight at my side. I trust only you with my life." He pointed at the slit in the tent wall. "I could die without you."

Lada raised an eyebrow. "I suppose that is an acceptable risk."

Mehmed threw his hands in the air and started pacing. "I am offering you so much more. I am offering you the world. I am offering you myself." He pointed angrily at the bed. "You were happy enough to accept it a few minutes ago."

"That was different! You promised me soldiers."

Disgust squeezed his words. "Was this merely a transaction for you?"

Lada slammed her fist into his stomach. He doubled over, and she spoke right into his ear. "Do not *ever* talk to me that way." But his words had struck too close to home. Angry tears filled her eyes. She had not sold her body to him, and she hated him for thinking she had used it to manipulate him. But she *had* sold her determination to gain the throne on her own, as well as her relationship with Hunyadi. All for the false promise of a few hundred men.

Mehmed caught her hand and pressed it against his cheek. "Whatever else you believe, know that what I did, I did out of love. I love you. I have always loved you. Will you still choose Wallachia?"

Lada yanked her hand away and retrieved her knife from

the floor. "You betray my brother with your feigned ignorance of his feelings. You betrayed me. But I will never betray Wallachia." She lifted the knife, pointing it at him. "If you set foot on Wallachian soil again—*my* soil—I will kill you."

Ignoring Mehmed as he shouted her name, she left the tent through the same cut she had entered it. This time it seemed much deeper.

23

Early April

IN THE CLAMMY MORNING fog, Radu sweated. He leaned
against the stone steps for a few breaths, then continued
climbing. The awkward shape of the tombstone chunk he
held made his fingers cramp. When he finally reached the top
of the wall, he staggered to the mound of stones and added
his own.

"Funny, using tombstones of the dead to repair the walls."

Radu looked up into the well-worn but cheerful face of
Giovanni Giustiniani, the Italian man from his first, and so far
only, meeting with Constantine. Giustiniani was tall, broad-
shouldered, even powerful in the way he moved. A deep line
between his brows made them look set in a permanent scowl,
but all his other wrinkles told of smiling and laughter.

Radu wiped his forehead with the back of his arm and
straightened. He was only a couple of inches taller than the
older man. "Well, it is the least those citizens could contribute
to the city's defense."

Giustiniani laughed, a sound like a cannon shot. He clapped

a hand on Radu's shoulder. "I remember you. You brought us news of the infidels' preparations."

Radu nodded. It was always jarring to hear the Ottomans referred to as the infidels, since that was what they called the Christians. "I wish I had come armed with better tidings."

"All information, good or bad, helps us." Giustiniani sighed and turned toward a group of men shouting at each other. "The dead contributing their tombstones may yet do more than the living who cannot stop fighting with each other." He strode away, toward the fight.

Radu leaned over the edge of the wall and looked out onto the plain beneath. It had been cleared of anything that could hide the Ottoman forces. In front of them was a fosse, a large, deep ditch meant to slow down attackers and make them easy to pick off. Constantinople's defenses of a fosse, the outer wall where Radu stood, and an inner wall had repelled all attackers for more than a thousand years.

But none of those attackers had been Mehmed.

"Radu!" The voice triggered a wave of happiness even before Radu realized who had called to him.

Radu turned to find Cyprian walking next to the emperor. Radu bowed deeply, trying to look surprised, as though he had not overheard Cyprian saying that he would be touring the walls with Constantine today, as though Radu had not deliberately stationed himself at one of the weakest points of the wall, knowing that the two men would end up here sooner rather than later. Cyprian had been so busy that he and Radu barely saw each other, even living in the same house.

But going out of his way to run into the other man was

tactical. It was not because he was lonely for conversation with anyone outside of the bedroom he shared with Nazira. She, too, was frequently gone, making social calls and leaving Radu with far too much time to think.

"Have you seen Giustiniani?" Cyprian asked.

"You only now missed him. There was a fight, and he went to see about it."

Constantine leaned out over the wall, itching at his beard. "If the Italians send us nothing else but Giustiniani, they have still done more to help than anyone. I cannot keep the Genoese from fighting with the Venetians, who fight with the Greeks, who suspect the Genoese, who hate the Orthodox, who hate the Catholics. Only the Turks under Orhan seem to get along with everyone." He smiled wryly at Radu.

"Orhan is still here?" Radu was surprised that he had not fled the city in advance of the siege.

"He has nowhere else to go. And I am glad for his help, and the help of his men. He is no Giustiniani, but no one is. Except perhaps Hunyadi."

Radu was eager to contribute to a topic he knew something about. "I had never heard of Giustiniani before, but if he is anything like Hunyadi, the Ottomans will fear and hate him."

"They fear Hunyadi that much?"

"He is a specter that haunts them. Even their victories against him count for little when stacked against how much he has cost them. His name alone would cause problems for Mehmed."

Constantine nodded thoughtfully. "He should have been here by now. I am afraid we have lost him."

"But you have more Venetians?" Radu hoped it sounded like he was trying to be positive rather than fishing for more information.

"Only a handful. We hope more are coming. Galata, our neighbor, will send no men. They are too afraid of being caught in the conflict. They are everyone's allies, and thus no one's. It was all we could do to make them attach the boom across the horn."

The giant chain that closed access to the Golden Horn bay was strung from Constantinople to Galata. Sitting along the swift water leading to the horn, Galata lacked Constantinople's natural defenses. If Mehmed attacked the city, it would fall. But he did not want to waste resources on Galata. If he took Constantinople, Galata would effectively be his.

During the day, people walked freely between the cities, but at night both closed and locked their gates. Radu wished everyone in Constantinople would walk across the bay to Galata and stay there. He did not understand why they stayed in Constantinople. When Mehmed arrived, Radu hoped they would finally see the futility.

"There," Constantine said, pointing. Cyprian was taking detailed notes. Radu moved closer, following the direction of Constantine's finger. "We need as many men as can be spared on the Lycus River section."

Though Constantinople was on a hill, there was one section of the wall that did not command high ground. The Lycus River cut straight through it, making a fosse impossible to dig, and lowering that section to a dangerously accessible level. Radu knew all this from Mehmed's maps, but it was still a strange thrill to see it in person, and from this side of the wall, too, where he had not expected to be until after the siege.

Constantine detailed which men and commanders should be stationed where. Radu committed it to memory, secreting it away with all the other information he heard. Everywhere they went, Constantine stood straight and confident, complimenting the men on the work in progress, giving suggestions for further improvements. He may have been jeered in the streets, but among the soldiers it was apparent that he was deeply respected—and returned the respect.

"Here," he said, stopping again. They had come to a patchwork section. Where the other walls were shining limestone with a red seam of brick running through, this one had a haphazard look to it. And, unlike the rest, there was only one wall, rather than two. It jutted out at a right angle, the palace where Constantine lived rising behind it.

"Why is this section so different?" Radu asked, though he knew the answer.

"We could not leave a shrine outside the walls." Constantine's tone hinted at annoyance, but his confident smile never left. "We are better protected by one wall and a holy shrine than by two walls without one. Or at least, that was the reasoning a few hundred years ago when they built the wall out to encompass the shrine."

Constantine noted several weakened and crumbling points as he talked with a foreman directing repairs. Finally, the three men descended the stairs and went back into the city through a sally port, a heavily guarded gate used to let soldiers in and out during attacks. "Tell me, Radu, what do you think of my walls?" Constantine asked.

"I think they deserve their tremendous reputation. They have stood for this long for a reason."

Constantine nodded thoughtfully. "They will protect us yet."

They had lasted a thousand years of unchanging siege warfare. But Mehmed was not the past. Mehmed was the future. He brought things no one else had yet imagined, and that no walls had yet seen.

Constantine spoke again, his thoughts apparently on the same man as Radu's. "I hear the sultan is repairing roads and bridges all over my lands. It is very generous of him to perform maintenance while I am busy. Do you think he would spare some of his men to help us repair the walls while he is at it?"

Radu laughed weakly. "I am afraid I am no longer in the position to make that request."

Constantine's face turned serious so quickly that Radu feared he had betrayed something. The emperor's hand came down on his shoulder, but instead of a blow, it was a reassuring weight. "I know why you fled. Everyone has heard of his depravity, his harems of both women and men. You are safe here, Radu. You never have to go back to that life."

Several moments passed while Radu worked through Constantine's words and tone. He looked at Cyprian, who was staring determinedly up at the palace. And then everything made sense. The sneering guard they had passed at the Rumeli Hisari. Everyone's willingness to accept that Radu would so easily turn from Mehmed. Eyes filled with scorn or with pity.

"I— Yes, thank you. I have to— Excuse me." Radu turned and walked stiffly away. When he had rounded a corner and was out of sight, he sank against the wall, pushing a fist into his mouth in horror.

Was that the rumor, then? That Mehmed had a male harem? And that Radu had been the jewel of it? *Radu the Handsome.* Someone else had called him that recently, before the soldier. Halil Vizier, back in Edirne. Was he the source? Was this another tactic of his to demean Mehmed, to make him seem evil?

Radu did not know which filled him with more despair— that everyone had heard this rumor except him, or that the mere suggestion of Mehmed loving women and men was seen as evil. His feelings for Mehmed had never felt evil or wicked. They had been the truest of his life, bordering on holy. To hear his love so casually profaned made him sick to his stomach.

And then another, more horrible thought occurred to him. Mehmed must know about these rumors. Surely he knew. Was the ruse of Radu's distance from Mehmed not simply for their enemies? The way Mehmed had jumped on the chance to send Radu away, too, with so little preparation or aid. Mehmed had been eager to take the opportunity without any information or guarantees. Radu had thought it was because Mehmed trusted him. Now he wondered.

Did Mehmed know the rumors *and* Radu's true feelings, and had he sent Radu here to end both of them?

———◆———

Radu collapsed into bed next to Nazira. He had spent a long day helping repair the walls. The irony of being sent behind the walls to undermine them while physically repairing them was not lost on Radu's aching muscles.

Sighing heavily, he put an arm over his face. "You first."

Nazira shoved him onto his stomach, then began kneading

the muscles in his back. Radu sank deeper into the uneven mattress, not caring about the feather spines that jabbed into him. Simple human contact with someone who cared about him did more healing than Nazira's small hands ever could. He realized how little anyone had actually touched him over the last few years. Lada had never been physically affectionate, unless he counted her fists. Lazar had frequently *accidentally* touched him, but Radu tried his best not to think about his dead friend. He could remember every moment of physical contact with Mehmed, but each was too short, too formal, never enough.

And then there had been the horrible kiss with Halil's son, Salih, a kiss that still filled Radu with self-loathing for how much he had liked being wanted, even when he did not return the feeling.

So this friendly intimacy with Nazira had its benefits. Of course, the downside to being married was that they were given the same room, and same bed, to share. Sometimes Radu woke up from dreams—aching, desperate dreams in which his mind somehow knew the sensations his actual body had yet to experience—in a state he *really* did not want Nazira to witness. Frequently, in spite of his exhaustion, he could not fall asleep for fear of what he might dream about while lying next to her.

Nazira worked on a tender knot and Radu grimaced. "Let me think of what I heard today," she said. "Mehmed is the Antichrist."

"Yes, I heard that one, too."

"Did you hear about the child who dreamed that the angel guarding the city walls abandoned his post?"

"No, that is a new one. I heard about a fisherman who drew up oysters that dripped blood."

"Good thing I never cared for oysters. And fish! So much fish in this city. If I never eat fish again when we leave, I will be happy. What else. Hmm. Oh! Helen, one of my new friends, is very bitter. Apparently the first emperor of the city was Constantine, son of Helen. And now this emperor is Constantine, son of Helen, which means the circle of history is closing and the city is doomed. It also means the name Helen is deeply unpopular, and she is taking it quite personally."

"Why are you friends with her?"

"She is currently entertaining one of the Venetian ship captains, a man named Coco. She talks about him constantly."

"Well done," Radu said, wincing as Nazira hit another particularly sore area of his shoulders. "Word from the walls is that with the relic of the true cross in the city, it cannot be taken by the Antichrist. On the other hand, they do not like the patterns of birds flying in the skies. However, Mary herself is protecting the city. Unfortunately, someone's uncle finally decoded the secret messages scrawled on a thousand-year-old pillar that declares this the last year of Earth. But the moon will be waxing soon, and the city cannot be taken on a waxing moon, so there you have it. The city is both utterly doomed and cannot possibly fall."

"These people are insane," Nazira said sadly.

"At least it saves us the trouble of trying to foment chaos within the walls. They need no help with that."

"How are you doing with getting close to Constantine?"

Radu shrugged, rolling back over. Nazira lay on her side,

propped up on an elbow. He had not told her the real reason why Constantine accepted his loyalty without question; he was too humiliated to speak it aloud. "I see him only in passing. He is everywhere in the city, constantly on the move to inspire people."

"I have seen him a few times. Helen hates him. I think he looks nice. What about the other important men?"

"Right now they are trying to organize, and waiting for further aid before they decide where to commit. I do not see much of them. I never knew waiting could be such a wearying task."

"What about Cyprian?"

Radu shifted uncomfortably. "He is close to Constantine. He takes notes for him. I am sure he knows most of the organization of the city. But . . ."

"But what?"

Closing his eyes, Radu rubbed his face. There was a bigger issue where Cyprian was concerned, a nebulous one, the contours of which Radu had not yet traced out. He did not know if he wanted to or even could. "We are living with Cyprian. We eat meals with him, sleep next to his room." And they liked him. Nazira had not said it, but Radu could see in the smiles she gave Cyprian, the easy way she laughed at his stories over meals. Radu was not the only one with complicated feelings toward their enemy. But he rationalized them anyway. "It would be dangerous to abuse any information we get through him. Too immediately suspicious."

"True." Nazira drew the blanket up to her chin and snuggled into Radu's side. "We carry on, then."

Radu patted her arm, waiting for her breath to go steady

and deep. Then he rolled away, sitting on the edge of the bed with his head in his hands.

The only thing coming here had accomplished was getting Radu far away from Mehmed and the rumors spread about them. Radu knew if that was what Mehmed needed, he should be glad. He should be willing to sacrifice himself to protect Mehmed's vision, to protect his reputation. But he could not—would not—be willing to sacrifice Nazira.

He would stay the course. He would make something of their time here. And he would get her out alive, no matter what.

24

Early April

O ANA—THE ONLY ONE WHO knew about Lada's meeting with Mehmed—said nothing as Lada commanded
her men to pack up camp the next morning. Lada was grateful
to her for that. She could not have handled questions about the
soldiers she should have returned with.

Bogdan stayed closer to her side than ever. He never asked
where she had gone. At least his unquestioning acceptance of
her actions had not changed. But even if he asked, she would
never tell him.

Or anyone.

Lada's mind chased itself in angry circles. Mehmed—whom
she had always trusted—had deceived her. And he thought she
would choose Constantinople after that? How little he knew her.

The next night, though, lying on the frozen ground, her
mind betrayed her. Images of being empress next to Mehmed
haunted her when she closed her eyes. It was the worst part of
everything, knowing that, on some level, she wanted that much
power, even at that cost.

She awoke, gasping and aching. No. The worst were dreams of Mehmed at her side in an entirely different fashion.

She made her men move before dawn. Sleep was not her ally. She drove them hard toward Hunedoara, reassuring herself that at least she had done some good for Hunyadi. Constantinople would fall—of that she had no doubts, whatever else she might now doubt and hate about Mehmed—and Hunyadi would have died there. Her duplicity had spared him his life. She could take comfort in that.

"I hate Hungary," Petru grumbled, riding abreast of Lada, Nicolae, and Bogdan. "And that lord or noble or prince, Matthias? Whenever he is around me, he holds a handkerchief to his nose." Petru ducked his head to smell under his arms. "I smell nothing."

Nicolae leaned close, then feigned fainting. "That is because your sense of smell has killed itself out of despair."

"Matthias is not a prince," Lada said. "He is Hunyadi's son."

Petru's expression shifted in surprise. "How did Hunyadi's seed produce that weak politician?"

Nicolae's cheerful voice answered. "The same way Vlad Dracul's traitorous seed produced our valiant Lada!"

Lada stared straight ahead, numb. In that moment, she realized she was *exactly* like her father. Hunyadi had cautioned her not to discount the man who made her the way she was. Apparently her father had done his job well. She, too, had taken someone who trusted her and leveraged that trust for Ottoman aid—aid that benefitted her nothing. And she had been stupid enough to make it personal with Mehmed.

She was a fool.

"Lada?" Bogdan asked, his low, grumbling voice soft with concern.

She pushed her horse forward, outpacing them all so they could not see the first tears she had cried since she was a child.

Oana caught her, though. Lada wiped furiously at her face. "What do you want?"

"Where are we going?"

"Back to Hunyadi. He is my only ally."

Oana made a humming noise. "Not your only ally. You have other family besides your father."

"Mircea is dead, too. And none of the boyars are more closely related to the Dracul line than to the Danesti or Basarab."

"Not that side. Your mother. Last I heard, she was alive in Moldavia. And she is still royalty there."

Lada turned her head to the side and spat. "She is nothing to me."

"Be that as it may, you might not be nothing to her. Blood calls to blood. You could yet find your path to the throne through the support of her family. If nothing else, it is a place to rest and regroup. You need some rest."

Groaning, Lada rubbed her forehead. "I do not want to see her." There was a reason appealing to her Moldavian relatives had never crossed her mind. Her mother had ceased existing for her years ago. The idea of welcoming that woman back into her life, even if it got her the throne . . .

Oana leaned closer. "It cannot cost you more than whatever happened with the sultan."

"God's wounds, woman, very well." Lada ignored Oana's pleased smile as she turned her horse around. "New plan," she said when she rejoined her men.

"New plan?" Petru asked.

"Where are we off to now?" Nicolae asked.

"Moldavia."

"Moldavia?" Petru said.

"Is there an echo here?" Lada glared at Petru.

Though he ducked his head and blushed, excitement animated his voice. "Are we burning Moldavian cities? Like we did in Transylvania?"

Lada had not forgotten Matei and the waste of his death, traitor or not. She would not lose men to petty vengeance again. Only to vengeance worth taking. She shook her head.

"What, then?" Nicolae asked.

"We go to appeal to my blood. We go to see my—" She paused, feeling the edges of the next word sticking in her throat, threatening to choke her. "My mother."

———— ⚬ ————

"She is so beautiful," Petru whispered, peering through the hedge they hid behind. "You look nothing like her."

Nicolae cringed. "And that, Petru, is why your line will die with you."

Lada did not—could not—answer as her mother rode elegantly toward them down the dirt path of her country manor.

The only clear memory Lada had of the woman was one of lank hair hanging over her face, sharp shoulder blades, bowed back. Crawling. Weeping. She had expected to come here and find the same broken creature. She had not been able to picture her mother standing, much less riding.

This woman was small and fine-boned like a bird. Her hair, pinned elaborately beneath her hat, shone black with hints of silver threaded through. Her back was straight, her chin lifted, a veil of lace over her face.

Lada had been apprehensive about trying to leverage her connection to her mother to get help from the Moldavian king, her grandfather. But it had been easier to think of her mother that way, as a stepping-stone. Someone to climb over.

Here her mother was not on the ground. She was higher than Lada.

"We should leave," she said. "This was a bad idea."

"We should at least talk to her," Nicolae said.

"I do not even know if that *is* her. I have not seen her since I was three. Perhaps we were misdirected. My mother might be dead."

Bogdan pushed Petru aside, taking over his vantage point. "That is her."

"How do you know?"

He shrugged. "I was older than you when she left."

"By a year!"

He blinked at Lada, expression intractable. "I remember everything about our childhood." He said the word *our* with uncharacteristic tenderness. It made Lada feel unsettled, even more than she already was.

Lada crossed her arms over her chest. "Well, what are we supposed to do? Jump out of the hedge and scream, 'Hello, Mother!'"

Nicolae shook his head. "Of course not. She is not *our* mother. Only yours."

"She is barely even that. She will not recognize me." Lada would have to prove her identity to the woman who had fled when she was a child. She had no way of doing that.

"We could bring my mother," Bogdan said. "She was your mother's companion for many years."

They had left Oana at camp with the rest of the men, hidden along the mountain pass where they had crept into Moldavia. The whole journey Lada had longed to turn around, to flee, to go back home. But she could not. She needed help.

She *hated* needing.

"Fine." Lada stood and pushed through the hedge. She struggled out from it right as her mother's horse passed.

"God's wounds!" Vasilissa shouted, using Lada's father's favorite curse. "Where did you—" She stopped, her fingers going to her mouth, pressing at the veil.

"You should travel with guards." Lada wore her anger as armor against this woman. "We could have been anyone."

Vasilissa moved her trembling hand to her heart.

"We are not going to rob you." Lada sighed. "We are here to speak with you."

"Ladislav," Vasilissa whispered. "My little girl."

Lada had been prepared to be humiliated by introducing herself. She had not thought about what she would do if her mother knew her. She stepped back as though struck, her vision narrowing to a tunnel. Every muscle tensed, waiting for attack.

Vasilissa leaned down as far as she could from her horse. Her voice was barely discernable over the rush of blood in Lada's ears.

"Ladislav." She reached one tiny, gloved hand toward Lada's hair. Then she cleared her throat, looking Lada up and down in a way that made her feel naked. "Come. We will get you a bath and some new clothes." Her mother turned the horse back toward the manor and set off at a brisk pace.

"I have men with me!" Lada shouted, finally regaining her voice.

"No," Vasilissa said, not turning around. "Only you. No men."

At a loss, Lada gestured to Petru, Nicolae, and Bogdan, who watched her from the cover of the hedge. "Just . . . stay, for now. I will come back for you."

"Are you certain you will come to no harm?" Bogdan asked, narrowed eyes tracking Vasilissa's hasty exit.

Lada was certain of the opposite. But she did not expect the type of harm Bogdan feared. "Wait here."

When she got to the manor, the front door was closed. Barren ivy climbed over every surface, its tangled brown masses swallowing the angles and shape of the house. In the summer it would be green and lovely, but not now.

The least her mother could have done was wait for her. Lada laughed bitterly. No, her mother was skilled at doing far less than the least she could do for her daughter. Of course she would make Lada knock. Lada pounded her gloved fist against the door. It opened with such speed, the maid behind it must have been waiting there.

The girl curtsied awkwardly. She wore a shapeless brown dress and an ill-fitting black cap. "Welcome, mistress. My lady has prepared a room for you."

Lada frowned. Who else was her mother expecting? "I only met her just now on the road."

The girl cleared her throat, keeping her eyes on the floor. "My lady has prepared a room for you. Please come with me."

"Where is my moth—where is Vasilissa?"

"If you will come with me, I will show you your room and draw a bath for you. Her ladyship receives visitors after supper."

"But she already knows I am here. And I have my men waiting outside."

The maid finally looked up. Her eyes pointed in slightly different directions, one drifting to the left. She whispered, "Please, mistress, do not speak of the men to her. We do as she wishes. It is for the best. Allow me to take you to your room, and she will see you after supper."

Exasperated, Lada flung a hand out. "Fine. Take me to my room."

The girl flashed a quick, grateful smile, and led Lada into the house. The deeper they got, the more Lada's stomach clenched in fear.

There was something very wrong here.

25

Early April

CHRIST STARED MOURNFULLY DOWN at Radu. No matter how Radu shifted or where he looked, the round eyes of Jesus followed him.

"Are you well?" Cyprian whispered out the side of his mouth, leaning close.

Radu stopped fidgeting under the giant mosaic. "Yes. Just tired."

In front of them, standing behind a giant wood postern, a priest ran through liturgy after liturgy. Radu's Greek was good, but he could barely understand the antiquated phrasings and words. Even if he could, he would not care. Being in this church made him feel like a child again. Radu had not enjoyed his childhood, and it was deeply uncomfortable to be reminded of it.

Everything was larger than life in the church. Though it was not as big or beautiful as the Hagia Sophia, gilt covered all possible surfaces. The priest wore elaborate robes, stitched and embroidered with pounds of history and tradition. A censer

filled the room with scented smoke that made Radu's eyes water
and his head spin.

On the raised dais next to the priest, Constantine sat on
a throne. Radu envied him a seat. All the other men stood,
packed in too tightly, still and listening. Radu yearned for the
movement of true prayer, for the simplicity and beauty and
companionship of it.

The liturgy continued, as cold and uncaring as the murals
of various saints meeting violent ends that decorated the walls.
Lada would like those at least. Radu smiled, remembering
when they had visited a monastery on the island of Snagov in
Wallachia. Lada had been chastised for laughing at the grue-
some death scene of Saint Bartholomew. An elaborate painting
of him with half his skin already off adorned one of the monastery walls. Radu could never look at that mural without shivering in fear. Lada had told him to think instead of how cold
poor Saint Bartholomew must have been without any skin on.

He wished Lada were with him now. But even if she were,
she would be up in the gallery with Nazira and all the other
women. And she would be blisteringly angry about it.

Radu avoided Jesus's gaze yet again and found himself staring at an equally mournful mosaic of Mary. Her head was tilted
down and to one side, a miniature Christ child solemn and
staring on her lap. *Will you protect your city?* Radu silently asked
her. He knew there was one God. But in this city of mysticism
steeped in so much religious fervor, he could not escape the fear
that the other god, the god of his childhood, lurked in the mist
and the rain and the tremors of the earth. Radu was trapped behind these walls, separated from who he had become. With his

tongue he cursed Muslim infidels and with his heart he prayed for constant forgiveness.

Surely the true God, the God of his heart, knew what Radu was doing here. Even if Radu himself did not.

When the liturgy finally ended, Radu wanted nothing more than to go back to Cyprian's house and sleep for a day. But Cyprian grabbed his arm and pulled him toward a group that was milling about near Constantine.

"I wanted to introduce you to—ah, here they are!" Cyprian clasped hands warmly with two boys who shared the round-eyed, mournful faces of the mosaics around them. Radu half expected them to tilt their heads and lift their hands in various saintlike poses. Instead, they smiled shyly.

"This is John, and his brother, Manuel. My cousins. Their father was John, the emperor before Constantine."

The older boy looked to be around eight, the younger five. They wore purple robes and gold circlets. The clasps of the chains securing their robes glittered like jewels, but as Radu looked closer, he saw they were made of glass.

Radu bowed. "I am Radu."

The younger boy, Manuel, perked up, his round eyes growing even rounder. "From the sultan's palace?"

"Who told you about me?" Radu asked, with a puzzled smile.

"Cyprian has told us all about you!"

Cyprian cleared his throat. "Not all about you. Just . . . that you saved me."

Manuel nodded. "Is it true what they say about the sultan?"

Radu smiled to hide the pit that had opened up in his stomach. Had even this small boy heard that Radu was the sultan's shameful plaything? Why would Cyprian have told him that? "They say many things. I am afraid you will have to be more specific."

"That the sultan kills a man before every meal and sprinkles his food with the blood to protect himself against death."

Radu was so relieved he had to choke back a laugh. He covered it by pretending to cough. "No, unless things have changed dramatically since I left. He prefers his food without blood, like most men."

"I heard he is so wealthy that he had all his teeth replaced with jewels." John, the older boy, said it with a studied casualness, but he leaned forward just as intently as his brother.

"That would make eating all his blood-sprinkled meals quite a task! But no, that is not true, either. Though he does sometimes wear a turban so large it nearly brushes the ceiling!" That was an exaggeration, but both boys nodded in wonder. "He has fountains of clear water in all his rooms, and his fingers are so heavy with jewels that he cannot sign his own name without removing his rings first."

Manuel scowled. "I do not know why he wants our dumb city, then."

John elbowed him sharply in the side. "You are just jealous because I am the heir to the throne and you are not."

Manuel stuck out his tongue. "Not if you die first!"

Cyprian put a hand on both their shoulders. "No talk like that, boys." They deflated, looking shamefacedly at the floor. "And I am going to have a word with your nurse about the rumors she is letting you hear."

John looked up first. He lifted his chin bravely, but it trembled slightly. "Is the sultan as cruel as they say?"

Radu wanted to deny it, but he had to remember he was playing a part. "He is . . . very smart, and very focused. He will do whatever it takes to get what he wants. So, yes, he can be cruel."

John nodded, then set his jaw determinedly. "Well, it does not matter. The walls will save us. And even if he gets past them, an angel will come down from heaven with flaming swords before they can pass the statue of Justinian. The infidels will never have my city."

A loud, deep laugh sounded next to them. Constantine ruffled the boy's brown curls, skewing the circlet to the side. "Your city? I am fairly certain it is still mine."

John smiled, blushing. "I only meant—"

"Have no fear, John. I will take good care of it until it is your turn."

They turned their smiles on Radu. The combined weight of their love and hope with the heavy gaze of Jesus above them nearly knocked Radu to the floor. He bowed to cover his feelings, then straightened.

"Will you join us for a meal?" Constantine asked. "It will be nice to have someone else to answer their infinite questions for once."

"I would love to," Radu said, still exhausted but with a spike of excitement. This was his first personal invitation to spend time with the emperor. It was a good thing. A step in the right direction. A way to feel like he was actually accomplishing something, even though he feared there was no point.

Then a tiny hand slipped into Radu's own, and he looked down into the saintly eyes of Manuel. The little boy beamed up at him, and Radu felt his soul wilt as he smiled back.

———

Everything had been so *normal* at dinner. Even Radu had managed to relax, enjoying the food and laughter and stories. All his hopes to hear something useful were dashed in the middle of bread and meat and preserved fruit.

And that was when he had his idea.

Mehmed might have sent him in without a plan, but he could destroy the city's chances at surviving a siege before the Ottomans ever got to Constantinople. If food made them feel normal, allowed them to continue on as though their city were not under imminent threat, the absence of food would finally make it clear they could not survive.

It would be an act of mercy, destroying the food supplies. People would be forced to flee. Even if it did not lead directly to surrender, at least it would empty the city of innocent citizens.

Orhan, the pretend heir to the Ottoman throne, proved the key to discovering the location of one of the major food supplies. Because his men were not allowed at the wall—for fear soldiers would confuse them for Turks loyal to Mehmed— they had other assignments throughout the city. And one of those assignments was patrolling and checking all the locks on a warehouse. Radu could think of no reason for its protection other than that it housed food.

It had been a simple enough task for Radu to shadow the

men and find his target. But now the bigger question: how to eliminate it?

Lada would burn it down. Radu did not doubt that. But the warehouse was in the middle of a relatively populated section of the city. If he set the building on fire, the fire would spread. He could end up killing innocent citizens—and part of his motivation in doing this was to save them. He could not live with collateral damage.

Poison would have the same effect, because they would not know the food was poisoned until people were dead. And Radu had no real means of obtaining large quantities of poison, much less doing so in secret.

He was in the kitchen tearing apart bread, pondering the problem of the food, when Nazira shrieked in terror from their bedroom. He raced upstairs to find her standing on the bed. "A rat!" She pointed to a corner where a large, mangy rat seemed equally terrified of her. "Kill it!"

Radu sighed, looking for something large enough to smash the rodent. And then he stopped. A smile lit his face. "No. I am going to catch it."

———•———

Though rats were in plentiful supply in the city, catching a significant number of them was no small task. Or rather, it was many, many small, wearying tasks. And because Radu could not risk being missed at the wall, he had to sacrifice sleep. Nazira loved the plan, but was physically incapable of interacting with rats without screaming. Screaming did not lend itself well to secrecy.

So Radu spent all night, every night, catching rats. It was a far cry from his life at the side of the sultan, but not so far from what his role had always been. Sneaking around, gathering supplies, building toward an ultimate goal.

It would have been thrilling if it did not involve so many damned rats.

"What happened to your hands?" Cyprian asked a couple of mornings into the rat adventures. He and Radu were eating together on the wall, shoulder to shoulder as they looked out on the empty field that was filled nonetheless with the looming threat of the future.

Radu looked down at his fingers. "Vermin cemetery residents do not like sharing gravestones with trespassers."

Cyprian set down his bread and took Radu's hands in his own. He carefully examined them. Radu's stomach fluttered. It felt like something more than fear of discovery, but he could not say what.

"Be careful," Cyprian said, running a finger as soft as a whisper along Radu's palm. "We need these hands." Cyprian looked up and Radu found himself unable to bear the intensity of his gaze. Cyprian released his hands, laughing awkwardly. "We need all the hands we can get."

"Yes," Radu murmured, still feeling Cyprian's finger tracing his palm.

———— ⋅◦⋅ ————

That night, Radu had enough rats. Any more and he would not be able to carry them in secret. He waited for Orhan's men to finish their patrol past the back doors of the warehouse. They never went inside, only checked the locks. He crept silently across the street, a wriggling, repulsive burlap sack filled to bursting slung across his back. He set the sack down and picked the lock, cursing his bitten fingers for their slowness. Cyprian had been right. They needed these hands.

Finally, shivering with nerves, Radu got the door open. Slipping inside, he made his way to the center of the vast space. Crates and barrels loomed like gravestones in the darkness. Everything smelled warm and dusty. He had guessed right about the contents of the warehouse. He used the metal rod he had brought to pry open lids, then he dumped rats into crates and barrels until his sack held only the rats that had not survived captivity. But he had managed to hit barely a third of the containers. He would have to do this every night for weeks to actually destroy all the supplies.

Burn it, Lada whispered in his mind.

"There's always another way," Radu answered. Thunder rumbled overhead as though agreeing with him. The city was prone to torrential downpours. Radu would need to hurry home to avoid getting caught in one. He looked up at the ceiling—

And he had another idea.

Back out in the night, he examined his options. The buildings in Constantinople were old and built close together. He hurried down the alley, looking for what he needed. Three buildings over, he found it: a ladder. The first drops of rain hit him as he climbed onto the building's roof. Taking a deep breath, he ran as fast as he could and jumped over the alley, slamming into the next roof so hard he nearly slid off. Lada would be so much better at this. But she also would not have bothered. Everything would already be burning.

Steeling himself against thoughts of his far more capable sister, Radu ran for the next roof and sailed over the alley. Landing softly this time, he collapsed onto his back and laughed as rain pattered down around him. Beneath him, warm and dusty and dry, was the city's food.

He clambered to the peak of the shallowly angled roof. The key was to pry enough shingles and thatch free to make small holes, but not so many that the damage would be noticed until it was too late. The shingles were heavy and tightly nailed down. He used his lever to pry them up. He focused on areas where it was obvious water had pooled in the many years of the roof's life.

The rain began pouring in earnest. The shingles were slick; Radu clung to them carefully. He could afford neither discovery nor injury. He allowed himself a few moments of quiet triumph as he watched water stream from the sky onto the roof and through the holes he had created.

Tearing up as many shingles on his way as he could, he crawled to the far end of the building. But he had a new problem.

He could not run to gather momentum. With the roof this slick, he would certainly slip and fall to his death. The drop to the ground was far—three times his height—and if he crashed down with any speed he did not like his chances.

There was a narrow ledge along the edge of the roof. Rain poured around him; the storm was picking up speed and force. He left the lever on the roof and grasped the ledge. Then he lowered himself, hanging on by only his fingertips. Praying silently, he dropped. When he hit the ground, he collapsed, trying not to let any one part of his body absorb too much of the impact. It was a trick he had learned long ago, running and hiding from his cruel older brother, Mircea. He had had to jump from many windows and walls in his childhood.

Mircea was dead now, and Radu did not mourn him. But

as he stood, checking his body for injuries, he was momentarily grateful for the lessons. One ankle was complaining and would be sore in the morning. It was a small price to pay. Radu pulled his hood up over his head.

"Hey! You!"

Radu turned in surprise. It was too dark for them to see his face, but Orhan's men had circled back on their patrol. And Radu was standing right next to the door of the storage warehouse. If they looked inside, all his work would be for nothing.

He quickly pulled a flint from his pocket and dropped it. Then, cursing loudly in Turkish, he ran.

"He was trying to burn the food! Spy! Sabotage!" The cry went up behind him, followed by the pounding of footsteps.

Radu ran for his life.

Bells began clanging the warning, chasing him with their peals. Radu cut through alleys and streets. He jumped over walls and kept to the darkest parts of the city. Soon he was in an abandoned area. But still he heard the sounds of pursuit. It was like a nightmare: running through a dead city, pursued in the darkness with nowhere to hide.

Desperate, Radu considered the outer wall. If he could make it to the wall, he could make it outside. He could find Mehmed.

But if he disappeared the same night a saboteur had been spotted in the city, it would not take much thought to connect the events. Nazira would be left in harm's way. Radu turned and ran into an empty stable. Rain poured in from the collapsed roof. He huddled in the corner of a stall.

Once, he had hidden with Lada in a stable. She had promised no one would kill him but her. *Please*, Radu thought, *please let that be prophetic.*

After he had waited for so long that his heart no longer pounded and he shivered with cold rather than fear, Radu stood and crept through the night. The rain was tapering off as he slowly found his way from the abandoned section of the city back to a part with life. He left his long black cloak on a washing line and combed his hair into a neat ponytail. Then he walked, unhurried, hunched against the rain.

His hand was on the doorknob when someone grabbed his shoulder roughly from behind. He was spun around—and embraced.

"Radu!" Cyprian said, holding him tightly. "I have been looking everywhere for you. There is a saboteur in the city. They caught him trying to light a fire. I was so worried about you."

Radu took a deep breath, trying to calm his voice. "I heard the bells and went out to see what was wrong. I feared the Ottomans had finally arrived. But why would you worry about me?"

Cyprian lingered in the hug, then pulled back, his hands still on Radu's shoulders. "If the sultan's man had discovered you . . ." His eyes were wrinkled with concern. "I feared for your safety."

Radu embraced Cyprian again, both because it was warm and comforting against the weariness of this long night, and because it was the only way he could hide how touched and sad he was that Cyprian's first fear had been for Radu's traitorous life.

26

Early April

A CLOUD OF DUST HUNG in front of the window, where musty drapes had been hastily tugged aside. The room was in the back of the house, on the second floor. Lada could see across a fallow field to the hedge where she had watched for her mother. But it was not clear enough to make out where her men waited for her.

She hoped they were still waiting for her. She felt so cut off. What if they left her, too? Radu was lost to her. Mehmed was a traitor. She had separated herself from Hunyadi. She could not lose her men.

The maid cleared her throat. Lada expected the girl to leave, but she just stood there next to the steaming bath she had filled.

"Well?" Lada snapped.

"I will help you undress?"

"No!"

The girl recoiled as if struck. "I am supposed to."

"You are *not* supposed to."

"But—I was to wash your hair, and plait it for you after, and help you into one of her ladyship's dresses." The girl frowned worriedly, looking at Lada's thick waist and large chest.

Lada laughed, the absurdity of it all finally getting to her. Here she was, seeing her mother for the first time in fifteen years, and her mother wanted to brush her hair and dress her up. No—her mother wanted someone else to do it for her. That made sense. At least Oana was not here. She would have been thrilled to volunteer.

"You may stand outside the door so that she thinks you are still in here. And then you may take a message and some food to my men outside. You will see their campfire."

The girl squeaked in fear. "Men! I could not. It is forbidden. Oh, please, do not ask it of me. If she knew, if she found out—"

Lada held up her hands. "Very well! They will last until I go back to them. Get out."

The girl nodded, wringing her hands, and slipped out the door. Lada followed, putting her ear to the door. She could hear the rapid, panicked breaths of the girl immediately outside.

What went on in this house?

Lada took a bath. Over the last year on the run, she had learned never to turn down a bath or a meal. But she did not wash her hair, or make any effort to tame it. She dressed again in her traveling clothes—breeches, a tunic, and a coat, all black. A red sash around her waist. When she was done putting her boots on, she opened the door. The maid was so close their noses nearly touched.

"Your hair?"

Lada shook her head, expression grim.

"I found some of her ladyship's old dresses. I could let out the seams, and . . ." The girl trailed off, hope dying on her face as Lada's expression did not change.

"When is supper?" Lada asked.

"She has already eaten."

"Without me?"

"Our schedule is very specific." The maid leaned forward, looking to either side as though fearful of discovery. "I will bring you some food from the kitchens later tonight," she whispered.

Lada did not know how to respond. With gratitude? Incredulity? Instead, she pushed forward with her goal. "If supper is over, I can see her now."

"Yes! She will be waiting to receive visitors in the drawing room."

"Does she receive many visitors?"

The maid shook her head. "Almost never."

"So she is only waiting to see me."

"After supper, she waits to receive visitors. You are a visitor. So you may see her now."

Lada followed the girl through the hall and down the stairs. She would much rather be facing a contingent of Bulgars, or a mounted cavalry. At least those she would understand.

Mehmed's mother, Huma, suddenly came to mind. Huma had been ferocious and terrifying. She had wielded her very womanhood like a weapon, one Lada did not understand and could not ever use. Was that what her mother was doing? Throwing Lada off guard to gain the upper hand? Huma had been able to manipulate Lada and Radu by forcing them to meet on her terms. Her mother must be doing the same thing.

It was comforting, in a way, girding herself to meet a challenge like Mehmed's formidable mother. Huma was a foe worth having. A murderer many times over, who had even had Mehmed's infant half brother drowned in a bath. Lada shuddered, the back of her hair wet against her neck. Was there a darker reason the maid had tried to insist on staying during Lada's bath?

She regarded the tiny, trembling thing ahead of her with new suspicion. Flexing her hands, Lada dismissed the notion. Though Lada *was* certain that if her mother wanted her dead, she would make someone else do it. This waif would have to resort to poison or murdering her in her sleep. She was glad she had missed supper, after all.

But everything Huma had done, she had done to further her son's place in life. What would Vasilissa stand to gain by killing Lada? And why did Lada find it more comfortable to think of Vasilissa as a potential assassin lying in wait than as her mother?

Before Lada could settle her mind, the maid opened a door to a sitting room. It was like being greeted by an open oven. The air was too close and heated past any reasonable degree. The windows were shuttered tightly, and a fire roared in a fireplace too large for a room this size.

The maid practically tugged Lada inside, closing the door as quickly as possible behind them. It took a moment for Lada's eyes to adjust to the dim room. Her mother sat in a high-backed chair, hands folded primly in her lap, voluminous skirt hiding her feet. Her hat had been replaced with a long veil pinned at the top of her head that completely obscured her face. She was not wearing the same dress as before. This one was white, with a ruffled neck so high it looked as though her veiled head sat on a platter. All the dress's folds and pleats nearly swallowed her whole.

"Oh," she said, an entire discourse in disappointment contained in that single word. "You did not change."

Lada longed to draw her knives, sheathed at her wrists. "These are my clothes." She took the chair opposite her mother without being invited. It sank under her weight, the stuffing worn and the velvet threadbare.

"Would you like something? Tea? Wine?"

"Wine."

Vasilissa nodded toward the maid, who poured two glasses and handed one to each of them. Lada took a sip. Or rather, she pretended to take a sip, preferring to wait until her mother drank first. Huma was too recently on her mind to risk otherwise. So far her mother was nothing like Huma, though. Huma had filled the space around her, no matter how large the room. Even in this small room, Lada's mother seemed to blend into the furniture.

Vasilissa lifted her veil and took a dainty sip. Lada followed suit. Her mother's eyes were large, like hers, but there was more of Radu in her face. It was startling, seeing her brother reflected in the face of a stranger. Lada could not place the exact similarities; they had something delicate and beautiful in common. But her mother's face was worn and broken at the edges. Was that what would happen to Radu, too? Would he fade with time, become a withered shadow of himself?

Lada longed for Radu at her side yet again. If he were here, she could focus on protecting him. Having only herself to protect made her feel so much more vulnerable.

"Tell me," her mother said, keeping a hand in front of her mouth. "What brings you to the countryside? It is not so lovely this time of year, I am afraid. Much nicer once spring has taken hold."

Lada frowned. "I am here to see you."

"That is sweet. We do not have many visitors." She lowered her hand, smiling with tightly shut lips. Then she simply stared. Lada wondered if her own large, hooded eyes were that disconcerting.

Lada had never been good at the games women played, the battles fought and won through incomprehensible conversations. So she pushed ahead. "I assume you have had news that my father is dead. So is Mircea."

Vasilissa lifted her hand to her mouth again. Lada thought it was in horror or mourning, but Vasilissa's tone was conversational. "Do you ride? I find a brisk ride in the afternoon settles my nerves and rouses my appetite. I have three horses. They have no names. I am so terrible with choosing names! But they are all gentle and sweet. Perhaps you can meet them tomorrow."

"Why are you speaking to me of horses?" Lada set aside her glass and leaned forward. "You have not seen me in so many years, since you abandoned us. At least do me the courtesy of speaking to me as an equal. Your husband, my father, is dead."

Her mother made a wounded face, a flash of truth breaking free. Her lips parted in an animal way, and Lada had a glimpse of a mouth full of broken teeth. Not rotted teeth—Lada had seen plenty of those—nor the gaps indicating lost teeth. Vasilissa's mouth was a graveyard of shattered teeth. Lada did not know what could have caused such damage.

Her mother, crawling away, weeping.

No. She *did* know what could have caused such damage.

Lada lowered her voice. "He is dead. Gone."

If her mother heard her, she did not indicate it. She drew her veil back down, making a repetitive clicking noise with her tongue. "Tell me, do you hunt? I find it abominable, but I have word that all the fashionable ladies do it now." Her laugh was high and trilling, like the panicked flight of a startled bird. "If you would like, I can have word sent to your cousin. He has an excellent falconer. I am certain he would give you a demonstration, should you wish it. He visits every summer. He has to stay in town, of course, several leagues away, but he always stops by when I receive visitors! We can expect him in a few months."

"I will not be here then. I am not here for a visit. I need help."

Vasilissa laughed again, the same terrible noise. "I should say so! But my maid works wonders on hair. We will have you settled in no time. Do you like your room?"

Lada stood. "I need to speak to your father."

Vasilissa shook her head. "He is— He has— I believe he is dead?"

With a defeated sigh, Lada sat back down. "Who leads Moldavia?"

"Your cousin, I think. Oh." Vasilissa wrung her hands in her lap. "Do you suppose that means he will not come this summer? I am sorry. I promised you a falcon demonstration."

"I do not care about falcons! I need men. I need alliances." Lada shook, a wave of unacknowledged anger and grief overwhelming her. Her father had given her a knife, and her mother had left her with nothing. She desperately wanted something to hold on to. Or, barring that, something to fight against. "I need you to ask me where I have been the last fifteen years! I need you to ask where your *son* is!"

Her mother stood, her dress-draped frame trembling. "It is time for me to retire for the night. The maid will see to you. Your room is the nicest in the house. You will be happy. And you will be safe; this is a very safe house."

Vasilissa held out a hand. The maid rushed to her side. Lada saw, for the first time, that her mother walked with a pronounced limp. One of her feet, when it peeked from beneath her skirts, was twisted at an odd angle. The way Vasilissa moved without cringing spoke of it as an old, permanent injury. Lada did not know what to say, how to talk to this strange, ruined creature. Her impression of Vasilissa on the horse had been wrong. Her mother was exactly the same person who had left them behind. The only difference was that she had found a safe place to hide.

Perhaps Radu would feel tenderly toward her. Lada knew he would urge compassion.

She felt only rage.

"You never came back for us," Lada said. "He sold us. To the Turks. We were tortured. We were raised in a foreign land by heathens. Radu stayed behind. They broke him."

"Well." Vasilissa reached out as though she would pat Lada's arm as she passed. Her hand hovered in the air, then moved back to the maid's arm for support. "You are welcome to stay forever. We are all safe here."

"I belong in Wallachia."

Her mother's voice was as harsh as Lada had ever heard it, finally filled with true emotion. "No one belongs there."

The maid was loath to part with any information, but as far as Lada could determine, her mother was mad. They had lived together in this house, far away from everyone and everything, for the last ten years. Vasilissa had been given the manor by her father, who doubtless could not stand the broken shell of a woman she was.

Every day was the same. The maid smiled as she described it, saying over and over how pleasant it was, to be safe and to always know what to expect. This was what Lada's mother had chosen. Safety. Seclusion. The woman had abandoned her children, utterly and completely, to live in pampered isolation instead of dealing with the harsh realities of life.

The harsh realities of her own children's desperate attempts to survive without anyone to aid them.

Lada did not say goodbye. She stopped in the kitchen and stole as much food as she could carry. Then she closed the front door behind her and walked along the dark lane to where the campfire of her men—her friends—called to her. She sat next to them, drawing heat and strength from their shoulders. Bogdan shifted closer and she leaned against him.

"Well?" Nicolae asked.

"She is mad."

"Then you do have something in common after all!"

His attempt at levity met with no reaction from Lada. His voice got quieter. "Will there be any aid from Moldavia?"

"None that she can provide. We can go to the capital and appeal to the new king. But I do not think these people will help us. She is just like all the nobility, the boyars. They are sick with the same disease. They lock themselves in finery and wealth, and they refuse to see anything that might jeopardize their comfort." Lada paused, remembering her mother's teeth, her mother's foot. Perhaps she should not begrudge the small measure of comfort a powerless woman had managed to find in a cruel world.

But she would absolutely begrudge her mother the failure to empower herself. Running and abandoning those who needed her was the weakest, lowest thing possible. Lada would not do that. She could not. Whatever else she was, Lada was nothing like the class who could go on living after turning their backs on those who depended upon them.

"What, then?" Nicolae asked. "Do we try to convince more boyars that you are a tame princess and not a warlord prince?"

Lada picked up a canteen of water and poured it on the flames, watching them sizzle and die. "I do not know. I have tried—" Her voice caught. She had tried everything. She had pledged loyalty to foreign kings, she had betrayed an ally, she had trusted that love was the same as honesty. "I have tried everything."

"The little zealot was always unlikely. None of us blame you for looking for help there, though."

Lada sat up straight, alarmed. "What do you mean?"

Nicolae's expression was without reproach. "We are all *very* good soldiers and scouts, Lada. Did you really think we would fail to notice the sultan camped within miles of us?"

She hung her head, the weight of her shame pulling her down. "I told you I was freeing you. But when he offered help, I leapt at the opportunity."

"We do not care," Petru said.

The way Bogdan sat perfectly still next to her indicated that he, perhaps, did.

"We know you fight for us. For Wallachia." Nicolae shrugged. "The little zealot was a means to an end. It did not work. So we find more means for the same end."

Lada held out her hands. "I have exhausted my means. I am sorry you have followed me this far."

"We still have Hunyadi," Bogdan said.

Nicolae rubbed his beard, leaning back with a thoughtful expression. "No, Hunyadi is not our best option. We have our own Hunyadi in Lada. What we need is someone who can work new angles of power. What we need is Matthias."

"He is the same as all the other leaders," Lada said, shaking her head.

"That is precisely the point." Nicolae smiled, the fire illuminating his face in the midst of the darkness. "He is the same as them. So if we get him . . ."

Lada took a deep breath filled with smoke. It seared her lungs. She wanted nothing to do with Matthias, and knew his help—if she could get it—would not be without a price. How much more of herself would she have to lose to get where she belonged?

"For Wallachia," Bogdan said.

Lada nodded. "For Wallachia."

27

April 4–6

A THICK FOG OVER THE city muffled all life: muting church bells, softening footfalls, cloaking the streets in a layer of damp and stifling mystery.

Radu turned from staring out his window into the blank white that had settled over the distance like a sickness coming ever closer. Taking a deep breath, he knelt on the floor facing Mecca. Letting go of his fear and questions, he hoped his prayer could find its way out of the fogged-in city even if nothing else could. He was so lost in the ritual he failed to notice an increase in the frequency and number of church bells until his door burst open.

For a split second, Radu froze. He was upright on his knees, so he clasped his hands in front of himself like he had been caught in an acceptably Christian form of prayer. Cyprian, breathing hard, had been scanning the room at eye level. By the time he looked down at Radu, Radu was *almost* certain everything appeared as it should.

"What is it?" Radu asked, standing.

"The Turks." Cyprian steadied himself against the door-frame. "They are here."

Without a word Radu pulled on his cloak. Nazira was in the kitchen preparing the afternoon meal with anemic vegetables and some lumpy bread. "While you are out, try to buy some meat!" she called as they rushed by.

"The Turks are here!" Cyprian shouted. Nazira was at their side as they ran out the front door. She wore only slippers and a layered dress. Radu unfastened his cloak and threw it around her shoulders. She held it shut, keeping pace with the two men as they raced through the streets toward the walls.

If Cyprian had not been with them, Radu was certain they would have gotten lost. The fog changed the character of the city, obscuring landmarks, leeching the already faded colors. With no church steeples visible, bells rang out as though from the world of spirits, their metallic warnings hanging lonely in the air.

"When did they arrive?" Radu nearly slipped on a slick portion of road. Cyprian grabbed his elbow to steady him.

"I do not know. I only now heard word of it."

By the time they bypassed several religious processions and made it to the walls, Nazira was winded and Radu was exhausted. They were allowed through a postern, one of the gates between the walls that let soldiers in and out of the city. Pulled down by the weight of fear, fog had settled heavily in this no-man's-land, curling and pulsing like a living thing. Radu kept brushing at his arms, trying to rub it off.

They were not the only ones who had come running. They had to wait several minutes before there was an opening for them to climb a narrow ladder to the top of the outer wall. As he searched for a good position for them, Radu bumped into Giustiniani. The Italian nodded, shuffling to the side to let them squeeze in.

There, shoulder to shoulder with their enemies, Radu and Nazira looked out on their countrymen. Tents had sprung up out of the mist like a growth of perfectly spaced mushrooms. Movement stirred the white tendrils of fog, offering glimpses of men who were then swallowed again.

"We are beset by an army of ghosts," Cyprian whispered.

"Do not let anyone hear you say that," Giustiniani said, his tone sharp. "We have more than enough superstition to contend with."

"When did they arrive?" Radu asked. He leaned forward and squinted, even though he knew it would not magically help him pierce the moisture-laden air. Knew he would not see what—who—he wanted to. But he tried nonetheless.

"It must have been in the night," Giustiniani said. "The damn fog has been so thick we did not even see them. I got reports of strange noises, and then it finally cleared some."

"What should we do?" Cyprian asked.

"Wait until we can see something. And then we will start collecting information."

Giustiniani had been right—visibility was poor, but sounds hung in the dead air. At times the noises were muted, as though coming from a very great distance. And sometimes they broke through with such startling clarity that everyone spooked, looking around in fear that the Ottomans were already behind the wall.

"Shovels," Nazira said, pointing toward the camp. "You hear that rhythmic scraping?"

Giustiniani nodded. "They will be digging their own moat, a protective line for themselves. Building up a bulwark to hide their lines behind. And generating material to try to fill in our fosse."

Another sound cut through the air. Radu had half turned before he realized what he was doing. The call to prayer, and Radu could not answer. He had prayed too early. Nazira's hand found his, gripping tightly. They stood, frozen, until it was over.

"Filthy infidels," a man to Giustiniani's right said, spitting over the wall. "The devil's own horde." Then the man straightened, brightening. "You hear that? Christians! I know that liturgy. We are answering them! I—" He stopped, his eyebrows drawing low. "Where is it coming from?"

"Outside of the wall," Cyprian said, his voice as heavy and blank as the fog.

"Mercenaries?" Giustiniani asked.

Radu realized the Italian had been addressing him. "Probably men pressed into service from vassal states: Serbs, Bulgars, maybe even some Wallachians. And then anyone who came willingly when they heard of the attack."

"Why would Christians come against us?" The soldier's face was twisted with despair. He turned to Radu as though he held all the answers.

It was Giustiniani who spoke, though. "For the same reason they sent us no aid. Money." This time he spat over the wall. "How will he organize?"

Radu leaned against the wall, turning his back on the Ottoman camps and staring toward the blank white bank of fog. Only one thing rose up high enough to pierce it—the spire of the Hagia Sophia. The cathedral the city left dark. "Irregulars and Christians at the fronts on most areas of the wall. Places he thinks are less important. He does not trust anyone who is here solely for money. Janissaries and spahi forces at the weakest points—the Lycus River, and the Blachernae Palace wall section."

"So he will be weak where the other forces are weak. If we sallied out, broke through—"

Radu shook his head. "He will have enough men to spare to make certain the irregulars maintain as much order and discipline as possible. There will be no breaking point in his lines. He will concentrate his attacks on your weaknesses, but he will have no weaknesses vulnerable to direct attack."

Giustiniani sighed. "So we wait."

"So we wait," Radu echoed.

—◆—

The next day dawned bright and clear. From the looks on the soldiers' faces, they wished it had not.

Radu was once again at Giustiniani's side, along with Cyprian. Nazira had stayed home. Her parting embrace had been too tight, her whispered caution tucked around him. Radu had to be more careful than ever.

Giustiniani handed him a spyglass. He pointed toward the back of the camp, in a corner where smoke was billowing upward. "What are they doing there?"

It took a moment for Radu to focus, and another few moments for him to train the glass on what he was trying to find. Familiarity warmed him, and he hid his affection behind a grim look. "Forges," he said, handing back the glass.

"What do they need forges that big for?" Cyprian asked.

"Cannons."

"They are going to make cannons on the battlefield?" Cyprian laughed. "Are they also planning on a brick kiln? Building a wall of their own while they are at it?"

"I think it is to repair cannons, mostly."

"They would need a tremendous amount of supplies." Giustiniani frowned. "The logistical aspects would be a nightmare. Do you think they could actually do it?"

"I do. Mehmed—" Radu cringed, and started over. "The sultan is organized and methodical. He has resources he can pull from two continents. If he needs it, it is already here or on its way. I have been in an Ottoman siege before, under the sultan Murad. This will be even bigger, cleaner, more efficient. Mehmed watched and learned. He will have enough supplies to last as long as he needs. The men will be limited to one meal a day to preserve food. He will keep things meticulously ordered and clean to prevent sickness."

Giustiniani pointed toward the rows of tents. "By my estimations, there are almost two hundred thousand men out there."

Cyprian let out a breath, as though he had been hit in the stomach. "That many?"

Radu nodded. "But roughly two men in support for every one man fighting."

"That still leaves sixty thousand? Seventy thousand?"

Cyprian covered his mouth with his hand. Radu was shocked to see tears pooling in his gray eyes. "So many. What could Christianity accomplish with a mere fraction of the unity Islam has? How can our God ever withstand the ferocity of this faith?"

"Do not blaspheme, young man." Giustiniani's tone was sharp, but it softened when he spoke again. "And do not despair. The odds are not so against us as they look." He patted the stone in front of them with one thick, callused hand. "With a handful of men and these walls, I could hold back the very forces of hell itself."

"Good," Cyprian said, his voice hollow as he looked back over the Ottoman camp. "Because it looks like we will have to."

Giustiniani left, but Radu and Cyprian stayed where they were. Cyprian waved his hand in disgust. "Look at those animals in that pen. That one, there. Those are not even war animals! That lord brought those to show off!"

Radu's eyes never left the red and gold tent in the center— Mehmed's. "A pasha, probably. Or a ghazi from the Eastern regions. They do not see each other often, so they would want to use this as a show of wealth and strength."

Cyprian laughed. "They do not even care about scaring us. They are here to impress each other." He sighed, finally turning and sinking down to sit with his back against the stones. Radu knew Mehmed was not here yet, that the tent was empty. Still, it was all he could do to look away and sit next to Cyprian.

"If they have all that—if they can do this much on a *military campaign*—why do they even want our city? That camp is nicer than anything we have in here."

Radu sighed, resting his head against the cold limestone

that stood between him and his people. "They think Constantinople is paved in gold."

"They are two hundred years too late. How can the sultan not know that?"

"He knows." Radu was certain of it. Mehmed was too careful, too meticulous not to know the true state of the city. "He lets them believe the city is wealthy so they are willing to fight. But he wants the city for itself. For its history. For its position. For his capital."

"And so he will take it."

Radu nodded, echoing Cyprian. "And so he will take it."

"What is life like under the Ottomans? For the vassal states and conquered people?"

Radu closed his eyes and saw a red and gold tent in the darkness. Saw the face of the man who would be there, so soon. Saw himself, where he should have been, in the tent next to Mehmed.

To impress his loyalty on Cyprian, he should probably talk of horrors. But the look of despair in Cyprian's eyes haunted him. There was comfort in the truth, so Radu extended it. "Honestly? It is better than many other things." Radu blinked away the images of what would not be, focusing on the city on a hill in front of him. "The Ottomans do not believe in the feudal systems. People are far freer under their rule. Industry and trade flourish. They let their vassal subjects continue to worship how they wish, without persecution."

"They do not force conversion?"

"Christians are free to remain Christians. The Ottomans actually prefer it, because they have to tax Muslims at a lower rate."

Cyprian laughed, surprising Radu. "Well, that is very ... practical of them."

Radu smiled grimly. "I do not know if it will comfort you, but when I compare the people in Wallachia to the people in the Ottoman Empire, the Ottomans have it better."

Cyprian swallowed, his throat shifting with the movement. He looked down at his hands, which were clasped in front of him. "But it was not better for you."

Radu turned his head away as though struck, remembering what they thought he was to Mehmed. What shame and pain they must think he carried over what he was rumored to be. What he would gladly have been, had Mehmed so much as hinted that it was a possibility.

"No," Radu said, his voice a cold shadow in the clear sunlight. He stood just in time to see Mehmed's procession arrive, the walls of the city the least impossible barrier between Radu and his heart's desire. "Not for me."

28

Mid-April

LADA STOOD, PARALYZED WITH rage and grief, next to the bed where Hunyadi lay dying.

Three weeks ago when she left him, he had been robust and thick with power. Now he was a wasted shadow of himself.

Mehmed had managed to kill him after all.

Hunyadi wheezed a laugh. "He sends any men with the plague to the front lines. It is clever, really. He could not get me with a sword, but he got me with—" His words were cut off as he struggled to breathe, gasping.

Lada had never before felt so powerless. She wanted to kill something.

She wanted to kill Mehmed.

"Where is Matthias?" she asked the girl attending Hunyadi in the dark, cramped room in a humble home a good distance from the castle.

The girl kept her eyes averted, tending the fire as though keeping it alive would do anyone any good. "He does not come."

"His father is dying. Send someone to fetch him."

The girl shook her head, locks of hair falling in front of her face. "He will not come."

"It is better," Hunyadi said, finally able to speak again. He smiled. His gums were pale, his lips cracked. "I was gone when my father died. Too busy fighting to watch a sick old farmer die. And now my son is too busy in the castle to watch a sick old soldier die. It is good."

Lada hated this talk. She wanted more time with Hunyadi. She wanted back the time she had squandered that had cost them both so dearly. She could still learn so much from him. She helped him sip some water, then adjusted his pillow. "How did you manage it? How did you come so far from such a humble start?"

"I always chose the path of most resistance. Did things no one else was willing to. Took risks no one else dared take. I was smarter. More determined. Stronger." He lifted one shaking hand in the air and wheezed a laugh. "Well, some things change. But I was always brutal. I was the most brutal. When you start lower, you have to fight for every scrap of space you occupy in the world." He patted Lada's cheek, his palm too warm, and thin like parchment. "Even starting from nothing, I had more luck than you. If you had been born a boy, the whole world would tremble before you."

Lada scowled. "I have no wish to be a man." Then she cringed, the memory of Mehmed's hands and tongue and lips on her body. She had never been happier to be a woman than she had been in that falsely precious space. Her body had not felt like a stranger to her then. She wanted to reclaim that feeling.

Hunyadi's eyes narrowed thoughtfully. "No. You are right.

I think if you had been born a boy, perhaps you would have been satisfied with what the world offered you. That is how we are alike. We saw everything that was not ours, and we hungered. Do not lose that hunger. You will always have to fight for everything. Even when you already have it, you will have to keep fighting to maintain it. You will have to be more ruthless, more brutal, more *everything*. Any weakness will undo everything you have accomplished. They will see any crack as evidence that they were right that a woman cannot do what you do."

Hunyadi knew what he spoke of. Her merits, her accomplishments, her strength would never speak for themselves. She would have to cut her way through the world, uphill, for the rest of her life. She showed all her small teeth in a vicious smile. "I will make you proud. No one will be more brutal than me. No one will be more ruthless. And I will never stop fighting."

Hunyadi laughed, wheezing and gasping until he was so pale he looked dead already. Lada helped him drink. He choked, spitting most of the water out, but managed to swallow some. Finally, he closed his eyes. "No rest for the wicked. But this wicked soul will have some now, I think."

"Sleep." She wanted to give him assurances that he would get better, but she could not bring herself to lie to him. Not again.

"Promise me," he whispered. "Promise me you will watch out for my Matthias. Be his ally."

"I swear it." She did not mention that she already intended to be just that.

"Your father is dying," Lada said as she sat in a private room with Matthias. It came out as an accusation, though she knew Matthias was not to blame. *She* was, at least in part.

"I never understood him," Matthias said, toying with a goblet of wine. "I never even really knew him. He sent me away as soon as I could talk. When he visited, he watched me with this look—this look like he could not believe I was his. All I heard of him was stories of his conquests, his bravery, his triumphs. And when he visited, I recited *poetry* for him. I asked him, once, to teach me to fight. He had never lost his temper with me, never been around long enough to, but that day I feared he would strike me. He told me he had not fought his whole life so his son could learn to swing a sword." Matthias touched a worn hilt at his side. "Now I have his sword and no idea how to use it. That is his legacy to me."

"You do not need a sword. All you need is to work with people who know what to do with them." Lada leaned forward, forcing him to meet her eyes. "You want to be king."

Matthias smiled slyly. "I am loyal to our blessed king, long may he rule."

Lada brushed his false sentiment from the air with a wave of her hand. "If I wanted shit, I would have visited the privy, not asked for an audience with you."

Matthias laughed. "I think you have been living with soldiers for too long."

"And I think you and I have something to offer each other. You want Hungary. I want Wallachia. I will do whatever you need to secure your throne. And, once you have it, you will help me to mine."

Matthias raised his eyebrows. "Will I? Tell me, why would I want that?"

"A strong Wallachia means a more secure Hungary. We both know the current prince has given the sultan rights to move through the country. They walk straight to your borders without so much as a blade to bar their way. If you help me gain Wallachia, I promise no Ottoman army will make it through alive."

Matthias's hand traced the air above his head, lingering on something Lada could not see. "Do you know, Poland has the crown? They took it for 'safekeeping.' No one can be a legitimate king of Hungary without that crown."

"What does that matter? It is an object."

"It is a symbol."

"Dependence on symbols breeds weakness. If you are king, you do not need a crown."

"Hmm." Matthias dropped his hand and looked Lada up and down in a way that made her feel more like livestock than a person. "My father has left you in charge while he is on the mend."

How little did Matthias know of his father's condition? Lada was not equipped to break the news gently to him. He should have already been told. "Your father will never mend."

Matthias shook his head. "No, that will not do. My father is in seclusion for his health, but while he rests, he has entrusted you with his most private concerns and important charges."

Lada caught his meanings like the beginning of a cold. "Yes," she said. "He has left me in charge."

"And he tasked you with rooting out threats to the throne. Such as treason."

"Treason." Lada had expected to argue with Matthias, to

convince him of her utility. She had underestimated his willingness to grasp at any advantage.

"Yes. It would appear that Ulrich, the protector of the king and my chief rival, has been committing treason. You and your men will go to his home and find all the evidence you need." Matthias smiled, teeth stained dark with wine. "And then you will execute him on behalf of my father."

Lada raised an eyebrow. "Without trial?"

"You are Wallachians. Everyone knows how vicious you are." He watched Lada for her reaction. Balking at being asked to commit murder. Taking offense at being called vicious. He would get no such reactions from her. She met his look with a hint of a smile. He seemed to think she would dislike her people being spoken of this way. Instead, it filled her with pride.

Satisfied with her lack of objections, Matthias continued. "After Ulrich is dead, the king will need a new protector and regent."

Lada nodded. It was simple enough. "And then?"

"And then the king will succumb to his weaknesses, and the protector will be the most obvious choice for king. A king who can connect you with those who will secure your own throne." Matthias held out his hand. It hung in the air between them like a chain. The chain was weighted with the deaths of two innocent men. Ulrich, whom Lada did not know, but whose reputation was one of fairness and morality. And the child king, who had done nothing wrong but be born to power he could not wield.

Two deaths. Two thrones.

Lada took his hand.

29

April 9

RADU CREPT INTO THE kitchen, a knife in his hand. The noise that had awakened him in the middle of the night was revealed by a candle, which threw the room into sharp relief. A few golden glows, a multitude of black shadows.

One of the glowing points was Cyprian's face, but it did not have its usual light. "What is wrong?" Radu crossed the room to him and felt his forehead, fearing Cyprian was ill.

Then he smelled the alcohol, and Cyprian's malady was explained. "Come on." Radu took Cyprian's elbow to steady him. "You should go to bed."

"No. No! I cannot sleep. Not now. I fear what dreams will dance before me after tonight's meeting with my uncle."

The withered part of Radu that still hoped to make some difference jolted alert. "Then we should go for a walk. The night air will help sober you."

Cyprian mumbled assent. Radu found the other man's cloak discarded on the floor and helped Cyprian fasten it. Cyprian stayed close to Radu, one hand on his shoulder. The weight of it suggested Cyprian could not quite stay upright without Radu's support. "What about Nazira?"

"She will not miss me." Radu opened the door and helped Cyprian navigate the short distance to the street. They walked in silence for some time, Cyprian leaning against Radu for support. The night was bitterly cold and as still as the grave.

"You love Nazira," Cyprian said.

"Yes."

"Like a sister."

Radu stopped, causing Cyprian to stumble. Radu forced a quiet laugh. "You have never met my sister if you think I could ever adore her as I do Nazira."

Cyprian gestured emphatically. "But there is no passion."

Radu began walking again, his mind whirling. Cyprian saw too much. They should never have agreed to live with him. If someone suspected Nazira was anything other than his beloved wife, they were in more danger than ever. She had come to sell his story beyond doubt. But if people doubted the marriage itself . . . "She is my wife, and my concern. And now you are my concern, too. What is wrong? I have never seen you like this." In the weeks that they had known him, Cyprian had never been drunk. Even when he had learned of the deaths of his fellow ambassadors, he had remained focused and collected in his grief. Something must have happened tonight to effect such a change.

"Eight thousand," Cyprian said, his voice a whisper.

"Eight thousand what?"

"Eight thousand men. That is all we have."

Radu paused, causing Cyprian to stumble again. Radu

caught him and held his arms. "Eight thousand?" That was fewer than Radu had suspected. He had seen how bleak the city was, but not even that was enough to indicate just how few men they had to call on.

"Eight thousand men for twelve miles of wall. Eight thousand men against sixty thousand."

"But surely more help will come."

Cyprian shook his head, listing to the side with the movement. "My uncle holds out hope, but I have none. The Turks are already here. You told us they have a navy on the way. Who will send aid? How will they get here? Who will look at the hordes at our gates and dare stand with us?"

"But you heard Giustiniani on the walls. You are still fighting from a place of strength." Radu did not know whether he was trying to press Cyprian for more details on the city's defenses or to comfort him. "You were able to repel that attack yesterday!"

Mehmed had sent a small force against one of the weaker sections of the wall. It was a sudden, ferocious attack. But after a couple of hours, two hundred Ottomans were dead and only a handful of defenders had been lost. It was a huge victory for Giustiniani, evidence that his claims of being able to defend the city had some weight.

Or at least, that was what was being said. Radu suspected that Mehmed had been playing, like a cat with its prey. Because what no one knew, what they did not take into account, was that throwing men at the walls was not how Mehmed meant to break them. The cannons had not arrived yet. Until then, he was content to bat at the walls and watch the mice scramble.

Radu saw a familiar building in front of them. He steered Cyprian toward the Hagia Sophia and propped him against the wall while he picked the lock. The door clicked open. Radu grabbed Cyprian and pushed him into the church. Cyprian stumbled, looking up at the ceiling instead of at his feet. "Why are we here?"

"Because it is quiet."

"Have you come here before? You picked that lock very easily."

Radu smiled, because Cyprian could not see it in the dark. "It took me forever to pick the lock. You are too drunk to remember. You fell asleep in the middle."

"I did not!"

Laughing, Radu guided Cyprian toward a corner, where the drunk man slid down against the wall and leaned his head back. Radu sat next to him, mimicking his posture.

"I am so sorry," Cyprian said.

"For what?"

"For bringing you here. I condemned you to death. I should have— I thought of taking us somewhere else. To Cyprus. I should have talked you out of this madness. Now you are trapped here, and it is all my fault."

Radu put a hand on Cyprian's arm, hating the anguish in his friend's voice—no, not his friend. He could not view him as a friend—would not. He quickly pulled his hand back. "You saved us from Mehmed. Do not apologize for that. We came because we wanted to help the city. We would not have accepted running and hiding, just as you could not bring yourself to do it."

"You call him Mehmed."

Radu turned toward Cyprian, but the other man was staring straight ahead into the darkness. Radu could not make out his expression. "What do you mean?" he asked, his voice careful.

"The sultan. You try not to, but when you are not being careful, you call him Mehmed. You were close to him."

Radu searched the shadows around them for the right way to answer. Cyprian spoke before he could, though. "It was not all bad, was it? Being with him?"

Now Radu was fully alert. Could Cyprian's drunkenness have been an act to lull Radu into security, to get him to reveal something he should not? Was this a follow-up to the prying questions about Radu's relationship with Nazira? He chose his words with as much care as he had ever given anything. "The sultan was kind to me when we were boys. I looked up to him. I thought he had saved me from the pain we endured from his father's tutors. He was all I had."

"Your sister was with you, though."

Radu laughed drily. "Again, you have never met my sister. She responded to our torments by getting harder, crueler, further away. It made her stronger, but it was breaking me. So when Mehmed—the sultan—offered me kindness, it was like someone had offered me the sun in the midst of the longest, coldest winter of my life." Radu cleared his throat. He walked as close to the truth as he could, so that his lies would be masked in sincerity. "But as we grew older, he became different. More focused. More determined. The friend and protector I thought I had was not mine at all, and never had been. I valued him above everything else, and he— Well. Everything in the empire belongs to him, and he uses people as he sees fit."

Radu knew Cyprian would think he was referring to being part of a male harem. But the sadness in his voice was not hard to place there. Mehmed had used him—sent him away on a fool's errand. He would rather have been a shameful secret than a banished one.

"But did you love him?"

Radu stared hard at Cyprian. Cyprian, in turn, stared only at the frigid marble tiles beneath them, tracing his finger along a seam. The question sounded oddly earnest, not as though he were teasing or trying to provoke Radu.

Radu stood. "It does not matter, because I betrayed him. He never forgives betrayal." Radu held out his hand, and Cyprian took it. He pulled Cyprian heavily to his feet, and they both lost their balance and stumbled. Cyprian held on to his collar, his face against Radu's shoulder.

"I would forgive you," he whispered. There was a moment between several breaths where Radu thought, maybe, perhaps—

Then Cyprian bent over, hands on his stomach, and ran for the door. Radu followed, then wished he had not as Cyprian vomited into the street just outside the Hagia Sophia.

Confused and cold, Radu closed and locked the door behind them. *I would forgive you* echoed in his brain, sticking where it should not.

Would he really? If he knew?

Radu turned to help Cyprian, whose wretched retching noises were the only sound in the dark. A movement caught his eye. Across the street, in the shadows of a pillar, stood a boy. Radu peered through the darkness and then inhaled sharply with surprise.

It was Amal. The servant who had spied for him while

Murad died. The servant who had raced through the empire to bring word to Mehmed so he could claim the throne before it was taken from him. The servant who had most definitely been in the palace at Edirne when Radu left.

The boy smiled at Radu. Checking to make sure Cyprian was otherwise distracted, Radu hurried across the street. He whispered troop locations, numbers, and any other details he could recall that Amal would be able to remember. To take to Mehmed.

His Mehmed.

Then Radu went back to Cyprian and helped the other man home, his burden lifted by excitement and hope.

———◆———

Radu paced, the candle in his hand throwing his shadow on the wall behind him. Nazira sat on the bed.

"He did have a plan for us! That was why he told me to visit the Hagia Sophia. He always meant to send a scout to find us there. Amal is the perfect choice! The passage between Galata and Constantinople is open during the day. He can easily slip back and forth, meeting Mehmed's men beyond Galata and carrying information. Oh, Nazira, he did have a plan for us."

Radu finally sat, overcome with exhaustion and relief. Nazira got off the bed and knelt in front of him, placing the candle on a table and taking Radu's hands in her own. "Of course he had a plan for us. Did you really think he sent us here for nothing?"

"I feared it. I thought he wanted me gone. I was so scared. I thought I had risked your life without any purpose."

She tutted. "I would never do anything so foolish. And I would never accuse Mehmed of being wasteful with resources. Of course he would not fail to take advantage of you. We will have to be careful with Amal and not put him in any danger. But it is a good method."

Before Radu could stop himself, tears streamed down his face. He and Nazira would be useful. They would help Mehmed. And Mehmed would know and be glad. "He did not abandon me," Radu said, lowering his head onto Nazira's shoulder. "I can still help him."

Nazira patted his back, then lifted his chin so he looked her in the eyes. "We can help the empire. That is why we are here. To fulfill the words of the Prophet, peace be upon him, and to secure stability for our people. We fight for our brothers and sisters, for their safety. Do not lose sight of that. We are not here as a favor to Mehmed." She paused, her voice getting softer but cutting deeper. "He will not love you for what you do here."

Radu jerked back from her words. "Do not speak to me of it."

"You carry too much hope, and it will canker in your soul like an infection. Serve Mehmed because through serving him, you serve the empire. But do not do it out of some desperate hope that it will make him love you the way you love him. He cannot."

"You do not know him!"

Nazira raised an eyebrow. Radu lowered his voice, hissing instead of shouting. "You do not know him. Besides, I do not wish anything more from him than his friendship."

"You are welcome to lie to me, but please stop lying to

yourself. Whatever your hopes are with him, I promise they will never be realized."

"*You* have found love."

"Yes. With someone who could return it. But you refuse to let go of this festering love for a man who is incapable of loving you."

Radu blinked back tears. "Do I not deserve love?"

She put her hand on Radu's cheek. "Sweet Radu, you deserve the greatest love the world has ever seen. I simply do not think Mehmed is capable of loving *anyone* the way you love him."

"He loves Lada."

"I have met your sister, and I have met Mehmed. They love themselves and their ambition above all else. They love what feeds their ambition, and when it stops feeding that, the love will turn to hate with more passion than either could ever love with. You love with all your heart, Radu, and deserve someone who can answer that with all of theirs."

Radu's buoyant happiness was now a leaden weight, dragging his soul lower than it had ever been. "But Mehmed is all I have ever wanted. He is the greatest man in the world."

"I agree. He will be the greatest leader our people have ever seen. And he will do great things. He is more than a man—which also makes him less. He has nothing to offer you."

Radu stood, pushing past Nazira. He felt hemmed in on every side, claustrophobic and desperate for air. "It does not matter anyway! I cannot have the love I want under any religion. It is wrong."

Nazira grabbed his arm, spinning him around to face her. She was livid. "Do you think my love of Fatima is wrong?"

He held up his hands. "No! No."

"God encompasses more than any of us realize. The peace I feel in prayer is the same I feel when I am alone with Fatima. The clarity of fasting is the same I have when we work side by side. When I am with Fatima, what I feel is pure and good. I cannot imagine a god who hates anything that is love, any way we find to take tender care of each other. I want you to find that same love, and I never want you to hate yourself for any love that is in you." She pulled him close and he let her, wondering if it was possible for him to ever have the clarity and purity of love that she had.

Knowing that with Mehmed, it was not possible.

But how could he let go of the man written onto his very soul?

30

Mid-April

THEY SPREAD THROUGH THE manor like fire. Servants awoke to the sounds of crashing furniture and breaking glass. Some tried to fight. Lada had instructed her men to kill no one. It was not difficult to subdue half-asleep, unarmed people.

By the time they reached Ulrich's bedchambers, he had dressed and was waiting for them. His back was straight, his shoulders broad, his face impassive. There was no one else in the bedchamber. Lada was grateful his wife was not there to weep and beg, to bear witness. It was cleaner this way.

Ulrich had a sword sheathed at his side. He made no effort to draw the weapon.

"What is the meaning of this?" he asked, voice calm and assured.

Lada knew his fate already. She did not wish to engage with him. With no witnesses, she did not have to playact and accuse him of things they both knew he had not done. Watching him greet his end with such stoic resolve filled her with a measure of shame. He was a strong man. Possibly even a great one, according to Stefan's information.

So she said nothing. She walked past him, drawing the letter from Mehmed out of her vest. The seal was still intact, his elaborate signature unmistakable. She took tongs and pulled a coal from the fire. With a small thrill of vindictive pleasure, she burned away her own name and the poetry Mehmed had written with his false fingers. When she was finished, the only things that could be seen were Mehmed's signature and his promise to meet in Transylvania with a gift of men.

She held out the letter to Nicolae. "We found him trying to burn this."

Nicolae took it, an uneasy look shadowing his face. She had not told her men everything, merely that they were raiding the house on behalf of Matthias and Hunyadi. This alliance had been Nicolae's idea, after all. He had no right to question where the road he had set them on would lead.

Lada turned back to Ulrich. Now, at last, emotion shaped his warm brown eyes. But he did not look angry or afraid as she had expected. He looked sad. "He could be an excellent king, you know."

Lada wondered why Ulrich was talking about Matthias. But then Ulrich continued. "He is a good child. Smart. With a genuine kindness to his soul that is uncommon in anyone, much less royalty. If he is allowed to grow long enough to reach manhood, he will be a fair and just king. The type of king Hungary needs and deserves."

"I am sorry." And, to her surprise, Lada *was* sorry. She had been so focused on getting Matthias's bidding done, she had not stopped to think how it would feel. Securing the throne of Hungary for someone else was not so simple as she had imagined.

She shook her head. "But I cannot put the needs of Hungary over the needs of Wallachia."

The tears that pooled in Ulrich's eyes caught the light of the fire. He lowered his head, whispering a prayer. Then he held out his arms to either side. "Remember that he is a child. Give him a gentle death."

Lada's knife paused. She looked down at it as it trembled in her hand. This was the first time she would kill a man outside of battle. It was not a reaction to save her own life. It was a choice. She could let Ulrich—a good man—live. He would take this attack as proof of Matthias's treachery and use it to drive him out of the castle. The young king could grow into a man shaped by the strength of his genuine protector.

Lada looked up into Bogdan's face—the face of her childhood. It held no judgment. He simply watched her, waiting. The locket around her neck pressed heavy against her heart.

Wallachia.

She took a deep breath. When she plunged the knife into Ulrich's heart, her hand was steady.

————

The "evidence" was enough to justify Ulrich's death with only moderate outcry. And since Elizabeth had chosen him as the king's protector, her decisions were suspect as well. She was removed to a far distant castle, to be kept there in seclusion. Matthias was named regent—and heir, should the king die without issue.

Lada did not doubt that would be the case, and sooner rather than later. When she watched Matthias put a hand on the trembling child's shoulder, Lada remembered Ulrich's request.

"Kill him gently," she said when Matthias met her in a quiet hall of the castle that would be his. Lada hated Hunedoara, hated this castle, hated her ally. She needed to be free of Hungary.

Matthias laughed. "Are you giving me commands now?"

"It was Ulrich's last request."

"I will do as I see fit." He handed her a letter, sealed with his coat of arms, in which a raven figured prominently. That morning, Lada had seen a raven pull a pigeon from its own nest in the castle eaves, tearing it apart methodically and efficiently.

"This is an introduction to Toma Basarab. He will instruct and help you on your way to the throne. No one knows the Wallachian boyars better than Toma."

"And men?"

Matthias shook his head. "I have no men better than the ones you already possess, and besides, I cannot part with any. If my men were to accompany you and you failed, it would destroy relations between Hungary and Wallachia."

Lada smiled tightly. "So regardless of whether I win or if I die, you still have an ally on the throne." Matthias was born to this. The young king might have a core of kindness, but Matthias knew what it took to gain and keep power.

"You understand perfectly," he said. "I do hope you succeed, Lada Dracul. I am very curious to see what you can do. I look forward to a long and fruitful relationship."

Lada wanted no such thing from him. But he had given her another knife, and she would use it to cut her way to the throne.

She inclined her head, unwilling to bow or curtsy. "I will pay my respects to your father before I leave."

Matthias's expression turned briefly wistful before resuming its usual sharpness. "He is dead. His final act was rooting out the traitor Ulrich. I do not expect you to stay for the funeral."

Lada flinched. She had betrayed Hunyadi to his downfall, and then she had falsely betrayed a good man in his name. This was the thanks she gave Hunyadi for his love, for his trust, for his support.

She clutched the locket around her neck so tightly her knuckles went white, drained of blood.

"You are a strange girl," Matthias said fondly.

"I am a dragon," she answered. Then she turned and left the toxic castle for what she hoped was the last time.

31

April 12–19

As Radu and Nazira prayed in their room in the pre-
dawn light, the end of the world began.

They felt the rumblings beneath their knees, cutting off
their prayer. The church bells began pealing with all the urgency of angels ushering in the end of times. Radu heard
screaming in the streets.

"The cannons." He turned to Nazira. "The cannons are
here."

"Go," she said.

Radu yanked on his boots, nearly falling over in his haste.
Before he had finished fastening his cloak, there was pounding
on the bedroom door. Radu opened it to find Cyprian, as pale
and worn as the limestone walls. "The cannons," he said, shaking his head. "We are finished."

"We must go to the walls." Radu grabbed Cyprian's arm
and turned him around. "Have you been yet? What has fallen?
Are the Ottomans in the city?"

"I do not know what has happened since I left. I was with

my uncle and Giustiniani. They have requested you. I think they finally believe your account of the Turks' guns."

Radu almost laughed as they raced out of Cyprian's home and through the streets. They had to push past several mobs that had gathered outside churches, everyone trying to press in at the same time. Concussive blasts shook the whole city, bursts that punctuated the still-clanging bells and the desperate wailing.

"You!" Cyprian grabbed a monk by the collar. The man looked at Cyprian as though he were the devil himself. "Where are you going?"

"To the church!"

"You will do no one good there!"

The monk's conviction that Cyprian was the devil solidified. He glared, aghast. "That is the only place we *can* do any good!"

"Gather citizens, have them haul stones and material to the walls. We will need everyone's help if we are to survive the night. You can pray while you work."

The monk hesitated but nodded at last. "I will spread the word."

"That was good," Radu said as they continued their sprint toward the walls.

"It will not be enough. Promise me that if they get through, you will run."

"I must get Nazira first."

Cyprian nodded. "Go to Galata, if you can. You may be able to slip out undetected."

"What about you?"

"I will stay with my uncle."

Radu stopped. The walls were in sight. They could see plumes of smoke, and the dust of shattered stone hanging in the air like a vision of the future. "You do not owe this city your life. It is not even *your* city."

Cyprian stopped, too, and they stood side by side, chests heaving from their run. "My uncle has shown me every kindness."

"And you should be and are grateful. But if it comes to staying and dying, or running and living, choose the latter. He would want that for you."

"Would he?"

"If he does not, he should. The city will stand or fall depending on the whims of fate. It would be a tragedy if you fell with it." Radu realized as he said it how true it was. He could not bear the thought of Cyprian dying with the city.

Cyprian's gray eyes shifted from troubled to thoughtful. Then his smile, the one that nearly shut his eyes with its exuberance, the one Radu had not seen in some time, erased everything else. Cyprian shook his head as though trying to physically shift the smile into a more appropriate expression, but it lingered. "Thank you," he said. Radu had never really noticed Cyprian's mouth before, but for some reason he could not look away from it now.

With all the clanging and shouting, Radu was disoriented. His head felt light, and his heart was beating far faster than the run here should have made it.

The sound of a stone ball smashing against a stone wall shook him out of his stupor. Cyprian guided Radu through the chaos to where the emperor and Giustiniani waited. They stood beneath a tower, gesturing emphatically. The barrel of a very large cannon stuck out of the tower, pointed toward the Ottoman troops.

"No!" Radu shouted, sprinting toward them.

A cracking noise rendered him momentarily deaf. As though it were happening from a very great distance, he watched the unanchored force of the cannon shoot it backward. The heat and movement of the blast were too much for the gun. As it hit the back of the tower with shattering force, both gun and tower exploded. Radu turned and tackled Cyprian to the ground beneath them, covering his head as rubble rained down on them. Something slammed into his shoulder.

When only a fine shower of dust was left falling around them, Radu rolled off Cyprian, clutching his shoulder.

"Are you hurt?" Cyprian leaned over him, searching him for a wound.

"Look for the emperor! He was closer."

Cyprian stood, dodging around the remains of the tower. "Uncle? Uncle!"

With a pained groan, Radu pushed himself up to a seated position. The tower was gone. Only its stone base was left. Several broken bodies were half buried in the rubble.

"Over here!" Cyprian shouted. Radu grimaced as he tried to stand. Cyprian must have found the emperor. Or his body. Radu knew he should feel relief or even joy that the emperor had been killed this soon—and by his own men's folly, no less. But it made him sad.

"Oh!" he exclaimed, looking up in wonder as Constantine held out a hand to help him stand. "I thought— You were so close to the tower!"

"Giustiniani heard your shout and we jumped free. How did you know it would come down?" Constantine looked toward the remains with murder written on his face. "Is my weapons master a traitor? Did he sabotage us?"

Radu grabbed his shoulder as though that could ease the pain pounding through him. "Not a traitor. Simply a fool. You cannot fire a cannon that large without padding all around it. The force of the blast pushes it backward. He packed too much gunpowder, too. I told you I knew of the sultan's guns. Urbana, the engineer who made them, was from Transylvania. She was my friend. We spoke often."

"Let me see," Cyprian said. He turned Radu around and gently peeled Radu's shirt free from his injured shoulder. His fingers were as light as a promise where they traced Radu's skin. Radu shivered. "You are not bleeding. There will be a lot of bruising. But if you can still move your shoulder, it is probably not broken." Cyprian's fingers lingered for a few infinite seconds longer; then he replaced Radu's shirt. That sense of breathlessness was back.

Giustiniani cleared his throat, spitting. He had so much stone dust in his hair he looked as though he had aged thirty years. He considered Radu thoughtfully. "Are you an expert in cannons, then?"

"Not an expert. But none of these towers are equipped for cannons. They are not strong enough, and there is not enough room to support the guns. You will have to figure out another way to use them."

"We thought if we could fire back at the sultan's cannons, we could—"

"Too small a target. By the time you used enough shots to

get the range right, they would move their guns. You have seen their camp. If you managed to destroy even one cannon, they have the means to repair and cast new cannons. I am certain Urbana will be with them. No one is better than she. And I am guessing they have dug in and are firing from behind a bulwark."

Constantine nodded grimly. "That first shot at the Saint Romanus Gate—even I thought the world was ending. But it has not been repeated. Maybe the cannon broke?"

Radu tested his shoulder. He could move it, but the pain was excruciating. "The Basilica." He almost smiled, thinking how delighted Urbana would be. "It has to cool between firing, so it's limited to several shots a day. It was more to prove they *could* than for any practical use. It is the number of guns you should fear, not the size of one. Are the walls holding?"

Giustiniani shook some of the grit from his hair. "So far there are no holes big enough to threaten us. They fire wrong. They should fire in sets of three, one on each side and then one in the middle, to bring a whole section down. Instead, they fire at the same spot over and over again. They are doing damage, but not enough."

Giustiniani leaned out, watching without flinching as a massive ball shattered against the wall some ways down from them. The sound was louder than any Radu had ever heard, like thunder smashing against thunder.

"We cannot absorb these blows. The fragments from the wall are as likely to kill our men as the cannon shot itself." Giustiniani was silent for a while, deep in thought. "We cannot answer their cannons, nor can we trust the strength of the walls." He smiled grimly. "It is time to become more flexible."

Because of Radu's shoulder injury, he helped Cyprian with organizing rather than going to fix the walls. All day they ran, directing men to dump mortar paste down the walls to strengthen them. They attached rope to bales of wool and lowered them to absorb impacts. The palace was raided of all tapestries, the elegant stitching and bright depictions of the past now draped over the walls in a desperate attempt to secure a future.

By nightfall, everyone in the city was wide-eyed and trembling from the ceaseless bombardment. But they were ready. As soon as it was dark, Giustiniani sent the supplies up. At each significant breach in the wall, they put down stakes with stretches of leather hide nailed tightly between them. Into the space between the hides and the remains of the wall they dumped stones, timber, bushes, brushwood, and bucket after bucket of dirt.

A few stakes to save a city.

"Will they burn?" Radu asked Cyprian as they oversaw a patch along the Blachernae Palace wall.

"The hides will not light easily. But we will need to station guards with crossbows to keep men away, regardless." Cyprian paused to shout directions to men rolling large barrels packed with dirt toward them. "Along the top so we have something to hide behind!"

The men had only just finished placing the barrels when a stone ball came sailing out from the blackness. Radu did not have time to hold his breath as he watched it smash directly into the makeshift wall.

The loose materials held by the skins absorbed the cannonball's impact, and the ball rolled harmlessly to the ground.

The men around them cheered. Many dropped to their knees in prayer. Cyprian whooped joyfully, throwing his arms around Radu in a hug. Radu cringed at the pain in his shoulder, and at the shout of joy that had escaped his own lips before he realized he was cheering for the wrong side.

The next five days brought no rest, no change. The cannons fired, the sound of stone shattering stone so constant Radu stopped noticing it. The acrid scent of smoke was everywhere. When he came home to sleep for a few hours, Nazira made him dump water over his hair outside to try to rinse some of it away.

But as soon as sleep claimed him, the noise from the wall would jar him awake. He stopped trying to go home, instead slumping in the shadow of the inner wall for a few minutes of rest. The hours blurred, only the sun or the moon marking the passage of time. Even those were so obscured by smoke that they were hardly visible.

In addition to the ceaseless bombardment, Ottoman troops threw themselves against the walls at random. They used hooks to pull down the barrels of earth protecting the defenders. The Ottomans were packed so tightly that a single shot of a small cannon could kill several, yet still they came.

That was the part Radu wished he could block out, the acts that made him certain he could never wash the scent of the wall from his soul. Because he had to be on this side, and he had to play his part. And so, when the Ottoman soldiers—his brothers—ran up to try to retrieve the bodies of their compatriots, he sat on top of the wall with the enemy and picked them off one by one.

The first time he hit a man, he turned and vomited. But soon even his body was numb to the horror of what he was doing. That felt worse. With each shot he prayed he missed, and with each hit he prayed the walls would fall soon and spare them all.

On the sixth day of the bombardment, an explosion cracked through the air, echoing off the walls. It was notable only because it had not come from the walls—it had come from the Ottoman camp.

Radu ran to the top of the wall, leaning over. Black smoke billowed from the bank of earth that hid the Basilica. The location of the cannon had been identified on the first day, but Giustiniani had not been able to destroy it. They had not needed to, apparently.

Even from this distance the devastation was obvious. The gun must have finally succumbed to the heat and pressure of so many firings and exploded. Radu wiped furiously at his face, his hands leaving more grit than they cleared away. He had no doubt that Urbana had accompanied Mehmed to take care of her precious artillery. Had her greatest triumph been her end?

An exhausted and ragged cheer rose around him, but this time he could not even pretend to join in. The Basilica was gone. The wall still held. And his friend was more than likely dead.

Cyprian found him sitting with his back to the barrels, staring blankly at the city on the hill. How much more would this damnable city cost them all before the end?

"Come. Giustiniani is at the Lycus River Valley section of the wall. He is guaranteed to have some food worth eating." Cyprian led Radu down the line to the Italian. He ate the offered food in numb silence as the sun set, realizing too late that he had not even remembered to pray in his heart.

"You should go rest," Giustiniani said, his tired smile kind. "We have had a victory today, through no merit of our own. But we will take it."

Radu felt as though he could sleep for years. That was what he wanted. To fall asleep and wake up with the city already the Ottoman capital, everything changed and settled and peaceful once more. Because he still believed Constantinople should be and would be Mehmed's. The Prophet, peace be upon him, had declared it.

But Radu did not want to see anything more that happened before the city fell.

That was when a rhythmic pounding broke through the smoke-dimmed quiet of the night air. It was followed by the clashing of cymbals and the calls of pipes. Finally, the screams of men joined the chorus, a chilling cacophony promising death. The hair on Radu's arms stood. He had been on the other end of this tactic before, at Kruje, exhilarated to join with his brothers in a wall of noise.

He had never been on the receiving end. He understood now why it was so effective, to hear what was coming and be unable to flee. Flares bloomed to life in the valley beneath them. With a wave of noise, thousands of men surged forward to crash against the wall.

Radu followed Giustiniani's screamed commands. Men raced from other sections of the wall to help. Radu fired arrow after arrow, switching to a crossbow when his injured shoulder became too much.

Still the Ottomans came.

Where they breached the wall, Giustiniani was waiting. At

some places the bodies were piled so high they formed steps nearly to the top. Ottomans scrambled on top of Ottomans, clawing their way to the death that waited for them. And then their bodies became stepping-stones for the men behind them.

Everything was smoke and darkness, screaming and drums, blood and fire. Radu stared in a daze. How could these be men? How could this be real?

"Radu!" Cyprian shouted. He grabbed Radu's arm, spinning him out of range of a sword. Several Ottomans had breached the wall next to him. Radu wanted to tell them they were not enemies. But their blades were raised, and so Radu met them. Cyprian pressed his back to Radu's. A sword flashed toward Cyprian. *Not Cyprian* was Radu's only thought as he hacked off the arm holding the sword. It was then that he finally saw the face of the man. He looked at Radu, all rage draining away. He looked like Petru, that stupid Janissary Lada kept around. He could have been, had Lada not taken them to Wallachia. Then the man tipped off the edge of the wall and fell into the darkness.

Radu did not have time to think, to feel, because there was another sword and another arm. These were his brothers, but in the chaos and the fury, it did not matter. It was kill or be killed, and Radu killed.

And killed.

And killed.

Finally, the attack that had started like a wave receded like one, quietly fading back into the night. Giustiniani limped past Radu and Cyprian. "Burn the battering rams. Let them gather their dead."

Radu did not know how long it had lasted, or what it had cost them, but it was over. He did not realize he was crying until Cyprian embraced him, holding him close. "It is done. We did it. The wall stands."

Whether Radu was crying in relief or despair, he was too tired to know. He had had no choice—had he? He had kept Cyprian alive, and he had stayed alive. But it did not feel like a victory. Together, they stumbled from the wall and into the city, collapsing in the shadow of a church and falling into a sleep not even the angry increase of bombardment could disturb.

When Radu awoke, his head was resting against Cyprian's shoulder. A deep sense of well-being and relief flooded him. They had done it. They had made it.

And then horror chased away the relief. He had fought at this man's side, rejoiced in their survival, knowing full well that every Byzantine who survived was one more Mehmed had to fight to win. Knowing that every day the walls held, more of his Muslim brothers died.

Where was his heart? Where was his loyalty?

Radu staggered away from the still-sleeping Cyprian. He wandered, dazed and in mourning, once again finding himself at the Hagia Sophia. A small boy was curled into himself, asleep at the base of the building. Invisible in the midst of so much darkness.

Radu walked over to Amal, his steps heavy. He leaned down and shook the boy awake.

"Tell Mehmed he is firing the cannons wrong."

32

Mid-April

LADA RAN TO MEET the solitary form of Stefan making his unhurried way through the canyon toward them. He had shaved. Facial hair had helped him blend in at the castle in Hunedoara, but out here where only landed men could have beards, a bare face made him more invisible.

"No gossip precedes us," he said. "We should make camp this afternoon, and travel the rest of the way in the morning."

Lada sighed. "I would set up camp with the devil right now if it meant getting out of the cold."

"I believe the devil quite likes flames."

Lada started, narrowing her eyes. "Stefan, did you make a joke? I did not think you knew how."

His face betrayed no emotion. "I have many skills."

Lada laughed. "That, I already knew."

The path they took followed the Arges River, retracing the route Lada had taken with her father so many summers ago. This time Bogdan rode at her side instead of in the back with the servants. And Radu was lost to her, as was her father and any tenderness she might have held for him.

Radu would survive. He would be fine. He could not die at the walls of Constantinople, because he belonged to her and she would not allow it. Just like Wallachia belonged to her and she would not allow anyone else to have it.

"Why do you keep looking up at that peak?" Nicolae asked, following her line of sight. "You are making me nervous. Do you expect an attack?"

Lada glared. "No."

She had considered slipping out and making her way toward the ruins of the fortress on the peak. She wanted to stand at its edge to greet the dawn and feel the warmth of her true mother, Wallachia, greeting her and blessing her.

But the too-recent encounter with her other mother pulled at her, tearing at the edges of her certainty. What if she remembered the fortress wrong? What if she climbed up and the sun did not come out? What if it did, but it felt the same as any other sunrise?

She could not risk tainting that precious memory. She clutched the locket around her neck, the one Radu had given her to replace her old leather pouch. Inside were the dusty remains of an evergreen sprig and a flower from these same mountains. She had carried them with her as talismans through the lands of her enemies. Now she was home, and still in the land of her enemies.

She would climb that peak one day, soon. When it was all hers. She would come back, and she would rebuild the fortress to honor Wallachia.

They paused at the peak's base, refilling their canteens and watering the horses. Lada dismounted. She scrambled through a jumble of dark gray boulders, following a trickle of water that met the stream. Hidden behind the rocks was a cave. She ducked inside, where the frigid temperature dropped even lower. She could not see far, so she felt along the rough edges of the cave. But then something changed under her fingers. These were too smooth, no longer the natural shape of rocks. Someone had carved this out of the mountain. Which meant it was not a cave.

It was a secret passage.

Lada pushed forward blindly until she hit the end. There were no other tunnels, no branches. Why make a passage that led nowhere? Had someone been cutting to the heart of the mountain just like Ferhat in the old story, only to find that mountains have no hearts?

A drop of water fell on her head and she tipped her chin up. She shouted. The sound echoed upward, disappearing into the noise of frantic bats disturbed in their slumber. Lada flinched, but none came down toward her.

Which meant there was another way for them to escape. She felt the wall again until she found handholds carved into the stone. There was only one place this tunnel could lead: straight to her ruined fortress. Which meant it was a secret escape, a way to be free when all other ways were closed.

Wallachia always found a way.

Though it was spring—bitterly cold, but still spring—Lada saw more fallow fields than ones ready for planting. The land they traveled through had an air of stagnation.

Finally they reached farmland that was being used. Decrepit hovels with smoke rising from their chimneys dotted the edges of fields. On the horizon, the Basarab manor soared, two stories and large enough to house all the peasants in all the hovels they had passed. Lada and her men made no attempt to hide their approach. Matthias had promised to send notice. If he had betrayed them, they were going to have to fight regardless.

A child sat on the side of the road. His head was too big for his rail-thin body, which was visible through his rags. It was too cold to be out in anything less than a cloak. He watched them approach, listless.

Nicolae paused in front of him. "Where is your mother?"

The boy blinked dully.

"Your father?"

When there was no response, Nicolae held out a hand. "Come with me," he said. The boy stood, and Nicolae easily lifted him onto his horse.

"He is probably crawling with bugs," Petru said, frowning. "Leave him be."

Nicolae gave Petru a dangerous look, all his good humor gone. "If being infested disqualified someone from our company, you would have been out years ago."

Petru sat straighter in his saddle, hand going to the pommel of his sword. "I tire of being the butt of your jokes."

"If you do not want to be the butt, try to be less of an ass."

Petru's expression turned ferocious. Lada moved her horse between them. "If Nicolae wants to pick up strays, that is his choice."

Bogdan, next to Lada as always, nodded toward their party. "We are doing a lot of that." Behind the mounted men, straggling back for half a league, a weary but determined group of people was catching up.

In addition to her thirty remaining Janissaries, Lada had picked up more than two dozen young Wallachian men from her time in Transylvania and Hungary. They carried staffs, pitchforks, clubs. One had a rusty scythe. None of them had horses, but they marched in as near a formation as they could manage. Lada knew those men. But behind them were the fringes of the camp—women organized by Oana to run things, men too old to fall in easily with the eager young ones, even a man and his daughters who had followed them from Arges rather than take the dangerous roads alone.

"This is absurd," Lada said. "Why do they stay with us?" Her men, she understood. They had nothing better, nowhere else to go. They were loyal to her, and to the hope that perhaps she would find them a place in the world. They were soldiers, too, used to travel and hardship. But these people, they . . .

They had nothing better, nowhere else to go. They were loyal to her, and to the hope that perhaps she would find them a place in the world, too.

———— ◆ ————

An hour later Lada sat in a pleasantly furnished room, drinking hot wine, and warm for the first time since her mother's stifling sitting room. Bogdan was on one side, Nicolae the other. Petru and Stefan stood at the door, casually intimidating. Against the opposite wall, Toma Basarab's guards stood with snide confidence.

"The letter I received from Matthias Corvinas was . . . interesting." Toma Basarab's hair and beard were silver. He wore velvet and silk as dark as his wine, his buttons shining silver beacons that matched his hair.

"I want to be prince," Lada said.

Toma Basarab laughed, his mirth as bright as his buttons. "Why would you want that?"

"Our princes fail Wallachia. They are too busy appealing to foreign powers, pandering to boyars, desperately going over their own coffers. Meanwhile our country rots around them. I will change that."

Toma leaned back, tapping his fingers on his glass. "The system is what it is. It has worked for this long."

"Worked for whom?"

"I know you have big dreams, little Draculesti. But Wallachia is as Wallachia was and will ever be. What can you offer it?"

Lada understood immediately his true question was "What can you offer me?" She wished Radu were here. He would have this old fox eating out of his hand. Lada fixed a cold glare on him. "Your mistake is in thinking I care one whit about *offering* anything. The system is broken. I am going to change it."

"People who agitate for change end up dead."

Lada bared her teeth at him in a smile. "We will see who is dead at the end of all this."

Toma smiled, a slow spread of his mouth and ending with his dark eyes. "I think I see what you have to offer, then. Matthias was right to send you here. You have much potential. I will advise you. There are many boyars I can sweep into your support. A few will need . . . aggressive persuasion. But I suspect you excel at that. Under my guidance, you will get your throne in Tirgoviste. I would be proud to be at your side, serving a Draculesti prince." He held out his hands in offering, the fire in the hearth burning behind him.

Lada remembered her joke about making camp with the devil, and a sudden revulsion seized her. She did not want to have his help, or anyone's. But she needed it.

"Thank you." The words grated against her teeth like sand.

"My men will show yours where they can stay. Let us take a meal while we discuss the surrounding regions. Many of these boyars have done simply horrendous things to their people." He clucked his tongue in pity, but his eyes looked like they were tallying encouraging financial ledgers as he considered Lada.

33

April 19–21

RADU'S INFORMATION HAD LED to more successful cannon fire, and he paid the price. Every day he watched as the adjusted bombardment targeted the walls with more devastation, and every day he stumbled home, exhausted from trying to fix the holes. His aid to Mehmed put his own life in constant danger. Did Mehmed worry about that? Was he sorry?

Nazira's work was equally exhausting, but in other ways. "Helen cries constantly," she said in the morning, the only time they saw each other. "I have to spend half our time reassuring her that Coco, the Italian captain she is mistress to, really does love her and that when this is all over he will leave his wife in Venice for her. It is all I can do not to slap her and tell her she is wasting her life. The other women mostly spend their time in church praying. And when they are not there, they are complaining of how hard it is to get food and how they had to donate their tapestries to the walls. How is your work?"

Radu pulled on his boots. They were caked with dust from the walls. "The bombardment is going better, but there have been no gaps big enough for a full-scale assault yet. Mehmed sends skirmishing troops to harass the forces and make certain no one is able to rest. I wonder if we can do anything more."

Nazira sat next to him on the bed, leaning her head on his shoulder. "It is wearisome work, for both souls and bodies. If you want to leave, I will be at your side. But do you feel that if we fled the city and joined the camp, we would be able to say we had done everything we could? I know you will not be satisfied with anything less. Nor will Mehmed."

Radu sighed, running his hands through his hair and pulling it back at the base of his neck. He missed wearing turbans. They kept his hair out of his face and provided protection from the sun. There was something soothing, too, in wrapping one around and around his head in the morning. All his comforting rituals were taken from him here.

"You are right. We will stay."

Nazira patted his hand. "But I did hear something that will make you happy. Word is spreading that the Ottoman navy is approaching, with doom in its terrible wake. Our friend Suleiman will be here soon, and maybe that will signal a quick end."

Radu allowed himself a weary smile tinged with hope. It would do his soul good to see those boats. And it would not even hurt that he was not on them, because the sea was the one place he wanted to be even less than on the wall.

———◆———

"I have been looking everywhere for you!" Cyprian said, joining Radu at the wall overlooking the Golden Horn. Radu had avoided Cyprian ever since that night they fought side by side.

It was easier this way. Though he still caught himself watching the men for Cyprian's way of walking, with shoulders leading, arms swinging wide.

"You leave so early and are never there at mealtimes. I miss you." Cyprian looked out over the water and tugged at the cloak around his neck. "Nazira is good company, but it is not the same without you."

It had been three days since Nazira brought news of the approaching fleet. Every spare moment Radu had, he spent at this wall looking for the ships.

Today, his long wait was answered. He wished Cyprian were not here, were not leaning close. It made it so much more difficult to be truly elated. The massive chain held, an impassable barrier stretching between Constantinople and Galata. In the horn, Constantine's ships loomed, ready to repel any attempt at destroying the chain. They were Venetian merchant ships, mostly, far taller and wider than the swift Ottoman war galleys. They were also armed to the teeth and well practiced in repelling pirates.

On the other side of the chain, just outside of firing range, Radu's fleet made the water look like a forest of masts. His heart swelled with pride to see it, and he shifted guiltily away from Cyprian. The fleet had arrived the day before, but this had been his first chance to come and see it in person. He wondered which boat Suleiman was on, wished he could see the admiral in full command of the finest navy in the world.

Cyprian looked on, devastation marring his face. "So many more than we had planned for. You were right, as always. Where did they find sailors?"

"Greek mercenaries, mostly."

"We will be our own undoing yet."

Radu hoped that was true, but still wanted to extend some comfort to Cyprian. It was an impulse he could not deny, and he thought again how this would all have been easier had Cyprian abandoned them to their fortunes once they had reached the city. His insistence on friendship made everything tight and aching in Radu's chest.

Radu again opted for truth as a way to avoid lying. "But the Ottomans cannot get past the chain."

"And neither can anyone else. Which means we are cut off from help. Men, weapons, supplies—nothing more is coming. What we have now is what we will have at the end, whatever that may be."

"Still, the seawalls are safe. Even if the Ottomans get past the chain, launching an assault from this side is nearly impossible. The sultan knows that. He means to press from all sides to wear you down. But you will not have to spare too many extra men to guard this wall. The Lycus River is his avenue in."

Cyprian considered Radu wryly. "You still think more like an attacker than a defender."

Radu blushed, his sheepish expression unfeigned. "I spent many years looking at maps over Mehmed's shoulder."

"What is he like? As a person, not as a sultan."

"This past year the sultan and the person have become inseparable." As Radu had seen Mehmed grow into himself and his power, he had also seen Mehmed grow further away. He was both proud and dismayed. "Before that? Focused. Driven. He had a burning intensity that did not slacken no matter what area of his life he directed it toward. He saw something unobtainable, and that was the only thing he wanted."

"Like you?" Cyprian's tone was soft and without accusation. It was merely curious, as though he was trying to fill in parts to a story he had heard only a few passages of.

Radu shook his head, keeping his eyes fixed on the water. The skies were leaden above them, making the sea the same color as Cyprian's eyes. But the sea was safer to look at. "No, it was the other Draculesti sibling who was the challenge."

"Your sister? She was part of his harem?"

"No." Radu grinned ruefully, finally looking at his companion. "That was precisely the problem. She was not, and she never would be, and so he wanted her more than anything else."

"What happened?"

"She left."

"She should not have left you."

"I wanted her to. I pushed her toward it. I thought that if she was gone, Mehmed would finally see—" Radu bit off the end of the sentence. It was so easy to talk to Cyprian. Too easy. He should not be admitting these things, not to him, not to anyone.

Cyprian filled in the rest of the sentence for him. "But Mehmed could only see the things he did not have. He is blind."

Radu cleared his throat and looked away. "Well. She left me, and she left him, too. And because of that, I think he will always love her. Or at least want her. He cannot abide failure."

"She was his Constantinople."

Radu smiled, having entertained the same thought before. But it was not quite right. "I am afraid Constantinople is his Constantinople. Nothing could ever overtake this city in his heart."

A shout from the tower next to them drew their attention back to the water. The Ottoman ships had broken formation and were turning away from the chain. Radu could not understand why, until he saw four huge merchant ships, barreling through the water toward the horn.

And directly toward the Ottoman navy.

"Those are Italian ships!" Cyprian said, leaning out over the wall. "They are making a run for the horn!"

The ships safely in the horn edged closer to the chain, uselessly firing cannons at the Ottoman fleet. They were too far away to make a difference. Radu could almost feel the desperation from here. Everyone could see the Italian ships, but no one could help them.

"It is four ships against more than a hundred. They will never make it through."

Cyprian smiled grimly. "Do not discount them. They are born on the water. If the wind stays with them, if luck is on our side . . ." Cyprian's lips moved silently, whether in prayer or something else, Radu did not know.

Together they watched the battle play out from above. Radu did not even have to pretend to be emotionally invested in the other side—he could look on with the same intensity as everyone else, and no one would know his hopes were with the Ottoman navy.

It did not look promising. He had assumed the numbers would give them the advantage, but the tall, heavy merchant ships cut through the water as though it were nothing. The smaller galleys struggled to navigate the choppy sea, their inexperience showing immediately. They fired cannons at the Italian ships, but no cannons large enough to be effective could be placed on the lightweight galleys.

The four ships barreled straight through the middle of the entire might of the Ottoman navy.

Cyprian cheered with the crowd that had gathered on the wall. Excited chatter around them made it feel more like a sporting event than a battle. Radu was devastated to see that it was *not* anything like a battle after all. His navy was useless.

Then he realized the wind was no longer flinging sea air in his face. Everything had gone still around them—and around the merchant ships. As fast as they had been slicing through the water, they now drifted directionless.

And the galleys had oars.

Suleiman wasted no time. The larger galleys pulled in close, the smaller galleys edging between them to get right next to the merchant ships. With no wind, the ships were at the mercy of the water—which was causing them to drift, slowly but surely, across the horn to the Galata shore, where Mehmed already had men waiting.

But the Italian sailors would not go down easily. They lashed the four ships together to prevent them from being separated and picked off. So many of the Ottoman vessels had converged it looked like a sailor could walk from one end of the sea to the other without ever touching water.

The first small galleys to reach the merchant ships never had a chance at boarding. Large stones and barrels of water were dropped by the on-deck loading cranes, damaging some of the galleys and sinking others. The sounds of the battle—the snapping of wood, the shattering of stone, and the clash of steel against steel—rang through the horn.

And always, a sound Radu heard even in his sleep, the screams of men. There was a quality of voice, some subtle shift, that allowed him even at this distance to pick out which screams were screams of killing, and which were those of dying.

When the Ottomans managed to throw ropes up, the ropes were cut down. Hands were sliced off when they tried to find purchase. Burning pitch was thrown, and Radu watched as men fell into the water to be extinguished or onto their own boats, lighting them on fire with their bodies.

The Italians had the advantage of height and weight, but the Ottomans kept coming. For every galley sunk, two more pushed into its place. It was exhausting to watch. The sun, too hot for once, had shifted overhead, marking the endless passage of time. The crowd around Radu and Cyprian had gone quiet except for the occasional prayer or gasping sob. Though the Italians fought bravely, the outcome was inevitable. They drifted ever closer to the shore, where the Ottoman cannons would take them out if the galleys did not manage to first. It was only a matter of time.

Radu closed his eyes in relief as a breeze cut through the sun battering his face. And then he opened his eyes in horror. A breeze from the south that turned into a stiff wind. A ragged cheer went up along the wall as the Italian ships' sails caught. They plowed through the galleys around them, pushing them aside like branches, moving forward as one. Their escape was unavoidable, unassailable.

Radu looked to the Galata shore and his heart sank. There, astride a beautiful white horse, a tiny figure watched as his navy—more than a hundred ships, the best in the world—was bested by four merchant boats.

Radu's project. Radu's navy. He hung his head with shame. Against all odds, they had failed. Mehmed's horse reared, then he turned it and rode swiftly away. All along the wall the citizens cheered and jeered, ebullient with the miracle of the Italian boats. The chain had been slipped free to allow them through. No galleys could catch up to take advantage before the chain was closed again.

It was over.

For once, Radu was invited to a meeting with the emperor. But this one he wished he could avoid. The humiliation of his navy's defeat settled in his chest like a sickness. It was a kindness, then, that he was not with Mehmed. He could not bear to think of what Mehmed would say, how disappointed he would be. He had trusted this task to Radu, and Radu had failed utterly.

Though Radu knew he should not, he took some small comfort in Cyprian's coming with him. He was unmoored, worn down by time and failure. At least with Cyprian he would have to pretend to be okay. That was a good reason. That was the only reason. He would not allow any other reasons to crave Cyprian's smile or a touch of his hand.

In Constantine's meeting room, Radu and Cyprian joined Giustiniani, the pretend Ottoman heir Orhan, the Italian commander Coco (whom Radu knew only through Nazira's stories of the unfortunate Helen), and the emperor. Constantine moved with more lightness than Radu had seen. He was again barefoot, pacing with joyful energy. "Grain, arms, manpower. Two hundred archers! But that is not the true strength. They have brought us hope. More can come. More will come. That wind was the hand of God, delivering a blessing to this city. The first of many."

Coco nodded, unable to avoid Constantine's infectious joy. "One good Italian ship is worth a hundred infidel boats."

Giustiniani laughed, clapping Orhan on the back. "So you see, we Italians can do good things. I hear the sultan is furious. The admiral will pay for his failure."

"Suleiman?" Radu spoke before he thought better of it. He tried to shift his face into impassivity, but it was impossible. "I knew him. Is he— Will he be killed?" A gentle hand on his back startled him, but he did not turn around. Had Radu's grief been that obvious to Cyprian?

"He lost an eye in the battle. That alone probably saved him, as testament to how hard he fought." Giustiniani snorted. "For all the good it did him. Our scouts report he was flogged and stripped of all rank and authority. One of the pashas is in charge of the boats now. Not that it matters. We have nothing to fear from the sea."

"But do the Venetians know that?" Cyprian asked. "They must have heard of the size of the Ottoman navy. How can we get word to them that they are guaranteed safe passage to the horn?"

Radu wished desperately that Lada were here. She would not be sad; she would not let this failure derail her. She would figure out a way to turn it to her advantage. She would use the enemies' strength and confidence against them. Just as she had when they snuck into the palace under Halil Pasha's nose, putting Mehmed in place to take the throne when his father died.

A flicker of delight lit Radu's soul as he remembered that night, all Lada's fierce Janissaries dressed in veils and silk robes, trying to walk like women so they could sneak past the watching guard. And then he knew exactly what Lada would do.

"Do you have any Ottoman flags?" he asked.

Everyone turned to him, puzzled. Orhan, a quiet, delicate man who wore a turban along with his Byzantine styles, nodded. "I have a supply of them."

"What about uniforms?"

Constantine spoke. "We have over two hundred prisoners. They have no use of their uniforms in our dungeons."

"Send out three boats tonight under cover of darkness. Small, unthreatening ones. I will teach their crews a few common greetings in Turkish. Have them fly the Ottoman flag and sail as close to the Ottoman galleys as they can."

"Slip by in disguise." Constantine tugged at his beard thoughtfully.

"Three small boats could get out where one large ship cannot. Task them with finding the aid we need, and then they can return, heralding the ships that will follow so we can be prepared to welcome them."

Giustiniani stretched in his chair, leaning back. "It is a good plan. Coco, select the men. They leave tonight."

The Italian captain nodded. Orhan excused himself to get the flags, and Giustiniani went to find suitable uniforms.

"Well done." Cyprian beamed at Radu.

Radu could not meet that smile full on, so he looked at the floor. He would not have time to send word to Mehmed. He did not need to, though. He *wanted* the boats to escape. Because if they could escape, they could return.

And when they did, Radu would have first warning of a Venetian force. Then he could warn Mehmed, and find some sort of redemption.

34

Mid-April

THIS TIME, STEFAN DID not return alone from scouting.
He walked with a peculiar guilt, slinking back into camp
with a girl.

"What is this?" Lada barely glanced at the girl. "You were
supposed to bring information on Silviu's land and men." Toma
Basarab had sent them here first. Silviu did not have much in
the way of soldiers, but he was a Danesti and in the path of all
their future goals. They could not leave a close blood relative
of the prince behind. Lada was to negotiate his support. If that
was not possible, she was to place him under house arrest and
leave precious men here to watch him. Toma Basarab would
hear no arguments against it.

"Well?" she demanded.

Stefan shrugged, clearing his throat at the same time, as
though he could force the words out. Lada had never seen him
like this. Fear seized her—was he injured? She looked him up
and down, but he did not appear harmed.

His face flushed a deep red. "She caught me."

Lada finally looked at the girl. She was Lada's height, perhaps younger than her, but not by much. She met Lada's stare with a bold, unflinching one of her own. Her narrow jaw was set and her dark eyes burned. Rough cloth wrapped her hair, and her clothes seemed made for someone else. They hung all wrong on her body, loose in the shoulders and pulled tight across her stomach, which—

"Oh," Lada said, frowning.

The girl's hands jerked instinctively in front of her pregnant belly. Then she deliberately moved them away. "Caught your man spying. Told him I would turn him in unless he brought me here."

Lada raised her eyebrows at Stefan. He shrank farther into his cloak. No one ever noticed him. He drifted invisibly, a weary traveler no one wanted. That was his entire purpose.

"Well." Lada turned her attention back to the girl. "Here you are. What do you want?"

"You are that woman, right? I thought you would be taller. And older. You are very young."

Lada gave her a heavy look. "I assume there are many women in this country. You will have to be more specific."

"I heard rumors. You are staying with Toma Basarab. Took in men for soldiers. Peasants talk."

Lada shifted uneasily. Thanks to Toma's men—both his trained soldiers and the farmers they had conscripted—her ranks had swelled to over one hundred men. The peasants were poorly trained and poorly fed, but they had a gritty eagerness that could not be undervalued. And they did not eat much, which was good.

The girl leaned forward, burning with intensity. "Are you going to do that in more places? Take men for fighting the prince?"

"Yes," Lada said.

"Good." The girl's hands fisted over her stomach. "I want the Danesti dead."

It was a dangerous sentiment to voice aloud. Lada wondered at her daring. "Does your husband want to join? He should have come himself."

The girl let out a harsh laugh, a burst of bitterness more than humor. "I have no husband. Tell her what you saw, Stefan."

To Lada's surprise, he followed the girl's order without question. "Lots of girls. In the fields. Most—" He paused, then nodded toward the girl's stomach. "Most like her."

"And between us not a single husband. A few years ago we had a nasty bout of plague. Killed most of the boys. There weren't enough men to work the fields. None to marry daughters to. So our loving Danesti boyar decided he would take care of us himself." The girl paused, as though waiting for something. When Lada did not respond, she spoke again. "No husbands." The girl glared at Lada for her stupidity. "No husbands, but all our babies are bastard cousins."

Clarity finally caught Lada in its horrible grasp. "Oh."

"So you will not find many men here to swell your ranks. Our boyar worm Silviu will agree with whatever you want because he is a coward, but he will betray you to the prince at the first opportunity. And he has nothing to offer. You should kill him. If not, then leave. These lands are a waste of your time."

Lada felt anger rising within. "Why?"

"I told you, we have no men."

"No. Why did you let this happen? Why did all of you let this happen?"

The girl's face purpled with rage. "*Let* it happen? What choice did we have? We give ourselves or our families starve. What choice is there in that?"

"Does Silviu work the land?"

"No, of course not."

"Does he tend the animals?"

"No."

"Does he do a single thing that directly feeds you or your families?"

The girl looked as though she very much wanted to hit Lada. "He owns it. He owns it all."

Lada paused, weighing her options. Then she shrugged. She would negotiate her own way. "Not anymore."

They marched straight through the fields, past more than a dozen girls in the same condition as Daciana. The girls stood watching as the men passed. No one said anything.

Daciana walked next to Stefan's horse. Lada could tell the girl made him nervous, which she found perversely delightful. She had once seen Stefan slit a man's throat without blinking. That this pregnant slip of a girl could unnerve him when that had not was odd. Daciana talked softly to him. No one noticed Stefan until it was too late. But this girl had seen him, and would not stop seeing him.

Lada liked her.

An older woman ran from the middle of a field and caught up to them. She grabbed Daciana's hand and halted her. Daciana leaned close, whispering. Apparently satisfied with Daciana's explanation, the woman fell into step.

Silviu's manor was tucked into the side of a hill overlooking the farmland. Ten guards stood in front. Their helmets were slightly askew, swords and spears clutched so tightly they shook. Lada stopped her horse directly in front of them, well within striking distance. She remembered Hunyadi riding into an enemy city, broad-shouldered and armed with unassailable confidence. She wrapped the same around herself.

"I am here to see Silviu."

The guards looked at each other, at a loss.

Lada had seventy men at her back. The guards knew as well as she did that what she wanted, she would get. "Tell him I will receive him here. And then you are welcome to join my men, or to flee. Any other course of action will not end well for you."

The shortest man, broad-chested and of middle years, gave her an ugly sneer. "I do not take orders from women."

"My men do not have a similar problem." Lada lifted a hand. The man fell, a crossbow bolt sticking out of his chest.

A harelipped guard jumped away as though death were contagious. Which, in this case, it was. "I will go fetch him, Miss! Um, Madam. My lady. I— Right now!" Two of the guards turned and ran. The rest began edging toward Lada's men, hands far from their weapons.

"Hello, Miron," Daciana said. She stepped forward, blocking the path of one of the guards. There was something verminous about his face and his beady eyes that darted around. "You remember when we used to play together as children?"

He did not look at her. She held her hand out to the older

woman next to her. "You remember when my mother gave you some of our milk because you were starving?"

His lip curled in a snarl, but still he did not respond.

"You remember when I screamed and screamed, and you stood outside the door and did nothing? You remember when he offered you—what did he call them, 'seconds'? You remember what you did?"

The man had the gall to finally meet her gaze. He shrugged, face set in cruel indifference. He shoved his shoulder into her, to push her out of the way.

"I remember that, too," her mother said as she brought her hand between them. Lada's view was blocked by the soldier's body. He made an odd noise, twitching. Then he stumbled backward, blood-soaked hands tugging ineffectually at the rough wooden handle of a knife protruding from his stomach. He sank down against the stone wall of the house. His ratlike eyes looked up in shock and pain at the girl and her mother.

"And now we will never remember you again." Daciana turned her back on him.

Stefan pulled a handkerchief from his vest and offered it to her. She passed it to her mother, who wiped the blood from her hands.

"What is the meaning of this?" A portly man, face veined and splotchy with age and alcohol, stumbled out of the manor. He wore a velvet vest with a gold necklace, and a black cap on his large head.

"Silviu?" Lada asked. "I am here to negotiate your support." Lada drew her crossbow and shot him in the chest. One of Toma's men shouted in surprise.

Lada turned her horse. "That went well. We have the full support of this estate now. It is yours." She pointed to Daciana.

Daciana nodded, a dazed expression on her face. Her mother finished cleaning her hands and gave the handkerchief back to Daciana. "I will tell the men."

"No," Lada snapped. "I did not say the land was theirs. Or any of the fathers of this land. They forfeited their rights when they sold their daughters for food. Why did you let them live?"

Daciana's mother met Lada's gaze without shame. "I have three other daughters. I could not sacrifice myself without sacrificing them. Until today."

Lada wanted to argue, to chastise. Then she realized that this woman had come directly from working in the fields, where she had no need of a knife. How long had she carried it? How long had she treasured it in secret, waiting for the right moment? This woman was smart. She saw an opening and she took it.

Though why more people had not done this sooner, she did not understand. If the Wallachians could see past titles and velvet, they would see that the true strength of the land—the true power—was theirs. All they needed was a knife and an opportunity.

Lada would be both for them.

"You are in charge," she said to the old woman.

"You cannot do that," Toma's man said. "We need a boyar."

"Are you a boyar?" Lada snapped.

The man opened his mouth to argue further.

"I am the only royal blood here." She stared at him until he bowed his head and looked away. Then she pointed at the body of the murdered soldier and addressed Daciana's mother. "I trust you. Treat your daughters and granddaughters better than their fathers have treated them."

Daciana's mother nodded slowly, a determination settling around her eyes and replacing the shock. "What do we do when the prince finds out our boyar is dead?"

"Do what you have always done. Work the land. Let me worry about the prince."

The woman nodded, then dipped her head in a bow. "We owe you everything."

Lada smiled. "Do not forget it. I promise I will not."

35

April 21–28

"THERE YOU ARE!" CYPRIAN said brightly, in defiance of the weariness painted on his face in dust and soot and traces of blood.

Radu paused on the doorstep, trying his best to meet Cyprian's smile. He had just returned from a long night on the wall. A night of black punctuated by burning orange and darkest red. It was a relief to see Cyprian again. It was always a relief, because with the wall, reunions were never guaranteed.

Cyprian leaned past him to open the door, gesturing excitedly. "I found fruit preserves. I will not tell you what I had to do to get them, but—"

"Turks! Turks in the horn!" a boy screamed, running through the street.

Cyprian and Radu shared a look of confusion and concern. Radu was too tired to know whether this feeling was excitement or dread. He sprinted after the boy, caught his sleeve, and dragged him to a stop. "The chain has broken?"

The boy shook his head, eyes wide with excitement and fear.

"They sailed their ships over land!" The boy wriggled free and darted away, shouting his news with no further explanation.

Cyprian raised his eyebrows, concern overpowered by curiosity. He started walking in the direction of the seawall. Radu followed.

"Do you have any idea what he is talking about?" Cyprian asked.

"Maybe they were able to sneak in the same way our boats slipped out past them?"

"That worked because of the chaos. But there is no chaos on our side of the chain. No one sleeps. Watch is kept at all hours. There must be something else going on."

Radu trudged after Cyprian. He could not find the energy in himself to run anymore. He had spent half the night cutting down hooks that the Ottomans threw up to try to dislodge the barrels of earth that protected the defenders. It was wearying work. Even arrows singing past his ears barely registered after a few hours on barrel duty. But at least all he had done was remove hooks. He had not had to kill any of his brothers last night, which made it better than most.

His mind was on endless barrels of earth as they climbed to the top of the seawall and looked over.

"God's wounds," Radu whispered. Nothing had prepared him for this. The Ottomans were, in fact, inside the horn. And just as the boy had said, they were sailing their ships over land.

Three medium-sized galleys floated in the water, their crews laughing and waving their oars. Coming down a road of greased logs on the hill behind the horn, another galley slowly made its way toward the sea. The men aboard rowed their oars through the air, perfectly in sync. Oxen pulled from the front, and hundreds of men held ropes to control the descent. Cresting the hill behind the galley was yet another boat.

A striped tent had been set up overlooking the boats' progress. Radu could not see clearly from this distance, but he suspected it shaded Mehmed himself. Surrounding the tent, a Janissary band played music more suited to a party than to war. The bright brass notes drifted across the horn to Radu and Cyprian.

As the lower galley slid off the bank and into the sea, a cheer went up among the Ottomans.

"Why do our ships do nothing?" Cyprian asked. Radu pointed to a row of cannons set up along the shore, aimed at the chain where Constantine's fleet floated, useless. A few ships were edging closer, apparently debating whether or not to risk the cannon fire.

Without warning, a huge stone flew over the top of the city of Galata and came splashing into the water between the Byzantine fleet and the Ottoman galleys. It was so close to the nearest merchant ships that they bobbed in the waves from the impact.

Mehmed had also solved the problem of how to fire from Galata. He could not, under treaty, place cannons in the city. And so he had engaged the trebuchets from bygone years. They sat behind the city and flung rocks over into the water.

A crash and a plume of dust from the middle of Galata proved that the trebuchet aim was not perfect. Or perhaps it was deliberate, a warning to the people not to interfere. Radu was astonished at Mehmed's brilliance.

In the meantime, yet another galley had slipped into the water, with two more on the way.

Cyprian did not look at Radu. "This plan had to be in the

works for months. With all the supplies they would need, the logistics of it all ... Did you know?"

Radu's chest was heavy with the weight of failure. Not only had he failed Mehmed with the navy, Mehmed had anticipated the failure. He had made plans without Radu, plans to circumvent everything. How could Radu hope to offer such a man anything?

"I had no idea." Radu shook his head, the music from across the horn mocking him. "I fear there may be even more plans I was not privy to."

Cyprian put a gentle hand on his shoulder. "If Mehmed suspected a hair of his beard knew his secrets, he would pluck it out and burn it."

Radu refused the comfort. "I cannot help anymore."

He could not help anyone.

———◆———

Nazira picked out worms from the little grain they had left. "Do you suppose we could eat these?"

Radu grimaced. "If it came to it, we could. But if the siege lasts that long, Mehmed will have already lost. It is taking too long as it is."

"I wish your escapade with ruining the food stores had been less successful." Nazira gave him a wry smile.

"There is still food enough in Galata, though no one has the money to buy it. My sabotage has not ended the siege, only made it more miserable." Radu leaned forward, resting his head on the table. He was due back at the wall in the evening. His last few shifts had been uneventful. Lonely, too. And

Cyprian was gone more often than not by the time Radu returned home.

Evidently, Nazira was thinking of their host as well. "We could try to get more information from Cyprian."

Radu did not lift his head. He would not go there. Not yet. "Too dangerous."

Nazira sounded relieved. "I am glad you agree. Also, it feels . . . wrong. To use Cyprian any more than we already are."

"He is a good person, and I— Sometimes I cannot bear to even look at him, knowing what we are doing here. I cannot bear to look at any of them. Constantine is a good man, too. Giustiniani. All of them. The longer we are here, the harder it is to remember why it was so important that we take the city. I have fought alongside them, I have bled with them, I have stood shoulder to shoulder as we killed my Muslim brothers. How—" Radu's voice cracked, breaking on the last question. "How do we go on?" he whispered.

Nazira put a hand on his cheek. "You should ask to join Orhan and his men. They are kept away from the walls. You would not have to kill anyone. You should never have been put in that position. Your heart is too big for this work, Radu." She leaned in and kissed his forehead. "I cannot imagine what you have been forced to see and do. No one could have clear eyes in the midst of that."

"What does it matter? I have done no good."

"You have. And we may yet do more. The kindest thing we can do for both sides is hasten the end of this siege. The longer it carries on, the worse it will be for everyone." Nazira stood, pulling on her cloak. Though the days were warming up, the evenings were still cold. "I am going to meet with Helen. She complains that the last three days Coco has been even more on edge than usual, snapping at her and pacing incessantly."

Radu's interest was piqued. "He is their most important captain."

"Precisely. Something is in motion for the sea. I do not know what, though."

Radu stood, too, glad for something to do. "I will send Amal to Galata. I can signal him from the roof of the Hagia Sophia if something might be coming, and he can signal the galleys. I will watch Coco's house through the night."

"It may be nothing."

Radu smiled grimly. "Then it will fit in perfectly well with all my other contributions so far."

Radu settled into the shadows of a stoop three houses down from Coco's. Amal had sprinted away to make the crossing to Galata before the gates closed for the evening. He knew of a tower with guards under Mehmed's pay where he could watch for a signal.

It would probably amount to nothing, but it was better than being on the walls. Anything was better than being on the walls.

Radu let his mind drift, his thoughts punctuated by the distant beat of the bombardment. It never ceased, but in the heart of the city it was merely background noise. The scent of smoke and burning, too, drifted as afterthoughts. And there was no scent of blood. Merely the constant memory of it.

Because Radu did not want to think—not about Mehmed,

not about boats, not about Cyprian—he recited sections of the Koran, lost himself to the beauty and rhythm of them. There was still some peace to be found there.

He was interrupted two hours before dawn. The door to Coco's house opened, and several cloaked figures stepped out, hurrying through the streets. Toward the horn.

Radu ran in the opposite direction. The lock to the Hagia Sophia was as easy to pick now as though he had a key. He raced to the roof, where he pulled out a lantern. Three sides were polished metal, while the fourth was a pane of clear glass. He lit the wick inside, then pointed it toward Galata. He released a prayer of gratitude like a breath. The night was clear enough for the warning to be seen.

Just as Radu began to fear that Amal had not made it, a light answered him. It flashed three times in quick succession, then went dark. Radu blew his own light out. He did not know what, if anything, he had accomplished.

Then a shooting star, burning brightly, moved slowly across the sky. It left a trail of light in its wake, like a signal to him from the heavens themselves. Radu lifted a hand toward it, remembering that night so long ago when he had watched stars fall with Mehmed and Lada. He closed his eyes, gratitude and warmth filling him. Perhaps the superstitious city was finally getting to him, but he could not help but see this as a sign. He had done a good thing. He had helped Mehmed.

He went to the wall near the Romanus Gate, sliding among the men as though he had been there all night. He made certain to say a few words to some of them, taking a place in their memories. Although he faced out toward the Ottomans, all his thoughts were focused on the horn at his back and the city between them.

The bells began ringing an hour before dawn. Radu acted as surprised as everyone, looking up and down the wall as though he, too, suspected the attack was on this side.

As soon as relief came, Radu joined the other men heading to the seawall. Brief flashes of cannon fire illuminated the end of a battle. A small galley burned. Radu's stomach dropped. But as the galley drifted slowly in the water, its flames revealed one of the big merchant ships half sunk and listing heavily. The merchant ship dragged itself away, flanked by two others.

"What happened?" Radu asked a guard on the wall. "Did they try an attack?"

The man shook his head. "We did. Somehow they knew we were coming, started firing before our ships had gotten close enough to surprise them. They sank one of our small ships."

Radu could have laughed with relief. Mehmed would know now that Radu still had use. The Italians would not risk another attack on the galleys, not after this. The Golden Horn was effectively neutralized.

Dawn broke, illuminating the remains of the battle. Though several galleys smoked, there were no significant losses on the Ottoman side. Radu saw more masts than should have been in the water though.

And then he realized they were not masts. The wooden poles reaching up to the sky to greet the dawn were stakes. And on each of them, slowly revealed as the light touched them, an Italian sailor was impaled. In the middle, on the highest stake, Radu recognized Coco himself.

On the hill above them, surrounded by Janissaries, a white-turbaned figure in a purple cloak sat on a horse.

Radu could not understand the scene in front of him. The Ottomans had won! They had decisively defeated the sneak attack. There was no reason for this, none, except to torment the city. It felt needless.

It felt . . . cruel.

Troubled, Radu watched the bodies as though his vigil could bring them peace. Or bring him peace. This seemed less like war and more like murder. And it was all because of him.

A commotion farther down the wall finally drew his attention away from the stakes. He leaned out just in time to see the first battered Ottoman prisoner dropped over the side. A length of rope secured around the prisoner's neck went taut, and the body swung limply.

Before Radu could shout, another prisoner had been hanged. And then another. And then another. He watched in horror as Ottoman prisoners were dropped like decorations, a tapestry of terror along the wall in response to the brutality across the horn.

Unable to stand it, he ran toward the hanging men. Someone had to end this. These soldiers would be held accountable for such cruelty to prisoners.

He stopped, though, when he saw the line of Ottoman prisoners waiting their turn. They were on their knees, some praying, some weeping, some too bloody and broken to do either. And standing behind them, staring out as tall and still as a pillar directly across from Mehmed, was Constantine.

Radu had been wrong. There were no good men in this city. And there were no good men outside of it, either.

36

Mid-April

LADA EMERGED FROM HER tent to find her fire already lit and a pot of water boiling. She had forced Oana to stay behind to help run their base at Toma's estate, in part because she trusted Oana to do it well, and in part because she did not want anyone fussing over her wretched hair. Since then, Lada had not woken to a fire.

"What are you doing?" Lada asked Daciana.

Daciana pointed to the pot. "Your options are weak pine tea or weak pine tea. You really need better provisions."

"You know what I meant." Lada sat, taking a cup of blisteringly hot pine tea. It was weak, as promised. "I am not riding through the country, charitably adopting all those who want to join my merry band. I am taking men who can fight. Besides, it is important that the land be tended to."

"Why do you care so much about the land?"

"Because it is mine. I have no desire to be prince of a country with no crops. People need to eat."

Daciana laughed. "You will be *prince*, then?"

Lada did not share her mirth. "There is no other title. I will be vaivode, prince of Wallachia. And I will make the land into the country my people deserve."

Daciana eased herself down, moving awkwardly with her swollen belly. "Very well, then. You take the men for soldiers and you leave the women to plant so that we do not all starve. And what will you do with the boyars?"

As though summoned, a letter from Toma Basarab was delivered at that moment by a smooth-faced boy.

Lada read the letter with a scowl. Nicolae sat next to her, trying to read over her shoulder. "What does he say?"

"He disagrees with my negotiating tactics." Her temper bubbled hotter than the tea. "And he says he is joining us to make certain I do not negotiate like that with any more boyars."

She threw the letter to the ground, standing and pacing. "Who is he to tell me what to do? You saw Silviu! You saw his land, what he was doing. Was I not right?"

Nicolae read over the letter with a resigned expression. "I am not saying you were not right. But . . . perhaps more thought and care should be taken with future boyars."

"Why?" Daciana said.

"We need them."

Lada snorted. "We need them? No one needs them. They are maggots, feeding on my land and doing nothing for it!"

Nicolae wore a long-suffering expression. "They are necessary for organization. They collect taxes. They run the farmlands. They muster troops from the men living in their provinces."

Lada leaned forward. "Tell me, Nicolae. Does it look like they are doing a good job?"

Nicolae smiled. "The roads are impassable with thieves. The fields are fallow or untended. The boyars are fat and wealthy while the people starve. The prince has no military support unless they decide to give it—which they never do. But the fact remains, that is how the country runs. Figure out how to use them better. Control them better. But you cannot get to the throne without them."

Lada sat in disgust. "Why not?"

"You are already using Toma Basarab. Trust that he knows what he is doing."

"I do not trust him at all."

Nicolae rubbed his scar. "Did you think he could just hand you the throne? You need allies. You need the boyars. You cannot skip past them, and to get them, you need him." Nicolae put an arm around Lada, drawing her close. "Make a deal with the devil until you are both over the bridge."

"Am I the devil, or are they?"

Nicolae laughed again, but he did not answer.

Bogdan sat on Lada's other side. His eyes lingered on Nicolae's arm around her shoulder. He offered her the inside of his bread. It was the softest part, her favorite. He took the crusts without expecting thanks. He simply did it, as he did everything for her. As he always had.

It sparked an idea.

"What if I take land—if I give the land to the people who deserve it, like Daciana's mother? I get their loyalty. The boyars claim things based on centuries of blood. The land is theirs by birthright. So I *take* it from those who oppose us. I give it to people whose vision for Wallachia matches my own. They have nothing to claim other than my favor, and they owe all allegiance to me." She met Bogdan's approving stare and offered him a smile. He ducked his head, a pleased flush spreading across his cheeks.

"You cannot kill *all* the boyars." Nicolae helped himself to some tea.

"Oh?"

Nicolae looked up sharply, narrowing his eyes. "They did not ask for their birthright. They have done nothing to you, and you have no guarantee that they ever will. I do not think you were wrong to kill that last pig, but slaughtering every noble in the country will have repercussions even you cannot handle." When Lada did not respond, he threw his hands up in exasperation, spilling his tea. "They are related to nobility in other countries. You will draw too much attention and too much ire. Someone will retaliate. Besides, they have families. They have influence. And they are *people*."

Lada gazed into the flames, letting them fill her vision. "Of course. I will listen to Toma Basarab and accept allegiance from those who offer it. But no one keeps anything without meriting it. That goes for every Wallachian." She blinked, spots of light dancing in front of her eyes. "Including you, Daciana. So I ask again: why are you here?"

"You have no lady's maid."

Nicolae snorted. "You are mistaken. Our Lada is no lady. She is a dragon."

Bogdan growled low and angry in his throat. Lada laughed, patting Bogdan's knee. Then she tossed a handful of dirt and dry evergreen needles at Nicolae. "No one asked for your opinion."

"My opinions are gifts I distribute freely, asking neither permission nor payment."

"Take your gifts elsewhere," Bogdan grumbled.

Lada waved her hand. "Nicolae is right. I need no lady's maid, because I am not a lady. I am a soldier."

Daciana smiled, smug and self-satisfied. "Precisely. A soldier does not have time to wash her monthly courses from her clothes."

Lada's cheeks burned, and she looked at the ground rather than at Nicolae and Bogdan. Daciana's stomach loomed in the edge of her vision. And then she had a thought.

A terrible thought.

Lada stood, nearly falling into the fire. She grabbed Daciana's hand. "Come with me." The girl yelped, struggling to her feet. Lada dragged her away from the camp and into the trees.

"Tell me about being with child. How did it happen? How long did it take until you knew there was a—" Lada swept her hand toward Daciana's stomach, unable to tear her eyes away from it now. "How long until you knew that thing was in there?"

Daciana's dark eyes betrayed no emotion. "When was your last bleeding?"

Lada turned her back, stalking several feet away. "I am not asking about that, I only want to know—"

"I am neither stupid nor a gossip. When was your last bleeding?"

"Weeks. Maybe eight? Or nine." It had been before Hunyadi, when they were in the mountains of Transylvania. Her underclothes had frozen when she hung them to dry after washing.

"Do you bleed regularly?"

Lada shook her head. "No. Only a few times a year."

"That is fortunate. I am—" Daciana paused, taking a deep breath. "I was so steady you could track the moon by my blood. And when did a man last know you?"

Lada whipped around, snarling, "No man knows me."

Again, Daciana did not respond with any apparent emotion. "Your breasts would be tender and swelling already. You would be sick. Exhausted beyond anything you have ever known."

Lada shook her head in relief, then realized she was confirming Daciana's assumptions. Of course she was. She was a fool. Moving with Mehmed in the darkness, the feel of his skin, the feel of him inside her . . .

She closed her eyes, because she had worked so hard not to think of it. But as soon as she allowed the memories back in, she wanted to kill him. And she wanted to be with him again.

She did not know which impulse was stronger.

"My sister is like you." Daciana spoke as though they were discussing the weather. "She bleeds rarely. She is one of the only ones who has never been with child, despite many visits from our boyar, may his soul be damned forever." Daciana spat on the ground. "She was the lucky one. You will probably have similar fortunes."

Lada swallowed down some of her fear. It tasted like blood and bile. Daciana turned to go back to camp.

"You may stay with me," Lada said.

The girl smiled. "I know."

"You can sleep in my tent, if it makes you feel safer."

"That is very generous of you. I will be sharing Stefan's tent soon, though."

"You will?" She had never known Stefan to take up with a

woman. Though, of all her men, he would be most likely to do it without being noticed.

Daciana's smile grew into something sly and sharp. "He does not know it yet."

Lada laughed, and then the two women walked back together. It was a pity no one had given Daciana a knife when she was a little girl. Lada suspected she was as formidable as any of the men in camp.

37

May 5–16

UNWILLING TO SPEND MORE time repairing the wall—a huge section of which had fallen the day before with losses on both sides but no real change—Radu visited Orhan's tower, where all the Turks in the city were stationed. Here, at least, were Ottomans he did not have to kill.

Radu stopped to sit with the guard. He knew them all by sight, if not by name. They were outsiders here, committed to the city but never truly a part of it. Everyone viewed them with some measure of distrust.

"There is little food," the guard, Ismael, complained. "And no coin to buy it with. Orhan does as well by us as he can, but it is not easy."

Radu nodded. "The Venetians tried to flee yesterday. Giustiniani barely stopped them. Men are missing their shifts on the walls, staying in the city to try to find food for their families."

"Such is the nature of a siege. Death from without, rot from within." Ismael smiled ruefully. "We may yet make it out of this, though. Back to the way things were before. How I miss walking the streets and having mud thrown at me simply because I am Turkish. Now we cannot leave our tower for fear people will think we are the sultan's men, inside the city."

Radu leaned back, the crate he sat on groaning in protest. Something inside caught his eye—an Ottoman flag. The crate held the rest of the flags they had not used for their messenger boat deception. Now, sitting here, useless and abandoned. Radu felt a surge of solidarity with the flags.

"Why did you stay?" Radu asked. If Mehmed won, Orhan's men were all dead. And even if Mehmed failed, they would still be pariahs in the city. Orhan would never be able to claim the Ottoman throne, not now that Mehmed had heirs. He was useless politically.

Ismael rubbed his chin thoughtfully. "Orhan is a good man. He has grown up as a pawn, but he never let it turn him cruel or bitter. I have not heard the same of the sultan." He shrugged. "Either way, my fate was always at this city. Die inside the walls or against them. We chose to stay with a man we respect."

A few weeks ago, Radu would have wanted to strike Ismael for accusing Mehmed of cruelty. Now every time Radu closed his eyes, he saw a forest of stakes bearing their monstrous fruit.

The two men looked up as a procession of horses trudged through the mud in front of them. In the middle was Constantine. His shoulders drooped and his head hung heavy. The day before it had been his presence at the walls that kept the defenders fighting long enough to repel the attack. But Radu could see he was cracking under the pressure.

Mud flew through the air, landing on the flank of Constantine's horse. The soldiers at his side were immediately alert, looking for the assailant. Constantine sighed and shook his head.

"Heretic!" someone shouted from an alley. "Our children starve because you betrayed God!"

Constantine glanced to the side and saw Radu. He smiled ruefully. "Our children starve because the only silver left in the city belongs to God himself."

Once the emperor's procession had passed, Radu bid Ismael farewell. As he walked back to Cyprian's house, he saw evidence of suffering everywhere. It was one thing to see men die on the walls, and another entirely to see their children sitting on stoops listless and dull-eyed with hunger. There was food in Galata, and they still traded during the day with Constantinople. But if no one had money, all the food in the world was still out of reach.

Constantine's words trailed along in Radu's wake, nagging at him. *The only silver left in the city belongs to God himself.* Radu could do nothing to force an end to the siege. But perhaps he could alleviate some suffering in the meantime. Suffering he had helped cause by destroying food. Perhaps he could still do some good for his own soul.

Cyprian and Nazira were both in the sitting room when Radu burst through the door, reenergized.

"What are you so pleased about?" Cyprian asked.

"There is silver in the churches, yes?"

Cyprian nodded. "The collection plates are all made of it."

"And they are used to collect money for the poor. I think we should collect those plates to create money for the poor. Surely God would look kindly on such an endeavor." Radu could not

imagine either god—the Christian one or the true God—
would frown upon charity, no matter to whom it was given. It
was one of the pillars of Islam, after all. He had not felt this
genuinely happy about anything since he had come to the city.

Cyprian shook his head. "My uncle cannot take anything
from the churches, not with his reputation. They barely let him
worship there as it is. If he began demanding holy silver, the
city would riot."

Radu smiled wickedly, holding out a hand to help Nazira
up. "Your uncle will not demand anything, nor will he take it.
I know my way around a foundry."

Cyprian bit his lips, his gray eyes dancing in delight. "I
know where they mint the royal coins. It has not been in operation much lately."

"I know someone who is very adept at picking locks."

Nazira laughed, grabbing a black shawl and draping it
over her head. "And I know someone who will be cleaning
the churches, should anyone happen upon our merry band of
thieves."

It was foolish, but it felt so good to be doing something
other than fighting at the walls or hating himself. Radu practically skipped through the streets. Nazira was on one side,
Cyprian on the other, and the night was as sweet as any he
had known. They found a dim, unused church not far from
Cyprian's house.

Nazira held her bucket of supplies in plain view, tapping
a foot impatiently as though she wanted to get on with her
work. The bucket conveniently blocked any view of Radu's lock
picking. The door clicked open and they tiptoed inside. Radu

loved churches best when they were dark. The lavish, sumptu-ous decorations were muted, the silence holier than any liturgy could be.

Cyprian made his way confidently to the altar, where he pulled out a plate and held it up in triumph. Nazira tucked it into the bottom of her bucket and covered it with rags.

Within three hours they had hit several churches. Nazira's bucket was nearly full. Radu was too tired to skip, but he and Cyprian kept laughing at the other's fumbling in the dark. In one church, Cyprian tripped and fell backward over a bench, his legs straight up in the air. Radu held himself, bent over, trying not to laugh so loudly that they got caught. Rather than getting up immediately, Cyprian had remained on his back, kicking his legs, until tears streamed down Radu's face.

When the tenth church was stripped, they agreed to one more. They weaved through the streets with secret laughter as muffled as the city by fog. Radu did not know how it felt to be drunk, but he suspected it felt something like this.

"I need it!" a woman screamed. They stopped, startled. Two women pulled at a basket. Each had a child or two at their legs, tugging on their skirts and crying. "My children are starving!" one of the women shouted.

"We are all starving!" a man said, shoving between the two women. One of them fell into the muddy street, taking a child down with her. The other scrambled for the basket, but the man got to it first.

"Give it to me," she begged, picking up her small child and holding him in front of her as proof of her desperation.

"I have my own hungry children."

Cyprian and Radu stepped forward, unsure what to do but knowing something needed to be done. "You should be at the walls," Cyprian said to the man.

The man's face shifted into something ugly and brutal. "So you can take this food for your own? I will go back to the wall when I know my family is eating." He shoved past them, nearly knocking Nazira down. He did not so much as look back at the women he had stolen the food from. The one still standing stomped away, one child in her arms and the other hurrying after her.

Radu reached out to help the fallen woman up. She took his hand and stood, brushing off her skirt and using a clean section to wipe her child's face.

"You should go to Galata," Radu said, as gently as he could. "They have more food there, and your children will be safer."

"God will protect us," she said, and Radu did not know if it sounded like a prayer or a condemnation.

"But God is not feeding you."

She looked at him, aghast, then bundled her child into her skirts and hurried away, as though Radu's blasphemy were contagious.

She might as well have carried off all their easy happiness, too. But at least they knew this night was worthwhile. Necessary. "One more," Cyprian said, sounding tired. He pointed the way. "The monastery where they house the Hodegetria."

"What is that?" Nazira asked, linking one arm through Radu's and the other through Cyprian's. It did not feel quite right, with her in the middle. Less balanced. Radu had preferred when he was between them. But he carried the now-heavy bucket.

"The Hodegetria is the holiest icon in the city," Cyprian said. "A painting of the Virgin Mary holding the child Jesus at her side. Said to be brought back from the Holy Land by the apostle Luke. They parade it around the walls sometimes as protection, though the monks have been withholding it as punishment for my uncle's dealings with the Catholics."

"Do they really think a painting will save them?" Nazira asked, no sting in her criticism, merely curiosity. Radu cringed at her choice of words—*them* instead of *us*—but Cyprian took no notice. At least Radu was not the only one too comfortable around Cyprian.

"They say it has saved the city before," Cyprian said.

"Do you believe it?" Nazira asked.

Cyprian looked up at the stars peeking through the low cover of cloud and smoke that never really cleared. "I believe that the Virgin Mary would rather see us take care of our own than take care of a painting of her. Which is why I am going to go distract the guard so you two can sneak in and take what silver you find." He bowed jauntily, trying to recapture some of their fun, then walked around the corner of the monastery.

Radu leaned up against a small outer door, working the lock as quickly as he could. They entered through a pitch-dark back hallway. Feeling their way along the wall, they came to another door. It was locked.

"That is promising," Nazira whispered.

Radu picked this last lock. The air inside stung his nose with the remains of censer smoke. Radu dared to light a candle in the windowless room. As the light flared to life, the image of the Virgin Mary appeared in front of them. The icon, nearly as tall as Radu, was mounted on a pallet with poles extending for carrying.

"Too bad we cannot melt it down," Nazira said thoughtfully, looking at the heavy gold frame. Radu searched for silver. There were a few small pieces, and he pocketed them. Nazira stayed where she was, staring at the icon.

"I think that is Constantinople's problem," she said. "They look to a painting to save them, instead of to each other. They argue and debate over the state of their souls for the afterlife, while letting the needy in this life go hungry. No wonder this city is dying."

Radu put a hand on her shoulder. "I have what we came for."

Nazira did not move. Her eyes shone heavy with tears in the candlelight. "I hate them. I hate everyone in this city. I walk among them, I talk to them, and it is like conversing with ghosts. I want to wear mourning clothes every day." She was crying now. Reaching into one of the jars in the bucket, she pulled out a glopping handful of grease.

Radu grasped her hand before she could fling the grease at the icon. "No," he said softly.

"We should burn it. We should punish them."

"They are being punished enough."

"Your sister would burn it to demoralize them."

"My sister would do much more than that." He smiled, imagining what Lada would do if she were here in his place. Nothing in the city would be safe. "But Cyprian is outside. He would know."

Sniffling, Nazira nodded. She rubbed her hands along the pallet handles, trying to wipe off the grease. "I am sorry. I miss

Fatima so much it feels like ice has entered my soul. And it is hard remembering not to care about these people. I was so sure when we came that it would not be a problem. I wanted— I wanted them to suffer. I wanted to watch them fall."

Radu had never heard her talk like that. "To protect Islam?"

"For revenge," she whispered. "For Fatima. Her family was killed by crusaders when she was very young. They did horrible things. Things she cannot talk about even now. I wanted Constantinople to be ours to prevent more crusades, yes. But also to punish them." She dabbed at her eyes with a corner of her shawl. "I know it is not rational. None of the people here were responsible for what happened to Fatima. But their mindless hatred of us, their demonizing of Islam, is what let those men do what they did. It was wicked of me to come here with so much hatred in my heart. Hatred makes monsters of us all."

Radu pulled her close, hugging her tightly. "You could never be a monster," he said, as the Virgin Mary pointed solemnly at her son. Her face betrayed no emotion, no hint of judgment or mercy.

"I still think we are doing the right thing." Nazira fixed her shawl. "And I am trying to set my heart in line with God."

Radu nodded, taking her hand. Together, they left the monastery.

Cyprian met them outside. "The foundry is not far. No one will be there."

When they got to the foundry, the forge's fires were cold. It would take a while for them to be hot enough to melt down the metal. Nazira excused herself to go home and sleep.

Radu saw now that she wore her sadness like a cloak. She smiled so brightly, it was too easy to miss the sorrow swirling around her. Radu wished he could take it from her. But he knew that leaving this city and being reunited with Fatima would be what began her healing.

As they started the furnace, Cyprian found the molds for coins. "My father told me I would never make any money for the family. I wish he could see me now."

"My father did not even think about me enough to wonder whether I was worth anything."

"He sounds like more of a bastard than I am."

Radu laughed, and was rewarded with one of Cyprian's precious genuine smiles. They took turns stoking the fire. Cyprian leaned close, looking over Radu's shoulder to watch the flames. He had washed, and did not smell like the walls anymore. He smelled like clothing dried in the sun, with a hint of the breeze blowing off the sea. Radu found himself breathing in so deeply he was dizzy.

"You are very good at this," Cyprian said, his breath tickling Radu's ear.

Radu would have blushed at the praise—after his broken childhood, he devoured praise like a starving man took bread—but it was so warm he was already flushed. Soon the room was stifling. Cyprian peeled off his outer layers, finally taking off even his undershirt.

It really is uncomfortably hot, Radu thought, looking everywhere but at the other man.

When the fire was bright enough, they fed the silver pieces to it one by one, collecting the molten metal. The coins they cast were rough, obviously inferior to genuine money. But no one would examine them too closely right now.

Cyprian sprawled out on the floor, arms behind his head. Radu did not look.

Until he did.

Cyprian was lean and tall, with broad shoulders. Radu's eyes lingered on the space where his torso dipped from his ribs toward the line of his trousers.

No. He was tired, and it was—something. It was all *something*. He did not know what, could not form a coherent thought. Looking at Cyprian made him remember seeing Mehmed that night in Mehmed's bedroom, before Mehmed had known he was there. Radu felt an odd surge of guilt, like he had somehow betrayed Mehmed tonight. When he thought of how miserable he had been in Edirne, he wanted to laugh. He would give anything for that small distance from Mehmed, as opposed to the tangle of emotions and questions the walls separating them had introduced.

Except he did not think he wanted to give up this night, even with everything getting here had cost him.

Still, he kept his eyes on the table after that. If Cyprian caught him looking, how would he react? How would Radu want him to react? Radu focused intently on the coins. "How will you explain them to your uncle?"

"A dowry from a withered old crone who wants to marry me."

"You would be more believable if you said it was buried treasure."

"I happen to be very appealing to women of advanced age. My eyes, you see. They cannot get enough of my eyes."

Radu finally tugged his own shirt off, because the room kept getting hotter. He tried very hard not to look at Cyprian. He sometimes succeeded. All the while, he stayed on the other side of the table, glad it was between him and Cyprian. And glad his trousers were thick enough to hide the feelings his body would not accept should not be there.

Bodies were traitorous things.

38

Mid-April

"WE NEED DORIN," TOMA said. He sat tall and regal on his horse. "And he is a Basarab."

Lada pointed toward where they had come from. "He attacked us!" They had been met on the edge of Dorin Basarab's forest by three dozen poorly armed and terrified farmers. Ten well-trained soldiers with weapons had stood at the farmers' backs, leaving them no option but to fight. Before Lada had been able to open her mouth, one of the farmers had shot an arrow at her. Bogdan immediately cut the man down, then went after the next. It was a few minutes of bloody, screaming work to dispatch them. It was a waste of her time, and a waste of the farmers' lives.

Toma did not mind. He sniffed lightly, eyeing the manor ahead of them appraisingly. "Dorin will agree to back us. And we will not have another *incident.*" He looked sharply at Lada. "I will placate him by offering him Silviu's lands when you are on the throne."

"No. I gave them to someone already."

Toma laughed. "To a peasant woman? Yes, I heard. That was amusing. Please leave land distribution to me. In fact, perhaps it is best if you stay out here with your men. I will handle everything."

He rode away, his men following. Lada watched his back with all the tension of a nocked arrow.

Nicolae put a hand on her arm.

"What?" she snapped.

He jerked his head behind them. She turned to see a line of peasants. A line of very angry peasants. They made no move toward her—probably owing to the mounted soldiers behind her—but she had no doubt they would kill her if they could.

"Who is in charge?" she asked, pacing her horse in front of them.

"My brother," one man grunted.

"Where is he?"

"Dead in the field back there."

Lada stopped her horse, glaring down her long, hooked nose at the man. "And you think that is my fault?"

"Your swords have blood on them."

Lada drew her sword. It gleamed, well polished. "My sword is clean. My sword was not behind your brothers and cousins, forcing them into a fight they were not prepared for. My sword was not hanging over your necks, forcing you to serve a man who cared nothing for your lives. My sword was not held by the guards of your boyar to ensure none of your sons and friends could run when they should have."

Nicolae cleared his throat. "Maybe not the best tactic to encourage them to fight with us," he said under his breath.

Lada turned her horse, disgusted and angry. "We are going to Tirgoviste," she said. "Join us."

The man looked to the side, rubbing his stubbled cheek. "Not right, a lady having a sword."

Lada knew that killing him would set a bad precedent. She knew that, yet her sword inched closer to him anyway.

"Why should we?" asked an old man with white and wispy hair like the clouds overhead. Loose skin beneath his chin wobbled as he spoke. "We were fine before you came. We want no trouble from Tirgoviste."

Lada turned toward him, sparing the other man. "And Tirgoviste has never troubled itself about you. It does not care. It does not care about your lives, or your families, or your welfare. What has the prince ever given you?"

The old man shrugged his sharp shoulders. "Nothing."

"If you are happy with nothing, by all means, flee and find another boyar to serve. Dorin Basarab will be with me. And when I am on the throne, I will remember every man who helped get me there, no matter his station."

"You want to be prince?" the first man asked. He was not angry anymore. He was confused. Lada preferred angry.

"I *will* be prince."

"What family are you from? Do they have no sons left?" he asked.

She opened her mouth to declare her lineage. Then she stopped. She did not deserve the throne because of her family. Because of her father. Because her brother would not take it. She did what she did not for herself or her family name but for Wallachia. She would *earn* the throne. "I am Lada Dracul, and

I will be prince." She lowered her voice, leaning toward the man and speaking like the sound of swords being drawn. "Do you doubt that?"

He shuffled back a step, finally seeing the truth in her face. She was not a lady. She was a dragon, and this whole country would know it before the end.

"If you fail?" the old man asked.

"Then you are no worse off than you are now. Your boyar will come crawling back. They always manage. But if I succeed—and I will succeed—I will remember *you*. Do you understand?"

The men nodded, some more grudgingly than others. The old man grinned toothlessly. "I think you are mad. But I will not say no to this offer." He bowed to her.

Lada looked over their heads toward the horizon. The effect was rather ruined by one of Toma's men riding up. "My lord says you can make camp behind the manor. You may join them for dinner, if you wish to."

Lada did not wish to. She gritted her teeth and nodded anyway.

39

May 16–24

As May passed its zenith and began slipping toward June, no end to the siege was in sight. The weariness with which Radu wandered through the days was broken only by scarlet bursts of horror. Everything else about that time was dirty—the dust, the clouds, his soul.

After the night in the forge, he had again done his best to avoid Cyprian. Nazira had few useful contacts left; Helen's disgrace at being associated with poor impaled Coco left her a pariah, and Nazira was swept along in that wake. Most of her time was spent trying to find food and delivering it to those in need. Radu never asked what the latter accomplished. He understood the need to extend kindness even as the very act devoured the soul with guilt. He understood the desire for penance, as well.

When Radu made it home to sleep, he and Nazira lay in the bed, not touching, not talking. Side by side, and alone together. The only thing Radu was certain of anymore in the sea of endless smoke was that Nazira would make it out alive. Everything else was negotiable.

On May nineteenth, the bells of the city jangled out their now-familiar call to the wall. *Panic!* they said. *Death!* they said. *Destruction!* they said. They were no longer instruments of worship, only proclaimers of doom.

Radu trudged past the Hagia Sophia. A sharp tug on his shirt startled him. He turned to find Amal. "I do not have anything for him," Radu said.

Amal shook his head. "He has a message for you."

Radu's weary heart stepped up its pace. Mehmed! His Mehmed. "Yes?"

"He says to stay away from the walls today. Find somewhere else to be."

Radu did not know whether to laugh in delight or cry in relief. Mehmed remembered him—and cared whether or not he was safe. "Why?"

Amal shrugged. "That is the message."

"Tell him thank you. Tell him—" *Tell him I miss him. Tell him I wish things could go back to how they were. Tell him I am terrified they never can. Tell him even if they could, I do not know if I will ever be satisfied with it again.* "Tell him my thoughts and prayers are with him."

Amal nodded, then held out his hand as though begging. Radu dug free a single coin and placed it in the boy's palm.

Radu turned to go back home, happy he could at least report to Nazira that Mehmed thought of them and had sent a warning. And then he remembered: Cyprian was already at the wall.

The wall Mehmed thought was dangerous enough it merited risking sending a message.

Radu could go home. He could wait and see what happened. He could stand at the window, watching for Cyprian. And if Cyprian did not return . . .

Radu ran for the wall. He would think of some reason, some excuse to pull Cyprian away. He did not question why it was worth the risk. He simply knew he had to.

When he got there, though, he stopped in shock. There were *towers* on the other side of the wall. Made of wood, they were covered in sheets of metal and leather hides to protect them from fire and arrows. Huge wheels stuck out from their bases. And they were making their way toward the city.

Where Mehmed had been keeping the towers was a mystery. No one around Radu knew where they had come from or when they had appeared. But their purpose was already being served. As the towers moved forward, the shielded men within them threw dirt and rocks and bushes into the fosse. Slowly but surely they were filling up the protective ditch.

Radu hurried past a line of archers, desperate to find Cyprian. Mehmed had not wanted him here, and he saw why now. The walls would fall today.

The archers shot burning arrows, but they bounced harmlessly off the towers' shielded exteriors. Small cannons were fired to little effect. The towers carried on without pause. Giustiniani pushed his way to the center of the wall, a few men down from where Radu crouched behind barrels. A constant barrage of arrows flew at the wall, preventing any concerted counterattack.

"What new hell is this?" Giustiniani said, peering between barrels. He noticed Radu and crawled over to him, gesturing toward the towers. "Did you know he had these?"

Radu shook his head, leaning back against the barrels, unable to face the towers.

All his previous anger at Mehmed had fallen away, like an

arrow bouncing off the armor Mehmed's message had supplied. But Mehmed protecting him and Mehmed trusting him were two different things. The towers had to have been in the works since the beginning. And Mehmed had never breathed a word about them to Radu.

Which meant one of two things: either Mehmed did *not* trust him, or Mehmed had deliberately withheld information because he had been looking for a way to get Radu into the city from the very beginning, and he had suspected Radu would be caught and tortured.

Even with the armor of Mehmed's warning, either option broke Radu's battered heart.

By nightfall the ditches were filled enough for the towers to cross them. Their progress was as slow and inevitable as the passage of the sun. As near as anyone could tell, men in the bottom pushed, inching them forward. The rain of arrows from the towers had not stopped. No counterattack could be launched, no run on the towers was possible. They crept forward at an agonizing pace, slowly bringing the city's doom. And still Radu had not found Cyprian. At this point he could not leave—because he did not have his friend, and because it would look as though he was running away.

Someone rode across the space between the walls on a horse pulling a heavily laden cart.

"Giustiniani!"

It was Cyprian. Radu perked up. The city was going to fall, but Cyprian was here! Radu could get him out, and they could get to Nazira and flee. Radu crouched, running along the wall to the ladder, then climbed down.

Cyprian was standing in the cart, arrows falling around him as he pushed a barrel off the end. Radu grabbed a discarded shield and ran forward, climbing on next to Cyprian and covering him while he worked. "We need to go!" Radu shouted.

"Almost finished!" An arrow thunked against the shield over their heads. Cyprian paused, giving Radu that smile that changed his whole face. "Well, that is another life I owe you. One of these days you will have to determine how I can repay you."

"What is this?" Radu asked as a few other men who had come to help lifted barrels down.

"Gunpowder."

"The cannons are too small to do enough damage to the towers."

Cyprian's grin shifted to something less warm but more appropriate to their surroundings. "Not for the cannons. Get these on the wall!" he shouted.

Radu jumped down, still shielding Cyprian as he directed the men. He kept looking toward the gate, wondering how he could get himself and Cyprian out. Meanwhile, Cyprian continued, oblivious to Radu's desperation. It was no small task leveraging the heavy barrels up the narrow ladders. They managed awkwardly, losing one man to an arrow. Radu followed Cyprian as they rolled the barrels along until they were positioned directly in front of the tower. Maybe if he helped Cyprian accomplish whatever he was doing, Radu could trick him into leaving.

Giustiniani gestured with concern. "This is nearly all the gunpowder we have left."

"It is doing us no good in the cannons," Cyprian said. "This is our best chance."

"But we do not have enough to take out *all* the towers. There are several more."

"The sultan does not know that, does he?"

Understanding dawned on Radu as Cyprian worked long fuses into the tops of the barrels. "You are going to blow up the towers." Radu laughed, his throat hoarse from exhaustion and smoke. It was exactly what Lada would have done. He should have thought of it himself.

No. He was not actually on this side. Radu tapped his head against the stones beside him, trying to knock some sense into himself. He should do something to prevent it. But he was trapped. He could not do anything for Mehmed, and he could not do anything to risk Cyprian's life.

Cyprian patted his vest, swearing. "I do not have a flint."

Radu held out his own. When Cyprian's fingers met his, there was a spark unrelated to the flint. Radu swallowed the mess of emotions blocking his throat and his breath.

Cyprian grinned at him, then struck the flint and lit the fuse. "If it bursts open when it hits the ground, we are blowing ourselves up."

Radu shrugged, sitting back. Perhaps that would be a kindness at this point. "At least I will have good company in hell."

Cyprian laughed. Giustiniani glared at them both. "On three," Cyprian said. The two other barrels were a few feet away. "One . . . two . . . three!"

Radu and Cyprian pushed the barrel up and over the wall while other soldiers did the same with theirs. They braced for an explosion, but none came. They peered over, holding their breath and watching as the barrels tumbled and rolled away from the wall and toward the tower. Giustiniani's veered too far to the right, lodging in debris. The third barrel lost momentum halfway there. But Cyprian's kept going, rolling right to the base of the tower.

"Get down!" Cyprian shouted, pulling Radu flat. Radu covered his ears, but the explosion was still deafening. He felt the concussive force of the blast passing right through him. The world hung in stillness for one soundless moment. Then debris pinged against the barrels, against his back, falling everywhere.

The tower was on its side, ripped open. Men ran forward to help the fallen Ottomans, not accounting for the other barrels. Radu and Cyprian ducked again, two more blasts coming in quick succession.

The scent of gunpowder almost covered the stench of burning flesh.

Giustiniani stood, pointing to a group of soldiers standing at the ready behind a sally port. "Burn everything! Kill anyone still moving!"

The port was flung open and men ran out. It was quick work, killing any Ottomans still alive and stunned from the last explosion. They poured pitch onto what was left of the tower's wooden frame and wheels. When lit, it burned so brightly that Radu could feel the flames warm his face.

Cyprian turned away from the killing, pulling his knees up and resting his head on them. His shoulders were shaking.

"Are you hurt?" Radu's hand hovered above the other man's arm. He did not dare touch him. Not on purpose, not in tenderness. He had defied Mehmed's order to stay safe because he could not abandon Cyprian. And in doing so, he had helped defeat this newest, best chance at the end of the siege. How many ways could a man turn traitor in one lifetime?

Cyprian looked up. Radu could not tell if he was laughing or crying. "I really thought that would blow us up. I thought there was a very good chance I was taking down our own walls and letting him in."

"But you tried it anyway?"

Cyprian wiped under his eyes, which left his face smeared with soot. "He is attacking us from every possible angle. Below the walls, outside them, above them. From the land, from the sea. He does not need everything to work. Just one thing. And eventually, something will." Cyprian leaned his head back, looking up at the smoke above them. "But not tonight," he whispered.

"But not tonight," Radu echoed. He did not know if he said it in relief or in mourning.

———— ·•· ————

Cyprian's gamble paid off. When one tower fell, Mehmed pulled them all back. The bombardment continued unabated, but by now that felt almost normal.

Two days after the towers retreated, Cyprian received a summons to the palace. Radu was pulling on his boots to go back to the wall. Amal had not been at his place outside the Hagia Sophia. Radu had nothing but confessions and confusions to send to Mehmed anyway.

"My uncle has asked you to come, too," Cyprian said.

Radu frowned, surprised. "Why?"

"He does not say."

The small part of Radu's soul that had not been beaten down under the bombardment feared that he had been discovered. Perhaps he was walking to his death. He caught Nazira's eye from across the room. "Nazira, it seems quieter at the walls today. You should go over to Galata and see if there is any food you can buy there. Cyprian is losing weight."

"I am not!" Cyprian forced his stomach forward and patted it.

"He looks terrible." Radu smiled as though in jest but levied a meaningful look at Nazira. "Bring him some food from those beautiful fat Italians."

"*You* look terrible." Nazira narrowed her eyes and shook her head at Radu. "I am not going to Galata for anyone or anything. I will be right here when you come back from the palace."

Radu walked up to her and placed a kiss on her forehead. "Please," he whispered against her skin.

"Not without you." Then she pulled back and smiled, reaching up to rub at the stubble on his face. "Both of you eat at the palace. Save me the trouble of making you a meal. And while you are at it, see if the emperor can spare a razor, too."

With one last pleading look, Radu joined Cyprian. They walked in silence through the muddy streets. Though there were more religious processions than ever, they were fortunate enough not to run into any. Sometimes in his dreams Radu was stuck in the middle of one. Around the sound of the priest's liturgy, the women wailed and the children cried, while the smoke of the censer clogged his eyes and nose until he could neither see nor breathe. When the smoke finally cleared, everyone around him was dead. But the liturgy continued.

"Are you well?" Cyprian asked. "You keep shuddering."

Radu nodded. "Cold for May."

"Do not tell anyone else that. They will find some prophecy or other that states that a cold May signals the end of the world."

Radu tried to laugh but could not. If only Nazira had agreed to leave, he would feel at peace with facing his end. It was inevitable, at this point. He was always going to die here. He did not want her to.

At least he trusted that Cyprian was not the one who had figured it out. Cyprian wore his honesty painted across his face. If Radu was going to his death, Cyprian did not know it. It was poor comfort, but enough to give Radu the strength to keep moving, keep walking in this precious space before Cyprian found out the truth and never again looked at him with those beautiful gray eyes.

They passed several women and children dragging sacks full of rocks and rubble to repair the walls. When a stone cannonball shattered the wall of a house next to them, Radu and Cyprian ducked instinctively, before they had even processed what caused the noise.

The women and children had no such experience. One of the children lay in the street, broken and unmoving. A woman knelt over the child. She picked up the body and tucked it against the wall. "I will be back," she said, her hands bloody. Then she retrieved her bag and the bag of the child, and continued on to the wall.

"How can we go on?" Cyprian whispered. "Is this hell?"

Radu took Cyprian's hand, turning him away from the body of the child. The palace was before them. Radu knew it did not matter what he hoped or feared would happen. Death was unfeeling and random, as likely to strike down an innocent child as a guilty man.

They were met by two soldiers who escorted them past Constantine's study. They moved deeper into the palace, and then through a courtyard into another building. It was colder than the palace, the rocks leeching warmth from the day. The air smelled of mildew and despair.

"Why are we going to the dungeons?" Cyprian asked.

Radu allowed himself one moment of true sorrow for Nazira. He had failed. At everything, at all of it, but at this one most important thing he had promised himself and God. *I am sorry,* he thought as a prayer. *I am sorry. Save her.*

"Prisoners," one of the soldiers said, as though that explained everything.

When they emerged through a door at the bottom of a winding set of stairs, Constantine turned to face them. His face was hard. Next to him was Giustiniani. Radu took a deep breath, praying for strength. He met their gazes unflinchingly. He might still be able to barter for Nazira's life.

"There you are. Come on." Giustiniani gestured impatiently. Radu stepped forward, finally able to see past them.

Kneeling on the floor chained, bloodied, and dazed, was a man Radu had last seen being berated by his mother while delivering gunpowder. Tohin's son, Timur. How was he here?

"He has been speaking Arabic," Giustiniani said, "and we cannot understand him. Can you translate?"

"I should be able to. Where did he come from?" Radu asked, trying to control his voice.

"We caught him digging a tunnel under the walls. The rest were killed with Greek fire. Burned alive."

"I am the lucky one," Timur mumbled around a bloody, swollen tongue and broken teeth. He looked up at Radu and smiled. Radu did not know if the smile was one of recognition or madness.

Radu was not here to be tortured and killed. He was here to aid in the torture of a man he knew. A man with a family. Two children, he had spoken of. Or was it three? Radu could not remember. It seemed very important now to remember. *I am sorry,* he prayed again, this time with even more anguish. But Nazira was still safe. He held on to that light as a way to keep out of the darkness threatening to claim him.

Radu cleared his throat. "I know this man. His name is Timur. I met him briefly before fleeing the court."

Giustiniani grunted. "We need the locations of all the other tunnels. My men have been working on him for a while, but he has not given us any information." He pointed at a map of the walls. "Do whatever you can think of to get him to talk."

Blood dripped slowly down Timur's face, pooling on the stained stones beneath him.

Radu crouched in front of him. He only knew Arabic from the Koran, and he would not bring those sacred verses here. He did not want to use Turkish for fear Constantine and Cyprian would understand. "Do you speak Hungarian?" he asked in that language. He knew Cyprian did not speak it, and he was fairly certain none of the other men did. He looked at them, but they did not seem to understand.

Timur dragged his head up. His eyes widened for the briefest moment in recognition, then he hung his head again. "Yes," he answered in the same language. "A little. Can you save me." It was not spoken like a question. A question implied hope. Timur knew there was none.

"I can guarantee you a quick death. And—" Radu's voice caught. He took a deep breath, then pressed on. "And I will send word to Mehmed of your bravery. Your family will be taken care of forever. I swear it."

Timur shuddered, the last of the tension in his shoulders leaving. "What do they want?"

"The location of all the other tunnels. Will there be any men in them now?"

"Not now. Tonight."

"If we give them the information, they will act on it immediately. No more of your men have to die. The tunnels did not work. You tried your best. I am sorry it ended this way."

A sigh escaped the other man's lips. It smelled like blood, but it sounded like relief. "I did my part. God knows. You will tell the sultan that."

"I will." Radu gestured for the map. Timur pointed to several locations, tracing lines. The blood on his fingers worked as ink.

"He is telling the truth," Giustiniani said. "I suspected these two. This one we found this morning. But the others we did not know about." He rolled up the blood-marked map and handed it to a waiting guard who ran out of the cell.

With his back to the other men, Radu mouthed a benediction in Arabic that only he and Timur could see. Timur's face relaxed, and he closed his eyes. Radu pulled out a knife and drove it into the base of Timur's neck. He slumped to the floor, dead. There was very little blood. Whatever had been done to him before Radu arrived had already drained him of most of his blood.

Cyprian exclaimed in surprise. Radu pulled out a handkerchief and wiped his knife clean. His hands looked steadier than he felt. "I promised him a quick death in exchange for the information. He upheld his end of the bargain."

"But we might have needed him for something else," Giustiniani said, frowning.

Radu feigned his own look of surprise. "I am sorry. You told me to do whatever it took to get him to give us what he knew. That was what it took." He avoided Cyprian's eyes and bowed to Constantine. "Unless you have further use for me, I am due at the walls."

Constantine scratched at his beard. This close, Radu could see that the skin beneath his beard was red and irritated. "May we all meet such mercy at the hands of our enemies," he said, his voice so quiet he might have been speaking to himself.

The sound of boots racing down the stairs drew their attention to the door. A soldier burst into the cell, out of breath. "The boats," he said. "The boats we sent out. They have returned."

"And?" Constantine stepped toward the soldier.

The soldier shook his head, his face devoid of hope. "No one is coming."

Constantine dropped to his knees, hanging his head in the same pose Timur had been in when Radu arrived. There were no chains on Constantine, but he had only the same option of release as Timur. Radu watched as though from a great distance, and time seemed to slow, the space between heartbeats stretching out to eternity.

If Lada were here, Radu asked himself yet again, *what would she do?*

The door was right there. Giustiniani and Cyprian had turned away out of respect for Constantine's grief. Radu could jam the knife into the emperor's neck the same way he had into Timur's. He could end Constantine right now. The emperor held Constantinople together through sheer force of will. With his death, the walls meant nothing. The city would surrender immediately.

Lada would do it. She would have already done it instead of standing around, wondering. Radu was certain she had never in her life asked herself what he would do in her situation. He closed his eyes, despair washing over him. Mehmed had sent the wrong sibling into the city. Because he could end it all, right here, right now, and maybe even get out alive. Even knowing Constantine, even respecting him, Radu could do it. He had killed Lazar, after all. He had stuck his knife into his best friend to save Mehmed.

If he did the same now, it would end the siege. It would be almost a kindness to a man suffering under a burden too large for anyone to bear. The city would surrender and fall without looting or further damage.

The broken body of the child in the street loomed before him. Accusing. Pleading. If he killed Constantine, no one else had to die.

But as Radu ran through what he could do, what he should

do, he kept pausing on another image—the gray eyes that would never look at him the same if he did it. Radu was looking at Constantine, but all he could feel was Cyprian's presence.

Maybe if Cyprian were not here, maybe if Cyprian were not *Cyprian*, Radu could have done the right thing. Instead, he watched, impotent and useless.

The emperor wept, the innocent died around them, and Radu was incapable of offering anyone mercy. It was with this guilt looped like a noose around his neck that Radu followed the other men out of the dungeon and into the palace.

A visibly trembling servant shuffled up. "There is someone here for you, my lord."

Constantine waved them all to accompany him. It was doubtless the captain of the boat, ready to make a full report of his findings. Radu did not want to go. But there might be important information he could pass to Amal to atone for not killing Constantine when he had the chance.

The door opened to reveal no weary sailors. Instead, Halil Pasha stood in the center of the room.

40

Late April

TOMA BASARAB LOOKED THROUGH letter after letter, smiling or humming thoughtfully depending on the contents. "Sit down before you pace a hole into that rug. It is worth more than anything you own." He paused for effect. "But then again, you do not own anything, do you?"

Lada glared at him, but she stopped prowling. "Well?"

Toma leaned back in his chair. They had taken residence in another Basarab family boyar's home. The study might as well have always belonged to Toma. His letters covered the desk, his wine next to his hand. Only Lada's sword was out of place.

They were close to Tirgoviste. So close Lada could not stand being cooped up in this house with these people, knowing how near her throne was.

Toma held up a letter. "The prince knows what we are up to."

"And?"

Toma smiled, the expression transforming him from a well-mannered boyar into something Lada understood far better: a predator. "And it does not matter. We have all the support we need. More than half the boyars are on my side." He paused, his smile shifting generously. "Our side. Most that are not will do nothing until they see where the advantage falls. He will not be able to draw a significant force in time to save himself. His sons and all the men he could ask for help are fighting at the walls of Constantinople at the sultan's request."

Lada closed her eyes, taking a deep breath. "I can go to Tirgoviste."

"Yes, my dear, you can," Toma answered, as though she had been asking permission. "I will follow."

"But not too closely." She opened her eyes and raised a knowing eyebrow.

He laughed. "No, not too closely. But you take all my hopes and prayers with you."

Lada picked up her sword where it leaned against a chair. "Keep your prayers. I do not need them."

⸺•⸺

They had made it only a couple of hours before the scouts ahead of them shouted a warning. Lada spurred her horse to a gallop, quickly closing the distance between herself and her scouts.

It was too late. The two men, who had been with her since Edirne, were bleeding their lives out into the dirt. A band of a dozen dirty men surrounded them, pawing through their clothes.

They looked up at Lada. Their faces twisted with cruel pleasure, dead eyes greeting her. She drew her sword and killed two before the rest could react. By the time they realized she was no easy prey, Bogdan and a score of her men had caught up.

Several of the robbers scattered for the trees. "Kill them all," Lada said. She paused, thinking. One of the robbers had curled into a ball on the ground, arms over his head. "Leave this one."

She dismounted. Kicking him in the side, she pushed him over so he was forced to look up at her. His face was covered with the angry red spots of youth. He was probably only a couple of years younger than her.

"Are there any other thieves?" she asked, jerking her head down the road.

"No. No. Just us in this part."

"And in other parts?"

He nodded desperately. "Yes, miss. All over."

She leaned close, resting her sword against his throat. "Would you like a job?"

He could not nod. He could not even swallow. He whispered a tortured "Yes."

"Go down this road ahead of us. Find every thief, every robber, everyone preying on my people, and give them a message. These roads belong to Lada Dracul now. I declare them safe. And anyone who defies that will die."

She eased her sword away. The boy scrambled to his feet, bowing. "Yes. Yes, miss. I will."

She thought for a moment. Words were one thing. Evidence was another. She bent down and cut the ears off the nearest bodies. The first she mangled. The second she found the right place to slice. Nicolae blanched. The sound and sensation was unpleasant, but Lada rolled her eyes at him. "Take these." She held the ears out to the boy.

He looked as though he would lose his stomach, but he took the ears in trembling hands.

"Tokens of my sincerity. If you run, if you fail to deliver my message, I will know. And I will find you."

The boy squeaked an assurance that he would not fail, then, stumbling once, ran down the road away from them.

Bogdan returned a few minutes later, wiping his sword clean. "We got them all."

"Good." Lada stared at the quickly receding silhouette of the fleeing boy. It was a good message. But it was not quite enough. She had spent years in a land where every road was safe. The Ottomans were free to travel and trade, and their country flourished. She had not forgotten her lessons on the subject.

She had learned something from her tutors there, after all.

"These roads need clearer directions. Hang the bodies from the trees. Write 'thieves' on them." Several of the recent recruits looked worried. Most of them could not read or write. "Nicolae will write it," she said.

"This all seems excessive." Nicolae paused, halfway through dragging one of their scouts' bodies to the side of the road, where another soldier had started on a shallow grave.

Lada shrugged. "They are already dead. They may as well serve a purpose in death, as they did nothing with their lives."

After a full day on the road and with Tirgoviste within reach on the morrow, they set up camp. Daciana had not yet moved into Stefan's tent, but Lada had no doubts it would happen soon.

Stefan watched Daciana move around camp with a sort of

confused fear tightening his eyes. He was so twitchy and nervous that Lada worried about sending him ahead to scout. Daciana paid him only the barest attentions, occasionally pausing in her work to comment to him, or to straighten his vest, or to remark on the color or length of his stubble, casually brushing her hand against it.

Lada did not understand the strange dance Daciana was performing. It seemed deeply inefficient. But seeing the way Stefan watched the girl, Lada became twitchy herself.

The place between her legs nagged at her at the strangest times, reminding her of how it had felt and could feel again in the future. She cursed Mehmed for introducing her to those sensations. Before, she had not known they existed. Now, she longed for them.

Daciana leaned close to Stefan, whispering something in his ear and then laughing.

Bogdan joined Lada at her fire. He was thick and menacing where Mehmed was lithe. Bogdan was a hammer to Mehmed's graceful sword. But hammers had good qualities, too. Lada looked at him, narrowing her eyes. "You would do anything for me." It was not a question.

He looked at her as though she had taken the time to inform him the sky was blue. "Yes."

"Come with me." She stood and walked into her tent. Bogdan followed.

It was much more efficient than Daciana's methods. And if she did not feel the same with Bogdan as with Mehmed, if the spark and the fire and the need were not overwhelming, Bogdan was as he had always been: loyal and serviceable.

Their second day on the road they met with no further thieves. They found evidence of campsites, hastily abandoned. Lada felt a stirring of something like what she imagined maternal pride to be. Her little robber boy was obeying her.

Bogdan rode closer to her than before, and occasionally in the midst of his inelegant protectiveness she caught a hint of newfound tenderness. It made her deeply uncomfortable. She knew Bogdan felt more for her than she did for him. She had always accepted it as natural, good even. He belonged to her, but she did not belong to him. Perhaps she had crossed a line she should not have.

Her discomfort was soon replaced with an inconvenient relief when she felt a gush of warm blood between her legs. She nearly prayed, she was so grateful. But she doubted that God cared one way or the other about the continued emptiness of her womb.

Lada pulled her horse to a stop and dismounted. In her bag she had extra strips of cloth. She peeled off her chain mail and draped it across her saddle.

"What is it?" Bogdan asked, halfway through dismounting.

"No!" She gestured impatiently for him to stay. "I will be back."

"You should not go alone," Nicolae said.

Lada glared at all of them. She could feel the blood still flowing. If she did not catch it soon, her trousers would be stained. Daciana, who rode on Stefan's horse with him, looked at how Lada walked with stiff legs. "Let her go. Lada is more frightening than anything in the forest."

Lada turned her back and marched toward the trees. "God's wounds, you are all ridiculous. Rest. Eat. I will be back."

She moved quickly through the trees, putting as much distance as possible between the massive party of men and her immediately pressing, deeply private needs.

She found a clear stream and squatted next to it. The water was freezing, but at least there was some warmth in the air. While she cleaned herself, she cursed the fact that she had to deal with this at such an important time.

But the blood was a welcome sight. Perhaps Bogdan had been a lucky thing, dislodging whatever had blocked her since being with Mehmed. She took it as confirmation that Daciana's thoughts were correct. Her body was not made for carrying babies. She hummed to herself as she rinsed out her underclothes and set them on a rock to dry next to her trousers. She took care to place the extra strips of cloth in her new underclothes to absorb the blood. Then, because she was happy and the day was warmer than any had been for a long time, she pulled off her tunic and rinsed it as well.

That was when she heard the sound of furtive footsteps. She froze, ready to curse Bogdan or Nicolae or whoever had disobeyed her. And then she realized the footsteps were coming from the opposite direction where her men were. For a moment the memory of other trees in another place, of another man sneaking up on her, paralyzed Lada. Her breath would not come. The memory of Ivan's weight on her, his hands . . .

She snatched her tunic out of the water, looking around desperately for somewhere to hide. The trees were too thin to climb, the stream was open and exposed. And she was alone, because of her stupid woman's body. She looked down at her arms clutching the dripping tunic against her chest. Her woman's body. Ivan had seen it as a weakness, as something he had power over.

The footsteps were getting closer.

Ivan was *dead.* Her body was a weapon. She could kill whoever approached, but ... Unbidden, Huma drifted across her mind's eye. The way she draped herself across furniture. The way she moved. Lada tried to recall everything about it, because Huma had been a weapon just as much as Lada was.

Lada picked up a knife where it lay next to her boots, holding it hidden behind her back. And then she let her tunic fall as three men appeared at the opposite end of the stream. Their tense grips on their weapons relaxed as their jaws dropped in shock.

"Oh!" Lada squealed, a poor imitation of what she thought a girl would sound like in this circumstance. She drew one arm across her unwieldy breasts.

One of the men averted his eyes, blushing. The other two had no such decency. "What are you doing here?" one of them asked, a puzzled smile on his face.

"I ..." Lada leaned down, picking up her tunic and hiding the knife beneath it. "I live there"—she gestured vaguely to her right—"and I was washing."

"You should not be here." The blushing soldier looked behind himself at something she could not see. "There are a lot more men coming."

"Oh! Oh no." Lada gathered up her trousers and her boots, feigning embarrassed clumsiness. She was grateful she had not put her trousers back on. Bundled as they were, it was not obvious that she did not have skirts.

"Go home," the man said, his voice tense but gentle.

The leering soldier grinned even bigger. "We will visit you after we take care of some trouble."

Lada did not know how to smile demurely, but she gave it her best shot. Then she hurried in the direction she had told them she lived. As soon as she thought it was safe, she yanked on her boots, shoving the rest of her things in her bag. She cut back toward the road, running as fast as she could. Her men would not be ready. They had gotten too used to being unchallenged. She had no idea how many soldiers were in the trees, but if they had the element of surprise, she did not like her forces' odds.

She burst onto the road much farther ahead of the troops than where she had left. Sprinting toward them, she waved her trousers in the air. She could not shout for fear the enemy was close enough to hear.

Nicolae noticed, waving tentatively back.

She pointed frantically toward the trees. Nicolae did not move for several agonizing seconds. Then he acted with all the practiced efficiency of a true soldier. Before Lada reached her men, they had all slid from the road and onto the opposite side, leaving an open expanse between themselves and the trees that hid the enemy. Lada joined them there, out of breath. She drew her sword from where it hung from her saddle.

"Lada," Nicolae hissed.

"Men. From Tirgoviste, I think. They are looking for us. I do not know how many, but they will be here soon. Spread word down the line. Crossbows first. We will surprise them."

"Lada," he said again. "Your . . ." He gestured wordlessly toward her chest. Bogdan moved so he was blocking Lada from view of anyone else. She looked down at where her breasts, still uncovered, moved up and down with her breathing.

Glaring, she yanked her tunic out of her bag and pulled it on. "Well, you can thank my"—she gestured wordlessly toward her chest as she tugged on her trousers—"for saving us."

Nicolae did not have time to inquire further about how, exactly, Lada's breasts had saved her men. The first enemy soldiers had begun coming out of the trees, moving with exaggerated stillness. Still believing the element of surprise was theirs, they looked up and down the road, then gestured for the others to join them.

It was not as big a force as her own, but if they had been able to use the cover of the trees and catch her men unaware, Lada did not want to think how it might have devastated her numbers. She lifted a fist, then lowered it. Crossbow bolts sang through the trees onto the road, cutting down half the men. The other half scrambled to load their own crossbows and form a rank, but by then it was too late. Lada's men roared out of the trees, an unbreakable wave of swords and strength.

When it was over and only a handful of their enemies remained, Lada joined them on the road. The men sat in a miserable circle, stripped of their weapons. Some bled. Bleeding was not always a weakness, though. Lada laughed to herself.

One of the soldiers on the road was the man who had had the decency to blush and look away. Lada pointed to him. "That one lives. Kill the rest." She ignored the messy work going on around the blushing man. "Did the prince send you?"

He cringed at the sound of sword separating soul from body. "Yes. We were supposed to kill you."

"And even though you were coming for me, you did not wonder if the girl in the woods was the one you hunted?"

He did not meet her eyes. "We assumed you would be somewhere safe. In a carriage, with guards. You are not what I expected. The prince said it would be easy."

"I am not so easy to get rid of." She offered him a hand. "You can go back and tell him that. Or you can stay and join my men."

He trembled from head to toe. "I will stay?" He finally glanced up to meet her eyes, and she knew he looked for confirmation of whether or not he had made the right choice. She had not lied to him—she would have let him go. But doubtless he thought that would have resulted in his death.

She nodded. "Very well."

"That was lucky," Nicolae said, leading Lada's horse out of the trees alongside his own horse. "You were right. Sometimes you do need to be alone."

Lada could not quite smile. It could have ended much differently. She pulled the reassuring weight of the chain mail around herself. Better to be a soldier than a woman.

Better to be a prince than anything.

41

May 24–25

"THIS MAN IS A snake and a liar," Halil said, sneering at Radu. "I wondered where he had slithered off to."

Radu took a steadying breath, reminding himself of all the times he had played a part to manipulate his old foe. He could do it here. He had to. "I should think, given your peaceful views of the city, you would envy those of us who had the courage to leave the tyrant sultan and serve the cause of the emperor."

Halil snorted. "If you have courage, I am a donkey."

"That has always been my personal opinion of you, but I never expected you to agree with me."

Halil's face turned a violent shade of red. "Get him out of here."

Constantine held out his hands in placation. "I do not know your history, but Radu has been instrumental to us. His advice and information are testament enough of his loyalty." Constantine raised a single eyebrow. "And he has no towers named after him in fortresses on my land."

Halil's scowl deepened. "You know I had no choice."

"There is always a choice. We appreciate your information and friendship, but you remain safely outside the walls. Radu is here."

"My position is not safe! No one's is. The camp is on the edge of riot. Daily we meet, and I urge negotiating peace, while others demand we give no quarter. I could not do that if I had not stayed with the sultan!"

Constantine rubbed his face wearily. "Tell me why you are here."

Halil threw a single piece of parchment on the table next to him. "Mehmed offers you terms of surrender. I will await your response." Leveling a murderous glare at Radu, Halil stomped out of the room.

Constantine read the letter, scratching absently at his beard. Droplets of blood broke through the skin. "He will let me go into the Peloponnese and be a governor there."

"We have wanted you to leave the city," Giustiniani said gently. "We need you safe, and then we can gather allies."

Constantine sighed. "If I leave the city, I am never getting back in. I cannot do it. But . . ." He paused, tracing a finger over the bottom half of the letter. "If we open the gates, they will march through peacefully, leaving all citizens and property unmolested." He looked up at Radu. "Do you think he will honor that?"

"He will." Radu felt the first true spark of hope in ages. He had been right not to kill Constantine! Another way to end this siege had been given to him. "It is Muslim law. If you surrender, they have to respect that. There will be no prisoners, no slaves, no looting."

Giustiniani scoffed. "I doubt that very much."

"You have seen the order of his camp, the control he has over his men. He wants the city itself, not anything in it. He does not want to destroy it—he wants to own it. I will stake my life on his truthfulness in this matter. He will honor these terms. All your people will be spared."

"And the Christian capital of the world will be handed over to their god."

Radu chose his next words carefully. "If they take the city by force, they have three days for looting and doing anything else they wish. But if you surrender, the Ottomans treat their vassal states well. We would all have to run or risk death, but your people would not suffer under the sultan's rule."

Constantine's smile was as brittle as spring ice on a river. "The same cannot be said for my rule. How my people have suffered. How my city has darkened." He looked at Cyprian, fondness in his expression. "What is your counsel, nephew?"

Today Cyprian's eyes were not gray like the sea or the clouds. They were gray like the ancient, weary rocks of the city. Radu knew that the nameless child dead in the streets had come into the room with them. "We have lost so much. Perhaps this is a way to avoid losing everything. Our people would not be slaughtered or sold into slavery. You would live." He put a hand on his uncle's shoulder, his voice breaking. "I want you to live."

Constantine looked to Giustiniani, the other reason the city had survived for as long as it had. "You?"

Giustiniani shook his head. "If Halil is right, all we need to do is hold on for a little longer and Mehmed will be forced to leave. He may even lose the throne." After a pause, Giustiniani looked at the floor. "But I cannot promise we can hold on for even a day more. We have fewer than half of the forces we started with. The men are hungry and weary and frightened. The Venetians want to leave. My men do, too. I will not let them, but it may come to a point where I can no longer prevent them. With one victory, they could topple us—or with one victory, we could have enough momentum to sustain ourselves. We are balanced on the edge of a knife. I do not know whom the knife will cut. The choice is yours."

Constantine sat, his broad shoulders sloping as he picked up a quill and stroked the length of it. "I cannot do it," he said. Radu leaned heavily against the wall, all hope extinguished. "I will send Halil with an offer of peace. We will increase our tribute, and give the sultan the land under the Rumeli Hisari. We will give him Orhan, too, and abandon all attempts at destabilizing his throne."

Constantine was willing to sacrifice Orhan, a man he had used to manipulate the Ottomans for decades, even though Orhan had chosen to stay and fight. He would sacrifice Orhan, but not his pride. Not his throne. Radu shook his head, trying to keep the anger out of his voice. "Mehmed will not accept."

"I know. But I cannot abandon my city. I am sorry, my friends. I will fight until my last breath before I will see Ottoman flags in this palace and hear their call to prayer from the Hagia Sophia. It is in God's hands now."

But which god? Radu thought. With so many men on both sides sending up so many prayers, how could any god sift through the noise?

That night, the air was sweet with the promise of summer around the corner. The wind had blown strong from the horn, clearing the smoke from the city for once. Radu and Cyprian sat on the Blachernae Palace wall, facing the Hagia Sophia. Though they had not discussed it, neither man had gone to his scheduled position at the wall after leaving Constantine. They had ended up out here, silent, side by side.

It was almost quiet enough to pretend the world was not ending around them.

"The moon begins waning tonight," Cyprian said.

Radu remembered the prophecy that the city could not be taken on a waxing moon. "Do you believe in that one?"

"I believe in very little these days."

Radu looked toward the Hagia Sophia, where the full moon would rise over the city. A full circle of gold, like their coins, the moon was a protector of the city along with the Virgin Mary. Would the waning finally shift the tide of war?

Next to him, Cyprian sat up straight, a sharp intake of breath like a hiss puncturing the quiet of the night. In place of the full moon rising over the Hagia Sophia, there was only a sliver of a crescent moon.

The crescent moon of Islam.

"How is this possible?" Cyprian whispered.

Radu shook his head in disbelief. The moon was full tonight—*had* to be full tonight. But slowly lifting itself above the city's holiest building, the moon remained a crescent. The dark part was not as dark as normal, but rather a deep red. Stained like blood.

For hours Radu and Cyprian watched as the crescent moon hung over the city, promising an end to everything. Wails and cries from the streets drifted on the sweet breeze. For once the church bells did not ring warning. What could bells do against the moon? Finally, agonizingly slowly, the moon returned to the fullness it should have had all along.

"I might believe in prophecies now," Cyprian said in awe and wonder. "But I do not think I like this one."

Radu wondered what it must have been like to see the moon in the Ottoman camps. Surely Mehmed would have capitalized on it, claiming it as a prophecy of victory, even as the citizens of Constantinople saw it as a portent of doom.

It was just the moon. The moon did not take sides. But the blood-washed expanse of the Byzantine full moon seemed to promise otherwise.

—————— ⁃ ——————

They spent the night on the palace wall, not moving. Sometime in the small hours of the morning, clouds rolled in, obscuring the moon. "Where were you when we could have used you?" Cyprian muttered.

Dawn dragged itself free from sludge of night, bringing with it a smattering of rain and the promise of more to come. After Radu prayed in his heart, they began to walk toward a gate that would lead them to the wall over the Lycus River.

"Oh, hell." Cyprian cringed. "Oh, damn, I am going to be damned for swearing about this." They were near the monastery they had broken into that housed the Hodegetria. A massive crowd had gathered outside. Priests were already swinging censers, chanting and singing the liturgy. More people came in the street behind Radu and Cyprian, blocking them in.

"See if you can push through," Cyprian said. "They are

going to take the Hodegetria around the walls. If we get stuck in the middle, we will be trapped for hours."

A team of men exited the monastery, the pallet lifted onto their shoulders. One of them nearly lost his grip, struggling to keep hold. Radu remembered Nazira wiping her hands clean of grease—on the poles of the icon.

"God's wounds," he whispered, fighting an urge to laugh born of nerves and exhaustion.

Another man's hands slipped. He adjusted quickly, lifting the icon higher. A crossbearer in front began walking, followed by the priests. Men, women, and children surrounded them, all barefoot. A man near the front cried out in a voice loud enough to be heard over the low rumbling of thunder.

"Do thou save thy city, as thou knowest and willest! We put thee forward as our arms, our rampart, our shield, our general!"

Radu leaned close to Cyprian. "Someone should tell Giustiniani he has been replaced by a centuries-old painting."

Cyprian snorted, covering his laugh behind a hand.

The man continued. "Do thou fight for our people!"

"Do you think she will take our place at the wall?" Cyprian whispered.

Radu laughed. A man nearby gave them a furious glare, crossing himself.

"We are going to hell for blasphemy," Cyprian said.

"We are already in hell," Radu said, shrugging. "And with so much company." They tried to edge away from the crowd, but the street was narrow and clogged with people. The two men were carried forward in the surge of religious zeal, pushed along a seemingly random path.

"There!" Radu said, pointing to a narrow alley. If they could duck into it, they could wait until the crowd had passed and then backtrack.

Someone cried out in horror from the front. The Hodegetria was slipping. Though the men carrying it scrambled to counter its momentum, they could not get a good grip on the poles. The icon, the holiest artifact in the city, slid off into a thick patch of mud.

Everyone was silent for a few disbelieving heartbeats. Then the men sprang into action, trying to lift it. Though it was only a painting and there were several men, they could not seem to pull it up. The earth had decided to reclaim the Virgin Mary and would not relinquish her.

Several children started crying, their mothers doing nothing to shush them. A murmur like a tiny earthquake rolled through the crowd. Whispers of doom, damnation, the Virgin abandoning them. Of God judging them and deeming them unclean.

Radu was half tempted to tell them God had nothing to do with this—it had been a young woman with grease on her hands and sorrow in her heart. But it would do no good.

Finally, after far too long, the men managed to leverage the icon out of the mud and back onto their shoulders. A ragged cheer went up, but it would not have felt out of place at a funeral for all the happiness it held.

Then the world was lit for a single second in blinding white. Radu had time only to wonder if he truly was being struck down for blasphemy before a clap of thunder louder than any bombardment followed an instant later, shaking the ground. Screams and cries went up. A rushing sound moved toward them. Radu saw the rain before it hit. It was a solid wall of water, so thick and fast that it slammed into the crowd with the force of a river.

Something stung Radu's face. He touched his cheek to make certain he was not bleeding. Then another piece of hail struck him, and another. The hail fell with more fury than the arrows of the Ottomans. Another brilliant bolt of lightning struck nearby, the thunder accompanying it so powerful Radu could hear nothing for nearly a minute afterward.

All around him people were falling to their knees, unable to see or walk in the middle of the tempest. Radu knew God had nothing to do with the icon slipping. This, however, was difficult to attribute to anything else. The water fell so furiously that it began streaming down the street, rising to Radu's ankles and then to his knees. The narrow streets were funneling it, channeling it into a sudden river.

"We have to get out of this!" Cyprian shouted. Radu could barely hear him, though Cyprian's mouth was right next to his ear. He pointed at the alley they had been aiming for. Because of the slope, the water did not travel far up it. The two men pushed through the street, mud sucking at their boots, the hungry water pulling eagerly. A child in front of them went down, disappearing beneath the brown water.

Radu dove to his knees, pushing his hands down blindly. He caught a foot and pulled the child into the air. A woman rushed toward them. Radu handed her the child. Cyprian shouted, pointing to an old man who had gone down. They hurried to him, helping him up and dragging him through the water to the alley.

"There!" Cyprian waved toward a woman in the middle of the street holding an infant to her breast and unable to move. He started forward, but another blinding flash of lightning and an overpowering burst of thunder cracked through the alley.

Some of the cracking noises were not the thunder. The stones from the roof above them that had been struck fell in a jumble, taking Cyprian down beneath them.

42

April 28

WALLACHIA WAS FATALLY FLAWED when it came to keeping princes alive. The boyars were tasked with protecting the prince. They controlled all the manpower, all the troops, all the blades that stood between life and death. In theory, the purpose was to keep the prince loyal to the country and the people whom he depended on for survival.

It may have worked, were the boyars ever loyal to a prince. But the roads were open and clear in front of Lada like a field after harvest. She was grateful now that the boyars were never loyal to a prince. The few men the prince had been able to rally were dead on the road behind them.

"So, what is the plan?" Nicolae asked.

Lada shrugged.

"That—that is not a plan. You have no plan? Really? None?"

"We go in. We take the throne. That is all the plan we need."

"No, I definitely need more plan than that."

Bogdan grunted. "She told you the plan. Shut up."

Lada kept her eyes on the city growing ever larger in front of them. Homes were closer together as farmland gave way to life clinging to the edge of the city and the opportunity it provided. Which, judging by the condition of the homes, was not much.

Lada did not smile at the people who huddled in the dark doorways, watching her procession. But she could feel their stares, feel their whispers. Nicolae shifted defensively. She shook her head at him. She would not cower.

"Look," Petru said, pointing up at the sky.

Among the first stars beginning to pierce the night, there was one falling. It burned, light trailing behind it as it slowly moved through the gathering darkness.

"It is an omen," Daciana said from her seat in front of Stefan on his horse, her voice quiet with wonder.

Lada closed her eyes, remembering another night when stars fell from the heavens. She had almost been happy then, with the two men she loved. Now she had neither of them. But she had known that night what she knew now: nothing but Wallachia would ever be enough.

The stars saw her. They knew.

She lifted a hand in the air toward the burning sign as she rode forward, letting everyone see her pointing to the omen of her coming. Everyone would witness it.

They were her people. This was her country. This was her throne. She needed no intrigues, no elaborate plans. Wallachia was her mother. After everything she had been through, all she had done in pursuit of the throne, she was left with one thing only: herself.

She was enough.

The gates to the city were closed when they came to them.

Two men illuminated by torches stood at the top, a faint metallic clinking puzzling Lada until she realized they were trembling in their chain mail.

"Open the gates," she said.

The men looked at each other, unsure what to do. They looked over her shoulder, where her men lined up behind her. A murmur of noise like pebbles signaling an avalanche accompanied her.

"I come like that star, burning in the night." She raised her voice so everyone could hear. "Anyone on my side before I take the throne will be a salaried soldier. I reward merit, and there will be much opportunity for advancement of fortunes."

"How?" one of the men asked.

"Because anyone who opposes me will be dead. Those are my terms. They will not be offered again."

The gate opened.

Several men fell into line with her own as they rode into the city. "You," she said, pointing at one of them. "Deliver my terms to every guard you meet."

He sprinted eagerly ahead of Lada's troops. They continued at an unhurried pace. The streets were narrow, like spokes in a wheel going toward the castle. She looked back only once, to see her party stretching back to the gate and beyond, everyone squeezing in to follow. Their numbers had swelled to more than double the soldiers. Men, women, even children. The children danced and laughed in the torchlight like it was a parade. The men and women were warier, but an intensity shone in their eyes that had not been there before. She had done that.

She faced forward again. She had not romanticized Tirgoviste when she lived here, but after all these years and her time in the Ottoman Empire, it was not only smaller than she remembered, but also dingier, bleaker. Even the manors were pale and haphazard imitations of stateliness. Paint had chipped away to reveal the brown and gray stone skeletons of houses like flesh rotting from bone.

No one exited the boyar manors to join the procession. Their windows were curtained and shuttered against the night. Against Lada. They passed a fountain that she remembered running with clear water. She had dunked her head there once, trying to wash away the fear that living in the castle had bred within her. Now, fetid water lay still and stinking in it. But she was not afraid anymore, and had nothing to wash away.

The gates to the castle wall were open. Guards stood to either side, eyes on the ground, heads lowered as she passed. Nicolae and Bogdan looked around rapidly, shifting behind her, but she had no fear of assassins' arrows. Just as Hunyadi had ridden into the city wearing his confidence and rightness around him, so would she. No one could shoot her. No one could stop her.

She nodded toward the door to the castle. The guard who had run ahead opened it for her. She rode her horse straight through, its hooves clattering against the stone floor. No pretty tiles here, no rugs, nothing between the teeth of the castle and the people it devoured.

She liked it that way. Her horse plodded forward, tentative in the narrow halls with their burning torches. Behind her, she heard Bogdan and Nicolae trying to calm their horses. She did not stop or wait for them to reassure the nervous beasts. The throne room was ahead of her. The last time she had been here, she had watched her father pretend he had any power left as he addressed Hunyadi.

It felt right that as she entered high on the back of her horse, the Danesti prince sat stiff and sweating on the throne. A phantom memory of the scent of her father's beard oil teased her nose. She wished for one heartbeat that the man on the throne were her father. That he could see what she had become, in spite of him. Because of him.

The Danesti was saying something, but she had not bothered to start listening. Her eyes were caught on the curved length of the Ottoman sword still hanging above the throne. It was framed by two torches, flickering hypnotically. She guided her horse closer, entranced.

"I said, explain yourself!"

Startled, she looked down at the sputtering prince. His face was red, a sheen of sweat making his skin glow. She did not remember him from her time here as a girl. He had not mattered to her then, and he did not matter to her now.

She glanced around the room. There were several guards, but none moved toward her. She heard voices in the hall, someone swearing about a horse. She was alone.

It did not matter.

She addressed the sword. "I have delivered my terms already."

"I have heard no terms!" the prince huffed.

"They are not for you. They are for the Wallachians in this room. Land and wealth for those on my side. Death for those opposed."

"You have no right to offer them such things!"

She nudged her horse forward so that the Danesti had to scramble to the side of the throne to avoid the horse's long, velvety nose. Lada stood in the stirrups, reaching for the sword on the wall. She tugged it free, pulling it out of its sheath. It was dimmed by age but sharp enough. The sword of their enemies. The sword of their vassalage. The sword of their weakness.

Her sword now. She lifted it in the air, turning it to play with the torchlight. "I have the only right there is." She put the sword through the usurper's chest before he could answer her. He had nothing to say she cared about. She turned her horse, pulling the sword free.

"It is going to be a nightmare to clean that throne," Nicolae said as he walked into the room, followed by Bogdan and the rest of her men.

Lada smiled. "I *am* the throne. Put his body on a stake in the square as proof that I keep my promises. Loyalty rewarded. Cowardice cut down."

The gate guard ran forward eagerly, dragging the body from the throne. It left a trail of blood, black in the dim light. The only legacy this prince would ever have, his weakness written across stones as testament to Lada's superiority.

Bogdan took a knee, his deep voice booming through the room. "All hail Lada the dragon, prince of Wallachia!"

Lada's horse shifted, putting her directly in line with one of the narrow, high windows. Through it, perfectly framed, the falling star finally burned out. She lifted her face, closing her eyes, as her mother blessed her. A warmth settled deep inside, and she clutched the locket she always wore.

She was home.

43

May 25–26

"Do you think he will recover?" Radu asked, pacing anxiously. He had half carried, half dragged Cyprian back to the house. Though Cyprian did not appear to have suffered any significant visible damage, a cut on his head bled freely, and he had not yet woken up.

"Time will tell." Nazira finished cleaning up the blood. She gave Radu a concerned look that managed to pull her full lips nearly flat. "Sit down. You cannot worry him back to health."

Radu collapsed into a chair and put his head in his hands. "I know we greased the poles of the icon. But the way it refused to be picked up again—and then the storm. I have never been in a storm of such sudden fury. They brought out the Hodegetria to guide them, and instead they were swept away, carried off in the middle of a tempest."

"This city is getting to you, Radu. Even you see signs in everything now."

Radu nodded, rubbing his eyes and leaning back. "I know. I feel sorry for them. To see your own destruction reflected in everything around you—the moon, the weather, the shaking of the earth itself—I am amazed that anyone remains in this city. Why could they not leave?"

Nazira smiled sadly. "I persuaded Helen to. I know there was no reason for me to continue my friendship with her, but she was so sad and lost. I gave her the last of our money. Yesterday she slipped into Galata, where she has distant relations who can help her get to Athens."

"That was a good thing."

The door opened and Valentin appeared with a bowl of water and some clean rags. Nazira took them; then Radu held up a hand to keep Valentin from leaving. "Do you have any family in the city?"

Valentin shook his head. "My parents died two years ago. My sister, too."

"Aunts? Uncles?"

"No, sir."

"What about outside the city? Do you have anywhere to go?"

Valentin stood straighter, puffing up his chest. "No, sir, and if I did, I would not go anyway. My place is serving Cyprian, and I will stay where he is until the end."

"What if I needed to send a letter to my sister in Hungary? One that I could send only with someone I trust absolutely?"

Valentin smiled, with an expression too knowing and weary for a boy as young as he. "Then I would say I suspect you of tricking me, and anyway, I have heard your stories of your sister and would rather take my chances here."

Radu laughed, shocked at how much the boy had picked up

on. "Very well. But promise me one thing: If the city is falling around you, you do everything you can to get out. Do you understand? And if I am not here, you help Nazira and Cyprian get out."

Valentin stood even straighter, giving a dignified nod. "I will protect them with my life."

"Good boy."

Valentin left, closing the door softly behind him.

Cyprian moaned. Radu rushed to the bedside. "Cyprian? Can you hear me?"

Cyprian tried to lift a hand to his head, his eyes squeezed shut. "Radu?"

"Yes! You are safe, at home."

"I think—" he croaked, his voice cracking.

"I will get him something to drink!" Nazira hurried from the room.

Cyprian swallowed, still not opening his eyes. "I think the city fell down on my head."

Radu laughed in relief. "It did. But you Byzantines are remarkably hardheaded."

Squinting, Cyprian looked at Radu. "Radu! You are here!"

"Yes. I am right here."

Cyprian lifted a hand, searching in the air. Radu took it in his own.

"I went back for you." Cyprian's eyes drifted shut again.

"No," Radu said, gently. "I was not hurt. I brought you home. Remember?"

Cyprian shook his head, then cringed, crying out in pain. He squinted again. "No, I went back to Edirne for you."

What if the blow had permanently damaged Cyprian's mind? "We are not in Edirne. We are in Constantinople."

"I know that," Cyprian snapped, rolling his eyes. "You are very confused."

Radu tried not to smile. "You are right. I am the confused one."

"We never spoke, but your face ... The look you shared with him about the book. I never stopped thinking of you."

"What book?" Radu wanted to keep Cyprian awake and talking, even if it was nonsense.

Cyprian waved his free hand. "The book we gave the sultan. You understood how funny it was. The dragon book. I wished so much I could laugh with you. Even then I knew you would have a wonderful laugh. He did not want me to go back, you know."

Radu searched his memory, trying to figure out what Cyprian was talking about. Books and dragons? And then it rushed back. Last year. The delegation from Constantinople after Mehmed's coronation. It was the first time Radu had seen Cyprian. Back when Cyprian was a nameless ambassador delivering a book on Saint George and the dragon as a gift. Radu remembered that moment perfectly, too. That startling jolt when he had met Cyprian's clear gray eyes and seen the hidden laughter there.

"Who did not want you to go back to Edirne?" Radu asked, suddenly very interested in the conversation.

"My uncle. Too dangerous. I insisted, though. I wanted to speak to you."

Radu's heart was racing. "To ask me to come here and give information on Mehmed?"

"No." Cyprian's voice went far away and quiet. "I just wanted to speak to you. I wanted to hear you laugh." He smiled, lifting their clasped hands toward Radu's cheek. Radu leaned his head down, letting Cyprian's fingers brush against his skin. Though his fingers were cold, the touch felt like fire.

"I regret nothing," Cyprian murmured, and then his face relaxed into sleep.

The door clicked shut and Radu startled, looking up guiltily.

"Oh, husband." Nazira sighed, already in the room, for how long Radu did not know. "You almost make me believe in fate, for how unfortunate yours is."

She set down a bowl of broth and a mug of watered-down wine. Adjusting Cyprian's blankets, she knelt across the bed from Radu and looked up at him. "First a man with no heart to give you, and now a man who can never know your truths."

Radu stood, his pulse still racing, his cheeks flushed. "I— He was— I am not—"

Nazira looked tenderly at Cyprian, brushing some hair from his forehead. "I suspected, but I hoped I was wrong. It seemed too cruel, too absurd an irony."

"You know I am loyal to Mehmed!"

Nazira's face darkened faster than the tempest in the streets. "You owe him nothing more than your loyalty. Certainly not your love. Normally I would rejoice that your heart had stirred in another direction. But this . . ." She lowered her head onto the bed, hiding her face from him. "Oh, Radu. What will we do?"

A bell in the distance tolled *doom, doom, doom.*

Radu could not sit at Cyprian's bedside. He wandered the streets until nightfall. The storm had disappeared as suddenly as it came, the clouds taking residence on the earth instead. The air was still and dead, the city shrouded as if for burial.

As night fell, the fog thickened, masking all lights and making the city as dark as a cave. Radu had started toward home when muted cries of "Fire, fire!" broke through the fog. He turned, running in their direction, wondering if this was it, if the wall had finally fallen. Instead, he saw the roof of the Hagia Sophia flickering with light.

Horrified, he ran several steps toward the church before stopping. It was not fire. The light danced and moved along the roof, but it was the wrong hue for fire, more white and blue than yellow. And there was no smoke. Radu watched, transfixed, as the light gathered around the main spire and then shot upward into the sky.

He stared, blinking in the darkness, the afterimage playing across his vision. He had never seen anything like this, never heard of anything like it. But no—had not God appeared to Moses as fire? A cloud during the day—like the impenetrable fog—and a pillar of fire at night.

Radu could not breathe, could not comprehend what he had seen. Because the only way he could explain it was that he had seen the spirit of God himself. And God had left Constantinople behind.

But the fire had gone into the sky, not to the camps of the Ottomans. Perhaps all their prayers had canceled each other out. It was only men against men now.

God was right to abandon them. If anyone had decided on

mercy and reason over stubbornness, all these lives could have been spared. If Mehmed had allowed the city to continue its natural, slow death rather than needing to claim it. If Constantine had bowed to the impossible odds and opted to save his people over his pride.

Radu was so angry with both of them. Different possibilities spun through his mind. Killing Constantine, as he had considered. It would lead to surrender.

Using Mehmed's trust and sending a message into the Ottoman camps that Hunyadi was on his way with an army from the pope. That would tip things out of Mehmed's favor, forcing him to accept a new peace treaty.

Either was a bigger betrayal than Radu had it in him to commit, and for that he was as culpable as emperor or sultan. He could not make the hard decision, could not solve this where they refused to.

Radu wandered, lost in the fog. It clung to him, questioning, nagging. Radu was sorrier than he had ever believed possible. Somewhere in the past months he had grown to love this odd, superstitious, worn-down city. Somewhere in the past months he had grown to love the man who brought them here.

But an end was coming. If Mehmed did not take the city, it would be his end. Halil would see to that. More Muslims would die in Christian crusades, like Fatima's family had. And the city would still fall eventually. But if Radu helped the city fall now, he could save Mehmed. Radu could be at his side to see the future Mehmed would create.

Lada had despised Radu for the fact that he would always choose Mehmed. Nazira had told him that he did not owe Mehmed his love.

But he did owe Mehmed his life. And Mehmed was the only man who could fill the destiny laid out by the Prophet, peace be upon him.

He had imagined Constantinople, had wanted it for Mehmed. It had been simple and straightforward. But now he knew the true cost of things, the murky horrors of the distance between wanting something and getting it.

He had wanted Mehmed in ways he could never have him, and that, too, had slowly been destroying him.

What, then, did he have left?

Radu closed his eyes, remembering the light. God might have left the city, but Radu would never leave his God. And Constantinople as it was would always be a threat to Islam, bringing crusades, destabilizing the Ottoman Empire.

Some lives are worth more than others, Lada had told him. He had wondered when the scales would tip out of their favor, had thought her a monster for valuing their lives above all others. But he had valued Mehmed above all. He valued Nazira more than any innocents in this city. And the value he had to admit he held for Cyprian would break his own heart.

It was wrong, this weighing and measuring lives as though they were coins that could be spent or saved. He longed to be free of it all, to live among men seeing everyone as his brother, to view no one as his enemy.

But his choice was made. He walked toward the Hagia Sophia to find Amal. He would do everything in his power to give Constantinople to Mehmed, to the true and only God, and let his own heart break or stop as it would after.

44

Early May

"THE CASTLE IN EDIRNE was nicer," Petru said, looking dubiously at the whitewashed walls and plain stone floors of the dining hall.

"There were pigpens in Edirne nicer than this castle," Lada said. "You are welcome to go back and live in one of them."

"I like this castle! Really!" Petru said, scrambling to repair the damage he feared he had done.

Lada sighed and shook her head. "No one hates this castle more than I do. But this is the capital, so we live here now." She sat back, looking around the table. Nicolae, Petru, Stefan, Daciana, and Bogdan were with her. Lada had sent for Oana. If her old nurse was in charge of the kitchen, Lada knew she would be safe from any attempts to poison her food.

"Has anyone checked the treasury yet? Do we even have a treasury?" Lada realized how little of the actual running of a castle she had witnessed as a child. Mehmed had a legion of men employed to keep charge of his empire's finances. Lada did not even know where her resources were physically located—or whether she had any.

"I can hunt for treasure in the castle," Nicolae said.

"Me too!" Petru sat up, excited. Sometimes Lada forgot how young he was.

How young she was, too. She felt it more now, in the three days since she had taken the throne. She had focused for so long on getting here, that she was not quite sure what to do now that her only goal was behind her.

"I doubt there is much to find," Daciana said. "Would the previous prince have kept his family wealth here? Our boyar"— she turned her head to the side and spit—"and his family kept their wealth on their own land. The Danesti was not always prince. His wealth would be held by his family."

"You need taxes," Stefan said. Lada noticed that his right hand and Daciana's left hand were not on the table. Were they holding hands beneath it?

"You do need taxes," a man's voice said. "And for that, you need boyars. And for that, you need me."

She looked up to see Toma beaming at her, his arms open wide as though expecting her to run to him. At his side was Oana, who shifted away from him with a look on her face like she smelled something foul. Bogdan stood and embraced his mother. She patted his arm, then looked Lada up and down. Nodding, she tightened the apron around her waist and walked toward the kitchen muttering about getting things in shape.

Lada was surprised at how relieved she was to have Oana here again. It felt right.

Toma, on the other hand ...

He sat down in the chair Bogdan had vacated, the one to Lada's immediate right. "Why are you meeting in here?" He looked derisively around the room. "You should be holding court in the throne room, or your chambers. I looked for you there first."

Lada had been staying in the tiny barracks with her men. That felt more like home than this castle. "I have not taken chambers yet."

"You must. And stop sitting with your men like a commoner. They should be standing at the ready near the doors, not treated like advisors. Appearances matter, Lada."

"Speaking of appearances," Nicolae interrupted—Lada suspected to spite Toma's pronouncement that her men were merely guards—"why are you here?"

Toma smiled, showing all his stained teeth. "Before I deliver the good news to Matthias, we need to discuss finances. Castles do not run themselves, I am afraid. And we will have to extend quite a few favors to secure the loyalty of the remaining Danesti boyars after what you did to their prince."

Lada sighed, making herself listen as Toma instructed her. The last time she had been forced to sit through tedious instruction in Tirgoviste, at least she had been able to demand to learn outside. Now she did not have even that luxury.

———◆———

The castle reminded Lada of a tomb, heavy stones waiting to claim her as they had her father before her. She did not want to live there—already, she craved escape, thinking longingly of the mountain peak in Arges. But she was the prince, and the prince lived in the castle.

She took her father's old rooms, throwing out everything

that had belonged to the dead Danesti. Some of it might have been left over from her father. She did not care either way. Daciana took over after Lada had cleared the rooms, securing enough furnishings for them to feel livable.

"Are you sure you do not want curtains?" she asked, hands on her hips, her belly jutting out.

Lada stared thoughtfully at the empty space above the narrow window. "My brother and I once used a curtain rod to push an assassin off a balcony. Maybe we *should* add them."

"Well, I thought they might be pretty. But, certainly, they can double as weapons. You are very practical."

Lada shook her head. "I hate this castle and every room in it. I do not care what it looks like."

Daciana nodded, not asking any questions. Lada liked that about her. She asked questions when she needed to and otherwise let memories lie where they would. Lada suspected it was because Daciana was equally reticent to talk about her own past. She seemed quite content in the present. She had appointed herself Lada's personal maid, but, contrary to convention, she did not sleep in Lada's rooms. Judging by the new expression of bemused happiness on Stefan's formerly blank face, Lada knew where Daciana had settled.

Daciana had decided what she wanted and had secured it. In spite of carrying another man's child, in spite of her circumstances, in spite of everything. Lada felt a pang of jealousy. To be able to want a man and claim him, heedless of anything else? She could have claimed Mehmed. She *had* claimed him. But it did not satisfy her. Why could Daciana find happiness when Lada could not?

No. That was wrong. Lada had decided what she wanted, and she had secured it. The throne was hers.

Mehmed's face and the feeling of his hands on her body still haunted her, though. She wished she could carve out his memory with a knife. Trace the lines of him that would not leave her, then cut them free. She would bleed, but she would not die. Still, he lingered in places no knife could ever reach.

Daciana gasped, bringing Lada back to the present. She was bent over, hands on her belly.

"Are you ill?" Lada asked.

"I think the baby is coming."

Lada was struck with a terror deeper than any battlefield could have presented. The need to flee was overwhelming. "I will go get the nurse. Oana, I mean."

Daciana nodded, breathing deeply against some internal pain Lada did not want to imagine.

The nurse was easy to find. After laughing at Lada's obvious horror, Oana escorted Daciana to another room. Lada waited outside with Stefan, who paced with nerves as though the child were his. Lada wondered idly what they would do with the newborn bastard. That was none of her business, though.

The hope on Stefan's face grew increasingly pained. It was obvious he loved Daciana. Lada wondered what that must feel like, to know someone loved you enough to take everything you were. To wait. To hope.

She wondered what it would feel like to be the person who loved that much, too.

She found Bogdan and invited him to her bedroom, but it did nothing to take the ache away from the edges of her memory of Mehmed. After, Bogdan wanted to linger. Lada dressed hurriedly and left her rooms. She did not have space in her heart for that. Not after last time. Not after loving Mehmed so much, and being so deeply betrayed by him.

No. Bogdan was safe. Bogdan was steady. And she did not and would never love Bogdan as she had Mehmed, which was both a relief and an agony.

When Oana told her that Daciana had safely delivered a little girl, Lada was unmoved. "They want to see you," the nurse said.

Lada did not want to see them. But Stefan was one of her oldest and most trusted men. So she entered the room, ready for the scent of blood and sweat and fear. Instead, she found a cozy, warm space. Daciana was curled in a nest of blankets, the babe at her breast. Stefan sat next to them, gazing in wonder at the tiny, mewling creature. Daciana looked up, beaming.

"Thank you," she said.

Lada frowned. "For what?"

"For giving me a world where I can raise my daughter how I wish. For giving us this Wallachia."

Lada felt something tender and sweet unfurling in her chest. It was a vulnerable feeling. A dangerous one. She cleared her throat. "Well. I guess I will have to find another maid."

Daciana laughed. "There is a boyar woman who has already hired me on as a wet nurse. It is amazing what they will pay for. But as soon as I am able, I will be back to fill your room with deadly curtains. You will help me, right, my little Lada?"

The endearment was very confusing. Stefan smiled up at her, nodding toward the baby. "We wanted to give her a name of strength."

Lada's face flushed. She had to clear her throat again. She leaned closer, trying to see the little bundle. "Is she pretty?"

Daciana held out the baby. Her face was red, squished and bruised from its violent entrance into the world. Dark hair sprouted from the top of her head, and one tiny fist was balled tightly and raised in the air. She was not pretty. But she screamed, and the sound was piercing and strong. "Do you want to hold her?"

"No!" Lada put her arms behind her back just in case Daciana and Stefan tried to force the baby on her. But Daciana seemed content to hold the baby herself. Lada tentatively smiled. "When she is old enough, I will give her a knife."

Daciana and Stefan both laughed, and though Lada had been serious, she laughed, too. But watching the tiny life, she promised herself she would do exactly that for this little girl and every other Wallachian under her rule.

She would make them strong.

45

May 28–29

THE LITURGY WAS PUNCTUATED by the ceaseless bombardment strikes. Radu wished they could have coordinated with Mehmed somehow, so that the distant sound and vibration of rock meeting stone could have matched up perfectly. As it was, the beats fell too soon or too late, a jarring mess guaranteeing no one could truly lose themselves to the worship service.

But that was never a possibility, anyway. Not tonight.

For the first time since Constantine had attempted to unite the churches, the Hagia Sophia was lit up. All their angry clinging to dogma and notions of religious purity had been abandoned, and they appealed to every icon, every relic, every link to God they had. If the Hagia Sophia could save them, they were finally ready to try it.

Outside the walls, the Ottoman camps were quiet. The bombardment had increased, everything they had left being flung at the city in anticipation of one final burst. Arrows came over the walls with scrawled warnings from sympathetic Christian soldiers:

The end is coming.

But they did not need the information written on arrows. It was already written in the massive stone cannonballs hitting the walls, in the day of rest and prayer Mehmed had given his men. One last assault, one last chance to defend or attack, to stand or fall, to live or die.

And so the people of the city came to church. The Hagia Sophia was packed, claustrophobic; people stood shoulder to shoulder. Radu breathed the same air as everyone around him. They exhaled terror and resignation, and he inhaled it until he could not catch his breath. He much preferred the Hagia Sophia dark, with the sound of birds fluttering near the roof. That had felt closer to worship than this.

Constantine stood at the front, looking upward as though he were already an icon himself. Nearby, Giustiniani stood, pale and sweating. He should have been sitting, but appearances were everything. He had been injured in the bombardment yesterday. The panic that spread through the city at the idea of losing him had been more dangerous than any cannon. And so Giustiniani stood when he should have been resting, prayed when he should have been sleeping, all so the people could see their emperor and their military commander and have some semblance of hope.

When the service ended, no one moved. Radu was desperate to get outside, to be away from all this. A hand tugged on his vest and he whirled around, ready to strike.

He looked down into the eyes of the little heir, Manuel. "Where is my cousin?" Manuel asked. Something in the way his lip trembled but his chin stayed firm stabbed Radu to the core. Manuel was expecting to hear that Cyprian was dead, and he was preparing himself not to cry over the news. Radu dropped into a crouch so he was face to face with the boy.

"Cyprian is resting at home. He was hit on the head with some rocks, but he will get better."

Manuel let out a breath of relief, grinning to reveal his first few lost teeth. "He promised to take me fishing when the siege is over."

"Well then, there you have it. He will heal quickly, because he would never break a promise like that."

Manuel nodded, quick to accept comfort. He slipped his tiny hand into Radu's hand, anchoring Radu with the weight of his innocence. John and their nurse soon joined them, the older boy solemn and ashen-faced. He nodded to Radu and Radu formally dipped his head.

"You will protect us," he said. Radu wanted to sink into the ground. John nodded again, and Radu realized the boy was reassuring himself. "The men and the walls will protect us."

Everyone turned, watching as Constantine, stately and regal, marched out of the church. As the door closed behind him, there was a whoosh of collectively held breaths released, along with wails and cries of despair. People scattered in every direction. Radu overheard snatches of plans to hide, places that might be safe, cisterns underground that no Turk would think to look in. At least they knew the limits of their faith.

Radu grabbed the nurse's arm as she tried to herd the boys away. "Stay here," he said.

She scowled in offense. "I am to take the boys back to the palace."

"If the walls are breached, the palace will be the first place the soldiers go looking for loot."

She lifted her nose defiantly in the air as though Radu's dour prediction were foul to smell. "Those filthy Turks cannot come past the columns. The angel of the Lord will descend from heaven and drive them away with a flaming sword."

Radu held back an exasperated huff, though it cost him dearly. Instead he smiled encouragingly. "Yes, of course. Which is why you should stay here. The Hagia Sophia is farther in the city than the angel will let the Turks get, so you will be safest here."

She frowned, weighing his words.

"And it will do the boys good to pray more."

No Byzantine nurse could resist the lure of forcing her charges to pray. She took both boys' hands and marched back into the center of the Hagia Sophia. Radu wished he could do more. But he knew Mehmed would want the Hagia Sophia intact, and would send soldiers to protect it if and when they breached the walls. It was safer than anywhere else in the city.

He walked out the doors, breathing the evening air with relief. Another little hand tugged on his shirt. He glanced down to see Amal. Taking a coin—his last—he placed it in the boy's palm. "Tell him to look to the gates at the palace wall. I will—"

"Where is my nephew?"

Radu whirled around. Constantine stared wearily back at him. Radu stammered in surprise and guilt. "He—he—he is resting. I think he will recover, but he is not fit to fight." He glanced to the side. Amal was gone.

Constantine nodded, something like relief in his eyes. "Take his place at my side, then."

Radu was swept along with Constantine's party. Stuck in the middle next to Giustiniani, he was unable to slip free. This was not where he wanted to be tonight. He had planned to position himself at the Circus Gate—a small gate opening into Blachernae Palace. He *needed* to be there. But there was nothing he could do to get away without looking suspicious. Constantine led them through the city, past the inner wall, and to the masses of soldiers clustered in front of the Lycus River section of the wall. It was here and at the Blachernae Palace section that their final stand would be made. The palace was visible in the distance. Nazira was there, as planned, and he was stuck here.

Constantine climbed onto a pile of rubble, looking out in the twilight over the heads of his men. "Do not fear the evil Turks!" His booming voice was punctuated by a distant impact. "Our superior armor will protect us. Our superior fighting will protect us. Our God will protect us! Their evil sultan started the war by breaking a treaty. He built a fortress on the Bosporus, on *our* land, all while pretending at peace. He looked on us with envy, lusting after the city of Constantine the Great, your homeland, the true homeland of all Christians and the protection of all Greeks! He has seen the glory of our God and wants it for himself. Will we let him take our city?"

The men shouted no angrily.

"Will we let the call to prayer corrupt the air good Christians have breathed for more than a thousand years?"

Another roar, even louder.

"Will we let them rape our women, murder our children

and elders, and profane the sacred temples of God by turning them into stables for their horses?"

This time the roar of anger was accompanied by the slamming of spear butts into the ground and the pounding of fists on shields. Radu could not point out that it had been a *Christian* crusade two hundred years before that had been guilty of all the above.

Constantine continued on. "Today is your day of triumph. If you shed even one drop of blood, you will prepare for yourself a martyr's crown and immortal glory!" He raised a fist in the air. "With God's help we will gain the victory! We will slaughter the infidels! We will bear the standard of Christ and earn our eternal rewards!"

The sound of the cheering and screaming was almost enough to drown out the bombardment. Constantine held his arms in the air, then lowered them and turned. His face was haggard and drawn, losing light as quickly as the day turned to night around them. "We lock the gates back into the city," he said quietly to Giustiniani. "We stand or fall where we are. No one gets out. If the wall falls, we all die together."

Giustiniani nodded grimly.

Radu watched the two men with a disconnected sense of farewell. In his time here, he had seen them be truly great, holding together a city against impossible odds. And he had seen them commit atrocities while doing it. He respected them, and he hated them, and he knew the world would be lesser for their deaths.

If they died.

He both hoped for and dreaded that outcome, impossible

to reconcile, just like everything else in this accursed city. He took a place on the wall next to Giustiniani. Although it was night, the Ottomans had lit so many fires the light bounced off the low clouds, creating an ominous orange haze everywhere. The defenders could not repair the walls, because there was no cover of darkness.

From his vantage point Radu could see the mustering area for the Ottoman troops. Somewhere nearby, Mehmed waited to find out whether his grand design would succeed or fail, whether he would fill the prophecies of generations. Maybe if Radu were out there with Mehmed, this would have all been exciting. It made him ill to think of it, to imagine who he could have been. How easily he could have wanted the end of this city and everyone in it.

It also filled him with longing, knowing it could have been simple. But he released that thought to the night, too, along with everything else. He would die on the wall tonight, between his brothers and his enemies, because he could no longer distinguish between the two. They had finally come to the end. Whichever side won, neither would triumph.

A stone cannonball slammed into the wall beneath Radu and Giustiniani. They fell to their knees, the impact jarring Radu from his toes to his teeth. He shook his head, trying to clear the strange ringing noise in his ears.

No. Not ringing. Screaming. He looked up past the defensive barrels to see a shouting horde rushing toward them. There was no order or sense to the approach. They ran like a swarm of locusts, over each other, pushing and shoving, each trying to get there first.

Those that did were cut down. But it did not matter. The ones behind them climbed over the bodies. When they, too, were killed by arrows, their bodies added to the pile. Radu shot into the melee, watching in disgusted horror as the irregular forces of Mehmed's army used the corpses—and sometimes the living injured—as steps. They clawed over each other, death itself a tool to crest the wall.

There were so many men that Radu could not help but hit someone with every arrow he fired. It was as effective as shooting at waves of the sea. The men never stopped coming. Giustiniani directed his own forces, anticipating whenever a group of irregulars would breach the wall. "There!" he shouted, pointing toward a stretch not far from Radu. Radu ran toward it, watching as the first few soldiers clawed and tumbled their way on top.

There were not enough men behind Radu. He had gotten there too fast. He hacked and slashed and blocked, but there was no hope. A man screaming in Wallachian barreled into him, tripping him. Radu fell flat on his back, looking up into the face of death. No matter where he went, his childhood followed. And now it would kill him.

Then the man was gone. Except for his torso, which fell across Radu's feet. Radu blinked away the dust and smoke. All the irregulars who had breached the wall had been cut down by one of their own cannonballs. Radu kicked the man's body away, laying his head back onto the wall and laughing.

Urbana and her cannons had saved his life after all.

He pushed himself up, rushing to Giustiniani. He was certain that he had been fated to die just then. But he was still here.

Which meant he could still accomplish something. This time, if an opportunity presented itself, he would not falter.

Much farther along the wall, Constantine threw a man over the side. He pointed and a spray of Greek fire lit up the night, burning the bodies of the living and the dead against the wall. The Greek fire moved up and down, consuming everything that wasn't stone. Men ran screaming, the attack's momentum gone.

"They are retreating!" Giustiniani roared. The men around Radu cheered, some crying and some praying. Between Constantine and Giustiniani, the city still stood a chance. Giustiniani clapped Radu on the shoulder. "You made it! I am glad." They ducked as a cannonball whistled overhead, falling somewhere in the space between the two walls. "Do you think we have them on the run?"

"They were intended to wear us down. Next he will send Janissaries." Mehmed would have saved his best men for last. And Radu knew without question that the next wave really would be the last. If numbers could not overwhelm the wall, only the Janissaries stood a chance. And if they could not win ... Mehmed was finished. He had nothing left to throw at them.

"We can hold. We will hold." Giustiniani favored his wounded leg as he limped toward a ladder. "Get something to drink and eat. You men, pick up the wounded. Take them to rest against the inner wall. We will shift positions to compensate, then—"

Everyone stopped as the music started. Radu watched as faces of weary happiness shifted into exhausted terror. They would have no break tonight. The metre music of the Janissaries crashed against the wall with as much force and intimidation as any bombardment. The white flaps of their caps glowed like skulls in the firelight as they rushed, screaming, toward the wall.

This was it. This last wave would overcome the wall and flood the city, or it would recede, taking Mehmed's chances with it.

Mehmed himself rode back and forth, just out of crossbow range. Radu could see him, would have known him anywhere. But his heart did not sing, did not yearn for him. So little land separated them, but that distance was soaked in blood and lit by flames.

Giustiniani shouted for Radu. "Cut the ropes! Throw down the hooks!"

Radu ran back and forth, hacking at ropes, dislodging hooks. Every man under Giustiniani followed his commands without hesitation or question. Radu could not see or hear Constantine, but he was certain that section of the wall was the same. Two men to hold back an empire.

Radu stopped, sitting with his back against a barrel and watching. All the men around him were Italians, Giustiniani's men. They were as good as the Janissaries, and they had the high ground. What could he do? Even if he stopped helping, stopped throwing down hooks and ropes, he would do nothing to turn the tide.

A man jumped over the wall next to Radu. Radu looked up at him in surprise, seeing Lazar's face under the Janissary cap.

No. Lazar was dead. Radu had killed him to save Mehmed. Radu pushed himself up, stabbing the Janissary and letting his body fall. But there were more. Janissaries leapt over this section of the wall, led by a giant of a man. He towered over everyone, the white of his cap gleaming above the mass of bodies. He held a broadsword. Unusual for an Ottoman, but fitting for his size. The man swung the sword from side to side, cutting down everyone who came at him with eerily silent efficiency. Protected by his fury, more and more Janissaries climbed onto the wall.

"With me!" Giustiniani slashed his way through to the giant. Radu followed in his wake, protecting his back. Not even Giustiniani could take the giant in hand-to-hand combat, though. As he got close, the man swung his sword. At the last moment, Giustiniani dropped to his knees. He swung his own sword with all the strength he had in him. The giant stopped, looking down in surprise. Then he slid to the ground, both his legs cut off at the knees.

The Janissaries around them stopped in shock. Giustiniani stood, raising his sword in triumph. And this time, when he knew what Lada would do, Radu did not hesitate. He swept his sword across the backs of Giustiniani's legs. Straight through the muscles and tendons. One swift cut to turn the tide.

Giustiniani fell. Radu caught him. "Giustiniani!" he shouted. "He is wounded! Help!"

The Italian's men rushed to them with all the energy they had left. The Janissaries remaining on the wall were quickly overwhelmed.

"What should we do?" one of the Italian soldiers asked, tears streaming down his face as he looked at the man he had followed in defense of a foreign city.

"We have to get him to the boats!" Radu stood, grasping Giustiniani under the arms.

"No," Giustiniani moaned, shaking his head. He was white

with shock and blood loss, eyes wild. "We cannot open the gate."

"We have to! To save him!" Radu nodded to the crying soldier, who carefully took Giustiniani's ruined legs. They maneuvered him down from the wall with the help of the rest of the Italians, passing him from one man to the other. Giustiniani groaned and cried out in pain, all the while telling them to stop.

They rushed across the open stretch, dodging arrows and cannonballs. All the Italians had followed, more than a hundred men this section of the wall could not afford to lose.

"The key!" Radu shouted. "Who has the key?"

"Giustiniani does!"

Radu heard shouting over everything else. On top of the wall, Constantine stood, gesturing. He was frantic, waving his hands and shaking his head. If that gate opened and men went through, it would be a mortal wound to the city. Too many would choose to flee if given the option. Men ran toward them to stop them, swords drawn.

"If they keep us here, Giustiniani will die!" Radu shouted.

The Italians, ever loyal to Giustiniani, drew their swords against the soldiers they had fought shoulder to shoulder with all these long weeks. Everyone stopped, waiting to see what would happen.

Radu reached into Giustiniani's blood-splattered vest and pulled out a heavy iron key. Giustiniani grabbed his hand. "Please," he said. His face was pale and bathed in sweat, but his eyes were lucid. "Do not do this."

Radu looked up at the wall. Constantine stood silhouetted

against the glowing night sky. His shoulders drooped. Then he took off his cloak, throwing it off the wall. His helmet, with a metal circlet on it, followed. He turned and joined the fight at the wall as one of the men he had lived with. As one of the men he would die with.

"It is the only thing I can do," Radu whispered. He tugged his hand free, then opened the gate. As soon as he was through, he ran toward Blachernae Palace. If any of Giustiniani's men noticed he did not stay with them, they were too busy saving themselves to stop him.

There were not many men left at the palace. Just a handful to guard the Circus Gate. And, in a stroke of luck or providence, they were all Italians. "Giustiniani has been wounded!" Radu shouted. "His only chance is to get to the boats! They need your help!"

The men stood still for a few seconds, then ran. The gate was his alone. Radu walked to it, his feet dragging. The bar across the door carried the weight of a thousand betrayals. He managed to lift it, and left the door open. He had chosen this one because it was the most poorly guarded, but it was not big enough to let a whole army in. He needed something more. If anyone could still claim victory in the midst of this, it was Constantine. Radu needed to break the defenders' spirits. If he did, the city would fall. He climbed back along the wall to the palace itself, where Nazira was waiting with a cloth-wrapped bundle.

She threw her arms around him, pressing her face into his shoulder. "I feared you were dead."

"Not yet." He pulled out the Ottoman flags they had stolen from Orhan's tower. They ran through the echoing palace, climbing and climbing until they reached the top. From there they heard the sounds of dying, the clash of metal, the screams of fury.

They tore down the emperor's flag, and in its place they hung the flag of the Ottoman Empire. Splitting up, they found every place they could hang a flag where the combatants would see it, finally meeting back on the wall above the gate that Radu had left open. He waved the last flag he had, before draping it over the wall above the way in.

He looked, then, at where Constantine stood between his city and destruction. Though it was too dark and Radu knew it was not possible, he felt as though they locked eyes one last time. A cry went up among the men; the desperate push at the gate to the city intensified. They thought the Ottomans were inside, and would abandon all to go save their families, or die alongside them.

Radu turned away. He had done his part. The pendulum had swung in Mehmed's favor and would never return to the defenders'. He had managed to kill Constantine after all. But too late to be merciful to any of them.

"What now?" Nazira whispered.

"Cyprian," Radu said.

They clasped hands and ran from the palace into the dark city, racing against the coming flood.

46

Mid-May

THE BODY OF LADA's brother Mircea rotted in a shallow grave a short ride from Tirgoviste. He had been heading for Snagov, the monastery island where their father had once taken them. He had not ridden fast or far enough to find sanctuary. Where he lay, the earth was nearly indistinguishable from that around it. Lada had only found his body because one of the soldiers who had run him down was now hers.

Ah, the loyalty of men.

She dismounted and kicked idly at the finally thawed ground. The morning mist had settled in the depression, softening everything. It was a beautiful morning, damp, with the slow promise of heat on the way. Petru and Bogdan stayed on their horses, scanning the field and distant trees for threats. Lada was prince now, which made her an even bigger target. But this was something she had felt she needed to do.

She could not share her victory with the brother she loved, so she would resolve the fate of the one she had hated.

Now that she was here, she did not know what she had

expected to accomplish. Rebury him? Bring his remains back to the castle? Say a prayer over his body, one that might as well be blasphemy for all the sincerity it held? She finally had to admit that she had seized on this adventure mainly as a way of escaping the city. Toma had been pestering her, wanting to talk about various Danesti boyars and their loyalties—how to gain them, why she needed them, what marriages might cement them. The other boyar lines were not thrilled with her ascension, but they would not object as long as they profited. The Danesti lines took it personally, though. Toma never passed up an opportunity to circle back to the subject of marriage with a Danesti, dangling the possibility in front of Lada with all the subtlety of a noose.

Finally she had told him she would meet with every Danesti boyar at the same time, and left him to plan it for her. She was certain his letter-writing skills far surpassed her own; he would know what to say to get the boyars to come. Her idea had been to tell them to come or forfeit their land and their lives. Toma had laughed like she had made a wonderful joke.

At least Mircea was dead, and she did not have to listen to him. That made him preferable to Toma. "How did he die?" she asked.

"He died well," the soldier said, voice tight as he stared straight ahead.

Lada snorted. "You are a liar. My brother was a bully and a coward. He would not have died well. He would have died fighting, or begging for his life. Which was it?"

The soldier shifted uncomfortably. "He died fighting."

"If he died fighting, why did you not say that to begin with?"

The soldier swallowed, saying nothing further.

"Dig him up."

The man finally met her eyes, horror shifting his dull expression into something childlike. "But—"

"Dig him up."

The man looked from the grave to Lada, then back again. "But we have no shovels, no tools."

Lada reached into her saddlebag and pulled out a hard loaf of bread. She broke off pieces and passed them to Bogdan and Petru. They dismounted and dragged an old stump over for Lada to sit on. She made herself comfortable. The soldier still stared dumbly. Lada pulled out a knife, setting it on the stump. "You have your hands. For now."

The man began digging.

The sun was directly overhead by the time he finished. His fingernails bled and he cradled his hands to his chest as he backed away from the body he had unearthed. Lada held her cloak over her nose. It would have been better had she taken the throne in the winter. It was warm enough now for her to smell him.

But that was not the troubling part. Her brother—Mircea the cruel, Mircea the hated, Mircea the dead—did not stare up at her with the accusing eyes of the dead. He did not stare up at all.

She was looking at the back of his head.

"Turn him over," she said.

Gagging, the soldier reached into the grave and maneuvered the corpse so it was faceup. Mircea's skin was waxy and thin where it had not been eaten away to the bone. His fingers, too, looked like the soldier's—nails broken and caked with dirt. Mircea's mouth was open in a scream, black with rot. Lada leaned closer. No—it was black with dirt, all the way down as far as she could see.

"You buried him alive," she said.

The soldier shook his head frantically. "I had nothing to do with it. It was Hunyadi's men and the Danesti prince."

"But you were there."

The man shook his head, then nodded, foolish tears of desperation leaking from his eyes. "But I did not kill him!"

Lada sighed, kicking the corpse of her brother back over so he could not see her. It was a terrible way to die. She imagined him twisting and turning, the weight of dirt suffocating him as he grew more and more disoriented. In the end, he had been clawing deeper into the earth, instead of toward the sun and freedom.

She wondered how her father had died. No one in Tirgoviste knew where he had been killed. Or, if they did, they were smart enough to say nothing. And she wondered about her own loyalty—and disloyalty—to Hunyadi, the man who had helped the Danesti boyars kill both her brother and father. The boyars whose support she was still courting. Guilt and regret warred with resigned exhaustion. She did not know how to feel about this. Why could she have no easy relationships? Why was there no man in her life she could feel only one way about?

"I did not kill him, I did not kill him," the soldier whispered, chant-like, as he rocked back and forth.

Lada *did* know how to feel about the soldier. She latched onto it with a startling ferocity. It offered her a lifeline, something solid and secure to react against. "I do not care if you killed him. He is dead. That problem is past us."

The soldier slumped in relief. "Thank you, my lady."

Lada sheathed her knife. "I am not your lady. I am your prince. And while the death of Mircea is not our problem, your lying to me is."

The soldier looked up, fear curling his lips to reveal his teeth, sticking out just like those in Mircea's agonized skull.

"Bogdan, a rope."

Bogdan took a rope out of his saddlebag. Lada tied it tightly around the soldier's wrists. She tossed the free end to Petru. He nodded grimly, then tied it to his saddle.

"What are you going to do to me?" the soldier asked through clattering teeth.

"We are taking you back to Tirgoviste as an example of what happens to those who do not honor the truth."

"What if he cannot keep up with the horses?" Petru asked.

Lada looked at the open grave of her brother, where his corpse once again faced the dirt that had claimed him. "That is what the rope is for."

She spurred her horse forward, going too fast for any man to run long enough to keep from being dragged to his death.

She did not look back.

47

May 29

Dawn came at last. Birds circled overhead, dark silhouettes against the sky, drawn by the carnage beneath. Soon they would descend.

Nazira and Radu ran as quickly as they could. The streets had filled with groups of citizens, clustered together and panicking. "Is it true?" a man shouted as they sprinted past. "Are they in the city?"

"Run!" Nazira screamed.

The man dropped to his knees and began praying instead. Behind them, they heard the sounds of conflict drawing closer. There were no Byzantine soldiers in the city—no one left to fight—but the Ottomans surging over the wall did not know that. They would come ready to fight in the streets, and when they realized there was no one left to bar their way ...

"We have to get Cyprian out," Radu said, gasping for air. "Valentin, too."

"How?"

The way to Galata would be closed. The Ottomans would

NOW I RISE

anticipate that. The bells on the seawall began clanging a warning. If the Ottoman soldiers in the galleys knew the city had been taken, they would be eager to join the pillaging. The seawalls were barely manned now, and with word spreading through the city that the walls had fallen, everyone would abandon their posts, leaving the sailors free to climb over. No one wanted to miss out on the looting. Nothing was off-limits—gold, jewelry, people. Anything that could be moved and sold would be.

But if the seawalls were not manned, and all the sailors rushed into the city—

"The horn," Radu said. "We make for the horn. There are still the Italian ships. We may even be able to steal one of the Ottoman galleys."

"Are you certain we will meet no resistance?" Nazira asked.

Radu could not be certain of anything. "It is our best chance."

"What about Mehmed? You could ride out to meet him."

They collapsed against Cyprian's door. His home was deep enough in the city that no sounds of fighting had reached it yet. "I will not leave you and Cyprian here, not for anything," Radu said. "I can come back when the three days of looting are over and everything has settled."

Nazira squeezed his hand; then they ran into the house. "Valentin!" Nazira shouted.

The boy rushed down the stairs, nearly falling. "We heard the bells. Cyprian is getting dressed to fight. I told him not to, but—"

Nazira handed Valentin his cloak. "The city is falling. We are running."

Radu looked up to see Cyprian standing at the top of the stairs. His injury had left him unable to get out of bed for more than a few minutes at a time without becoming dizzy. He was as pale and bleak as the dawn. "My uncle?"

Radu shook his head. "It is over. If we do not run now, we will not get out alive."

Cyprian closed his eyes, taking a deep breath. Then he nodded, resolve hardening all his features. "Where do we go?"

"The horn." Radu turned to leave, then paused. "Wait!" He sprinted up the stairs, throwing open the chest in the room he had shared with Nazira. At the bottom, carefully folded, were the clothes they had worn on their journey to Constantinople. Radu yanked his robes on over what he already wore, then hastily wrapped a turban around his hair. Better to look like friend than foe to the invading army.

Cyprian nodded. "Like the flags," he said. For a terrible moment Radu thought Cyprian knew what they had done at the palace. But then he remembered the flags on the boats to help them sneak past the Ottoman fleet.

"Yes. Speak in Turkish," Radu cautioned. "Valentin, you say nothing."

The four of them paused on the threshold of the house. They had been happy here, after a manner. As much happiness as could be found in the slow, agonizing death of a city falling around them. Then they ran. Cyprian was in the lead, taking them on a winding route around the edges of the city, skirting populated areas in favor of abandoned ones. They were nearly to a gate on the seawall when they came across the first group of Ottoman soldiers.

A clump of citizens had been caught in the alley, and the soldiers ran at them, screaming and brandishing swords. Half of the group had been cut down before the soldiers realized there was no resistance and stopped. Radu thought nothing could be more horrifying than watching unarmed people hewn down.

Until the soldiers began claiming them. One young woman, her clothes already torn, was being tugged between two men. "I had her first!" one shouted.

"She is mine! Find your own!"

"There will be plenty," their commander said, going through the bags of the dead. He did not even look at the girl as the soldiers pulled off what remained of her clothes, arguing over who could keep her and how much she would be worth. The girl stared at Radu, her eyes already blank and dead, though she still lived.

If Radu were truly good, if he were not a coward, if he valued all life the same, he would risk drawing the soldier's attention and kill her right now. But he had to save Nazira, and he had to save Cyprian. "Come on," Radu whispered. They slipped back the way they had come.

At a gate to the thin shore of the horn, two remaining Greek soldiers huddled, debating whether or not to open it. Cyprian stalked up without pausing. "They are already in the city," he said.

"We will drive them out!" A small soldier, barely past his youth, stood in Cyprian's way. "The angel will come! We must hold them off until then."

"Does he have the key?" Cyprian asked the lanky soldier next to the boy. He nodded. Cyprian punched the boy in the face, then pulled the key from his vest. "The city has fallen. Do what you see best."

Crying, the young soldier stumbled away. The lanky soldier slipped out the gate as soon as Cyprian unlocked it. They followed him onto a narrow stretch of rocky beach lining the seawall. No boats were docked here. The Venetian boats had not fled yet, but from the movement onboard, they would soon. And, just as Radu had predicted, several Ottoman galleys were drifting not far from shore, completely abandoned. Someone had dumped logs into the water, where they floated by the hundreds, bobbing gently on the waves.

No.

Not logs.

Radu watched as a man who had managed to swim as far as the Venetian ships attempted to climb up the side. A sailor on the deck reached down with a long pole, pushing him off into the water.

"Why? Why not help him?" Nazira whispered, her hands covering her mouth.

Cyprian leaned back against the wall, the hollows beneath his eyes nearly as gray as his irises. "They fear being swamped. There are too many people trying to get on the boats."

Valentin shook his head in disbelief. "All these people. They could have saved them."

Many of the bodies in the water had wounds no pole could cause, though. The Ottomans must have gotten here at the same time as those people who had figured out the horn was a means of escape. The delay to get Cyprian and Valentin had likely saved all their lives.

"What do we do?" Nazira asked, turning to Radu.

"Can you swim?"

"A little."

He looked at Cyprian, who nodded. Valentin nodded, too, eyeing the corpse-strewn water with resigned weariness that had no place on such a young face.

"The smallest galley. We can row it out until we catch the wind. Once we have that in our sails, we can slip down and away."

"And then?" Cyprian asked.

"And then we keep going."

The bells of the Hagia Sophia, deeper and older than any others in the city, began clanging. Radu bade the church a silent farewell. Valentin slipped his hand into Radu's.

And Radu remembered two young boys. Still in the church, where he had left them. *You will protect us,* John had said.

Radu looked at Nazira, and Valentin, and Cyprian, and he knew then that the scales would never be back in his favor. But he could do this one thing. He could die trying to save two boys who meant nothing to him. Who meant everything to him.

"I am staying," Radu said.

"What? No!" Nazira grabbed his free hand, tugging him toward the water. "We need to leave now."

"I have to go back."

Her full lips trembling, Nazira nodded. "Fine. We go back."

Radu kissed her hand, then held it out to Cyprian. "No woman is safe in the city. Not today, not for the next three days. I cannot let anything happen to you. I promised Fatima. You have to go home."

Nazira stamped her foot, tears streaming down her face. "We have to go home together."

"You cannot go back in." Cyprian stepped past Nazira. He ignored her hand and grabbed Radu's, the intensity of his gaze overwhelming. "You will die."

"I know where John and Manuel are. I can save them."

Cyprian looked as though he had been struck. He closed his eyes, then stepped even closer, pressing his forehead to Radu's. "Their fate is in God's hands now."

"It was never in God's hands."

"No, it was in my uncle's, damn him and his pride. *He* has killed them, not you. Not us. If you stay, Mehmed will find you, and he will kill you."

Radu's final punishment was announced by a new bell pealing nearby, harsh and unyielding. He would not be allowed any mercy for the things he had done. He could not escape, and he could not keep anything he hoped to. Radu shifted his face, resting his cheek against Cyprian's for the space of one eternally breaking heartbeat. "He will not kill me," Radu whispered. Then he pulled back, forcing himself to look Cyprian in the eyes. Those eyes that had caught his attention even when Mehmed was his whole world. Those eyes that had somehow become the foundation of a hope that maybe, someday, Radu could have love.

"He will not kill me," Radu repeated, waiting for Cyprian to understand. The foundation in Cyprian's eyes crumbled like the walls around them.

Cyprian stumbled back, shaking his head. "All this time," he whispered.

"Will you still keep her safe?" Radu asked.

Cyprian stared at the rocks beneath them, as mute and stunned as he had been when lightning nearly killed him. "You could have escaped," he finally whispered. "You did not have to tell me. I would have— We could have—we could have been happy. We could have?" he asked.

Radu knew what Cyprian was asking, and if he had not already lost all hope it would have ended him. "I do not deserve happiness." The bells of the Hagia Sophia rang out more insistently. "John and Manuel are running out of time. Will you still keep Nazira safe?"

A single tear ran down Cyprian's face. He did not look at Radu. But he nodded. "I will," he said.

This one good thing, then, Radu had managed to do. He had not broken all his promises. Nazira threw herself forward, hugging him fiercely. "You come back to us," she hissed in his ear.

"Be safe," he answered. Then, his heart breaking all the more for knowing that he could trust Cyprian even now, Radu fled back into the city.

———◆———

The street was slick beneath Radu's boots. He slipped, going down on his hands and knees. When he rose again, his hands were bloody. He had not felt them get cut, had not thought he had fallen hard. Then he realized that the blood was not a result of his fall, but rather the cause of it. The streets ran with it.

And so he, too, ran. He ran past soldiers throwing everything portable out of houses. He ran past women and children being dragged screaming from hiding places. He ran, and he ran, and he ran. He tried his best not to look, but he knew that what he saw that day would be seared in his memory.

Today, he saw the true cost of two men's immovable wills. He saw what happened when men were forced to fight each other for months on end. It was not merely sickness of the body that plagued sieges, but sickness of the soul that turned men into monsters.

Radu was nearly at the Hagia Sophia when he saw a boy thrown to the ground. A soldier flipped the boy onto his back, reaching down to undo his trousers. Radu slit the soldier's throat from behind.

He reached down and hauled the boy up, only to see the tearstained face of Amal. "Why are you back here?" Radu asked, shocked and despairing.

Amal shook his head, unable to answer. Radu dragged him along. That, with his turban, bloody clothes, and sword, were enough to make him blend in with all the other soldiers dragging people and things through the streets.

In the square outside the Hagia Sophia, soldiers not interested in immediately partaking of spoils secured their prizes. Beautiful children, girls and boys, were highly prized as slaves, as were young women. Anyone who looked wealthy was also carefully bound for future ransom. All around them were the bodies of those deemed too old or too sick to be of any worth.

Radu dragged Amal through the center of the fall of Byzantium, through the center of prophecy. Everything was profaned and ruined. There was nothing holy in this victory. God had truly left the city.

God was not here, but Radu was. And he still had a mission. His suspicion that Mehmed would send men ahead to protect the Hagia Sophia had proved correct. Several Janissaries stood in front of the church's barred door. But a growing mob of irregulars and other soldiers shouted and screamed for their right to three days' pillaging of everything. The guards and the bar would not last long. If Radu was not in the first wave of men inside, he did not want to think what would happen to two small, beautiful boys. There was the side door he had broken in through, but there were too many soldiers around to do anything unseen.

He shoved directly through the mob to the Janissary guards. One lowered his sword at him, but Radu brushed it impatiently aside. "Do you know what is in this building?" he asked.

The Janissary hesitated. "We are to leave it unspoiled. Mehmed does not want anything burned."

"All the wealthiest people in the city are hiding behind those doors. All the gold, the silver, the riches we were promised are behind those doors. We are not here to burn." He raised his voice to a shout. "We are here to grow rich on the fat of these unholy infidels!"

The mob behind him roared, pushing forward. The Janissaries, smart enough to know when they were going to lose, ran. Radu himself hacked through the bar, then pushed the doors open. The looters were greeted with screams and shrieks of despair. The mob fanned out, running to be the first to grab someone or something worthwhile. Radu scanned the faces, looking for the two he had come for. Amal stayed on his heels.

In the corner near the stairs leading up to the gallery, Radu saw the two boys. They stood in front of their nurse with straight backs. Radu ran, shoving several others out of the way to get there first.

"Please." The nurse pushed the two boys forward. "Spare me. These are the heirs! Constantine's heirs. I give them to you." The boys lifted their chins bravely.

A man nudged Radu. "They yours?" he asked, breathing heavily over Radu's shoulder.

"The boys are. You can do whatever you want with that woman." He reached out a hand to either boy, crouching down so he was eye level with them. Recognition dawned on their faces. Manuel burst into tears. John threw himself forward, looping his arms tightly around Radu's neck.

"Come on," Radu whispered. "We do not have much time. I know you are both very, very brave, but pretend you are scared and do not wish to go with me."

John released him and took Manuel's hand. Amal tentatively reached out and took John's other hand. Radu walked behind them, pushing them toward the stairs. "Why are we going up?" John whispered as they climbed past the gallery.

"There is no way out of the city now," Radu said. "I am going to hide you."

Fortunately no one had made it past the main floor. With so many people in the Hagia Sophia, the soldiers were busy grabbing as many of them as they could. Radu ushered the boys down the hall, then up the familiar ladders until they passed through a trapdoor and onto the roof.

Once they were on the roof, Radu jammed his sword into the trapdoor's hinges. It would not hold against any serious attempt to break through, but he doubted that men looking for the spoils of war would think to check the roof of a cathedral.

He led the boys away from the edge, where they could be seen from the street—and where they could see what was happening. John and Manuel, at least, had been spared those memories so far. Radu would keep it that way. They found a sheltered area and sat together. One heir huddled against each of Radu's sides, with Amal curled by his legs.

"Thank you for saving us," John said, trembling.

Radu looked up to heaven and closed his eyes, because he could not accept those thanks. He had not saved them. He had no way to get them out, no way to leave the city unnoticed. All he had done was delay the inevitable.

But unlike him, they were innocent. And so he would keep them safe for as long as he was breathing.

And he prayed that, somewhere out there, Cyprian would do the same for Nazira.

48

Late May

IN THE WEEKS AFTER her ascension, Lada spent as much time as possible outside. They were waiting for the end of May, when all the Danesti boyars had been invited to a feast. Anticipating it was a burden. Toma had taken over most of the planning, for which she was both grateful and annoyed. She knew she needed the boyars' permanent support if she was to keep her throne, but she did not know how to get it. If only she had Radu.

Radu.

She had received word that the siege against Constantinople was in progress. Where was he? Was he safe? Of all the things she held against Mehmed, jeopardizing Radu's safety was the greatest. If Radu was hurt, she would never forgive Mehmed. Radu was not an acceptable sacrifice, not for any city.

Though Lada herself had sacrificed her relationship with him to come here. Wallachia was different, though. Wallachia was hers. It was bigger and more important than any city. Besides, she had not put Radu directly in harm's way. Other than leaving him with a man he loved who would never love him back. Who would willingly send Radu into danger, never seeing that Radu would give up anything and everything for what Mehmed could never return.

If Radu had been harmed, she would avenge him. She would kill Mehmed. Thinking about that made her feel slightly better. She spent nearly as much time dreaming of killing Mehmed as she did of doing . . . other things to him.

But she needed Radu. She still did not know what to do with the boyars. There were some already in Tirgoviste. The ones who had supported her had come to pay their respects, but she suspected all the payments were forgeries, imitations of actual respect.

She often rode in the poorer parts of the city. Always she had men with her—the ones she knew, the ones she trusted. Bogdan and Nicolae. Petru. Stefan, if he could be found, and others of her old Janissaries when needed. She told herself it was because the Wallachian men who had joined her were not as well trained, but the truth was she still felt more at home among Janissaries than Wallachians. That preference filled her with gnawing guilt, but she reassured herself that it was because all her Janissaries had been Wallachian first. Just like her.

On this trip into the city, they stopped at a well to get a drink. Lada had noticed that none of the wells in the city had cups or ladles. Many of them did not even have buckets for drawing up water. Her bag clinked metallically at her side.

"Why is there no cup here?" Lada asked, projecting her voice.

A tiny girl, whose curiosity won out over others' wariness,

sidled closer. "No cups, Prince." She smiled shyly around the title, obviously delighted to address a girl that way. "People always take them."

Lada frowned. "You cannot even keep a cup here for the good of the people?"

The little girl shook her head. Lada knew all this. She had counted on it. Turning to the men with her, she continued talking, loud enough for the people lingering on the edges to hear. "Interview everyone. Discover any thieves. People cannot prosper if they cannot so much as get a drink without fearing theft."

"And when we find them?" Bogdan asked.

Lada jerked her head toward the castle. "Then they can go in the courtyard and join the soldier who represents dishonesty and the imposter prince who represents theft." There had been a steady parade of citizens come to gawk at the impaled bodies. Lada knew word of the prince's fate and the soldier's punishment had spread through all Tirgoviste. It had been the right thing to do.

She pushed the soldier's face from her mind. It mingled now with Mircea's rotting, dirt-covered face, staring at her in accusation.

She was doing the right thing.

"That seems a bit harsh," Nicolae said, his voice soft. He moved closer so no one could hear him. "These people are poor. They have nothing."

Lada raised an eyebrow. "They have me now. And they should know that things are changing." She reached into her bag, pulling out one of ten silver cups. The treasury at the castle was as sparse and depressing as everything else in this city. But she had no need for fine things. Out here they served a purpose.

They had attracted quite a crowd, people come to look at their new prince and whisper of her ascension and promises. Lada held the cup in the air. "This is from my treasury. My wealth is your wealth. I give you a cup for your well." The people gasped, murmurs of curiosity—and derision—rippling through them. Lada smiled. "This cup belongs to everyone. It is everyone's responsibility. I will not tolerate theft in my land, nor anyone who supports theft."

The grumbling grew louder. Lada held up a hand to silence it. "Theft cannot flourish in a country that cuts it out with swift and sharp vengeance. Thieves prosper among you because you allow it, which makes you complicit. I am tired of seeing Wallachia weak. We are better than that. Together, we are stronger than anything. We are stronger than any*one*."

There was more nodding than grumbling now. Lada smiled bigger. "This cup stays at this well." She handed it down to the little girl, who took it reverently. "It is everyone's responsibility to ensure it remains safe to serve your community." Lada's smile turned sharp and cold as steel. "I will come back to check on it. I expect it to be here the next time I want a drink."

There was no denying the threat in her words or her eyes. She saw it settle on the people. Some met it with fear. Some stood straighter, nodding, her own fierceness catching in their eyes.

As they rode away, Nicolae leaned close once more. "That was . . . dramatic."

Lada turned to him, exasperated. "Say what you mean, Nicolae."

"You know that cup will be stolen."

"No, it will not."

"What will you do if it is?"

"Make an example."

Nicolae scowled, his scar puckering where it separated his eyebrows. "You cannot fix a whole country in a few days, Lada. It will take time."

"Have you seen how long the average reign of a prince is? We have no time. I have to change things now."

"If you are so certain we have no time, why bother? Someone else will come and undo everything you have done."

Lada shook her head, tightening her grasp on the reins. She thought of Mehmed, all his careful planning. He had taken power and immediately made sure his empire was streamlined, efficient, and safe. He knew everything had to be settled at home before he could look outward.

Lada did not want to look outward. But she had to have safety and security here before she could hope to defend Wallachia—and her throne. If she could make the country stable for the common people, they would be hers. She did not understand the subtlety and machinations of the boyars. She *did* understand swift, assured justice. Her people would, too.

"Everything has to change now so that I *do* have time. We cannot go on as we always have. And the only way I know to shift our course is through severely fulfilled promises." She closed her eyes, remembering all her lessons at the hands of her early Ottoman tutors. The head gardener. The prisons. The corpses hung for everyone to see their crimes and learn from their punishments. If that was how her country would move toward prosperity, then so be it.

Mercy and patience were not options, not for her. The blood

of a few would water the land for the bounty of many. *Some lives are worth more than others,* she thought. *How many lives until the balance tips out of our favor?* Radu whispered back.

———

They found the castle's stores of wine. Nicolae presented them to her, with none of his usual good humor. "Should we sell it?" he asked. "Or keep them for when the boyars come?"

Lada stared at the barrels in front of her. It had taken them so long to get here, and now that they were, nothing felt the way it should. She was tired of being in control all the time, tired of worrying, tired of waiting. Tired of making hard decisions and wondering if they were the right ones.

"No," she said. She smiled at her friend. "We should get very, very drunk."

For the first time since they had arrived, Nicolae's smile was the same that had greeted her all those long years ago in a Janissary practice ring in Amasya. With Stefan, Petru, Bogdan, and a handful of Lada's other first Janissaries, they dragged the barrels up to one of the towers. It was the same tower from which Lada, with Radu at her side, had watched Hunyadi ride into the city. That day had heralded the end of her life as she knew it. This one, she hoped, would herald the beginning of her life as she demanded it to be.

Lada cleared her throat, holding a cup full of sour liquid. "I wanted to thank you. You rode with me. You stayed with me. And we won."

Nicolae cheered, raising his cup high, sloshing wine on Petru's arm. Petru laughed and licked it off, then hit Nicolae roughly so that even more wine spilled. Stefan almost smiled at her, which made Lada embarrassed at his effusiveness.

Bogdan gave her a heavy, meaningful stare. She raised her cup to cut it off, drinking deeply. She did not know if he knew how she really felt about him, but it was obvious what he felt was more. Longer. Deeper. Truer. That made her feel powerful, and she would not give it up.

The more they drank, the louder they got. Everyone traded stories, most about Lada and some outrageous thing she had done.

"Do you remember when we were outside Sighisoara, the goat I found?" Nicolae asked.

"Yes! That thing was so mean, and its milk was sour. But at least we had milk."

Nicolae tipped his head back, scar puckered and pulled tight as his cheeks shifted into a delighted smile. "I did not steal it like I told you I did. Well, not exactly like I told you. Though I suppose I did end up stealing it."

Lada knew he wanted her to demand he tell the real story. Normally she would have avoided asking just to tease him, but she was too warm and happy to pretend. "What really happened?"

"Do you remember the old farmer we ran into earlier that day? The one with the—"

"The long fingernails!" Lada finished, finally remembering. It took a lot to stand out in her memory of that time. But that particular man had had fingernails nearly as long again as his fingers. Each nail was twisted, yellowed, and cracked. He had offered to sell them food, but she could not stop looking at his nails and imagining what something they had touched would taste like. They had ridden on and camped nearby.

"Yes! I ran into him again as I was hunting. He had a goat with him that he had no need of."

"So he gave it to you?" Petru asked.

Nicolae shook his head, his smile growing even bigger. "He had no need of a goat, but he did have need . . . of a wife."

"No," Lada said, finally seeing where the story was going.

"Yes!" Nicolae doubled over with laughter. "I sold you to him! For a single goat! I told him I would take the goat back to camp and get you ready to be his bride!"

Lada shuddered, imagining being touched by those hands. "If I had known, I would have stabbed you."

"That is why I never told you. I think of him sometimes, staring forlornly out of his shack, still holding out hope that someday his bride will come."

"I cannot believe you sold me for a single goat."

Bogdan huffed indignantly. "Lada is worth all the goats in the world."

She knew he meant it sweetly, but she really would rather not be valued in terms of goats. "Next story," she said, throwing her empty cup at Nicolae. He ducked just in time, and it shattered against the stone tower.

Nicolae refilled Bogdan's cup. "What was she like as a child?"

"Smaller," Bogdan replied.

Lada laughed until her stomach hurt. "Tell them about the time Radu—" She stopped, cutting herself off. Because saying his name, bringing him into this space, made her realize that she would trade any of these men—her men, her friends—for Radu to be here with her.

Nicolae filled in the space her silence created, recounting the abuse she had hurled at the Janissaries in the woods to distract them from Hunyadi's forces. But soon they ran out of stories from the past year. When they had finally circled so far back in their history that the stories started taking place in the Ottoman Empire, everyone got quiet.

They had left it behind, but they still brought it with them everywhere. What they had learned. What they had done. What they had lost. Lada knew that was why she kept these men closest. Not because they were better trained, but because they had been hardened in the same fire she had. Only they understood the strange space of hating what a country made them, while being grateful for it at the same time.

Lada looked at the Radu-sized hole next to her. Then she looked up at the stars beginning to shine above them. "We are never going back to the Ottomans," she said.

"They will come for us," Bogdan said. "They always do."

Mehmed would not come. She had made it very clear what she would do if he did. But now, with the softening and dulling of the wine, she doubted her rash declaration. If he came to her, maybe she would not kill him. No one made her feel the way he did. He haunted her dreams. If he came to her, she would make him make her feel those things Bogdan could not manage.

And *then* she would kill him, if she still wanted to.

"Let them come," she said. "I will drink their blood and dance on their corpses."

Petru raised his cup. "I will drink to that!"

Nicolae was staring at the horizon, frowning. "Either I am far, far drunker than I thought I was, or something is wrong with the moon."

Lada was about to tell him to stop criticizing the poor moon, when she realized he was right. The moon had been almost full the night before. But tonight it rose as a slender crescent, barely there. The rest of the moon was washed darkest red.

"You see that, right?" Nicolae asked.

"It looks like blood," Petru whispered.

They sat on the tower and watched the moon in silence. Lada wondered what it meant, that the night she chose to herald the beginning of her new life was bathed in the light of a moon stained with blood.

49

May 29–June 12

Tʜᴀᴛ ᴇᴠᴇɴɪɴɢ, ᴡɪᴛʜ ᴛʜᴇ boys sleeping curled up around each other like puppies, Radu went to the edge of the roof and watched. He could tell from the activity in various neighborhoods that something was changing. Someone was coming.

Mehmed.

But Radu did not *know* the way he used to, when Mehmed had felt like a current running through his body pulling him swiftly in the right direction. He knew now because he saw the effects of the man rippling outward. Soldiers coming through, clearing the streets, dragging bodies to the side.

Finally, Radu could see him. Mehmed rode straight and proud through the city, his horse sidestepping occasionally around a remaining body. Perhaps Mehmed was not riding so straight-backed out of pride, but rather out of stiff revulsion. His triumphant entry into the city of his dreams was paved with bodies and decorated with death.

Mehmed picked his way slowly toward the Hagia Sophia,

and Radu wondered what to do. Go down and appeal to Mehmed's mercy? Wait and try to sneak the boys out of the city once things had calmed down? Find Cyprian and Nazira and live a fantasy life where they could all forget and forgive everything they had seen and done?

Sick and exhausted, Radu decided to sleep instead. He walked past the trapdoor—only to find his sword placed to the side. Horror clawing through his chest, he raced to where he had left the boys. Manuel and John were still there, sleeping.

Amal was gone.

Radu had not spoken with Amal, had not given him any instructions. But Radu had not been the one to send Amal into the city in the first place. Radu finally felt the tugging sensation of his connection to Mehmed return, and he walked slowly back to the edge of the roof.

Mehmed had entered the square. The soldiers there lifted their swords, cheering and yelling, praising God and Mehmed. Then a boy darted between them, running directly to Mehmed's horse. Mehmed's guards drew close, but Mehmed waved them off.

Amal pointed, and Mehmed looked up at Radu. Mehmed smiled, a look of relief and joy lighting his face. Once, Radu would have given anything to have Mehmed look at him that way. Now, Radu *had* given everything, only to find he was still empty. He sat on the edge of the roof, dangling his legs over the side. Doubtless Amal would have told Mehmed about the heirs, too. Radu could not hide them from Mehmed. He had saved them for nothing. They would meet the same fate as Mehmed's infant half brother, sacrificed for the security of the future.

Radu should do what he should have done to Constantine. He should get up and swiftly kill them as they slept.

Instead, he hung his head and wept.

———•———

Small fires burning throughout the city gave it a cheery glow as, sometime later, the trapdoor opened. Radu did not turn around when Mehmed sat next to him, shoulder to shoulder.

"I am glad you are here," Mehmed said.

Radu smiled bitterly. "That makes one of us."

"The flags in the palace—that was brilliant."

Radu imagined himself before his time in Constantinople, how that person would have exulted in this moment. How he would have been filled to the brim with joy and pride to be recognized by Mehmed, to be truly seen. To be the more valuable Dracul.

He could not answer.

Mehmed put a hand on Radu's shoulder. It felt cold. "You turned the tide. You saw exactly what was needed, and you did it. As you always have, my dearest, my truest friend."

Several men climbed onto the roof behind them, bringing lanterns that cast sharp shadows.

"Where are the heirs?" Mehmed asked, standing and offering Radu a hand.

Radu did not take it. "What will you do with them?"

"Get them off this roof, to start with. It is no place for children."

Radu looked up at Mehmed, raising an eyebrow. "And down there is?"

Uncertainty turned Mehmed's expression angry. "Where are they, Radu?"

Radu stood on his own, then crossed the roof to where the boys still slept. Mehmed gestured, and one of the men handed him a bag. He reached in and, to Radu's immediate relief, pulled out a loaf of bread and a leather canteen. Mehmed knelt in front of the boys, who were now sitting up, blinking against the lantern light.

"Hello." Mehmed's voice was gentle as he held out the food. He spoke Greek. "You must be very hungry and thirsty after being up here all day. That was clever and good of you to stay out of the way. You are very smart boys."

Manuel looked up, finding Radu, his eyebrows drawn tight in concern. John, too, searched Radu's face. Radu put everything he had left into giving the boys a smile of reassurance. He had no idea whether or not the smile was the most damning lie he had ever told.

John reached out and took the bread, then handed it to Manuel. "Thank you," he said.

Mehmed sat across from the boys, passing the canteen after taking a small drink himself. "John, is it? And Manuel?"

The boys nodded, still wary.

"I am so glad I have found you. I sent my friend Radu to keep you safe." Mehmed smiled up at Radu. Radu looked off into the night, unable to play along. "You see, our city is hurting. I need your help. I want to rebuild Constantinople, to make it into the city it was always meant to be. To honor its past and bring it into its glorious future. Will you help me do that?"

John and Manuel looked at each other; then John nodded.

Manuel followed his example, his head bobbing with enthusiasm. Mehmed clapped his hands. "Oh, thank you! I am so glad to have you on my side." He stood, holding out a hand to help them stand. Each boy took his hand in turn, smiling up at their new savior.

Radu knew precisely how they felt. He knew how much they must worship Mehmed now, for coming in the darkness and saving them from it. Radu had *been* them, many years before. He wished he could accept Mehmed's hand with the same warm relief again.

Mehmed gave the boys into the care of his guards, promising he would see them again when they had gotten some rest, safe and sound in a real bed. Radu went back to the edge of the roof. Already dawn was approaching. The hours here moved all wrong—some crawling by and lasting days, others slipping like water through his fingers.

Mehmed joined him again.

"Will they really be safe?" Radu asked.

"Why would you ask me that?" Mehmed replied, his tone troubled.

"That was not an answer."

"Of course they will be safe. I will make them part of my household. They will be given the finest tutors and raised to be part of my empire. This is my city now, and they are part of my city. I never wanted to destroy Constantinople, or anything in it."

"We cannot always get what we want."

Side by side but further from Mehmed than he had ever been, Radu watched as the sun rose on the broken city. He shifted to look at Mehmed. Rather than pride, a slow expression of despair crept across Mehmed's beloved features. What he had sought for so long as the jewel of his empire was finally laid out before him in all its crumbling, dying glory. Even without the looting, the city was devastated, and had been for generations.

Perhaps, looking out over it, Mehmed saw what the beginning of his legacy would eventually lead to. Whatever Mehmed did, whatever he built, the greatest city in the world was irrefutable evidence that all things died.

"I thought this would feel different," Mehmed said, melancholy shaping his words like a song. He leaned against Radu, finally giving him the contact he had craved for so long.

"So did I," Radu whispered.

After a single day of looting, rather than the traditional three, Mehmed declared an end. He kicked all the soldiers out of the city, banishing them to the camp to go over their spoils and leave what remained of the city unmolested. The camp itself swelled to accommodate the nearly forty thousand citizens taken captive to be ransomed or sold as slaves.

Most of the churches had been protected by the guards Mehmed sent in, and all the fires that had been set were already extinguished. Mehmed himself had killed a soldier found tearing up the marble tiles of the Hagia Sophia. Then he had brought in his own holy men, and the jewel of the Orthodox religion was gently and respectfully converted into a mosque.

Orhan had died fighting in his tower, as had all the men

who attempted to hold out. One other tower had fought so long and so determinedly, though, that Mehmed visited and granted the soldiers there safe passage out of the city.

Two communities within Constantinople survived without harm. One was a fortified city within the city that had negotiated its own terms of surrender; the other, the tiny Jewish sector. Mehmed met with the leaders there and asked them to write to their relatives in Spain and invite all the Jewish refugees to relocate and settle their own quarter of the city. He even offered to help them build new synagogues.

Once the soldiers were back at the camp, word was sent throughout the city that anyone who had not been captured had full amnesty. Whether driven out by hope or starvation or simply exhaustion, slowly the survivors appeared.

Mehmed vowed to build something better, and Radu knew that he would.

He simply could not shake the cost of what it had taken to get there.

In the days that followed, Radu wandered the streets in a daze, listening to Turkish in the place of Greek and finding he missed the latter. Over and over he returned to Cyprian's house, but he could never bring himself to go inside. It would not be the same. He would never see Cyprian again, and Cyprian certainly would never want to see him again. Not now, not after what he had done.

In a city filled with the dead, where tens of thousands now suffered horrible fates outside its walls, Radu knew it was horrendous to mourn the loss of his relationship with Cyprian. And yet he could not stop.

Kumal found him sitting outside the Hagia Sophia. His old friend ran up to him, embracing him and crying for joy. Then he looked around. "Where is my sister?"

Radu felt dead inside as he answered. "I do not know."

Kumal sat heavily next to Radu. "Is she . . . ?"

"I sent her from the city on a boat with a trusted friend. But whether they got out, and where they went if they did, I do not know." He had inquired after the boat and received no concrete word of its fate. His only hope was that once news traveled that Constantinople was open to Christian refugees and Ottoman citizens alike, Nazira would return.

"God will protect her." Kumal took Radu's hand and squeezed it. "We have fulfilled the words of the Prophet, peace be upon him. Her work in helping us will not be forgotten, nor go unrewarded by God."

"How can you say that? How can you be so sure of the rightness of this? Did you not see what it cost? Were you not at the same battles I was?"

Kumal's kind smile was sad. "I have faith because I must. At times like this, it is only through God that we can find comfort and meaning."

Radu shook his head. "I despair that my time here has cost me even that. I do not know how to live in a world where everyone is right and everyone is wrong. Constantine was a good man, and he was also a fool who threw away the lives of his people. I have loved Mehmed with everything I am since I was a child, and I have longed to enter this city triumphant with him. But now that we are here, I cannot look at him without hearing the cries of the dying, without seeing the blood on my hands.

Nazira and I—we ate and dreamed and walked and bled with these people. And now they are gone, and my people are here, but I do not know who I am anymore."

Kumal said nothing, but he held Radu close as Radu cried.

"Give yourself some time," Kumal whispered. "All will come right in the end. All these experiences will lead you to new ways to serve God on earth."

Radu did not see how that was possible. He loved Kumal for trying to comfort and guide him, but he was no longer a lost little boy in a strange new city. Now he was a lost man in a broken old city, and no amount of prayers and kindness could undo what had been done.

* * *

Two weeks after the city fell, Mehmed asked Radu to meet him in the palace. He had set up a temporary residence there, already beginning construction on what would be his grand palace. A home to rival all others, a refuge from the world.

Radu passed a woman in the hallway.

"Radu?"

He blinked, focusing on her. "Urbana? I thought you were dead!"

Half her face was shiny with new scars, but she smiled. "No. And I got the forges at Constantinople, after all. I won!"

Radu tried to meet her happiness, but it was too large a task for him. "I am glad for you."

"You are welcome to help me any time you want." She patted his arm, already distracted and doubtless planning her next cannon. Radu watched her walk away, glad she had survived.

Then he saw two other familiar faces. Aron and Andrei Danesti. "Radu," Andrei said. "I know you now."

Radu did not bother bowing or showing respect. He was too tired for pretense. "Yes."

"It is good to see you," Aron said. "Will you take a meal with us later?"

"Do you mean that, or do you want something from me?"

Aron's face and voice were soft. "Only the company of someone who speaks Wallachian and understands some of what we have been through these last months. And I want to apologize for our youth together. We were cruel. There is no excuse for that. It does my heart good, though, to see the man you have grown into. I would like to get to know you."

Radu thought he would like to know himself, too. He felt like a stranger in his own skin. Sighing, he nodded. "Send word when you want me to come."

Andrei nodded silently, and Aron clasped Radu's hand. Then there was no one between Radu and the room that held Mehmed.

"Ah, Radu!" Mehmed stood when Radu entered, embracing him. Radu noted that they were alone. No stool bearer, no guards.

"What can I do for you, my sultan?"

Mehmed drew back, frowning. "Your sultan? Is that all I am to you?"

Radu passed a hand over his eyes. "I do not know. Forgive me, Mehmed. I am tired, and I have been pretending for so long, I can no longer remember what I am supposed to be and whom I am supposed to be it for."

Mehmed took Radu's hand and led him to sit in his own chair. "Well, that is part of what we are doing today. I know who you are, and you need a new title to reflect it. How do you feel about Radu Pasha?" Mehmed grinned. He was making it official that Radu was someone important in the empire.

Before he could think better of it, Radu answered, "I thought I was known as Radu the Handsome."

In the shadow that passed over Mehmed's face and the way he immediately looked away, it was confirmed. Mehmed had known about the rumors. He had known, and he had said nothing to Radu.

"Is that why you sent me away? To kill the whispers about us?"

"No! I never sent you away. You were always close to me. Every day I looked at the city and trained my thoughts on you, wishing you well and worrying for you. I am so sorry that your time in the city was terrible. Soon it will be as a dream."

"It was not all terrible," Radu said. Something in the way Mehmed's expression shifted to deliberate casualness made his next question anything but innocent.

"The ambassador, you mean? He quite liked you. I could see it at Edirne."

Radu realized with a sickening lurch of his stomach that Mehmed was dancing around a question, trying to determine whether or not Radu cared for Cyprian in the same way. Which meant that Mehmed knew Radu had the feelings for men that he was supposed to have for women.

Which meant Mehmed could not possibly be unaware of the feelings Radu had nurtured for him all these years.

Shame welled up in him, but a new feeling came, too. Radu felt . . . used. If Mehmed had known all this time, but had never acknowledged it, not even to gently tell Radu it was impossible . . . Nazira had said Mehmed would never fail to pursue an advantage. And having a friend so deeply in love with him that the friend would do anything in his service was certainly useful to any leader.

But even now, as angry and hurt as he was, Radu could not look on Mehmed's face without love. He was still Mehmed, Radu's Mehmed, his oldest friend. And in spite of everything, Radu would not give him up. Radu had made his choice. He had chosen to save Mehmed at the expense of an entire city.

Mehmed smiled, and it was the sun. Nazira was right. Mehmed was both more and less than a man. He was the greatest leader of generations, he was brilliant, he was a man other men would follow to their deaths.

And because of that, just like Constantine, he was a man who would leave death in his wake as he built greatness around himself.

"I have a surprise for you," Mehmed said, his eyes dancing.

Radu had one last dark spike of hope that finally, finally he could have what he wanted. They were reunited. The city was Mehmed's, and Radu had given it to him. They both knew how Radu felt. Maybe if Radu could have Mehmed, he could forget everything it took to get there. The same way Mehmed could forget what it took to get Constantinople, now that he had it.

Radu leaned forward. Mehmed turned, clapping his hands together. A guard opened the door. "Bring him in!" Mehmed said, his tone and expression gleeful.

Halil Vizier entered the room, the hems of his robes betraying the trembling of his knees. He bowed deeply. "How can I serve you, my sultan?"

"Not merely sultan anymore. Caesar of Rome. Emperor. The Hand of God on Earth."

Halil bowed deeper. "All this and more is your right."

Mehmed winked at Radu, then began pacing in circles around Halil, prowling like a cat. "You asked how you can serve me. I have an idea. I would like a member of your family for my harem."

Halil straightened, swallowing so hard Radu heard it. Even now Radu could see the wheels turning in the man's head. He nodded eagerly. "I have two daughters, both lovely, and—"

"No," Mehmed said, holding up a hand. "Not *that* harem. The other one."

Halil turned pale. "I do not understand."

"Yes, you do. My other harem. The one you were so fond of telling people I had. The one that would ask for sons instead of daughters. I heard all about that harem. Didn't you, too, Radu?"

Radu had so long nurtured a hatred of the detestable man now visibly shaking in the middle of the room. He had devoted so much time to defeating him, had played a game in which Halil was the spider and Radu the valiant friend protecting Mehmed from the spider's web. But now, seeing Halil finally fall, Radu felt neither pleasure nor triumph.

"Halil Vizier," Mehmed said, not waiting for an answer from Radu, "you have worked against me from the beginning. I sentence you to death for your crimes. I will grant you this one kindness: you may choose whether your family dies before you, or whether they watch you die before dying themselves."

Halil hung his head, then lifted it, his eyes staring straight ahead. "Please kill them first so they have less time to be afraid."

Mehmed nodded in approval. "A noble choice." He gestured and the guards moved forward, taking Halil away. Mehmed watched until the door closed, and then he spun around, robes and cape flaring. "One more enemy defeated! Your reputation is restored, Radu Pasha!" He beamed with pride, waiting for Radu to thank him.

"No," Radu said.

"What do you mean?" Mehmed's eyebrows drew together. He looked at Radu as though looking upon a stranger. And perhaps he was. Radu was not the same person Mehmed had sent into the city.

"Do not kill his family. They should not be held account-able for his guilt." Radu knew Halil's second son, Salih. Had used him. Had taken advantage of Salih's attraction to him to get what he needed. He looked at the floor in deepest shame. He was no better than Mehmed in this matter.

"But if I kill Halil, his family will be against me."

"Send them away. Banish them. Strip them of their titles and forbid anyone in power to marry into that family. But if you do this for me, spare them."

"If that is what pleases you," Mehmed said, waving his hand with a puzzled expression. He spared their lives as easily as he had condemned them.

Radu bowed to hide his expression of sorrow. Sorrow for Halil's family. Sorrow for Constantine and Constantinople.

Sorrow for the person he had left behind when he crossed the wall for the first time. Sorrow for leaving Lada to pursue her own fate, while he stayed with someone who saw it as a gift to protect Radu's "reputation" against the truth of his actual affections.

Mehmed put his hand on Radu's head, like a benediction. Then with one finger under Radu's chin, Mehmed lifted Radu's face to look searchingly in his eyes.

"Do you still believe in me?" he asked, suddenly the boy at the fountain again. His brown eyes were warm and alive, the cold distance of the sultan gone.

"I do," Radu answered. "I always will." It was the truth. He knew Mehmed would build something truly amazing. He knew that Constantinople needed to fall for Mehmed to hold on to his empire. He knew that Mehmed was the greatest sultan his people had ever known. But, like his love for Mehmed, it was no longer simple.

Radu had seen what it took to be great, and he never again wanted to be part of something bigger than himself.

50

May 29

"LET ME HANDLE ANY talk of the prince," Toma Basarab said. He eyed Lada critically.

Lada had dressed for battle. Over her black tunic and trousers, she wore chain mail. It rippled down her body, the weight familiar and comforting. At her waist, she buckled the sword she had ripped free from the wall. On her wrists, she slid knives into her cuffs. *The daughter of Wallachia wants her knife back.*

She shuddered. She was not her father. She would not become him.

Her only concession to finery was a bloodred hat in the style of the courts. In the center of it, she pinned a glittering star, with a single feather sticking up from it. Her comet. Her omen. Her symbol.

Her country.

"Do you have a dress?" Toma asked.

She did not answer him, so he continued. "They will demand reparations, and of course we will make them. Every Danesti boyar will be at this meal. It may be overwhelming for you. I will handle everything."

"I do not need you to do that."

He smiled and set his dry, warm hand on hers. Lada pulled her hand away. "I have also had word from Matthias. He is very pleased with your success. The king of Hungary has taken ill, and Matthias has stepped in to make all decisions."

Lada felt a small stab of guilt. She had promised Ulrich that the boy would have a quick and painless death. Another promise broken.

"I am drafting our letter to the sultan right now. We feel it is best to continue in the vassalage—appraising Matthias of any developments or troop movements."

"Continue in our vassalage? I have no intentions of paying anything to Mehmed, or anyone else."

"Oh, that will not work. We already owe money to the throne of Hungary and several Transylvanian governors. They will expect to collect soon."

"Do *you* have debts to them?" Lada raised an eyebrow. "You keep saying 'we,' but I have no debts to those countries."

"I believe you burned a church and slaughtered sheep? If you want good relations with our neighbors, we must make amends. Just like tonight is for making amends to the Danesti families." Toma opened the door. "Come, they should be eating now. We cannot keep them waiting."

Toma insisted a show of wealth was as necessary as a show of strength, and so the food they served was finer than any Lada had swallowed since Edirne. Finer than any her starving people ate. She resented every mouthful she imagined going into the boyars' privileged bellies. The smells of roasted meat and sour wine assailed her as she walked into the room. Somehow Toma had managed to enter before her.

The massive table, lined with Danesti boyars, stretched from one end of the room to the other.

Lada had expected cold glares and hard looks as she threw her shoulders back and strode through the room behind Toma. Instead, she was met with a few curious, even amused glances. Most of the boyars did not stop eating or speaking to their neighbor.

She had dressed for battle and was met with indifference. Would she have to fight the battle to be seen her whole life?

The walk to the head of the table took an eternity. She wished she had not insisted she be alone for this. She wanted someone trusted by her side. Nicolae, with his incessant questions? Bogdan, with his dogged loyalty? Petru, or Stefan, or even Daciana?

She realized with a pang whom it was she missed. She wanted Radu on her right. And she wanted Mehmed on her left. They had made her feel strong, and smart, and seen. They had made her feel like a dragon. Without their belief in her, who was she?

She stood at the head of the table and waited. And waited. Nothing changed. No one ceased conversation, or bowed.

"Welcome," she said. Her voice was lost among the general buzz of activity. She cleared her throat and shouted it, the meaning of the word probably lost with her angry tone.

Finally, taking their time, the boyars' chatter quieted and then stopped. All eyes turned toward her. Eyebrows lifted. Corners of mouths turned up or down. Nowhere did she see the anticipated anger. Most of the boyars looked . . . bored.

She looked desperately to a side door, where Nicolae stood smartly at attention. He mouthed *Thank you for coming.*

"Thank you for coming," Lada blurted, then immediately

regretted it. She cleared her throat again, standing straighter. "We have much to discuss."

"I want compensation for the death of my cousin," a boyar near her said, his tone flat.

"I— We will get to that, but—"

"Yes, of course," Toma said. He sat next to the head of the table, on her right. "I think we can work out payments, and extra land as redress."

Lada froze, grasping for words. Why had he answered for her? Already they had put her on the defensive. This was not how it was supposed to go. How could they come in here, demanding compensation for the deaths of their relatives, while her own father and brother rotted because of their betrayal?

Toma smiled encouragingly, as though nudging her. "That is how you will answer for the deaths, right?"

Lada closed her eyes, then opened them, smoothing her expression to match Toma's tone. "I will answer the same way they will answer for my brother lying facedown in a grave outside the city. Or my father, who has no grave."

Toma cleared his throat, giving her a minute shake of his head and a small, disappointed frown. "This is all very bleak talk for the dinner table. We should speak of something else. How will you disperse your men?"

"You mean to clear the roads?" She had not had a chance to finalize her plans for making the roads safe for travel and commerce. Why was Toma pushing her to talk about those ideas now? "I had thought we would divide it by area, and—"

Toma held up a hand to cut her off. "No. You misunderstand. As prince, you are not allowed to have a standing military force. It is part of our treaties with Hungary and the Turks both. Matthias Corvinas specifically mentioned it in his most recent letter." He smiled patronizingly. "I know this is all very new, and you were so young when you left us. Of course you did not know, but your men far outnumber a traditional guard. You may keep . . ." He paused as though thinking, stroking his beard. "Oh, twenty? That should more than meet your needs. The rest we will divide among our estates. Since I already have a relationship with them, I volunteer to house the bulk of your forces."

Lada had more than three hundred men now. Good men. Men who had given up everything to follow her. "They are *my* men," she snapped. "I have made no promises to Hungary or to the Ottomans, but I have made promises to my men."

A dark-haired, rat-faced boyar near the middle of the table spoke up. "Promises you were never entitled to make. *Princes*," he said with a sneer that made it clear what he thought of a woman holding the title, "cannot defend themselves. It is not done. A prince is the servant of the people. It is the duty of the boyars to hold soldiers to be called upon in times of need. If we decide the need is urgent, we will organize our men."

Toma nodded, reaching out to pat Lada's hand. "You have been gone too long. A prince is a vassal, a figurehead. Any attempt to build an army or even so much as a tower to defend yourself is seen as an act of aggression. You have nothing to fear now, though. The boyars are your support."

"So your strength is my strength," Lada said, eyes half closing as she let the sea of faces in front of her blur. "That is comforting."

Some of the men and women laughed. Many went back

to their conversations. None of this had gone as she thought it would. She had expected opposition, challenges, arguments. Instead, they all seemed perfectly willing to accept her as their prince.

And then she realized why. They were happy to have her because they were happy with weakness. The more pliable the prince, the more power they had. And who could be more pliable than a simple girl, playing at the throne? No wonder Toma had supported her. He could not have designed a better avenue to power for himself than a female prince. If Lada died, the Danesti line would put their own back on the throne. And until then, they would do whatever they saw fit.

If she had Radu, if she had a way to manipulate them, then maybe she could manage all this. But they worked with weapons she had no training in. Despair washed over her.

Toma leaned forward conspiratorially. "You did very well. I will stay on as your advisor. No one expects you to understand everything."

All the change she saw sweeping the country in the shadow of her wings had been an illusion. These people ran everything, and nothing had changed for them.

"Which one will she marry?" a woman a few seats down asked.

The man sitting next to her snorted into his cup of wine. "Aron or Andrei, whichever one, what a pity for them. First they lose their father, and then they have to marry the ugliest murderess in existence."

"Still, it will be good to get the Draculesti line under control."

Lada stood. Her chair scraped back loudly. "Lada," someone said from the door nearest her. She turned to see Bogdan. Something was wrong. She could see it in his pale face and downturned mouth. She hurried to him.

"What is it?"

"Come with me."

No one called after her. She followed Bogdan down the hall and into the kitchen, where a large wooden table had been cleared of food. It was now laden with a body.

Petru's body.

Lada stumbled forward. His eyes were closed, his face still. His shirt had been pulled up to reveal a ragged hole of a wound that was no longer bleeding, because his heart no longer pumped. Bogdan turned him gently on his side. The origin of the wound was his back. Someone had stabbed him from behind.

"How did this happen?" Lada touched Petru's cheek; it was still warm. He had been with her since Amasya. She had watched him grow up, into himself, into a man. One of her men. One of her best.

"We found him behind the stables," Stefan said.

"Were there any witnesses?"

Bogdan's voice was grim. "Two Danesti family guards who were arguing with him earlier said they saw and heard nothing. They suggested perhaps he fell on his own sword. Backward."

Lada clenched her jaw. She stared at the body on the table until her vision blurred. Petru was *hers.* He represented her. And he had been stabbed in the back by men who represented the Danesti boyars. "Kill the guards. All of them, not just those two. Then bring my first men—those who have been with us since before we were free—into the dining hall."

Lada turned around. She walked back toward the room holding the Danesti boyars. Dining with boyars. Dealing with Hungary. Pleading with the Ottomans for aid. Had she become her father this quickly?

She slammed through the door, the noise drawing the attention of everyone who had not noticed her absence. "Someone's guards killed one of my men. I want to know who allowed it."

"Why?" Toma asked.

"Because an attack on my men is an attack on me, and I punish treason with death."

Toma grimaced a smile at the table, then leaned close. "I am certain it was a misunderstanding. Besides, you cannot ask for a noble life in exchange for a soldier's."

"I can do anything I want," Lada said.

Toma's expression became sharp. "Sit down," he commanded. "You are embarrassing me. We will talk about this later."

Lada did not sit. "How many princes have you served under?"

Toma narrowed his eyes even more. "I would have to count."

She leaned forward against the table, gesturing toward everyone. "I wish to know how many princes you have all served under."

"Four," the rat-faced boyar said with a shrug of his shoulders.

Many nodded. "Eight," another said. "Nine!" someone else countered.

A wizened old man near the back shouted out, "I have you all beat. Twenty-one princes have I seen in my lifetime!"

Everyone laughed. Lada laughed loudest and sharpest. She

kept laughing long after everyone else stopped, her laugh ringing alone through the room. She laughed until everyone stared at her, confused and pitying.

She stopped abruptly, the room echoing with the silence left in the wake of her laughter. "Princes come and go, but you all remain."

Toma nodded. "We are the constants. Wallachia depends on us."

"Yes, I have seen Wallachia. I have seen what your constant care has created." Lada thought of the fields empty of crops. The roads empty of commerce. The hollow eyes and the hollow stomachs. The boys missing from the fields, their corpses against the walls of Constantinople now. The lands eaten away by Transylvania and Hungary.

So many things missing, so many things lost. And always, ever, the boyars remained exactly as they were.

She, too, had been lost. Sold to another land, for what? For her father to be betrayed and murdered by the men and women in front of her now, eating her food. Patting her hand. Calculating how long this prince would best serve their needs until they found another.

The Danesti boyars were a poison that would be her eventual end. In the meantime, they would try to marry her into their families, and would siphon the life from *her* Wallachia. She had promised the people a better country. A stronger country. And now, finally, she understood how to create it. There were no compromises, no gentle pathways. She could not keep power the way anyone else had before her, because she was like no one else before her.

"Your mistake is in assuming that because I have been far away, I do not understand how things work." She reached over and plucked the knife from beside Toma's plate. "I *have* been far away. And because of that, I understand perfectly how things work. I have learned at the feet of our enemies. I have seen that sometimes the only way forward is to destroy everything that came before. I have learned that if what you are doing is not working, you try something else."

She stabbed the knife into the top of the table, embedding it in the wood. Then she looked up to see her men entering the room and lining the walls of the hallway. "Who killed my father and brother? And who is responsible for the death of my soldier Petru? I demand justice."

No one spoke.

"Very well. Lock the doors," she said, her voice cold.

A murmur arose among the boyars. They shifted in their seats, watching as each exit was closed and locked. Finally, they had the sense to look uncomfortable. Finally, they truly saw her.

Lada drew her sword, looking down the curve of it. She had thought it like a smile, before. Now she saw what it was: a scythe. Without a word she shifted and plunged it into the chest of Toma. The man who had used *we* to talk about their plans, when he meant himself and a foreign king. The man who had thought that through words and advice, he could take Lada's soldiers, Lada's power, Lada's *country* without ever fighting her. She watched his face as he died, committing it to memory.

A woman screamed. Several chairs clattered as people hastily stood. Lada pulled her sword from Toma's chest, then gestured to the table.

"Kill them all," she said.

Her men did not move, until Bogdan drew his sword and stepped forward, swiftly killing two boyars. Then the work of harvesting began in earnest.

Lada picked up a cloth napkin and used it to wipe the blood off the length of her sword. The screams were distracting, but she was used to distractions. *Hold hands with the devil until you are both over the bridge.*

Or kill the devil and burn the bridge so no one can get to you.

It took a few moments for her to notice the screaming had finally stopped. She looked up. Bodies littered the room. Men and women slumped over the table or lay in their blood on the floor where they had tried to escape. Her men had not even broken a sweat.

It was good that Radu was not here after all. She did not want him to see this. Maybe it would not have been necessary if he had been here. Maybe, together, they could have found another way.

But he had chosen Mehmed, and she had chosen this. She could not stop now. Lada sheathed her sword. "Take the bodies to the courtyard. Everyone needs to know a new Wallachia has been born tonight. After they have been displayed, we will give Petru the memorial he deserves."

"What about their families?" Bogdan asked.

"Kill any Danesti heirs. They have nothing to inherit now. I will give their titles and land to those who actually serve me."

"Lada." Nicolae grasped her elbow. His sword was still sheathed. "Do not do this."

"It is already done."

"But their children—"

"We cut out the corruption so we can grow. I am making Wallachia strong." She turned to face him, her eyes as hard as her blade. "Do you disagree with me? They killed my family. They would have killed me, too, when it suited them. And they wanted us to continue under the Ottomans. They would sell our children to the Turkish armies, just like you. Just like *Petru*. You know I am right."

Nicolae looked down, scar twisting. "I— Yes, I know. I wish we could have done it another way, but I think you are right. The Danesti boyars would never have supported a new Wallachia under you. But their children are innocent. You can afford to show mercy."

She remembered the choice Huma made to assassinate Mehmed's infant half brother to avoid future civil war. Kill a child, save an empire. It was terrible. Sometimes terrible things were necessary. But unlike Mehmed, who had his vicious mother, no one would make these choices for Lada. No one would save her from this. She had to be strong. "Mercy is the one thing I cannot afford. Not yet. When Wallachia is stable, when we have rebuilt, then yes. What we do now, we do so that someday mercy will be able to survive here."

"But the children." Nicolae's voice was as empty as a boyar's promise.

"You said you would follow me to the ends of the earth."

"God's wounds, Lada," he whispered, shaking his head. "Someday you will go further than I can follow." He let go of her arm, then grabbed Toma's body and dragged it from the room.

She had done what was necessary. She watched as each body was removed. She would mark their passing, and acknowledge their unwilling sacrifice. Because with each body they drew closer to her goal. She clutched her locket so tightly that her fingers ached.

She was a dragon. She was a prince. She was the only hope Wallachia had of ever prospering.

And she would do whatever it took to get there.

51

To Lada Dracul, Vaivode of Wallachia, Beloved Sister,

Constantinople has fallen. Mehmed is sultan, emperor, caesar of Rome, the new Alexander. He has united East and West in his new capital. As his vassal, I ask your presence to celebrate his victory and to negotiate new terms for Wallachia's taxes and Janissary contributions.

He wishes to see you, as do I. I think of you often, and wonder whether I chose right after all. Please come. Mehmed will offer you good terms, and I dearly wish to spend time with you. I have much to talk about with you.

Your visit is eagerly anticipated.

With all my love, and the official order of the sultan, emperor, and caesar of Rome,

Radu Pasha

52

To Radu, my brother,

I do not acknowledge your new title, nor Mehmed's. Tell the lying coward I send no congratulations. He sent none to me when I took my throne
in spite of him.

You did not choose right.

Tell Mehmed Wallachia is mine.

With all defiance,
Lada Dracul, Prince of Wallachia

DRAMATIS PERSONAE

Draculesti Family, Wallachian Nobility

Vlad Dracul: Deceased vaivode of Wallachia, father of Lada and Radu, father of Mircea, husband of Vasilissa

Vasilissa: Mother of Lada and Radu, princess of Moldavia

Mircea: Deceased oldest son of Vlad Dracul and his first, deceased wife

Lada: Daughter and second legitimate child of Vlad Dracul

Radu: Son and third legitimate child of Vlad Dracul

Vlad: Illegitimate son of Vlad Dracul with a mistress

Wallachian Court and Countryside Figures

Nurse: Oana, Mother of Bogdan, childhood caretaker of Lada and Radu

Bogdan: Son of the nurse, childhood best friend of Lada

Andrei: Boyar from rival Danesti family, son of the replacement prince

Aron: Brother of Andrei

Danesti family: Rival family for the Wallachian throne

Daciana: Peasant girl living under a Danesti boyar's rule

Toma Basarab: Boyar from Basarab family

Ottoman Court Figures

Murad: Deceased Ottoman sultan, father of Mehmed

Halima: One of Murad's wives, mother of murdered infant heir Ahmet

Mara Brankovic: One of Murad's wives, returned to Serbia

Huma: Deceased mother of Mehmed and concubine of Murad

Mehmed: The Ottoman sultan

Halil Vizier: Formerly Halil Pasha, an important advisor in the Ottoman courts whose loyalties are to Constantinople

Salih: The second son of Halil Vizier, formerly a friend of Radu

Kumal: Devout bey in Mehmed's inner circles, brother of Nazira, brother-in-law and friend to Radu

Nazira: Radu's wife in name only, Kumal's sister

Fatima: Nazira's maid in name only

Amal: A young servant who has aided Radu and Mehmed in the past

Suleiman: The admiral of the Ottoman navy

Timur: An Ottoman citizen working for Mehmed

Tohin: An Ottoman citizen expert in gunpowder, mother of Timur

Urbana of Transylvania: An expert in cannons and artillery

Lada Dracul's Inner Military Circle

Matei: An experienced former Janissary, one of Lada's oldest men

Nicolae: Lada's closest friend

Petru: Lada's youngest soldier from the Janissary troop

Stefan: Lada's best spy

The Hungarian Court

John Hunyadi: Hungary's most brilliant military commander, responsible for Vlad Dracul's and Mircea's deaths

Matthias: John Hunyadi's son, high up in court politics

Elizabeth: The mother of the young king, Ladislas Posthumous

Ladislas Posthumous: The ill young king

Ulrich: The king's regent, advisor, and protector

Constantinople Court Figures

Constantine: The emperor of Constantinople

John: The heir of Constantinople, nephew of Constantine

Manuel: John's brother, nephew of Constantine

Coco: An important naval captain

Cyprian: An ambassador for the court, bastard nephew of Constantine

Giustiniani: An Italian, Constantine's most important military advisor

Helen: A citizen of Constantinople, Coco's mistress and Nazira's friend

GLOSSARY

bey: A governor of an Ottoman province

boyars: Wallachian nobility

censer: A metal ball with slits or small holes into which one puts burning incense, then swings through the air on a chain; used during religious processions and worship

concubine: A woman who belongs to the sultan and is not a legal wife but could produce legal heirs

dracul: *Dragon,* also *devil,* as the terms were interchangeable

fosse: A ditch dug around the exterior of Constantinople's walls to prevent easy attack

Galata: A city-state across the Golden Horn from Constantinople, ostensibly neutral

galley: A warship of varying size, with sails and oars for maneuvering in battle

Golden Horn: The body of water surrounding one side of Constantinople, blocked off by a chain and nearly impossible to launch an attack from

Greek fire: A method of spraying compressed, liquid fire known only to the Greeks and highly effective in battles

Hagia Sophia: A cathedral built at the height of the Byzantine era, the jewel of the Christian world

harem: A group of women consisting of wives, concubines, and servants that belongs to the sultan

Hodegetria: A holy relic, said to have been painted by an apostle and used for religious protection in Constantinople

infidels: A term used for anyone who does not practice the religion of the speaker

irregulars: Soldiers in the Ottoman Empire who are not part of officially organized troops, often mercenaries or men looking for spoils

Janissary: A member of an elite force of military professionals, taken as boys from other countries, converted to Islam, educated, and trained to be loyal to the sultan

liturgy: Religious worship performed in Latin or Greek, depending on whether the church is Catholic or Orthodox

metre: Loud music performed by Janissary troops as they attack, extremely effective at demoralizing and disorienting enemy troops

Order of the Dragon: Order of Crusaders anointed by the pope

pasha: A noble in the Ottoman Empire, appointed by the sultan

pashazada: A son of a pasha

postern: A small gate designed to let troops in and out of Constantinople through the inner walls

regent: An advisor appointed to help rule on behalf of a king too young to be fully trusted

Rumeli Hisari: A fortress built on one side of the Bosporus Strait as companion to the Anadolu Hisari

spahi: A military commander in charge of local Ottoman soldiers called up during war

Transylvania: A small country bordering Wallachia and Hungary; includes the cities of Brasov and Sibiu

trebuchet: A medieval engine of war with a sling for hurling large stones

vaivode: Warlord prince of Wallachia

vassal state: A country allowed to retain rulership but subject to the Ottoman Empire, with taxes of both money and slaves for the army

vizier: A high-ranking official, usually advisor to the sultan

Wallachia: A vassal state of the Ottoman Empire, bordered by Transylvania, Hungary, and Moldavia

AUTHOR'S NOTE

Please see the author's note in *And I Darken* for more information on resources for further study on the fascinating lives of Vlad Tepes, Mehmed II, and Radu cel Frumos.

As a note in this book, I would like to personally apologize to the nation of Hungary and its incredible history. The Hunyadi family legacy is worthy of its own trilogy, but in the interest of not writing three-thousand-page-long books, I had to dramatically simplify and compress things to suit my narrative needs. In the end, these books are works of fiction. I try to incorporate as much history as respectfully as I can, and encourage anyone intrigued to further study this time period and region.

The characters in the series each interact with religion, and more specifically Islam, in various ways. I have nothing but respect for the rich history and beautiful legacy of that gospel of peace. Individual characters' opinions on the complexities of faith, both Islamic and Christian, do not reflect my own.

Spelling varies between languages and over time, as do place names. Any errors or inconsistencies are my own. Though the main characters speak a variety of languages, I made an editorial decision to present all common terms in English.

ACKNOWLEDGMENTS

First, in correction to an error of omission for *And I Darken:*
Thank you to Mihai Eminescu, the brilliant Romanian poet
who wrote " Trecut-au anii" (translated into English as "Years
Have Trailed Past"), a beautiful and deeply affecting poem that
ends with the line that inspired the titles for these books: "Behind me time gathers . . . and I darken!"

Thank you to Michelle Wolfson, my tireless agent. I
couldn't do this without you, plain and simple. Here is to many
more years of me sending you "I wrote a strange thing, please
figure out how to sell it" emails.

Thank you to Wendy Loggia, my brilliant editor, whose
guiding hand is on every page of these books. I'm so deeply
fortunate to have you shaping my words and my career.

Special thanks to Cassie McGinty, who somehow escaped
being thanked in book one, but who was a phenomenal publi-
cist and champion of the series. And thank you to the devastat-
ingly lovely Aisha Cloud, who called dibs on Lada and Radu's
publicity, much to my everlasting delight.

Thank you to Beverly Horowitz, Audrey Ingerson, the
First In Line team, the copy editors, the cover designers, the

marketing department, and everyone at Delacorte Press and Random House Children's Books. You are the absolute best team and absolute best house I could have asked for. I'm constantly amazed by your dedication, innovation, and intelligence.

Thank you to Penguin Random House worldwide, in particular Ruth Knowles and Harriet Venn, for getting our vicious Lada into the UK and Australia with such style. I'm so jealous she gets to hang out with you.

Thank you to my first and last critique partners (that sounds more ominous than it is), Stephanie Perkins for the save-me-please emergency reads and Natalie Whipple for the save-me-please emergency moral support. We all know I wouldn't be here without you.

Thank you as always to my incredible husband, Noah, without whom these books would have never existed, and without whom my life would suck. I'll never get over how lucky I am to have you. And to our three beautiful children, thank *me* for marrying your father and passing along such excellent genes. (But also thank you all for being the delightful center of my life.)

Finally, I always feared people wouldn't connect with my brutal, vicious Lada and my tender, clever Radu. I should never have doubted you. To everyone who embraced the Dracul siblings and these books: thank you, thank you, thank you. A girl could take over the world with you on her side.

ABOUT THE AUTHOR

KIERSTEN WHITE is the *New York Times* bestselling author of *And I Darken* and *Now I Rise*. She lives with her family near the ocean in San Diego, which, in spite of its perfection, spurs her to dream of faraway places and even further away times.

Visit her at kierstenwhite.com and follow @kierstenwhite on

THE ENGLISH PATIENT

PICADOR

THIRTY

Also by Michael Ondaatje

Coming Through Slaughter

The Collected Works of Billy the Kid

The Cinnamon Peeler

Running in the Family

In the Skin of a Lion

Handwriting

Anil's Ghost

MICHAEL ONDAATJE

THE ENGLISH PATIENT

PICADOR

First published 1992 by Bloomsbury Publishing Limited

First published in paperback 1993 by Picador

This edition published 2002 by Picador
an imprint of Pan Macmillan Ltd
Pan Macmillan, 20 New Wharf Road, London N1 9RR
Basingstoke and Oxford
Associated companies throughout the world
www.panmacmillan.com

ISBN 0 330 49191 1

Copyright © Michael Ondaatje 1992

The right of Michael Ondaatje to be identified as the
author of this work has been asserted by him in accordance
with the Copyright, Designs and Patents Act 1988.

Pages 326 and 327 constitute an extension of this copyright page.

3 5 7 9 8 6 4 2

A CIP catalogue record for this book is available from
the British Library.

Typeset by SX Composing DTP, Rayleigh, Essex
Printed and bound in Great Britain by
Mackays of Chatham plc, Chatham, Kent

In memory of
Skip and Mary Dickinson

For Quintin and Griffin

And for Louise Dennys,
with thanks

"Most of you, I am sure, remember the tragic circumstances of the death of Geoffrey Clifton at Gilf Kebir, followed later by the disappearance of his wife, Katharine Clifton, which took place during the 1939 desert expedition in search of Zerzura.

"I cannot begin this meeting tonight without referring very sympathetically to those tragic occurrences.

"The lecture this evening . . ."

From the minutes of the
Geographical Society meeting
of November 194-, London

Contents

I The Villa *1*

II In Near Ruins *27*

III Sometimes a Fire *71*

IV South Cairo 1930–1938 *141*

V Katharine *159*

VI A Buried Plane *171*

VII In Situ *193*

VIII The Holy Forest *219*

IX The Cave of Swimmers *243*

X August *281*

I

The Villa

SHE STANDS UP in the garden where she has been working and looks into the distance. She has sensed a shift in the weather. There is another gust of wind, a buckle of noise in the air, and the tall cypresses sway. She turns and moves uphill towards the house, climbing over a low wall, feeling the first drops of rain on her bare arms. She crosses the loggia and quickly enters the house.

In the kitchen she doesn't pause but goes through it and climbs the stairs which are in darkness and then continues along the long hall, at the end of which is a wedge of light from an open door.

She turns into the room which is another garden – this one made up of trees and bowers painted over its walls and ceiling. The man lies on the bed, his body exposed to the breeze, and he turns his head slowly towards her as she enters.

Every four days she washes his black body, beginning at the destroyed feet. She wets a washcloth and holding it above his ankles squeezes the water onto him, looking up as he murmurs, seeing his smile. Above the shins the burns are worst. Beyond purple. Bone.

She has nursed him for months and she knows the body well, the penis sleeping like a sea horse, the thin tight hips. Hipbones of Christ, she thinks. He is her despairing saint. He lies flat on his back, no pillow, looking up at the foliage painted onto the ceiling, its canopy of branches, and above that, blue sky.

She pours calamine in stripes across his chest where he is less burned, where she can touch him. She loves the hollow below the lowest rib, its cliff of skin. Reaching his shoulders she blows cool air onto his neck, and he mutters.

What? she asks, coming out of her concentration.

He turns his dark face with its grey eyes towards her. She puts her hand into her pocket. She unskins the plum with her teeth, withdraws the stone and passes the flesh of the fruit into his mouth.

He whispers again, dragging the listening heart of the young nurse beside him to wherever his mind is, into that well of memory he kept plunging into during those months before he died.

There are stories the man recites quietly into the room which slip from level to level like a hawk. He wakes in the painted arbour that surrounds him with its spilling flowers, arms of great trees. He remembers picnics, a woman who kissed parts of his body that now are burned into the colour of aubergine.

I have spent weeks in the desert, forgetting to look at the moon, he says, as a married man may spend days never looking into the face of his wife. These are not sins of omission but signs of preoccupation.

4

His eyes lock on to the young woman's face. If she moves her head, his stare will travel alongside her into the wall. She leans forward. How were you burned?

It is late afternoon. His hands play with a piece of sheet, the back of his fingers caressing it.

I fell burning into the desert.

They found my body and made me a boat of sticks and dragged me across the desert. We were in the Sand Sea, now and then crossing dry riverbeds. Nomads, you see. Bedouin. I flew down and the sand itself caught fire. They saw me stand up naked out of it. The leather helmet on my head in flames. They strapped me into a cradle, a carcass boat, and feed thudded along as they ran with me. I had broken the spareness of the desert.

The Bedouin knew about fire. They knew about planes that since 1939 had been falling out of the sky. Some of their tools and utensils were made from the metal of crashed planes and tanks. It was the time of the war in heaven. They could recognize the drone of a wounded plane, they knew how to pick their way through such shipwrecks. A small bolt from a cockpit became jewellery. I was perhaps the first one to stand up alive out of a burning machine. A man whose head was on fire. They didn't know my name. I didn't know their tribe.

Who are you?

I don't know. You keep asking me.

You said you were English.

At night he is never tired enough to sleep. She reads to him from whatever book she is able to find in the library downstairs. The candle flickers over the page and over the young nurse's talking face, barely revealing at this hour the trees and vista that decorate the walls. He listens to her, swallowing her words like water.

If it is cold she moves carefully into the bed and lies beside him. She can place no weight upon him without giving him pain, not even her thin wrist.

Sometimes at two a.m. he is not yet asleep, his eyes open in the darkness.

He could smell the oasis before he saw it. The liquid in the air. The rustle of things. Palms and bridges. The banging of tin cans whose deep pitch revealed they were full of water.

They poured oil into large pieces of soft cloth and placed them on him. He was anointed.

He could sense the one silent man who always remained beside him, the flavour of his breath when he bent down to unwrap him every twenty-four hours at nightfall, to examine his skin in the dark.

Unclothed he was once again the man naked beside the blazing aircraft. They spread the layers of grey felt over him. What great nation had found him, he wondered. What country invented such soft dates to be chewed by the man beside him and then passed from that mouth into his. During this time with these people, he could not remember where he was from. He could have been, for all he knew, the enemy he had been fighting from the air.

Later, at the hospital in Pisa, he thought he saw beside him the face that had come each night and chewed and softened the dates and passed them down into his mouth.

There was no colour during those nights. No speech or song. The Bedouin silenced themselves when he was awake. He was on an altar of hammock and he imagined in his vanity hundreds of them around him and there may have been just two who had found him, plucked the antlered hat of fire from his head. Those two he knew only by the taste of saliva that entered him along with the date or by the sound of their feet running.

She would sit and read, the book under the waver of light. She would glance now and then down the hall of the village that had been a war hospital, where she had lived with the other nurses before they had all transferred out gradually, the war moving north, the war almost over.

This was the time in her life that she fell upon books as the only door out of her cell. They became half her world. She sat at the night table, hunched over, reading of the young boy in India who learned to memorize diverse jewels and objects on a tray, tossed from teacher to teacher – those who taught him dialect those who taught him memory those who taught him to escape the hypnotic.

The book lay on her lap. She realized that for more than five minutes she had been looking at the porousness of the paper, the crease at the corner of page 17 which someone had folded over as a mark. She brushed her hand over its skin. A scurry in her mind like a mouse in the ceiling, a moth on the night window. She looked down the hall, though there was no one else living there now, no one except the English patient and herself in the Villa San Girolamo. She had enough vegetables planted in the bombed-out orchard above the house for them to survive, a man coming now and then from the town with whom she would trade soap and sheets and whatever there was left in this war hospital for other essentials. Some beans, some meats. The man had left her two bottles of wine, and each night after she had lain with the Englishman and he was asleep, she would ceremoniously pour herself a small beaker and carry it back to the night table just outside the three-quarter-closed door and sip away further into whatever book she was reading.

So the books for the Englishman, as he listened intently or not, had gaps of plot like sections of a road washed out by storms, missing incidents as if locusts had consumed a section of tapestry, as if plaster loosened by the bombing had fallen away from a mural at night.

The villa that she and the Englishman inhabited now was much like that. Some rooms could not be entered because of rubble. One bomb crater allowed moon and rain into the library downstairs – where there was in one corner a permanently soaked armchair.

She was not concerned about the Englishman as far as the gaps in plot were concerned. She gave no summary of the missing chapters. She simply brought out the book and said "page ninety-six" or "page one hundred and eleven." That was the only locator. She lifted both of his hands to her face and smelled them – the odour of sickness still in them.

Your hands are getting rough, he said.

The weeds and thistles and digging.

Be careful. I warned you about the dangers.

I know.

Then she began to read.

Her father had taught her about hands. About a dog's paws. Whenever her father was alone with a dog in a house he would lean over and smell the skin at the base of its paw. This, he would say, as if coming away from a brandy snifter, is the greatest smell in the world! A bouquet! Great rumours of travel! She would pretend disgust, but the dog's paw *was*

8

a wonder: the smell of it never suggested dirt. It's a cathedral! her father had said, so-and-so's garden, that field of grasses, a walk through cyclamen – a concentration of hints of all the paths the animal had taken during the day.

A scurry in the ceiling like a mouse, and she looked up from the book again.

They unwrapped the mask of herbs from his face. The day of the eclipse. They were waiting for it. Where was he? What civilization was this that understood the predictions of weather and light? El Ahmar or El Abyadd, for they must be one of the northwest desert tribes. Those who could catch a man out of the sky, who covered his face with a mask of oasis reeds knitted together. He had now a bearing of grass. His favourite garden in the world had been the grass garden at Kew, the colours so delicate and various, like levels of ash on a hill.

He gazed onto the landscape under the eclipse. They had taught him by now to raise his arms and drag strength into his body from the universe, the way the desert pulled down planes. He was carried in a palanquin of felt and branch. He saw the moving veins of flamingos across his sight in the half-darkness of the covered sun.

Always there were ointments, or darkness, against his skin. One night he heard what seemed to be wind chimes high in the air, and after a while it stopped and he fell asleep with a hunger for it, that noise like the slowed-down sound from the throat of a bird, perhaps flamingo, or a desert fox, which one of the men kept in a sewn-half-closed pocket in his burnoose.

9

The next day he heard snatches of the glassy sound as he lay once more covered in cloth. A noise out of the darkness. At twilight the felt was unwrapped and he saw a man's head on a table moving towards him, then realized the man wore a giant yoke from which hung hundreds of small bottles on different lengths of string and wire. Moving as if part of a glass curtain, his body enveloped within that sphere.

The figure resembled most of all those drawings of archangels he had tried to copy as a schoolboy, never solving how one body could have space for the muscles of such wings. The man moved with a long, slow gait, so smoothly there was hardly a tilt in the bottles. A wave of glass, an archangel, all the ointments within the bottles warmed from the sun, so when they were rubbed on to skin they seemed to have been heated especially for a wound. Behind him was translated light – blues and other colours shivering in the haze and sand. The faint glass noise and the diverse colours and the regal walk and his face like a lean dark gun.

Up close the glass was rough and sandblasted, glass that had lost its civilisation. Each bottle had a minute cork the man plucked out with his teeth and kept in his lips while mixing one bottle's contents with another's, a second cork also in his teeth. He stood over the supine burned body with his wings, sank two sticks deep into the sand and then moved away free of the six-foot yoke, which balanced now within the crutches of the two sticks. He stepped out from under his shop. He sank to his knees and came towards the burned pilot and put his cold hands on his neck and held him there.

He was known to everyone along the camel route from the Sudan north to Giza, the Forty Days Road. He met the caravans, traded spice and liquid, and moved between oases and water camps. He walked through sandstorms with this coat of bottles, his ears plugged with two other small corks so he seemed a vessel to himself, this merchant doctor, this king of oils and perfumes and panaceas, this baptist. He would enter a camp and set up the curtains of bottles in front of whoever was sick.

He crouched by the burned man. He made a skin cup with the soles of his feet and leaned back to pluck, without even looking, certain bottles. With the uncorking of each tiny bottle the perfumes fell out. There was an odour of the sea. The smell of rust. Indigo. Ink. River-mud arrow-wood formaldehyde paraffin ether. The tide of airs chaotic. There were screams of camels in the distance as they picked up the scents. He began to rub green-black paste on to the rib cage. It was ground peacock bone, bartered for in a medina to the west or the south – the most potent healer of the skin.

Between the kitchen and the destroyed chapel a door led into an oval-shaped library. The space inside seemed safe except for a large hole at portrait level in the far wall, caused by mortar-shell attack on the village two months earlier. The rest of the room had adapted itself to this wound, accepting the habits of weather, evening stars, the sound of birds. There was a sofa, a piano covered in a grey sheet, the head of a stuffed bear and high walls of books. The shelves nearest the torn wall bowed with the rain, which had doubled the weight of the books. Lightning came into the room too, again and again, falling across the covered piano and carpet.

At the far end were French doors that were boarded up. If they had been open she could have walked from the library to the loggia, then down thirty-six penitent steps past the chapel towards what had been an ancient meadow, scarred now by phosphorus bombs and explosions. The German army had mined many of the houses they retreated from, so most rooms not needed, like this one, had been sealed for safety, the doors hammered into their frames.

She knew these dangers when she slid into the room, walking into its afternoon darkness. She stood conscious suddenly of her weight on the wooden floor, thinking it was probably enough to trigger whatever mechanism was there. Her feet in dust. The only light poured through the jagged mortar circle that looked onto the sky.

With a crack of separation, as if it were being dismantled from one single unit, she pulled out *The Last of the Mohicans* and even in this half-light was cheered by the aquamarine sky and lake on the cover illustration, the Indian in the foreground. And then, as if there were someone in the room who was not to be disturbed, she walked backwards, stepping on her own footprints, for safety, but also as part of a private game, so it would seem from the steps that she had entered the room and then the corporeal body had disappeared. She closed the door and replaced the seal of warning.

She sat in the window alcove in the English patient's room, the painted walls on one side of her, the valley on the other. She opened the book. The pages were joined together in a stiff wave. She felt like Crusoe finding a drowned book that had washed up and dried itself on the shore. *A Narrative of 1757.* Illustrated by N. C. Wyeth. As in all of the best books, there was the important page with the list of illustrations, a line of text for each of them.

She entered the story knowing she would emerge from it feeling she had been immersed in the lives of others, in plots that stretched back twenty years, her body full of sentences and moments, as if awaking from sleep with a heaviness caused by unremembered dreams.

Their Italian hill town, sentinel to the northwest route, had been besieged for more than a month, the barrage focusing upon the two villas and the monastery surrounded by apple and plum orchards. There was the Villa Medici, where the generals lived. Just above it the Villa San Girolamo, previously a nunnery, whose castlelike battlements had made it the last stronghold of the German army. It had housed a hundred troops. As the hill town began to be torn apart like a battleship at sea, by fire shells, the troops moved from the barrack tents in the orchard into the now crowded bedrooms of the old nunnery. Sections of the chapel were blown up. Parts of the top storey of the villa crumbled under explosions. When the Allies finally took over the building and made it a hospital, the steps leading to the third level were sealed off, though a section of chimney and roof survived.

She and the Englishman had insisted on remaining behind when the other nurses and patients moved to a safer location in the south. During this time they were very cold, without electricity. Some rooms faced on to the valley with no walls at all. She would open a door and see just a sodden bed huddled against a corner, covered with leaves. Doors opened into landscape. Some rooms had become an open aviary.

The staircase had lost its lower steps during the fire that was set before the soldiers left. She had gone into the library, removed twenty books and nailed them to the floor and then on to each other, in this way rebuilding the two lowest steps. Most of the chairs had been used for fires. The armchair in the library was left there because it was always wet, drenched by evening storms that came in through the mortar hole. Whatever was wet escaped burning during that April of 1945.

There were few beds left. She herself preferred to be nomadic in the house with her pallet or hammock, sleeping sometimes in the English patient's room, sometimes in the hall, depending on temperature or wind or light. In the morning she rolled up her mattress and tied it into a wheel with string. Now it was warmer and she was opening more rooms, airing the dark reaches, letting sunlight dry all the dampness. Some nights she opened doors and slept in rooms that had walls missing. She lay on the pallet on the very edge of the room, facing the drifting landscape of stars, moving clouds, wakened by the growl of thunder and lightning. She was twenty years old and mad and unconcerned with safety during this time, having no qualms about the dangers of the possibly mined library or the thunder that startled her in the night. She was restless after the cold months, when she had been limited to dark, protected spaces. She entered rooms that had been soiled by soldiers, rooms whose furniture had been burned within them. She cleared out leaves and shit and urine and charred tables. She was living like a vagrant, while elsewhere the English patient reposed in his bed like a king.

From outside, the place seemed devastated. An outdoor staircase disappeared in midair, its railing hanging off. Their life was foraging and tentative safety. They used only essential candlelight at night because of the brigands who annihilated everything they came across. They were protected by the simple fact that the villa seemed a ruin. But she felt safe here, half adult and half child. Coming out of what had happened to her during the war, she drew her own few rules to herself. She would not be ordered again or carry out duties for the greater good. She would care only for the burned patient. She would read to him and bathe him and give him his doses of morphine – her only communication was with him.

She worked in the garden and orchard. She carried the six-foot crucifix from the bombed chapel and used it to build a scarecrow above her seedbed, hanging empty sardine cans from it which clattered and clanked whenever the wind lifted. Within the village she would step from rubble to a candlelit alcove where there was her neatly packed suitcase, which held little besides some letters, a few rolled-up clothes, a metal box of medical supplies. She had cleared just small sections of the villa, and all this she could burn down if she wished.

She lights a match in the dark hall and moves it onto the wick of the candle. Light lifts itself on to her shoulders. She is on her knees. She puts her hands on her thighs and breathes in the smell of the sulphur. She imagines she also breathes in light.

She moves backwards a few feet and with a piece of white chalk draws a rectangle onto the wood floor. Then continues backwards, drawing more rectangles, so there is a pyramid of them, single then double then single, her left hand braced flat on the floor, her head down, serious. She moves farther and farther away from the light. Till she leans back onto her heels and sits crouching.

She drops the chalk into the pocket of her dress. She stands and pulls up the looseness of her skirt and ties it around her waist. She pulls from another pocket a piece of metal and flings it out in front of her so it falls just beyond the farthest square.

She leaps forward, her legs smashing down, her shadow behind her curling into the depth of the hall. She is very quick, her tennis shoes skidding on the numbers she has drawn into each rectangle, one foot landing, then two feet, then one again, until she reaches the last square.

She bends down and picks up the piece of metal, pauses

in that position, motionless, her skirt still tucked up above her thighs, hands hanging down loose, breathing hard. She takes a gulp of air and blows out the candle.

Now she is in darkness. Just a smell of smoke.

She leaps up and in midair turns so she lands facing the other way, then skips forward even wilder now down the black hall, still landing on squares she knows are there, her tennis shoes banging and slamming onto the dark floor – so the sound echoes out into the far reaches of the deserted Italian villa, out towards the moon and the scar of a ravine that half circles the building.

Sometimes at night the burned man hears a faint shudder in the building. He turns up his hearing aid to draw in a banging noise he still cannot interpret or place.

She picks up the notebook that lies on the small table beside his bed. It is the book he brought with him through the fire – a copy of *The Histories* by Herodotus that he has added to, cutting and gluing in pages from other books or writing in his own observations – so they all are cradled within the text of Herodotus.

She begins to read his small gnarled handwriting.

There is a whirlwind in southern Morocco, the *aajej*, against which the fellahin defend themselves with knives. There is the *africo*, which has at times reached into the city of Rome. The *alm*, a fall wind out of Yugoslavia. The *arifi*, also christened *aref* or *rifi*, which scorches with numerous tongues. These are permanent winds that live in the present tense.

There are other, less constant winds that change direction, that can knock down horse and rider and realign themselves anticlockwise. The *bist roz* leaps into Afghanistan for 170 days – burying villages. There is the hot, dry *ghibli* from Tunis, which rolls and rolls and produces a nervous condition. The *haboob* – a Sudan dust storm that dresses in bright yellow walls a thousand metres high and is followed by rain. The *harmattan*, which blows and eventually drowns itself into the Atlantic. *Imbat*, a sea breeze in North Africa. Some winds that just sigh towards the sky. Night dust storms that come with the cold. The *khamsin*, a dust in Egypt from March to May, named after the Arabic word for "fifty," blooming for fifty days – the ninth plague of Egypt. The *datoo* out of Gibraltar, which carries fragrance.

There is also the ——, the secret wind of the desert, whose name was erased by a king after his son died within it. And the *nafhat* – a blast out of Arabia. The *mezzar-ifoullousen* – a violent and cold southwesterly known to Berbers as "that which plucks the fowls." The *beshabar*, a black and dry north-easterly out of the Caucasus, "black wind." The *Samiel* from Turkey, "poison and wind," used often in battle. As well as the other "poison winds", the *simoom*, of North Africa, and the *solano*, whose dust plucks off rare petals, causing giddiness.

Other, private winds.

Travelling along the ground like a flood. Blasting off paint, throwing down telephone poles, transporting stones and statue heads. The *harmattan* blows across the Sahara filled with red dust, dust as fire, as flour, entering and coagulating in the locks of rifles. Mariners called this red wind the "sea of darkness." Red sand fogs out of the Sahara were deposited as far north as Cornwall and Devon, producing showers of mud so great this was also mistaken for blood. "Blood rains were widely reported in Portugal and Spain in 1901."

There are always millions of tons of dust in the air, just as there are millions of cubes of air in the earth and more living flesh in the soil (worms, beetles, underground creatures) than there is grazing and existing on it. Herodotus records the death of various armies engulfed in the *simoom* who were never seen again. One nation was "so enraged by this evil wind that they declared war on it and marched out in full battle array, only to be rapidly and completely interred."

Dust storms in three shapes. The whirl. The column. The sheet. In the first the horizon is lost. In the second you are surrounded by "waltzing Ginns." The third, the sheet, is "copper-tinted. Nature seems to be on fire."

She looks up from the book and sees his eyes on her. He begins to talk across the darkness.

The Bedouin were keeping me alive for a reason. I was useful, you see. Someone there had assumed I had a skill when my plane crashed in the desert. I am a man who can recognize an unnamed town by its skeletal shape on a map. I have always had information like a sea in me. I am a person who if left alone in someone's home walks to the bookcase, pulls down a volume and inhales it. So history enters us. I knew maps of the sea floor, maps that depict weaknesses in the shield of the earth, charts painted on skin that contain the various routes of the Crusades.

So I knew their place before I crashed among them, knew when Alexander had traversed it in an earlier age, for this cause or that agreed. I knew the customs of nomads besotted by silks or wells. One tribe dyed a whole valley floor, blackening it to increase convection and thereby the possibility of rainfall, and built high structures to pierce the belly of a cloud. There were some tribes who held up their open palm against the beginnings of wind. Who believed that if this was done at the right moment they could deflect a storm into an adjacent sphere of the desert, towards another, less loved tribe. There were continual drownings, tribes suddenly made historical with sand across their gasp.

In the desert it is easy to lose a sense of demarcation. When I came out of the air and crashed into the desert, into those troughs of yellow, all I kept thinking was, I must build a raft. . . . I must build a raft.

And here, though I was in the dry sands, I knew I was among water people.

In Tassili I have seen rock engravings from a time when the Sahara people hunted water horses from reed boats. In Wadi Sura I saw caves whose walls were covered with paintings of swimmers. Here there had been a lake. I could draw its shape on a wall for them. I could lead them to its edge, six thousand years ago.

Ask a mariner what is the oldest known sail, and he will describe a trapezoidal one hung from the mast of a reed boat that can be seen in rock drawings in Nubia. Pre-dynastic. Harpoons are still found in the desert. These were water people. Even today caravans look like a river. Still, today it is water who is the stranger here. Water is the exile, carried back in cans and flasks, the ghost between your hands and your mouth.

When I was lost among them, unsure of where I was, all I needed was the name of a small ridge, a local custom, a cell of this historical animal, and the map of the world would slide into place.

What did most of us know of such parts of Africa? The armies of the Nile moved back and forth – a battlefield eight hundred miles deep into the desert. Whippet tanks, Blenheim medium-range bombers. Gladiator biplane fighters. Eight thousand men. But who was the enemy? Who were the allies of this place – the fertile lands of Cyrenaica, the salt marshes of El Agheila? All of Europe were fighting their wars in North Africa, in Sidi Rezegh, in Baguoh.

He travelled on a skid behind the Bedouin for five days in darkness, the hood over his body. He lay within this oil-doused cloth. Then suddenly the temperature fell. They had reached the valley within the red high canyon walls, joining the rest of the desert's water tribe that spilled and slid over sand and stones, their blue robes shifting like a spray of milk or a wing. They lifted the soft cloth off him, off the suck of his body. He was within the larger womb of the canyon. The buzzards high above them slipping down a thousand years into this crack of stone where they camped.

In the morning they took him to the far reach of the *siq*. They were talking loudly around him now. The dialect suddenly clarifying. He was here because of the buried guns.

He was carried towards something, his blindfolded face looking straight ahead, and his hand made to reach out a yard or so. After days of travel, to move this one yard. To lean towards and touch something with a purpose, his arm still held, his palm facing down and open. He touched the Sten barrel and the hand let go of him. A pause among the voices. He was there to translate the guns.

"Twelve-millimetre Breda machine gun. From Italy."

He pulled back the bolt, inserted his finger to find no bullet, pushed it back and pulled the trigger. *Puht.* "Famous gun," he muttered. He was moved forward again.

"French seven-point-five-millimetre Châtterlarault. Light machine gun. Nineteen twenty-four."

"German seven-point-nine-millimetre MG-Fifteen air service."

He was brought to each of the guns. The weapons seemed to be from different time periods and from many countries, a museum in the desert. He brushed the contours of the stock and magazine or fingered the sight. He spoke out the gun's name, then was carried to another gun. Eight weapons formally handed to him. He called the names out loud, speaking in French and then the tribe's own language. But what did that matter to them? Perhaps they needed not the name but to know that he knew what the gun was.

He was held by the wrist again and his hand sunk into a box of cartridges. In another box to the right were more shells, seven-millimetre shells this time. Then others.

When he was a child he had grown up with an aunt, and on the grass of her lawn she had scattered a deck of cards face down and taught him the game of Pelmanism. Each player allowed to turn up two cards and, eventually, through memory pairing them off. This had been in another landscape, of trout streams, birdcalls that he could recognize from a halting fragment. A fully named world. Now, with his face blindfolded in a mask of grass fibres, he picked up a shell and moved with his carriers, guiding them towards a gun, inserted the bullet, bolted it, and holding it up in the air fired. The noise cracking crazily down the canyon walls. *"For echo is the soul of the voice exciting itself in hollow places."* A man thought to be sullen and mad had written that sentence down in an English hospital. And he, now in this desert, was sane, with clear thought, picking up the cards, bringing them together with ease, his grin flung out to his aunt, and firing each successful combination into the air, and gradually the unseen men around him replied to each rifle shot with a cheer. He would turn to face one direction, then move back to the Breda this time on his strange human palanquin, followed by a man with a knife who carved a parallel code on shell box and gun stock. He thrived on it – the movement and the cheering after the solitude. This was payment with his skill for the men who had saved him for such a purpose.

There are villages he will travel into with them where there are no women. His knowledge is passed like a counter of usefulness from tribe to tribe. Tribes representing eight thousand individuals. He enters specific customs and specific music. Mostly blindfolded he hears the water-drawing songs of the Mzina tribe with their exultations, *dahhiya* dances, pipe-flutes which are used for carrying messages in times of emergency, the *makruna* double pipe (one pipe constantly sounding a drone). Then into the territory of five-stringed lyres. A village or oasis of preludes and interludes. Hand-clapping. Antiphonal dance.

He is given sight only after dusk, when he can witness his

23

captors and saviours. Now he knows where he is. For some he draws maps that go beyond their own boundaries and for other tribes too he explains the mechanics of guns. The musicians sit across the fire from him. The *simsimiya* lyre notes flung away by a gust of breeze. Or the notes shift towards him over the flames. There is a boy dancing, who in this light is the most desirable thing he has seen. His thin shoulders white as papyrus, light from the fire reflecting sweat on his stomach, nakedness glimpsed through openings in the blue linen he wears as a lure from neck to ankle, revealing himself as a line of brown lightning.

The night desert surrounds them, traversed by a loose order of storms and caravans. There are always secrets and dangers around him, as when blind he moved his hand and cut himself on a double-edged razor in the sand. At times he doesn't know if these are dreams, the cut so clean it leaves no pain, and he must wipe the blood on his skull (his face still untouchable) to signal the wound to his captors. This village of no women he has been brought into in complete silence, or the whole month when he did not see the moon. Was this invented? Dreamed by him while wrapped in oil and felt and darkness?

They had passed wells where water was cursed. In some open spaces there were hidden towns, and he waited while they dug through sand into the buried rooms or waited while they dug into nests of water. And the pure beauty of an innocent dancing boy, like sound from a boy chorister, which he remembered as the purest of sounds, the clearest river water, the most transparent depth of the sea. Here in the desert, which had been an old sea where nothing was strapped down or permanent, everything drifted like the shift of linen across the boy as if he were embracing or

24

freeing himself from an ocean or his own blue afterbirth. A boy arousing himself, his genitals against the colour of fire.

Then the fire is sanded over, its smoke withering around them. The fall of musical instruments like a pulse or rain. The boy puts his arm across, through the lost fire, to silence the pipe-flutes. There is no boy, there are no footsteps when he leaves. Just the borrowed rags. One of the men crawls forward and collects the semen which has fallen on the sand. He brings it over to the white translator of guns and passes it into his hands. In the desert you celebrate nothing but water.

She stands over the sink, gripping it, looking at the stucco wall. She has removed all mirrors and stacked them away in an empty room. She grips the sink and moves her head from side to side, releasing a movement of shadow. She wets her hands and combs water into her hair till it is completely wet. This cools her and she likes it when she goes outside and the breeze hits her, erasing the thunder.

II

In Near Ruins

THE MAN WITH BANDAGED HANDS had been in the military hospital in Rome for more than four months when by accident he heard about the burned patient and the nurse, heard her name. He turned from the doorway and walked back into the clutch of doctors he had just passed, to discover where she was. He had been recuperating there for a long time, and they knew him as an evasive man. But now he spoke to them, asking about the name, and startled them. During all that time he had never spoken, communicating by signals and grimaces, now and then a grin. He had revealed nothing, not even his name, just wrote out his serial number, which showed he was with the Allies.

His status had been double-checked, and confirmed in messages from London. There was the cluster of known scars on him. So the doctors had come back to him, nodded at the bandages on him. A celebrity, after all, wanting silence. A war hero.

That was how he felt safest. Revealing nothing. Whether they came at him with tenderness or subterfuge or knives. For more than four months he had not said a word. He was a large animal in their presence, in near ruins when he was brought in and given regular doses of morphine for the pain in his hands. He would sit in an armchair in the darkness, watching the tide of movement among patients and nurses in and out of the wards and stockrooms.

But now, walking past the group of doctors in the hall, he heard the woman's name, and he slowed his pace and turned and came up to them and asked specifically which hospital she was working in. They told him it was in an old nunnery, taken over by the Germans, then converted into a hospital after the Allies had laid siege to it. In the hills north of Florence. Most of it torn apart by bombing. Unsafe. It had been just a temporary field hospital. But the nurse and the patient had refused to leave.

Why didn't you force the two of them down?

She claimed he was too ill to be moved. We could have brought him out safely, of course, but nowadays there is no time to argue. She was in rough shape herself.

Is she injured?

No. Partial shell shock probably. She should have been sent home. The trouble is, the war here is over. You cannot make anyone do anything anymore. Patients are walking out of hospital. Troops are going AWOL before they get sent back home.

Which villa? he asked.

It's one they say has a ghost in the garden. San Girolamo. Well, she's got her own ghost, a burned patient. There is a face, but it is unrecognizable. The nerves all gone. You can pass a match across his face and there is no expression. The face is asleep.

Who is he? he asked.

We don't know his name.

He won't talk?

The clutch of doctors laughed. No, he talks, he talks all the time, he just doesn't know who he is.

Where did he come from?

The Bedouin brought him into Siwa Oasis. Then he was in Pisa for a while, then . . . One of the Arabs is probably wearing his name tag. He will probably sell it and we'll get it one day, or perhaps they will never sell it. These are great charms. All pilots who fall into the desert – none of them come back with identification. Now he's holed up in a Tuscan villa and the girl won't leave him. Simply refuses. The Allies housed a hundred patients there. Before that the Germans held it with a small army, their last stronghold. Some rooms are painted, each room has a different season. Outside the village is a gorge. All this is about twenty miles from Florence, in the hills. You will need a pass, of course. We can probably get someone to drive you up. It is still terrible out there. Dead cattle. Horses shot dead, half eaten. People hanging upside down from bridges. The last vices of war. Completely unsafe. The sappers haven't gone in there yet to clear it. The Germans retreated burying and installing mines as they went. A terrible place for a hospital. The smell of the dead is the worst. We need a good snowfall to clean up this country. We need ravens.

Thank you.

He walked out of the hospital into the sun, into open air for the first time in months, out of the green-lit rooms that lay like glass in his mind. He stood there breathing everything in, the hurry of everyone. First, he thought, I need shoes with rubber on the bottom. I need *gelato*.

He found it difficult to fall asleep on the train, shaking from side to side. The others in the compartment smoking.

His temple banging against the window frame. Everyone was in dark clothes, and the carriage seemed to be on fire with all the lit cigarettes. He noticed that whenever the train passed a cemetery the travellers around him crossed themselves. *She's in rough shape herself.*

Gelato for tonsils, he remembered. Accompanying a girl and her father to have her tonsils out. She had taken one look at the ward full of other children and simply refused. This, the most adaptable and genial of children, suddenly turned into a stone of refusal, adamant. No one was ripping anything out of *her* throat though the wisdom of the day advised it. She would live with it in, whatever "it" looked like. He still had no idea what a tonsil was.

They never touched my head, he thought, that was strange. The worst times were when he began to imagine what they would have done next, cut next. At those times he always thought of his head.

A scurry in the ceiling like a mouse.

He stood with his valise at the far end of the hall. He put the bag down and waved across the darkness and the intermittent pools of candlelight. There was no clatter of footsteps as he walked towards her, not a sound on the floor, and that surprised her, was somehow familiar and comforting to her, that he could approach this privacy of hers and the English patient's without loudness.

As he passed the lamps in the long hall they flung his shadow forward ahead of him. She turned up the wick on the oil lamp so it enlarged the diameter of light around her. She sat very still, the book on her lap, as he came up to her and then crouched beside her like an uncle.

"Tell me what a tonsil is."

Her eyes staring at him.

"I keep remembering how you stormed out of the hospital followed by two grown men."

She nodded.

"Is your patient in there? Can I go in?"

She shook her head, kept shaking it until he spoke again.

"I'll see him tomorrow, then. Just tell me where to go. I don't need sheets. Is there a kitchen? Such a strange journey I took in order to find you."

When he had gone along the hall she came back to the table and sat down, trembling. Needing this table, this half-finished book in order to collect herself. A man she knew had come all the way by train and walked the four miles uphill from the village and along the hall to this table just to see her. After a few minutes she walked into the Englishman's room and stood there looking down on him. Moonlight across the foliage on the walls. This was the only light that made the trompe l'oeil seem convincing. She could pluck that flower and pin it onto her dress.

The man named Caravaggio pushes open all the windows in the room so he can hear the noises of the night. He undresses, rubs his palms gently over his neck and for a while lies down on the unmade bed. The noise of the trees, the breaking of moon into silver fish bouncing off the leaves of asters outside.

The moon is on him like skin, a sheaf of water. An hour later he is on the roof of the villa. Up on the peak he is aware of the shelled sections along the slope of roofs, the two acres of destroyed gardens and orchards that neighbour the villa. He looks over where they are in Italy.

In the morning by the fountain they talked tentatively.

"Now you are in Italy you should find out more about Verdi."

"What?" She looks up from the bedding that she is washing out in the fountain.

He reminds her. "You told me once you were in love with him."

Hana bows her head, embarrassed.

Caravaggio walks around, looking at the building for the first time, peering down from the loggia into the garden.

"Yes, you used to love him. You used to drive us all *mad* with your new information about Giuseppe. What a man! The best in every way, you'd say. We all had to agree with you, the cocky sixteen-year-old."

"I wonder what happened to her." She spreads the washed sheet over the rim of the fountain.

"You were someone with a dangerous will."

She walks over the paved stones, grass in the cracks. He watches her black-stockinged feet, the thin brown dress. She leans over the balustrade.

"I think I did come here, I have to admit, something at

the back of my mind made me, for Verdi. And then of course you had left and my dad had left for the war. . . . Look at the hawks. They are here every morning. Everything else is damaged and in pieces here. The only running water in this whole villa is in this fountain. The Allies dismantled water pipes when they left. They thought that would make me leave."

"You should have. They still have to clear this region. There are unexploded bombs all over the place."

She comes up to him and puts her fingers on his mouth.

"I'm glad to see you, Caravaggio. No one else. Don't say you have come here to try and persuade me to leave."

"I want to find a small bar with a Wurlitzer and drink without a fucking bomb going off. Listen to Frank Sinatra singing. We have to get some music," he says. "Good for your patient."

"He's still in Africa."

He is watching her, waiting for her to say more, but there is nothing more about the English patient to be said. He mutters, "Some of the English love Africa. A part of their brain reflects the desert precisely. So they're not foreigners there."

He sees her head nod slightly. A lean face with hair cut short, without the mask and mystery of her long hair. If anything, she seems calm in this universe of hers. The fountain gurgling in the background, the hawks, the ruined garden of the villa.

Maybe this is the way to come out of a war, he thinks. A burned man to care for, some sheets to wash in a fountain, a room painted like a garden. As if all that remains is a capsule from the past, long before Verdi, the Medicis considering a balustrade or window, holding up a candle at night in the presence of an invited architect – the best architect in the fifteenth century – and requesting something more satisfying to frame that vista.

"If you are staying," she says, "we are going to need more food. I have planted vegetables, we have a sack of beans, but we need some chickens." She is looking at Caravaggio, knowing his skills from the past, not quite saying it.

"I lost my nerve," he says.

"I'll come with you, then," Hana offers. "We'll do it together. You can teach me to steal, show me what to do."

"You don't understand. I lost my nerve."

"Why?"

"I was caught. They nearly chopped off my fucking hands."

At night sometimes, when the English patient is asleep or even after she has read alone outside his door for a while, she goes looking for Caravaggio. He will be in the garden lying along the stone rim on a lower terrace. In this early-summer weather he finds it difficult to stay indoors at night. Most of the time he is on the roof beside the broken chimney, but he slips down silently when he sees her figure cross the terrace looking for him. She will find him near the headless statue of a count, upon whose stub of neck one of the local cats likes to sit, solemn and drooling when humans appear. She is always made to feel that she is the one who has found him, this man who knows darkness, who when drunk used to claim he was brought up by a family of owls.

Two of them on a promontory, Florence and her lights in the distance. Sometimes he seems frantic to her, or he will be too calm. In daylight she notices better how he moves, notices the stiffened arms above the bandaged hands, how

37

his whole body turns instead of just the neck when she points to something farther up the hill. But she has said nothing about these things to him.

"My patient thinks peacock bone ground up is a great healer."

He looks up into the night sky. "Yes."

"Were you a spy then?"

"Not quite."

He feels more comfortable, more disguised from her in the dark garden, a flicker of the lamp from the patient's room looking down. "At times we were sent in to steal. Here I was, an Italian and a thief. They couldn't believe their luck, they were falling over themselves to use me. There were about four or five of us. I did well for some time. Then I was accidentally photographed. Can you imagine that?

"I was in a tuxedo, a monkey suit, in order to get into this gathering, a party, to steal some papers. Really I was still a thief. No great patriot. No great hero. They had just made my skills official. But one of the women had brought a camera and was snapping at the German officers, and I was caught in mid-step, walking across the ballroom. In mid-step, the beginning of the shutter's noise making me jerk my head towards it. So suddenly everything in the future was dangerous. Some general's girlfriend.

"All photographs taken during the war were processed officially in government labs, checked by the Gestapo, and so there I would be, obviously not part of any list, to be filed away by an official when the film went to the Milan laboratory. So it meant having to try and steal that film back somehow."

She looks in on the English patient, whose sleeping body is probably miles away in the desert, being healed by a man who continues to dip his fingers into the bowl made with the joined soles of his feet, leaning forward, pressing the dark paste against the burned face. She imagines the weight of the hand on her own cheek.

She walks down the hall and climbs into her hammock, giving it a swing as she leaves the ground.

Moments before sleep are when she feels most alive, leaping across fragments of the day, bringing each moment into the bed with her like a child with schoolbooks and pencils. The day seems to have no order until these times, which are like a ledger for her, her body full of stories and situations. Caravaggio has for instance given her something. His motive, a drama, and a stolen image.

He leaves the party in a car. It crunches over the slowly curving gravel path leading out of the grounds, the automobile purring, serene as ink within the summer night. For the rest of the evening during the Villa Cosima gathering he had been looking at the photographer, spinning his body away whenever she lifted the camera to photograph in his direction. Now that he knows of its existence he can avoid it. He moves into the range of her dialogue, her name is Anna, mistress to an officer, who will be staying here in the villa for the night and then in the morning will travel north through Tuscany. The death of the woman or the woman's sudden disappearance will only arouse suspicion. Nowadays anything out of the ordinary is investigated.

Four hours later, he runs over the grass in his socks, his shadow curled under him, painted by the moon. He stops at the gravel path and moves slowly over the grit. He looks up at the Villa Cosima, at the square moons of window. A palace of war-women.

A car beam – like something sprayed out of a hose – lights up the room he is in, and he pauses once again in mid-step, seeing that same woman's eyes on him, a man moving on top of her, his fingers in her blonde hair. And she has seen, he knows, even though now he is naked, the same man she photographed earlier in the crowded party, for by accident he stands the same way now, half turned in surprise at the light that reveals his body in the darkness. The car lights sweep up into a corner of the room and disappear.

Then there is blackness. He doesn't know whether to move, whether she will whisper to the man fucking her about the other person in the room. A naked thief. A naked assassin. Should he move – his hands out to break a neck – towards the couple on the bed?

He hears the man's lovemaking continue, hears the silence of the woman – no whisper – hears her thinking, her eyes aimed toward him in the darkness. The word should be *thinkering*. Caravaggio's mind slips into this consideration, another syllable to suggest collecting a thought as one tinkers with a half-completed bicycle. Words are tricky things, a friend of his has told him, they're much more tricky than violins. His mind recalls the woman's blonde hair, the black ribbon in it.

He hears the car turning and waits for another moment of light. The face that emerges out of the dark is still an arrow upon him. The light moves from her face down onto the body of the general, over the carpet, and then touches and slides over Caravaggio once more. He can no longer see her. He shakes his head, then mimes the cutting of his throat. The camera is in his hands for her to understand. Then he is in darkness again. He hears a moan of pleasure now from her towards her lover, and he is aware it is her agreement with him. No words, no hint of irony, just a contract with him, the morse of understanding, so he knows he can now move safely to the verandah and drop out into the night.

Finding her room had been more difficult. He had entered the villa and silently passed the half-lit seventeenth-century murals along the corridors. Somewhere there were bedrooms like dark pockets in a gold suit. The only way he could get past guards was to be revealed as an innocent. He had stripped completely and left his clothes on a flower bed.

He ambles naked up the stairs to the second floor, where the guards are, bending down to laugh at some privacy, so his face is almost at his hip, nudging the guards about his evening's invitation, *al fresco*, was that it? Or seduction *a cappella*?

One long hall on the third floor. A guard by the stair and one at the far end twenty yards away, too many yards away. So a long theatrical walk, and Caravaggio now having to perform it, watched with quiet suspicion and scornfully by the two bookend sentries, the ass-and-cock walk, pausing at a section of mural to peer at a painted donkey in a grove. He leans his head on the wall, almost falling asleep, then walks again, stumbles and immediately pulls himself together into a military gait. His stray left hand waves to the ceiling of cherubs bum-naked as he is, a salute from a thief, a brief waltz while the mural scene drifts haphazardly past him, castles, black-and-white duomos, uplifted saints on this Tuesday during the war, in order to save his disguise and his life. Caravaggio is out on the tiles looking for a photograph of himself.

He pats his bare chest as if looking for his pass, grabs his penis and pretends to use it as a key to let him into the room that is being guarded. Laughing, he staggers back, peeved at his woeful failure, and slips into the next room humming.

He opens the window and steps out onto the verandah. A dark, beautiful night. Then he climbs off it and swings on to the verandah one level below. Only now can he enter the room of Anna and her general. Nothing more than a perfume in their midst. Printless foot. Shadowless. The story he told someone's child years ago about the person who searched for his shadow – as he is now looking for this image of himself on a piece of film.

In the room he is immediately aware of the beginnings of sexual movement. His hands within her clothing thrown onto chair backs, dropped upon the floor. He lies down and rolls across the carpet in order to feel anything hard like a camera, touching the skin of the room. He rolls in silence in the shape of fans, finding nothing. There is not even a grain of light.

He gets to his feet and sways his arms out slowly, touches a breast of marble. His hand moves along a stone hand – he understands the way the woman thinks now – off which the camera hangs with its sling. Then he hears the vehicle and simultaneously as he turns is seen by the woman in the sudden spray of car light.

Caravaggio watches Hana, who sits across from him looking into his eyes, trying to read him, trying to figure the flow of thought the way his wife used to do. He watches her sniffing him out, searching for the trace. He buries it and looks back at her, knowing his eyes are faultless, clear as any river, unimpeachable as a landscape. People, he knows, get lost in them, and he is able to hide well. But the girl watches him quizzically, tilting her head in a question as a dog would when spoken to in a tone or pitch that is not human. She sits across from him in front of the dark, blood-red walls, whose colour he doesn't like, and in her black hair and with that look, slim, tanned olive from all the light in this country, she reminds him of his wife.

Nowadays he doesn't think of his wife, though he knows he can turn around and evoke every move of her, describe any aspect of her, the weight of her wrist on his heart during the night.

He sits with his hands below the table, watching the girl eat. He still prefers to eat alone, though he always sits with Hana during meals. Vanity, he thinks. Mortal vanity. She has seen him from a window eating with his hands as he sits on one of the thirty-six steps by the chapel, not a fork or a knife in sight, as if he were learning to eat like someone from the East. In his greying stubble-beard, in his dark jacket, she sees the Italian finally in him. She notices this more and more.

He watches her darkness against the brown-and-red walls, her skin, her cropped dark hair. He had known her and her father in Toronto before the war. Then he had been a thief, a married man, slipped through his chosen world with a lazy confidence, brilliant in deceit against the rich, or charm towards his wife Giannetta or with this young daughter of his friend.

But now there is hardly a world around them and they are forced back on themselves. During these days in the hill town near Florence, indoors during the days of rain, daydreaming in the one soft chair in the kitchen or on the bed or on the roof, he has no plots to set in motion, is interested only in Hana. And it seems she has chained herself to the dying man upstairs.

During meals he sits opposite this girl and watches her eat.

Half a year earlier, from a window at the end of the long hall in Santa Chiara Hospital in Pisa, Hana had been able to see a white lion. It stood alone on top of the battlements, linked by colour to the white marble of the Duomo and the Camposanto, though its roughness and naive form seemed part of another era. Like some gift from the past that had to be accepted. Yet she accepted it most of all among the things surrounding this hospital. At midnight she would look through the window and know it stood within the curfew blackout and that it would emerge like her into the dawn shift. She would look up at five or five-thirty and then at six to see its silhouette and growing detail. Every night it was her sentinel while she moved among patients. Even through the shelling the army had left it there, much more concerned about the rest of the fabulous compound – with its mad logic of a tower leaning like a person in shell shock.

Their hospital buildings lay in old monastery grounds. The topiary carved for thousands of years by too careful monks was no longer bound within recognizable animal forms, and during the day nurses wheeled patients among the lost shapes. It seemed that only white stone remained permanent.

Nurses too became shell-shocked from the dying around them. Or from something as small as a letter. They would carry a severed arm down a hall, or swab at blood that never stopped, as if the wound were well, and they began to believe

44

in nothing, trusted nothing. They broke the way a man dismantling a mine broke the second his geography exploded. The way Hana broke in Santa Chiara Hospital when an official walked down the space between a hundred beds and gave her a letter that told her of the death of her father.

A white lion.

It was sometime after this that she had come across the English patient – someone who looked like a burned animal, taut and dark, a pool for her. And now, months later, he is her last patient in the Villa San Girolamo, their war over, both of them refusing to return with the others to the safety of the Pisa hospitals. All the coastal ports, such as Sorrento and Marina di Pisa, are now filled with North American and British troops waiting to be sent home. But she washed her uniform, folded it and returned it to the departing nurses. The war is not over everywhere she was told. The war is over. This war is over. The war here. She was told it would be like desertion. This is not desertion. I will stay here. She was warned of the uncleared mines, lack of water and food. She came upstairs to the burned man, the English patient, and told him she would stay as well.

He said nothing, unable even to turn his head towards her, but his fingers slipped into her white hand, and when she bent forward to him he put his dark fingers into her hair and felt it cool within the valley of his fingers.

How old are you?

Twenty.

There was a duke, he said, who when he was dying wanted to be carried halfway up the tower in Pisa so he could die looking out into the middle distance.

A friend of my father's wanted to die while Shanghai-dancing. I don't know what it is. He had just heard of it himself.

What does your father do?

He is . . . he is in the war.

You're in the war too.

She does not know anything about him. Even after a
month or so of caring for him and allotting him the needles
of morphine. There was shyness at first within both of them,
made more evident by the fact that they were now alone.
Then it was suddenly overcome. The patients and doctors
and nurses and equipment and sheets and towels – all went
back down the hill into Florence and then to Pisa. She had
salted away codeine tablets, as well as the morphine. She
watched the departures, the line of trucks. Good-bye, then.
She waved from his window, bringing the shutters to a close.

Behind the villa a rock wall rose higher than the house.
To the west of the building was a long enclosed garden,
and twenty miles away was the carpet of the city of Florence, which often disappeared under the mist of the valley.
Rumour had it one of the generals living in the old Medici
villa next door had eaten a nightingale.

The Villa San Girolamo, built to protect inhabitants from
the flesh of the devil, had the look of a besieged fortress, the
limbs of most of the statues blown off during the first days of
shelling. There seemed little demarcation between house and
landscape, between damaged building and the burned and
shelled remnants of the earth. To Hana the wild gardens were
like further rooms. She worked along the edges of them aware
always of unexploded mines. In one soil-rich area beside the
house she began to garden with a furious passion that could
come only to someone who had grown up in a city. In spite
of the burned earth, in spite of the lack of water. Someday
there would be a bower of limes, rooms of green light.

Caravaggio came into the kitchen to find Hana sitting hunched over the table. He could not see her face or her arms tucked in under her body, only the naked back, the bare shoulders.

She was not still or asleep. With each shudder her head shook over the table.

Caravaggio stood there. Those who weep lose more energy than they lose during any other act. It was not yet dawn. Her face against the darkness of the table wood.

"Hana," he said, and she stilled herself as if she could be camouflaged by stillness.

"Hana."

She began to moan so the sound would be a barrier between them, a river across which she could not be reached.

He was uncertain at first about touching her in her nakedness, said "Hana," and then lay his bandaged hand on her shoulder. She did not stop shaking. The deepest sorrow, he thought. Where the only way to survive is to excavate everything.

She raised herself, her head down still, then stood up

against him as if dragging herself away from the magnet of the table.

"Don't touch me if you're going to try and fuck me."

The skin pale above her skirt, which was all she wore in this kitchen, as if she had risen from the bed, dressed partially and come out here, the cool air from the hills entering the kitchen doorway and cloaking her.

Her faced was red and wet.

"Hana."

"Do you understand?"

"Why do you adore him so much?"

"I love him."

"You don't love him, you adore him."

"Go away, Caravaggio. Please."

"You've tied yourself to a corpse for some reason."

"He is a saint. I think. A despairing saint. Are there such things? Our desire is to protect them."

"He doesn't even care!"

"I can love him."

"A twenty-year-old who throws herself out of the world to love a ghost!"

Caravaggio paused. "You have to protect yourself from sadness. Sadness is very close to hate. Let me tell you this. This is the thing I learned. If you take in someone else's poison – thinking you can cure them by sharing it – you will instead store it within you. Those men in the desert were smarter than you. They assumed he could be useful. So they saved him, but when he was no longer useful they left him."

"Leave me alone."

When she is solitary she will sit, aware of the nerve at her ankle, damp from the long grasses of the orchard. She peels a plum from the orchard that she has found and carried in the dark cotton pocket of her dress. When she is solitary she tries to imagine who might come along the old road under the green hood of the eighteen cypress trees.

As the Englishman wakes she bends over his body and places a third of the plum into his mouth. His open mouth holds it, like water, the jaw not moving. He looks as if he will cry from this pleasure. She can sense the plum being swallowed.

He brings his hand up and wipes from his lip the last dribble, which his tongue cannot reach, and puts his finger in his mouth to suck it. Let me tell you about plums, he says. When I was a boy . . .

After the first nights, after most of the beds had been burned for fuel against the cold, she had taken a dead man's hammock and begun to use it. She would bang spikes into whatever walls she desired, whichever room she wanted to wake in, floating above all the filth and cordite and water on the floors, the rats that had started to appear coming down from the third storey. Each night she climbed into the khaki ghostline of hammock she had taken from a dead soldier, someone who had died under her care.

A pair of tennis shoes and a hammock. What she had taken from others in this war. She would wake under the slide of moonlight on the ceiling, wrapped in an old shirt she always slept in, her dress hanging on a nail by the door. There was more heat now, and she could sleep this way. Before, when it had been cold, they had to burn things.

Her hammock and her shoes and her frock. She was secure in the miniature world she had built; the two other men seemed distant planets, each in his own sphere of memory and solitude. Caravaggio, who had been her father's gregarious friend in Canada, in those days was capable of standing still and causing havoc within the caravan of women he seemed to give himself over to. He now lay in his darkness. He had been a thief who refused to work with men, because he did not trust them, who talked with men but who preferred talking to women and when he began talking to women was soon caught in the nets of relationship. When she would sneak home in the early hours of the morning she would find him asleep on her father's armchair, exhausted from professional or personal robberies.

She thought about Caravaggio – some people you just had to embrace, in some way or another, had to bite into the muscle, to remain sane in their company. You needed to grab their hair and clutch it like a drowner so they would pull you into their midst. Otherwise they, walking casually down the street towards you, almost about to wave, would leap over a wall and be gone for months. As an uncle he had been a disappearer.

Caravaggio would disturb you by simply enfolding you in his arms, his wings. With him you were embraced by character. But now he lay in darkness, like her, in some outpost of the large house. So there was Caravaggio. And there was the desert Englishman.

Throughout the war, with all of her worst patients, she survived by keeping a coldness hidden in her role as nurse. I will survive this. I won't fall apart at this. These were buried sentences all through her war, all through the towns they crept towards and through, Urbino, Anghiari, Monterchi, until they entered Florence and then went farther and finally reached the other sea near Pisa.

In the Pisa hospital she had seen the English patient for the first time. A man with no face. An ebony pool. All identification consumed in a fire. Parts of his burned body and face had been sprayed with tannic acid, that hardened into a protective shell over his raw skin. The area around his eyes was coated with a thick layer of gentian violet. There was nothing to recognize in him.

Sometimes she collects several blankets and lies under them, enjoying them more for their weight than for the warmth they bring. And when moonlight slides onto the ceiling it wakes her, and she lies in the hammock, her mind skating. She finds rest as opposed to sleep the truly pleasurable state. If she were a writer she would collect her pencils and notebooks and favourite cat and write in bed. Strangers and lovers would never get past the locked door.

To rest was to receive all aspects of the world without judgement. A bath in the sea, a fuck with a solider who never knew your name. Tenderness towards the unknown and anonymous, which was a tenderness to the self.

Her legs move under the burden of military blankets. She swims in their wool as the English patient moved in his cloth placenta.

What she misses here is slow twilight, the sound of familiar trees. All through her youth in Toronto she learned to read the summer night. It was where she could be herself, lying in a bed, stepping onto a fire escape half asleep with a cat in her arms.

In her childhood her classroom had been Caravaggio. He had taught her the somersault. Now, with his hands always in his pockets, he just gestures with his shoulders. Who knew what country the war had made him live in. She herself had been trained at Women's College Hospital and then sent overseas during the Sicilian invasion. That was in 1943. The First Canadian Infantry Division worked its way up Italy, and the destroyed bodies were fed back to the field hospitals like mud passed back by tunnellers in the dark. After the battle of Arezzo, when the first barrage of troops recoiled, she was surrounded day and night by their wounds. After three full days without rest, she finally lay down on the floor beside a mattress where someone lay dead, and slept for twelve hours, closing her eyes against the world around her.

When she woke, she picked up a pair of scissors out of the porcelain bowl, leaned over and began to cut her hair, not concerned with shape or length, just cutting it away – the irritation of its presence during the previous days still in her mind – when she had bent forward and her hair had touched blood in a wound. She would have nothing to link her, to lock her, to death. She gripped what was left to make sure there were no more strands and turned again to face the rooms full of the wounded.

She never looked at herself in mirrors again. As the war got darker she received reports about how certain people she had known had died. She feared the day she would remove blood from a patient's face and discover her father or someone who had served her food across a counter on Danforth Avenue. She grew harsh with herself and the patients. Reason was the only thing that might save them, and there was no reason. The thermometer of blood moved up the country. Where was and what was Toronto anymore in her mind? This was treacherous opera. People hardened against those around them – soldiers, doctors, nurses, civilians. Hana bent closer to the wounds she cared for, her mouth whispering to soldiers.

She called everyone "Buddy," and laughed at the song that had the lines

> *Each time I chanced to see Franklin D.*
> *He always said "Hi, Buddy" to me.*

She swabbed arms that kept bleeding. She removed so many pieces of shrapnel she felt she'd transported a ton of metal out of the huge body of the human that she was caring for while the army travelled north. One night when one of the patients died she ignored all rules and took the pair of tennis shoes he had with him in his pack and put them down. They were slightly too big for her but she was comfortable.

Her face became tougher and leaner, the face Caravaggio would meet later. She was thin, mostly from tiredness. She was always hungry and found it a furious exhaustion to feed a patient who couldn't eat or didn't want to, watching the bread crumble away, the soup cool, which she desired to swallow fast. She wanted nothing exotic, just bread, meat. One of the towns had a bread-making section attached to the hospital and in her free time she moved among the bakers, inhaling the dust and the promise of food. Later, when they were east of Rome, someone gave her a gift of Jerusalem artichoke.

It was strange sleeping in the basilicas, or monasteries, or wherever the wounded were billeted, always moving north. She broke the small cardboard flag off the foot of the bed when someone died, so that orderlies would know glancing from a distance. Then she would leave the thick-stoned building and walk outside into spring or winter or summer, seasons that seemed archaic, that sat like old gentlemen throughout the war. She would step outside whatever the weather. She wanted air that smelled of nothing human, wanted moonlight even if it came with a rainstorm.

Hello Buddy, good-bye Buddy. Caring was brief. There was a contract only until death. Nothing in her spirit or past had taught her to be a nurse. But cutting her hair was a contract, and it lasted until they were bivouacked in the

Villa San Girolamo north of Florence. Here there were four other nurses, two doctors, one hundred patients. The war in Italy moved farther north and they were what had been left behind.

Then, during the celebrations of some local victory, somewhat plaintive in this hill town, she had said she was not going back to Florence or Rome or any other hospital, her war was over. She would remain with the one burned man they called "the English patient," who, it was now clear to her, should never be moved because of the fragility of his limbs. She would lay belladonna over his eyes, give him saline baths for the keloided skin and extensive burns. She was told the hospital was unsafe – the nunnery that had been for months a German defence, barraged with shells and flares by the Allies. Nothing would be left for her, there would be no safety from brigands. She still refused to leave, got out of her nurse's uniform, unbundled the brown print frock she had carried for months, and wore that with her tennis shoes. She stepped away from the war. She had moved back and forth at their desire. Till the nuns reclaimed it she would sit in this villa with the Englishman. There was something about him she wanted to learn, grow into, and hide in, where she could turn away from being an adult. There was some little waltz in the way he spoke to her and the way he thought. She wanted to save him, this nameless, almost faceless man who had been one of the two hundred or so placed in her care during the invasion north.

In her print dress she walked away from the celebration. She went into the room she shared with the other nurse and sat down. Something flickered in her eye as she sat, and she caught the eye of a small round mirror. She got up slowly and went towards it. It was very small but even so seemed a luxury. She had refused to look at herself for more than a year, now and then just her shadow on walls. The mirror revealed only her cheek, she had to move it back to arm's length, her hand wavering. She watched the little portrait of herself as if within a clasped brooch. She. Through the window there was the sound of the patients being brought out into the sunlight in their chairs, laughing and cheering with the staff. Only those who were seriously ill were still indoors. She smiled at that. Hi Buddy, she said. She peered into her look, trying to recognize herself.

Darkness between Hana and Caravaggio as they walk in the garden. Now he begins to talk in his familiar slow drawl.

"It was someone's birthday party late at night on Danforth Avenue. The Night Crawler restaurant. Do you remember, Hana? Everyone had to stand and sing a song. Your father, me, Giannetta, friends, and you said you wanted to as well – for the first time. You were still at school then, and you had learned the song in a French class.

"You did it formally, stood on the bench and then one more step up on to the wooden table between the plates and the candles burning.

" *'Alonson fon!'*

"You sang out, your left hand to your heart. *Alonson fon!* Half the people there didn't know what the hell you were singing, and maybe you didn't know what the exact words meant, but you knew what the song was about.

"The breeze from the window was swaying your skirt over so it almost touched a candle, and your ankles seemed fire-white in the bar. Your father's eyes looking up at you, miraculous with this new language, the cause pouring out so

57

distinct, flawless, no hesitations, and the candles swerving away, not touching your dress but almost touching. We stood up at the end and you walked off the table into his arms."

"I would remove those bandages on your hands. I *am* a nurse, you know."

"They're comfortable. Like gloves."

"How did this happen?"

"I was caught jumping from a woman's window. That woman I told you about, who took the photograph. Not her fault."

She grips his arm, kneading the muscle. "Let me do it." She pulls the bandaged hands out of his coat pockets. She has seen them grey in daylight, but in this light they are almost luminous.

As she loosens the bandages he steps backwards, the white coming out of his arms as if he were a magician, till he is free of them. She walks towards the uncle from childhood, sees his eyes hoping to catch hers to postpone this, so she looks at nothing but his eyes.

His hands held together like a human bowl. She reaches for them while her face goes up to his cheek, then nestles in his neck. What she holds seems firm, healed.

"I tell you I had to negotiate for what they left me."

"How did you do that?"

"All those skills I used to have."

"Oh, I remember. No, don't move. Don't drift away from me."

"It is a strange time, the end of a war."

"Yes. A period of adjustment."

"Yes."

He raises his hands up as if to cup the quarter-moon.

"They removed both thumbs, Hana. See."

He holds his hands in front of her. Showing her directly what she has glimpsed. He turns one hand over as if to reveal that it is no trick, that what looks like a gill is where the thumb has been cut away. He moves the hand towards her blouse.

She feels the cloth lift in the area below her shoulder as he holds it with two fingers and tugs it softly towards him.

"I touch cotton like this."

"When I was a child I thought of you always as the Scarlet Pimpernel, and in my dreams I stepped onto the night roofs with you. You came home with cold meals in your pockets, pencil cases, sheet music off some Forest Hill piano for me."

She speaks into the darkness of his face, a shadow of leaves washing over his mouth like a rich woman's lace. "You like women, don't you? You liked them."

"I like them. Why the past tense?"

"It seems unimportant now, with the war and such things."

He nods and the pattern of leaves rolls off him.

"You used to be like those artists who painted only at night, a single light on in their street. Like the worm-pickers with their old coffee cans strapped to their ankles and the helmet of light shooting down into the grass. All over the city parks. You took me to that place, that café where they sold them. It was like the stock exchange, you said, where the price of worms kept dropping and rising, five cents, ten cents. People were ruined or made fortunes. Do you remember?"

"Yes."

"Walk back with me, it's getting cold."

"The great pickpockets are born with the second and third fingers almost the same length. They do not need to go as deep into a pocket. The great distance of half an inch!"

They move towards the house, under the trees.

"Who did that to you?"

"They found a woman to do it. They thought it was more trenchant. They brought in one of their nurses. My wrists handcuffed to the table legs. When they cut off my thumbs my hands slipped out of them without any power. Like a wish in a dream. But the man who called her in, he was really in charge – he was the one. Ranuccio Tommasoni. She was an innocent, knew nothing about me, my name or nationality or what I may have done."

When they came into the house the English patient was shouting. Hana let go of Caravaggio and he watched her run up the stairs, her tennis shoes flashing as she ascended and wheeled around with the banister.

The voice filled the halls. Caravaggio walked into the kitchen, tore off a section of bread and followed Hana up the stairs. As he walked towards the room the shouts became more frantic. When he stepped into the bedroom the Englishman was staring at a dog – the dog's head angled back as if stunned by the screaming. Hana looked over to Caravaggio and grinned.

"I haven't seen a dog for *years*. All through the war I saw no dog."

She crouched and hugged the animal, smelling its hair and the odour of hill grasses within it. She steered the dog towards Caravaggio, who was offering it the heel of bread. The Englishman saw Caravaggio then and his jaw dropped.

It must have seemed to him that the dog – now blocked by Hana's back – had turned into a man. Caravaggio collected the dog in his arms and left the room.

I have been thinking, the English patient said, that this must be Poliziano's room. This must have been his villa we are in. It is the water coming out of that wall, that ancient fountain. It is a famous room. They all met here.

It was a hospital, she said quietly. Before that, long before that a nunnery. Then armies took it over.

I think this was the Villa Bruscoli. Poliziano – the great protégé of Lorenzo. I'm talking about 1483. In Florence, in Santa Trinità Church, you can see the painting of the Medicis with Poliziano in the foreground, wearing a red cloak. Brilliant, awful man. A genius who worked his way up into society.

It was long past midnight and he was wide awake again.

Okay, tell me, she thought, take me somewhere. Her mind still upon Caravaggio's hands. Caravaggio, who was by now probably feeding the stray dog something from the kitchen of the Villa Bruscoli, if that was what its name was.

It was a bloody life. Daggers and politics and three-decker hats and colonial padded stockings and wigs. Wigs of silk! Of course Savonarola came later, not much later, and there was his Bonfire of the Vanities. Poliziano translated Homer. He wrote a poem on Simonetta Vespucci, you know her?

No, said Hana, laughing.

Paintings of her all over Florence. Died of consumption at twenty-three. He made her famous with *Le Stanze per la Giostra* and then Botticelli painted scenes from it. Leonardo painted scenes from it. Poliziano would lecture every day for two hours in Latin in the morning, two hours in Greek in the afternoon. He had a friend called Pico della Mirandola, a wild socialite who suddenly converted and joined Savonarola.

That was my nickname when I was a kid. *Pico*.

Yes, I think a lot happened here. This fountain in the wall. Pico and Lorenzo and Poliziano and the young Michelangelo. They held in each hand the new world and the old world. The library hunted down the last four books of Cicero. They imported a giraffe, a rhinoceros, a dodo. Toscanelli drew maps of the world based on correspondence with merchants. They sat in this room with a bust of Plato and argued all night.

And then came Savonarola's cry out of the streets: "*Repentance! The deluge is coming!*" And everything was swept away – free will, the desire to be elegant, fame, the right to worship Plato as well as Christ. Now came the bonfires – the burning of wigs, books, animal hides, maps. More than four hundred years later they opened up the graves. Pico's bones were preserved. Poliziano's had crumbled into dust.

Hana listened as the Englishman turned the pages of his commonplace book and read the information glued in from other books – about great maps lost in the bonfires and the burning of Plato's statue, whose marble exfoliated in the heat, the cracks across wisdom like precise reports across the valley as Poliziano stood on the grass hills smelling the future. Pico down there somewhere as well, in his grey cell, watching everything with the third eye of salvation.

He poured some water into a bowl for the dog. An old mongrel, older than the war.

He sat down with the carafe of wine the monks from the monastery had given Hana. It was Hana's house and he moved carefully, rearranging nothing. He noticed her civilization in the small wildflowers, the small gifts to herself. Even in the overgrown garden he would come across a square foot of grass snipped down with her nurse's scissors. If he had been a younger man he would have fallen in love with this.

He was no longer young. How did she see him? With his wounds, his unbalance, the grey curls at the back of his neck. He had never imagined himself to be a man with a sense of age and wisdom. They had all grown older, but he still did not feel he had wisdom to go with his aging.

He crouched down to watch the dog drinking and he rebalanced himself too late, grabbing the table, upsetting the carafe of wine.

Your name is David Caravaggio, right?

They had handcuffed him to the thick legs of an oak table. At one point he rose with it in his embrace, blood pouring away from his left hand, and tried to run with it through the thin door and falling. The woman stopped, dropping the knife, refusing to do more. The drawer of the table slid out and fell against his chest, and all its contents, and he thought perhaps there was a gun that he could use. Then Ranuccio Tommasoni picked up the razor and came over to him. *Caravaggio, right?* He still wasn't sure.

As he lay under the table, the blood from his hands fell into his face, and he suddenly thought clearly and slipped the handcuff off the table leg, flinging the chair away to drown out the pain and then leaning to the left to step out of the other cuff. Blood everywhere now. His hands already useless. For months afterwards he found himself looking at only the thumbs of people, as if the incident had changed him just by producing envy. But the event had produced age, as if during the one night when he was locked to that table they had poured a solution into him that slowed him.

He stood up dizzy above the dog, above the red wine-soaked table. Two guards, the woman, Tommasoni, the telephones ringing, ringing, interrupting Tommasoni, who would put down the razor, caustically whisper *Excuse me* and pick up the phone with his bloody hand and listen. He had, he thought, said nothing of worth to them. But they let him go, so perhaps he was wrong.

Then he had walked along the Via di Santo Spirito to the one geographical location he had hidden away in his brain. Walked past Brunelleschi's church towards the library of the German Institute, where he knew a certain person would look after him. Suddenly he realized this was why they had let him go. Letting him walk freely would fool him into revealing this contact. He arced into a side street, not looking back, never looking back. He wanted a street fire so he could stanch his wounds, hang them over the smoke from a tar cauldron so black smoke would envelop his hands. He was on the Santa Trinità Bridge. There was nothing around, no traffic, which surprised him. He sat on the smooth balustrade of the bridge, then lay back. No sounds. Earlier, when he had walked, his hands in his wet pockets, there had been the manic movement of tanks and jeeps.

As he lay there the mined bridge exploded and he was flung upwards and then down as part of the end of the world. He opened his eyes and there was a giant head beside him. He breathed in and his chest filled with water.

He was underwater. There was a bearded head beside him in the shallow water of the Arno. He reached towards it but couldn't even nudge it. Light was pouring into the river. He swam up to the surface, parts of which were on fire.

When he told Hana the story later that evening she said, "They stopped torturing you because the Allies were coming. The Germans were getting out of the city, blowing up bridges as they left."

"I don't know. Maybe I told them everything. Whose head was it? There were constant phone calls into that room. There would be a hush, and the man would pull back from me, and all of them would watch him on the phone listening to the silence of the *other* voice, which we could not hear. Whose voice? Whose head?"

"*They were leaving*, David."

She opens *The Last of the Mohicans* to the blank page at the back and begins to write in it.

> There is a man named Caravaggio, a friend of my father's. I have always loved him. He is older than I am, about forty-five, I think. He is in a time of darkness, has no confidence. For some reason I am cared for by this friend of my father.

She closes the book and then walks down into the library and conceals it in one of the high shelves.

The Englishman was asleep, breathing through his mouth as he always did, awake or asleep. She got up from her chair and gently pulled free the lit candle held in his hands. She walked to the window and blew it out there, so the smoke went out of the room. She disliked his lying there with a candle in his hands, mocking a deathlike posture, wax falling unnoticed on to his wrist. As if he was preparing himself, as if he wanted to slip into his own death by imitating its climate and light.

She stood by the window and her fingers clutched the hair on her head with a tough grip, pulling it. In darkness, in any light after dusk, you can slit a vein and the blood is black.

She needed to move from the room. Suddenly she was claustrophobic, untired. She strode down the hall and leapt down the stairs and went out onto the terrace of the villa, then looked up, as if trying to discern the figure of the girl she had stepped away from. She walked back into the building. She pushed at the stiff swollen door and came into the library and then removed the boards from the French doors at the far end of the room, opening them, letting in the night air. Where Caravaggio was, she didn't know. He was out most evenings now, usually returning a few hours before dawn. In any case there was no sign of him.

She grabbed the grey sheet that covered the piano and walked away to a corner of the room hauling it in after her, a winding-cloth, a net of fish.

No light. She heard a far grumble of thunder.

She was standing in front of the piano. Without looking down she lowered her hands and started to play, just chording sound, reducing melody to a skeleton. She paused after each set of notes as if bringing her hands out of water to see what she had caught, then continued, placing down the main bones of the tune. She slowed the movements of her fingers even more. She was looking down as two men slipped through the French doors and placed their guns on the end of the piano and stood in front of her. The noise of chords still in the air of the changed room.

Her arms down her sides, one bare foot on the bass pedal, continuing with the song her mother had taught her, that she practised on any surface, a kitchen table, a wall while she walked upstairs, her own bed before she fell asleep. They had had no piano. She used to go to the community centre on Saturday mornings and play there, but all week she practised wherever she was, learning the chalked notes that her mother had drawn onto the kitchen table and then wiped off later. This was the first time she had played on the villa's piano, even though she had been here for three months, her eye catching its shape on her first day there through the French doors. In Canada pianos needed water. You opened up the back and left a full glass of water, and a month later the glass would be empty. Her father had told her about the dwarfs who drank only at pianos, never in bars. She had never believed that but had at first thought it was perhaps mice.

A lightning flash across the valley, the storm had been coming all night, and she saw one of the men was a Sikh. Now she paused and smiled, somewhat amazed, relieved anyway, the cyclorama of light behind them so brief that it was just a quick glimpse of his turban and the bright wet guns. The high flap of the piano had been removed and used as a hospital table several months earlier, so their guns lay on the far side of the ditch of keys. The English patient could have identified the weapons. Hell. She was surrounded by foreign men. Not one pure Italian. A villa romance. What would Poliziano have thought of this 1945 tableau, two men and a woman across a piano and the war almost over and the guns in their wet brightness whenever the lightning slipped itself into the room filling everything with colour and shadow as it was doing now every half-minute thunder crackling all over the valley and the music antiphonal, the press of chords, *When I take my sugar to tea . . .*

Do you know the words?

There was no movement from them. She broke free of the chords and released her fingers into intricacy, tumbling into what she had held back, the jazz detail that split open notes and angles from the chestnut of melody.

> *When I take my sugar to tea*
> *All the boys are jealous of me,*
> *So I never take her where the gang goes*
> *When I take my sugar to tea.*

Their clothes wet while they watched her whenever the lightning was in the room among them, her hands playing now against and within the lightning and thunder, counter to it, filling up the darkness between light. He face so con- centrated they knew they were invisible to her, to her brain

69

struggling to remember her mother's hand ripping newspaper and wetting it under a kitchen tap and using it to wipe the table free of the shaded notes, the hopscotch of keys. After which she went for her weekly lesson at the community hall, where she would play, her feet still unable to reach the pedals if she sat, so she preferred to stand, her summer sandal on the left pedal and the metronome ticking.

She did not want to end this. To give up these words from an old song. She saw the places they went, where the gang never went, crowded with aspidistra. She looked up and nodded towards them, and acknowledgement that she would stop now.

Caravaggio did not see all this. When he returned he found Hana and the two soldiers from a sapper unit in the kitchen making up sandwiches.

III

Sometimes a Fire

THE LAST MEDIAEVAL WAR was fought in Italy in 1943 and 1944. Fortress towns on great promontories which had been battled over since the eighth century had the armies of new kings flung carelessly against them. Around the outcrops of rocks were the traffic of stretchers, butchered vineyards, where if you dug deep beneath the tank ruts, you found blood-axe and spear. Monterchi, Cortona, Urbino, Arezzo, Sansepolcro, Anghiaria. And then the coast.

Cats slept in the gun turrets looking south. English and Americans and Indians and Australians and Canadians advanced north, and the shell traces exploded and dissolved in the air. When the armies assembled at Sansepolcro, a town whose symbol is the crossbow, some soldiers acquired them and fired them silently at night over the walls of the untaken city. Field Marshal Kesselring of the retreating German army seriously considered the pouring of hot oil from battlements.

Mediaeval scholars were pulled out of Oxford colleges and flown into Umbria. Their average age was sixty. They were billeted with the troops, and in meetings with strategic command they kept forgetting the invention of the airplane. They spoke of towns in terms of the art in them. At Monterchi there was the *Madonna del Parto* by Piero della Francesca, located in the chapel next to the town grave-yard. When the thirteenth-century castle was finally taken during the spring rains, troops were billeted under the high dome of the church and slept by the stone pulpit where Hercules slays the Hydra. There was only bad water. Many died of typhoid and other fevers. Looking up with service binoculars in the Gothic church at Arezzo soldiers would come upon their contemporary faces in the Piero della Francesca frescoes. The Queen of Sheba conversing with King Solomon. Nearby a twig from the Tree of Good and Evil inserted into the mouth of the dead Adam. Years later this queen would realize that the bridge over the Siloam was made from the wood of this sacred tree.

It was always raining and cold, and there was no order but for the great maps of art that showed judgement, piety and sacrifice. The Eighth Army came upon river after river of destroyed bridges, and their sapper units clambered down banks on ladders of rope within enemy gunfire and swam or waded across. Food and tents were washed away. Men who were tied to equipment disappeared. Once across the river they tried to ascend out of the water. They sank their hands and wrists into the mud wall of the cliff face and hung there. They wanted the mud to harden and hold them.

The young Sikh sapper put his cheek against the mud and thought of the Queen of Sheba's face, the texture of her skin. There was no comfort in this river except for his desire for her, which somehow kept him warm. He would pull the veil off her hair. He would put his right hand between her neck and olive blouse. He too was tired and sad, as the wise king and guilty queen he had seen in Arezzo two weeks earlier.

·

He hung over the water, his hands locked into the mud-bank. Character, that subtle art, disappeared among them during those days and nights, existed only in a book or on a painted wall. Who was sadder in that dome's mural? He leaned forward to rest on the skin of her frail neck. He fell in love with her downcast eye. This woman who would somehow know the sacredness of bridges.

At night in the camp bed, his arms stretched out into distance like two armies. There was no promise of solution or victory except for the temporary pact between him and that painted fresco's royalty who would forget him, never acknowledge his existence or be aware of him, a Sikh, halfway up a sapper's ladder in the rain, erecting a Bailey bridge for the army behind him. But he remembered the painting of their story. And when a month later the battalions reached the sea, after they had survived everything and entered the coastal town of Cattolica and the engineers had cleared the beach of mines in a twenty-yard stretch so the men could go down naked into the sea, he approached one of the mediaevalists who had befriended him – who had once simply talked with him and shared some Spam – and promised to show him something in return for his kindness.

The sapper signed out a Triumph motorbike, strapped a crimson emergency light onto his arm, and they rode back the way they had come – back into and through the now innocent towns like Urbino and Anghiari, along the winding crest of the mountain ridge that was a spine down Italy, the old man bundled up behind him hugging him, and down the western slope towards Arezzo. The piazza at night was empty of troops, and the sapper parked in front of the church. He helped the mediaevalist off, collected his equipment and walked into the church. A colder darkness.

A greater emptiness, the sound of his boots filling the area. Once more he smelled the old stone and wood. He lit three flares. He slung block and tackle across the columns above the nave, then fired a rivet already threaded with rope into a high wooden beam. The professor was watching him bemused, now and then peering up into the high darkness. The young sapper circled him and knotted a sling across his waist and shoulders, taped a small lit flare to the old man's chest.

He left him there by the communion rail and noisily climbed the stairs to the upper level, where the other end of the rope was. Holding onto it, he stepped off the balcony into the darkness, and the old man was simultaneously swung up, hoisted up fast until, when the sapper touched ground, he swung idly in midair within three feet of the frescoed walls, the flare brightening a halo around him. Still holding the rope the sapper walked forward until the man swung to the right to hover in front of *The Flight of Emperor Maxentius*.

Five minutes later he let the man down. He lit a flare for himself and hoisted his body into the dome within the deep blue of the artificial sky. He remembered its gold stars from the time he had gazed on it with binoculars. Looking down he saw the mediaevalist sitting on a bench, exhausted. He was now aware of the depth of this church, not its height. The liquid sense of it. The hollowness and darkness of a well. The flare sprayed out of his hand like a wand. He pulleyed himself across to her face, his Queen of Sadness, and his brown hand reached out small against the giant neck.

The Sikh sets up a tent in the far reaches of the garden, where Hana thinks lavender was once grown. She has found dry leaves in that area which she has rolled in her fingers and identified. Now and then after a rain she recognizes the perfume of it.

At first he will not come into the house at all. He walks past on some duty or other to do with the dismantling of mines. Always courteous. A little nod of his head. Hana sees him wash at a basin of collected rainwater, placed formally on top of a sundial. The garden tap, used in previous times for the seedbeds, is now dry. She sees his shirtless brown body as he tosses water over himself like a bird using its wing. During the day she notices his arms in the short-sleeved army shirt and the rifle which is always with him, even though battles seem now to be over for them.

He has various postures with the gun – half-staff, half a crook for his elbows when it is over his shoulders. He will turn, suddenly realizing she is watching him. He is a survivor of his fears, will step around anything suspicious, acknowledging her look in this panorama as if claiming he can deal with it all.

He is a relief to her in his self-sufficiency, to all of them in the house, though Caravaggio grumbles at the sapper's continuous humming of Western songs he has learned for himself in the last three years of the war. The other sapper, who had arrived with him in the rainstorm, Hardy he was called, is billeted elsewhere, nearer the town, though she has seen them working together, entering a garden with their wands of gadgetry to clear mines.

The dog has stuck by Caravaggio. The young soldier, who will run and leap with the dog along the path, refuses to give it food of any kind, feeling it should survive on its own.

If he finds food he eats it himself. His courtesy goes only so far. Some nights he sleeps on the parapet that overlooks the valley, crawling into his tent only if it rains.

He, for his part, witnesses Caravaggio's wanderings at night. On two occasions the sapper trails Caravaggio at a distance. But two days later Caravaggio stops him and says, Don't follow me again. He begins to deny it, but the older man puts his hand across his lying face and quiets him. So the soldier knows Caravaggio was aware of him two nights before. In any case, the trailing was simply a remnant of a habit he had been taught during the war. Just as even now he desires to aim his rifle and fire and hit some target precisely. Again and again he aims at a nose on a statue or one of the brown hawks veering across the sky of the valley.

He is still very much a youth. He wolfs down food, jumps up to clear away his plate, allowing himself half an hour for lunch. She has watched him at work, careful and timeless as a cat, in the orchard and within the overgrown garden that rises behind the house. She notices the darker brown skin of his wrist, which slides freely within the bangle that clinks sometimes when he drinks a cup of tea in front of her.

He never speaks about the danger that comes with this kind of searching. Now and then an explosion brings her and Caravaggio quickly out of the house, her heart taut from the muffled blast. She runs out or runs to a window seeing Caravaggio too in the corner of her vision, and they will see the sapper waving lazily towards the house, not even turning around from the herb terrace.

Once Caravaggio entered the library and saw the sapper up by the ceiling, against the trompe l'oeil – only Caravaggio would walk into a room and look up into the high corners to see if he was alone – and the young soldier, his eyes not leaving their focus, put out his palm and snapped his fingers, halting Caravaggio in his entrance, a warning to leave the room for safety as he unthreaded and cut a fuze wire he had traced to that corner, hidden above the valance.

He is always humming or whistling. "Who is whistling?" asks the English patient one night, having not met or even seen the newcomer. Always singing to himself as he lies upon the parapet looking up at a shift of clouds.

When he steps into the seemingly empty villa he is noisy. He is the only one of them who has remained in uniform. Immaculate, buckles shined, the sapper appears out of his tent, his turban symmetrically layered, the boots clean and banging into the wood or stone floors of the house. On a dime he turns from a problem he is working on and breaks into laughter. He seems unconsciously in love with his body, and his physicalness, bending over to pick up a slice of bread, his knuckles brushing the grass, even twirling the rifle absent-mindedly like a huge mace as he walks along the path of cypresses to meet the other sappers in the village.

He seems casually content with this small group in the villa, some kind of loose star on the edge of their system. This is like a holiday for him after the war of mud and rivers and bridges. He enters the house only when invited in; just a tentative visitor, the way he had done that first night when he had followed the faltering sound of Hana's piano and come up the cypress-lined path and stepped into the library.

He had approached the villa on that night of the storm not out of curiosity about the music but because of a danger to the piano player. The retreating army often left pencil mines within musical instruments. Returning owners opened up pianos and lost their hands. People would revive the swing on a grandfather clock, and a glass bomb would blow out half a wall and whoever was nearby.

He followed the noise of the piano, rushing up the hill with Hardy, climbed over the stone wall and entered the villa. As long as there was no pause it meant the player would not lean forward and pull out the thin metal band to set the metronome going. Most pencil bombs were hidden in these – the easiest place to solder the thin layer of wire upright. Bombs were attached to taps, to the spines of books, they were drilled into fruit trees so an apple falling on to a lower branch would detonate the tree, just as a hand gripping that branch would. He was unable to look at a room or field without seeing the possibilities of weapons there.

He had paused by the French doors, leaned his head against the frame, then slid into the room and except for moments of lightning remained within the darkness. There was a girl standing, as if waiting for him, looking down at the keys she was playing. His eyes took in the room before they took her in, swept across it like a spray of radar. The metronome was ticking already, swaying innocently back and forth. There was no danger, no tiny wire. He stood there in his wet uniform, the young woman at first unaware of his entrance.

Besides his tent the antenna of a crystal set is strung up into the trees. She can see the phosphorus green from the radio dial if she looks over there at night with Caravaggio's field glasses, the sapper's shifting body covering it up suddenly if he moves across the path of vision. He wears the portable contraption during the day, just one earphone attached to his head, the other loose under his chin, so he can hear sounds from the rest of the world that might be important to him. He will come into the house to pass on whatever information he has picked up that he thinks might be interesting to them. One afternoon he announces that the bandleader Glenn Miller has died, his plane having crashed somewhere between England and France.

So he moves among them. She sees him in the distance of a defunct garden with the diviner or, if he has found something, unravelling that knot of wires and fuzes someone has left him like a terrible letter.

He is always washing his hands. Caravaggio at first thinks he is too fussy. "How did you get through a war?" Caravaggio laughs.

"I grew up in India, Uncle. You wash your hands all the time. Before all meals. A habit. I was born in the Punjab."

"I'm from Upper America," she says.

He sleeps in and half out of the tent. She sees his hands remove the earphone and drop it onto his lap.

Then Hana puts down the glasses and turns away.

They were under the huge vault. The sergeant lit a flare, and the sapper lay on the floor and looked up through the rifle's telescope, looked at the ochre faces as if he were searching for a brother in the crowd. The cross hairs shook along the biblical figures, the light dousing the coloured vestments and flesh darkened by hundred of years of oil and candle smoke. And now this yellow gas smoke, which they knew was outrageous in this sanctuary, so the soldiers would be thrown out, would be remembered for abusing the permission they received to see the Great Hall, which they had come to, wading up beachheads and the one thousand skirmishes of small wars and the bombing of Monte Cassino and then walking in hushed politeness through the Raphael Stanze till they were here, finally seventeen men who had landed in Sicily and fought their way up the ankle of the country to be here – where they were offered just a mostly dark hall. As if being in the presence of the place was enough.

And one of them had said, "Damn. Maybe more light, Sergeant Shand?" And the sergeant released the catch of the flare and held it up in his outstretched arm, the niagara of its light pouring off his fist, and stood there for the length of its burn like that. The rest of them stood looking up at the figures and faces crowded onto the ceiling that emerged in the light. But the young sapper was already on his back, the rifle aimed, his eye almost brushing the beards of Noah and Abraham and the variety of demons until he reached the great face and was stilled by it, the face like a spear, wise, unforgiving.

The guards were yelling at the entrance and he could hear the running steps, just another thirty seconds left on the flare. He rolled over and handed the rifle to the padre. "That one. Who is he? At three o'clock northwest, who is he? Quick, the flare is almost out."

The padre cradled the rifle and swept it over to the corner, and the flare died.

He returned the rifle to the young Sikh.

"You know we shall all be in serious trouble over this lighting of weapons in the Sistine Chapel. I should not have come here. But I also must thank Sergeant Shand, he was heroic to do it. No real damage has been done, I suppose."

"Did you see it? The face. Who was it?"

"Ah yes, it *is* a great face."

"You saw it."

"Yes. Isaiah."

When the Eighth Army got to Gabbice on the east coast, the sapper was head of night patrol. On the second night he received a signal over the shortwave that there was enemy movement in the water. The patrol sent out a shell and the water erupted, a rough warning shot. They did not hit anything, but in the white spray of the explosion he picked up a darker outline of movement. He raised the rifle and held the drifting shadow in his sights for a full minute, deciding not to shoot in order to see if there would be other movement nearby. The enemy was still camped up north, in Rimini, on the edge of the city. He had the shadow in his sights when the halo was suddenly illuminated around the head of the Virgin Mary. She was coming out of the sea.

She was standing in a boat. Two men rowed. Two other men held her upright, and as they touched the beach the people of the town began to applaud from their dark and opened windows.

The sapper could see the cream-coloured face and the halo of small battery lights. He was lying on the concrete pillbox, between the town and the sea, watching her as the four men climbed out of the boat and lifted the five-foot-tall plaster statue into their arms. They walked up the beach, without pausing, no hesitation for the mines. Perhaps they had watched them being buried and charted them when the Germans had been there. Their feet sank into the sand. This was Gabicce Mare on May 29, 1944. Marine Festival of the Virgin Mary.

Adults and children were on the streets. Men in band uniforms had also emerged. The band would not play and break the rules of curfew, but the instruments were still part of the ceremony, immaculately polished.

He slid from the darkness, the mortar tube strapped to his back, carrying the rifle in his hands. In his turban and with the weapons he was a shock to them. They had not expected him to emerge too out of the no-man's-land of the beach.

He raised his rifle and picked up her face in the gun sight

– ageless, without sexuality, the foreground of the men's dark hands reaching into her light, the gracious nod of the twenty small light bulbs. The figure wore a pale blue cloak, her left knee raised slightly to suggest drapery.

They were not romantic people. They had survived the Fascists, the English, Gauls, Goths and Germans. They had been owned so often it meant nothing. But this blue and cream plaster figure had come out of the sea, was placed in a grape truck full of flowers, while the band marched ahead of her in silence. Whatever protection he was supposed to provide for this town was meaningless. He couldn't walk among their children in white dresses with these guns.

He moved one street south of them and walked at the speed of the statue's movement, so they reached the joining streets at the same time. He raised his rifle to pick up her face once again in his sights. It all ended on a promontory over-looking the sea, where they left her and returned to their homes. None of them was aware of his continued presence of the periphery.

Her face was still lit. The four men who had brought her by boat sat in a square around her like sentries. The battery attached to her back began to fade; it died at about four-thirty in the morning. He glanced at his watch then. He picked up the men with the rifle telescope. Two were asleep. He swung the sights up to her face and studied her again. A different look in the fading light around her. A face which in the darkness looked more like someone he knew. A sister. Someday a daughter. If he could have parted with it, the sapper would have left something as his gesture. But he had his own faith after all.

Caravaggio enters the library. He has been spending most afternoons there. As always, books are mystical creatures to him. He plucks one out and opens it to the title page. He is in the room about five minutes before he hears a slight groan.

He turns and sees Hana asleep on the sofa. He closes the book and leans back against the thigh-high ledge under the shelves. She is curled up, her left cheek on the dusty brocade and her right arm up towards her face, a fist against her jaw. Her eyebrows shift, the face concentrating within sleep.

When he had first seen her after all this time she had looked taut, boiled down to just body enough to get her through this efficiently. Her body had been in a war and, as in love, it had used every part of itself.

He sneezed out loud, and when he looked up from the movement of his tossed-down head she was awake, the eyes open staring ahead at him.

"Guess what time it is."

"About four-oh-five. No, four-oh-seven," she said.

It was an old game between a man and a child. He slipped out of the room to look for the clock, and by his movement and assuredness she could tell he had recently taken morphine, was refreshed and precise, with his familiar confidence. She sat up and smiled when he came back shaking his head with wonder at her accuracy.

"I was born with a sundial in my head, right?"

"And at night?"

"Do they have moondials? Has anyone invented one? Perhaps every architect preparing a villa hides a moondial for thieves like a necessary tithe."

"A good worry for the rich."

"Meet me at the moondial, David. A place where the weak can enter the strong."

"Like the English patient and you?"

"I was almost going to have a baby a year ago."

Now that his mind is light and exact with the drug, she can whip around and he will be with her, thinking alongside her. And she is being open, not quite realizing she is awake and conversing, as if still speaking in a dream, as if his sneeze had been the sneeze in a dream.

Caravaggio is familiar with this state. He has often met people at the moondial. Disturbing them at two a.m. as a whole bedroom cupboard came crashing down by mistake. Such shocks, he discovered, kept them away from fear and violence. Disturbed by owners of houses he was robbing, he would clap his hands and converse frantically, flinging an expensive clock into the air and catching it in his hands, quickly asking them questions, about where things were.

"I lost the child. I mean, I had to lose it. The father was already dead. There was a war."

"Were you in Italy?"

"In Sicily, about the time this happened. All through the time we came up the Adriatic behind the troops I thought of it. I had continued conversations with the child. I worked very hard in the hospitals and retreated from everybody around me. Except the child, who I shared everything with. In my head. I was talking to him while I bathed and nursed patients. I was a little crazy."

"And then your father died."

"Yes. Then Patrick died. I was in Pisa when I heard."

She was awake. Sitting up.

"You knew, huh?"

"I got a letter from home."

"Is that why you came here, because you knew?"

"No."

"Good. I don't think that he believed in wakes and such things. Patrick used to say he wanted a duet by two women on musical instruments when he died. Squeeze-box and violin. That's all. He was so damn sentimental."

"Yes. You could really make him do anything. Find him a woman in distress and he was lost."

The wind rose up out of the valley to their hill so the cypress trees that lined the thirty-six steps outside the chapel wrestled with it. Drops of earlier rain nudged off, falling with a ticking sound upon the two of them sitting on the balustrade by the steps. It was long after midnight. She was lying on the concrete ledge, and he paced or leaned out looking down into the valley. Only the sound of the dislodged rain.

"When did you stop talking to the baby?"

"It all got too busy, suddenly. Troops were going into battles at the Moro Bridge and then into Urbino. Maybe in Urbino I stopped. You felt you could be shot anytime there, not just if you were a solider, but a priest or nurse. It was a rabbit warren, those narrow tilted streets. Soldiers were coming in with just bits of their bodies, falling in love with me for an hour and then dying. It was important to remember their names. But I kept seeing the child whenever they died. Being washed away. Some would sit up and rip all their dressings off trying to breathe better. Some would be worried about tiny scratches on their arms when they died. Then the bubble in the mouth. That little pop. I leaned forward to close a dead soldier's eyes, and he opened them and sneered, 'Can't wait to have me dead? You *bitch*!' He sat up and swept everything on my tray to the floor. So furious. Who would want to die like that? To die with that kind of anger. You *bitch*! And after that I always waited for the bubble in their mouths. I know death now, David. I know all the smells. I know how to divert them from agony. When to give the quick jolt of morphine in a major vein. The saline solution. To make them empty their bowels before they die. Every damn general should have had my job. Every damn general. It should have been a prerequisite for any river crossing. Who the hell were we to be given this responsibility, expected to be wise as old priests, to know how to lead people towards something no one wanted and somehow make them feel comfortable. I could never believe in all those services they gave for the dead. Their vulgar rhetoric. How dare they! How dare they talk like that about a human being dying."

There was no light, all lamps out, the sky mostly cloud-hidden. It was safer not to draw attention to the civilization of existing homes. They were used to walking the grounds of the house in darkness.

"You know why the army didn't want you to stay here, with the English patient? Do you?"

"An embarrassing marriage? My father complex?" She was smiling at him.

"How's the old guy?"

"He still hasn't calmed down about that dog."

"Tell him he came with me."

"He's not really sure you are staying here either. Thinks you might walk off with the china."

"Do you think he would like some wine? I managed to scrounge a bottle today."

"From?"

"Do you want it or not?"

"Let's just have it now. Let's forget him."

"Ah, the breakthrough!"

"Not the breakthrough. I badly need a serious drink."

"Twenty years old. By the time I was twenty . . ."

"Yes, yes, why don't you scrounge a gramophone some-day. By the way, I think this is called looting."

"My country taught me all this. It's what I did for them during the war."

He went through the bombed chapel into the house.

Hana sat up, slightly dizzy, off balance. "And look what they did to you," she said to herself.

Even among those she worked closely with she hardly talked during the war. She needed an uncle, a member of the family. She needed the father of the child, while she waited in this hill town to get drunk for the first time in years, while a burned man upstairs had fallen into his four hours of sleep and an old friend of her father's was now rifling through her medicine chest, breaking the glass tab, tightening a boot-lace round his arm and injecting the morphine quickly into himself, in the time it took for him to turn around.

At night, in the mountains around them, even by ten o'clock, only the earth is dark. Clear grey sky and the green hills.

"I was sick of the hunger. Of just being lusted at. So I stepped away, from the dates, the jeep rides, the courtship. The last dances before they died – I was considered a snob. I worked harder than others. Double shifts, under fire, did anything for them, emptied every bedpan. I became a snob because I wouldn't go out and spend their money. I wanted to go home and there was no one at home. And I was sick of Europe. Sick of being treated like gold because I was female. I courted one man and he died and the child died. I mean, the child didn't just die, I was the one who destroyed it. After that I stepped so far back no one could get near me. Not with talk of snobs. Not with anyone's death. Then I met him, the man burned black. Who turned out to be, close up, an Englishman.

"It has been a long time, David, since I thought of anything to do with a man."

After a week of the Sikh sapper's presence around the villa they adapted to his habits of eating. Wherever he was – on the hill or in the village – he would return around twelve-thirty and join Hana and Caravaggio, pull out the small bundle of blue handkerchief from his shoulder bag and spread it onto the table alongside their meal. His onions and his herbs – which Caravaggio suspected he was taking from the Franciscans' garden during the time he spent there sweeping the place for mines. He peeled the onions with the same knife he used to strip rubber from a fuze wire. This was followed by fruit. Caravaggio suspected he had gone through the whole invasion never eating from a mess canteen.

In fact he had always been dutifully in line at the crack of dawn, holding out his cup for the English tea he loved, adding to it his own supply of condensed milk. He would drink slowly, standing in sunlight to watch the slow move-ment of troops who, if they were stationary that day, would already be playing canasta by nine a.m.

Now, at dawn, under the scarred trees in the half-bombed gardens of the Villa San Girolamo, he takes a mouthful of water from his canteen. He pours tooth powder onto the brush and begins a ten-minute session of lackadaisical brushing as he wanders around looking down into the valley still buried in the mist, his mind curious rather than awestruck at the vista he happens now to be living above. The brushing of teeth, since he was a child, has always been for him an outdoor activity.

The landscape around him is just a temporary thing, there is no permanence to it. He simply acknowledges the possibility of rain, a certain odour from a shrub. As if his mind, even when used, is radar, his eyes locating the choreography of inanimate objects for the quarter-mile around him, which is the killing radius of small arms. He studies the two onions he has pulled out of the earth with care, aware that gardens too have been mined by retreating armies.

At lunch there is Caravaggio's avuncular glance at the objects on the blue handkerchief. There is probably some rare animal, Caravaggio thinks, who eats the same foods that this young soldier eats with his right hand, his fingers carrying it to his mouth. He uses the knife only to peel the skin from the onion, to slice fruit.

The two men take a trip by cart down into the valley to pick up a sack of flour. Also, the soldier has to deliver maps of the cleared areas to headquarters at San Domenico. Finding it difficult to ask questions about each other, they speak about Hana. There are many questions before the older man admits having known her before the war.

"In Canada?"

"Yes, I knew her there."

They pass numerous bonfires on the sides of the road and Caravaggio diverts the young soldier's attention to them.

The sapper's nickname is Kip. "Get Kip." "Here comes Kip." The name had attached itself to him curiously. In his first bomb disposal report in England some butter had marked his paper, and the officer had exclaimed, "What's this? Kipper grease?" and laughter surrounded him. He had no idea what a kipper was, but the young Sikh had been thereby translated into a salty English fish. Within a week his real name, Kirpal Singh, had been forgotten. He hadn't minded this. Lord Suffolk and his demolition team took to calling him by his nickname, which he preferred to the English habit of calling people by their surname.

That summer the English patient wore his hearing aid so he was alive to everything in the house. The amber shell hung within his ear with its translations of casual noises – the chair in the hall scraping against the floor, the click of the dog's claws outside his room so he would turn up the volume and even hear its damn breathing, or the shout on the terrace from the sapper. The English patient within a few days of the young soldier's arrival had thus become aware of his presence around the house, though Hana kept them separate, knowing they would probably not like each other.

But she entered the Englishman's room one day to find the sapper there. He was standing at the foot of the bed, his arms hung over the rifle that rested across his shoulders. She disliked this casual handling of the gun, his lazy spin towards her entrance as if his body were the axle of a wheel, as if the weapon had been sewn along his shoulders and arms and into his small brown wrists.

The Englishman turned to her and said, "We're getting along famously!"

She was put out that the sapper had strolled casually into this domain, seemed able to surround her, be everywhere. Kip, hearing from Caravaggio that the patient knew about guns, had begun to discuss the search for bombs with the Englishman. He had come up to the room and found him a reservoir of information about Allied and enemy weaponry. The Englishman not only knew about the absurd Italian fuzes but also knew the detailed topography of this region of Tuscany. Soon they were drawing outlines of bombs for each other and talking out the theory of each specific circuit.

"The Italian fuzes seem to be put in vertically. And not always at the tail."

"Well, that depends. The ones made in Naples are that way, but the factories in Rome follow the German system. Of course, Naples, going back to the fifteenth century . . ."

It meant having to listen to the patient talk in his circuitous way, and the young soldier was not used to remaining still and silent. He would get restless and kept interrupting the pauses and silences the Englishman always allowed himself, trying to energize the train of thought. The soldier rolled his head back and looked at the ceiling.

"What we should do is make a sling," the sapper mused, turning to Hana as she entered, "and carry him around the house." She looked at both of them, shrugged and walked out of the room.

When Caravaggio passed her in the hall she was smiling. They stood in the hall and listened to the conversation inside the room.

Did I tell you my concept of Virgilian man, Kip? Let me . . . Is your hearing aid on?

What?
Turn it—

She walks out into the sunlight and the courtyard. At noon the taps deliver water into the villa's fountain and for twenty minutes it bursts forth. She removes her shoes, climbs into the dry bowl of the fountain and waits.

At this hour the smell of hay grass is everywhere. Blue-bottles stumble in the air and bang into humans as if slamming into a wall, then retreat unconcerned. She notices where water spiders have nested beneath the upper bowl of the fountain, her face in the shade of its overhang. She likes to sit in this cradle of stone, the smell of cool and dark hidden air emerging from the still empty spout near her, like air from a basement opened for the first time in late spring so the heat outside hangs in contrast. She brushes her arms and toes free of dust, of the crimp of shoes, and stretches.

Too many men in the house. Her mouth leans against the bare arm of her shoulder. She smells her skin, the familiarity of it. One's own taste and flavour. She remembered when she had first grown aware of it, somewhere in her teens – it seemed a place rather than a time – kissing her forearm to practise kissing, smelling her wrist or bending down to her thigh. Breathing into her own cupped hands so breath would bounce back towards her nose. She rubs her bare white feet now against the brindle colour of the fountain. The sapper has told her about statues he came across during the fighting, how he had slept beside one who was a grieving angel, half male, half female, that he had found beautiful. He had lain back, looking at the body, and for the first time during the war felt at peace.

She sniffs the stone, the cool moth smell of it.

Did her father struggle into his death or die calm? Did he lie the way the English patient reposes grandly on his cot? Was he nursed by a stranger? A man not of your own blood can break upon your emotions more than someone of your own blood. As if falling into the arms of a stranger you discover the mirror of your choice. Unlike the sapper, her father was never fully comfortable in the world. His conversations lost some of their syllables out of shyness. In any of Patrick's sentences, her mother had complained, you lost two or three crucial words. But Hana liked that about him, there seemed to be no feudal spirit around him. He had a vagueness, an uncertainty that allowed him tentative charm. He was unlike most men. Even the wounded English patient had the familiar purpose of the feudal. But her father was a hungry ghost, liking those around him to be confident, even raucous.

Did he move towards his death with the same casual sense of being there at an accident? Or in fury? He was the least furious man she knew, hating argument, just walking out of a room if someone spoke baldy of Roosevelt or Tim Buck or praised certain Toronto mayors. He had never attempted to convert anyone in his life, just bandaging or celebrating events that occurred near him. That was all. A novel is a mirror walking down a road. She had read that in one of the books the English patient recommended, and that was the way she remembered her father – whenever she collected the moments of him – stopping his car under one specific bridge in Toronto north of Pottery Road at midnight and telling her that this was where the starlings and pigeons uncomfortably and not too happily shared the rafters during the night. So they had paused there on a summer night and leaned their heads out into the racket of noise and sleepy chirpings.

I was told Patrick died in a dove-cot, Caravaggio said.

Her father loved a city of his own invention, whose streets and walls and borders he and his friends had painted. He never truly stepped out of that world. She realizes everything she knew about the real world she learned on her own or from Caravaggio or, during the time they lived together, from her stepmother, Clara. Clara, who had once been an actress, the articulate one, who had articulated fury when they all left for the war. All through the last year in Italy she has carried the letters from Clara. Letters she knows were written on a pink rock on an island in Georgian Bay, written with the wind coming over the water and curling the paper of her notebook before she finally tore the pages out and put them in an envelope for Hana. She carried them in her suitcase, each containing a flake of pink rock and that wind. But she has never answered them. She has missed Clara with a woe but is unable to write to her, now, after all that has happened to her. She cannot bear to talk of or even acknowledge the death of Patrick.

And now, on this continent, the war having travelled elsewhere, the nunneries and churches that were turned briefly into hospitals are solitary, cut off in the hills of Tuscany and Umbria. They hold the remnants of war societies, small moraines left by a vast glacier. All around them now is the holy forest.

She tucks her feet under her thin frock and rests her arms along her thighs. Everything is still. She hears the familiar hollow churn, restless in the pipe that is buried in the central column of the fountain. Then silence. Then suddenly there is a crash as the water arrives bursting around her.

The tales Hana had read to the English patient, travelling with the old wanderer in *Kim* or with Fabrizio in *The Charterhouse of Parma*, had intoxicated them in a swirl of armies and horses and wagons – those running away from or running towards a war. Stacked in one corner of his bedroom were other books she had read to him whose landscapes they have already walked through.

Many books open with an author's assurance of order. One slipped into their waters with a silent paddle.

> *I begin my work at the time when Servius Galba was Consul. . . . The histories of Tiberius, Caligula, Claudius and Nero, while they were a power, were falsified through terror and after their death were written under a fresh hatred.*

So Tacitus began his *Annals*.

But novels commenced with hesitation or chaos. Readers were never fully in balance. A door a lock a weir opened and they rushed through, one hand holding a gunnel, the other a hat.

When she begins a book she enters through stilted

doorways into large courtyards. Parma and Paris and India spread their carpets.

He sat, in defiance of municipal orders, astride the gun of Zam-Zammah on her brick platform opposite the old Ajaib-Gher – the Wonder House, as the natives called the Lahore Museum. Who hold Zam-Zammah, that "fire-breathing dragon," hold the Punjab; for the great green-bronze piece is always first of the conqueror's loot.

"Read him slowly, dear girl, you must read Kipling slowly. Watch carefully where the commas fall so you can discover the natural pauses. He is a writer who used pen and ink. He looked up from the page a lot, I believe, stared through his window and listened to birds, as most writers who are alone do. Some do not know the names of birds, though he did. Your eye is too quick and North American. Think about the speed of his pen. What an appalling, barnacled old first paragraph it is otherwise."

That was the English patient's first lesson about reading. He did not interrupt again. If he happened to fall asleep she would continue, never looking up until she herself was fatigued. If he had missed the last half-hour of plot, just one room would be dark in a story he probably already knew. He was familiar with the map of the story. There was Benares to the east and Chilianwallah in the north of the Punjab. (All this occurred before the sapper entered their lives, as if out of this fiction. As if the pages of Kipling had been rubbed in the night like a magic lamp. A drug of wonders.)

She had turned from the ending of *Kim*, with its delicate and holy sentences – and now clean diction – and picked up the patient's notebook, the book he had somehow managed to carry with him out of the fire. The book splayed open, almost twice its original thickness.

There was thin paper from a Bible, torn out and glued into the text.

King David was old and stricken in years and they covered him with clothes but he received no heat.

Whereupon his servants said, Let there be sought for the King a young virgin: and let her cherish him, and let her lie in this bosom, that our King may have heat.

So they sought for a fair damsel throughout all the coasts of Israel, and found Abishag a Shunammite. And the damsel cherished the King, and ministered to him: but the King knew her not.

The —— tribe that had saved the burned pilot brought him into the British base at Siwa in 1944. He was moved in the midnight ambulance train from the Western Desert to Tunis, then shipped to Italy. At that time of the war there were hundreds of soldiers lost from themselves, more innocent than devious. Those who claimed to be uncertain of their nationalities were housed in compounds in Tirrenia, where the sea hospital was. The burned pilot was one more enigma, with no identification, unrecognizable. In the criminal compound nearby they kept the American poet Ezra Pound in a cage, where he hid on his body and pockets, moving it daily for his own image of security, the propeller of eucalyptus he had bent down and plucked from his traitor's garden when he was arrested. *"Eucalyptus that is for memory."*

"You should be trying to trick me," the burned pilot told his interrogators, "make me speak German, which I can, by the way, ask me about Don Bradman. Ask me about Marmite, the great Gertrude Jekyll." He knew where every Giotto was in Europe, and most of the places where a person could find convincing trompe l'oeil.

The sea hospital was created out of bathing cabins along the beach that tourists had rented at the turn of the century. During the heat the old Campari umbrellas were placed once more into their table sockets, and the bandaged and the wounded and the comatose would sit under them in the sea air and talk slowly or stare or talk all the time. The burned man noticed the young nurse, separate from the others. He was familiar with such dead glances, knew she was more patient than nurse. He spoke only to her when he needed something.

He was interrogated again. Everything about him was very English except for the fact that his skin was tarred black, a bogman from history among the interrogating officers.

They asked him where the Allies stood in Italy, and he said he assumed they had taken Florence but were held up by the hill towns north of them. The Gothic Line. "Your division is stuck in Florence and cannot get past bases like Prato and Fiesole for instance because the Germans have barracked themselves into villas and convents and they are brilliantly defended. It's an old story – the Crusaders made the same mistake against the Saracens. And like them you now need the fortress towns. They have never been abandoned except during times of cholera."

He had rambled on, driving them mad, traitor or ally, leaving them never quite sure who he was.

Now, months later in the Villa San Girolamo, in the hill

town north of Florence, in the arbour room that is his bed-room, he reposes like the sculpture of the dead knight in Ravenna. He speaks in fragments about oasis towns, the later Medicis, the prose style of Kipling, the woman who bit into his flesh. And in his commonplace book, his 1890 edition of Herodotus' *Histories*, are other fragments – maps, diary entries, writings in many languages, paragraphs cut out of other books. All that is missing is his own name. There is still no clue to who he actually is, nameless, without rank or battalion or squadron. The references in his book are all pre-war, the deserts of Egypt and Libya in the 1930s, interspersed with references to cave art or gallery art or journal notes in his own small handwriting. "There are no brunettes," the English patient says to Hana as she bends over him, "among Florentine Madonnas."

The book is in his hands. She carries it away from his sleeping body and puts it on the side table. Leaving it open she stands there, looking down, and reads. She promises herself she will not turn the page.

May 1936.
I will read you a poem, Clifton's wife said, in her formal voice, which is how she always seems unless you are very close to her. We were all at the southern campsite, within the firelight.

> *I walked in a desert.*
> *And I cried:*
> *"Ah, God, take me from this place!"*
> *A voice said: "It is no desert."*
> *I cried: "Well, but—*
> *The sand, the heat, the vacant horizon."*
> *A voice said: "It is no desert."*

No one said anything.

She said, That was by Stephen Crane, he never came to the desert.

He came to the desert, Madox said.

July 1936.

There are betrayals in war that are childlike compared with our human betrayals during peace. The new lover enters the habits of the other. Things are smashed, revealed in new light. This is done with nervous or tender sentences, although the heart is an organ of fire.

A love story is not about those who lose their heart but about those who find that sullen inhabitant who, when it is stumbled upon, means the body can fool no one, can fool nothing – not the wisdom of sleep or the habit of social graces. It is a consuming of oneself and the past.

It is almost dark in the green room. Hana turns and realizes her neck is stiff from stillness. She has been focused and submerged within the crabbed handwriting in his thick-leaved sea-book of maps and texts. There is even a small fern glued into it. *The Histories.* She doesn't close the book, hasn't touched it since she laid it on the side table. She walks away from it.

Kip was in a field north of the villa when he found the large mine, his foot – almost on the green wire as he crossed the orchard – twisting away, so he lost his balance and was on his knees. He lifted the wire until it was taut, then followed it, zigzagging among the trees.

He sat down at the source with the canvas bag on his lap. The mine shocked him. They had covered it with concrete. They had laid the explosive there and then plastered wet concrete over it to disguise its mechanism and what its strength was. There was a bare tree about four yards away. Another tree about ten yards away. Two months' grass had grown over the concrete ball.

He opened his bag and with scissors clipped the grass away. He laced a small hammock of rope around it and after attaching a rope and pulley to the tree branch slowly lifted the concrete into the air. Two wires led from the concrete towards the earth. He sat down, leaned against the tree and looked at it. Speed did not matter now. He pulled the crystal set out of the bag and placed the earphones to his head. Soon the radio was filling him with American music from the AIF station. Two and a half minutes average for each song or dance number. He could work his way back along "A String of Pearls," "C-Jam Blues" and other tunes to discover how long he had been there, receiving the background music subconsciously.

Noise did not matter. There would be no faint tickings or clickings to signal danger on this kind of bomb. The distraction of music helped him towards clear thought, to the possible forms of structure in the mine, to the personality that had laid the city of threads and then poured wet concrete over it.

The tightening of the concrete ball in midair, braced with a second rope, meant the two wires would not pull away, no matter how hard he attacked it. He stood up and began to chisel the disguised mine gently, blowing away loose grain with his mouth, using the feather stick, chipping more concrete off. He stopped his focus only when the music slipped off the wavelength and he had to realign the station, bringing clarity back to the swing tunes. Very slowly he unearthed the series of wires. There were six wires jumbled up, tied together, all painted black.

He brushed the dust off the mapboard the wires lay on.

Six black wires. When he was a child his father had bunched up his fingers and, disguising all but the tips of them, made him guess which was the long one. His own small finger would touch his choice, and his father's hand would unfold, blossoming, to reveal the boy's mistake. One could of course make a red wire negative. But this opponent had not just concreted the thing but painted all the characters black. Kip was being pulled into a psychological vortex. With the knife he began to scrape the paint free, revealing a red, a blue, a green. Would this opponent have also switched them? He'd have to set up a detour with black wire of his own like an oxbow river and then test the loop for positive or negative power. Then he would check it for fading power and know where the danger lay.

Hana was carrying a long mirror in front of her down the hall. She would pause because of the weight of it and then move forward, the mirror reflecting the old dark pink of the passageway.

The Englishman had wanted to see himself. Before she stepped into the room she carefully turned the reflection upon herself, not wanting the light to bounce indirectly from the window onto his face.

He lay there in his dark skin, the only paleness the hearing aid in his ear and the seeming blaze of light from his pillow. He pushed the sheets down with his hands. Here, do this, pushing as far as he could, and Hana flicked the sheet to the base of the bed.

She stood on a chair at the foot of the bed and slowly tilted the mirror down at him. She was in this position, her hands braced out in front of her, when she heard the faint shouts.

She ignored them at first. The house often picked up noise from the valley. The use of megaphones by the clearance military had constantly unnerved her when she was living alone with the English patient.

"Keep the mirror still, my dear," he said.

"I think there is someone shouting. Do you hear it?"

His left hand turned up the hearing aid.

"It's the boy. You'd better go and find out."

She leaned the mirror against the wall and rushed down the corridor. She paused outside waiting for the next yell. When it came she took off through the garden and into the fields above the house.

He stood, his hands raised above him as if he were holding a giant cobweb. He was shaking his head to get free of the earphones. As she ran towards him he yelled at her to circle to the left, there were mine wires all over the place. She stopped. It was a walk she had taken numerous times with no sense of danger. She raised her skirt and moved forward, watching her feet as they entered the long grass.

His hands were still up in the air as she came alongside him. He had been tricked, ending up holding two live wires he could not put down without the safety of a descant chord. He needed a third hand to negate one of them and he needed to go back once more to the fuze head. He passed the wires carefully to her and dropped his arms, getting blood back into them.

"I'll take them back in a minute."

"It's okay."

"Keep very still."

He opened up his satchel for the Geiger counter and magnet. He ran the dial up and along the wires she was holding. No swerve to negative. No clue. Nothing. He stepped backwards, wondering where the trick could be.

"Let me tape those to the tree, and you leave."

"No. I'll hold it. They won't reach the tree."

"No."

"Kip – I can hold them."

"We have an impasse. There's a joke. I don't know where to go from here. I don't know how complete the trick is."

Leaving her, he ran back to where he had first sighted the wire. He raised it and followed it all the way this time, the Geiger counter alongside it. Then he was crouched about ten yards from her, thinking, now and then looking up, looking right through her, watching only the two tributaries of wire she held in her hands. I don't know, he said out loud, slowly, *I don't know*. I think I have to cut the wire in your left hand, you must leave. He was pulling the radio earphones on over his head, so the sound came back into him fully, filling him with clarity. He schemed along the different paths of the wire and swerved into the convolutions of their knots, the sudden corners, the buried switches that translated them from positive to negative. The tinderbox. He remembered the dog, whose eyes were as big as saucers. He raced with the music along the wires, and all the while he was staring at the girl's hands, which were very still holding on to them.

"You'd better go."

"You need another hand to cut it, don't you?"

"I can attach it to the tree."

"I'll hold it."

He picked the wire like a thin adder from her left hand. Then the other. She didn't move away. He said nothing more, he now had to think as clearly as he could, as if he were alone. She came up to him and took back one of the wires. He was not conscious of this at all, her presence erased. He travelled the path of the bomb fuze again, alongside the mind that had choreographed this, touching all the key points, seeing the X-ray of it, the band music filling everything else.

Stepping up to her, he cut the wire below her left fist before the theorem faded, the sound like something bitten through with a tooth. He saw the dark print of her dress along her shoulder, against her neck. The bomb was dead. He dropped the cutters and put his hand on her shoulder, needing to touch something human. She was saying something he couldn't hear, and she reached forward and pulled the earphones off so silence invaded. Breeze and a rustle. He realized the click of the wire being cut had not been heard at all, just felt, the snap of it, the break of a small rabbit bone. Not letting go of her, he moved his hand down her arm and pulled the seven inches of wire out of her still tight grip.

She was looking at him, quizzical, waiting for his answer to what she had said, but he hadn't heard her. She shook her head and sat down. He started collecting various objects around himself, putting them into his satchel. She looked up into the tree and then only by chance looked back down and saw his hands shaking, tense and hard like an epileptic's, his breathing deep and fast, over in a moment. He was crouched over.

"Did you hear what I said?"

"No. What was that?"

"I thought I was going to die. I wanted to die. And I thought if I was going to die I would die with you. Someone like you, young as I am, I saw so many dying near me in the last year. I didn't feel scared. I certainly wasn't brave just now. I thought to myself, We have this villa this grass, we should have lain down together, you in my arms, before we died. I wanted to touch that bone at your neck, collarbone, it's like a small hard wing under your skin. I wanted to place my fingers against it. I've always liked flesh the colour of rivers and rocks or like the brown eye of a Susan, do you know what that flower is? Have you seen them? I am so tired, Kip, I want to sleep. I want to sleep under this tree, put my eye against your collarbone I just want to close my eyes without thinking of others, want to find the crook of a tree and climb into it and sleep. What a careful mind! To know which wire to cut. How did you know? You kept saying I don't know I don't know, but you did. Right? Don't shake, you have to be a still bed for me, let me curl up as if you were a good grandfather I could hug, I love the world 'curl,' such a slow word, you can't rush it. . . ."

Her mouth was against his shirt. He lay with her on the ground as still as he had to, his eyes clear, looking up into a branch. He could hear her deep breath. When he had put his arm around her shoulder she was already asleep but had gripped it against herself. Glancing down he noticed she still had the wire, she must have picked it up again.

It was her breath that was most alive. Her weight seemed so light she must have balanced most of it away from him. How long could he lie like this, unable to move or turn to busyness. It was essential to remain still, the way he had relied on statues during those months when they moved up the coast fighting into and beyond each fortress until there was no difference in them, the same narrow streets everywhere that became sewers of blood so he would dream that if he lost balance he would slip down those slopes on the red liquid and be flung off the cliff into the valley. Every night he had walked into the coldness of a captured church and found a statue for the night to be his sentinel. He had given his trust only to this race of stones, moving as close as possible against them in the darkness, a grieving angel whose thigh was a woman's perfect thigh, whose line and shadow appeared so soft. He would place his head on the lap of such creatures and release himself into sleep.

She suddenly let more weight onto him. And now her breathing stretched deeper, like the voice of a cello. He watched her sleeping face. He was still annoyed the girl had stayed with him when he defused the bomb, as if by that she had made him owe her something. Making him feel in retrospect responsible for her, though there was no thought of that at the time. As if *that* could usefully influence what he chose to do with a mine.

But he felt he was now within something, perhaps a painting he had seen somewhere in the last year. Some secure couple in a field. How many he had seen with their laziness of sleep, with no thought of work or the dangers of the world. Beside him there were the mouslike movements within Hana's breath; her eyebrows rode upon argument, a small fury in her dreaming. He turned his eyes away, up towards the tree and the sky of white cloud. Her hand gripped him as mud had clung along the bank of the Moro River, his fist plunging into the wet earth to stop himself slipping back into the already crossed torrent.

If he were a hero in a painting, he could claim a just sleep. But as even she had said, he was the brownness of a rock, the brownness of a muddy storm-fed river. And something in him made him step back from even the naive innocence of such a remark. The successful defusing of a bomb ended novels. Wise white fatherly men shook hands, were acknowledged, and limped away, having been coaxed out of solitude for this special occasion. But he was a professional. And he remained the foreigner, the Sikh. His only human and personal contact was this enemy who had made the bomb and departed brushing his tracks with a branch behind him.

Why couldn't he sleep? Why couldn't he turn towards the girl, stop thinking everything was still half lit, hanging fire? In a painting of his imagining the field surrounding this embrace would have been in flames. He had once followed a sapper's entrance into a mined house with binoculars. He had seen him brush a box of matches off the edge of a table and be enveloped by light for the half-second before the crumpling sound of the bomb reached him. What lightning was like in 1944. How could he trust even this circle of elastic on the sleeve of the girl's frock that gripped her arm? Or the rattle in her intimate breath as deep as stones within a river.

She woke when the caterpillar moved from the collar of her dress onto her cheek, and she opened her eyes, saw him crouched over her. He plucked it from her face, not touching her skin, and placed it in the grass. She noticed he had already packed up his equipment. He moved back and sat against the tree, watching her as she rolled slowly onto her back and then stretched, holding that moment for as long as she could. It must have been afternoon, the sun over there. She leaned her head back and looked at him.

"You were supposed to hold onto me!"

"I did. Till you moved away."

"How long did you hold me?"

"Until you moved. Until you needed to move."

"I wasn't taken advantage of, was I?" Adding, "Just joking," as she saw him beginning to blush.

"Do you want to go down to the house?"

"Yes, I'm hungry."

She could hardly stand up, the dazzle of sun, her tired legs. How long they had been there she still didn't know. She could not forget the depth of her sleep, the lightness of the plummet.

A party began in the English patient's room when Caravaggio revealed the gramophone he had found somewhere.

"I will use it to teach you to dance, Hana. Not what your young friend there knows. I have seen and turned my back on certain dances. But this tune, 'How Long Has This Been Going On,' is one of the great songs because the introduction's melody is purer than the song it introduces. And only great jazzmen have acknowledged that. Now, we can have this party on the terrace, which would allow us to invite the dog, or we can invade the Englishman and have it in the bedroom upstairs. Your young friend who doesn't drink managed to find bottles of wine yesterday in San Domenico. We have not just music. Give me your arm. No. First we must chalk the floor and practise. Three main steps – one-two-three – now give me your arm. What happened to you today?"

"He dismantled a large bomb, a difficult one. Let him tell you about it."

The sapper shrugged, not modestly, but as if it was too complicated to explain. Night fell fast, night filled up the

114

valley and then the mountains and they were left once more with lanterns.

They were shuffling together in the corridors towards the English patient's bedroom, Caravaggio carrying the gramophone, one hand holding its arm and needle.

"Now, before you begin on your histories," he said to the static figure in the bed, "I will present you with 'My Romance.'"

"Written in 1935 by Mr. Lorenz Hart, I believe," muttered the Englishman. Kip was sitting at the window, and she said she wanted to dance with the sapper.

"Not until I've taught you, dear worm."

She looked up at Caravaggio strangely; that was her father's term of endearment for her. He pulled her into his thick grizzled embrace and said "dear worm" again, and began the dancing lesson.

She had put on a clean but unironed dress. Each time they spun she saw the sapper singing to himself, following the lyrics. If they had had electricity they could have had a radio, they could have had news of the war somewhere. All they had was the crystal set belonging to Kip, but he had courteously left it in his tent. The English patient was discussing the unfortunate life of Lorenz Hart. Some of his best lyrics to "Manhattan," he claimed, had been changed and he now broke into those verses

"We'll bathe at Brighton;
The fish we'll frighten
When we're in.
Your bathing suit so thin
Will make the shellfish grin
Fin to fin.

"Splendid lines, and erotic, but Richard Rodgers, one suspects, wanted more dignity."

"You must guess my moves, you see."

"Why don't you guess mine?"

"I will when you know what to do. At present I'm the only one who does."

"I bet Kip knows."

"He may know but he won't do it."

"I shall have some wine," the English patient said, and the sapper picked up a glass of water, flung the contents through the window and poured wine for the Englishman.

"This is my first drink in a year."

There was a muffled noise, and the sapper turned quickly and looked out of the window, into the darkness. The others froze. It could have been a mine. He turned back to the party and said, "It's all right, it wasn't a mine. That seemed to come from a cleared area."

"Turn the record over, Kip. Now I will introduce you to 'How Long Has This Been Going On,' written by—" He left an opening for the English patient, who was stymied, shaking his head, grinning with the wine in his mouth.

"This alcohol will probably kill me."

"Nothing will kill you, my friend. You are pure carbon."

"Caravaggio!"

"George and Ira Gershwin. Listen."

He and Hana were gliding to that sadness of the saxophone. He was right. The phrasing so slow, so drawn out, she could sense the musician did not wish to leave the small parlour of the introduction and enter the song, kept wanting to remain there, where the story had not yet begun, as if enamoured by a maid in the prologue. The Englishman murmured that the introductions to such songs were called "burdens."

Her cheek rested against the muscles of Caravaggio's shoulder. She could feel those terrible paws on her back against the clean frock, and they moved in the limited space between the bed and the wall, between bed and door, between the bed and the window alcove that Kip sat within. Every now and then as they turned she would see his face. His knees up and his arms resting on them. Or he would be looking out of the window into darkness.

"Do any of you know a dance called the Bosphorus hug?" the Englishman asked.

"No such thing."

Kip watched the large shadows slide over the ceiling, over the painted wall. He struggled up and walked to the English patient to fill his empty glass, and touched the rim of his glass with the bottle in a toast. West wind coming into the room. And he turned suddenly, angry. A frail scent of cordite reaching him, a percentage of it in the air, and then he slipped out of the room, gesturing weariness, leaving Hana in the arms of Caravaggio.

There was no light with him as he ran along the dark hall. He scooped up the satchel, was out of the house and racing down the thirty-six chapel steps to the road, just running, cancelling the thought of exhaustion from his body.

Was it a sapper or was it a civilian? The smell of flower and herb along the road wall, the beginning stitch at his side. An accident or wrong choice. The sappers kept to themselves for the most part. They were an odd group as far as character went, somewhat like people who worked with jewels or stone, they had a hardness and clarity within them, their decisions frightening even to others in the same trade. Kip had recognized that quality among gem-cutters but never in himself, though he knew others saw it there. The sappers never became familiar with each other. When they talked they passed only information along, new devices, habits of the enemy. He could step into the town hall, where they were billeted, and his eyes would take in the three faces and be aware of the absence of the fourth. Or there would be four of them and in a field somewhere would be the body of an old man or a girl.

He had learned diagrams of order when he joined the army, blueprints that became more and more complicated, like great knots or musical scores. He found out he had the skill of the three-dimensional gaze, the rogue gaze that could look at an object or page of information and realign it, see all the false descants. He was by nature conservative but able also to imagine the worst devices, the capacity for accident in a room – a plum on a table, a child approaching and eating the pit of poison, a man walking into a dark room and before joining his wife in bed brushing loose a paraffin lamp from its bracket. Any room was full of such choreography. The rogue gaze could see the buried line under the surface, how a knot might weave when out of sight. He turned away from mystery books with irritation, able to pinpoint villains with too much ease. He was most comfortable with men who had the abstract madness of autodidacts, like his mentor, Lord Suffolk, like the English patient.

He did not yet have a faith in books. In recent days, Hana had watched him sitting beside the English patient, and it seemed to her a reversal of *Kim*. The young student was now Indian, the wise old teacher was English. But it was Hana in the night who stayed with the old man, who guided him over the mountains to the sacred river. They had even read that book together, Hana's voice slow when wind flattened the candle flame beside her, the page dark for a moment.

He squatted in a corner of the clanging waiting-room,
rapt from all other thoughts; hands folded in lap, and
pupils contracted to pin-points. In a minute – in another
half second – he felt he would arrive at the solution of the
tremendous puzzle . . .

And in some way on those long nights of reading and listening, she supposed, they had prepared themselves for the young soldier, the boy grown up, who would join them. But it was Hana who was the young boy in the story. And if Kip was anyone, he was the officer Creighton.

A book, a map of knots, a fuze board, a room of four people in an abandoned villa lit only by candlelight and now and then light from a storm, now and then the possible light from an explosion. The mountains and hills and Florence blinded without electricity. Candlelight travels less than fifty yards. From a greater distance there was nothing here that belonged to the outside world. They had celebrated in this evening's brief dance in the English patient's room their own simple adventures – Hana her sleep, Caravaggio his "finding" of the gramophone, and Kip a difficult defusing, though he had almost forgotten such a moment already. He was someone who felt uncomfortable in celebrations, in victories.

Just fifty yards away, there had been no representation of them in the world, no sound or sight of them from the valley's eyes as Hana's and Caravaggio's shadows glided across the walls and Kip sat comfortably encased in the alcove and the English patient sipped his wine and felt its spirit percolate through his unused body so it was quickly drunk, his voice bringing forth the whistle of a desert fox bringing forth a flutter of the English wood thrush he said was found only in Essex, for it thrived in the vicinity of lavender and wormwood. All of the burned man's desire was in the brain, the sapper had been thinking to himself, sitting in the stone alcove. Then he turned his head suddenly, knowing everything as he heard the sound, certain of it. He had looked back at them and for the first time in his life lied – "It's all right, it wasn't a mine. That seemed to come from a cleared area" – prepared to wait till the smell of the cordite reached him.

Now, hours later, Kip sits once again in the window alcove. If he could walk the seven yards across the Englishman's room and touch her he would be sane. There was so little light in the room, just the candle at the table where she sat, not reading tonight; he thought perhaps she was slightly drunk.

He had returned from the source of the mine explosion to find Caravaggio asleep on the library sofa with the dog in his arms. The hound watched him as he paused at the open door, moving as little of its body as it had to, to acknowledge it was awake and guarding the place. Its quiet growl rising above Caravaggio's snore.

He took off his boots, tied the laces together and slung them over his shoulder as he went upstairs. It had started to rain and he needed a tarpaulin for his tent. From the hall he saw the light still on in the English patient's room.

She sat in the chair, one elbow on the table where the low candle sprayed its light, her head leaning back. He lowered his boots to the floor and came silently into the room, where the party had been going on three hours earlier. He could smell alcohol in the air. She put her fingers to her lips as he entered and then pointed to the patient. He wouldn't hear Kip's silent walk. The sapper sat in the well of the window again. If he could walk across the room and touch her he would be sane. But between them lay a treacherous and complex journey. It was a very wide world. And the Englishman woke at any sound, the hearing aid turned to full level when he slept, so he could be secure in his own awareness. The girl's eyes darted around and then were still when she faced Kip in the rectangle of window.

He had found the location of the death and what was left there and they had buried his second-in-command, Hardy. And afterwards he kept thinking of the girl that afternoon, suddenly terrified for her, angry at her for involving herself. She had tried to damage her life so casually. She stared. Her last communication had been the finger to her lips. He leaned over and wiped the side of his cheek against the lanyard on his shoulder.

He had walked back through the village, rain falling into pollarded trees of the town square untrimmed since the start of the war, past the strange statue of two men shaking hands on horseback. And now he was here, the candlelight swaying, altering her look so he could not tell what she thought. Wisdom or sadness or curiosity.

If she had been reading or if she had been bending over the Englishman, he would have nodded to her and probably left, but he is now watching Hana as someone young and alone. Tonight, gazing at the scene of the mine blast, he had begun to fear her presence during the afternoon dismantling. He had to remove it, or she would be with him each time he approached a fuze. He would be pregnant with her. When he worked, clarity and music filled him, the human world extinguished. Now she was within him or on his shoulder, the way he had once seen a live goat being carried by an officer out of a tunnel they were attempting to flood.

No.

That wasn't true. He wanted Hana's shoulder, wanted to place his palm over it as he had done in the sunlight when she slept and he had lain there as if in someone's rifle sights, awkward with her. Within the imaginary painter's landscape. He did not want comfort but he wanted to surround the girl with it, to guide her from this room. He refused to believe in his own weaknesses, and with her he had not found a weakness to fit himself against. Neither of them was willing to reveal such a possibility to the other. Hana sat so still. She looked at him, and the candle wavered and altered her look. He was unaware that for her he was just a silhouette, his slight body and his skin part of the darkness.

Earlier, when she saw that he had left the window alcove, she had been enraged. Knowing that he was protecting them like children from the mine. She had clung closer to Caravaggio. It had been an insult. And tonight the growing exhilaration of the evening didn't permit her to read after Caravaggio had gone to bed, stopping to rifle through her medicine box first, and after the English patient had plucked at the air with his bony finger and, when she had bent over, kissed her cheek.

She had blown out the other candles, lit just the night stub at the bedside table and sat there, the Englishman's body facing her in silence after the wildness of his drunken speeches. *"Sometime a horse I'll be, sometime a hound. A hog, a headless bear, sometimes a fire."* She could hear the spill of the wax into the metal tray beside her. The sapper had gone through town to some reach of the hill where the explosion had taken place, and this unnecessary silence still angered her.

She could not read. She sat in the room with her eternally

dying man, the small of her back still feeling bruised from an accidental slam against the wall during her dance with Caravaggio.

Now if he moves towards her she will stare him out, will treat him to a similar silence. Let him guess, make a move. She has been approached before by soldiers.

But what he does is this. He is halfway across the room, his hand sunk to the wrist in his open satchel which still hangs off his shoulder. His walk silent. He turns and pauses beside the bed. As the English patient completes one of his long exhalations he snips the wire of his hearing aid with the cutters and drops them back into the satchel. He turns and grins towards her.

"I'll rewire him in the morning."

He puts his left hand on her shoulder.

"David Caravaggio – an absurd name for you, of course . . ."

"At least I have a name."

"Yes."

Caravaggio sits in Hana's chair. Afternoon sun fills the room, revealing the swimming motes. The Englishman's dark lean face with its angular nose has the appearance of a still hawk swaddled in sheets. The coffin of a hawk, Caravaggio thinks.

The Englishman turns to him.

"There's a painting by Caravaggio, done late in his life. *David with the Head of Goliath*. In it, the young warrior holds at the end of his outstretched arm the head of Goliath, ravaged and old. But that is not the true sadness in the picture. It is assumed that the face of David is a portrait of the youthful Caravaggio and the head of Goliath is a portrait of him as an older man, how he looked when he did the painting. Youth judging age at the end of its outstretched hand. The judging of one's own mortality. I think when I see him at the foot of my bed that Kip is my David."

Caravaggio sits there in silence, thoughts lost among the floating motes. War has unbalanced him and he can return to no other world as he is, wearing these false limbs that morphine promises. He is a man in middle age who has never become accustomed to families. All his life he has avoided permanent intimacy. Till this war he has been a better lover than husband. He has been a man who slips away, in the way lovers leave chaos, the way thieves leave reduced houses.

He watches the man in the bed. He needs to know who this Englishman from the desert is, and reveal him for Hana's sake. Or perhaps invent a skin for him, the way tannic acid camouflages a burned man's rawness.

Working in Cairo during the early days of the war, he had been trained to invent double agents or phantoms who would take on flesh. He had been in charge of a mythical agent named "Cheese," and he spent weeks clothing him with facts, giving him qualities of character – such as greed and a weakness for drink when he would spill false rumours to the enemy. Just as some in Cairo he worked for invented whole platoons in the desert. He had lived through a time of war when everything offered up to those around him was a lie. He had felt like a man in the darkness of a room imitating the calls of a bird.

But here they were shedding skins. They could imitate nothing but what they were. There was no defence but to look for the truth in others.

She pulls down the copy of *Kim* from the library shelf and, standing against the piano, begins to write into the flyleaf in its last pages.

> *He says the gun – the Zam-Zammah cannon – is still there outside the museum in Lahore. There were two guns, made up of metal cups and bowls taken from every Hindu household in the city – as* jizya, *or tax. These were melted down and made into the guns. They were used in many battles in the eighteenth and nineteenth centuries against Sikhs. The other gun was lost during a battle crossing in the Chenab River—*

She closes the book, climbs on to a chair and nestles the book into the high, invisible shelf.

She enters the painted bedroom with a new book and announces the title.

"No books now, Hana."

She looks at him. He has, even now, she thinks, beautiful eyes. Everything occurs there, in that grey stare out of his darkness. There is a sense of numerous gazes that flicker on to her for a moment, then shift away like a lighthouse.

"No more books. Just give me the Herodotus."

She puts the thick, soiled book into his hands.

"I have seen editions of *The Histories* with a sculpted portrait on the cover. Some statue found in a French museum. But I never imagine Herodotus this way. I see him more as one of those spare men of the desert who travel from oasis to oasis, trading legends as if it is the exchange of seeds, consuming everything without suspicion, piecing together a mirage. 'This history of mine,' Herodotus says, 'has from the beginning sought out the supplementary to the main argument.' What you find in him are cul-de-sacs within the sweep of history – how people betray each other for the sake of nations, how people fall in love. . . . How old did you say you were?"

"Twenty."

"I was much older when I fell in love."

Hana pauses. "Who was she?"

But his eyes are away from her now.

"Birds prefer trees with dead branches," said Caravaggio. "They have complete vistas from where they perch. They can take off in any direction."

"If you are talking about me," Hana said, "I'm not a bird. The real bird is the man upstairs."

Kip tried to imagine her as a bird.

"Tell me, it is possible to love someone who is not as smart as you are?" Caravaggio, in a belligerent morphine rush, wanted the mood of argument. "This is something that has concerned me most of my sexual life – which began late, I must announce to this select company. In the same way the sexual pleasure of conversation came to me only after I was married. I had never thought words erotic. Sometimes I really do like to talk more than fuck. Sentences. Buckets of this buckets of that and then buckets of this again. The trouble with words is that you can really talk yourself into a corner. Whereas you can't fuck yourself into a corner."

"That's a man talking," muttered Hana.

"Well, I haven't," Caravaggio continued, "maybe you have, Kip, when you came down to Bombay from the hills, when you came to England for military training. Has anyone, I wonder, fucked themselves into corner. How old are you, Kip?"

"Twenty-six."

"Older than I am."

"Older than Hana. Could you fall in love with her if she wasn't smarter than you? I mean, she may not be smarter than you. But isn't it important for you to *think* she is smarter than you in order to fall in love? Think now. She can be obsessed by the Englishman because he knows more. We're in a huge field when we talk to that guy. We don't even know if he's English. He's probably not. You see, I think it is easier to fall in love with *him* than with *you*. Why is that? Because we want to *know* things, how the pieces fit. Talkers seduce, words direct us into corners. We want more than anything to grow and change. Brave new world."

"I don't think so," said Hana.

"Neither do I. Let me tell you about people my age. The worst thing is others assume you have developed your character by now. The trouble with middle age is they think you are fully formed. *Here*."

Here Caravaggio lifted up his hands, so they faced Hana and Kip. She got up and went behind him and put her arm around his neck.

"Don't do this, okay, David?"

She wrapped her hands softly around his.

"We've already got one crazy talker upstairs."

"Look at us – we sit here like the filthy rich in their filthy villas up in the filthy hills when the city gets too hot. It's nine in the morning – the old guy upstairs is asleep. Hana's obsessed with him. I am obsessed with the sanity of Hana, I'm obsessed with my 'balance,' and Kip will probably get blown up one of these days. Why? For whose sake? He's twenty-six years old. The British army teaches him the skills and the Americans teach him further skills and the team of sappers are given lectures, are decorated and sent off into the rich hills. You are being used, boyo, as the Welsh say. I'm not staying here much longer. I want to take you home. Get the hell out of Dodge City."

"Stop it, David. He'll survive."

"The sapper who got blown up the other night, what was his name?"

Nothing from Kip.

"What was his name?"

"Sam Hardy." Kip went to the window and looked out, leaving their conversation.

"The trouble with all of us is we are where we shouldn't be. What are we doing in Africa, in Italy? What is Kip doing dismantling bombs in orchards, for God's sake? What is he doing fighting English wars? A farmer on the western front cannot prune a tree without ruining his saw. Why? Because of the amount of shrapnel shot into it during the *last* war. Even the trees are thick with diseases we brought. The armies indoctrinate you and leave you here and they fuck off somewhere else to cause trouble, inky-dinky parlez-vous. We should all move out together."

"We can't leave the Englishman."

"The Englishman left months ago, Hana, he's with the Bedouin or in some English garden with its phlox and shit. He probably can't even remember the woman he's circling around, trying to talk about. He doesn't know where the fuck he is.

"You think I'm angry at you, don't you? Because you have fallen in love. Don't you? A jealous uncle. I'm terrified

130

for you. I want to kill the Englishman, because that is the only thing that will save you, get you out of here. And I am beginning to like him. Desert your post. How can Kip love you if you are not smart enough to make him stop risking his life?"

"Because. Because he believes in a civilized world. He's a civilized man."

"First mistake. The correct move is to get on a train, go and have babies together. Shall we go and ask the Englishman, the bird, what he thinks?"

"Why are you not smarter? It's only the rich who can't afford to be smart. They're compromised. They got locked years ago into privilege. They have to protect their belongings. No one is meaner than the rich. Trust me. But they have to follow the rules of their shitty civilized world. They declare war, they have honour, and they can't leave. But you two. We three. We're free. How many sappers die? Why aren't you dead yet? Be irresponsible. Luck runs out."

Hana was pouring milk into her cup. As she finished she moved the lip of the jug over Kip's hand and continued pouring the milk over his brown hand and up his arm to his elbow and then stopped. He didn't move it away.

There are two levels of long, narrow garden to the west of the house. A formal terrace and, higher up, the darker garden, where stone steps and concrete statues almost disappear under the green mildew of the rains. The sapper has his tent pitched here. Rain falls and mist rises out of the valley, and the other rain from the branches of cypress and fir falls upon this half-cleared pocket on the side of the hill.

Only bonfires can dry the permanently wet and shadowed upper garden. The refuse of planks, rafters from prior shellings, dragged branches, weeds pulled up by Hana during the afternoons, scythed grass and nettles – all are brought here and burned by them during the late afternoon's pivot into dusk. The damp fires steam and burn, and the plant-odoured smoke sidles into the bushes, up into the trees, then withers on the terrace in front of the house. It reaches the window of the English patient, who can hear the drift of voices, now and then a laugh from the smoky garden. He translates the smell, evolving it backwards to what had been burned. Rosemary, he thinks, milkweed, wormwood, something else is also there, scentless, perhaps the dog violet, or the false sunflower, which loves the slightly acidic soil of this hill.

The English patient advises Hana on what to grow. "Get your Italian friend to find seeds for you, he seems capable in that category. What you want are plum leaves. Also fire pink and Indian pink – if you want the Latin name for your Latin friend, it is *Silene virginica*. Red savory is good. If you want finches get hazel and chokecherries."

She writes everything down. Then puts the fountain pen into the drawer of the small table where she keeps the book she is reading to him, along with two candles. Vesta matches. There are no medical supplies in this room. She hides them in other rooms. If Caravaggio is to hunt them out, she doesn't want him disturbing the Englishman. She puts the slip of paper with the names of plants into the pocket of her dress to give to Caravaggio. Now that physical attraction has raised its head, she has begun to feel awkward in the company of the three men.

If it is physical attraction. If all this has to do with love of Kip. She likes to lay her face against the upper reaches of his arm, that dark brown river, and to wake submerged within it, against the pulse of an unseen vein in his flesh beside her. The vein she would have to locate and insert a saline solution into if he were dying.

At two or three in the morning, after leaving the Englishman, she walks through the garden towards the sapper's hurricane lamp, which hangs off the arm of St Christopher. Absolute darkness between her and the light, but she knows every shrub and bush in her path, the location of the bonfire she passes, low and pink in its near completion. Sometimes she cups a hand over the glass funnel and blows out the flame, and sometimes she leaves it burning and ducks under it and enters through the open flaps, to crawl in against his body, the arm she wants, her tongue instead of a swab, her tooth instead of a needle, her mouth instead of the mask with the codeine drops to make him sleep, to make his immortal ticking brain slow into sleepiness. She folds her paisley dress and places it on top of her tennis shoes. She knows that for him the world burns around them with only a few crucial rules. You replace TNT with steam, you drain it, you— all this she knows is in his head as she sleeps beside him virtuous as a sister.

The tent and the dark wood surround them.

They are only a step past the comfort she has given others in the temporary hospitals in Ortona or Monterchi. Her body for last warmth, her whisper for comfort, her needle for sleep. But the sapper's body allows nothing to enter him that comes from another world. A boy in love who will not eat the food she gathers, who does not need or want the drug in a needle she could slide into his arm, as Caravaggio does, or those ointments of desert invention the Englishman craves, ointments and pollen to reassemble himself the way the Bedouin had done for him. Just for the comfort of sleep.

There are ornaments he places around himself. Certain leaves she has given him, a stub of candle, and in his tent the crystal set and the shoulder bag full of the objects of discipline. He has emerged from the fighting with a calm which, even if false, means order for him. He continues his strictness, following the hawk in its float along the valley within the V of his rifle sight, opening up a bomb and never taking his eyes off what he is searching for as he pulls a

Thermos towards him and unscrews the top and drinks, never even looking at the metal cup.

The rest of us are just periphery, she thinks, his eyes are only on what is dangerous, his listening ear on whatever is happening in Helsinki or Berlin that comes over the short-wave. Even when he is a tender lover, and her left hand holds him above the *kara*, where the muscles of his forearm tense, she feels invisible to that lost look till his groan when his head falls against her neck. Everything else, apart from danger, is periphery. She has taught him to make a noise, desired it of him, and if he is relaxed at all since the fighting it is only in this, as if finally willing to admit his whereabouts in the darkness, to signal out his pleasure with a human sound.

How much she is in love with him or he with her we don't know. Or how much it is a game of secrets. As they grow intimate the space between them during the day grows larger. She likes the distance he leaves her, the space he assumes is their right. It gives each of them a private energy, a code of air between them when he passes below her window without a word, walking the half-mile to assemble with the other sappers in the town. He passes a plate or some food into her hands. She places a leaf across his brown wrist. Or they work with Caravaggio between them mortaring up a collapsing wall. The sapper sings his Western songs, which Caravaggio enjoys but pretends not to.

"Pennsylvania six-five-oh-oh-oh," the young soldier gasps.

She learns all the varieties of his darkness. The colour of his forearm against the colour of his neck. The colour of his palms, his cheek, the skin under the turban. The darkness of fingers separating red and black wires, or against bread he picks off the gunmetal plate he still uses for food. Then he stands up. His self-sufficiency seems rude to them, though no doubt he feels it is excessive politeness.

She loves most the wet colours of his neck when he bathes. And his chest with its sweat which her fingers grip when he is over her, and the dark, tough arms in the darkness of his tent, or one time in her room when light from the valley's city, finally free of curfew, rose among them like twilight and lit the colour of his body.

Later she will realize he never allowed himself to be beholden to her, or her to him. She will stare at the word in a novel, lift it off the book and carry it to a dictionary. *Beholden. To be under obligation.* And he, she knows, never allowed that. If she crosses the two hundred yards of dark garden to him it is her choice, and she might find him asleep, not from a lack of love but from necessity, to be clear-minded towards the next day's treacherous objects.

He thinks her remarkable. He wakes and sees her in the spray of the lamp. He loves most her face's smart look. Or in the evenings he loves her voice as she argues Caravaggio out of a foolishness. And the way she crawls in against his body like a saint.

They talk, the slight singsong of his voice within the canvas smell of their tent, which has been all through the Italian campaign, which he reaches up to touch with his slight fingers as if it too belonged to his body, a khaki wing he folds over himself during the night. It is his world. She feels displaced out of Canada during these nights. He asks her why she cannot sleep. She lies there irritated at his self-sufficiency, his ability to turn so easily away from the world.

She wants a tin roof for the rain, two poplar trees to shiver outside her window, a noise she can sleep against, sleeping trees and sleeping roofs that she grew up with in the east end of Toronto and then for a couple of years with Patrick and Clara along the Skootamatta River and later Georgian Bay. She has not found a sleeping tree, even in the density of this garden.

"Kiss me. It's your mouth I'm most purely in love with. Your teeth." And later, when his head has fallen to one side, towards the air by the tent's opening, she has whispered aloud, heard only by herself, "Perhaps we should ask Caravaggio. My father told me once that Caravaggio was a man always in love. Not just *in* love but always sinking within in. Always confused. Always happy. Kip? Do you hear me? I'm so happy with you. To be with you like this."

Most of all she wished for a river they could swim in. There was a formality in swimming which she assumed was like being in a ballroom. But he had a different sense of rivers, had entered the Moro in silence and pulled the harness of cables attached to the folding Bailey bridge, the bolted steel panels of it slipping into the water behind him like a creature, and the sky then had lit up with shell fire and someone was sinking beside him in mid-river. Again and again the sappers dove for the lost pulleys, grappling hooks in the water among them, mud and surface and faces lit up by phosphorus flares in the sky around them.

All through the night, weeping and shouting, they had to stop each other going crazy. Their clothes full of winter river, the bridge slowly eased into a road above their heads. And two days later another river. Every river they came to was bridgeless, as if its name had been erased, as if the sky were starless, homes doorless. The sapper units slid in with ropes, carried cables over their shoulders and spannered the bolts, oil-covered to silence the metals, and then the army marched over. Drove over the prefabricated bridge with the sappers still in the water below.

So often they were caught in midstream when the shells came, flaring into mudbanks, breaking apart the steel and iron into stones. Nothing would protect them then, the brown river thin as silk against metals that ripped through it.

He turned from that. He knew the trick of quick sleep against this one who had her own rivers and was lost from them.

Yes, Caravaggio would explain to her how she could sink into love. Even how to sink into cautious love. "I want to take you to the Skootamatta River, Kip," she said. "I want to show you Smoke Lane. The woman my father loved lives out on the lakes, slips into canoes more easily than into a car. I miss thunder that blinks out electricity. I want you to meet Clara of the canoes, the last one in my family. There are no others now. My father forsook her for a war."

She walks towards the night tent without a false step or any hesitation. The trees make a sieve of moonlight, as if she is caught within the light of a dance hall's globe. She enters his tent and puts an ear to his sleeping chest and listens to his beating heart, the way he will listen to a clock on a mine. Two a.m. Everyone is asleep but her.

IV

South Cairo 1930–1938

THERE IS, after Herodotus, little interest by the Western world towards the desert for hundreds of years. From 425 B.C. to the beginning of the twentieth century there is an averting of eyes. Silence. The nineteenth century was an age of river seekers. And then in the 1920s there is a sweet postscript history on this pocket of earth, made mostly by privately funded expeditions and followed by modest lectures given at the Geographical Society in London at Kensington Gore. These lectures are given by sunburned, exhausted men who, like Conrad's sailors, are not too comfortable with the etiquette of taxis, the quick, flat wit of bus conductors.

When they travel by local trains from the suburbs towards Knightsbridge on their way to Society meetings, they are often lost, tickets misplaced, clinging only to their old maps and carrying their lecture notes – which were slowly and painfully written – in their ever present knapsacks which will always be a part of their bodies. These men of all nations travel at that early evening hour, six o'clock, when there is the light of the solitary. It is an anonymous time, most of the city is going home. The explorers arrive too early at Kensington Gore, eat at the Lyons Corner House and then enter the Geographical Society, where they sit in the upstairs hall next to the large Maori canoe, going over their notes. At eight o'clock the talks begin.

Every other week there is a lecture. Someone will introduce the talk and someone will give thanks. The concluding speaker usually argues or tests the lecture for hard currency, is pertinently critical but never impertinent. The main speakers, everyone assumes, stay close to the facts, and even obsessive assumptions are presented modestly.

My journey through the Libyan Desert from Sokum on the Mediterranean to El Obeid in the Sudan was made over one of the few tracks of the earth's surface which present a number and variety of interesting geographical problems . . .

The years of preparation and research and fund-raising are never mentioned in these oak rooms. The previous week's lecturer recorded the loss of thirty people in ice in Antarctica. Similar losses in extreme heat or windstorm are announced with minimal eulogy. All human and financial behaviour lies on the far side of the issue being discussed – which is the earth's surface and its "interesting geographical problems."

Can other depressions in this religion, besides the much-discussed Wadi Rayan, be considered possible of utilization in connection with irrigation or drainage of the Nile Delta? Are the artesian water supplies of the oases gradually diminishing? Where shall we look for the mysterious "Zerzura"? Are there any other "lost" oases

> *remaining to be discovered? Where are the tortoise*
> *marshes of Ptolemy?*

John Bell, director of Desert Surveys in Egypt, asked these questions in 1927. By the 1930s the papers grew even more modest. *"I should like to add a few remarks on some of the points raised in the interesting discussion on the 'Prehistoric Geography of Kharga Oasis.'"* By the mid-1930s the last oasis of Zerzura was found by Ladislaus de Almásy and his companions.

In 1939 the great decade of Libyan Desert expeditions came to an end, and this vast and silent pocket of the earth became one of the theatres of war.

In the arboured bedroom the burned patient views great distances. The way that dead knight in Ravenna, whose marble body seems alive, almost liquid, has his head raised upon a stone pillow, so it can gaze beyond his feet into vista. Farther than the desired rain of Africa. Towards all their lives in Cairo. Their works and days.

Hana sits by his bed, and she travels like a squire beside him during these journeys.

In 1930 we had begun mapping the greater part of the Gilf Kebir Plateau, looking for the lost oasis that was called Zerzura. The City of Acacias.

We were desert Europeans. John Bell had sighted the Gilf in 1917. Then Kemal el Din. Then Bagnold, who found his way south into the Sand Sea. Madox, Walpole of Desert Surveys, His Excellency Wasfi Bey, Casparius the photographer, Dr. Kadar the geologist and Bermann. And the Gilf Kebir – that large plateau resting in the Libyan Desert, the size of Switzerland, as Madox liked to say – was our heart, its escarpments precipitous to the east and west, the plateau sloping gradually to the north. It rose out of the desert four hundred miles west of the Nile.

For the early Egyptians there was supposedly no water west of the oasis towns. The world ended out there. The interior was waterless. But in the emptiness of deserts you are always surrounded by lost history. Tebu and Senussi tribes had roamed there possessing wells that they guarded with great secrecy. There were rumours of fertile lands that nestled within the desert's interior. Arab writers in the thirteenth century spoke of Zerzura. "The Oasis of Little Birds." "The City of Acacias." In *The Book of Hidden Treasures*, the *Kitab al Kanuz*, Zerzura is depicted as a white city, "white as a dove."

Look at a map of the Libyan Desert and you will see names. Kemal el Din in 1925, who, almost solitary, carried out the first great modern expedition. Bagnold 1930–1932. Almásy–Madox 1931–1937. Just north of the Tropic of Cancer.

We were a small clutch of a nation between the wars, mapping and re-exploring. We gathered at Dakhla and Kufra as if they were bars or cafés. An oasis society, Bagnold called it. We knew each other's intimacies, each other's skills and weaknesses. We forgave Bagnold everything for the way he wrote about dunes. *"The grooves and the corrugated sand resemble the hollow of the roof of a dog's mouth."* That was the real Bagnold, a man who would put his inquiring hand into the jaws of a dog.

1930. Our first journey, moving south from Jaghbub into the desert among the preserve of Zwaya and Majabra's tribes. A seven-day journey to El Taj. Madox and Bermann, four others. Some camels a horse and a dog. As we left they told us the old joke. "To start a journey in a sandstorm is good luck."

We camped the first night twenty miles south. The next morning we woke and came out of our tents at five. Too cold to sleep. We stepped towards the fires and sat in their light in the larger darkness. Above us were the last stars. There would be no sunrise for another two hours. We passed around hot glasses of tea. The camels were being fed, half asleep, chewing the dates along with the date stones. We ate breakfast and then drank three more glasses of tea.

Hours later we were in the sandstorm that hit us out of clear morning, coming from nowhere. The breeze that had been refreshing had gradually strengthened. Eventually we looked down, and the surface of the desert was changed. Pass me the book . . . here. This is Hassanein Bey's wonderful account of such storms—

"It is as though the surface were underlaid with steam-pipes, with thousands of orifices through which tiny jets of steam are puffing out. The sand leaps in little spurts and whirls. Inch by inch the disturbance rises as the wind increases its force. It seems as though the whole surface of the desert were rising in obedience to some upthrusting force beneath. Larger pebbles strike against the skins, the knees, the thighs. The sand-grains climb the body till it strikes the face and goes over the head. The sky is shut out, all but the nearest objects fade from view, the universe is filled."

We had to keep moving. If you pause sand builds up as it would around anything stationary, and locks you in. You are lost forever. A sandstorm can last five hours. Even when we were in trucks in later years we would have to keep driving with no vision. The worst terrors came at night. Once, north of Kufra, we were hit by a storm in the darkness. Three a.m. The gale swept the tents from their moorings and we rolled with them, taking in sand like a sinking boat takes in water, weighed down, suffocating, till we were cut free by a camel driver.

We travelled through three storms during nine days. We missed small desert towns where we expected to locate more supplies. The horse vanished. Three of the camels died. For the last two days there was no food, only tea. The last link with any other world was the clink of the fire-black tea urn and the long spoon and the glass which came towards us in the darkness of the mornings. After the third night we gave up talking. All that mattered was the fire and the minimal brown liquid.

Only by luck did we stumble on the desert town of El Taj. I walked through the souk, the alley of clocks chiming, into the street of barometers, past the rifle-cartridge stalls, stands of Italian tomato sauce and other tinned food from Benghazi, calico from Egypt, ostrich-tail decorations, street dentists, book merchants. We were still mute, each of us dispersing along our own paths. We received this new world slowly, as if coming out of a drowning. In the central square of El Taj we sat and ate lamb, rice, *badawi* cakes, and drank milk with almond pulp beaten into it. All this after the long wait for three ceremonial glasses of tea flavoured with amber and mint.

Sometime in 1931 I joined a Bedouin caravan and was told there was another one of us there. Fenelon-Barnes, it turned out. I went to his tent. He was out for the day on some small expedition, cataloguing fossil trees. I looked around his tent, the sheaf of maps, the photos he always carried of his family, et cetera. As I was leaving I saw a mirror tacked up high against the skin wall, and looking at it I saw the reflection of the bed. There seemed to be a small lump, a dog possibly, under the covers. I pulled back the *djellaba* and there was a small Arab girl tied up, sleeping there.

By 1932, Bagnold was finished and Madox and the rest of us were everywhere. Looking for the lost army of Cambyses. Looking for Zerzura. 1932 and 1933 and 1934. Not seeing each other for months. Just the Bedouin and us, crisscrossing the Forty Days Road. There were rivers of desert tribes, the most beautiful humans I've met in my life. We were German, English, Hungarian, African – all of us insignificant to them. Gradually we became nationless. I came to hate nations. We are deformed by nation-states. Madox died because of nations.

The desert could not be claimed or owned – it was a piece of cloth carried by winds, never held down by stones, and given a hundred shifting names long before Canterbury existed, long before battles and treaties quilted Europe and the East. Its caravans, those strange rambling feasts and cultures, left nothing behind, not an ember. All of us, even those with European homes and children in the distance, wished to remove the clothing of our countries. It was a place of faith. We disappeared into landscape. Fire and sand. We left the harbours of oasis. The places water came to and touched . . . *Ain, Bir, Wadi, Foggara, Khottara, Shaduf*. I didn't want my name against such beautiful names. Erase the family name! Erase nations! I was taught such things by the desert.

Still, some wanted their mark there. On that dry watercourse, on this shingled knoll. Small vanities in this plot of land northwest of the Sudan, south of Cyrenaica. Fenelon-Barnes wanted the fossil trees he discovered to bear his name. He even wanted a tribe to take his name, and spent a year on the negotiations. Then Bauchan outdid him, having a type of sand dune named after him. But I wanted to erase my name and the place I had come from. By the time war arrived, after ten years in the desert, it was easy for me to slip across borders, not to belong to anyone, to any nation.

1933 or 1934. I forget the year. Madox, Casparius, Bermann, myself, two Sudanese drivers and a cook. By now we travel in A-type Ford cars with box bodies and are using for the first time large balloon tyres known as air wheels. They ride better on sand, but the gamble is whether they will stand up to stone fields and splinter rocks.

We leave Kharga on March 22. Bermann and I have theorized that three wadis written about by Williamson in 1838 make up Zerzura.

Southwest of the Gilf Kebir are three isolated granite massifs rising out of the plain – Gebel Arkanu, Gebel Uweinat, and Gebel Kissu. The three are fifteen miles apart from each other. Good water in several of the ravines, though the wells are Gebel Arkanu are bitter, not drinkable except in an emergency. Williamson said three wadis formed Zerzura, but he never located them and this is considered fable. Yet even one rain oasis in these crater-shaped hills would solve the riddle of how Cambyses and his army could attempt to cross such a desert, of the Senussi raids during the Great War, when the black giant raiders crossed a desert which supposedly has no water or pasture. This was a world that had been civilised for centuries, had a thousand paths and roads.

We find jars at Abu Ballas with the classic Greek amphora shape. Herodotus speaks of such jars.

Bermann and I talk to a snakelike mysterious old man in the fortress of El Jof – in the stone hall that once had been the library of the great Senussi sheik. An old Tebu, a caravan guide by profession, speaking accented Arabic. Later Bermann says "like the screeching of bats," quoting Herodotus. We talk to him all day, all night, and he gives nothing away. The Senussi creed, their foremost doctrine, is still not to reveal the secrets of the desert to strangers.

At Wadi el Melik we see birds of an unknown species.

On May 5, I climb a stone cliff and approach the Uweinat plateau from a new direction. I find myself in a broad wadi full of acacia trees.

There was a time when mapmakers named the places they travelled through with the names of lovers rather than their own. Someone seen bathing in a desert caravan, holding up muslin with one arm in front of her. Some old Arab poet's woman, whose white-dove shoulders made him describe an oasis with her name. The skin bucket spreads water over her, she wraps herself in the cloth, and the old scribe turns from her to describe Zerzura.

So a man in the desert can slip into a name as if within a discovered well, and in its shadowed coolness be tempted never to leave such containment. My great desire was to remain there, among those acacias. I was walking not in a place where no one had walked before but in a place where there were sudden, brief populations over the centuries – a fourteenth-century army, a Tebu caravan, the Senussi raiders of 1915. And in between these times – nothing was there. When no rain fell the acacias withered, the wadis dried out . . . until water suddenly reappeared fifty or a hundred years later. Sporadic appearances and disappearances, like legends and rumours through history.

In the desert the most loved waters, like a lover's name, are carried blue in your hands, enter your throat. One swallows absence. A woman in Cairo curves the white length of her body up from the bed and leans out of the window into a rainstorm to allow her nakedness to receive it.

Hana leans forwards, sensing his drifting, watching him, not saying a word. Who is she, this woman?

The ends of the earth are never the points on a map that colonists push against, enlarging their sphere of influence. On one side servants and slaves and tides of power and correspondence with the Geographical Society. On the other the first step by a white man across a great river, the first sight (by a white eye) of a mountain that has been there forever.

When we are young we do not look into mirrors. It is when we are old, concerned with our name, our legend, what our lives will mean to the future. We become vain with the names we own, our claims to have been the first eyes, the strongest army, the cleverest merchant. It is when he is old that Narcissus wants a graven image of himself.

But we were interested in how our lives could mean something to the past. We sailed into the past. We were young. We knew power and great finance were temporary things. We all slept with Herodotus. *"For those cities that were great in earlier times must have now become small, and those that were great in my time were small in the time before. . . . Man's good fortune never abides in the same place."*

In 1936 a young man named Geoffrey Clifton had met a friend at Oxford who mentioned what we were doing. He contacted me, got married the next day, and two weeks later flew with his wife to Cairo.

The couple entered our world – the four of us, Prince Kemal el Din, Bell, Almásy and Madox. The name that still filled our mouths was Gilf Kebir. Somewhere in the Gilf nestled Zerzura, whose name occurs in Arab writings as far back as the thirteenth century. When you travel that far in time you need a plane, and young Clifton was rich and he could fly and he had a plane.

Clifton met us in El Jof, north of Uweinat. He sat in his two-seater plane and we walked towards him from the base camp. He stood up in the cockpit and poured a drink out of his flask. His new wife sat beside him.

"I name this site the Bir Messaha Country Club," he announced.

I watched the friendly uncertainty scattered across his wife's face, her lionlike hair when she pulled off the leather helmet.

They were youth, felt like our children. They climbed out of the plane and shook hands with us.

That was 1936, the beginning of our story. . . .

They jumped off the wing of the Moth. Clifton walked towards us holding out the flask, and we all sipped the warm alcohol. He was one for ceremonies. He had named his plane *Rupert Bear*. I don't think he loved the desert, but he had an affection for it that grew out of awe at our stark order, into which he wanted to fit himself – like a joyous undergraduate who respects silent behaviour in a library. We had not expected him to bring his wife, but we were I suppose courteous about it. She stood there while the sand collected in her mane of hair.

What were we to this young couple? Some of us had

written books about dune formation, the disappearance and reappearance of oases, the lost culture of deserts. We seemed to be interested only in things that could not be bought or sold, of no interest to the outside world. We argued about latitudes, or about an event that had happened seven hundred years earlier. The theorems of exploration. That Abd el Melik Ibrahim el Zwaya who lived in Zuck oasis pasturing camels was the first man among those tribes who could understand the concept of photographs.

The Cliftons were on the last days of their honeymoon. I left them with the others and went to join a man in Kufra and spent many days with him, trying out theories I had kept secret from the rest of the expedition. I returned to the base camp at El Jof three nights later.

The desert fire was between us. The Cliftons, Madox, Bell and myself. If a man leaned back a few inches he would disappear into darkness. Katharine Clifton began to recite something, and my head was no longer in the halo of the camp's twig fire.

There was classical blood in her face. Her parents were famous, apparently, in the world of legal history. I am a man who did not enjoy poetry until I heard a woman recite it to us. And in that desert she dragged her university days into our midst to describe the stars – the way Adam tenderly taught a woman with gracious metaphors.

> *These then, though unbeheld in deep of night,*
> *Shine not in vain, nor think, though men were none,*
> *That Heav'n would want spectators. God want praise:*
> *Millions of spiritual Creatures walk the Earth*
> *Unseen, both when we wake, and when we sleep:*
> *All these with ceaseless praise his works behold*
> *Both day and night: how often from the steep*

> *Of echoing Hill or Thicket have we heard*
> *Celestial voices to the midnight air,*
> *Sole or responsive each to other's note*
> *Singing their great Creator . . .*

That night I fell in love with a voice. Only a voice. I wanted to hear nothing more. I got up and walked away.

She was a willow. What would she be like in winter, at my age? I see her still, always, with the eye of Adam. She had been these awkward limbs climbing out of a plane, bending down in our midst to prod at a fire, her elbow up and pointed towards me as she drank from a canteen.

A few months later, she waltzed with me, as we danced as a group in Cairo. Though slightly drunk she wore an unconquerable face. Even now the face I believe that most revealed her was the one she had that time when we were both half drunk, not lovers.

All these years I have been trying to unearth what she was handing me with that look. It seemed to be contempt. So it appeared to me. Now I think she was studying me. She was an innocent, surprised at something in me. I was behaving the way I usually behave in bars, but this time with the wrong company. I am a man who kept the codes of my behaviour separate. I was forgetting she was younger than I.

She was *studying* me. Such a simple thing. And I was watching for one wrong move in her statue-like gaze, something that would give her away.

Give me a map and I'll build you a city. Give me a pencil and I will draw you a room in South Cairo, desert charts on the wall. Always the desert was among us. I could wake and raise my eyes to the map of old settlements along the Mediterranean coast – Gazala, Tobruk, Mersa Matruh – and south of that the hand-painted wadis, and surrounding those the shades of yellowness that we invaded, tried to lose ourselves in. *"My task is to describe briefly the several expeditions which have attacked the Gilf Kebir. Dr. Bermann will later take us back to the desert as it existed thousands of years ago. . . ."*

That is the way Madox spoke to other geographers at Kensington Gore. But you do not find adultery in the minutes of the Geographical Society. Our room never appears in the detailed reports which chartered every knoll and every incident of history.

In the street of imported parrots in Cairo one is hectored by almost articulate birds. The birds bark and whistle in rows, like a plumed avenue. I knew which tribe had travelled which silk or camel road carrying them in their petite palanquins across the deserts. Forty-day journeys, after the birds were caught by slaves or picked like flowers in equatorial gardens and then placed in bamboo cages to enter the river that is trade. They appeared like brides in a mediaeval courtship.

We stood among them. I was showing her a city that was new to her.

Her hand touched me at the wrist.

"If I gave you my life, you would drop it. Wouldn't you?"

I didn't say anything.

V

Katharine

THE FIRST TIME she dreamed of him she woke up beside her husband screaming.

In their bedroom she stared down onto the sheet, mouth open. Her husband put his hand on her back.

"Nightmare. Don't worry."

"Yes."

"Shall I get you some water?"

"Yes."

She wouldn't move. Wouldn't lie back into that zone they had been in.

The dream had taken place in this room – his hand on her neck (she touched it now), his anger towards her that she had sensed the first few times she had met him. No, not anger, a lack of interest, irritation at a married woman being among them. They had been bent over like animals, and he had yoked her neck back so she had been unable to breathe within her arousal.

Her husband brought her the glass on a saucer but she could not lift her arms, they were shaking, loose. He put the glass awkwardly against her mouth so she could gulp the chlorinated water, some coming down her chin, falling to her stomach. When she lay back she hardly had time to think of what she had witnessed, she fell into a quick deep sleep.

That had been the first recognition. She remembered it sometime during the next day, but she was busy then and she refused to nestle with its significance for long, dismissed it; it was an accidental collision on a crowded night, nothing more.

A year later the other, more dangerous, peaceful dreams came. And even within the first one of these she recalled the hands at her neck and waited for the mood of calmness between them to swerve to violence.

Who lays the crumbs of food that tempt you? Towards a person you never considered. A dream. Then later another series of dreams.

He said later it was propinquity. Propinquity in the desert. It does that here, he said. He loved the word – the propinquity of water, the propinquity of two or three bodies in a car driving the Sand Sea for six hours. Her sweating knee beside the gearbox of the truck, the knee swerving, rising with the bumps. In the desert you have time to look everywhere, to theorize on the choreography of all things around you.

When he talked like that she hated him, her eyes remaining polite, her mind wanting to slap him. She always had the desire to slap him, and she realized even that was sexual. For him all relationships fell into patterns. You fell into propinquity or distance. Just as, for him, the histories in Herodotus clarified all societies. He assumed he was experienced in the ways of the world he had essentially left years earlier, struggling ever since to explore a half-invented world of the desert.

At Cairo, aerodrome they loaded the equipment into the vehicles, her husband staying on to check the petrol lines of the Moth before the three men left the next morning. Madox went off to one of the embassies to send a wire. And *he* was going into town to get drunk, the usual final evening in Cairo, first at Madame Badin's Opera Casino, and later to disappear into the streets behind the Pasha Hotel. He would pack before the evening began, which would allow him to just climb into the truck the next morning, hung over.

So he drove her into town, the air humid, the traffic bad and slow because of the hour.

"It's so hot. I need a beer. Do you want one?"

"No, I have to arrange for a lot of things in the next couple of hours. You'll have to excuse me."

"That's all right," she said. "I don't want to interfere."

"I'll have one with you when I come back."

"In three weeks, right?"

"About that."

"I wish I were going too."

He said nothing in answer to that. They crossed the Bulaq Bridge and the traffic got worse. Too many carts, too many pedestrians who owned the streets. He cut south along the Nile towards the Semiramis Hotel, where she was staying, just beyond the barracks.

"You're going to find Zerzura this time, aren't you."

"I'm going to find it this time."

He was like his old self. He hardly looked at her on the drive, even when they were stalled for more than five minutes in one spot.

At the hotel he was excessively polite. When he behaved this way she liked him even less; they all had to pretend this pose was courtesy, graciousness. It reminded her of a dog in clothes. To hell with him. If her husband didn't have to work with him she would prefer not to see him again.

He pulled her pack out of the rear and was about to carry it into the lobby.

"Here, I can take that." Her shirt was damp at the back when she got out of the passenger seat.

The doorman offered to take the pack, but he said, "No, she wants to carry it," and she was angry again at his assumption. The doorman left them. She turned to him and he passed her the bag so she was facing him, both hands awkwardly carrying the heavy case in front of her.

"So. Good-bye. Good luck."

"Yes. I'll look after them all. They'll be safe."

She nodded. She was in shadow, and he, as if unaware of the harsh sunlight, stood in it.

Then he came up to her, closer, and she thought for a moment he was going to embrace her. Instead he put his right arm forward and drew it in a gesture across her bare neck so her skin was touched by the whole length of his damp forearm.

"Good-bye."

He walked back to the truck. She could feel his sweat now, like blood left by a blade which the gesture of his arm seemed to have imitated.

She picks up a cushion and places it onto her lap as a shield against him. "If you make love to me I won't lie about it. If I make love to you I won't lie about it."

She moves the cushion against her heart, as if she would suffocate that part of herself which has broken free.

"What do you hate most?" he asks.

"A lie. And you?"

"Ownership," he says. "When you leave me, forget me."

Her fist swings towards him and hits hard into the bone just below his eye. She dresses and leaves.

Each day he would return home and look at the black bruise in the mirror. He became curious, not so much about the bruise, but about the shape of his face. The long eyebrows he had never really noticed before, the beginning of grey in his sandy hair. He had not looked at himself like this in a mirror for years. That was a long eyebrow.

Nothing can keep him from her.

When he is not in the desert with Madox or with Bermann in the Arab libraries, he meets her in Groppi Park – beside the heavily watered plum gardens. She is happiest here. She is a woman who misses moisture, who has always loved low green hedges and ferns. While for him this much greenery feels like a carnival.

From Groppi Park they are out into the old city, South Cairo, markets where few Europeans go. In his rooms maps cover the walls. And in spite of his attempts at furnishing there is still a sense of base camp to his quarters.

They lie in each other's arms, the pulse and shadow of the fan on them. All morning he and Bermann have worked in the archaeological museum placing Arabic texts and European histories beside each other in an attempt to recognize echo, coincidence, name changes – back past Herodotus to the *Kitab al Kanuz*, where Zerzura is named after the bathing woman in a desert caravan. And there too the slow blink of a fan's shadow. And here too the intimate exchange and echo of a childhood history, of scar, of manner of kiss.

"I don't know what to do. I don't know what to do! How can I be your lover? He will go mad."

A list of wounds.

The various colours of the bruise – bright russet leading to brown. The plate she walked across the room with, flinging its contents aside, and broke across his head, the blood rising up into the straw hair. The fork that entered the back of his shoulder, leaving its bite marks the doctor suspected were caused by a fox.

He would step into an embrace with her, glancing first to see what moveable objects were around. He would meet her with others in public with bruises or a bandaged head and explain about the taxi jerking to a halt so that he had hit the open side window. Or with iodine on his forearm that covered a welt. Madox worried about his becoming suddenly accident-prone. She sneered quietly at the weakness of his explanation. Maybe it's his age, maybe he needs glasses, said her husband, nudging Madox. Maybe it's a woman he met, she said. Look, isn't that a woman's scratch or bite?

It was a scorpion, he said. *Androctonus australis*.

A postcard. Neat handwriting fills the rectangle.

> *Half my days I cannot bear not to touch you.*
> *The rest of the time I feel it doesn't matter*
> *if I ever see you again. It isn't the morality,*
> *it is how much you can bear.*

No date, no name attached.

Sometimes when she is able to spend the night with him they are wakened by the three minarets of the city beginning their prayers before dawn. He walks with her through the indigo markets that lie between South Cairo and her home. The beautiful songs of faith enter the air like arrows, one minaret answering another, as if passing on a rumour of the two of them as they walk through the cold morning air, the smell of charcoal and hemp already making the air profound. Sinners in a holy city.

He sweeps his arm across plates and glasses on a restaurant table so she might look up somewhere else in the city hearing this cause of noise. When he is without her. He, who has never felt alone in the miles of longitude between desert towns. A man in a desert can hold absence in his cupped hands knowing it is something that feeds him more than water. There is a plant he knows of near El Taj, whose heart, if one cuts it out, is replaced with a fluid containing herbal goodness. Every morning one can drink the liquid the amount of a missing heart. The plant continues to flourish for a year before it dies from some lack or other.

He lies in his room surrounded by the pale maps. He is without Katharine. His hunger wishes to burn down all social rules, all courtesy.

Her life with others no longer interests him. He wants only her stalking beauty, her theatre of expressions. He wants the minute and secret reflection between them, the depth of field minimal, their foreignness intimate like two pages of a closed book.

He has been disassembled by her.

And if she has brought him to this, what has he brought her to?

When she is within the wall of her class and he is beside her in larger groups he tells jokes he doesn't laugh at himself. Uncharacteristically manic, he attacks the history of exploration. When he is unhappy he does this. Only Madox recognizes the habit. But she will not even catch his eye. She smiles to everyone, to the objects in the room, praises a flower arrangement, worthless impersonal things. She misinterprets his behaviour, assuming this is what he wants, and doubles the size of the wall to protect herself.

But now he cannot bear this wall in her. You built your walls too, she tells him, so I have my wall. She says it glittering in a beauty he cannot stand. She with her beautiful clothes, with her pale face that laughs at everyone who smiles at her, with the uncertain grin for his angry jokes. He continues his appalling statements about this and that in some expedition they are all familiar with.

The minute she turns away from him in the lobby of Groppi's bar after he greets her, he is insane. He knows the only way he can accept losing her is if he can continue to hold her or be held by her. If they can somehow nurse each other out of this. Not with a wall.

Sunlight pours into his Cairo room. His hand flabby over the Herodotus journal, all the tension in the rest of his body, so he writes words down wrong, the pen scrawling as if without spine. He can hardly write down the word *sunlight*. The words *in love*.

In the apartment there is light only from the river and the desert beyond it. It falls upon her neck her feet the vaccination scar he loves on her right arm. She sits on the bed hugging nakedness. He slides his open palm along the sweat of her shoulder. This is my shoulder, he thinks, not her husband's, this is my shoulder. As lovers they have offered parts of their bodies to each other, like this. In this room on the periphery of the river.

In the few hours they have, the room has darkened to this pitch of light. Just river and desert light. Only when there is the rare shock of rain do they go towards the window and put their arms out, stretching, to bathe as much as they can of themselves in it. Shouts towards the brief downpour fill the streets.

"We will never love each other again. We can never see each other again."

"I know," he says.

The night of her insistence on parting.

She sits, enclosed within herself, in the armour of her terrible conscience. He is unable to reach through it. Only his body is close to her.

"Never again. Whatever happens."

"Yes."

"I think he will go mad. Do you understand?"

He says nothing, abandoning the attempt to pull her within him.

An hour later they walk into a dry night. They can hear the gramophone songs in the distance from the Music for All cinema, its windows open for the heat. They will have to part before that closes up and people she might know emerge from there.

They are in the botanical garden, near the Cathedral of All Saints. She sees one tear and leans forward and licks it, taking it into her mouth. As she has taken the blood from his hand when he cut himself cooking for her. Blood. Tear. He feels everything is missing from his body, feels he contains smoke. All that is alive is the knowledge of future desire and want. What he would say he cannot say to this woman whose openness is like a wound, whose youth is not mortal yet. He cannot alter what he loves most in her, her lack of compromise, where the romance of the poems she loves still sit with ease in the real world. Outside these qualities he knows there is no order in the world.

This night of her insistence. Twenty-eighth of September. The rain in the trees already dried by hot moonlight. Not one cool drop to fall down upon him like a tear. This parting at Groppi Park. He has not asked if her husband is home in that high square of light, across the street.

He sees the tall row of traveller's palms above them, their outstretched wrists. The way her head and hair were above him, when she was his lover.

Now there is no kiss. Just one embrace. He untugs himself from her and walks away, then turns. She is still there. He comes back within a few yards of her, one finger raised to make a point.

"I just want you to know. I don't miss you yet."

His face awful to her, trying to smile. Her head sweeps away from him and hits the side of the gatepost. He sees it hurt her, notices the wince. But they have separated already into themselves now, the walls up at her insistence. Her jerk, her pain, is accidental, is intentional. Her hand is near her temple.

"You will," she says.

From this point on in our lives, she had whispered to him earlier, we will either find or lose our souls.

How does this happen? To fall in love and be disassembled.

I was in her arms. I had pushed the sleeve of her shirt up to the shoulder so I could see her vaccination scar. I love this, I said. This pale aureole on her arm. I see the instrument scratch and then punch the serum within her and then release itself, free of her skin, years ago, when she was nine years old, in a school gymnasium.

VI

A Buried Plane

HE GLARES OUT, each eye a path, down the long bed at the end of which is Hana. After she has bathed him she breaks the tip off an ampoule and turns to him with the morphine. An effigy. A bed. He rides the boat of morphine. It races in him, imploding time and geography the way maps compress the world into a two-dimensional sheet of paper.

The long Cairo evenings. The sea of night sky, hawks in rows until they are released at dusk, arcing towards the last colour of the desert. A unison of performance like a handful of thrown seed.

In that city in 1936 you could buy anything – from a dog or a bird that came at one pitch of a whistle, to those terrible leashes that slipped over the smallest finger of a woman so she was tethered to you in a crowded market.

In the northeast section of Cairo was the great courtyard of religious students, and beyond it the Khan el Khalili bazaar. Above the narrow streets we looked down upon cats on the corrugated tin roofs who also looked down the next ten feet to the street and stalls. Above all this was our room. Windows open to minarets, feluccas, cats, tremendous noise. She spoke to me of her childhood gardens. When she couldn't sleep she drew her mother's garden for me, word by word, bed by bed, the December ice over the fish pond, the creak of rose trellises. She would take my wrist at the confluence of veins and guide it onto the hollow indentation at her neck.

March 1937, Uweinat. Madox is irritable because of the thinness in the air. Fifteen hundred feet above sea level and he is uncomfortable with even this minimal height. He is a desert man after all, having left his family's village of Marston Magna, Somerset, altered all customs and habits so he can have the proximity to sea level as well as regular dryness.

"Madox, what is the name of that hollow at the base of a woman's neck? At the front. *Here*. What is it, does it have an official name? That hollow about the size of an impress of your thumb?"

Madox watches me for a moment through the noon glare.

"Pull yourself together," he mutters.

"Let me tell you a story," Caravaggio says to Hana. "There was a Hungarian named Almásy, who worked for the Germans during the war. He flew a bit with the Africa Korps, but he was more valuable than that. In the 1930s he had been one of the great desert explorers. He knew every water hole and had helped map the Sand Sea. He knew all about the desert. He knew all about dialects. Does this sound familiar? Between the two wars he was always on expeditions out of Cairo. One was to search for Zerzura – the lost oasis. Then when war broke out he joined the Germans. In 1941 he became a guide for spies, taking them across the desert into Cairo. What I want to tell you is, I think the English patient is not English."

"Of course he is, what about all those flower beds in Gloucestershire?"

"Precisely. It's all a perfect background. Two nights ago, when we were trying to name the dog. Remember?"

"Yes."

"What were his suggestions?"

"He was strange that night."

"He was very strange, because I gave him an extra dose

175

of morphine. Do you remember the names? He put out about eight names. Five of them were obvious jokes. Then three names. Cicero. Zerzura. Delilah."

"So?"

"'Cicero' was a code name for a spy. The British unearthed him. A double then triple agent. He got away. 'Zerzura' is more complicated."

"I know about Zerzura. He's talked about it. He also talks about gardens."

"But it is mostly the desert now. The English garden is wearing thin. He's dying. I think you have the spy-helper Almásy upstairs."

They sit on the old cane hampers of the linen room looking at each other. Caravaggio shrugs. "It's possible."

"I think he is an Englishman," she says, sucking in her cheeks as she always does when she is thinking or considering something about herself.

"I know you love the man, but he's not an Englishman. In the early part of the war I was working in Cairo – the Tripoli Axis. Rommel's Rebecca spy—"

"What do you mean, 'Rebecca spy'?"

"In 1942 the Germans sent a spy called Eppler into Cairo before the battle of El Alamein. He used a copy of Daphne du Maurier's novel *Rebecca* as a code book to send messages back to Rommel on troop movements. Listen, the book became bedside reading with British Intelligence. Even I read it."

"You read a book?"

"Thank you. The man who guided Eppler through the desert into Cairo on Rommel's personal orders – from Tripoli all the way to Cairo – was Count Ladislaus de Almásy. This was a stretch of desert that, it was assumed, no one could cross.

"Between the wars Almásy had English friends. Great explorers. But when war broke out he went with the Germans. Rommel asked him to take Eppler across the desert into Cairo because it would have been too obvious by plane or parachute. He crossed the desert with the guy and delivered him to the Nile delta."

"You know a lot about this."

"I was based in Cairo. We were tracking them. From Gialo he led a company of eight men into the desert. They had to keep digging the trucks out of the sand hills. He aimed them towards Uweinat and its granite plateau so they could get water, take shelter in the caves. It was a halfway point. In the 1930s he had discovered caves with rock paintings there. But the plateau was crawling with Allies and he couldn't use the wells there. He struck out into the sand desert again. They raided British petrol dumps to fill up their tanks. In the Kharga Oasis they switched into British uniforms and hung British army number plates on their vehicles. When they were spotted from the air they hid in the wadis for as long as three days, completely still. Baking to death in the sand.

"It took them three weeks to reach Cairo. Almásy shook hands with Eppler and left him. This is where we lost him. He turned and went back into the desert alone. We think he crossed it again, back towards Tripoli. But that was the last time he was ever seen. The British picked up Eppler eventually and used the Rebecca code to feed false information to Rommel about El Alamein."

"I still don't believe it, David."

"The man who helped catch Eppler in Cairo was named Sansom."

"Delilah."

"Exactly."

"Maybe he's Sansom."

"I thought that at first. He was very like Almásy. A desert lover as well. He had spent his childhood in the Levant and knew the Bedouin. But the thing about Almásy was, he could fly. We are talking about someone who crashed in a plane. Here is this man, burned beyond recognition, who somehow ends up in the arms of the English at Pisa. Also, he can get away with sounding English. Almásy went to school in England. In Cairo he was referred to as the English spy."

She sat on the hamper watching Caravaggio. She said, "I think we should leave him be. It doesn't matter what side he was on, does it?"

Caravaggio said, "I'd like to talk with him some more. With more morphine in him. Talking it out. Delilah. Zerzura. You will have to give him the altered shot."

"No, David. You're too obsessed. It doesn't matter who he is. The war's over."

"I will then. I'll cook up a Brompton cocktail. Morphine and alcohol. They invented it at Brompton Hospital in London for their cancer patients. Don't worry, it won't kill him. It absorbs fast into the body. I can put it together with what we've got. Give him a drink of it. Then put him back on straight morphine."

She watched him sitting on the hamper, clear-eyed, smiling. During the last stages of the war Caravaggio had become one of the numerous morphia thieves. He had sniffed out her medical supplies within hours of his arrival. The small tubes of morphine were now a source for him. Like toothpaste tubes for dolls, she had thought when she first saw them, finding them utterly quaint. Caravaggio carried two or three in his pocket all day long, slipping the fluid into his flesh. She had stumbled on him once vomiting from its excess, crouched and shaking in one of the dark corners of the villa, looking up and hardly recognizing her. She had tried speaking with him and he had stared back. He had found the metal supply box, torn it open with God knows what strength. Once when the sapper cut open the palm of his hand on an iron gate, Caravaggio broke the glass tip off with his teeth, sucked and spat the morphine into the brown hand before Kip even knew what it was. Kip pushing him away, glaring in anger.

"Leave him alone. He's my patient."

"I won't damage him. The morphine and alcohol will take away the pain."

(3 CC's BROMPTON COCKTAIL. 3:00 P.M.)

Caravaggio slips the book out of the man's hands.

"When you crashed in the desert – where were you flying from?"

"I was leaving the Gilf Kebir. I had gone there to collect someone. In late August. Nineteen forty-two."

"During the war? Everyone must have left by then."

"Yes. There were just armies."

"The Gilf Kebir."

"Yes."

"Where is it?"

"Give me the Kipling book . . . here."

On the frontispiece of *Kim* was a map with a dotted line for the path the boy and the Holy One took. It showed just a portion of India – a darkly cross-hatched Afghanistan, and Kashmir in the lap of the mountains.

He traces his black hand along the Numi River till it enters the sea at 23° 30′ latitude. He continues sliding his finger seven inches west, off the page, onto his chest; he touches his rib.

"Here. The Gilf Kebir, just north of the Tropic of Cancer. On the Egyptian–Libyan border."

What happened in 1942?

I had made the journey to Cairo and was returning from there. I was slipping between the enemy, remembering old maps, hitting the pre-war caches of petrol and water, driving towards Uweinat. It was easier now that I was alone. Miles from the Gilf Kebir, the truck exploded and I capsized, rolling automatically into the sand, not wanting a spark to touch me. In the desert one is always frightened of fire.

The truck exploded, probably sabotaged. There were spies among the Bedouin, whose caravans continued to drift like cities, carrying spice, rooms, government advisors wherever they went. At any given moment among the Bedouin in those days of the war, there were Englishmen as well as Germans.

Leaving the truck, I started walking towards Uweinat, where I knew there was a buried plane.

Wait. What do you mean, a buried plane?

Madox had an old plane in the early days, which he had shaved down to the essentials – the only "extra" was the closed bubble of cockpit, crucial for desert flights. During our times in the desert he had taught me to fly, the two of us walking around the guy-roped creature theorizing on how it hung or veered in the wind.

When Clifton's plane – *Rupert* – flew into our midst, the ageing plane of Madox's was left where it was, covered with a tarpaulin, pegged down in one of the northeast alcoves of Uweinat. Sand collected over it gradually for the next few years. None of us thought we would see it again. It was another victim of the desert. Within a few months we would pass the northeast gully and see no contour of it.

By now Clifton's plane, ten years younger, had flown into our story.

So you were walking towards it?

Yes. Four nights of walking. I had left the man in Cairo and turned back into the desert. Everywhere there was war. Suddenly there were "teams." The Bermanns, the Bagnolds, the Slatin Pashas – who had at various times saved each other's lives – had now split into camps.

I walked towards Uweinat. I got there about noon and climbed up into the caves of the plateau. Above the well named Ain Dua.

"Caravaggio thinks he knows who you are," Hana said.

The man in the bed said nothing.

"He says you are not English. He worked with intelligence out of Cairo and Italy for a while. Till he was captured. My family knew Caravaggio before the war. He was a thief. He believed in 'the movement of things.' Some thieves are collectors, like some of the explorers you scorn, like some men with women or some women with men. But Caravaggio was not like that. He was too curious and generous to be a successful thief. Half the things he stole never came home. He thinks you are not English."

She watched his stillness as she spoke it; it appeared that he was not listening carefully to what she was saying. Just his distant thinking. The way Duke Ellington looked and thought when he played "Solitude."

She stopped talking.

He reached the shallow well named Ain Dua. He removed all of his clothes and soaked them in the well, put his head and then his thin body into the blue water. His limbs exhausted from the four nights of walking. He left his clothes spread on the rocks and climbed up higher into the boulders, climbed out of the desert, which was now, in 1942, a vast battlefield, and went naked into the darkness of the cave.

He was among the familiar paintings he had found years earlier. Giraffes. Cattle. The man with his arms raised, in a plumed headdress. Several figures in the unmistakeable posture of swimmers. Bermann had been right about the presence of an ancient lake. He walked farther into the coldness, into the Cave of Swimmers, where he had left her. She was still there. She had dragged herself into a corner, had wrapped herself tight in the parachute material. He had promised to return for her.

He himself would have been happier to die in a cave, with its privacy, the swimmers caught in the rock around them. Bermann had told him that in Asian gardens you could look at rock and imagine water, you could gaze at a still pool and believe it had the hardness of rock. But she was a woman who had grown up within gardens, among moistness, with words like *trellis* and *hedgehog*. Her passion for the desert was temporary. She'd come to love its sternness because of him, wanting to understand his comfort in its solitude. She was always happier in rain, in bathrooms steaming with liquid air, in sleepy wetness, climbing back in from his window that rainy night in Cairo and putting on her clothes while still wet, in order to hold it all. Just as she loved family traditions and courteous ceremony and old memorized poems. She would have hated to die without a name. For her there was a line back to her ancestors that was tactile; whereas he had erased the path he had emerged from. He was amazed she had loved him in spite of such qualities of anonymity in himself.

She was on her back, positioned the way the mediaeval dead lie.

I approached her naked as I would have done in our South Cairo room, wanting to undress her, still wanting to love her.

What is terrible in what I did? Don't we forgive everything of a lover? We forgive selfishness, desire, guile. As long as we are the motive for it. You can make love to a woman with a broken arm, or a woman with fever. She once sucked blood from a cut on my hand as I had tasted and swallowed her menstrual blood. There are some European words you can never translate properly into another language. *Félhomály.* The dusk of graves. With the connotation of intimacy there between the dead and the living.

I lifted her into my arms from the shelf of sleep. Clothing like cobweb. I disturbed all that.

I carried her out into the sun. I dressed. My clothes dry and brittle from the heat in the stones.

My linked hands made a saddle for her to rest on. As soon as I reached the sand I jostled her around so her body was facing back, over my shoulder. I was conscious of the airiness of her weight. I was used to her like this in my arms, she had spun around me in my room like a human reflection of the fan – her arms out, fingers like starfish.

We moved like this towards the northeast gully, where the plane was buried. I did not need a map. With me was the tank of petrol I had carried all the way from the capsized truck. Because three years earlier we had been impotent without it.

"What happened three years earlier?"

"She had been injured. In 1939. Her husband had crashed his plane. It had been planned as a suicide-murder by her husband that would involve all three of us. We were not even lovers at the time. I suppose information of the affair trickled down to him somehow."

"So she was too wounded to take with you."

"Yes. The only chance to save her was for me to try and reach help alone."

In the cave, after all those months of separation and anger, they had come together and spoken once more as lovers, rolling away the boulder they had placed between themselves for some social law neither had believed in.

In the botanical garden she had banged her head against the gatepost in determination and fury. Too proud to be a lover, a secret. There would be no compartments in her world. He had turned back to her, his finger raised, *I don't miss you yet.*

You will.

During their months of separation he had grown bitter and self-sufficient. He avoided her company. He could not stand her calmness when she saw him. He phoned her house and spoke to her husband and heard her laughter in the background. There was a public charm in her that tempted everyone. This was something he had loved in her. Now he began to trust nothing.

He suspected she had replaced him with another lover. He interpreted her every gesture to others as a code of promise. She gripped the front of Roundell's jacket once in a lobby and shook it, laughing at him as he muttered something, and he followed the innocent government aide for two days to see if there was more between them. He did not trust her last endearments to him anymore. She was with him or against him. She was against him. He couldn't stand even her tentative smiles at him. If she passed him a drink he would not drink it. If at a dinner she pointed to a bowl with a Nile lily floating in it he would not look at it. Just another fucking flower. She had a new group of intimates that excluded him and her husband. No one goes back to the husband. He knew that much about love and human nature.

He bought pale brown cigarette papers and glued them into sections of *The Histories* that recorded wars that were of no interest to him. He wrote down all her arguments against him. Glued into the book – giving himself only the voice of the watcher, the listener, the "he."

During the last days before the war he had gone for a last time to the Gilf Kebir to clear out the base camp. Her husband was supposed to pick him up. The husband they had both loved until they began to love each other.

Clifton flew up on Uweinat to collect him on the appointed day, buzzing the lost oasis so low the acacia shrubs dismantled their leaves in the wake of the plane, the Moth slipping into the depressions and cuts – while he stood on the high ridge signalling with blue tarpaulin. Then the plane pivoted down and came straight towards him, then crashed into the earth fifty yards away. A blue line of smoke uncoiling from the undercarriage. There was no fire.

A husband gone mad. Killing all of them. Killing himself and his wife – and him by the fact there was now no way out of the desert.

Only she was not dead. He pulled the body free, carrying it out of the plane's crumpled grip, this grip of her husband.

How did you hate me? she whispers in the Cave of Swimmers, talking through her pain of injuries. A broken wrist. Shattered ribs. You were terrible to me. That's when my husband suspected you. I still hate that about you – disappearing into deserts or bars.

You left *me* in Groppi Park.

Because you didn't want me as anything else.

Because you said your husband was going mad. Well, he went mad.

Not for a long time. I went mad before he did, you killed everything in me. Kiss me, will you. Stop defending yourself. Kiss me and call me by my name.

Their bodies had met in perfumes, in sweat, frantic to get under that thin film with a tongue or a tooth, as if they each could grip character there and during love pull it right off the body of the other.

Now there is no talcum on her arm, no rose water on her thigh.

You think you are an iconoclast, but you're not. You just move, or replace what you cannot have. If you fail at something you retreat into something else. Nothing changes you. How many women did you have? I left you because I knew I could never change you. You would stand in the room so still sometimes, so wordless sometimes, as if the greatest betrayal of yourself would be to reveal one more inch of your character.

In the Cave of Swimmers we talked. We were only two latitudes away from the safety of Kufra.

He pauses and holds out his hand. Caravaggio places a morphine tablet into the black palm, and it disappears into the man's dark mouth.

I crossed the dry bed of the lake towards Kufra Oasis, carrying nothing but robes against the heat and night cold, my Herodotus left behind with her. And three years later, in 1942, I walked with her towards the buried plane, carrying her body as if it was the armour of a knight.

In the desert the tools of survival are underground – troglodyte caves, water sleeping within a buried plant, weapons, a plane. At longitude 25, latitude 23, I dug down towards the tarpaulin, and Madox's old plane gradually emerged. It was night and even in the cold air I was sweating. I carried the naphtha lantern over to her and sat for a while, beside the silhouette of her nod. Two lovers and desert – starlight or moonlight, I don't remember. Everywhere else out there was a war.

The plane came out of the sand. There had been no food and I was weak. The tarp so heavy I couldn't dig it out but had simply to cut it away.

In the morning, after two hours' sleep, I carried her into the cockpit. I started the motor and it rolled into life. We moved and then slipped, years too late, into the sky.

The voice stops. The burned man looks straight ahead in his morphine focus.

The plane is now in his eye. The slow voice carries it with effort above the earth, the engine missing turns as if losing a stitch, her shroud unfurling in the noisy air of the cockpit, noise terrible after his days of walking in silence. He looks down and sees oil pouring onto his knees. A branch breaks free of her shirt. Acacia and bone. How high is he above the land? How low is he in the sky?

The undercarriage brushes the top of a palm and he pivots up, and the oil slides over the seat, her body slipping down into it. There is a spark from a short, and the twigs at her knee catch fire. He pulls her back into the seat beside him. He thrusts his hands up against the cockpit glass and it will not shift. Begins punching the glass, cracking it, finally breaking it, and the oil and the fire slop and spin everywhere. How low is he in the sky? She collapses – acacia twigs, leaves, the branches that were shaped into arms uncoiling around him. Limbs begin disappearing in the suck of air. The odour of morphine on his tongue. Caravaggio reflected in the black lake of his eye. He goes up and down now like a well bucket. There is blood somehow all over his face. He is flying a rotted plane, the canvas sheetings on the wings ripping open in the speed. They are carrion. How far back had the palm tree been? How long ago? He lifts his legs out of the oil, but they are so heavy. There is no way he can lift them again. He is old. Suddenly. Tired of living without her. He cannot lie back in her arms and trust her to stand guard all day all night while he sleeps. He has no one. He is exhausted not from the desert but from solitude. Madox gone. The woman translated into leaves and twigs, the broken glass to the sky like a jaw above him.

He slips into the harness of the oil-wet parachute and pivots upside down, breaking free of glass, wind flinging his body back. Then his legs are free of everything, and he is in the air, bright, not knowing why he is bright until he realizes he is on fire.

Hana can hear the voices in the English patient's room and
stands in the hall trying to catch what they are saying.

How is it?
Wonderful!
Now it's my turn.
Ahh! Splendid, splendid.
This is the greatest of inventions.
A remarkable find, young man.

When she enters she sees Kip and the English patient
passing a can of condensed milk back and forth. The Englishman sucks at the can, then moves the tin away from his
face to chew the thick fluid. He beams at Kip, who seems
irritated that he does not have possession of it. The sapper
glances at Hana and hovers by the bedside, snapping his
fingers a couple of times, managing finally to pull the tin
away from the dark face.

"We have discovered a shared pleasure. The boy and I.
For me on my journeys in Egypt, for him in India."

"Have you ever had condensed-milk sandwiches?" the
sapper asks.

Hana glances back and forth between the two of them.

Kip peers into the can. "I'll get another one," he says, and leaves the room.

Hana looks at the man in the bed.

"Kip and I are both international bastards – born in one place and choosing to live elsewhere. Fighting to get back to or get away from our homelands all our lives. Though Kip doesn't recognize that yet. That's why we get on so well together."

In the kitchen Kip stabs two holes into the new can of condensed milk with his bayonet, which, he realizes, is now used more and more for only this purpose, and runs back upstairs to the bedroom.

"You must have been raised elsewhere," the sapper says. "The English don't suck it out that way."

"For some years I lived in the desert. I learned everything I knew there. Everything that ever happened to me that was important happened in the desert."

He smiles at Hana.

"One feeds me morphine. One feeds me condensed milk. We may have discovered a balanced diet!" He turns back to Kip.

"How long have you been a sapper?"

"Five years. Mostly in London. Then Italy. With the unexploded-bomb units."

"Who was your teacher?"

"An Englishman in Woolwich. He was considered eccentric."

"The best kind of teacher. That must have been Lord Suffolk. Did you meet Miss Morden?"

"Yes."

At no point does either of them attempt to make Hana

comfortable in their conversation. But she wants to know about his teacher, and how he would describe him.

"What was he like, Kip?"

"He worked in Scientific Research. He was head of an experimental unit. Miss Morden, his secretary, was always with him, and his chauffeur, Mr Fred Harts. Miss Morden would take notes, which he dictated as he worked on a bomb, while Mr. Harts helped with the instruments. He was a brilliant man. They were called the Holy Trinity. They were blown up, all three of them, in 1941. At Erith."

She looks at the sapper leaning against the wall, one foot up so the sole of his boot is against a painted bush. No expression of sadness, nothing to interpret.

Some men had unwound their last knot of life in her arms. In the town of Anghiari she had lifted live men to discover they were already being consumed by worms. In Ortona she had held cigarettes to the mouth of the boy with no arms. Nothing had stopped her. She had continued her duties while she secretly pulled her personal self back. So many nurses had turned into emotionally disturbed handmaidens of the war, in their yellow-and-crimson uniforms with bone buttons.

She watches Kip lean his head back against the wall and knows the neutral look on his face. She can read it.

VII

In Situ

WESTBURY, ENGLAND, 1940

Kirpal Singh stood where the horse's saddle would have lain across its back. At first he simply stood on the back of the horse, paused and waved to those he could not see but who he knew would be watching. Lord Suffolk watched him through binoculars, saw the young man wave, both arms up and swaying.

Then he descended, down into the giant white chalk horse of Westbury, into the whiteness of the horse, carved into the hill. Now he was a black figure, the background radicalizing the darkness of his skin and his khaki uniform. If the focus on the binoculars was exact, Lord Suffolk would see the thin line of crimson lanyard on Singh's shoulder that signalled his sapper unit. To them it would look like he was striding down a paper map cut out in the shape of an animal. But Singh was conscious only of his boots scuffing the rough white chalk as he moved down the slope.

Miss Morden, behind him, was also coming slowly down the hill, a satchel over her shoulder, aiding herself with a rolled umbrella. She stopped ten feet above the horse, unfurled the umbrella and sat within its shade. Then she opened up her notebooks.

"Can you hear me?" he asked.

"Yes, it's fine." She rubbed the chalk off her hands onto her skirt and adjusted her glasses. She looked up into the distance and, as Singh had done, waved to those she could not see.

Singh liked her. She was in effect the first Englishwoman he had really spoken with since he arrived in England. Most of his time had been spent in a barracks at Woolwich. In his three months there he had met only other Indians and English officers. A woman would reply to a question in the NAAFI canteen, but conversations with women lasted only two or three sentences.

He was the second son. The oldest son would go into the army, the next brother would be a doctor, a brother after that would become a businessman. An old tradition in his family. But all that had changed with the war. He joined a Sikh regiment and was shipped to England. After the first months in London he had volunteered himself into a unit of engineers that had been set up to deal with delayed-action and unexploded bombs. The word from on high in 1939 was naive: *"Unexploded bombs are considered the responsibility of the Home Office, who are agreed that they should be collected by A.R.P. wardens and police and delivered to convenient dumps, where members of the armed forces will in due course detonate them."*

It was not until 1940 that the War Office took over responsibility for bomb disposal, and then, in turn, handed it over to the Royal Engineers. Twenty-five bomb disposal units were set up. They lacked technical equipment and had in their possession only hammers, chisels and road-mending tools. There were no specialists.

A bomb is a combination of the following parts:
1. *A container or bomb case.*
2. *A fuze.*
3. *An initiating charge, or gaine.*
4. *A main charge of high explosive.*
5. *Superstructional fittings – fins, lifting lugs, kopfrings, etc.*

Eighty per cent of bombs dropped by airplanes over Britain were thin-walled, general-purpose bombs. They usually ranged from a hundred pounds to a thousand. A 2,000-pound bomb was called a "Hermann" or an "Esau." A 4,000-pound bomb was called a "Satan."

Singh, after long days of training, would fall asleep with diagrams and charts still in his hands. Half dreaming, he entered the maze of a cylinder alongside the picric acid and the gaine and the condensers until he reached the fuze deep within the main body. Then he was suddenly awake.

When a bomb hit a target, the resistance caused a trembler to activate and ignite the flash pellet in the fuze. The minute explosion would leap into the gaine, causing the penthrite wax to detonate. This set off the picric acid, which in turn caused the main filling of TNT, amatol and aluminized powder, to explode. The journey from trembler to explosion lasted a microsecond.

The most dangerous bombs were those dropped from low altitudes, which were not activated until they had landed. These unexploded bombs buried themselves in cities and fields and remained dormant until their trembler contacts were disturbed – by a farmer's stick, a car wheel's nudge, the bounce of a tennis ball against the casing – and then they would explode.

Singh was moved by lorry with the other volunteers to the research department in Woolwich. This was a time when the casualty rate in bomb disposal units was appallingly high, considering how few unexploded bombs there were. In 1940, after France had fallen and Britain was in a state of siege, it got worse.

By August the blitz had begun, and in one month there were suddenly 2,500 unexploded bombs to be dealt with. Roads were closed, factories deserted. By September the number of live bombs had reached 3,700. One hundred new bomb squads were set up, but there was still no understanding of how the bombs worked. Life expectancy in these units was ten weeks.

"This was a Heroic Age of bomb disposal, a period of individual prowess, when urgency and a lack of knowledge and equipment led to the taking of fantastic risks. . . . It was, however, a Heroic Age whose protagonists remained obscure, since their actions were kept from the public for reasons of security. It was obviously undesirable to publish reports that might help the enemy to estimate the ability to deal with weapons."

In the car, driving down to Westbury, Singh had sat in front with Mr. Harts while Miss Morden rode in the back with Lord Suffolk. The khaki-painted Humber was famous. The mudguards were painted bright signal red – as all bomb disposal travel units were – and at night there was a blue filter over the left sidelight. Two days earlier a man walking near the famous chalk horse on the Downs had been blown up.

When engineers arrived at the site they discovered that another bomb had landed in the middle of the historic location – in the stomach of the giant white horse of Westbury carved into the rolling chalk hills in 1778. Shortly after this event, all the chalk horses on the Downs – there were seven – had camouflage nets pegged down over them, not to protect them so much as stop them being obvious landmarks for bombing raids over England.

From the backseat Lord Suffolk chatted about the migration of robins from the war zones of Europe, the history of bomb disposal, Devon cream. He was introducing the customs of England to the young Sikh as if it was a recently discovered culture. In spite of being Lord Suffolk he lived in Devon, and until war broke out his passion was the study of *Lorna Doone* and how authentic the novel was historically and geographically. Most winters he spent puttering around the villages of Brandon and Porlock, and he had convinced authorities that Exmoor was an ideal location for bomb-disposal training. There were twelve men under his command – made up of talents from various units, sappers and engineers, and Singh was one of them. They were based for most of the week at Richmond Park in London, being briefed on new methods or working on unexploded bombs while fallow deer drifted around them. But on weekends they would go down to Exmoor, where they would continue training during the day and afterwards be driven by Lord Suffolk to the church where Lorna Doone was shot during her wedding ceremony. "Either from this window or from that back door . . . shot right down the aisle – into her shoulder. Splendid shot, actually, though of course reprehensible. The villain was chased onto the moors and had his muscles ripped from his body." To Singh it sounded like a familiar Indian fable.

Lord Suffolk's closest friend in the area was a female aviator who hated society but loved Lord Suffolk. They went shooting together. She lived in a small cottage in Countisbury on a cliff that overlooked the Bristol Channel. Each village they passed in the Humber had its exotica described by Lord Suffolk. "This is the very best place to buy blackthorn walking sticks." As if Singh were thinking of stepping into the Tudor corner store in his uniform and turban to chat casually with the owners about canes. Lord Suffolk was the best of the English, he later told Hana. If there had been no war he would never have roused himself from Countisbury and his retreat, called Home Farm, where he mulled along with the wine, with the flies in the old back laundry, fifty years old, married but essentially bachelor in character, walking the cliffs each day to visit his aviator friend. He liked to fix things – old laundry tubs and plumbing generators and cooking spits run by a waterwheel. He had been helping Miss Swift, the aviator, collect information on the habits of badgers.

The drive to the chalk horse at Westbury was therefore busy with anecdote and information. Even in wartime he knew the best place to stop for tea. He swept into Pamela's Tea Room, his arm in a sling from an accident with guncotton, and shepherded in his clan – secretary, chauffeur and sapper – as if they were his children. How Lord Suffolk had persuaded the UXB Committee to allow him to set up his experimental bomb disposal outfit no one was sure, but with his background in inventions he probably had more qualifications than most. He was an autodidact, and he believed his mind could read the motives and spirit behind any invention. He had immediately invented the pocket shirt, which allowed fuzes and gadgets to be stored easily by a working sapper.

They drank tea and waited for scones, discussing the in situ defusing of bombs.

"I trust you, Mr. Singh, you know that, don't you?"

"Yes, sir." Singh adored him. As far as he was concerned, Lord Suffolk was the first real gentleman he had met in England.

"You know I trust you to do as well as I. Miss Morden will be with you to take notes. Mr. Harts will be farther back. If you need more equipment or more strength, blow on the police whistle and he will join you. He doesn't advise but he understands perfectly. If he won't do something it means he disagrees with you, and I'd take his advice. But you have total authority on the site. Here is my pistol. The fuzes are probably more sophisticated now, but you never know, you might be in luck."

Lord Suffolk was alluding to an incident that had made him famous. He had discovered a method for inhibiting a delayed action fuze by pulling out his army revolver and firing a bullet through the fuze head, so arresting the movement of the lock body. The method was abandoned when the Germans introduced a new fuze in which the percussion cap and not the clock was uppermost.

Kirpal Singh had been befriended, and he would never forget it. So far, half of his time during the war had taken place in the slipstream of this lord who had never stepped out of England and planned never to step out of Countisbury once the war ended. Singh had arrived in England knowing no one, distanced from his family in the Punjab. He was twenty-one years old. He had met no one but soldiers. So that when he read the notice asking for volunteers with an experimental bomb squad, even though he heard other sappers speak of Lord Suffolk as a madman, he had already decided that in a war you have to take control, and there was a greater chance of choice and life alongside a personality or an individual.

He was the only Indian among the applicants, and Lord Suffolk was late. Fifteen of them were led into a library and asked by the secretary to wait. She remained at the desk, copying out names, while the soldiers joked about the interview and the test. He knew no one. He walked over to a wall and stared at a barometer, was about to touch it but pulled back, just putting his face close to it. *Very Dry* to *Fair* to *Stormy*. He muttered the words to himself with his new English pronunciation. "Wery dry. *Very* dry." He looked back at the others, peered around the room and caught the gaze of the middle-aged secretary. She watched him sternly. An Indian boy. He smiled and walked towards the bookshelves. Again he touched nothing. At one point he put his nose close to a volume called *Raymond*, or *Life and Death* by Sir Oliver Lodge. He found another, similar title. *Pierre, or the Ambiguities*. He turned and caught the woman's eyes on him again. He felt as guilty as if he had put the book in his pocket. She had probably never seen a turban before. The English! They expect you to fight for them but won't talk to you. Singh. And the ambiguities.

They met a very hearty Lord Suffolk during lunch, who poured wine for anyone who wanted it, and laughed loudly at every attempt at a joke by the recruits. In the afternoon they were all given a strange exam in which a piece of machinery had to be put back together without any prior information of what it was used for. They were allowed two hours but could leave as soon as the problem was solved.

Singh finished the exam quickly and spent the rest of the time inventing other objects that could be made from the various components. He sensed he would be admitted easily if it were not for his race. He had come from a country where mathematics and mechanics were natural traits. Cars were never destroyed. Parts of them were carried across a village and readapted into a sewing machine or water pump. The backseat of a Ford was reupholstered and became a sofa. Most people in his village were more likely to carry a spanner or screwdriver than a pencil. A car's irrelevant parts thus entered a grandfather clock or irrigation pulley or the spinning mechanism of an office chair. Antidotes to mechanized disaster were easily found. One cooled an overheating car engine not with new rubber hoses but by scooping up cow shit and patting it around the condenser. What he saw in England was a surfeit of parts that would keep the continent of India going for two hundred years.

He was one of three applicants selected by Lord Suffolk. This man who had not even spoken to him (and had not laughed with him, simply because he had not joked) walked across the room and put his arm around his shoulder. The severe secretary turned out to be Miss Morden, and she bustled in with a tray that held two large glasses of sherry, handed one to Lord Suffolk and, saying, "I know you don't drink," took the other one for herself and raised her glass to him. "Congratulations, your exam was splendid. Though I was sure you would be chosen, even before you took it."

"Miss Morden is a splendid judge of character. She has a nose for brilliance and character."

"Character, sir?"

"Yes. It is not really necessary, of course, but we *are* going to be working together. We are very much a family here. Even before lunch Miss Morden had selected you."

"I found it quite a strain being unable to wink at you, Mr Singh."

Lord Suffolk had his arm around Singh again and was walking him to the window.

"I thought, as we do not have to begin till the middle of next week, I'd have some of the unit come down to Home Farm. We can pool our knowledge in Devon and get to know each other. You can drive down with us in the Humber."

So he had won passage, free of the chaotic machinery of the war. He stepped into a family, after a year abroad, as if he were the prodigal returned, offered a chair at the table, embraced with conversations.

It was almost dark when they crossed the border from Somerset into Devon on the coastal road overlooking the Bristol Channel. Mr. Harts turned down the narrow path bordered with heather and rhododendrons, a dark blood colour in this last light. The driveway was three miles long.

Apart from the trinity of Suffolk, Morden and Harts, there were six sappers who made up the unit. They walked the moors around the stone cottage over the weekend. Miss Morden and Lord Suffolk and his wife were joined by the aviatrix for the Saturday-night dinner. Miss Swift told Singh she had always wished to fly overland to India. Removed from his barracks, Singh had no idea of his location. There was a map on a roller high up on the ceiling. Alone one morning he pulled the roller down until it touched the floor. *Countisbury and Area. Mapped by R. Fones. Drawn by desire of Mr. James Halliday.*

"Drawn by desire . . ." He was beginning to love the English.

He is with Hana in the night tent when he tells her about the explosion in Erith. A 250-kilogram bomb erupting as Lord Suffolk attempted to dismantle it. It also killed Mr. Fred Harts and Miss Morden and four sappers Lord Suffolk was training. May 1941. Singh had been with Suffolk's unit for a year. He was working in London that day with Lieutenant Blackler, clearing the Elephant and Castle area of a Satan bomb. They had worked together at defusing the 4,000-pound bomb and were exhausted. He remembered halfway through he looked up and saw a couple of bomb disposal officers pointing in his direction and wondered what that was about. It probably meant they had found another bomb. It was after ten at night and he was dangerously tired. There was another one waiting for him. He turned back to work.

When they had finished with the Satan he decided to save time and walked over to one of the officers, who had at first half turned away as if wanting to leave.

"Yes. Where is it?"

The man took his right hand, and he knew something was wrong. Lieutenant Blackler was behind him and the officer told them what had happened, and Lieutenant Blackler put his hands on Singh's shoulders and gripped him.

He drove to Erith. He had guessed what the officer was hesitating about asking him. He knew the man would not have come there just to tell him of the deaths. They were in a war, after all. It meant there was a second bomb somewhere in the vicinity, probably the same design, and this was the only chance to find out what had gone wrong.

He wanted to do this alone. Lieutenant Blackler would stay in London. They were the last two left of the unit, and it would have been foolish to risk both. If Lord Suffolk had failed, it meant there was something new. He wanted to do this alone, in any case. When two men worked together there had to be a base of logic. You had to share and compromise decisions.

He kept everything back from the surface of his emotions during the night drive. To keep his mind clear, they still had to be alive. Miss Morden drinking one large and stiff whisky before she got to the sherry. In this way she would be able to drink more slowly, appear more ladylike for the rest of the evening. "You don't drink, Mr Singh, but if you did, you'd do what I do. One full whisky and then you can sip away like a good courtier." This was followed by her lazy, gravelly laugh. She was the only woman he was to meet in his life who carried two silver flasks with her. So she was still drinking, and Lord Suffolk was still nibbling at his Kipling cakes.

The other bomb had fallen half a mile away. Another SC-250kg. It looked like the familiar kind. They had defused hundreds of them, most by rote. This was the way the war progresses. Every six months or so the enemy altered something. You learned the trick, the whim, the little descant, and taught it to the rest of the units. They were at a new stage now.

He took no one with him. He would just have to remember each step. The sergeant who drove him was a man named Hardy, and he was to remain by the jeep. It was suggested he wait till the next morning, but he knew they would prefer him to do it now. The 250-kilogram SC was too common. If there was an alteration they had to know quickly. He made them telephone ahead for lights. He didn't mind working tired, but he wanted proper lights, not just the beams of two jeeps.

When he arrived in Erith the bomb zone was already lit. In daylight, on an innocent day, it would have been a field. Hedges, perhaps a pond. Now it was an arena. Cold, he borrowed Hardy's sweater and put it on top of his. The lights would keep him warm, anyway. When he walked over to the bomb they were still alive in his mind. Exam.

With the bright light, the porousness of the metal jumped into precise focus. Now he forgot everything except distrust. Lord Suffolk had said you can have a brilliant chess player at seventeen, even thirteen, who might beat a grand master. But you can never have a brilliant bridge player at that age. Bridge depends on character. Your character and the character of your opponents. You must consider the character of your enemy. This is true of bomb disposal. It is two-handed bridge. You have one enemy. You have no partner. Sometimes for my exam I make them play bridge. People think a bomb is a mechanical object, a mechanical enemy. But you have to consider that somebody made it.

The wall of the bomb had been torn open in its fall to earth, and Singh could see the explosive material inside. He felt he was being watched, and refused to decide whether it was by Suffolk or the inventor of this contraption. The freshness of the artificial light had revived him. He walked around the bomb, peering at it from every angle. To remove the fuze, he would have to open the main chamber and get past the explosive. He unbuttoned his satchel and, with a universal key, carefully twisted off the plate at the back of the bomb case. Looking inside he saw that the fuze pocket had been knocked free of the case. This was good luck – or bad luck; he couldn't tell yet. The problem was that he didn't know if the mechanism was already at work, if it had already been triggered. He was on his knees, leaning over it, glad he was alone, back in the world of straightforward choice. Turn left or turn right. Cut this or cut that. But he was tired, and there was still anger in him.

He didn't know how long he had. There was more danger in waiting too long. Holding the nose of the cylinder firm with his boots, he reached in and ripped out the fuze pocket, and lifted it away from the bomb. As soon as he did this he began to shake. He had got it out. The bomb was essentially harmless now. He put the fuze with its tangled fringe of wires down on the grass; they were clear and brilliant in this light.

He started to drag the main case towards the truck, fifty yards away, where the men could empty it of the raw explosive. As he pulled it along, a third bomb exploded a quarter of a mile away and the sky lit up, making even the arc lights seem subtle and human.

An officer gave him a mug of Horlicks, which had some kind of alcohol in it, and he returned alone to the fuze pocket. He inhaled the fumes from the drink.

There was no longer serious danger. If he were wrong, the small explosion would take off his hand. But unless it was clutched to his heart at the moment of impact he wouldn't die. The problem was now simply the problem. The fuze. The new "joke" in the bomb.

He would have to reestablish the maze of wires into its original pattern. He walked back to the officer and asked him for the rest of the Thermos of the hot drink. Then he returned and sat down again with the fuze. It was about one-thirty in the morning. He guessed, he wasn't wearing a watch. For half an hour he just looked at it with a magnified circle of glass, a sort of monocle that hung off his buttonhole. He bent over and peered at the brass for any hint of other scratches that a clamp might have made. Nothing.

Later he would need distractions. Later, when there was a whole personal history of events and moments in his mind, he would need something equivalent to white sound to burn or bury everything while he thought of the problems in front of him. The radio or crystal set and its loud band music would come later, a tarpaulin to hold the rain of real life away from him.

But now he was aware of something in the far distance, like some reflection of lightning on a cloud. Harts and Morden and Suffolk were dead, suddenly just names. His eyes focused back onto the fuze box.

He began to turn the fuze upside down in his mind, considering the logical possibilities. Then turned it horizontal again. He unscrewed the gaine, bending over, his ear next to it so the scrape of brass was against him. No little clicks. It came apart in silence. Tenderly he separated the clockwork sections from the fuze and set them down. He picked up the fuze-pocket tube and peered down into it again. He saw nothing. He was about to lay it on the grass when he hesitated and brought it back up to the light. He wouldn't have noticed anything wrong except for the weight. And he would never have thought about the weight if he wasn't looking for the joke. All they did, usually, was listen or look. He tilted the tube carefully, and the weight slipped down towards the opening. It was a second gaine – a whole separate device – to foil any attempt at defusing.

He eased the device out towards him and unscrewed the

gaine. There was a white-green flash and the sound of a whip from the device. The second detonator had gone off. He pulled it out and set it beside the other parts on the grass. He went back to the jeep.

"There was a second gaine," he muttered. "I was very lucky, being able to pull out those wires. Put a call in to headquarters and find out if there are other bombs."

He cleared the soldiers away from the jeep, set up a loose bench there and asked for the arc lights to be trained on it. He bent down and picked up the three components and placed them each a foot along the makeshift bench. He was cold now, and he breathed out a feather of his warmer body air. He looked up. In the distance some soldiers were still emptying out the main explosive. Quickly he wrote down a few notes and handed the solution for the new bomb to an officer. He didn't fully understand it, of course, but they would have this information.

When sunlight enters a room where there is a fire, the fire will go out. He had loved Lord Suffolk and his strange bits of information. But his absence here, in the sense that everything now depended on Singh, meant Singh's awareness swelled to all bombs of this variety across the city of London. He had suddenly a map of responsibility, something, he realized, that Lord Suffolk carried within his character at all times. It was this awareness that later created the need in him to block so much out when he was working on a bomb. He was one of those never interested in the choreography of power. He felt uncomfortable in the ferrying back and forth of plans and solutions. He felt capable only of reconnaissance, of locating a solution. When the reality of the death of Lord Suffolk came to him, he concluded the work he was assigned to and reenlisted into the anonymous machine of the army. He was on the troopship *Macdonald*, which carried a hundred other sappers towards the Italian campaign. Here they were used not just for bombs but for building bridges, clearing debris, setting up tracks for armoured rail vehicles. He hid there for the rest of the war. Few remembered the Sikh who had been with Suffolk's unit. In a year the whole unit was disbanded and forgotten, Lieutenant Blackler being the only one to rise in the ranks with his talent.

But that night as Singh drove past Lewisham and Blackheath towards Erith, he knew he contained, more than any other sapper, the knowledge of Lord Suffolk. He was expected to be the replacing vision.

He was still standing at the truck when he heard the whistle that meant they were turning off the arc lights. Within thirty seconds metallic light had been replaced with sulphur flares in the back of the truck. Another bomb raid. These lesser lights could be doused when they heard the planes. He sat down on the empty petrol can facing the three components he had removed from the SC-250kg, the hisses from the flares around him loud after the silence of the arc lights.

He sat watching and listening, waiting for them to click. The other men silent, fifty yards away. He knew he was for now a king, a puppet master, could order anything, a bucket of sand, a fruit pie for his needs, and those men who would not cross an uncrowded bar to speak with him when they were off duty would do what he desired. It was strange to him. As if he had been handed a large suit of clothes that he could roll around in and whose sleeves would drag behind him. But he knew he did not like it. He was accustomed to his invisibility. In England he was ignored in the various barracks, and he came to prefer that. The self-sufficiency and privacy Hana saw in him later were caused not just by his being a sapper in the Italian campaign. It was as much a result of being the anonymous member of another race, a part of the invisible world. He had built up defences of character against all that, trusting only those who befriended him. But that night in Erith he knew he was capable of having wires attached to him that influenced all around him who did not have his specific talent.

A few months later he had escaped to Italy, had packed the shadow of his teacher into a knapsack, the way he had seen the green-clothed boy at the Hippodrome do it on his first leave during Christmas. Lord Suffolk and Miss Morden had offered to take him to an English play. He had selected *Peter Pan*, and they, wordless, acquiesced and went with him to a screaming child-full show. There were such shadows of memory with him when he lay in his tent with Hana in the small hill town in Italy.

Revealing his past or qualities of his character would have been too loud a gesture. Just as he could never turn and inquire of her what deepest motive caused this relationship. He held her with the same strength of love he felt for those three strange English people, eating at the same table with them, who had watched his delight and laughter and wonder when the green boy raised his arms and flew into the darkness high above the stage, returning to teach the young girl in the earthbound family such wonders too.

In the flare-lit darkness of Erith he would stop whenever planes were heard, and one by one the sulphur torches were sunk into buckets of sand. He would sit in the droning darkness, moving the seat so he could lean forward and place his ear close to the ticking mechanisms, still timing the clicks, trying to hear them under the throb of the German bombers above him.

Then what he had been waiting for happened. After exactly one hour, the timber tripped and the percussion cap exploded. Removing the main gaine had released an unseen striker that activated the second, hidden gaine. It had been set to explode sixty minutes later – long after a sapper would normally have assumed the bomb was safely defused.

This new device would change the whole direction of Allied bomb disposal. From now on, every delayed-action bomb would carry the threat of a second gaine. It would no longer be possible for sappers to deactivate a bomb by simply removing the fuze. Bombs would have to be neutralized with the fuze intact. Somehow, earlier on, surrounded by arc lights, and in his fury, he had withdrawn the sheared second fuze out of the booby trap. In the sulphureous darkness under the bombing raid he witnessed the white-green flash the size of his hand. One hour late. He had survived only with luck. He walked back to the officer and said, "I need another fuze to make sure."

They lit the flares around him again. Once more light poured into his circle of darkness. He kept testing the new fuzes for two more hours that night. The sixty-minute delay proved to be consistent.

He was in Erith most of that night. In the morning he woke up to find himself back in London. He could not remember being driven back. He woke up, went to a table and began to sketch the profile of the bomb, the gaines, the detonators, the whole ZUS-40 problem, from the fuze up to the locking rings. Then he covered the basic drawing with all the possible lines of attack to defuse it. Every arrow drawn exactly, the text written out clear the way he had been taught.

What he had discovered the night before held true. He had survived only through luck. There was no possible way to defuse such a bomb in situ without just blowing it up. He drew and wrote out everything he knew on the large blueprint sheet. At the bottom he wrote: *Drawn by desire of Lord Suffolk, by his student Lieutenant Kirpal Singh, 10 May 1941.*

He worked flat-out, crazily, after Suffolk's death. Bombs were altering, with new techniques and devices. He was barracked in Regent's Park with Lieutenant Blackler and three other specialists, working on solutions, blueprinting each new bomb as it came in.

In twelve days, working at the Directorate of Scientific Research, they came up with the answer. Ignore the fuze entirely. Ignore the first principle, which until then was "defuse the bomb." It was brilliant. They were all laughing and applauding and hugging each other in the officers' mess. They didn't have a clue what the alternative was, but they knew in the abstract they were right. The problem would not be solved by embracing it. That was Lieutenant Blackler's line. "If you are in a room with a problem don't talk to it." An offhand remark. Singh came towards him and held the statement from another angle. "Then we don't touch the fuze at all."

Once they came up with that, someone worked out the solution in a week. A steam sterilizer. One could cut a hole into the main case of a bomb, and then the main explosive could be emulsified by an injection of steam and drained away. That solved that for the time being. But by then he was on a ship to Italy.

"There is always yellow chalk scribbled on the side of bombs. Have you noticed that? Just as there was yellow chalk scribbled onto our bodies when we lined up in the Lahore courtyard.

"There was a line of us shuffling forward slowly from the street into the medical building and out into the courtyard as we enlisted. We were signing up. A doctor cleared or rejected our bodies with his instruments, explored our necks with his hands. The tongs slid out of Dettol and picked up parts of our skin.

"Those accepted filled up the courtyard. The coded results written into our skin with yellow chalk. Later, in the lineup, after a brief interview, an Indian officer chalked more yellow on to the slates tied around our necks. Our weight, age, district, standard of education, dental condition and what unit we were best suited for.

"I did not feel insulted by this. I am sure my brother would have been, would have walked in fury over to the well, hauled up the bucket, and washed the chalk markings away. I was not like him. Though I loved him. Admired him. I had this side to my nature which saw reason in all things. I was the one who had an earnest and serious air at school, which he would imitate and mock. You understand, of course, I was far less serious than he was, it was just that I hated confrontation. It didn't stop me doing whatever I wished or doing things the way I wanted to. Quite early on I had discovered the overlooked space open to those of us with a silent life. I didn't argue with the policeman who said I couldn't cycle over a certain bridge or through a specific gate in the fort – I just stood there, still, until I was invisible, and then I went through. Like a cricket. Like a hidden cup of water. You understand? That is what my brother's public battles taught me.

"But to me my brother was always the hero in the family. I was in the slipstream of his status as firebrand. I witnessed his exhaustion that came after each protest, his body gearing up to respond to this insult or that law. He broke the tradition of our family and refused, in spite of being the oldest brother, to join the army. He refused to agree to any situation where the English had power. So they dragged him into their jails. In the Lahore Central Prison. Later the Jatnagar jail. Lying back on his cot at night, his arm raised within plaster, broken by his friends to protect him, to stop him trying to escape. In jail he became serene and devious. More like me. He was not insulted when he heard I had signed up to replace him in the enlistment, no longer to be a doctor, he just laughed and sent a message through our father for me to be careful. He would never go to war against me or what I did. He was confident that I had the trick of survival, of being able to hide in silent places."

He is sitting on the counter in the kitchen talking with Hana. Caravaggio breezes through it on his way out, heavy ropes swathed over his shoulders, which are his own personal business, as he says when anyone asks him. He drags them behind him and as he goes out the door says, "The English patient wants to see you, boyo."

"Okay, boyo." The sapper hops off the counter, his Indian accent slipping over into the false Welsh of Caravaggio.

"My father had a bird, a small swift I think, that he kept beside him, as essential to his comfort as a pair of spectacles or a glass of water during a meal. In the house, even if he just was entering his bedroom he carried it with him. When he went to work the small cage hung off the bicycle's handle-bars."

"Is your father still alive?"

"Oh, yes. I think. I've not had letters for some time. And it is likely that my brother is still in jail."

He keeps remembering one thing. He is in the white horse. He feels hot on the chalk hill, the white dust of it swirling up all around him. He works on the contraption, which is quite straightforward, but for the first time he is working alone. Miss Morden sits twenty yards above him, higher up the slope, taking notes on what he is doing. He knows that down and across the valley Lord Suffolk is watching through the glasses. He works slowly. The chalk dust lifts, then settles on everything, his hands, the con-traption, so he has to blow it off the fuze caps and wires continually to see the details. It is hot in the tunic. He keeps putting his sweating wrists behind himself to wipe them on the back of his shirt. All the loose and removed parts fill the various pockets across his chest. He is tired, checking things repetitively. He hears Miss Morden's voice. "Kip?" "Yes." "Stop what you're doing for a while, I'm coming down." "You'd better not, Miss Morden." "Of course I can." He does up the buttons on his various vest pockets and lays a cloth over the bomb; she clambers down into the white horse awkwardly and then sits next to him and opens up her satchel. She douses a lace handkerchief with the contents of a small bottle of eau de cologne and passes it to him. "Wipe

your face with this. Lord Suffolk uses it to refresh himself."
He takes it tentatively and at her suggestion dabs his forehead and neck and wrists. She unscrews the Thermos and pours each of them some tea. She unwraps oil paper and brings out strips of Kipling cake.

She seems to be in no hurry to go back up the slope, back to safety. And it would seem rude to remind her that she should return. She simply talks about the wretched heat and the fact that at least they have booked rooms in town with baths attached, which they can all look forward to. She begins a rambling story about how she met Lord Suffolk. Not a word about the bomb beside them. He had been slowing down, the way one, half asleep, continually rereads the same paragraph, trying to find a connection between sentences. She has pulled him out of the vortex of the problem. She packs up her satchel carefully, lays a hand on his right shoulder and returns to her position on the blanket above the Westbury horse. She leaves him some sunglasses, but he cannot see clearly enough through them so he lays them aside. Then he goes back to work. The scent of eau de cologne. He remembers he had smelled it once as a child. He had a fever and someone had brushed it onto his body.

VIII

The Holy Forest

KIP WALKS OUT of the field where he has been digging, his left hand raised in front of him as if he has sprained it.

He passes the scarecrow for Hana's garden, the crucifix with its hanging sardine cans, and moves uphill towards the villa. He cups the hand held in front of him with the other as if protecting the flame of a candle. Hana meets him on the terrace, and he takes her hand and holds it against his. The ladybird circling the nail on his small finger quickly crosses over onto her wrist.

She turns back into the house. Now her hand is held out in front of her. She walks through the kitchen and up the stairs.

The patient turns to face her as she comes in. She touches his foot with the hand that holds the ladybird. It leaves her, moving onto the dark skin. Avoiding the sea of white sheet, it begins to make the long trek towards the distance of the rest of his body, a bright redness against what seems like volcanic flesh.

In the library the fuze box is in midair, nudged off the counter by Caravaggio when he turned to Hana's gleeful yell in the hall. Before it reaches the floor Kip's body slides underneath it, and he catches it in his hand.

Caravaggio glances down to see the young man's face blowing out all the air quickly through his cheeks.

He thinks suddenly he owes him a life.

Kip begins to laugh, losing his shyness in front of the older man, holding up the box of wires.

Caravaggio will remember the slide. He could walk away, never seeing him again, and he would never forget him. Years from now on a Toronto street Caravaggio will get out of a taxi and hold the door open for an East Indian who is about to get into it, and he will think of Kip then.

Now the sapper just laughs up towards Caravaggio's face and up past that towards the ceiling.

"I know all about sarongs." Caravaggio waves his hand towards Kip and Hana as he spoke. "In the east end of Toronto I met these Indians. I was robbing a house and it turned out to belong to an Indian family. They woke from their beds and they were wearing these cloths, sarongs, to sleep in, and it intrigued me. We had lots to talk about and they eventually persuaded me to try it. I removed my clothes and stepped into one, and they immediately set upon me and chased me half naked into the night."

"Is that a true story?" She grinned.

"One of many!"

She knew enough about him to almost believe it. Caravaggio was constantly diverted by the human element during burglaries. Breaking into a house during Christmas, he would become annoyed if he noticed the Advent calendar had not been opened up to the date to which it should have been. He often had conversations with the various pets left alone in houses, rhetorically discussing meals with them, feeding them large helpings, and was often greeted by them with considerable pleasure if he returned to the scene of a crime.

She walks in front of the shelves in the library, eyes closed, and at random pulls out a book. She finds a clearing between two sections in a book of poetry and begins to write there.

He says Lahore is an ancient city. London is a recent town compared with Lahore. I say, Well, I come from an even newer country. He says they have always known about gunpowder. As far back as the seventeenth century, court paintings recorded fireworks displays.

He is small, not much taller than I am. An intimate smile up close that can charm anything when he displays it. A toughness to his nature he doesn't show. The Englishman says he's one of those warrior saints. But he has a peculiar sense of humour that is more rambunctious than his manner suggests. Remember "I'll rewire him in the morning." Ooh la la!

He says Lahore has thirteen gates – named for saints and emperors or where they lead to.

The word bungalow *comes from Bengali.*

At four in the afternoon they had lowered Kip into the pit in a harness until he was waist-deep in the muddy water, his body draped around the body of the Esau bomb. The casing from fin to tip ten feet high, its nose sunk into the mud by his feet. Beneath the brown water his thighs embraced the metal casing, much the way he had seen soldiers holding women in the corner of NAAFI dance floors. When his arms tired he hung them upon the wooden struts at shoulder level, which were there to stop mud collapsing in around him. The sappers had dug the pit around the Esau and set up the wood-shaft walls before he had arrived on the site. In 1941, Esau bombs with a new Y fuze had started coming in; this was his second one.

It was decided during planning sessions that the only way around the new fuze was to immunize it. It was a huge bomb in ostrich posture. He had come down barefoot and he was already sinking slowly, being caught within the clay, unable to get a firm hold down there in the cold water. He wasn't wearing boots – they would have locked within the clay, and when he was pulleyed up later the jerk out of it could break his ankles.

He laid his left cheek against the metal casing, trying to think himself into warmth, concentrating on the small touch of sun that reached down into the twenty-foot pit and fell on the back of his neck. What he embraced could explode at any moment, whenever tumblers tremored, whenever the gaine was fired. There was no magic or X ray that would tell anyone when some small capsule broke, when some wire would stop wavering. Those small mechanical semaphores were like a heart murmur or a stroke within the man crossing the street innocently in front of you.

What town was he in? He couldn't even remember. He heard a voice and looked up. Hardy passed the equipment down in a satchel at the end of a rope, and it hung there while Kip began to insert the various clips and tools into the many pockets of his tunic. He was humming the song Hardy had been singing in the jeep on the way to the site –

> They're changing guard at Buckingham Palace –
> Christopher Robin went down with Alice.

He wiped the area of fuze head dry and began moulding a clay cup around it. Then he unstopped the jar and poured the liquid oxygen into the cup. He taped the cup securely onto the metal. Now he had to wait again.

There was so little space between him and the bomb he could feel the change in temperature already. If he were on dry land he could walk away and be back in ten minutes. Now he had to stand there beside the bomb. They were two suspicious creatures in an enclosed space. Captain Carlyle had been working in a shaft with frozen oxygen and the whole pit had suddenly burst into flames. They hauled him out fast, already unconscious in his harness.

Where was he? Lisson Grove? Old Kent Road?

Kip dipped cotton wool into the muddy water and touched it to the casing about twelve inches away from the fuze. It fell away, so it meant he had to wait longer. When the cotton wool stuck, it meant he had to wait longer. When the cotton wool stuck, it meant enough of the area around the fuze was frozen and he could go on. He poured more oxygen into the cup.

The growing circle of frost was a foot in radius now. A few more minutes. He looked at the clipping someone had taped onto the bomb. They had read it with much laughter that morning in the update kit sent to all bomb disposal units.

When is explosion reasonably permissible?

If a man's life could be capitalized as X, the risk at Y, and the estimated damage from explosion at V, then a logician might contend that if V is less than X or over Y, the bomb should be blown up; but if V over Y is greater than X, an attempt should be made to avoid explosion in situ.

Who wrote such things?

He had by now been in the shaft with the bomb for more than an hour. He continued feeding in the liquid oxygen. At shoulder height, just to his right, was a hose pumping down normal air to prevent him from becoming giddy with oxygen. (He had seen soldiers with hangovers use the oxygen to cure headaches.) He tried the cotton wool again and this time it froze on. He had about twenty minutes. After that the battery temperature within the bomb would rise again. But for now the fuze was iced up and he could begin to remove it.

He ran his palms up and down the bomb case to detect any rips in the metal. The submerged section would be safe, but oxygen could ignite if it came into contact with exposed explosive. Carlyle's flaw. X over Y. If there were rips they would have to use liquid nitrogen.

"It's a two-thousand-pound bomb, sir. Esau." Hardy's voice from the top of the mud pit.

"Type-marked fifty, in a circle, B. Two fuze pockets, most likely. But we think the second one is probably not armed. Okay?"

They had discussed all this with each other before, but things were being confirmed, remembered for the final time.

"Put me on a microphone now and get back."

"Okay, sir."

Kip smiled. He was ten years younger than Hardy, and no Englishman, but Hardy was happiest on the cocoon of regimental discipline. There was always hesitation by the soldiers to call him "sir," but Hardy barked it out loud and enthusiastically.

He was working fast now to prise out the fuze, all the batteries inert.

"Can you hear me? Whistle. . . . Okay, I heard it. A last topping up with oxygen. Will let it bubble for thirty seconds. Then start. Freshen the frost. Okay, I'm going to remove the *dam*. . . . Okay, *dam* gone."

Hardy was listening to everything and recording it in case something went wrong. One spark and Kip would be in a shaft of flames. Or there could be a joker in the bomb. The next person would have to consider the alternatives.

"I'm using the quilter key." He had pulled it out of his breast pocket. It was cold and he had to rub it warm. He began to remove the locking ring. It moved easily and he told Hardy.

"They're changing guard at Buckingham Palace," Kip

whispered. He pulled off the locking ring and the locating ring and let them sink into the water. He could feel them roll slowly at his feet. It would all take another four minutes.

"Alice is marrying one of the guard. 'A soldier's life is terrible hard,' says Alice!"

He was singing it out loud, trying to get more warmth into his body, his chest painfully cold. He kept trying to lean back far enough away from the frozen metal in front of him. And he had to keep moving his hands up to the back of his neck, where the sun still was, then rub them to free them of the muck and grease and frost. It was difficult to get the collet to grip the head. Then to his horror the fuze head broke away, came off completely.

"Wrong, Hardy. Whole fuze head snapped off. Talk back to me, okay? The main body of the fuze is jammed down there, I can't get to it. There's nothing exposed I can grip."

"Where is the frost at?" Hardy was right above him. It had been a few seconds but he had raced to the shaft.

"Six more minutes of frost."

"Come up and we'll blow it up."

"No, pass me down some more oxygen."

He raised his right hand and felt an icy canister being placed in it.

"I'm going to dribble the muck onto the area of exposed fuze – where the head separated – then I'll cut into the metal. Chip through till I can grip something. Get back now, I'll talk it through."

He could hardly keep his fury back at what had happened. The muck, which was their name for oxygen, was going all over his clothes, hissing as it hit the water. He waited for the frost to appear and then began to shear metal off with a chisel. He poured more on, waited and chiselled deeper. When nothing came off he ripped free a bit of his shirt, placed it between the metal and the chisel, and then banged the chisel dangerously with a mallet, chipping off fragments. The cloth of his shirt his only safety against a spark. What was more of a problem was the coldness on his fingers. They were no longer agile, they were inert as the batteries. He kept cutting sideways into the metal around the lost fuze head. Shaving it off in layers, hoping the freezing would accept this kind of surgery. If he cut down directly there was always a chance he would hit the percussion cap that flashed the gaine.

It took five more minutes. Hardy had not moved from the top of the pit, instead was giving him the approximate time left in the freezing. But in truth neither of them could be sure. Since the fuze head had broken off, they were freezing a different area, and the water temperature though cold to him was warmer than the metal.

Then he saw something. He did not dare chip the hole any bigger. The contact of the circuit quivering like a silver tendril. If he could reach it. He tried to rub warmth into his hands.

He breathed out, was still for a few seconds, and with the needle pliers cut the contact in two before he breathed in again. He gasped as the freeze burned part of his hand when he pulled it back out of the circuits. The bomb was dead.

"Fuze out. Gaine off. Kiss me." Hardy was already rolling up the winch and Kip was trying to clip on the halter; he could hardly do it with the burn and the cold, all his muscles cold. He heard the pulley jerk and just held tight onto the leather straps still half attached around him. He began to feel his brown legs being pulled from the grip of the mud, removed like an ancient corpse out of a bog.

His small feet rising out of the water. He emerged, lifted out of the pit into the sunlight, head and then torso.

He hung there, a slow swivel under the tepee of poles that held the pulley. Hardy was now embracing him and unbuckling him simultaneously, letting him free. Suddenly he saw there was a large crowd watching from about twenty yards away, too close, far too close, for safety; they would have been destroyed. But of course Hardy had not been there to keep them back.

They watched him silently, the Indian, hanging onto Hardy's shoulder, scarcely able to walk back to the jeep with all the equipment – tools and canisters and blankets and the recording instruments still wheeling around, listening to the nothingness down in the shaft.

"I can't walk."

"Only to the jeep. A few yards more, sir. I'll pick up the rest."

They kept pausing, then walking on slowly. They had to go past the staring faces who were watching the slight brown man, shoeless, in the wet tunic, watching the drawn face that didn't recognize or acknowledge anything, any of them. All of them silent. Just stepping back to give him and Hardy room. At the jeep he started shaking. His eyes couldn't stand the glare off the windshield. Hardy had to lift him, in stages, into the passenger seat.

When Hardy left, Kip slowly pulled off his wet trousers and wrapped himself in the blanket. Then he sat there. Too cold and tired even to unscrew the Thermos of hot tea on the seat beside him. He thought: I wasn't even frightened down there. I was just angry – with my mistake, or the possibility that there was a joker. An animal reacting just to protect myself.

Only Hardy, he realized, keeps me human now.

When there is a hot day at the Villa San Girolamo they all wash their hair, first with kerosene to remove the possibility of lice, and then with water. Lying back, his hair spread out, eyes closed against the sun, Kip seems vulnerable. There is a shyness within him when he assumes this fragile posture, looking more like a corpse from a myth than anything living or human. Hana sits beside him, her dark brown hair already dry. These are the times he will talk about his family and his brother in jail.

He will sit up and flip his hair forward, and begin to rub the length of it with a towel. She imagines all of Asia through the gestures of this one man. The way he lazily moves, his quiet civilization. He speaks of warrior saints and she now feels he is one, stern and visionary, pausing only in these rare times of sunlight to be godless, informal, his head back again on the table so the sun can dry his spread hair like grain in a fan-shaped straw basket. Although he is a man from Asia who has in these last years of war assumed English fathers, following their codes like a dutiful son.

"Ah, but my brother thinks me a fool for trusting the English." He turns to her, sunlight in his eyes. "One day, he says, I will open my eyes. Asia is still not a free continent,

232

and he is appalled at how we throw ourselves into English wars. It is a battle of opinion we have always had. 'One day you will open your eyes,' my brother keeps saying."

The sapper says this, his eyes closed tight, mocking the metaphor. "Japan is a part of Asia, I say, and the Sikhs have been brutalized by the Japanese in Malaya. But my brother ignores that. He says the English are now hanging Sikhs who are fighting for independence."

She turns away from him, her arms folded. The feuds of the world. The feuds of the world. She walks into the daylight darkness of the villa and goes in to sit with the Englishman.

At night, when she lets his hair free, he is once more another constellation, the arms of a thousand equators against his pillow, waves of it between them in their embrace and in their turns of sleep. She holds an Indian goddess in her arms, she holds wheat and ribbons. As he bends over her it pours. She can tie it against her wrist. As he moves she keeps her eyes open to witness the gnats of electricity in his hair in the darkness of the tent.

He moves away in relation to things, beside walls, raised terrace hedges. He scans the periphery. When he looks at Hana he sees a fragment of her lean cheek in relation to the landscape behind it. The way he watches the arc of a linnet in terms of the space it gathers away from the surface of the earth. He has walked up Italy with eyes that tried to see everything except what was temporary and human.

The one thing he will never consider is himself. Not his twilit shadow or his arm reaching for the back of a chair or the reflection of himself in a window or how they watch him. In the years of war he has learned that the only thing safe is himself.

He spends hours with the Englishman, who reminds him of a fir tree he saw in England, its one sick branch, too weighted down with age, held up by a crutch made out of another tree. It stood in Lord Suffolk's garden on the edge of the cliff, overlooking the Bristol Channel like a sentinel. In spite of such infirmity he sensed the creature within it was noble, with a memory whose power rainbowed beyond ailment.

He himself has no mirrors. He wraps his turban outside in his garden, looking about at the moss on trees. But he notices the swath scissors have made in Hana's hair. He is familiar with her breath when he places his face against her body, at the clavicle, where the bone lightens her skin. But if she asked him what colour her eyes are, although he has come to adore her, he will not, she thinks, be able to say. He will laugh and guess, but if she, black-eyed, says with her eyes shut that they are green, he will believe her. He may look intently at eyes but not register what colour they are, the way food already in his throat or stomach is just texture more than taste or specific object.

When someone speaks he looks at a mouth, not eyes and their colours, which, it seems to him, will always alter depending on the light of a room, the minute of the day. Mouths reveal insecurity or smugness or any other point on the spectrum of character. For him they are the most intricate aspect of faces. He's never sure what an eye reveals. But he can read how mouths darken into callousness, suggest tenderness. One can often misjudge an eye from its reaction to a simple beam of sunlight.

Everything is gathered by him as part of an altering harmony. He sees her in differing hours and locations that alter her voice or nature, even her beauty, the way the background power of the sea cradles or governs the fate of lifeboats.

They were in the habit of rising with daybreak and eating dinner in the last available light. Throughout the late evening there would be only one candle flaring into the darkness beside the English patient, or a lamp half filled with oil if Caravaggio had managed to forage any. But the corridors and other bedrooms hung in darkness, as if in a buried city. They became used to walking in darkness, hands out, touching the walls on either side with their fingertips.

"No more light. No more colour." Hana would sing the phrase to herself again and again. Kip's unnerving habit of leaping down the stairs one hand halfway down the rail had to be stopped. She imagined his feet travelling through air and hitting the returning Caravaggio in the stomach.

She had blown out the candle in the Englishman's room an hour earlier. She had removed her tennis shoes, her frock was unbuttoned at the neck because of summer heat, the sleeves unbuttoned as well and loose, high up at the arm. A sweet disorder.

On the main floor of the wing, apart from the kitchen, library and deserted chapel, was a glassed-in indoor courtyard. Four walls of glass with a glass door that let you into where there was a covered well and shelves of dead plants that at one time must have flourished in the heated room. This indoor courtyard reminded her more and more of a book opened to reveal pressed flowers, something to be glanced at during passing, never entered.

It was two a.m.

Each of them entered the villa from a different doorway, Hana at the chapel entrance by the thirty-six steps and he at the north courtyard. As he stepped into the house he removed his watch and slid it into an alcove at chest level where a small saint rested. The patron of this village hospital. She would not catch a glance of phosphorus. He had already removed his shoes and wore just trousers. The lamp strapped to his arm was switched off. He carried nothing else and just stood there for a while in darkness, a lean boy, a dark turban, the *kara* loose on his wrist against the skin. He leaned against the corner of the vestibule like a spear.

Then he was gliding through the indoor courtyard. He came into the kitchen and immediately sensed the dog in the dark, caught it and tied it with a rope to the table. He picked up the condensed milk from the kitchen shelf and returned to the glass room in the indoor courtyard. He ran his hands along the base of the door and found the small sticks leaning against it. He entered and closed the door behind him, at the last moment snaking his hand out to prop the sticks up against the door again. In case she had seen them. Then he climbed down into the well. There was a cross-plank three feet down he knew was firm. He closed the lid over himself and crouched there, imagining her searching for him or hiding herself. He began to suck at the can of condensed milk.

She suspected something like this from him. Having made her way to the library, she turned on the light on her arm and walked beside the bookcases that stretched from her ankles to unseen heights above her. The door was closed, so no light could reveal itself to anyone in the halls. He would be able to see the glow on the other side of the French doors only if he was outside. She paused every few feet, searching once again through the predominantly Italian books for the odd English one that she could present to the English patient. She had come to love these books dressed in their Italian spines, the frontispieces, the tipped-in colour illustrations with a covering of tissue, the smell of them, even the sound of the crack if you opened them too fast, as if breaking some minute unseen series of bones. She paused again. *The Charterhouse of Parma.*

"If I ever get out of my difficulties," he said to Celia, "I shall pay a visit to the beautiful pictures of Parma, and then will you deign to remember the name: Fabrizio del Dongo."

Caravaggio lay on the carpet at the far end of the library. From his darkness it seemed that Hana's left arm was raw phosphorus, lighting the books, reflecting redness onto her dark hair, burning against the cotton of her frock and its puffed sleeve at her shoulder.

He came out of the well.

The three-foot diameter of light spread from her arm and then was absorbed into blackness, so it felt to Caravaggio that there was a valley of darkness between them. She tucked the book with the brown cover under her right arm. As she moved, new books emerged and others disappeared.

She had grown older. And he loved her more now than he loved her when he had understood her better, when she was the product of her parents. What she was now was what she herself had decided to become. He knew that if he had passed Hana on a street in Europe she would have had a familiar air but he wouldn't have recognized her. The night he had first come to the villa he had disguised his shock. Her ascetic face, which at first seemed cold, had a sharpness. He realized that during the last two months he had grown towards who she now was. He could hardly believe his pleasure at her translation. Years before, he had tried to imagine her as an adult but had invented someone with qualities moulded out of her community. Not this wonderful stranger he could love more deeply because she was made up of nothing he had provided.

She was lying on the sofa, had twisted the lamp inward so she could read, and had already fallen deep into the book. At some point later she looked up, listening, and quickly switched off the light.

Was she conscious of him in the room? Caravaggio was aware of the noisiness of his breath and the difficulty he was having breathing in an ordered, demure way. The light went on for a moment and then was quickly shut off again.

Then everything in the room seemed to be in movement but Caravaggio. He could hear it all around him, surprised he wasn't touched. The boy was in the room. Caravaggio walked over to the sofa and placed his hand down towards Hana. She was not there. As he straightened up, an arm went around his neck and pulled him down backwards in a grip. A light glared harshly into his face, and there was a gasp from them both as they fell towards the floor. The arm with the light still holding him at the neck. Then a naked foot emerged into the light, moved past Caravaggio's face and stepped on to the boy's neck beside him. Another light went on.

"Got you. *Got you.*"

The two bodies on the floor looked up at the dark outline of Hana above the light. She was singing it, "*I got you, I got you.* I used Caravaggio – who really does have a bad wheeze! I knew he would be here. He was the trick."

Her foot pressed down harder on to the boy's neck. "Give up. *Confess.*"

Caravaggio began to shake within the boy's grip, sweat already all over him, unable to struggle out. The glare of light from both lamps now on him. He somehow had to climb and crawl out of this terror. *Confess.* The girl was laughing. He needed to calm his voice before he spoke, but they were hardly listening, excited at their adventure. He worked his way out of the boy's loosening grip and, not saying a word, left the room.

They were in darkness again. "Where are you?" she asks. Then moves quickly. He positions himself so she bangs into his chest, and in this way slips her into his arms. She puts her hand to his neck, then her mouth to his mouth. "Condensed milk! During our contest? Condensed milk?" She puts her mouth at his neck, the sweat of it, tasting him where her bare foot had been. "I want to see you." His light goes on and he sees her, her face streaked with dirt, her hair spiked up in a swirl from perspiration. Her grin towards him.

He puts his thin hands up into the loose sleeves of her dress and cups her shoulders with his hands. If she swerves now, his hands go with her. She begins to lean, puts all her weight into her fall backwards, trusting him to come with her, trusting his hands to break the fall. Then he will curl himself up, his feet in the air, just his hands and arms and his mouth on her, the rest of his body the tail of a mantis. The lamp is still strapped against the muscle and sweat of his left arm. Her face slips into the light to kiss and lick and taste. His forehead towelling itself in the wetness of her hair.

Then he is suddenly across the room, the bounce of his sapper lamp all over the place, in this room he has spent a week sweeping of all possible fuzes so it is now cleared. As if the room has now finally emerged from the war, is no longer a zone or territory. He moves with just the lamp, swaying his arm, revealing the ceiling, her laughing face as he passes her standing on the back of the sofa looking down at the glisten of his slim body. The next time he passes her he sees she is leaning down and wiping her arms on the skirt of her dress. "But I got you, I got you," she cants. "I'm the Mohican of Danforth Avenue."

Then she is riding on his back and her light swerves into the spines of books in the high shelves, her arms rising up and down as he spins her, and she dead-weights forward, drops and catches his thighs, then pivots off and is free of him, lying back on the old carpet, the smell of the past ancient rain still in it, the dust and grit on her wet arms. He bends down to her, she reaches out and clicks off his light. "I won, right?" He still has said nothing since he came into the room. His head goes into that gesture she loves which is partly a nod, partly a shake of possible disagreement. He cannot see her for the glare. He turns off her light so they are equal in darkness.

There is the one month in their lives when Hana and Kip sleep beside each other. A formal celibacy between them. Discovering that in lovemaking there can be a whole civilization, a whole country ahead of them. The love of the idea of him or her. I don't want to be fucked. I don't want to fuck you. Where he had learned it or she had who knows, in such youth. Perhaps from Caravaggio, who had spoken to her during those evenings about his age, about the tenderness towards every cell in a lover that comes when you discover your mortality. This was, after all, a mortal age. The boy's desire completed itself only in his deepest sleep while in the arms of Hana, his orgasm something more to do with the pull of the moon, a tug of his body by the night.

All evening his thin face lay against her ribs. She reminded him of the pleasure of being scratched, her fingernails in circles raking his back. It was something an ayah had taught him years earlier. All comfort and peace during childhood, Kip remembered, had come from her, never from the mother he loved or from his brother or father, whom he played with. When he was scared or unable to sleep it was the ayah who recognized his lack, who would ease him into sleep with her hand on his small thin back, this intimate stranger from South India who lived with them, helped run a household, cooked and served them meals, brought up her own children within the shell of the household, having comforted his older brother too in earlier years, probably knowing the character of all of the children better than their real parents did.

It was a mutual affection. If Kip had been asked whom he loved most he would have named his ayah before his mother. Her comforting love greater than any blood love or sexual love for him. All through his life, he would realize later, he was drawn outside the family to find such love. The platonic intimacy, or at times the sexual intimacy, of a stranger. He would be quite old before he recognized that about himself, before he could ask even himself that question of whom he loved most.

Only once did he feel he had given her back any comfort, though she already understood his love for her. When her mother died he had crept into her room and held her suddenly old body. In silence he lay beside her mourning in her small servant's room where she wept wildly and formally. He watched as she collected her tears in a small glass cup held against her face. She would take this, he knew, to the funeral. He was behind her hunched-over body, his nine-year-old hands on her shoulders, and when she was finally still, just now and then a shudder, he began to scratch her through her sari, then pulled it aside and scratched her skin – as Hana now received this tender art, his nails against the million cells of her skin, in his tent, in 1945, where their continents met in a hill town.

IX

The Cave of Swimmers

I PROMISED to tell you how one falls in love.

A young man named Geoffrey Clifton had met a friend at Oxford who had mentioned what we were doing. He contacted me, got married the next day, and two weeks later flew with his wife to Cairo. They were on the last days of their honeymoon. That was the beginning of our story.

When I met Katharine she was married. A married woman. Clifton climbed out of the plane and then, unexpected, for we had planned the expedition with just him in mind, she emerged. Khaki shorts, bony knees. In those days she was too ardent for the desert. I liked his youth more than the eagerness of his new young wife. He was our pilot, messenger, reconnaissance. He was the New Age, flying over and dropping codes of long coloured ribbon to advise us where we should be. He shared his adoration of her constantly. Here were four men and one woman and her husband in his verbal joy of honeymoon. They went back to Cairo and returned a month later, and it was almost the same. She was quieter this time but he was still the youth.

She would squat on some petrol cans, her jaw cupped in her hands, her elbows on her knees, staring at some constantly flapping tarpaulin, and Clifton would be singing her praises. We tried to joke him out of it, but to wish him more modest would have been against him and none of us wanted that.

After that month in Cairo she was muted, read constantly, kept more to herself, as if something had occurred or she realized suddenly that wondrous thing about the human being, it can change. She did not have to remain a socialite who had married an adventurer. She was discovering herself. It was painful to watch, because Clifton could not see it, her self-education. She read everything about the desert. She could talk about Uweinat and the lost oasis, had even hunted down marginal articles.

I was a man fifteen years older than she, you understand. I had reached that stage in life where I identified with cynical villains in a book. I don't believe in permanence, in relationships that span ages. I was fifteen years older. But she was smarter. She was hungrier to change than I expected.

What altered her during their postponed honeymoon on the Nile estuary outside Cairo? We had seen them for a few days – they had arrived two weeks after their Cheshire wedding. He had brought his bride along, as he couldn't leave her and he couldn't break the commitment to us. To Madox and me. We would have devoured him. So her bony knees emerged from the plane that day. That was the burden of our story. Our situation.

Clifton celebrated the beauty of her arms, the thin lines of her ankles. He described witnessing her swim. He spoke about the new bidets in the hotel suite. Her ravenous hunger at breakfast.

To all that, I didn't say a word. I would look up sometimes as he spoke and catch her glance, witnessing my unspoken exasperation, and then her demure smile. There was some irony. I was the older man. I was the man of the world, who had walked ten years earlier from Dakhla Oasis to the Gilf Kebir, who charted the Farafra, who knew Cyrenaica and had been lost more than twice in the Sand Sea. She met me when I had all those labels. Or she could twist a few degrees and see the labels on Madox. Yet apart from the Geographical Society we were unknown; we were the thin edge of a cult she had stumbled onto because of this marriage.

The words of her husband in praise of her meant nothing. But I am a man whose life in many ways, even as an explorer, has been governed by words. By rumours and legends. Charted things. Shards written down. The tact of words. In the desert to repeat something would be to fling more water into the earth. Her nuance took you a hundred miles.

Our expedition was about forty miles from Uweinat, and Madox and I were to leave alone on a reconnaissance. The Cliftons and the others were to remain behind. She had consumed all her reading and asked me for books. I had nothing but maps with me. "That book you look at in the evenings?" "Herodotus. Ahh. You want that?" "I don't presume. If it is private." "I have my notes within it. And cuttings. I need it with me." "It was forward of me, excuse me." "When I return I shall show it to you. It is unusual for me to travel without it."

All this occurred with much grace and courtesy. I explained it was more a commonplace book, and she bowed to that. I was able to leave without feeling in any way selfish. I acknowledged her graciousness. Clifton was not there.

We were alone. I had been packing in my tent when she had approached me. I am a man who has turned my back on much of the social world, but sometimes I appreciate the delicacy of manner.

We returned a week later. Much had happened in terms of findings and piecings together. We were in good spirits. There was a small celebration at the camp. Clifton was always one to celebrate others. It was catching.

She approached me with a cup of water. "Congratulations, I heard from Geoffrey already—" "Yes!" "Here, drink this." I put out my hand and she placed the cup in my palm. The water was very cold after the stuff in the canteens we had been drinking. "Geoffrey has planned a party for you. He's writing a song and wants me to read a poem, but I want to do something else." "Here, take the book and look through it." I pulled it from my knapsack and handed it to her.

After the meal and herb teas Clifton brought out a bottle of cognac he had hidden from everyone till this moment. The whole bottle was to be drunk that night during Madox's account of our journey, Clifton's funny song. Then she began to read from *The Histories* – the story of Candaules and his queen. I always skim past that story. It is early in the book and has little to do with the places and period I am interested in. But it is of course a famous story. It was also what she had chosen to talk about.

This Candaules had become passionately in love with his own wife; and having become so, he deemed that his wife was fairer by far than all other women. To Gyes, the son of Daskylus (for he of all his spearmen was the most pleasing to him), he used to describe the beauty of his wife, praising it above all measure.

"Are you listening, Geoffrey?"

"Yes, my darling."

He said to Gyges: "Gyges, I think that you do not believe me when I tell you of the beauty of my wife, for it happens that men's ears are less apt of belief than their eyes. Contrive therefore means by which you may look upon her naked."

There are several things one can say. Knowing that eventually I will become her lover, just as Gyges will be the queen's lover and murderer of Candaules. I would often open Herodotus for a clue to geography. But Katharine had done that as a window to her life. Her voice was wary as she read. Her eyes only on the page where the story was, as if she were sinking within quicksand while she spoke.

"I believe indeed that she is of all women the fairest and I entreat you not to ask of me that which it is not lawful for me to do." But the King answered him thus: "Be of good courage, Gyges, and have no fear, either of me, that I am saying these words to try you, or my wife, lest any harm may happen to you from her. For I will contrive it so from the first that she shall not perceive that she has been seen by you."

This is a story of how I fell in love with a woman, who read me a specific story from Herodotus. I heard the words she spoke across the fire, never looking up, even when she teased her husband. Perhaps she was just reading it to him. Perhaps there was no ulterior motive in the selection except for themselves. It was simply a story that had jarred her in its familiarity of situation. But a path suddenly revealed itself in real life. Even though she had not conceived it as a first errant step in any way. I am sure.

*"I will place you in the room where we will sleep, behind
the open door; and after I have gone in, my wife will also
come to lie down. Now there is a seat near the entrance
of the room and on this she lays her garments as she takes
them off one by one; and so you will be able to gaze at
her at full leisure."*

But Gyges is witnessed by the queen when he leaves the
bedchamber. She understands then what has been done by
her husband; and though ashamed, she raises no outcry . . .
she holds her peace.

It is a strange story. Is it not, Caravaggio? The vanity of
a man to the point where he wishes to be envied. Or he
wishes to be believed, for he thinks he is not believed. This
was in no way a portrait of Clifton, but he became a part of
this story. There is something very shocking but human in
the husband's act. Something makes us believe it.

The next day the wife calls in Gyges and gives him two
choices.

*"There are now two ways open to you, and I will give
you the choice which of the two you will prefer to take.
Either you must slay Candaules and possess both me and
the Kingdom of Lydia, or you must yourself here on the
spot be slain, so that you mayest not in future, by obeying Candaules in all things, see that which you should
not. Either he must die who formed this design, or you
who have looked upon me naked."*

So the king is killed. A New Age begins. There are poems
written about Gyges in iambic trimesters. He was the first of
the barbarians to dedicate objects at Delphi. He reigned as
King of Lydia for twenty-eight years, but we still remember
him as only a cog in an unusual love story.

She stopped reading and looked up. Out of the quick-sand. She was evolving. So power changed hands. Meanwhile, with the help of an anecdote, I fell in love.

Words, Caravaggio. They have a power.

When the Cliftons were not with us they were based in Cairo. Clifton doing other work for the English, God knows what, an uncle in some government office. All this was before the war. But at that time the city had every nation swimming in it, meeting at Groppi's for the soirée concerts, dancing into the night. They were a popular young couple with honour between them, and I was on the periphery of Cairo society. They lived well. A ceremonial life that I would slip into now and then. Dinners, garden parties. Events I would not normally have been interested in but now went to because she was there. I am a man who fasts until I see what I want.

How do I explain her to you? With the use of my hands? The way I can arc out in the air the shape of a mesa or rock? She had been part of the expedition for almost a year. I saw her, conversed with her. We had each been continually in the presence of the other. Later, when we were aware of mutual desire, these previous moments flooded back into the heart, now suggestive, that nervous grip of an arm on a cliff, looks that had been missed or misinterpreted.

I was at that time seldom in Cairo, there about one month in three. I worked in the Department of Egyptology on my own book, *Récentes Explorations dans le Désert Libyque*, as the days progressed, coming closer and closer to the text as if the desert were there somewhere on the page, so I could even smell the ink as it emerged from the fountain pen. And simultaneously struggled with her nearby presence, more obsessed if truth be known with her possible mouth, the tautness behind the knee, the white plain of stomach, as I wrote my brief book, seventy pages long, succinct and to the point, complete with maps of travel. I was unable to remove her body from the page. I wished to dedicate the monograph to her, to her voice, to her body that I imagined rose white out of a bed like a long bow, but it was a book I dedicated to a king. Believing such an obsession would be mocked, patronized by her polite and embarrassed shake of the head.

I began to be doubly formal in her company. A characteristic of my nature. As if awkward about a previously revealed nakedness. It is a European habit. It was natural for me – having translated her strangely into my text of the desert – now to step into metal clothing in her presence.

The wild poem is a substitute
For the woman one loves or ought to love,
One wild rhapsody a fake for another.

On Hassanein Bey's lawn – the grand old man of the 1923 expedition – she walked over with the government aide Roundell and shook my hand, asked him to get her a drink, turned back to me and said, "I want you to ravish me." Roundell returned. It was as if she had handed me a knife. Within a month I was her lover. In that room over the souk, north of the street of parrots.

I sank to my knees in the mosaic-tiled hall, my face in the curtain of her gown, the salt taste of these fingers in her mouth. We were a strange statue, the two of us, before we began to unlock our hunger. Her fingers scratching against the sand in my thinning hair. Cairo and all her deserts around us.

Was it desire for her youth, for her thin adept boyishness? Her gardens were the gardens I spoke of when I spoke to you of gardens.

There was that small indentation at her throat we called the Bosphorus. I would drive from her shoulder into the Bosphorous. Rest my eye there. I would kneel while she looked down on me quizzical as if I were a planetary stranger. She of the quizzical look. Her cool hand suddenly against my neck on a Cairo bus. Taking a closed taxi and our quick-hand love between the Khedive Ismail Bridge and the Tipperary Club. Or the sun through her fingernails on the third-floor lobby at the museum when her hand covered my face.

As far as we were concerned there was only one person to avoid being seen by.

But Geoffrey Clifton was a man embedded in the English machine. He had a family genealogy going back to Canute. The machine would not necessarily have revealed to Clifton, married only eighteen months, his wife's infidelity, but it began to encircle the fault, the disease in the system. It knew every move she and I made from the first day of the awkward touch in the porte cochère of the Semiramis Hotel.

I had ignored her remarks about her husband's relatives. And Geoffrey Clifton was as innocent as we were about the great English web that was above us. But the club of bodyguards watched over her husband and kept him protected. Only Madox, who was an aristocrat with a past of regimental associations, knew about such discreet convolutions. Only Madox, with considerable tact, warned me about such a world.

I carried Herodotus, and Madox – a saint in his own marriage – carried *Anna Karenina*, continually rereading the story of romance and deceit. One day, far too late to avoid the machinery we had set in motion, he tried to explain Clifton's world in terms of Anna Karenina's brother. Pass me my book. Listen to this.

> *Half Moscow and Petersburg were relations of friends of Oblonsky. He was born into the circle of people who were, or who became, the great ones of this earth. A third of the official world, the older men, were his father's friends and had known him from the time he was a baby in petticoats. . . . Consequently, the distributors of the blessings of this world were all friends of his. They could not pass over one of their own. . . . It was only necessary not to raise objections or be envious, not to quarrel or take offence, which in accordance with his natural kindliness he never did.*

I have come to love the tap of your fingernail on the syringe, Caravaggio. The first time Hana gave me morphine in your company you were by the window, and at the tap of her nail your neck jerked towards us. I know a comrade. The way a lover will always recognize the camouflage of other lovers.

Women want everything of a lover. And too often I would sink below the surface. So armies disappear under sand. And there was her fear of her husband, her belief in her honour, my old desire for self-sufficiency, my disappearances, her suspicions of me, my disbelief that she loved me. The paranoia and claustrophobia of hidden love.

"I think you have become inhuman," she said to me.

"I'm not the only betrayer."

"I don't think you care – that this has happened among us. You slide past everything with your fear and hate of ownership, of being owned, of being named. You think this is a virtue. I think you are inhuman. If I leave you, who will you go to? Would you find another lover?"

I said nothing.

"Deny it, damn you."

She had always wanted words, she loved them, grew up on them. Words gave her clarity, brought reason, shape. Whereas I thought words bent emotions like sticks in water.

She returned to her husband.

From this point on, she whispered, we will either find or lose our souls.

Seas move away, why not lovers? The harbours of Ephesus, the rivers of Heraclitus disappear and are replaced by estuaries of silt. The wife of Candaules becomes the wife of Gyges. Libraries burn.

What had our relationship been? A betrayal of those around us, or the desire of another life?

She climbed back into her house beside her husband, and I retired to the zinc bars.

> *I'll be looking at the moon,*
> *but I'll be seeing you.*

That old Herodotus classic. Humming and singing that song again and again, beating the lines thinner to bend them into one's own life. People recover from secret loss variously. I was seen by one of her retinue sitting with a spice trader. She had once received from him a pewter thimble that held saffron. One of the ten thousand things.

And if Bagnold – having seen me sitting by the saffron trader – brought up the incident during dinner at the table where she sat, how did I feel about that? Did it give me some comfort that she would remember the man who had given her a small gift, a pewter thimble she hung from a thin dark chain around her neck for two days when her husband was out of town? The saffron still in it, so there was the stain of gold on her chest.

How did she hold this story about me, pariah to the group after some scene or other where I had disgraced myself, Bagnold laughing, her husband who was a good man worrying about me, and Madox getting up and walking to a window and looking out towards the south section of the city. The conversation perhaps moved to other sightings. They were mapmakers, after all. But did she climb down into the well we helped dig together and hold herself, the way I desired myself towards her with my hand?

We each now had our own lives, armed by the deepest treaty with the other.

"What are you doing?" she said running into me on the street. "Can't you see you are driving us all *mad*."

To Madox I had said I was courting a widow. But she was not a widow yet. When Madox returned to England she and I were no longer lovers. "Give my greetings to your Cairo widow," Madox murmured. "Would've liked to have met her." Did he know? I always felt more of a deceiver with him, this friend I had worked with for ten years, this man I loved more than any other man. It was 1939, and we were all leaving this country, in any case, to the war.

And Madox returned to the village of Marston Magna, Somerset, where he had been born, and a month later sat in the congregation of a church, heard the sermon in honour of war, pulled out his desert revolver and shot himself.

I, Herodotus of Halicarnassus, set forth my history, that time may not draw the colour from what Man has brought into being, nor those great and wonderful deeds manifested by both Greeks and Barbarians . . . together with the reason they fought one another.

Men had always been the reciters of poetry in the desert. And Madox – to the Geographical Society – had spoken beautiful accounts of our traversals and coursings. Bermann blew theory into the embers. And I? I was the skill among them. The mechanic. The others wrote out their love of solitude and meditated on what they found there. They were never sure of what I thought of it all. "Do you like that moon?" Madox asked me after he'd known me for ten years. He asked it tentatively, as if he had breached an intimacy. For them I was a bit too cunning to be a lover of the desert. More like Odysseus. Still, I was. Show me a desert, as you would show another man a river, or another man the metropolis of his childhood.

When we parted for the last time, Madox used the old farewell. "May God make safety your companion." And I strode away from him saying, "There is no God." We were utterly unlike each other.

Madox said Odysseus never wrote a word, an intimate book. Perhaps he felt alien in the false rhapsody of art. And my own monograph, I must admit, had been stern with accuracy. The fear of describing her presence as I wrote caused me to burn down all sentiment, all rhetoric of love. Still, I described the desert as purely as I would have spoken of her. Madox asked me about the moon during our last days together before the war began. We parted. He left for England, the probability of the oncoming war interrupting everything, our slow unearthing of history in the desert. Good-bye, Odysseus, he said grinning, knowing I was never that fond of Odysseus, less fond of Aeneas, but we had decided Bagnold was Aeneas. But I was not that fond of Odysseus either. Good-bye, I said.

I remember he turned back, laughing. He pointed his thick finger to the spot by his Adam's apple and said, "This is called the vascular sizood." Giving that hollow at her neck an official name. He returned to his wife in the village of Marston Magna, took only his favourite volume of Tolstoy, left all of his compasses and maps to me. Our affection left unspoken.

And Marston Magna in Somerset, which he had evoked for me again and again in our conversations, had turned its green fields into an aerodrome. The planes burned their exhaust over Arthurian castles. What drove him to the act I do not know. Maybe it was the permanent noise of flight, so loud to him now after the simple drone of the Gypsy Moth that had putted over our silences in Libya and Egypt. Someone's war was slashing apart his delicate tapestry of companions. I was Odysseus, I understood the shifting and temporary vetoes of war. But he was a man who made friends with difficulty. He was a man who knew two or three people in his life, and they had turned out now to be the enemy.

He was in Somerset alone with his wife, who had never met us. Small gestures were enough for him. One bullet ended the war.

It was July 1939. They caught a bus from their village into Yeovil. The bus had been slow and so they had been late for the service. At the back of the crowded church, in order to find seats they decided to sit separately. When the sermon began half an hour later, it was jingoistic and without any doubt in its support of the war. The priest intoned blithely about battle, blessing the government and the men about to enter the war. He pulled out the desert pistol, bent over and shot himself in the heart. He was dead immediately. A great silence. Desert silence. Planeless silence. They heard his body collapse against the pew. Nothing else moved. The priest frozen in a gesture. It was like those silences when a glass funnel round a candle in church splits and all faces turn. His wife walked down the centre aisle, stopped at his row, muttered something, and they let her in beside him. She knelt down, her arms enclosing him.

How did Odysseus die? A suicide, wasn't it? I seem to recall that. Now. Maybe the desert spoiled Madox. That time when we had nothing to do with the world. I keep thinking of the Russian book he always carried. Russia has always been closer to my country than to his. Yes, Madox was a man who died because of nations.

I loved his calmness in all things. I would argue furiously about locations on a map, and his reports would somehow speak of our "debate" in reasonable sentences. He wrote calmly and joyfully about our journeys when there was joy to describe, as if we were Anna and Vronsky at a dance. Still, he was a man who never entered those Cairo dance halls with me. And I was the man who fell in love while dancing.

He moved with a slow gait. I never saw him dance. He was a man who wrote, who interpreted the world. Wisdom grew out of being handed just the smallest sliver of emotion. A glance could lead to paragraphs of theory. If he witnessed a new knot among a desert tribe or found a rare palm, it would charm him for weeks. When we came upon messages on our travels – any wording, contemporary or ancient, Arabic on a mud wall, a note in English written in chalk on the fender of a jeep – he would read it and then press his hand upon it as if to touch its possible deeper meanings, to become as intimate as he could with the words.

He holds out his arm, the bruised veins horizontal, facing up, for the raft of morphine. As it floods him he hears Caravaggio drop the needle into the kidney-shaped enamel tin. He sees the grizzled form turn its back to him and then reappear, also caught, a citizen of morphia with him.

There are days when I come home from arid writing when all that can save me is "Honeysuckle Rose" by Django Reinhardt and Stéphane Grappelly performing with the Hot Club of France. 1935. 1936. 1937. Great jazz years. The years when it floated out of the Hôtel Claridge on the Champs-Élysées and into the bars of London, southern France, Morocco, and then slid into Egypt, where the rumour of such rhythms was introduced in a hush by an unnamed Cairo dance band. When I went back into the desert, I took with me the evenings of dancing to the 78 of "Souvenirs" in the bars, the women pacing like greyhounds, leaning against you while you muttered into their shoulders during "My Sweet." Courtesy of the Société Ultraphone Française record company 1938. 1939. There was the whispering of love in a booth. There was war around the corner.

During those final nights in Cairo, months after the affair was over, we had finally persuaded Madox into a zinc bar for his farewell. She and her husband were there. One last night. One last dance. Almásy was drunk and attempting an old dance step he had invented called the Bosphorus hug, lifting Katharine Clifton into his wiry arms and traversing the floor until he fell with her across some Nile-grown aspidistras.

Who is he speaking as now? Caravaggio thinks.

Almásy was drunk and his dancing seemed to the others a brutal series of movements. In those days he and she did not seem to be getting on well. He swung her from side to side as if she were some anonymous doll, and smothered with drink his grief at Madox's leaving. He was loud at the tables with us. When Almásy was like this we usually dispersed, but this was Madox's last night in Cairo and we stayed. A bad Egyptian violinist mimicking Stéphane Grappelly, and Almásy like a planet out of control. "To us – the planetary strangers," he lifted his glass. He wanted to dance with everyone, men and women. He clapped his hands and announced, "Now for the Bosphorus hug. You, Bernhardt? Hetherton?" Most pulled back. He turned to Clifton's young wife, who was watching him in a courteous rage, and she went forward as he beckoned and then slammed into her, his throat already at her left shoulder on that naked plateau above the sequins. A maniac's tango ensued till one of them lost the step. She would not back down from her anger, refused to let him win by her walking away and returning to the table. Just staring hard at him when he pulled his head back, not solemn but with an attacking face. His mouth muttering at her when he bent his face down, swearing the lyrics of "Honeysuckle Rose," perhaps.

In Cairo between expeditions no one ever saw much of Almásy. He seemed either distant or restless. He worked in the museum during the day and frequented the South Cairo market bars at night. Lost in another Egypt. It was only for Madox they had all come here. But now Almásy was dancing with Katharine Clifton. The line of plants brushed against her slimness. He pivoted with her, lifting her up, and then fell. Clifton stayed in his seat, half watching them. Almásy lying across her and then slowly trying to get up, smoothing back his blond hair, kneeling over her in the far corner of the room. He had at one time been a man of delicacy.

It was past midnight. The guests there were not amused, except for the easily amused regulars, accustomed to these ceremonies of the desert European. There were women with long tributaries of silver hanging off their ears, women in sequins, little metal droplets warm from the bar's heat that Almásy in the past had always been partial towards, women who in their dancing swung the jagged earrings of silver against his face. On other nights he danced with them, carrying their whole frame by the fulcrum of rib cage as he got drunker. Yes, they were amused, laughing at Almásy's stomach as his shirt loosened, not charmed by his weight, which leaned on their shoulders as he paused during the dance, collapsing at some point later during a schottische onto the floor.

It was important during such evenings to *proceed* into the plot of the evening, while the human constellations whirled and skidded around you. There was no thought or forethought. The evening's field notes came later, in the desert, in the landforms between Dakhla and Kufra. Then he would remember that doglike yelp at which he looked around for a dog on the dance floor and realized, now regarding the compass disc floating on oil, that it may have been a woman he had stepped on. Within sight of an oasis he would pride himself on his dancing, waving his arms and his wristwatch up to the sky.

Cold nights in the desert. He plucked a thread from the horde of nights and put it into his mouth like food. This was during the first two days of a trek out, when he was in the zone of limbo between city and plateau. After six days had passed he would never think about Cairo or the music or the streets or the women; by then he was moving in ancient time, had adapted into the breathing patterns of deep water. His only connection with the world of cities was Herodotus, his guidebook, ancient and modern, of supposed lies. When he discovered the truth to what had seemed a lie, he brought out his glue pot and pasted in a map or news clipping or used a blank space in the book to sketch men in skirts with faded unknown animals alongside them. The early oasis dwellers had not usually depicted cattle, though Herodotus claimed they had. They worshipped a pregnant goddess and their rock portraits were mostly of pregnant women.

Within two weeks even the idea of a city never entered his

mind. It was as if he had walked under the millimetre of haze just above the inked fibres of a map, that pure zone between land and chart between distances and legend between nature and storyteller. Sandford called it geomorphology. The place they had chosen to come to, to be their best selves, to be unconscious of ancestry. Here, apart from the sun compass and the odometer mileage and the book, he was alone, his own invention. He knew during these times how the mirage worked, the fata morgana, for he was within it.

He awakens to discover Hana washing him. There is a bureau at waist level. She leans over, her hands bringing water from the porcelain basin to his chest. When she finishes she runs her wet fingers through her hair a few times, so it turns damp and dark. She looks up and sees his eyes are open, and smiles.

When he opens his eyes again, Madox is there, looking ragged, weary, carrying the morphinic injection, having to use both hands because there are no thumbs. How does he give it to himself? he thinks. He recognizes the eye, the habit of the tongue fluttering at the lip, the clearness of the man's brain catching all he says. Two old coots.

Caravaggio watches the pink in the man's mouth as he talks. The gums perhaps the light iodine colour of the rock paintings discovered in Uweinat. There is more to discover, to divine out of this body on the bed, nonexistent except for a mouth, a vein in the arm, wolf-grey eyes. He is still amazed at the clarity of discipline in the man, who speaks sometimes in the first person, sometimes in the third person, who still does not admit that he is Almásy.

"Who was talking, back then?"

"'Death means you are in the third person.'"

All day they have shared the ampoules of morphine. To unthread the story out of him, Caravaggio travels within the code of signals. When the burned man slows down, or when Caravaggio feels he is not catching everything – the love affair, the death of Madox – he picks up the syringe from the kidney-shaped enamel tin, breaks the glass tip off an ampoule with the pressure of a knuckle and loads it. He is blunt about all this now with Hana, having ripped the sleeve off his left arm completely. Almásy wears just a grey singlet, so his black arm lies bare under the sheet.

Each swallow of morphine of the body opens a further door, or he leaps back to the cave paintings or to a buried plane or lingers once more with the woman beside him under a fan, her cheek against his stomach.

Caravaggio picks up the Herodotus. He turns a page, comes over a dune to discover the Gilf Kebir, Uweinat, Gebel Kissu. When Almásy speaks he stays alongside him reordering the events. Only desire makes the story errant, flickering like a compass needle. And this is the world of nomads in any case, an apocryphal story. A mind travelling east and west in the disguise of sandstorm.

On the floor of the Cave of Swimmers, after her husband had crashed their plane, he had cut open and stretched out the parachute she had been carrying. She lowered herself onto it, grimacing with the pain of her injuries. He placed his fingers gently into her hair, searching for other wounds, then touched her shoulders and her feet.

Now in the cave it was her beauty he did not want to lose,

the grace of her, these limbs. He knew he already had her nature tight in his fist.

She was a woman who translated her face when she put on makeup. Entering a party, climbing into a bed, she had painted on blood lipstick, a smear of vermilion over each eye.

He looked up to the one cave painting and stole the colours from it. The ochre went into her face, he daubed blue around her eyes. He walked across the cave, his hands thick with red, and combed his fingers through her hair. Then all of her skin, so her knee that had poked out of the plane that first day was saffron. The pubis. Hoops of colour around her legs so she would be immune to the human. There were traditions he had discovered in Herodotus in which old warriors celebrated their loved ones by locating and holding them in whatever world made them eternal – a colourful fluid, a song, a rock drawing.

It was already cold in the cave. He wrapped the parachute around her for warmth. He lit one small fire and burned the acacia twigs and waved smoke into all the corners of the cave. He found he could not speak directly to her, so he spoke formally, his voice against the bounce of the cave walls. *I'm going for help now, Katharine. Do you understand? There is another plane nearby, but there is no petrol. I might meet a caravan or a jeep, which means I will be back sooner. I don't know.* He pulled out the copy of Herodotus and placed it beside her. It was September 1939. He walked out of the cave, out of the flare of firelight, down through darkness and into the desert full of moon.

He climbed down the boulders to the base of the plateau and stood there.

No truck. No plane. No compass. Only moon and his shadow. He found the old stone marker from the past that located the direction of El Taj, north-northwest. He memorized the angle of his shadow and started walking. Seventy miles away was the souk with the street of clocks. Water in a skin bag he had filled from the *ain* hung from his shoulder and sloshed like a placenta.

There were two periods of time when he could not move. At noon, when the shadow was under him, and at twilight, between sunset and the appearance of the stars. Then everything on the disc of the desert was the same. If he moved, he might err as much as ninety degrees off his course. He waited for the live chart of stars, then moved forward reading them every hour. In the past, when they had had desert guides, they would hang a lantern from a long pole and the rest of them would follow the bounce of light above the star reader.

A man walks as fast as a camel. Two and a half miles an hour. If lucky, he would come upon ostrich eggs. If unlucky, a sandstorm would erase everything. He walked for three days without any food. He refused to think about her. If he got to El Taj he would eat *abra*, which the Goran tribes made out of colocynth, boiling the pips to get rid of bitterness and then crushing it along with dates and locusts. He would walk through the street of clocks and alabaster. May God make safety your companion, Madox had said. Good-bye. A wave. There is God only in the desert, he wanted to acknowledge that now. Outside of this there was just trade and power, money and war. Financial and military despots shaped the world.

He was in broken country, had moved from sand to rock. He refused to think about her. Then hills emerged like mediaeval castles. He walked till he stepped with his shadow into the shadow of a mountain. Mimosa shrubs. Colocynths. He yelled out her name into the rocks. *For echo is the soul of the voice exciting itself in hollow places.*

Then there was El Taj. He had imagined the street of mirrors for most of his journey. When he got to the outskirts of the settlements, English military jeeps surrounded him and took him away, not listening to his story of the woman injured at Uweinat, just seventy miles away, listening in fact to nothing he said.

"Are you telling me the English did not believe you? No one listened to you?"

"No one listened."

"Why?"

"I didn't give them a right name."

"Yours?"

"I gave them mine."

"Then what—"

"*Hers.* Her name. The name of her husband."

"What did you say?"

He says nothing.

"Wake up! What did you say?"

"I said she was my *wife.* I said *Katharine.* Her husband was dead. I said she was badly injured, in a cave in the Gilf Kebir at Uweinat, north of the Ain Dua well. She needed water. She needed food. I would go back with them to guide them. I said all I wanted was a jeep. One of their jeeps . . . Perhaps I seemed like one of those mad desert prophets after the journey, but I don't think so. The war was beginning already. They were just pulling spies in out of the desert. Everyone with a foreign name who drifted into these small oasis towns was suspect. She was just seventy miles away and they wouldn't listen. Some stray English outfit in El Taj. I must have gone berserk then. They were using these wicker prisons, size of a shower. I was put into one and moved by truck. I was flailing around in there until I fell off onto the street, still in it. I was yelling Katharine's name. Yelling the Gilf Kebir. Whereas the only name I should have yelled, dropped like a calling card into their hands, was Clifton's.

"They hauled me up into the truck again. I was just another possible second-rate spy. Just another international bastard."

Caravaggio wants to rise and walk away from this villa, the country, the detritus of a war. He is just a thief. What Caravaggio wants is his arms around the sapper and Hana or, better, people of his own age, in a bar where he knows everyone, where he can dance and talk with a woman, rest his head on her shoulder, lean his head against her brow, whatever, but he knows first he must get out of this desert, its architecture of morphine. He needs to pull away from the invisible road to El Taj. This man he believes to be Almásy has used him and the morphine to return to his own world, for his own sadness. It no longer matters which side he was on during the war.

But Caravaggio leans forward.

"I need to know something."

"What?"

"I need to know if you murdered Katharine Clifton. That is, if you murdered Clifton, and in so doing killed her."

"No. I never even imagined that."

"The reason I ask is that Geoffrey Clifton was with British Intelligence. He was not just an innocent Englishman, I'm afraid. Your friendly boy. As far as the English were concerned, he was keeping an eye on your strange group in the Egyptian–Libyan desert. They knew the desert would someday be a theatre of war. He was an aerial photographer. His death perturbed them, still does. They still raise the question. And Intelligence knew about your affair with his wife, from the beginning. Even if Clifton didn't. They thought his death may have been engineered as protection, hoisting up the drawbridge. They were waiting for you in Cairo, but of course you turned back into the desert. Later, when I was sent to Italy, I lost the last part of your story. I didn't know what had happened to you."

"So you have run me to earth."

"I came because of the girl. I knew her father. The last person I expected to find here in this shelled nunnery was Count Ladislaus de Almásy. Quite honestly, I've become more fond of you than most of the people I worked with."

The rectangle of light that had drifted up Caravaggio's chair was framing his chest and head so that to the English patient the face seemed a portrait. In muted light his hair appeared dark, but now the wild hair lit up, bright, the bags under his eyes washed out in the pink late daylight.

He had turned the chair around so he could lean forward on its back, facing Almásy. Words did not emerge easily from Caravaggio. He would rub his jaw, his face creasing up, the eyes closed, to think in darkness, and only then would he blurt out something, tearing himself away from his own thoughts. It was this darkness that showed in him as he sat in the rhomboid frame of light, hunched over a chair beside Almásy's bed. One of the two older men in this story.

"I can talk with you, Caravaggio, because I feel we are both mortal. The girl, the boy, they are not mortal yet. In spite of what they have been through. Hana was greatly distressed when I first met her."

"Her father was killed in France."

"I see. She would not talk about it. She was distant from

everybody. The only way I could get her to communicate was to ask her to read to me. . . . Do you realize neither of us has children?"

Then pausing, as if considering a possibility.

"Do you have a wife?" Almásy asked.

Caravaggio sat in the pink light, his hands over his face to erase everything so he could think precisely, as if this was one more gift of youth that did not come so easily to him any longer.

"You must talk to me, Caravaggio. Or am I just a book? Something to be read, some creature to be tempted out of a loch and shot full of morphine, full of corridors, lies, loose vegetation, pockets of stones."

"Thieves like us were used a great deal during this war. We were legitimized. We stole. Then some of us began to advise. We could read through the camouflage of deceit more naturally than official intelligence. We created double bluffs. Whole campaigns were being run by this mixture of crooks and intellectuals. I was all over the Middle East, that's where I first heard about you. You were a mystery, a vacuum on their charts. Turning your knowledge of the desert into German hands."

"Too much happened at El Taj in 1939, when I was rounded up, imagined to be a spy."

"So that's when you went over to the Germans."

Silence.

"And you still were unable to get back to the Cave of Swimmers and Uweinat?"

"Not till I volunteered to take Eppler across the desert."

"There is something I must tell you. To do with 1942, when you guided the spy into Cairo . . ."

"Operation Salaam."

"Yes. When you were working for Rommel."

"A brilliant man. . . . What were you going to tell me?"

"I was going to say, when you came through the desert avoiding Allied troops, travelling with Eppler – it *was* heroic. From Gialo Oasis all the way to Cairo. Only you could have gotten Rommel's man into Cairo with his copy of *Rebecca*."

"How did you know that?"

"What I want to say is that they did not just discover Eppler in Cairo. They knew about the whole journey. A German code had been broken long before, but we couldn't let Rommel know that or our sources would have been discovered. So we had to wait till Cairo to capture Eppler.

"We watched you all the way. All through the desert. And because Intelligence had your name, knew you were involved, they were even more interested. They wanted you as well. You were supposed to be killed. . . . If you don't believe me, you left Gialo and it took you twenty days. You followed the buried-well route. You couldn't get near Uweinat because of Allied troops, and you avoided Abu Ballas. There were times when Eppler had desert fever and you had to look after him, care for him, though you say you didn't like him. . . .

"Planes supposedly 'lost' you, but you were being tracked very carefully. You were not the spies, we were spies. Intelligence thought you had killed Geoffrey Clifton over the woman. They had found his grave in 1939, but there was no sign of his wife. You had become the enemy not when you sided with Germany but when you began your affair with Katharine Clifton."

"I see."

"After you left Cairo in 1942, we lost you. They were supposed to pick you up and kill you in the desert. But they lost you. Two days out. You must have been haywire, not rational, or we would have found you. We had mined the hidden jeep. We found it exploded later, but there was nothing of you. You were gone. That must have been your great journey, not the one to Cairo. When you must have been mad."

"Were you there in Cairo with them tracking me?"

"No, I saw the files. I was going into Italy and they thought you might be there."

"Here."

"Yes."

The rhomboid of light moved up the wall leaving Caravaggio in shadow. His hair dark again. He leaned back, his shoulder against the foliage.

"I suppose it doesn't matter," Almásy murmured.

"Do you want morphine?"

"No. I'm putting things into place. I was always a private man. It is difficult to realize I was so *discussed*."

"You were having an affair with someone connected with Intelligence. There were some people in Intelligence who knew you personally."

"Bagnold probably."

"Yes."

"Very English Englishman."

"Yes."

Caravaggio paused.

"I have to talk to you about one last thing."

"I know."

"What happened to Katharine Clifton? What happened

just before the war to make you all come to the Gilf Kebir again? After Madox left for England."

I was supposed to make one more journey to the Gilf Kebir, to pack up the last of the base camp at Uweinat. Our life there was over. I thought nothing more would happen between us. I had not me her as a lover for almost a year. A war was preparing itself somewhere like a hand entering an attic window. And she and I had already retreated behind our own walls of previous habit, into seeming innocence of relationship. We no longer saw each other very much.

During the summer of 1939 I was to go overland to the Gilf Kebir with Gough, pack up the base camp, and Gough would leave by truck. Clifton would fly in and pick me up. Then we would disperse, out of the triangle that had grown up among us.

When I heard the plane, saw it, I was already climbing down the rocks of the plateau. Clifton was always prompt.

There is a way a small cargo plane will come down to land, slipping from the level of horizon. It tips its wings within desert light and then sound stops, it drifts to earth. I have never fully understood how planes work. I have watched them approach me in the desert and I have come out of my tent always with fear. They dip their wings across the light and then they enter that silence.

The Moth came skimming over the plateau. I was waving the blue tarpaulin. Clifton dropped altitude and roared over me, so low the acacia shrubs lost their leaves. The plane veered to the left and circled, and sighting me again realigned itself and came straight towards me. Fifty yards away from me it suddenly tilted and crashed. I started running towards it.

I thought he was alone. He was supposed to be alone. But

when I got there to pull him out, she was beside him. He was dead. She was trying to move the lower part of her body, looking straight ahead. Sand had come in through the cockpit window and had filled her lap. There didn't seem to be a mark on her. Her left hand had gone forward to cushion the collapse of their flight. I pulled her out of the plane Clifton had called *Rupert* and carried her up into the rock caves. Into the Cave of Swimmers, where the paintings were. Latitude 23° 30' on the map, longitude 25° 15'. I buried Geoffrey Clifton that night.

Was I a curse upon them? For her. For Madox? For the desert raped by war, shelled as if it were just sand? The Barbarians versus the Barbarians. Both armies would come through the desert with no sense of what it was. *The deserts of Libya*. Remove politics, and it is the loveliest phrase I know. *Libya*. A sexual drawn-out word, a coaxed well. The *b* and the *y*. Madox said it was one of the few words in which you heard the tongue turn a corner. Remember Dido in the deserts of Libya? *A man shall be as rivers of water in a dry place.* . . .

I do not believe I entered a cursed land, or that I was ensnared in a situation that was evil. Every place and person was a gift to me. Finding the rock paintings in the Cave of Swimmers. Singing "burdens" with Madox during expeditions. Katharine's appearance among us in the desert. The way I would walk towards her over the red polished concrete floor and sink to my knees, her belly against my head as if I were a boy. The gun tribe healing me. Even the four of us, Hana and you and the sapper.

Everything I have loved or valued has been taken away from me.

I stayed with her. I discovered three of her ribs were

broken. I kept waiting for her wavering eye, for her broken wrist to bend, for her still mouth to speak.

How did you hate me? she whispered. You killed almost everything in me.

Katharine . . . you didn't—

Hold me. Stop defending yourself. Nothing changes you.

Her glare was permanent. I could not move out of the target of that gaze. I will be the last image she sees. The jackal in the cave who will guide and protect her, who will never deceive her.

There are a hundred deities associated with animals, I tell her. There are the ones linked to jackals – Anubis, Duamutef, Wepwawet. These are creatures who guide you into the afterlife – as my early ghost accompanied you, those years before we met. All those parties in London and Oxford. Watching you. I sat across from you as you did schoolwork, holding a large pencil. I was there when you met Geoffrey Clifton at two a.m. in the Oxford Union Library. Everybody's coats were strewn on the floor and you in your bare feet like some heron picking your way among them. He is watching you but I am watching you too, though you miss my presence, ignore me. You are at an age when you see only good-looking men. You are not yet aware of those outside your sphere of grace. The jackal is not used much at Oxford as an escort. Whereas I am the man who fasts until I see what I want. The wall behind you is covered in books. Your left hands hold a long loop of pearls that hangs from your neck. Your bare feet picking their way through. You are looking for something. You were more plump in those days, though aptly beautiful for university life.

There are three of us in the Oxford Union Library, but

you find only Geoffrey Clifton. It will be a whirlwind romance. He has some job with archaeologists in North Africa, of all places. "A strange old coot I'm working with." Your mother is quite delighted at your adventure.

But the spirit of the jackal, who was the "opener of the ways," whose name was Wepwawet or Almásy, stood in the room with the two of you. My arms folded, watching your attempts at enthusiastic small talk, a problem as you both were drunk. But what was wonderful was that even within the drunkenness of two a.m., each of you somehow recognized the more permanent worth and pleasure of the other. You may have arrived with others, will perhaps cohabit this night with others, but both of you have found your fates.

At three a.m. you feel you must leave, but you are unable to find one shoe. You hold the other in your hand, a rose-coloured slipper. I see one half buried near me and pick it up. The sheen of it. They are obviously favourite shoes, with the indentation of your toes. Thank you, you say accepting it, as you leave, not even looking at my face.

I believe this. When we meet those we fall in love with, there is an aspect of our spirit that is historian, a bit of a pedant, who imagines or remembers a meeting when the other had passed by innocently, just as Clifton might have opened a car door for you a year earlier and ignored the fate of his life. But all parts of the body must be ready for the other, all atoms must jump in one direction for desire to occur.

I have lived in the desert for years and I have come to believe in such things. It is a place of pockets. The trompe l'oeil of time and water. The jackal with one eye that looks back and one that regards the path you consider taking. In his jaws are pieces of the past that he delivers to you, and when all of that time is fully discovered it will prove to have been already known.

Her eyes looked at me, tired of everything. A terrible weariness. When I pulled her from the plane her stare had tried to receive all things around her. Now the eyes were guarded, as if protecting something inside. I moved closer, and sat on my heels. I leaned forward and put my tongue against the right blue eye, a taste of salt. Pollen. I carried that taste to her mouth. Then the other eye. My tongue against the fine porousness of the eyeball, wiping off the blue; when I moved back there was a sweep of white across her gaze. I parted the lips on her mouth, this time I let the fingers go in deeper and prised the teeth apart, the tongue was "withdrawn," and I had to pull it forward, there was a thread, a breath of death in her. It was almost too late. I leaned forward and with my tongue carried the blue pollen to her tongue. We touched this way once. Nothing happened. I pulled back, took a breath and then went forward again. As I met the tongue there was a twitch within it.

Then the terrible snarl, violent and intimate, came out of her upon me. A shudder through her whole body like a path of electricity. She was flung from the propped position against the painted wall. The creature had entered her and it leapt and fell against me. There seemed to be less and less light in the cave. Her neck flipping this way and that.

I know the devices of a demon. I was taught as a child about the demon lover. I was told about a beautiful temptress who came to a young man's room. And he, if he were wise, would demand that she turn around, because demons and witches have no back, only what they wish to present to you.

What had I done? What animal had I delivered into her? I had been speaking to her I think for over an hour. Had I been her demon lover? Had I been Madox's demon friend? This country – had I charted it and turned it into a place of war?

It is important to die in holy places. That was one of the secrets of the desert. So Madox walked into a church in Somerset, a place he felt had lost its holiness, and he committed what he believed was a holy act.

When I turned her around, her whole body was covered in bright pigment. Herbs and stones and light and the ash of acacia to make her eternal. The body pressed against sacred colour. Only the eye blue removed, made anonymous, a naked map where nothing is depicted, no signature of lake, no dark cluster of mountain as there is north of the Borkou-Ennedi-Tibesti, no lime-green fan where the Nile rivers enter the open palm of Alexandria, the edge of Africa.

And all the names of the tribes, the nomads of faith who walked in the monotone of the desert and saw brightness and faith and colour. The way a stone or found metal box or bone can become loved and turn eternal in a prayer. Such glory of this country she enters now and becomes part of. We die containing a richness of lovers and tribes, tastes we have swallowed, bodies we have plunged into and swum up as if rivers of wisdom, characters we have climbed into as if trees, fears we have hidden in as if caves. I wish for all this to be marked on my body when I am dead. I believe in such cartography – to be marked by nature, not just to label ourselves on a map like the names of rich men and women on buildings. We are communal histories, communal books. We are now owned or monogamous in our taste or experience. All I desired was to walk upon such an earth that had no maps.

I carried Katharine Clifton into the desert, where there is the communal book of moonlight. We were among the rumour of wells. In the palace of winds.

Almásy's face fell to the left, staring at nothing – Caravaggio's knees perhaps.

"Do you want some morphine now?"

"No."

"Can I get you something?"

"Nothing."

X

August

CARAVAGGIO CAME DOWN the stairs through darkness and into the kitchen. Some celery on the table, some turnips whose roots were still muddy. The only light came from a fire Hana had recently started. She had her back to him and had not heard his steps into the room. His days at the villa had loosened his body and freed his tenseness, so he seemed bigger, more sprawled out in his gestures. Only his silence of movement remained. Otherwise there was an easy inefficiency to him now, a sleepiness to his gestures.

He dragged out the chair so she would turn, realize he was in the room.

"Hello, David."

He raised his arm. He felt that he had been in deserts for too long.

"How is he?"

"Asleep. Talked himself out."

"Is he what you thought he was?"

"He's fine. We can let him be."

"I thought so. Kip and I are both sure he is English. Kip thinks the best people are eccentrics, he worked with one."

"I think Kip is the eccentric myself. Where is he, anyway?"

"He's plotting something on the terrace, doesn't want me out there. Something for my birthday." Hana stood up from her crouch at the grate, wiping her hand on the opposite forearm.

"For your birthday I'm going to tell you a small story," he said.

She looked at him.

"Not about Patrick, okay?"

"A little about Patrick, mostly about you."

"I still can't listen to those stories, David."

"Fathers die. You keep on loving them in any way you can. You can't hide him away in your heart."

"Talk to me when the morphia wears off."

She came up to him and put her arms around him, reached up and kissed his cheek. His embrace tightened around her, his stubble like sand against her skin. She loved that about him now; in the past he had always been meticulous. The parting in his hair like Yonge Street at midnight, Patrick had said. Caravaggio had in the past moved like a god in her presence. Now, with his face and his trunk filled out, and this greyness in him, he was a friendlier human.

Tonight dinner was being prepared by the sapper. Caravaggio was not looking forward to it. One meal in three was a loss as far as he was concerned. Kip found vegetables and presented them barely cooked, just briefly boiled into a soup. It was to be another purist meal, not what Caravaggio wished for after a day such as this when he had been listening to the man upstairs. He opened the cupboard beneath the sink. There, wrapped in damp cloth, was some dried meat, which Caravaggio cut and put into his pocket.

"I can get you off the morphine, you know. I'm a good nurse."

"You're surrounded by madmen. . . ."

"Yes. I think we are all mad."

When Kip called them, they walked out of the kitchen and onto the terrace, whose border, with its low stone balustrade, was ringed with light.

It looked to Caravaggio like a string of small electric candles found in dusty churches, and he thought the sapper had gone too far in removing them from a chapel, even for Hana's birthday. Hana walked slowly forward with her hands over her face. There was no wind. Her legs and thighs moved through the skirt of her frock as if it were thin water. Her tennis shoes silent on the stone.

"I kept finding dead shells wherever I was digging," the sapper said.

They still didn't understand. Caravaggio bent over the flutter of lights. They were snail shells filled with oil. He looked along the row of them; there must have been about forty.

"Forty-five," Kip said, "the years so far of this century. Where I come from, we celebrate the age as well as ourselves."

Hana moved alongside them, her hands in her pockets now, the way Kip loved to see her walk. So relaxed, as if she had put her arms away for the night, now in simple armless movement.

Caravaggio was diverted by the startling presence of three bottles of red wine on the table. He walked over and read the labels and shook his head, amazed. He knew the sapper wouldn't drink any of it. All three had already been opened. Kip must have picked his way through some etiquette book in the library. Then he saw the corn and the meat and the potatoes. Hana slid her arm into Kip's and came with him to the table.

They ate and drank, the unexpected thickness of the wine like meat on their tongues. They were soon turning silly in their toasts to the sapper – "the great forager" – and to the English patient. They toasted each other, Kip joining in with his beaker of water. This was when he began to talk about himself. Caravaggio pressing him on, not always listening, sometimes standing up and walking around the table, pacing and pacing with pleasure at all this. He wanted these two married, longed to force them verbally towards it, but they seemed to have their own strange rules about their relationship. What was he doing in *this* role. He sat down again. Now and then he noticed the death of a light. The snail shells held only so much oil. Kip would rise and refill them with pink paraffin.

"We must keep them lit till midnight."

They talked then about the war, so far away. "When the war with Japan is over, everyone will finally go home," Kip said. "And where will *you* go?" Caravaggio asked. The sapper rolled his head, half nodding, half shaking it, his mouth smiling. So Caravaggio began to talk, mostly to Kip.

The dog cautiously approached the table and laid its head on Caravaggio's lap. The sapper asked for other stories about Toronto as if it were a place of peculiar wonders. Snow that drowned the city, iced up the harbour, ferryboats in the summer where people listened to concerts. But what he was really interested in were the clues to Hana's nature, though she was evasive, veering Caravaggio away from stories that involved some moment of her life. She wanted Kip to know her only in the present, a person perhaps more flawed or more compassionate or harder or more obsessed than the girl or young woman she had been then. In her life there was her mother Alice her father Patrick her stepmother Clara and Caravaggio. She had already admitted these names to Kip as if they were her credentials, her dowry. They were faultless and needed no discussion. She used them like authorities in a book she could refer to on the right way to boil an egg, or the correct way to slip garlic into a lamb. They were not to be questioned.

And now – because he was quite drunk – Caravaggio told the story of Hana's singing the "Marseillaise," which he had told her before. "Yes, I have heard the song," said Kip, and he attempted a version of it. "No, you have to sing it *out*," said Hana, "you have to sing it standing up!"

She stood up, pulled her tennis shoes off and climbed on to the table. There were four small lights flickering, almost dying, on the table beside her bare feet.

"This is for you. This is how you must learn to sing it, Kip. This is for *you*."

She sang up into darkness beyond their snail light, beyond the square of light from the English patient's room and into the dark sky waving with shadows of cypress. Her hands came out of their pockets.

Kip had heard the song in the camps, sung by groups of men, often during strange moments, such as before an impromptu soccer match. And Caravaggio when he had heard it in the last few years of the war never really liked it, never liked to listen to it. In his heart he had Hana's version from many years before. Now he listened with a pleasure because she was singing again, but this was quickly altered by the way she sang. Not the passion of her at sixteen but echoing the tentative circle of light around her in the darkness. She was singing it as if it was something scarred, as if one couldn't ever again bring all the hope of the song together. It had been altered by the five years leading to this night of her twenty-first birthday in the forty-fifth year of the twentieth century. Singing in the voice of a tired traveller, alone against everything. A new testament. There was no certainty to the song anymore, the singer could only be one voice against all the mountains of power. That was the only sureness. The one voice was the single unspoiled thing. A song of snail light. Caravaggio realized she was singing with and echoing the heart of the sapper.

In the tent there have been nights of no talk and nights full of talk. They are never sure what will occur, whose fraction of past will emerge, or whether touch will be anonymous and silent in their darkness. The intimacy of her body or the body of her language in his ear – as they lie upon the air pillow he insists on blowing up and using each night. He has been charmed by this Western invention. He dutifully releases the air and folds it into three each morning, as he has done all the way up the landmass of Italy.

In the tent Kip nestles against her neck. He dissolves to her scratching fingernails across his skin. Or he has his mouth against her mouth, his stomach against her wrist.

She sings and hums. She thinks him, in this tent's darkness, to be half bird – a quality of feather within him, the cold iron at his wrist. He moves sleepily whenever he is in such darkness with her, not quite quick as the world, whereas in daylight he glides through all that is random around him, the way colour glides against colour.

But at night he embraces torpor. She cannot see his order and discipline without seeing his eyes. There isn't a key to him. Everywhere she touches braille doorways. As if organs,

289

the heart, the rows of rib, can be seen under the skin, saliva across her hand now a colour. He has mapped her sadness more than any other. Just as she knows the strange path of love he has for his dangerous brother. "To be a wanderer is in our blood. That is why jailing is most difficult for his nature and he would kill himself to get free."

During the verbal nights, they travel his country of five rivers. The Sutlej, Jhelum, Ravi, Chenab, Beas. He guides her into the great gurdwara, removing her shoes, watching as she washes her feet, covers her head. What they enter was built in 1601, desecrated in 1757 and built again immediately. In 1830 gold and marble were applied. "If I took you before morning you would see first of all the mist over the water. Then it lifts to reveal the temple in light. You will already be hearing the hymns of the saints – Ramananda, Nanak and Kabir. Singing is at the centre of worship. You hear the song, you smell the fruit from the temple gardens – pomegranates, oranges. The temple is a haven in the flux of life, accessible to all. It is the ship that crossed the ocean of ignorance."

They move through the night, they move through the silver door to the shrine where the Holy Book lies under a canopy of brocades. The *ragis* sing the Book's verses accompanied by musicians. They sing from four in the morning till eleven at night. The Granth Sahib is opened at random, a quotation selected, and for three hours, before the mist lifts off the lake to reveal the Golden Temple, the verses mingle and sway out with unbroken reading.

Kip walks her beside a pool to the tree shrine where Baba Gujhaji, the first priest of the temple, is buried. A tree of superstitions, four hundred and fifty years old. "My mother came here to tie a string onto a branch and beseeched the tree for a son, and when my brother was born returned and asked to be blessed with another. There are sacred trees and magic water all over the Punjab."

Hana is quiet. He knows the depth of darkness in her, her lack of a child and of faith. He is always coaxing her from the edge of her fields of sadness. A child lost. A father lost.

"I have lost someone like a father as well," he has said. But she knows this man beside her is one of the charmed, who has grown up an outsider and so can switch allegiances, can replace loss. There are those destroyed by unfairness and those who are not. If she asks him he will say he has had a good life – his brother in jail, his comrades blown up, and he risking himself daily in this war.

In spite of the kindnesses in such people they were a terrible unfairness. He could be all day in a clay pit dismantling a bomb that might kill him at any moment, could come home from the burial of a fellow sapper, his energy saddened, but whatever the trials around him there was always solution and light. But she saw none. For him there were the various maps of fate, and at Amristar's temple all faiths and classes were welcome and ate together. She herself would be allowed to place money or a flower onto the sheet spread upon the floor and then join in the great permanent singing.

She wished for that. Her inwardness was a sadness of nature. He himself would allow her to enter any of his thirteen gates of character, but she knew that if he were in danger he would never turn to face her. He would create a space around himself and concentrate. This was his craft. Sikhs, he said, were brilliant at technology. "We have a mystical closeness . . . what is it?" "Affinity." "Yes, affinity, with machines."

He would be lost among them for hours, the beat of music within the crystal set whacking away at his forehead and into his hair. She did not believe she could turn fully to him and be his lover. He moved at a speed that allowed him to replace loss. That was his nature. She would not judge it in him. What right did she have. Kip stepping out each morning with his satchel hanging off his left shoulder and walking the path away from the Villa San Girolamo. Each morning she watched him, seeing his freshness towards the world perhaps for the last time. After a few minutes he would look up into the shrapnel-torn cypresses, whose middle branches had been shelled away. Pliny must have walked down a path like this, or Stendahl, because passages in *The Charterhouse of Parma* had occurred in this part of the world too.

Kip would look up, the arch of the high wounded trees over him, the path in front of him mediaeval, and he a young man of the strangest profession his century had invented, a sapper, a military engineer who detected and disarmed mines. Each morning he emerged from the tent, bathed and dressed in the garden, and stepped away from the villa and its surroundings, not even entering the house – maybe a wave if he saw her – as if language, humanity, would confuse him, get, like blood, into the machine he had to understand. She would see him forty yards from the house, in a clearing of the path.

It was the moment he left them all behind. The moment the drawbridge closed behind the knight and he was alone with just the peacefulness of his own strict talent. In Siena there was that mural she had seen. A fresco of a city. A few yards outside the city walls the artist's paint had crumbled away, so there was not even the security of art to provide an orchard in the far acres for the traveller leaving the castle. That was where, she felt, Kip went during the day. Each morning he would step from the painted scene towards dark bluffs of chaos. The knight. The warrior saint. She would see the khaki uniform flickering through the cypresses. The Englishman had called him *fato profugus* – fate's fugitive. She guessed than these days began for him with the pleasure of lifting his eyes up to the trees.

They had flown the sappers into Naples at the beginning of October 1943, selecting the best from the engineering corps that were already in southern Italy, Kip among the thirty men who were brought into the booby-trapped city.

The Germans in the Italian campaign had choreographed one of the most brilliant and terrible retreats in history. The advance of the Allies, which should have taken a month, took a year. There was fire in their path. Sappers rode the mudguards of trucks as the armies moved forward, their eyes searching for fresh soil disturbances that signalled land mines or glass mines or shoe mines. The advance impossibly slow. Farther north in the mountains, partisan bands of Garibaldi communist groups, who wore identifying red handkerchiefs, were also wiring explosives over the roads which detonated when German trucks passed over them.

The scale of the laying of mines in Italy and in North Africa cannot be imagined. At the Kismaayo–Afmadu road junction, 260 mines were found. There were 300 at the Omo River Bridge area. On June 30, 1941, South African sappers laid 2,700 Mark II mines in Mersa Matruh in one day. For months later the British cleared Mersa Matruh of 7,806 mines and placed them elsewhere.

Mines were made out of everything. Forty-centimetre galvanized pipes were filled with explosives and left along military paths. Mines in wooden boxes were left in homes. Pipe mines were filled with gelignite, metal scraps and nails. South African sappers packed iron and gelignite into four-gallon petrol cans that could then destroy armoured cars.

It was worst in the cities. Bomb disposal units, barely trained, were shipped out from Cairo and Alexandria. The Eighteenth Division became famous. During three weeks in October 1941, they dismantled 1,403 high-explosive bombs.

Italy was worse than Africa, the clockwork fuzes nightmarishly eccentric, the spring-activated mechanisms different from the German ones that units had been trained in. As sappers entered cities they walked along avenues where corpses were strung from trees or the balconies of buildings. The Germans often retaliated by killing ten Italians for every German killed. Some of the hanging corpses were mined and had to be blown up in midair.

The Germans evacuated Naples on October 1, 1943. During an Allied raid the previous September, hundreds of citizens had walked away and begun living in the caves outside the city. The Germans in their retreat bombed the entrance to the caves, forcing the citizens to stay underground. A typhus epidemic broke out. In the harbour scuttled ships were freshly mined underwater.

The thirty sappers walked into a city of booby traps. There were delayed-action bombs sealed into the walls of public buildings. Nearly every vehicle was rigged. The sappers became permanently suspicious of any object placed casually in a room. They distrusted everything they saw on a table unless it was placed facing "four o'clock." Years after the war a sapper putting a pen on a table would position it with the thicker end facing four o'clock.

Naples continued as a war zone for six weeks and Kip was there with the unit for the whole period. After two weeks they discovered the citizens in the caves. Their skin dark with shit and typhus. The procession of them back into the city hospitals was one of ghosts.

Four days later the central post office blew up, and seventy-two were killed or wounded. The richest collection of mediaeval records in Europe had already burned in the city archives.

On the twentieth of October, three days before electricity was to be restored, a German turned himself in. He told authorities that there were thousands of bombs hidden in the harbour section of the city that were wired to the dormant electrical system. When power was turned on, the city would dissolve in flames. He was interrogated more than seven times, in differing stages of tact and violence – at the end of which the authorities were still uncertain about his confession. This time an entire area of the city was evacuated. Children and the old, those almost dead, those pregnant, those who had been brought out of the caves, animals, valuable jeeps, wounded soldiers out of the hospitals, mental patents, priests and monks and nuns out of the abbeys. By dusk on the evening of October 22, 1943, only twelve sappers remained behind.

The electricity was to be turned on at three p.m. the next day. None of the sappers had ever been in an empty city before, and these were to be the strangest and most disturbing hours of their lives.

During the evenings thunderstorms roll over Tuscany. Lightning drops towards any metal or spire that rises up out of the landscape. Kip always returns to the villa along the yellow path between the cypresses around seven in the evening, which is when the thunder, if there is going to be thunder, begins. The mediaeval experience.

He seems to like such temporal habits. She or Caravaggio will see his figure in the distance, pausing in his walk home to look back towards the valley to see how far away the rain is from him. Hana and Caravaggio return to the house. Kip continues his half-mile uphill walk on the path that curls slowly to the right and then slowly to the left. There is the noise of his boots on the gravel. The wind reaches him in bursts, hitting the cypresses broadside so they tilt, entering the sleeves of his shirt.

For the next ten minutes he walks, never sure if the rain will overtake him. He will hear the rain before he feels it, a clicking on the dry grass, on the olive leaves. But for now he is in the great refreshing wind of the hill, in the foreground of the storm.

If the rain reaches him before he gets to the villa, he continues walking at the same pace, snaps the rubber cape over his haversack and walks on within it.

In his tent he hears the pure thunder. Sharp cracks of it overhead, a coach-wheel wound as it disappears into the mountains. A sudden sunlight of lightning through the tent wall, always, it seems to him, brighter than sunlight, a flash of contained phosphorus, something machinelike, to do with the new word he has heard in the theory rooms and through his crystal set, which is "nuclear." In the event he unwinds the wet turban, dries his hair and weaves another around his head.

The storm rolls out of Piedmont to the south and to the east. Lightning falls upon the steeples of the small alpine chapels whose tableaux reenact the Stations of the Cross or the Mysteries of the Rosary. In the small towns of Varese and Varallo, larger-than-life terra-cotta figures carved in the 1600s are revealed briefly, depicting biblical scenes. The bound arms of the scourged Christ pulled back, the whip coming down, the baying dog, three soldiers in the next chapel tableau raising the crucifix higher towards the painted clouds.

The Villa San Girolamo, located where it is, also receives such moments of light – the dark halls, the room the Englishman lies in, the kitchen where Hana is laying a fire, the shelled chapel – all lit suddenly, without shadow. Kip will walk with no qualms under the trees in his patch of garden during such storms, the dangers of being killed by lightning pathetically minimal compared with the danger of his daily life. The naive Catholic images from those hillside shrines that he has seen are with him in the half-darkness, as he counts the seconds between lightning and thunder. Perhaps this villa is a similar tableau, the four of them in private movement, momentarily lit up, flung ironically against this war.

The twelve sappers who remained behind in Naples fanned out into the city. All through the night they have broken into sealed tunnels, descended into sewers, looking for fuze lines that might be linked with the central generators. They are to drive away at two p.m., an hour before the electricity is to be turned on.

A city of twelve. Each in separate parts of the town. One at the generator, one at the reservoir, still diving – the authorities most certain destruction will be caused by flooding. How to mine a city. It is unnerving mostly because of the silence. All they hear of the human world are barking dogs and bird songs that come from apartment windows above the streets. When the time comes, he will go into one of the rooms with a bird. Some human thing in this vacuum. He passes the Museo Archeologico Nazionale, where the remnants of Pompeii and Herculaneum are housed. He has seen the ancient dog frozen in white ash.

The scarlet sapper light strapped to his left arm is turned on as he walks, the only source of light on the Strada Carbonara. He is exhausted from the night search, and now there seems little to do. Each of them has a radiophone, but it is to be used only for an emergency discovery. It is the terrible silence in the empty courtyards and the dry fountains that makes him most tired.

At one p.m. he traces his way towards the damaged Church of San Giovanni a Carbonara, where he knows there is a chapel of the Rosary. He had been walking through the church a few evenings earlier when lightning filled the darkness, and he had seen large human figures in the tableau. An angel and a woman in a bedroom. Darkness replaced the brief scene and he sat in a pew waiting, but there was to be no more revelation.

He enters that corner of the church now, with the terra-cotta figures painted the colour of white humans. The scene depicts a bedroom where a woman is in conversation with an angel. The woman's curly brown hair reveals itself under the loose blue cape, the fingers of her left hand touching her breastbone. When he steps forward into the room he realizes everything is larger than life. His own head is no higher than the shoulder of the woman. The angel's raised arm reaches fifteen feet in height. Still, for Kip, they are company. It is an inhabited room, and he walks within the discussion of these creatures that represent some fable about mankind and heaven.

He slips his satchel from his shoulder and faces the bed. He wants to lie on it, hesitating only because of the presence of the angel. He has already walked around the ethereal body and noticed the dusty light bulbs attached to its back beneath the dark coloured wings, and he knows in spite of his desire that he could not sleep easily in the presence of such a thing. There are three pairs of stage slippers, a set designer's sub-tlety, peeking out from under the bed. It is about one-forty.

He spreads his cape on the floor, flattens the satchel into a pillow and lies down on the stone. Most of his childhood in Lahore he slept on a mat on the floor of his bedroom. And in truth he has never gotten accustomed to the beds of the West. A pallet and an air pillow are all he uses in his tent, whereas in England when staying with Lord Suffolk he sank claustrophobically into the dough of a mattress, and lay there captive and awake until he crawled out to sleep on the carpet.

He stretches out beside the bed. The shoes too, he notices, are larger than life. The feet of Amazonians slips into them. Above his head the tentative right arm of the woman. Beyond his feet the angel. Soon one of the sappers will turn on the city's electricity, and if he is going to explode he will do so in the company of these two. They will die or be secure. There is nothing more he can do, anyway. He has been up all night on a final search for caches of dynamite and time cartridges. Walls will crumble around him or he will walk through a city of light. At least he has found these parental figures. He can relax in the midst of this mime of conversation.

He has his hands under his head, interpreting a new toughness in the face of the angel he didn't notice before. The white flower it holds has fooled him. The angel too is a warrior. In the midst of this series of thoughts his eyes close and he gives in to tiredness.

He is sprawled out with a smile on his face, as if relieved finally to be sleeping, the luxuriousness of such a thing. The palm of his left hand facedown on the concrete. The colour of his turban echoes that of the lace collar at the neck of Mary.

At her feet the small Indian sapper, in uniform, beside the six slippers. There seems to be no time here. Each of them has selected the most comfortable of positions to forge time. So we will be remembered by others. In such smiling comfort when we trust our surroundings. The tableau now, with Kip at the feet of the two figures, suggest a debate over his fate. The raised terra-cotta arm a stay of execution, a promise of some great future for this sleeper, childlike, foreign-born. The three of them almost at the point of decision, agreement.

Under the thin layer of dust the angel's face has a powerful joy. Attached to its back are the six light bulbs, two of which are defunct. But in spite of that the wonder of electricity suddenly lights its wings from underneath, so that their blood-red and blue and goldness the colour of mustard fields shine animated in the late afternoon.

Wherever Hana is now, in the future, she is aware of the line of movement Kip's body followed out of her life. Her mind repeats it. The path he slammed through among them. When he turned into a stone of silence in their midst. She recalls everything of that August day – what the sky was like, the objects on the table in front of her going dark under the thunder.

She sees him in the field, his hand clasped over his head, then realizes this is a gesture not of pain but of his need to hold the earphones tight against his brain. He is a hundred yards away from her in the lower field when she hears a scream emerge from his body which had never raised its voice among them. He sinks to his knees, as if unbuckled. Stays like that and then slowly gets up and moves in a diagonal towards his tent, enters it, and closes the flaps behind him. There is the dry crackle of thunder and she sees her arms darken.

Kip emerges from the tent with the rifle. He comes into the Villa San Girolamo and sweeps past her, moving like a steel ball in an arcade game, through the doorway and up the stairs three steps at a time, his breath metronomed, the hit of his boots against the vertical sections of stairs. She hears his feet along the hallway as she continues to sit at the table in the kitchen, the book in front of her, the pencil, these objects frozen and shadowed in the pre-storm light.

He enters the bedroom. He stands at the foot of the bed where the English patient lies.

Hello, sapper.

The rifle stock is against his chest, its sling braced against his triangled arm.

What was going on outside?

Kip looks condemned, separate from the world, his brown face weeping. The body turns and fires into the old fountain, and the plaster explodes dust onto the bed. He pivots back so the rifle points at the Englishman. He begins to shudder, and then everything in him tries to control that.

Put down the gun, Kip.

He slams his back against the wall and stops his shaking. Plaster dust in the air around them.

I sat at the foot of this bed and listened to you, Uncle. These last months. When I was a kid I did that, the same thing. I believed I could fill myself up with what older people taught me. I believed I could carry that knowledge, slowly altering it, but in any case passing it beyond me to another.

I grew up with traditions from my country, but later, more often, from *your* country. Your fragile white island that with customs and manners and books and prefects and reason somehow converted the rest of the world. You stood for precise behaviour. I knew if I lifted a teacup with the wrong finger I'd be banished. If I tied the wrong kind of knot in a tie I was out. Was it just ships that gave you such power? Was it, as my brother said, because you had the histories and printing presses?

You and then the Americans converted us. With your missionary rules. And Indian soldiers wasted their lives as heroes so they could be *pukkah*. You had wars like cricket. How did you fool us into this? Here . . . listen to what you people have done.

He throws the rifle on the bed and moves towards the Englishman. The crystal set is at his side, hanging off his belt. He unclips it and puts the earphones over the black head of the patient, who winces at the pain on his scalp. But the sapper leaves them on him. Then he walks back and picks up the rifle. He sees Hana at the door.

One bomb. Then another. Hiroshima. Nagasaki.

He swerves the rifle towards the alcove. The hawk in the valley air seems to float intentionally into the V sight. If he closes his eyes he sees the streets of Asia full of fire. It rolls across cities like a burst map, the hurricane of heat withering bodies as it meets them, the shadows of humans suddenly in the air. This tremor of Western wisdom.

He watches the English patient, earphones on, the eyes focused inwards, listening. The rifle sight moves down the thin nose to the Adam's apple, above the collarbone. Kip stops breathing. Braced at exact right angles to the Enfield rifle. No waver.

Then the Englishman's eyes look back at him.

Sapper.

Caravaggio enters the room and reaches for him, and Kip wheels the butt of the rifle into his ribs. A swat from the paw of an animal. And then, as if part of the same movement, he is back in the braced right-angle position of those in firing

304

squads, drilled into him in various barracks in India and England. The burned neck in his sights.

Kip, talk to me.

Now his face is a knife. The weeping from shock and horror contained, seeing everything, all those around him, in a different light. Night could fall between them, fog could fall, and the young man's dark brown eyes would reach the new revealed enemy.

My brother told me. Never turn your back on Europe. The deal makers. The contract makers. The map drawers. Never trust Europeans, he said. Never shake hands with them. But we, oh, we were easily impressed – by speeches and medals and your ceremonies. What have I been doing these last few years? Cutting away, defusing, limbs of evil. For what? For *this* to happen?

What is it? Jesus, tell us!

I'll leave you the radio to swallow your history lesson. Don't move again, Caravaggio. All those speeches of civilization from kings and queens and presidents . . . such voices of abstract order. Smell it. Listen to the radio and smell the celebration in it. In my country, when a father breaks justice in two, you kill the father.

You don't know who this man is.

The rifle sight unwavering at the burned neck. Then the sapper swerves it up towards the man's eyes.

Do it, Almásy says.

The eyes of the sapper and the patient meet in this half-dark room crowded now with the world.

He nods to the sapper.

Do it, he says quietly.

Kip ejects the cartridges and catches it as it begins to fall. He throws the rifle onto the bed, a snake, its venom collected. He sees Hana on the periphery.

The burned man untugs the earphones off his head and slowly places them down in front of him. Then his left hand reaches up and pulls away the hearing aid, and drops it to the floor.

Do it, Kip. I don't want to hear anymore.

He closes his eyes. Slips into darkness, away from the room.

The sapper leans against the wall, his hands folded, head down. Caravaggio can hear air being breathed in and out of his nostrils, fast and hard, a piston.

He isn't an Englishman.

American, French, I don't care. When you start bombing the brown races of the world, you're an Englishman. You had King Leopold of Belgium and now you have fucking Harry Truman of the USA. You all learned it from the English.

No. Not him. Mistake. Of all people he is probably on your side.

He would say that doesn't matter, Hana says.

Caravaggio sits down in the chair. He is always, he thinks, sitting in this chair. In the room there is the thin squawking from the crystal set, the radio still speaking in its underwater voice. He cannot bear to turn and look at the sapper or look towards the blur of Hana's frock. He knows the young soldier is right. They would never have dropped such a bomb on a white nation.

The sapper walks out of the room, leaving Caravaggio and Hana by the bed. He has left the three of them to their world, is no longer their sentinel. In the future, if and when the patient dies, Caravaggio and the girl will bury him. Let the dead bury the dead. He has never been sure what that meant. Those few callous words in the Bible.

They will bury everything except the book. The body, the sheets, his clothes, the rifle. Soon he will be alone with Hana. And the motive for all this on the radio. A terrible event emerging out of the shortwave. A new war. The death of a civilization.

Still night. He can hear nighthawks, their faint cries, the muted thud of wings as they turn. The cypress trees rise over his tent, still on this windless night. He lies back and stares into the dark corner of the tent. When he closes his eyes he sees fire, people leaping into rivers into reservoirs to avoid flame or heat that within seconds burns everything, whatever they hold, their own skin and hair, even the water they leap into. The brilliant bomb carried over the sea in a plane, passing the moon in the east, towards the green archipelago. And released.

He has not eaten food or drunk water, is unable to swallow anything. Before light failed he stripped the tent of all military objects, all bomb disposal equipment, stripped all insignia off his uniform. Before lying down he undid the turban and combed his hair out and then tied it up into a topknot and lay back, saw the light on the skin of the tent slowly disperse, his eyes holding onto the last blue of light, hearing the drop of wind into windlessness and then hearing the swerve of the hawks as their wings thudded. And all the delicate noises of their air.

He feels all the winds of the world have been sucked into Asia. He steps away from the many small bombs of his career towards a bomb the size, it seems, of a city, so vast it lets the living witness the death of the population around them. He knows nothing about the weapon. Whether it was a sudden assault of metal and explosion or if boiling air scoured itself towards and through anything human. All he knows is, he feels he can no longer let anything approach him, cannot eat the food or even drink from a puddle on a stone bench on the terrace. He does not feel he can draw a match out of his bag and fire the lamp, for he believes the lamp will ignite everything. In the tent, before the light evaporated, he had brought out the photograph of his family and gazed at it. His name is Kirpal Singh and he does not know what he is doing here.

He stands now under the trees in the August heat, unturbaned, wearing only a *kurta*. He carries nothing in his hands, just walks alongside the outline of hedges, his bare feet on the grass or on terrace stone or in the ash of an old bonfire. His body alive in its sleeplessness, standing on the edge of a great valley of Europe.

In the early morning she sees him standing beside the tent. During the evening she had watched for some light among the trees. Each of them in the villa had eaten alone that night, the Englishman eating nothing. Now she sees the sapper's arm sweep out and the canvas walls collapse on themselves like a sail. He turns and comes towards the house, climbs the steps onto the terrace and disappears.

In the chapel he moves past the burned pews towards the apse, where under a tarpaulin weighted down with branches is the motorbike. He begins dragging the covering of the machine. He crouches down by the bike and begins nuzzling oil into the sprockets and cogs.

When Hana comes into the roofless chapel he is sitting there leaning his back and head against the wheel.

Kip.

He says nothing, looking through her.

Kip, it's *me*. What did we have to do with it?

He is a stone in front of her.

She kneels down to his level and leans forward into him, the side of her head against his chest, holding herself like that.

A beating heart.

When his stillness doesn't alter she rolls back onto her knees.

The Englishman once read me something, from a book: "Love is so small it can tear itself through the eye of a needle."

He leans to his side away from her, his face stopping a few inches from a rain puddle.

A boy and a girl.

While the sapper unearthed the motorcycle from under the tarpaulin, Caravaggio leaned forward on the parapet, his chin against his forearm. Then he felt he couldn't bear the mood of the house and walked away. He wasn't there when the sapper gunned the motorbike to life and sat on it while it half bucked, alive under him, and Hana stood nearby.

Singh touched her arm and let the machine roll away, down the slope, and then only revved it to life.

Halfway down the path to the gate, Caravaggio was waiting for him, carrying the gun. He didn't even lift it formally towards the motorbike when the boy slowed down, as Caravaggio walked into his path. Caravaggio came up to him and put his arms around him. A great hug. The sapper felt the stubble against his skin for the first time. He felt drawn in, gathered into the muscles. "I shall have to learn how to miss you," Caravaggio said. Then the boy pulled away and Caravaggio walked back to the house.

The machine broke into life around him. The smoke of the Triumph and dust and fine gravel fell away through the trees. The bike leapt the cattle grid at the gates, and then he was weaving down out of the village, passing the smell of gardens on either side of him that were tacked onto the slopes in their treacherous angle.

His body slipped into a position of habit, his chest parallel with, almost touching, the petrol tank, his arms horizontal in the shape of least resistance. He went south, avoiding Florence completely. Through Greve, across to Montevarchi and Ambra, small towns ignored by war and invasion. Then, as the new hills appeared, he began to climb the spine of them towards Cortona.

He was travelling against the direction of the invasion, as if rewinding the spool of war, the route no longer tense with military. He took only roads he knew, seeing the familiar castle towns from a distance. He lay static on the Triumph as it burned under him in its tear along the country roads. He carried little, all weapons left behind. The bike hurled through each village, not slowing for town or memory of war. *"The earth shall reel to and fro like a drunkard, and shall be removed like a cottage."*

She opened up his knapsack. There was a pistol wrapped in oilskin, so that its smell was released when she uncovered it. Toothbrush and tooth powder, pencil sketches in a note-book, including a drawing of her – she was sitting on the terrace and he had been looking down from the English-man's room. Two turbans, a bottle of starch. One sapper lamp with its leather straps, to be worn in emergencies. She flicked it on and the knapsack filled with crimson light.

In the side pockets she found pieces of equipment to do with bomb disposal, which she didn't wish to touch. Wrapped up in another small piece of cloth was the metal spile she had given him, which was used for tapping maple sugar out of a tree in her country.

From within the collapsed tent she unearthed a portrait that must have been of his family. She held the photograph in her palm. A Sikh and his family.

An older brother who was only eleven in this picture. Kip beside him, eight years old. *"When the war came my brother sided with whoever was against the English."*

There was also a small handbook that had a map of bombs. And a drawing of a saint accompanied by a musician.

She packed everything back in except the photograph, which she held in her free hand. She carried the bag through the trees, walked across the loggia and brought it into the house.

Each hour or so he slowed to a stop, spat into the goggles and wiped dust off with the sleeve of his shirt. He looked into the map again. He would go to the Adriatic, then south. Most of the troops were at the northern borders.

He climbed into Cortona, the high-pitched gunning of the bike all around him. He rode the Triumph up the steps to the door of the church and then walked in. A statue was there, bandaged in scaffold. He wanted to get closer to the face, but he had no rifle telescope and his body felt too stiff to climb up the construction pipes. He wandered around underneath like somebody unable to enter the intimacy of a home. He walked the bike down the church steps, and then coasted down through the shattered vineyards and went on to Arezzo.

At Sansepolcro he took a winding road into the mountains, into their mist, so he had to slow to minimal speed. The Bocca Trabaria. He was cold but locked the weather out of his mind. Finally the road rose above the whiteness, the mist a bed behind him. He skirted Urbino where the Germans had burned all the field horses of the enemy. They had fought here in this region for a month; now he slid through in minutes, recognizing only the Black Madonna shrines. The war had made all the cities and towns similar.

He came down towards the coast. Into Gabicce Mare, where he had seen the Virgin emerge from the sea. He slept on the hill, overlooking cliff and water, near where the statue had been taken. That was the end of his first day.

Dear Clara – Dear Maman,

Maman *is a French word, Clara, a circular word, suggesting cuddles, a personal word that can be even shouted in public. Something as comforting and as eternal as a barge. Though you, in spirit, I know are still a canoe. Can serve one around and enter a creek in seconds. Still independent. Still private. Not a barge responsible for all around you. This is my first letter in years, Clara, and I am not used to the formality of them. I have spent the last few months living with three others, and our talk has been slow, casual. I am not used to talking in any way but that now.*

The year is 194-. What? For a second I forget. But I know the month and the day. One day after we heard the bombs were dropped in Japan, so it feels like the end of the world. From now on I believe the personal will forever be at war with the public. If we can rationalize this we can rationalize anything.

Patrick died in a dove-cot in France. In France in the seventeenth and eighteenth centuries they built them huge, larger than most houses. Like this.

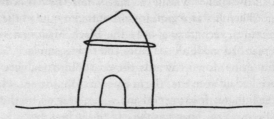

The horizontal line one-third of the way down was called the rat ledge – to stop rats running up the brick, so the doves would be safe. Safe as a dove-cot. A sacred place. Like a church in many ways. A comforting place. Patrick died in a comforting place.

At five a.m. he kicked the Triumph to life, and the rear wheel threw gravel in a skirt. He was still in darkness, still unable to distinguish sea in the vista beyond the cliff. For the journey from here to the south he had no maps, but he could recognize the war roads and follow the coast route. When sunlight came he was able to double his speed. The rivers were still ahead of him.

Around two in the afternoon he reached Ortona, where the sappers had laid the Bailey bridges, nearly drowning in the storm in mid-river. It began to rain and he stopped to put on a rubber cape. He walked around the machine in the wetness. Now, as he travelled, the sound in his ears changed. The *shush shush* replacing the whine and howl, the water flung onto his boots from the front wheel. Everything he saw through the goggles was grey. He would not think of Hana. In all the silence within the bike's noise he did not think of her. When her face appeared he erased it, pulled the handlebars so he would swerve and have to concentrate. If there were to be words they would not be hers; they would be names on this map of Italy he was riding through.

He feels he carries the body of the Englishman with him in this flight. It sits on the petrol tank facing him, the black body in an embrace with his, facing the past over his shoulder, facing the countryside they are flying from, that receding palace of strangers on the Italian hill which shall never be rebuilt. *"And my words which I have put in thy mouth shall not depart out of thy mouth. Nor out of the mouth of thy seed. Nor out of the mouth of thy seed's seed."*

The voice of the English patient sang Isaiah into his ear as he had that afternoon when the boy had spoken of the face on the chapel ceiling in Rome. "There are of course a hundred Isaiahs. Someday you will want to see him as an old man – in southern France the abbeys celebrate him as bearded and old, but the power is still there in his look." The Englishman had sung out into the painted room. *"Behold, the Lord will carry thee away with a mighty captivity, and He will surely cover thee. He will surely violently turn and toss thee like a ball into a large country."*

He was riding deeper into thick rain. Because he had loved the face on the ceiling he had loved the words. As he had believed in the burned man and the meadows of civilization he tended. Isaiah and Jeremiah and Solomon were in the burned man's bedside book, his holy book, whatever he had loved glued into his own. He had passed his book to the sapper, and the sapper had said we have a Holy Book too.

The rubber lining on the goggles had cracked during the past months and the rain now began filling each pocket of air in front of his eyes. He would ride without them, the *shush shush* a permanent sea in his ears, and his crouched body stiff, cold, so there was only the idea of heat from this machine he rode so intimately, the white spray of it as he slid through villages like a slipping star, a half-second of visitation when one could make a wish. *"For the heavens shall vanish away like smoke and the earth shall wax old like a garment. And they that dwell therein shall die in like manner. For the moth shall eat them up like a garment, and the worms shall eat them like wool."* A secret of deserts from Uweinat to Hiroshima.

He was removing the goggles as he came out of the curve

and onto the bridge over the Ofanto River. And with his left arm up holding the goggles free he began to skid. He dropped them and calmed the bike but was not prepared for the iron bounce onto the lip of the bridge, the bike lying down to the right underneath him. He was suddenly sliding with it along the skin of rainwater down the centre of the bridge, blue sparks from the scratching metal around his arms and face.

Heavy tin flew off and shouldered past him. Then he and the bike veered to the left, there was no side to the bridge, and they hurtled out parallel to the water, he and the bike sideways, his arms flung back above his head. The cape released itself away from him, from whatever was machine and mortal, part of the element of air.

The motorbike and the soldier stilled in midair, then pivoted down into the water, the metal body between his legs as they slammed into it, jarring a white path through it, disappearing, the rain too entering the river. *"He will toss thee like a ball into a large country."*

How did Patrick end up in a dove-cot, Clara? His unit had left him, burned and wounded. So burned the buttons of his shirt were part of his skin, part of his dear chest. That I kissed and you kissed. And how was my father burned? He who could swerve like an eel, or like your canoe, as if charmed, from the real world. In his sweet and complicated innocence. He was the most unverbal of men, and I am always surprised women liked him. We tend to like a verbal man around us. We are the rationalists, the wise, and he was often lost, uncertain, unspoken.

*He was a burned man and I was a nurse and I could
have nursed him. Do you understand the sadness of geography? I could have saved him or at least been with him
till the end. I know a lot about burning. How long was he
alone with doves and rats? With the last stages of blood
and life in him? Doves over him. The flutter when they
thrashed around him. Unable to sleep in the darkness. He
always hated darkness. And he was alone, without lover
or kin.*

*I am sick of Europe, Clara. I want to come home. To your
small cabin and pink rock in Georgian Bay. I will take a
bus up to Parry Sound. And from the mainland send a message over the shortwave radio out towards the Pancakes.
And wait for you, wait to see the silhouette of you in a canoe
coming to rescue me from this place we all entered, betraying you. How did you become so smart? How did you
become so determined? How were you not fooled like us?
You that demon for pleasure who became so wise. The
purest among us, the darkest bean, the greenest leaf.*

Hana.

The sapper's bare head comes out of the water, and he gasps
in all the air above the river.

Caravaggio has made a one-strand bridge with hemp rope
down to the roof of the next villa. The rope is tightened at

this end round the waist of the statue of Demetrius and then secured to the well. The rope barely higher than the tops of the two olive trees along his path. If he loses his balance he will fall into the rough dusty arms of the olive.

He steps onto it, his socked feet gripping the hemp. How valuable is that statue? he once asked Hana casually, and she told him the English patient had said all statues of Demetrius were worthless.

She seals the letter and stands up, moves across the room to close the window, and at that moment lightning slips through the valley. She sees Caravaggio in midair halfway across the gorge that lies like a deep scar alongside the villa. She stands there as if in one of her dreams, then climbs into the window alcove and sits there looking out.

Every time there is lightning, rain freezes in the suddenly lit night. She sees the buzzard hawks flung up into the sky, looks for Caravaggio.

He is halfway across when he smells the rain, and then it begins to fall all over his body, clinging to him, and suddenly there is the greater weight of his clothes.

She puts her cupped palms out of the window and combs the rain into her hair.

The villa drifts in darkness. In the hallway by the English patient's bedroom the last candle burns, still alive in the night. Whenever he opens his eyes out of sleep, he sees the old wavering yellow light.

For him now the world is without sound, and even light seems an unneeded thing. He will tell the girl in the morning he wants no candle flame to accompany him while he sleeps.

Around three a.m. he feels a presence in the room. He sees, for a pulse of a moment, a figure at the foot of his bed, against the wall or painted onto it perhaps, not quite discernible in the darkness of foliage beyond the candlelight. He mutters something, something he had wanted to say, but there is silence and the slight brown figure, which could be just a night shadow, does not move. A poplar. A man with plumes. A swimming figure. And he would not be so lucky, he thinks, to speak to the young sapper again.

He stays awake in any case this night, to see if the figure moves towards him. Ignoring the tablet that brings painlessness, he will remain awake till the light dies out and the smell of candle smoke drifts into his room and into the girl's room farther down the hall. If the figure turns around there will be paint on his back, where he slammed in grief against the mural of trees. When the candle dies out he will be able to see this.

His hand reaches out slowly and touches his book and returns to his dark chest. Nothing else moves in the room.

Now where does he sit as he thinks of her? These years later. A stone of history skipping over the water, bouncing up so she and he have aged before it touches the surface again and sinks.

Where does he sit in his garden thinking once again he should go inside and write a letter or go one day down to the telephone depot, fill out a form and try to contact her in another country. It is this garden, this square patch of dry cut grass that triggers him back to the months he spent with Hana and Caravaggio and the English patient north of Florence in the Villa San Girolamo. He is a doctor, has two children and a laughing wife. He is permanently busy in this city. At six p.m. he removes his white lab coat. Underneath he wears dark trousers and a short-sleeved shirt. He closes up the clinic, where all the paperwork has weights of various kinds – stones, inkpots, a toy truck his son no longer plays with – to keep it from being blown away by the fan. He climbs onto his bicycle and pedals the four miles home, through the bazaar. Whenever he can he swerves his bicycle over to the shadowed part of the street. He has reached an age when he suddenly realizes that the sun of India exhausts him.

He glides under the willows by the canal and then stops at a small neighbourhood of houses, removes his cycle clips and carries the bicycle down the steps into the small garden his wife has nurtured.

And something this evening has brought the stone out of the water and allowed it to move back within the air towards the hill town in Italy. It was perhaps the chemical burn on the arm of the girl he treated today. Or the stone stairway, where brown weeds grow ardently along the steps. He had been carrying his bicycle and was halfway up the steps before he remembered. This had been on the way to work, so the trigger of memory was postponed when he got to the hospital and ran into seven hours of constant patients and administration. Or it might have been the burn on the young girl's arm.

He sits in the garden. And he watches Hana, her hair longer, in her own country. And what does she do? He sees her always, he face and body, but he doesn't know what her profession is or what her circumstances are, although he sees her reactions to people around her, her bending down to children, a white fridge door behind her, but only her, in silence. He cannot discern the company she moves among, her judgement; all he can witness is her character and the lengthening of her dark hair, which falls again and then again into her eyes.

She will, he realizes now, always have a serious face. She has moved from being a young woman into having the angular look of a queen, someone who has made her face with her desire to be a certain kind of person. He still likes that about her. Her smartness, the fact that she did not inherit that look or that beauty, but that it was something searched for and that it will always reflect a present stage of her character. It seems every month or two he witnesses her this way, as if these moments of revelation are a continuation of the letters she wrote to him for a year, getting no reply, until she stopped sending them, turned away by his silence. His character, he supposed.

Now there are these urges to talk with her during a meal and return to that stage they were most intimate at in the tent or in the English patient's room, both of which contained the turbulent river of space between them. Recalling the time, he is just as fascinated at himself there as he is with her – boyish and earnest, his lithe arm moving across the air towards the girl he has fallen in love with. His wet boots are by the Italian door, the laces tied together, his arm reaches for her shoulder, there is the prone figure on the bed.

During the evening meal he watches his daughter struggling with her cutlery, trying to hold the large weapons in her small hands. At this table all of their hands are brown. They move with ease in their customs and habits. And his wife has taught them all a wild humour, which has been inherited by his son. He loves to see his son's wit in this house, how it surprises him constantly, going beyond even his and his wife's knowledge and humour – the way he treats dogs on the streets, imitating their stroll, their look. He loves the fact that this boy can almost guess the wishes of dogs from the variety of expressions at a dog's disposal.

And Hana moves possibly in the company that is not her choice. She, at even this age, thirty-four, has not found her own company, the ones she wanted. She is a woman of honour and smartness whose wild love leaves out luck, always taking risks, and there is something in her brow now that only she can recognize in a mirror. Ideal and idealistic in that shiny dark hair! People fall in love with her. She still remembers the lines of poems the Englishman read out loud to her from his commonplace book. She is a woman I don't know well enough to hold in my wing, if writers have wings, to harbour for the rest of my life.

And so Hana moves and her face turns and in a regret she lowers her hair. Her shoulder touches the edge of a cupboard and a glass dislodges. Kirpal's left hand swoops down and catches the dropped fork an inch from the floor and gently passes it into the fingers of his daughter, a wrinkle at the edge of his eyes behind his spectacles.

Acknowledgements

While some of the characters who appear in this book are based in historical figures, and while many of the areas described – such as the Gilf Kebir and its surrounding desert – exist, and were explored in the 1930s, it is important to stress that this story is a fiction and that the portraits of the characters who appear in it are fictional, as are some of the events and journeys.

I would like to thank the Royal Geographical Society, London, for allowing me to read archival material and to glean from their *Geographical Journals* the world of explorers and their journeys – often beautifully recorded by their writers. I have quoted a passage from Hassanein Bey's article "Through Kufra to Darfur" (1924), describing sandstorms, and I have drawn from him and other explorers to evoke the desert of the 1930s. I would like to acknowledge information drawn from Dr Richard A. Bermann's "Historical Problems of the Libyan Desert" (1934) and R. A. Bagnold's review of Almásy's monograph on his explorations in the desert.

Many books were important to me in my research. *Unexploded Bomb* by Major A. B. Hartley was especially useful in re-creating the construction of bombs and in describing the British bomb disposal units at the start of World War II. I have quoted directly from his book (the italicized lines in the "In Situ" section) and have based some of Kirpal Singh's methods of defusing on actual techniques that Hartley records. Information found in the patient's notebook on the nature of certain winds is drawn from Lyall Watson's wonderful book *Heaven's Breath*, direct quotes appearing in quotation marks. The section from the Candaules–Gyges story in Herodotus's *Histories* is from the 1890 translation by G. C. McCauley (Macmillan). Other quotations from Herodotus use the David Gene translation (University of Chicago Press). The line in italics on page 23 is by Christopher Smart; the lines in italics on pages 155–6 are from John Milton's *Paradise Lost*; the line Hana remembers on page 309 is by Anne Wilkinson. I would also like to acknowledge Alan Moorehead's *The Villa Diana*, which discusses the life of Poliziano in Tuscany. Other important books were Mary McCarthy's *The Stones of Florence*, Leonard Mosley's *The Cat and the Mice*: G. W. L. Nicholson's *The Canadians in Italy 1943–5* and *Canada's Nursing Sisters; The Marshall Cavendish Encyclopaedia of World II*; F. Yeats-Brown's *Martial India*; and three other books on the Indian military: *The Tiger Strikes* and *The Tiger Kills*, published in 1942 by the Directorate of Public Relations, New Delhi, India, and *A Roll of Honor*.

Thanks to the English department at Glendon College, York University, the Villa Serbelloni, the Rockefeller Foundation, and the Metropolitan Toronto Reference Library.

I would like to thank the following for their generous help: Elisabeth Dennys, who let me read her letters written from Egypt during the war; Sister Margaret at the Villa San Girolamo; Michael Williamson at the National Library of Canada, Ottawa; Anna Jardine; Rodney Dennys; Linda Spalding; Ellen Levine. And Lally Marwah, Douglas LePan, David Young and Donya Peroff.

Finally a special thanks to Ellen Seligman, Liz Calder and Sonny Mehta.

Permissions Acknowledgements

Grateful acknowledgement is made to the following for permission to reprint previously published material:

Famous Music Corporation: Excerpt from "When I Take My Sugar to Tea" by Sammy Fain, Irving Kahal and Pierre Norman. Copyright 1931 by Famous Music Corporation. Copyright renewed 1958 by Famous Music Corporation. Reprinted by permission.

Alfred A. Knopf, Inc.: Excerpt from "Arrival at the Waldorf" by Wallace Stevens from *The Collected Poems of Wallace Stevens*. Copyright 1954 by Wallace Stevens. Reprinted by permission.

326